THE DIVINE SPACE PIRATES TRILOGY

COLLECTOR SET

♦♦♦♦

Book 1, *THE HEIGHTS OF PERDITION*

Book 2, *THE BREADTH OF CREATION*

Book 3, *THE PRICE OF PARADISE*

C. S. Johnson

TABLE OF CONTENTS

Book 1, THE HEIGHTS OF PERDITION

Book 2, THE BREADTH OF CREATION

Book 3, THE PRICE OF PARADISE

THE HEIGHTS OF PERDITION

BOOK ONE OF *THE DIVINE SPACE PIRATES*

♦♦♦♦

C. S. Johnson

Per usual, this is for Sam. There is just no leaving you behind when it comes to a new adventure.

This is also for Tyler. You were a great student but you make a better friend. I have such hope for my children thanks to you.

I also feel a great deal owed toward my favorite friends. Esther and Jennifer, thanks for your support during the last few weeks of this novel's writing. I wouldn't have the drive if I didn't think where I was going was any fun, and you always make me have fun.

In addition, it is only fitting that my first "more romance" romance novel should be for my mother. I might live in a world splattered with fantasies, but there is nothing unreal that did not come into being without the solid reality of your love. I love you, Mommy!

♦1♦

At just the right angle, the dark blue and white orb, suspended in a sea of invisible shadows, held in place by a faith as impossible to believe in as it was to see, fit nicely between his fingers. Outside his window, Earth looked small and fragile, seemingly innocent, and mostly harmless. A hollowness slipped between his thumb and forefinger as he squashed them together, crushing the blueberry-sized circle.

Amused by the irony of the forced perspective before him, a rare, genuine smile formed on Exton Shepherd's face.

It was, he decided, almost a shame no one else was around to witness such an unusual event. He smooshed his fingers together, imagining the world completely decimated into dust.

But then, he recalled, he'd given plenty of smiles earlier, as all the hubbub went on about the ship. Surely the crew, his hodgepodge of adopted family and coworkers, would have been satisfied with those, even though they were inauthentic at best and mocking at worst.

Duty sometimes demanded playing happy. Exton knew that, and he followed it, even in instances he loathed.

Like today.

Between the thirteenth and fifteenth sunrises of his day, he'd watched the only other person he truly cared for in all the world—no, he mentally corrected himself, in all the universe—pledge her love, heart, and life to another man.

It was heartbreaking on some levels, but strangely freeing, too.

The wedding had been quaint, warm, and sweet. Its simplicity suggested nothing of its socially taxing nature.

Exton had no regrets about ducking out as soon as the bride and groom finished their vows and the Ecclesia had pronounced them husband and wife.

Once he had successfully slipped out of sight, Exton proceeded to the Captain's Lounge, the small room he'd claimed as his the day after launching the *Perdition* into space.

There was little to be said of the room's comfort; it was more like a tall elevator shaft than a room, empty of everything but the coldness of space and a small window hidden up near the far end. More than once, Exton wondered if he'd found a kind of kinship with it; hollow and bleak, with a tiny view looking out toward the fleeing horizon.

It was there, on a window seat built into the windowpane, where Exton tucked his legs under his chin and entered into his own world of privacy, where he was free to be who he wanted, even if it was for only a moment.

As captain of the ship, he didn't want his crew to see him in one of his more melancholy moods.

His frown returned when he opened his fingers again, only to see Earth was still hanging in space before him, its silence mocking and spiteful. Rearranging his hand, he made it seem like he was carrying the earth in the palm. Fleetingly, he toyed with the idea of pretending to toss the small pearl away into the dark recesses of space, into an imaginary hell.

But he knew that would not work.

Exton knew two things with startling clarity and unshakable certainty: The first was that hell was real, and the second was that it was his home.

"Having fun?" a voice asked from below him.

"Huh?" Exton jerked around in surprise, nearly falling off the window ledge. "Come on, Emery, don't do that," he groaned, while the young woman dressed all in white only laughed. His balance, already compromised by the pull of the starship's gravity, faltered again as Exton tried to adjust himself. "You know I don't like it when people interrupt me, especially when I'm here."

"But it's my wedding day," Emery insisted. "And I'd like to have a dance with the ship's captain before the night shift starts. Come on, we're up first."

Exton gave up on staying by the window and jumped down as gracefully as he could. "All the shifts up here are technically the night shift," he grumbled.

"Some would say we live in perpetual day up here on the

Perdition," Emery offered, her voice gentle even as she maintained her stance. "Sunrise and sunset are only ninety-two minutes apart for us now, when we're this close to Earth."

"Sunrises and sunsets do not make day and night up here," Exton told her, touching his forehead.

Emery reached out and took his hand, before she placed it over his heart. "I think your problem is too much night in here, not out there." She turned her attention back to the window, where six inches of steel-grade glass separated them from the vacuum of space.

Exton followed her gaze, wondering if she was looking for any sign of familiarity from their old home. He watched as the end of the ocean braced itself against the shore of the Old Republic; he felt his memory pull him in, and he could see it clearly inside his mind.

The chill of the old mountains where he would go work and play with his father, the spray of the salt water on his transport module, the warmth of his mother's arms as she welcomed him home from school—all of it embraced him, surrounding him and penetrating into the deep recesses of his heart.

And then there was pain, and then it was gone.

Exton shook his head. "I know it seems like a long time has passed, but it's time to cause the URS some trouble. It's almost the anniversary, you know."

"I know," she replied. A sudden sadness appeared in her gaze, and Exton wondered if she had been reminiscing as well.

Pushing aside his grief, he straightened his shoulders. "I have a plan that will really make them sorry this year, Em."

"I know you're a man of your word," Emery replied, "but I'm not sure it will be enough to convince them to give us what we want."

"They already cannot give us what we want." Exton shrugged. "Our game was never for power. It was for meaning."

"It's not a game, Exton."

"I know it's not!" Out of the corner of his eye, he saw Emery flinch. "I know it's not," he repeated carefully, reverting to his usual, detached tone. "It's not our fault that it became a quest for survival, Emery. I know that even more than you do."

"If it's survival you want," Emery scoffed, "there's no point in selling your soul in the process."

Before Exton could assure Emery he had no soul left that was worth saving, let alone selling, he stopped. Happy times, he reminded himself.

Emery's wedding was a special occasion, one that had excited her for the past several months, offering a glimmer of hope on a horizon of gloom and turmoil. Exton was determined not to let the past rob him—or her—of anything else, so long as it was in his power. "You're right," he acquiesced, momentarily giving in.

Emery smiled brightly, and Exton suddenly had a hard time believing she was only two years younger than he was. At twenty-two, she seemed much more innocent than the figure that gazed back at him when he looked in the mirror.

He slipped his hand out from under hers, before taking and squeezing it. "Are you sure you wouldn't like to have the first dance with your new husband?"

"Tyler is my heart's desire," Emery told him firmly, "but you will always be my hero."

Exton grimaced. He knew he was no hero. "It would be a shame to waste your time with me."

"Time with you is not a waste."

"Did Tyler approve of changing up the dancing order? The man might be in love, but there's no need to make him prove to be the fool."

"Hey, Tyler's your commander, and your best friend," Emery objected. "You know he's not a fool."

"Not where it concerns you. He would be smart to correct that, and I have been telling him since he received approval from the Ecclesia to start courting you," Exton told her. He gave her a devious look. "Should I make him walk the plank?"

Emery frowned and searched the darkened shadows of his face. "That's not funny, Exton."

"I know."

They walked in silence for a few moments before Exton spoke once more. "I don't want to dance. No offense, Em."

"Traditionally, it was the daughter's duty to dance with her father, first." Emery smiled. "But that's more of a cultural thing I've read about from the Old Republic."

"Yes, I remember that," Exton agreed. "Ironic, how the Revolutionary States would be appalled by it now."

Of course, he recalled, even the idea of using the term "father" might have some of the more militant protestors up in arms, as the beloved Daddy Dictator of the URS, Grant Osgood, did not encourage familial relationships, unless such feelings were directed toward government.

"If the URS is against it, you should be more inclined to appease me, then," Emery contended.

There was a breath of silence and stillness before Exton responded. "I'm not our father," he scoffed.

"You're more like him than you might wish."

As Exton scowled at her, Emery pointed her finger at him accusingly. "See? You even have the same exasperated look he used to get when he was frustrated."

"I'll have to take your word for it." Exton shrugged, scratching his head. He frowned as he realized it had been some time since he'd gotten a haircut. His father used to do the same thing, especially when he was planning his next engineering endeavor. Exton suddenly wondered if it was his own scruffy locks that had been making him shrink back from mirrors of late.

He missed his father too much to want to see him staring out of the mirror from the other side of the grave.

Emery chuckled again, drawing him out of his thoughts. "Well, I know at least one trait you share with him. He had a hard time telling me no to anything I wanted, if memory serves."

"You look too much like Mom for me to say no," Exton admitted. "I'm sure he had the same problem, but that's one I'm more willing to share with him."

With her dark brown hair, blue-green eyes, and petite form, Emery was the living memory of their mother. She even had the same dimple hovering above the left corner of her lips, a trait Exton knew was the extent of their common features. Their father's blue eyes, as clear and sharp as ice, had passed to him, along with his height, broad shoulders, and black hair.

"He always did want me to follow in his footsteps," Exton muttered as they headed out of the Captain's Lounge. "But I'm not sure he would have enjoyed the ghost of Captain Chainsword, the infamous space lumberjack pirate."

"I don't think he would have liked it, given how much he derided you for enjoying those fantasy adventures you used to read."

"It seemed fitting at the time, to create a new role for him to play, along with the rest of us."

"I suppose." Emery shrugged. "But Papa was a brilliant engineer, same as you, and a good man. I'm not sure he would have liked your emphasis on piracy and power."

"For the most part, I think you are right," Exton agreed. "But he was too idealistic by far. That was what got him killed." He looked out a nearby window, where, even as he could no longer see Earth, he still felt the pull of its shadow.

"In hindsight, you would prove to be correct on that point."

"That is why I will not make the same mistake as he did. While *Paradise* is out of reach, *Perdition* will do what it can to ensure a better life for us."

"And others, too," Emery added proudly.

"Maybe." Exton shrugged. "I only have a duty to you, and you're technically Tyler's problem now. Anyone else is just extra."

"Your duty to me hasn't ended."

Exton rolled his eyes. "I'm going to dance with you, aren't I? What else is there?"

"Your duty to me might include a dance tonight, but I wish for you to find someone you would love as I love Tyler." She smiled. "Someone you can spend your life trying to make happy."

"Even as life makes me miserable?"

Emery frowned and sighed. "I don't know why you do that."

"Do what?"

"Make it impossible for yourself to be happy."

"Happiness is fleeting, remember?" Exton rolled his eyes. "Even the leaders of the Ecclesia would agree with me there."

"They don't often agree with you, especially when it comes to your mandates," Emery concurred. "The only reason they would on this account is because the phrasing is vague enough to seem to agree on the meaning." She narrowed her gaze. "And the practice."

Exton wrinkled his nose. "We've been up here for too long if you know me so well."

"I still prefer this to when we were off at different universities, working on our studies," Emery admitted with a thoughtful smile. "But as for the argument, you don't seem to agree with the Ecclesia a whole lot, either. You don't share most of their beliefs. I find it hard to believe that you would try to garner support from among their teachings."

"Their teachings on wisdom and life, and how it should be, I respect. But it's different when you're trying to manage a pirate starship and ruin an empire."

"Not to mention when you insist so stubbornly on remaining miserable."

"I *am* going back to your wedding celebration, aren't I?" Exton groaned. "Please don't push it, Em. You know how I feel. If God would grant your wish for me, if he wanted so much for me to be 'happy,' he could have let me 'fall in love' with someone on the *Perdition*, like you and Tyler. But even when we send our smaller ships down to Earth for supplies, see Aunt Patty, or attack the URS, there's no one there for me. There are only people there who want the protection *Perdition* can offer to political dissents or refugees such as themselves."

After a moment of thought, he added, "Besides, my job is to protect and lead aboard the spaceship. The last thing I need is to be led around by the whims of a woman."

"There's no need to make it sound so deplorable," Emery scoffed, arching an eyebrow at him. "Do you honestly think dealing with the moods of a man are any easier?"

He flashed her a charming grin.

"You don't need to set yourself up for failure like that. We have only been up in space for six years now, hiding in the shadows of all the toxic clouds while playing war games with the URS."

"Not to mention watching destruction of all other sorts go unchecked," Exton added, his voice grim.

"It's not all 'unchecked,'" Emery reminded him. "Exton, you still can't lose hope. God is a supposed to be a god of miracles, remember? We have time."

Exton wondered how his sister could be worried about his heart, when his life, as well all the lives of his crew, faced the bigger risk. It was one thing to be aware of danger, but another to disregard it, especially for something as silly as true love.

He studied Emery's daydreaming smile in silence and decided he had the right of it: As much as she was ever his practical and precise sister, Emery's wedded bliss was affecting her judgment.

Exton was surprised at the sudden stab of jealousy. He squashed it down as he caught sight of the approaching Earth through the galley windows.

Didn't Emery see the coming battle? Exton wondered. *Didn't she feel the haunted air about the starship, with specters of the past lurking around every corner of the* Perdition?

They couldn't outlast the URS forever up in space. While

Exton and the Ecclesia had established the *Perdition* a safe haven over the past few years, it was only a matter of time before the URS would come for them, and he knew it would not be to make peace.

"What is it, Exton?" Emery asked, jolting him out of his gloomy thoughts.

Exton sighed. "It's not like God's just going to dump someone into the ship just for me. You might as well save your breath for dancing, Em."

♦2♦

All Aeris St. Cloud wanted to do was dance.

The musical fanfare surely had to resonate all throughout the URS, Aerie thought. From the auditorium of her school, the New Hope Education Center 616, the country's anthem surely had to echo out into even the bleakest ends of Earth.

It seemed wrong to resist the urge to jump up and down.

But she knew she had to present a respectable, stoic face to the brave new world before her. She *had* to. There were too many people in the large assembly before her, and the rest of her graduating class was counting on her not to make any mistakes or mess up.

For once.

Mara Fleming, the class president, had triple-checked Aerie's pinned-back hair, while Claire Luceno, the graduating class student coordinator, warned her that this time she was going to have to hold in her sneezes, no matter how powerful.

Similar reminders from her housing unit members—always her toughest critics—burned in the back of her mind like a warning flare, sending a wave of embarrassment rushing through her.

Luckily, the sheer power of it triggered the hidden reserves of her self-control.

But not before she wriggled her butt and smiled brightly.

"Ahem."

The quick, sharp cough came from a familiar shadow from far down the line. It was quiet enough that the Master of Ceremony marched on with his speech relentlessly, the small indiscretion unnoticed by the crowd beyond him.

Aerie let only a tiny sigh escape in protest. No one was allowed to break formation throughout the URS ceremonies, and even she knew she would never be the exception.

She leaned forward, watching her teacher's familiar nostrils flair as his large pair of eyebrows sank into their trademark frown. *How did Master Browning even see me from all the way over there?* Aerie wondered.

She knew it wouldn't be much longer before the ceremony was over.

And then everything in her life would be perfect.

Almost as if he could read her mind, the schoolmaster glared even more fiercely at her, his face suddenly blushing an angry purple.

Even as guilt sunk in, Aerie nearly giggled at the reproving look. After six years, she knew better than to disappoint her schoolmaster. But no one could really blame her for her slip-ups today, Aerie decided, though she knew the State wouldn't hesitate to punish her for them.

Today was the day when she would finally join the rest of her unit in the New Hope Military Academy. She would prove them wrong, at last, and they would finally accept her.

Sadness gently brushed through her. *This is the day I've been waiting for ever since Mom died.*

Aerie had heard the rebellious mutterings about Heaven, a place in the clouds where people would go when they died. She might have thought her mother was watching her from there if most of New Hope wasn't located underground, and if the Earth's ominous, gray clouds didn't look so opaque.

And if Heaven wasn't illegal, she added belatedly to herself.

But she hoped if her mother was watching, she would be proud. Aerie had put more care into her appearance than usual; her hair, a golden shade of ginger, was pulled back into the tightest bun she could manage, with her long bangs tucked underneath her URS student service hat. She was wearing her best uniform, and her boots, perpetually crinkled and scuffed, were buffed to an acceptable shine.

Of course, no one noticed. But at least no one teased her for looking sloppy or trying to draw attention to herself. Aerie decided that alone was a good sign.

Nothing is going to go wrong today.

Another smile slipped out.

"Aerie."

At the sound of her name, Aerie glanced over to her to

her left. She nearly melted at the sight of her longtime friend, Brock Rearden, until she saw he was signaling her to get her to be still.

She rolled her eyes at him, feeling unexpected irritation starting to push through her enthusiasm. She could understand the schoolmaster's rebuke, but Brock's was frustrating.

But then, she reasoned a moment later, there was a rumor going around that Brock was going to ask her to the Military Academy Ball, the opening gala where all the new recruits and accepted personnel were honored.

Maybe that was why he was concerned, Aerie thought. *He wouldn't want to go with me if I caused a scene at graduation.*

After all, Brock had an impressive reputation as one of the top students in their class. Other rumors she heard said that he had been talking with the Military Academy Board since the previous year.

While getting into the military academy would mean proving her worth to her unit, showing up with Brock Rearden would prove her value to her peers.

Not that that is really a major concern, Aerie told herself. There were other, more important, elements that went along with getting invited to the ball by the most handsome, cunning, and eligible military recruit.

She sighed silently and happily to herself. The ball was a tradition in the URS, and it was the perfect place for her to get her first date, her first dance, and even her first kiss.

Which Brock was perfect for, too, she thought, still pretending to pay attention to the speaker as she conjured up an image of her friend.

Like many military recruits, his hair was cut short, but its wheat color reminded Aerie of the surface, of the softness of soil or the warmth of fur. His eyes were a combination of green and brown, which made her think of her mother's small garden, with specks of life surrounded by the warmth and power of the earth.

Power, Aerie decided, was a word that matched Brock.

While his ruggedly handsome face and build were hard to miss, it was his strength and shrewdness that made him stand out among everyone else in the room. He projected an aura that was both protective and predatory.

It's hard to imagine Brock not *getting into the military*, Aerie thought appreciatively.

"—and now, comrades, please join with me in welcoming our graduates to their new ranking as full members of the United Revolutionary States."

Aerie, along with her class, automatically saluted the audience with the formal RSS, the Revolutionary State Salute. Her right hand closed into a fist and then covered her heart, before she bowed her head. It was the URS salute of the highest order, required as a sign of respect.

She'd always thought it was a bit odd, but she heard the legends and stories of the past—at first reluctantly, then insatiably—which told of ancient nations that showed respect by grasping hands, bowing deeply, and exchanging name cards. Before the URS rescued the citizens of Earth, there was so much diversity and so many differences it was impossible to maintain any working order. She could easily see the Founding Fighters working to compromise on a design for respect, and that was how they arrived at the Revolutionary State Salute, before the first dictator, Hal J. P. Rothsburton, approved and mandated it.

"Thank you for that warm welcome to our new graduates."

Aerie struggled not to break formation. If there was any time to ensure she was following orders perfectly, it was at that moment.

Dictator Osgood is here!

She peeked over at him, excited to see the leader of the fair world speaking at her school. It was a special occasion indeed, even if his wrinkles seemed deeper and he was shorter than when he was onscreen; he couldn't have been any taller than Brock.

Like all educated students, Aerie knew Dictator Osgood

had been the URS Dictator for about eleven years, ever since the previous ruler retired.

He just wasn't what she would call handsome, Aerie decided privately.

"—pleased at the new recruits for the Military Academy this year. It will prove to be an interesting year, too, as we have received a message from the so-called ghost of Captain Chainsword."

Silence remained, but stillness suddenly accompanied it.

Aerie glanced to the left side of the podium, where His Excellency stood. Posted up on the walls were several pictures of defectors. Some, long destroyed, were marked off with a large, red slash. Others had faded over time, forgotten to the passage of progress.

Except one.

Among the sea of criminals, Captain Chainsword's profile stood out. Aerie, having little to no desire to pay attention to the various lectures she'd been forced to attend in the auditorium, was familiar with the pirate's features. Under the crimson slash that crossed his profile, his expression remained steadfast. A pirate hat was perched crookedly on his head, while his hair was black as starless night, running into his gray and white beard. His eyes, clear and sharp despite their age, mocked the onlooker with an almost compassionate gaze, reminding them all that there were some who would have power at any price.

"Captain Chainsword, as you know, has taken it upon himself to declare war on us, despite his death ten years ago," Osgood continued. "He has cut our access to our satellite systems, making our scouting attempts to find survivors out in the nuclear and chemical minefields much more arduous and hazardous. His ship, the *Perdition*, has remained undetected. But last night, we received a transmission.

"I am here to warn you, and remind you of the great sacrifices our nation has made over the past decades. Ecological disaster, accelerated by war—not the least among the list the destruction of the Persian oil fields, the nuclear discharge compromising the Old Republic electric grids, the chemical warfare unleashed upon the oceans—has forced us to find a new way of life."

Osgood paused, and Aerie quickly glanced at Brock, who was eying the poster of Captain Chainsword with barely contained hatred.

"Fortunately for us, it was a better life. With all the capitalists and bankers"—a collective flinch went through the crowd at the mere mention of the former state's slave owners—"rounded up and routinely executed, we were free to begin again, and in a fair manner.

"But now, Captain Chainsword's ghost seeks to return us to the days of market competition and economic inequality. In his quest for power, he has continued over the years to reign down tyranny against us, saying the days of the dictators are nearly over. Captain Chainsword's message to us this time was simple: 'War is coming to New Hope.'"

As a collective wave of unmoving surprise rippled through the audience, Aerie gasped. Immediately, her face burned red. She quickly tried to quash her feelings of reflexive shame.

After years of training, even the most outraged of individuals would be able to restrain themselves, especially in the face of a credible threat.

You'd think I would have learned that by now!

Osgood cleared his throat loudly. "While it might surprise some of you, I want you to know I am pleased by this. Since Captain Chainsword has been living on his starship, he has allowed himself to remain focused on his quest for power. In attacking New Hope, he will find that we have changed much over the last ten years.

"Indeed, if you recall your lessons on our history, New Hope was chosen as the United Revolutionary States' great capital for its values and resistance. When unscrupulous villains would try to bomb or attack it, we would rise when knocked down, coming out more powerful than ever before," Osgood said, referencing the tranquil times before the URS had been born, before the nuclear ash and toxic clouds made a large part of Earth uninhabitable. "As a result, I am confident we will be able to withstand his attack."

Aerie puffed up with pride. She was honored to be a resident of New Hope. Even in the dark days of capitalism, New Hope, previously known as New York City, was a beacon of hope to people all over the world.

"To prepare for this," Dictator Osgood continued, "I am personally reminding all citizens of New Hope to remain in their underground living quarters."

Her heart stilled as her intuition flared.

Osgood gestured to the right side of the stage. "It is my pleasure to have with me today General St. Cloud, who, as my new Lieutenant Commander-in-Chief, in addition to overseeing the new graduate PARs today, will be recruiting and training Emergency Responders to help with any attack Captain Chainsword's ghost might be foolish enough to unleash on our city."

Aerie's gaze sharpened as her father briefly glanced in her direction. Her heart stopped as he caught her eyes with his.

Then he turned and took his position at the podium. Without so much as a word of welcome to his audience, General St. Cloud began listing off all sorts of reminders and procedures.

Aerie felt her heart slowly, but loudly, resume its beating.

If her father was here, maybe her brothers would need to leave before she saw them. As fighter pilots in the Air Force, they might be called to the first line of defense for the URS.

Her gaze went back to Brock. He'd always dreamed of flying.

If war is coming to New Hope, he might get his chance.

Aerie wasn't sure of the exact moment their graduation ceremony ended, but when she was finally allowed to smile, she suddenly had to force it.

♦3♦

Despite the events at graduation, Aerie reasoned that there was no reason to believe Dictator Osgood's appearance was cause for immediate concern. She could still have her perfect day.

After all, she had passed her classes with high marks in tactical and combat skills, both difficult and necessary requirements for entering the URS Military Academy. There was also her final graduation project, where she'd prepared and delivered a research project presentation. Her instructors had given her many good compliments on that.

Surely, that will be enough to get me into the military, she thought.

"Aerie!"

She turned and smiled brightly as Brock came up to her. "Hi, Brock."

"That was so intense back there," Brock said, nodding toward the stage. "I'm so glad you didn't slip up. Master Browning was about ready to blow, I'm sure."

"I'm sure he should be used to it after all these years," Aerie said with a laugh. She tried not to let the fact that it was true hurt her. "Besides, if he did, wouldn't he be the one who would need to be reeducated in self-control?"

"You're right," he agreed. "Though you could get penalized for it as well, for being the cause of it."

Does Brock have just absolutely no sense of humor today? Aerie wondered. She shrugged it off; maybe he was, like her, just too overwhelmed by the ceremony and the PARs coming up.

"So, when do you go in for your PAR?" Aerie asked, tucking her hands behind her back.

"My review is supposed to be soon."

"Oh, really? You're lucky. I'm expected to be called up close to last."

"Well, you do have to consider your privilege," Brock told her. "Being a member of General St. Cloud's unit and all."

"Ha!" Aerie laughed. "The General is hardly around for me to see him, let alone talk military strategies. I was lucky he remembered to enroll me in combat class this year."

She didn't mention that his appearance at the graduation ceremony was the first time she'd seen him since the mid-quarter retreat several weeks ago.

"Others might think you are at an advantage, and it's important to make sure these things are fair," Brock said.

"Are you feeling okay?" Aerie asked with a frown. "You're sounding an awful lot like my instruction manual on how to be an officer, instead of my comrade."

"Aerie, come on," Brock muttered. "We're graduates now. You know as well as I do that the facts are not more important than feelings on this sort of matter; in fact, that's pretty close to breaking the State Codes. That's how the laws are here."

Aerie sighed. "Speaking of facts," she said. "I heard a rumor that you were going to take someone from our class to the Military Academy Ball." She smiled again, trying to bat her eyelashes the way her older roommate and sister, Serena, did when flirting with one of her many admirers.

"I do have an idea of who I'd like to ask, if I get in," Brock said. He gave her a kind smile—*the first one all day from him*, she pathetically noted—and winked at her.

Aerie felt her heart race as she wondered if he was going to ask her to the ball then and there.

The rush of possibility was instantly derailed.

"I'm waiting. If I ask anyone to the ball, I'd hope she would be accepted into the academy, too."

"You wouldn't just want to ask any girl?" Aerie asked, surprised. "Even if she didn't get in?"

"Nearly all our classmates are hoping to get into the academy," Brock reminded her. "If I ask someone who didn't get it, can you imagine how awkward it would be to explain to everyone else at the ball why she didn't get in?" He shook his head. "It would be an insult."

"Not for your company," Aerie told him wistfully.

"It's no matter now. I haven't been accepted yet."

"You don't think you'll get in?" Aerie playfully risked punching his shoulder. "Come on, no one is going to get in if you don't. You've got the highest scores and your final presentation was phenomenal, I heard."

"Well, General Sootan and General Tanner were both very interested in my analysis of hand-to-hand fighting techniques from the pre-war era of the Old Republic," Brock admitted, some color coming to his cheeks.

Finally, Aerie mused. A topic she could get him to focus on that didn't make her angry in the process. "Oh, I heard it was the best!"

"Did you really?" Brock grinned. "Well, I do want to look into climbing up through the ranks of the military quickly. Maybe all that research will come in handy." He nodded toward the towering profile of Captain Chainsword. "Especially if that traitor decides to come and visit us. I'd love the chance to prove he's not a ghost."

"Let's not talk about him," Aerie said. "He's an unpleasant topic." There was more than one reason Aerie did not want to talk about Captain Chainsword. For all the scornful derision she saw in his picture's gaze, she could not shake the feeling he was more than just an enemy.

She'd heard the stories, the rumors—the ones the URS *never* encouraged. They said he'd been betrayed by those closest to him, and died of a broken heart more than the bullet that pierced it.

How evil did you have to be before the people who knew you best betrayed you? Aerie wondered. She shuddered at the thought, thinking of her own unit. They would not be happy to know she had been listening to rumors again.

"All right." Brock shrugged. "If you don't want to. I wouldn't want to make you uncomfortable on purpose." He cleared his throat. "Tell me again, what did you present on for the URS General Education Board?"

"I was given the assignment on weaponizing pollen," Aerie reminded him. "Master Harrick thought I would enjoy that topic since it was on plants. She thought weaponizing them would be a fun project for me, since I wanted to go into the military."

"What did you find out?" Brock asked politely.

"Nothing, really. It's a terrible idea, so I researched plant generations instead. It's really quite—"

"What?" Brock rounded on her. "You defied the Board's orders for your assignment?"

"I gave them a better one," Aerie insisted. "Breeding plants for war might not be technically chemical warfare, but it is still—"

"You *defied an order*," Brock interrupted.

"Come on, Brock. It's a matter of taking initiative. Besides, they seemed to like what I—"

"Aerie, I thought you *wanted* to get into military school," Brock interrupted.

"I do," Aerie insisted.

"You can't defy an order and expect to get into the URS Military Academy. It's just not possible."

"I thought *you* were supposed to be my friend, Brock."

"I am," he agreed hastily. "We are comrades for life."

"Then why are you being so difficult today?" Aerie countered. *This discussion is rapidly turning sour.*

"*I'm* the one being difficult?" Brock looked astounded. "You're the one who has defied an order set by the council. Do you think they'll let you slide into the academy I've worked my whole life to get into simply because you're the General's charge?"

"No," she snapped.

"And now you're denying you'll use the only possible privilege you have in getting what you want?"

"I don't believe in the whole 'privilege' concept when it comes to my unit," Aerie told him matter-of-factly. "I told you, I've barely seen the General since he was promoted to the URS's National Guard ten years ago after the last dictator retired—"

"The military academy has standards for a reason," Brock

insisted, ignoring her arguments.

"Well, I have standards, too," Aerie declared. "And I am not going to *stand* for this conversation anymore." With that, she turned on her heel and walked away, not even bothering to salute him before she left.

It was for the best. If she'd bowed to him, she would have been too tempted to spit on his perfectly shined shoes.

The nerve of him. Aerie clenched her fists. Why did he have to ruin her good mood?

She'd known Brock for many years, and they were friends, as he said. He helped her with her training, while she invited him over for dinner. She had even let him borrow the General's written accounts of his early-career battles against the Middle Eastern Nuclear Arms Coalition and Enterprise, also known as MENACE. The history of the nuclear attacks on the United Nations of America and her allies in the books were perfect for his studies, and Brock must have known books were still extremely rare, given the decimation of trees and plants since the Old Republic war began.

At that thought, she turned around and headed in the other direction, suddenly inspired.

Aerie checked the time on her wristwatch; it wouldn't do to be late for her final PAR.

Her stress gradually lessened as she climbed up through the back stairways and ducked inside the old air duct.

Finding her way up to the surface followed naturally after all her previous visits.

Aerie might have said, though in jest because she knew it was forbidden, that something supernatural seemed to call her attention to the secret way above ground.

She breathed in the air, unpurified and untreated, and smiled brightly before pushing the top of the duct portal free of its locked position.

And then she stepped out into what was left of New Hope's above-ground world.

The years of toxic rain, sharpened by nuclear attacks, ate at the metal and cement, leaving the city pockmarked with rust and rot. Rather than abandon it, the citizens of the Union of North America followed the rats underground, forsaking sunlight rather than their home. Aerie had heard the legend of New Yorkers, and she wondered at it, because as passionate as they were about their home, she felt somewhat trapped by their pride. Once the URS was born from UNA's remains, they continued the practice, enforcing it as part of the rule of law.

Which made sense in many cases. After all, their civilization could only survive if they were safe.

She made her way down the empty blocks, where occasionally a few homeless people were snuggled into corners, some crippled, some rejected by the government below.

None of them ever seemed to make a move to talk to her, for which she was partially grateful and partially saddened.

Aerie scanned her surroundings but did not see any other people around. She felt her excitement renew itself as she finally saw what she'd come for—the Memory Tree.

Nearly eighty feet tall, the grand oak tree had been a signature site in the city before war and ecological disaster had drastically transformed the outside world. While the rest of the manmade world around her looked decrepit, rusting over and wasting away, the tree seemed unaware that it was supposed to be dying as well.

Her steps increased in speed as she set her eyes on her intended destination. The tree was a survivor, and Aerie could more than identify with the loneliness accompanying the privilege of living in a broken world.

A small *mew!* sang out, calling to her.

"Moona!" Aerie reached down and picked up the small kitten at her heels. She petted the soft, black-and-white ball of fur before burying her face in it. The dirt clinging to its hair bristled her cheeks, but Aerie didn't mind. She was just glad to see Moona had survived, even if the cat's white coat was no match for city life. "I've missed you."

It had been awhile since she'd come back to see Moona

and the Memory Tree. At least two weeks.

"I've been busy with schoolwork," she told the kitten as she hoisted her up on her shoulder. "I have my PAR later today, but then I'll be finished with school."

"Mew," the cat replied.

"I should be able to come up here more frequently after I get accepted into the Academy," Aerie said. "As long as my father—sorry, the General—doesn't pay much attention to me." She paused. "Which he shouldn't, considering Dictator Osgood told us that Captain Chainsword's ghost is on his way to New Hope. That should keep him busy for a while."

The kitten purred in agreement next to her, and Aerie laughed, the sound hollow and strange against the silence of the rotting city remnants. The wind tickled against the Memory Tree, the only remaining tree in all of New Hope, and Aerie decided that was the tree's way of giving her a friendly response. She was near enough she could see the small breeze fluttering through its branches, making some of the burnt-brown leaves crinkle a small hello.

She finally reached the tree. "Hello, my friend," she whispered. Her hands reached down and pressed into the soil, studying its texture and the different sediments she found around the tree's roots.

"It's still doing well," she observed in wonder. "Even though the URS has been reporting higher concentrations of toxins lately." Aerie suddenly wished she'd brought her gardening tools and sampling kit. As much as she knew it was frivolous, Aerie had always loved working with her mother's small garden and learning different ways to care for plants.

Before she ended up dwelling on her final project, and Brock's unpleasant comments, Aerie shifted Moona to her arm and carried her like a small baby as she approached the tree.

Moona hissed in futile protest.

"Sorry," Aerie told her, "but if you're going to climb the tree with me, you're going to have to trust me."

The kitten gave only a hardened silence for a reply as

Aerie climbed up the spotted branches of the tree swiftly. It had been several months since she found this place; she knew instinctively which branches would hold her weight and which ones would be strengthened if only the sun would shine through the clouds.

She found her favorite branch about forty feet up from the ground and settled against the trunk. The leaves on the underside of the tree twinkled green at her, while the topside ones were a dark, rusty-looking brown.

"From here, Moona, you can almost see past the city's horizon," Aerie said. "I think Mom would've liked this place."

Moona yawned and curled up once more, kneading her paws into Aerie's leg.

"I miss her," Aerie admitted aloud. "Mom would have loved coming up here. I still take care of her small garden, you know."

Aerie giggled as the kitten stretched. "I know I'm not supposed to call her that, you know. But somehow 'Madame' or 'Unit Director' didn't seem right." She frowned. "She told me in secret, when I was old enough, I could call her 'Mom,' but then nothing else really fit. The General would punish me if he heard me call her that in front of anyone else. To say nothing of what he would do if he found me here."

Having grown up in the heart of the State, Aerie knew her allegiance to the State came first. But somehow, her loyalty to her mother insisted on taking those risks, and as time went on, it was more natural to do so.

A pungent smell wafted into Aerie's nose. Her eyes, already damp with unshed tears, flickered shut. "Something stinks," she muttered. She moved a reluctant Moona away and stood up, glancing around. *Was it rain?* Aerie glanced up at the sky.

"Captain Chainsword's ghost is supposed to be joining us here in New Hope," Aerie told Moona. "I wonder if this means the URS is going to launch an attack of its own?"

Probably.

It's what I would do, she thought. *Tell all the people to stay underground, and then blame all the blasts and booms on the enemy.*

Not that the URS would lie to their people, unless it was for their own good, she thought with a pinch of guilt.

Aerie gave the tree a loving pat as she scooped up Moona and tucked her into one of her coat pockets. "Sorry, Moona," she apologized. "But we'd better go. Between the rain and warfare, you'll be safer with me. We'll come back when it's clear."

The small kitten squirmed in initial protest, but once she realized the inside of Aerie's uniform jacket was dark and cozy, she settled down and went to sleep.

Aerie grinned, knowing it would be her last smile for some time. The URS required seriousness in all matters, it seemed. There was little time for fun and laughter.

When survival is the endgame, she thought, there is nothing funny.

She took one last look around, grateful for the small moments she had to herself; the city was far from peaceful, but being topside had settled her heart and renewed her determination to make a difference.

"Hold on, Moona," she muttered, before jumping skillfully into the abandoned air duct. "War might be coming, but even that can't stop me from getting into the Military Academy today."

♦4♦

Exton knew from his studies that the earth had once shone with a crystal blue, brown, and green face, covered with a sporadic white veil of clouds. As the *Perdition* passed through the ocean of satellites and other space electronics, including the Old Republic's International Space Station, he looked through the windshield of the *Perdition* and wondered if it ever would return to its previous state.

"Probably not," he murmured to himself, sickened yet transfixed by the sight before him. Flickers of grisly auroras snaked along the poles, shielding the darkened earth below while a relentless cloud cover, reaching from the Tropic of Cancer to the Tropic of Capricorn, sheltered the middle of the world, almost like a serpent had wound its way around the earth several times and was slowly squeezing it to death. He could clearly recall the gray underbelly of the beast from his days training in the URS.

"We've reached our intended altitude, Captain." Tyler Caldwell, the ship's Commander and his new brother-in-law, turned toward him. Before Exton could reply an affirmative response, Tyler frowned.

"What is it?" Exton asked.

"Did you just come from the Biovid?" Tyler asked.

"Uh … no."

"Really? Because you're tracking mud behind you."

Exton frowned. "Ignore it," he ordered. "And call for Olga. Tell her to send a crewmember to come and take care of it once I'm done here."

"Yes, Captain." Despite the exchange, Tyler smiled before he continued with his report. "I've put down the anchor on the ship's electro-fission core."

"Very good," Exton commended. "See to the preparations of Captain Chainsword's capsule."

"Already completed." Tyler pointed to another screen nearby. "Emery says everyone is ready to go down on the launch pad. The preflight tests are completed, the atmosphere's been checked … our analyst, Thora, says there is a storm brewing west of New Hope and moving eastward. It should work to our advantage, with the rain hitting their military base. Central and Western regions of the URS are clear."

"Excellent." Exton nodded. "Have them prepare a place for me on the ship."

Tyler raised his brows. "You're going to go down to Earth with them?"

"Surely you don't think just because you're married to my sister now, you think it's fine to challenge my decisions?"

"I've almost always challenged your decisions," Tyler reminded him. "As do most members of the Ecclesia. But you know we're always leery when you return to Earth."

"I know, and it never seems to stop me," Exton replied. He looked at the newest member of his family and faltered. Tyler was not just his best friend now; he was family, and family was family.

In all fairness, Exton knew he couldn't have asked for a better addition. Tyler had been at his side in the URS, and he'd been the first to rally behind Exton as captain of the *Perdition.*

But even as Tyler gave his fealty, Exton could see the uncertainty lingering behind his gaze.

"This is the tenth anniversary, Tyler. I want to honor my father," Exton explained. "I always go."

Tyler sighed. "I know." He ran a hand through his blond hair in frustration. "I guess this means I'm stuck at the helm, right?"

"You already knew that," Exton pointed out in a flat tone. "That's your job as Flight Commander."

"Jared's been coming along nicely with his flying exams," Tyler countered. "I could let him pilot the ship for a bit and come with you guys."

Behind them, a young man close to twenty years of age suddenly jolted and straightened upright, hearing his name. Exton shot a nod in the boy's direction. "The capsule crew has been briefed on the mission. I'll need you to keep *Perdition* targeted on the eastern point of New Hope."

"New Hope?" Tyler repeated. Several crewmembers suddenly glanced over in his direction, their eyes wide or mouths open.

Exton almost laughed at the sight, but decided against it. *No need to give them a reason to doubt me*, he thought. "Yes. *Perdition* will align to the coordinates of the city as we pass it in thirty minutes," he instructed. "I think a short stop will be enough to completely devastate and demoralize the URS this year."

He turned and walked out, knowing there were several delayed, robotic salutes and soft whispers following him.

"Captain," Tyler called, stepping up beside him. They headed down the tight hallways, with Exton only half a step in front of Tyler.

"I don't want to discuss this with you, Tyler," Exton told him. "I've already made up my mind."

"But I thought—" Tyler stopped, before he glanced around and lowered his voice. "I thought you were dead set against using the nukes."

Exton balked. "We're not going to use them. I didn't say we were, did I?"

"No, but how else would you 'completely devastate and demoralize' the URS?"

"When you are going up against an enemy," Exton told him, "and there is no winning him over, no agreeable compromise, and no possible way to get what you want, then what do you do?"

Tyler just stared at him, frowning.

"You crush his heart," Exton answered. "That is what we're going to do."

"How?"

"The same way we do our usual business—with charges and chainsaws. I've got a prize in mind, and I'll need the *Perdition* ready for backup."

"You know, Emery's worried about you."

The admission came out of nowhere. While it might have upset him, Exton was secretly pleased. Tyler had run out of logical arguments, so he was going to try to appeal to his softer emotions. *Nice try*, Exton thought. "My sister has already expressed her concern for me. I assured her there is no great need for it."

"But don't you think—"

"No, I don't think; I know." Exton's mouth twisted into a painful smile. "My heart is already crushed, remember? There's no need to worry for something that's already been lost."

As Tyler stumbled behind him, Exton kept walking, stopping only when he came to the deck elevator. "But the bombs—"

"I wouldn't worry about it, Tyler."

"You can't order me around like you do everyone else," Tyler insisted. "I'm not only your friend, but I was your partner in this business long before we knew what we were getting into."

"If you must know, we need some more supplies," Exton grumbled. "So I thought this was an excellent chance to kill two birds with one stone."

"You're sure you're not going to do anything crazy?"

"Crazy?" Exton repeated as he stepped into an elevator. "Oh, it'll be crazy. But I do promise it's not quite as extreme as you think. In fact, it'll be similar to our other missions."

"Well," Tyler remarked, clearly annoyed, "that's a relief."

Exton smiled at the sarcasm before the doors closed, and he found himself descending down to Level Ten, where the ship's transport hangar was located.

The hangar design had been smart, and the secret launch pad was nothing short of pure genius. While the *Perdition* had been modeled in mostly astronomic style, the aeronautic design allowed for full and efficient use in a four-dimensional flying field.

Emery came up beside him. "I know you're dramatic and everything, but it's things like this that the others and I don't like."

"Dramatic? I'm not dramatic."

Emery arched an eyebrow at him. "Yes, you are, Exton. Don't you think the ghost of Captain Chainsword is proof of that?"

She has me there. Exton gave her a playful sneer. "Speaking of which, I think it's time he made his appearance."

Pain, heady and nostalgic, shot through him as Exton remembered how proud and seemingly invincible their father was.

He quickly and quietly shook off his angry grief. There were more important things to worry about, after all.

It was only fitting that he would lead the crew down and steal the "hope" right out of New Hope.

Emery waved over to one of the cadets, a pretty, blonde-haired girl named Alice, who immediately came forward. In her hands was a large black bag. As Alice neared Emery and Exton, he could see the glowing smile on her face.

He sighed. Every year, more and more girls on the ship attempted to get his attention, and every year he found it more and more tiresome.

"Thank you, Alice," Emery said, saluting the girl as she reached for the bag. "That will be all." Alice's smile caved at being shooed away, but Emery paid no attention to her as she thrust the bag into Exton's arms.

As he hurried to catch it, Exton caught the look of triumph on his sister's face. He decided to let her savor it. *For now.*

"Well, there you go," Emery retorted.

He opened the bag and pulled out the familiar pirate hat. "You don't think this makes me look dashing?" he asked, putting it on his head.

"It's a romantic notion," Emery admitted, "but with the wig and the outfit, it's hardly close to what I would call dashing."

"It goes well with the weaponry, though," Exton told her, indicating the large portrait of Captain Chainsword's iconic weapon on the capsule's starboard side. "And it's a nice tribute to Papa."

She wrinkled her nose. "I'm not sure he would agree with the chainsaw sword."

"He liked it when I made a smaller one when we were younger, when we would go collect wood for building houses and boats."

"I don't think he intended you to actually threaten people with it."

"If you want to talk about actually threatening people, maybe I should send you down to have a nice chat with Dictator Osgood so he can tell you how he runs the States."

"Ha! I'd likely murder the man."

Exton sneered. "Good to see you're not against using force where force is due, Em."

"We are called to protect," Emery reminded him.

"And that's exactly what I'm going to do. I'm going to protect us."

"While provoking others."

"Well, there's always a price to pay when it comes to our pleasures, isn't there?" Exton asked. "Speaking of which, you did send out that message to Osgood, right?"

"Yes, I did send the message," Emery informed him. She frowned. "I'd hardly believe that this is a pleasure for you, Exton."

"Avenging our father is the only thing that can possibly give me any pleasure at all," Exton argued. "Dressing up as a the ghost of a fearsome space pirate while we knock out their satellites and play games with their weapon systems is hardly what I would call fun, I'll give you that, but there's nothing else like it." He tugged at the hat on his head, straightening it determinedly.

"You need to find something more amusing to do, Exton," Emery scolded. "Or maybe less amusing, depending."

"I'll have to work on that."

Emery frowned. "Your cynicism is just awful to deal with

some days, you know."

"My cynicism is the only thing that's really working to save people," Exton defended himself. "That's the reason we have the Biovid and the Ark, if you recall."

"Your intentions might be noble, if they weren't cloaked in causing so much trouble for the URS and everyone on Earth."

"Two things, Em. One, the URS has caused many more problems for Earth more than I have caused."

"They had a head start," Emery objected.

Exton ignored her. "And two, if I believed they were capable of change, do you think I would have gone through such drastic measures to fight them?"

"They did kill Papa," Emery reminded him. "That was enough of a reason for you to defect."

"And you as well."

"Yes, me as well." Emery sighed. "But—"

"Instead of this," Exton said, "I could have infiltrated their ranks, picked off our father's executioner, and worked to change the regime's views. But not only did they rob us of our father once they killed him, all true hope for regeneration died with him. Papa was the idealist. They have no interest in letting people's lives flourish; the URS just wants control, and we've seen how they've managed to keep it."

"I know," Emery bit back. "But still—"

"Still nothing." Exton shook his head. "This is the best chance we have to change the fate of the world, along with our own. They are done listening to the people. We must force them to listen."

Emery threw up her hands in exasperation. "I know."

"Yes, and I know you don't like combat. But we must fight. There are only two possible outcomes for us while we're out here on the *Perdition*, and neither of them are fun."

"Only two?"

"Yes," Exton asserted. "We will beat them, or they destroy us. But either way, we will live free."

"There might be other outcomes," Emery insisted.

"We're working on several other projects, and the Ecclesia has recruited several people for our cause."

"You're Papa's girl, through and through, with that idealism."

"Better than your cynicism."

"I disagree with that, but I will concede there's always a third possibility of sabotage," Exton considered. "That's another reason the pirate shtick is a good cover."

"Really?" Emery snorted. "How's that, exactly?"

"The fear's in the name, in the unknown."

Emery frowned. "I guess if we're going to go, you'd better get ready for takeoff." She nodded toward the bag and then, with one last sigh, headed off to start the launch.

Exton felt his fingers grip the bag even more tightly. Anticipation pulsated through him, and he knew, for the briefest moment, why the Ecclesia believed in the miraculous.

It was time.

♦5♦

It was time.

"Comrade St. Cloud!"

Aerie flinched as she heard her name called out just as she managed to slip back into the education center.

Looks like I'm not going to have time to drop Moona off somewhere safe, she thought with a grimace. She fervently hoped none of the Generals would notice the slight bulge in the side of her uniform as she made her way to the conference room.

She spied Brock in the crowd, talking with all of his fans excitedly. *No doubt reveling in his new position in the military academy*, she thought.

For a small second, she considered dropping Moona off with him, but immediately thought better of it.

He'd probably turn me in at this rate.

Tasting bile as she recalled their earlier conversation, Aerie strutted past him and his friends, blatantly ignoring them as she headed toward the small classroom where the Board of Generals would decide her fate.

A PAR, a Performance Assessment Review, was necessary at the end of every year of education for each student of the URS. Members of the Board of Generals, along with a schoolmaster or instructor, examined her collective school file, with records ranging from primary school to the completion of her educational career. They would question her regarding classwork, behavior, expectations, and federal laws.

After the final year, her eighteenth year, the Board would collectively consider and decide a future for her. She could end up in the working field, furthering her education, or going into the military.

Given her scores in her training and academic grades, Aerie rightfully anticipated a spot at the New Hope Military Academy. *I could even be assigned as one of the Emergency Responders, too*, she recalled, thinking of Osgood's speech at the graduation ceremony.

Her assurance increased as three top Generals—including her father—asked questions she answered with confidence and aplomb.

Aerie's first dose of doubt came when her general education teacher, Master Harrick, cleared her throat and spoke up at the end of the questioning.

Master Harrick did not have to raise her voice to command attention. As she stood, each of the generals seated around their table looked to her in expectancy.

"Comrade St. Cloud has been an excellent student when it comes to academia. This is part of the reason, rather than support her in her decision to pursue a military career path, I decline in favor of sending her to a university for further study."

Aerie smiled in relief when General St. Cloud, her father, frowned. "I do not agree."

I'll pay Master Harrick back for her impertinence one day, Aerie vowed angrily and silently, as the Master Instructor once more took her seat.

She was glad that her father had stood up against the teacher.

The General continued, "I recommend Comrade St. Cloud for immediate entrance into the working class."

"What?" Aerie gasped. The teacher's betrayal she could handle, but the General's denouncement of her dream was too much for her to remain silent. "But I don't want to do that!"

The other two generals suddenly nodded. "I see what you meant earlier," the one muttered as he thoughtfully stroked his beard.

"What are you talking about?" Aerie demanded to know.

"Comrade," General St. Cloud intoned. "Your PAR examination has revealed you have had several slips in character and your decision-making process. In the past, this was generally regarded as a phase, but this year in school has shown you are reluctant to grow out of it."

"I still don't know what you are talking about," Aerie

grumbled.

"Your final presentation to the board would be a good starting point." His eyes, a shade darker than her own amber-colored eyes, burned into her.

"That's ridiculous. All reports pointed to disastrous outcomes if we started breeding poisons into pollen. My research on promoting plant growth in hostile environments was much safer *and* beneficial to society." She took a step forward daringly. She knew they had to see her courage and insight for survival, rather than destruction, would serve the nation better.

"That's not the point of an assignment," the other general, General Lowell, said. "The point of an assignment is to follow orders. How would this look on a battlefield if we were to command you?"

"In the heat of battle, just like in doing research, circumstances change," Aerie argued. "You would do better to have someone who can react and adapt to the battlefield than someone who is blindly awaiting orders!"

"That's enough, Comrade!"

"You are students of warfare, not students in botany and horticulture. Weaponizing pollen seeds to spout poison would easily cause the collapse of *all* plant life and humanity. Allowing plants to adapt to the hostile environment on the surface of the earth, and helping them to grow, can help return the Earth to a fully habitable world. Several of my samples can even be used to help reverse-engineer cures for plant toxins. My project is not only more beneficial, but it went well beyond the requirements for the one given to me."

"Comrade St. Cloud has done exceptionally well in her gardening and horticulture electives," Master Harrick inserted, before the generals could respond.

"There is no need for a first-year working class graduate to worry about bigger projects," another general, General Zike, announced. "I also do not agree with your decision to pursue a military career at this time."

"Nor do I," General St. Cloud agreed.

"I see the merit of your demeanor," the final general, General Lowell, admitted, still rubbing his beard. "But following orders are foundational to any military concern. You have been training for this from the first day you entered into the Secondary Education Center's program at twelve." He nodded toward the Master Instructor. "I agree with your instructor in this. Further education might help society more than your combat skills—"

"But my combat skills are in the top ten percent of my class!" Aerie argued. "Top five, even."

General Lowell eyed her grievously. "As I was saying, you might benefit the URS more by going to university to learn more than going into the combat field, where your training has left much to be desired." His gaze softened. "Your research, while it is incorrect and against the rules, is underscored by a deep passion. I have to confess, I do not understand your desire to go to the military. While you are proficient in combat, your efforts are markedly different from your scholarly pursuits, especially in your scientific courses."

Aerie slumped over and stepped back, her posture one of defeat while her disposition was one of defiance. Strands of her hair, shining like fire against the bright lighting, caught her eye; the pins she'd meticulously stabbed into her head that morning were coming loose, along with her patience.

"If her disposition is this combative, perhaps we should consider the Reeducation Program," General Zike commented.

Aerie's eyes shot up, burning with rage as she looked at the man sitting next to her father.

Reeducation was a program designed for the most difficult of students. They were rigorously given repetitive orders until their full will was broken and given over to the State. *And done so rightfully*, Aerie added to herself, more out of reluctant duty than personal agreement.

"Such a process is likely too extreme," General St. Cloud observed calmly.

Aerie said nothing; she thought he'd taken her side

against the Master Instructor earlier, only to find out he was ready to punish her even more severely. She doubted he was *actually* trying to help her this time.

There is no point in getting disappointed more than you have to, Aerie decided.

"I advocate for placing her in the Communication Sector," General St. Cloud proposed. "Relaying information, finding solutions for different parties, and following instructions are all critical skills. We could easily have her learn her place while allowing her to fulfill her desire for more autonomy."

Aerie watched as the rest of the General Board shuttered, no doubt at the thought of personal responsibility.

The Master Instructor was the only one who nodded in agreement. "Her mind, while proficient in her studies, is unaccustomed to outside discipline. Working in the Communication Sector would help provide the necessary structure she would need to become a beneficial soldier later on," the teacher theorized. "Not to mention, working in that sector, with the demand for addressing complaints and concerns from the different regions of the State, she might overcome her persistent propensity to daydream."

Anger and shame reddened Aerie's cheeks, as several memories of getting punished for daydreaming in class automatically ran through her mind.

The General nodded. "It is another trait of hers that is ill-suited for combat and military life."

Aerie felt the last of her optimism crumble. Rage and anger, injustice and defeat, all took their toll on her as she stood there.

There has to be a way out of this. I am not going to do this on their terms.

She stepped forward once more. "Generals, I shall accept your decision." And then, without waiting to be dismissed, without saluting anyone, she turned on her heel and headed out the door.

Regret sank in as soon as the door shut behind her; she

argued with herself, finally deciding it was okay to allow herself a form of tame revolt.

Besides, Aerie thought, it wasn't as if she would have a choice to follow through on their decision. At least this way she could claim it was her choosing, rather than their commanding.

Wouldn't it be nice to believe this was a way to have some freedom? Aerie thought deviously. Freedom, or personal responsibility, was strongly discouraged by the State. When freedom was present, there was always the chance something could go wrong.

Aerie agreed with that, but the more she visited the world on the topside of the soil, the more she suspected freedom wasn't as bad as the Generals and Dictator Osgood made it sound.

Of course, she recalled bitterly, *there were people like Captain Chainsword who had to ruin it for everyone else*. Maybe if he wasn't around, the URS could actually let people choose the careers they wanted, rather than allowing them to pursue the path they were most likely to succeed in.

Immediate guilt set in.

There is no need to be treasonous because of a rough day.

A louder voice in the back of her head screamed that this was no mere "rough day," and she was allowed to have thoughts of her own, independent of the State's approval.

Aren't I? Aerie wondered, surprised she wasn't sure of the answer.

"Aeris!"

The voice of the General behind her made her snap to attention. She stopped in her tracks, not daring to turn around to face him.

He came up beside her and crossed his arms over his chest. "I suppose you think that was clever, leaving early?"

"No, sir," Aerie lied.

"You're lucky they all agreed Reeducation was too harsh of a punishment. Not to mention inefficient."

"I'm sorry to hear I caused disappointment."

"I've heard that line from you enough to know you don't really mean it."

"What do we *ever* mean down here, anyway?" Aerie scoffed. "We're told what to do, not *why*."

"Humanity has longed for these days, Aeris," the General replied. His eyes narrowed with confident scorn. "The best life possible is not only *easy* to achieve, but it is fulfilling. And there is more to come."

"By following orders?" Aerie asked. She wrinkled her nose. "How would you even know that to be true?"

"The State says it is true, and it has kept us alive," the General asserted. "We owe our allegiance to the State for everything it has done for us, and with the opportunities we have with the next stage of development, we will have even more, Aeris. Safety, resources, influence, and power. We owe more than our lives to the State for these, myself included. And you, too. As a result, you will obey your orders."

"But I don't really want to go work in the Comms Sec," Aerie argued. "I want to be free to make that choice myself."

"Freedom is dangerous," the General growled. "Fairness is better."

She blinked back tears. "I wanted to get into the military. I wanted to make you proud of me."

For the first time Aerie could ever remember, her father's eyes softened. "Aeris …"

"And I wanted to show the rest of the family unit, too," she added. "They're never going to take me seriously if I work in communications."

The General's gaze corrected its lapse. "It would be no more than you deserve," he said, shocking her with his cold tone. "You were lucky that I was there to protect you, otherwise the State *would* have punished you. They know, Aeris, about your visits to the Memory Tree."

Aerie knew from the General's expression her eyes easily betrayed her guilt.

"Yes, I know about that," he said. He gestured to the lump in her uniform. "Did you bring another cat down here?"

"No," Aerie quickly lied, mentally shouting at Moona to remain still. She put a protective hand over the bulge and said, "I had to pick up … some female things from our unit's storage today."

He frowned. "After you brought the last cat down, I had to file all sorts of papers to make sure you would graduate. Director Phoebe was angry."

"I didn't know about that," Aerie admitted softly, grimacing further at thought of displeasing her stepmother. Phoebe was a kind and gentle figure, so mindlessly graceful her presence was often overlooked, even by her husband and stepchildren.

"Listen, Aeris," the General said. "You are much more like your mother"—his jaw tightened and his face flushed over at his use of the term—"than me and the rest of us in the housing unit. She liked plants and animals too, and that was why they put her in the marriage career program. They thought her talent in nurturing would make her a good breeder."

He paused, glaring at her. "I know how you feel about that particular career. You're lucky you didn't end up there."

Aerie knew the General was right. *I don't want to end up in a situation like Mom did, or what Phoebe has to deal with now. What is the point of having a marriage if you aren't loved?*

Shame colored her cheeks. Love wasn't necessary for survival; it was just a poor term for pleasure in many cases.

Well, if you're not going to have pleasure from a family, why have one anyway?

Her familiar confusion with her thoughts about the unit/family situation were wiped away as her father continued.

"—heard Dictator Osgood earlier. We're up against a persistent enemy, and we need to focus on survival. Completely changing the project you are assigned by the State is wrong," he insisted. "You cannot win by making up your own rules."

"This isn't supposed to be a game," Aerie argued.

"Survival is not a game," he agreed, "so stop treating it like one."

"I'm not!"

"Fine. Then you will put in your time for your disintegration and nonconformity. You will work at the Comms Sec, and if you put in a good year of it, I will see to it that you have another chance to petition for the Military Academy."

"A whole year?"

That long?!

"It would be good for you, Aeris," he told her, surprising her with a softened, almost sympathetic, tone. "There have been a lot of developments with our communications program. The URS just released the newest version of NETech."

"NETech? You mean the NET?" Aerie asked. She frowned, recalling the various lectures she had attended on it. The technology had been specially designed with her horticulture instructor, Master Specter, as a lead consultant on the project.

"Yes. With your background in research and plants, it would be good for you to go and work with the Comms Sector. It's being further integrated in our battle gear as we speak." The General sighed. "That, of course, is classified information. But it could change our situation with the ghost of Captain Chainsword and our other enemies. Caledon and Dorian have tested it. Serena's even used it for Med Comms. I want you to get in where you can help not only the URS, but our unit as well."

The General's reasoning, while it was intended to make her feel better (she assumed), didn't sound promising. Instead, it made her feel used.

"Starting tomorrow, at 800 hours, young lady. Go get the address and stop by the uniform center for a proper worker's suit before you leave."

Aerie ducked her head in shame and reluctant obedience.

What other choice do I have? "Yes, sir."

"I'll see you in the dining hall with the other unit members. We'll celebrate your graduation and assignment."

"I'm not hungry."

"The rest of our unit will find out your assignment soon enough," the General told her. "You might as well show some humility. Remember, there is no reason to feel as though you have failed. You will be placed in a job where you will be of most use to the Revolutionary States until you will be considered for reassignment."

"I still don't want to eat with the family."

"Aeris."

The warning made her dip her head in quick apology. The terminological difference between "family" and "unit" had been permanently sealed off for discussion.

"I should hate to think you deserve to go to the Reeducation Center after all," the General remarked. Then surprisingly, his voice softened. "Why don't you invite Comrade Rearden to dinner? He's your best friend, isn't he? He's a good fighter. He's been given a ship in the same pilot test program Caledon and Dorian are in."

Aerie was a bit surprised by the suggestion, and even more by the realization the General knew Brock's name.

Brock's dreams came true. Seeing him at dinner, where her unit would look on her with proud disappointment, was too much to contemplate.

Aerie slumped over as she realized she wouldn't be able to go to the ball with him without embarrassing him.

She pursed her lips together tightly before abruptly turning around and hurrying away. Tears stung her eyes, but she refused to give in to the pressure to release them.

"Aeris, wait."

"General St. Cloud, sir," a voice called out from down the hall. Aerie could see a woman in uniform headed toward him. "Victor, we need you for the next PAR."

Aerie could barely hear the General's sigh as he turned away; she didn't have to look back to know he would let her go.

After her mother had died, he always managed to find a way to leave her.

It worked out for the best. She had no intention of following orders. At least, not right away.

"Aerie!" Brock's voice called out as he came up to her and took her hand, gripping it excitedly. "Did you hear? I've been accepted into the Academy, and I've performed enough in school to get preferential treatment. I begin pilot training tomorrow!"

"That's great, Brock." Aerie pulled away from him. "You'll have to tell me all about it sometime."

"Before you know it, I'll get a chance to blast Captain Chainsword right out of the sky!"

"I'm sure you will."

"This is the best day," Brock said with a grin. "Did you get your assignment?"

"Yes," she said. "It's not exactly what I wanted."

"You can still come with me to the Academy Ball, though, right?" His hand found hers once again. "Now that everything's finally settled, I can be a bit more open with you. I was worried if I told you that I wanted to escort you to the ball earlier, your—er, General St. Cloud—might have found a way to keep me from the military."

"What are you talking about?"

His eyes widened in surprise. "General St. Cloud has certain standards for the people that he lets you spend time with. I thought it was better to make sure my career was stable before I asked you to the ball."

"Wait, the General has standards for people who spend time with me? *And* you're asking me to the military ball?" Aerie blushed. "But I'm—"

"I mean, only if it's okay with General St. Cloud, of course. I wouldn't want to upset him. You're his youngest charge, and I know he probably isn't happy about just *anyone* taking you out."

Aerie tightened her hand around his, briefly, before

letting go. "I'll have to ask him about that," she said, before the pressure behind her eyes was too much. "Excuse me."

She rushed off before he could see her cry.

♦6♦

For the longest moment of her life, all she could think about was jumping.

Aerie didn't know when she started to contemplate that idea, but once she realized it, all the hurt and disappointment that had slowly seeped into her heart reached full maturation.

"Stupid. Don't think like that. Stupid." Aerie put her head in her hands, upset but still maintaining her balance perfectly on the upper branches of the Memory Tree. Her body adjusted into the large tree's sloppy hug, the pain of the tree's ridges more comforting to her than any pleasure she'd known.

The Memory Tree was a place of happiness for her. There was nothing she loved to do more than climb its limbs, take refuge under its wide branches, and curl up beside its strong trunk.

She traced the hardened bark, letting her fingers brush over some new lichens beginning to take root along the acid stains and patches where pollution had sunken in, almost as if her mother's memory would absorb her pain.

It was supposed to be a happy day.

She recoiled with shame, playing back the events of the day: The lackluster graduation, the intolerable PAR, her father's rebuke, Brock's attempts at securing a date and a future, and the nonexistent chances of accepting his invitation to the military ball …

Ending it, permanently, would just add to the overall horror.

And there was another reason why jumping would be idiotic, she thought. The General and the rest of her family unit would know she'd done it deliberately, especially after all the times they saw her climb in combat class. Then they would have even more reasons to hide their faces from public scrutiny at her wasted death.

Especially after today, she thought. *Doomed to work in the Comms Sec!*

Thunder crackled around her, startling Moona and making Aerie flinch.

Of course.

Of course it was going to rain, and of course she'd forgotten all about that from earlier. The rest of the day had been particularly and devastatingly uncooperative. Why not the weather, too?

Aerie gazed up through the tree branches, peering at the clouds. Their shadows darkened with the oncoming night. The air was not as sharp as she would have expected, but the rumbling in the distance could only mean rain.

Someone had once said that half of Earth should have been kept safe from human activity, protected from all human interaction. If the war of the Old Republic hadn't broken out, would most of the remaining humans still have found their way underground, leaving the top of the world to be largely reclaimed by nature?

She could only wonder as the sky darkened ominously.

The buildings, covered with their rusty moss and climbing vines, reflected off fragmented beams, making the world around her into a mirror of sorts, intensifying the hollowness surrounding her.

But all the loneliness in the empty world around her was more welcoming than the prospect of eating the evening meal with her housing unit. She knew what would happen. Her two older unit members, her brothers Dorian and Caledon, would come home from the military bases where they worked, and Serena, still working through her final year of military training, would stop by long enough to pretend she had nowhere else to go. Later, she would slip away to meet up with her friends or one of her many admirers.

They would find out Aerie failed to get into the academy, as she had been proclaiming she would do since she was twelve, and spend the rest of the time making slighted and veiled jabs at her. (In-fighting was discouraged by the State.)

It was even possible Brock would stop by, as he had been a frequent guest in the past two years. After finding out she was not accepted into the military, he'd probably promptly wish her a grand life and take his leave.

He might even offer his sympathies to the General on his way out, too.

Aerie paused in her critique. He *seemed* interested in asking her to the ball. Was it possible she was judging Brock too harshly? Aerie wondered.

Was it true what her Master Instructor said? Did she daydream too much? Too much to see the real world for what it really was?

"What do you think, Moona?" she asked, petting the kitten who once more purred out pure affection in her lap.

"Mew," was the only response she received, but Aerie embraced it.

"You're right," she agreed. "There has to be more to the world than just … this." Daydreaming is necessary to see the world as it could be.

Of course, there were other nation-states under the URS. Perhaps she could go live in one of those towns. They were not as centralized or militarized as the capital. Surely, out there, among all the other regions, there were places where housing units went by the actual name of "family," and no one bothered to correct her with a tone drenched in disgust when she called it such.

But how to get there? And what would happen if she couldn't find any place to truly call home?

She sighed. It was better to live with the hope of freedom than to actually go and try to find it.

Wasn't it?

A crackle of thunder rumbled across the sky, as lightning flashed, as if to answer her question.

Aerie winced. "Come on, Moona," she said, picking up the cat. "I can't take you down to weather out the storm with me, but I can try to find you a safe place before the storm hits."

Moona objected, swiping her claws at Aerie as she tried to move her.

"Hey!" Aerie frowned. "Come on, Moona, don't be like that."

Moona hissed at her, and then launched off Aerie's shoulder, heading up higher into the tree branches.

"Come back here!" Aerie demanded. She felt the wind pick up, and thunder roared in her ears. Her fingers tingled, and suddenly fear began to trickle through her. "Moona!" Her voice nearly cracked as she called.

Aerie glanced down at the ground, and then back up at her wayward cat, weighing her options.

"Mew," the kitten replied, nearly ten feet higher up in the tree.

Aerie sighed. "Hold still," she ordered in a tight voice. "I'm coming for you."

The smug expression on the kitten's face made Aerie frown, but a moment later she emerged triumphant. "Ah-ha! Got you!"

Sirens from the Military Base suddenly began to sound.

The thunder grew sharper, and its booming dwindled down into a piercing cry. Aerie almost dropped Moona as a gust of wind blew into the buildings around her; at the last second, she swiveled around and ducked into a small dip in the Memory Tree's trunk, fighting hard to breathe as dust and shards of all materials went flying by.

Several shots and missiles plunged into the nearby buildings, sending them crashing down to the ground below.

Aerie coughed and sputtered as ash and soot were slung into her mouth. Before she could move, a fireball came sprouting up behind her. The ground trembled and shook as the dust refused to settle down.

The familiar shriek of a URS fighter jet scorched through the air above as more bombs dropped around her.

"No," she gasped, tightening her grip on the tree. Moona struggled against her, but Aerie managed to tuck the kitten into her uniform jacket once more. "Stay!" she sputtered, as she scrambled to get a better look at the sight before her.

With the wind still pummeling her, Aerie started climbing

up to the top of the branches. She glanced down to see the slightest shadow of dirt and ground. A moment of vertigo set in, and she shut her eyes. To think she'd thought about jumping not twenty minutes before!

Of course, climbing up the tree had to be just as stupid as jumping from it.

As she finally caught a glimpse of the sight before her, she knew all the reason in the world could not have stopped her when it came to satisfying her curiosity.

A gray space shuttle was speeding through the fire and wreckage toward the Memory Tree. Aerie started to scream as death came hurdling toward her.

Suddenly, the shuttle's nose opened up to reveal several serrated drills, before it launched vigorously into the ground.

For a moment, Aerie's scream went silent, choked back by uncertainty. *What is going on?!*

The New Hope Military Base was off on the other side of the city, and the education and living quarters were scattered throughout underground. The only thing of any real importance around here was …

"No!" Aerie called out, as the tree underneath her buckled and started to fall over. The shuttle's impressive power surged underground, scooping up the roots of the tree, scattering its home from the dirt, and desecrating the rocks and sediment that harbored the source of its life.

Aerie clung to the tree as it shifted under the pressure. Her hands gripped onto the smaller branches as others snapped under the applied force. She almost thought of yelling for help, but between the dashes of darkness and the spurts of light and battle, she didn't know if she would survive—or if survival was even the better option between imprisonment and torture from the ghost of Captain Chainsword and his MENACE supporters.

A gush of air rushed out of the enemy's shuttle as its payload bay doors burst open and a large excavator unfolded.

Above all the noise—the sirens, the sky fighters, the rumbling of the earth, the crying of the sky, the last tremble of the Memory Tree as its top branches snapped—nothing was able to drown out his voice.

"Crush its heart!"

Aerie felt her own heart crumble in the process, and the tears she'd clung to so ardently before were released. "No," she whispered.

Several soldiers appeared, forming a circular barrier around the tree. Their weapons, ranging from smaller guns to larger bazookas, were all trained on the jets scorching the skies around them.

Another blast sounded out from the skies as a rocket rumbled into the earth not far from her. She could feel the shake of the foundations of the remaining buildings.

Aerie screamed as she scrambled, clinging to the tree with only her fingertips as it collapsed into the upheaval of dirt and rock. A blanket of rods suddenly smashed into her back. She cried out and felt her voice drown in the surrounding fury.

The excavator grasped onto the trunk of the tree and pulled.

Something warm and familiar matted her hair. Blood, she realized, as Moona squirmed in futile rebellion, trapped inside her uniform jacket. She tried to move her legs, only to realize they were caught in a pile of mud and sticks. Even her hair was getting tangled in the floppy twigs, the sodden rust, and soft buds.

"Collect the tree," the stranger's voice called out. "To the starboard side, rotate fifty-three degrees."

"Fighters, Captain, coming in!"

A sense of the surreal overtook Aerie. The ghost of Captain Chainsword had come. She shifted slightly to her right, trying to get a good look at him. Only a tall shadow, crowned with a pirate's hat, became clear in the flashes of bombs and laser strikes, surrounded by the guard of his warriors.

"Hold them off," the captain commanded. He raised his hand, revealing his long sword, decorated with a chainsaw down its length. Energy radiated from the hilt as the chainsword ignited with power.

Aerie felt pain unleash through her as he brought down the blade, like he was cutting her heart instead of her tree.

The excavator lifted and turned again, freeing Aerie's legs but forcing her to hold on once more as the tree was hoisted into the air. "I'm sorry, my friend," she whispered as tears filled her eyes.

The chainsword continued to whir. Branches dropped and leaves were cut down. Other shadows joined in, and soon the tree was free from the ground that had been its home for centuries.

Aerie remained silent, weakening as her grip and adrenaline faded. Her enthusiasm, her usual gusto for battle, and even the sounds of the battle itself, faded as blood continued to pour out from the gash on her head.

After what seemed to be an eternity, the buzzing of the enemy's swords faded.

"Contain it," the captain ordered, "and burn the remnants and the surrounding area. Not even a seedling must remain."

Aerie felt silence once more subdue her as the tree was packed into the shuttle. Robotic arms secured it, their straps binding her legs and torso under the layer of remaining branches. Aerie was trapped.

"Pull back," the captain called. "Prepare for takeoff!"

As Moona moaned a small *mew*! from her pocket, Aerie's survival instincts kicked in and she screamed.

But the pressure of takeoff, combined with the pain of her bleeding wound, fought against her. Aerie saw her vision blur before she slipped into the nothingness of unconscious slumber.

♦7♦

Once the capsule's payload doors shut, Exton turned to his crew. "Get us out of here," he shouted to Emery, who was at the controls.

Another fighter jet was making its run on the horizon.

"Launch prep," Emery called, while her co-pilot quickly complied.

The other crewmembers buckled in after securing the Memory Tree, while Exton hurried them along. Seconds later, the capsule's boosters fired up and they were off.

Just in time to avoid getting hit with an explosive charge.

"Activate cannons," Exton called to his gunners. "Return fire only if necessary."

"Yes, Captain," came the response.

A rare feeling of relief, mingled in with the barest traces of regret, settled into Exton. He was glad when the pulsar engines roared to life and the small ship began to speed against the atmosphere.

He hadn't been expecting such a show.

Grant Osgood was known for his frugality as much as his thoroughness. *It's almost a shame to have the man as an enemy*, Exton thought. The man's principles in economy, both in power and resources, strongly aligned with Exton's own.

"We're taking on heavy fire," Emery called. "Prep for evasive maneuvers!"

But then, Osgood's survival didn't depend on the use of his resources the way he and his crew did.

Still, the fighter strikes, with their fission charges and raid bombs, were still more excessive than he'd anticipated. It was decidedly out of character for the URS Dictator.

As Emery swerved to avoid the last of the attacks and the capsule's weapons pierced the last of the oncoming missiles, Exton decided the attack warranted further investigation.

"Approaching the mother ship," Emery announced.

Was it possible that Osgood *wanted* to cause a scene? Or was he really frightened by the thought of Captain

Chainsword's ghost making a mockery of his nation?

"Prepare for landing."

Something is wrong, Exton thought. He wasn't sure what exactly, but there was something wrong.

"Setting down in three … two … one." The small ship jolted as its landing gear made contact with the inner hangar of the *Perdition.*

As the other crew members unbuckled and began moving, Exton sat still, frowning at the monitor in front of him.

"What is it?" Emery asked as she came up beside him.

"Have the Capsule's record taken up to Tactics. I want it analyzed. Something's not right."

"You know, it is possible you feel bad about attacking the URS out of revenge," Emery told him. "Guilt is an appropriate response. I can see why that would feel wrong to you."

"It's not guilt," Exton assured her. "I'm not sorry to tell you that, either," he added, looking at her scrunched-up face. "The Ecclesia doesn't approve of the attacks, and I know it, Em. Remember? I approved the measure that says you don't have to come down with me when we go."

"I might not approve of your actions," Emery said, "but I still love you, Exton. You are my only brother and I want to be by your side."

He only shrugged.

"Besides," she added with a grin, "I'm the best pilot you have onboard the *Perdition.*"

Despite his concerns, Exton grinned. "Does Tyler agree with you on that?"

"Of course. We're well aware you promoted him to Commander just to keep him busy."

When Exton said nothing, Emery sighed. "You know," she said, "you can always return the tree if you're so worried about it."

"No, we needed more water," Exton said. "We'd been running low on new water since our last run down to see

Aunt Patty. And after that, there's nothing more fitting for this tree than a sacrificial death. Might as well be one worth remembering, don't you think?"

"You always did like irony just a bit too much," Emery told him as she switched off the engine and finalized the landing process. "I'm going to make my reports up in the Command Center."

"Tell Tyler we made it just fine for me," Exton called after her. "No nukes."

As she rolled her eyes and hurried down the exit ramp, Exton nearly laughed, but the feeling of discontent had only sunken into him more deeply.

A voice came over the intercom system. "Captain, there's a problem in the cargo hold of the capsule."

"On my way," Exton muttered as he stood up, more to himself than anyone in particular.

Is it possible something went wrong when we stole the Memory Tree? Exton wondered.

When he appeared through the entrance to the cargo hold a moment later, Exton saw the few members of the capsule crew were standing, motionless, at the base of the tree's roots. "Hey," he spoke up. "Are you going to move this to the Biovid for water stripping or not?"

The crewmembers visibly flinched at his voice. One crewmember stepped forward. "It's just we were … concerned about that, Captain," he said with a repentant gulp, pointing his finger at a small pair of shadowed eyes squinting from under the base of the trunk.

Exton sighed. He tried to recall how many years the crewmembers had been with him, and that not all of them had been around animals much before joining the ship. A moment later, he gave up; there was no point in using up all his energy for patience when he could put it into action. "It's just a cat."

"A cat we have not pre-screened for any bugs or insects or diseases," another crewmember spoke up. She nodded toward the decontamination suits hanging up in the hangar.

"Should we proceed to process it, sir?"

Exton reached down and let the cat sniff his fingers. "I think we'll be okay with a simple decontamination," he said. "No need to kill it."

"But sir—"

"It's just a cat," Exton said. "Barely that, even. It looks malnourished, and in need of a bath, but I don't see the harm in—ouch!" He snatched back his hand as the kitten's claws slashed across his knuckles.

The kitten meowed and scampered up the tree branches. Exton jumped up to follow it, determined to grab it as his subordinates suppressed their smiles. "Come back here!" Exton called. "This is no time for games … "

His voice faltered as the cat ceased its run and settled down on a snapped branch. As the cat snidely flicked its tail, Exton felt his breath inhale sharply.

Underneath the branch was a woman.

"What's wrong, Captain?" the second crewmember called out.

"There's a person up here," he said, moving toward her. He knelt down and grasped at the branches, then snapped them off. "She's trapped here in the tree."

Exton pushed further in. His first impression of the woman was similar to a sprite from his books and stories as a kid; with her eyes closed, she looked just like a fairy sleeping in the crevice of the old tree. Her long red hair fanned out behind her, while her arms were limp against the trunk.

When he saw the crewmembers only glance at each other, the same surprised expression on their faces, Exton felt his anger bubble. "What are you waiting for?" he growled. "Go and retrieve a medic. See if you can get a stretcher up here for her."

The crewmembers nodded as they hustled for the nearest exit.

"Alert my sister," Exton called after them. "She'll need to see to this lady's care." He watched as they exited the ship before going back to untangling the woman from the tree's protection.

"What did you do to my tree?"

Great, she's waking up, he thought as he stifled a groan. He freed her from the overlapping branches and brackets as she stirred, trying his best to pull her out of the jumbled mess.

"Ow," she muttered. "My hair."

"I'll get it," Exton muttered. "Give me a second." He saw her hair curled around some of the smaller lichens and buds. Reaching over, he gently tugged the twigs and leaves free.

He was surprised by her hair. It seemed to have a mind of its own as he patted it down and faced its refusal. "It's like it's growing out of the tree instead of you," he said, surprised to hear his thoughts said aloud as he finished breaking off the seedlings.

Exton watched in amusement as the cat took off after the broken twigs, batting at the loosened twigs with its paws.

He carefully pulled her up to a sitting position, before attempting to pick her up and put her on her feet. She stumbled as he stood her up. Instinctively, he pulled her against his chest as he steadied her.

Something inside his heart lurched uncomfortably, almost painfully, as she stood there in his arms. "It'll be okay," he told the woman. And himself.

The last thing he wanted to feel was guilt.

He loosened his grip and looked down at her, trying to get a good assessment. The flame-red hair was the first thing he'd noticed, and not just because of the color. With her uniform identifying her as a typical URS citizen, her long hair seemed out of place. Many soldiers and students kept their hair short, to keep it out of the way. When survival mattered most, he recalled, there was little time for extravagance.

She seemed young, too, though that could have been from her size; she was at least half a foot shorter than he was.

Through the various layers of his Captain Chainsword disguise, he could feel warmth radiating from her. Was it possible she had a fever?

"Thank you," the woman murmured, her arms curling

around him, her fragile grip reminding him she needed care.

"For what?" Exton asked, belatedly recalling he did not deserve any thanks. He was the one responsible for her being there in the first place.

The grip around his chest tightened painfully. "For freeing me," she said, before slamming her foot down on his instep.

"Ouch!" Exton scrambled back, but her grip on his outer coat remained constant. He rolled back onto the trunk of the tree, just in time for her to land a new blow to his rib cage.

"Can you just calm down?" he muttered, trying not to let the flustered, angry harpy he found straddling him get the better of his pride as well as his power.

"Take that," the woman cried out as she struck out again.

Exton slid to the side just in time to feel the power of her fist fly past him. "Hold on a moment," he called, grabbing her hands. "What are you doing?"

"What I was trained to do, *Captain!*" The sarcastic reply forced out the last of any possible sympathy he might have thought he had for her.

His grip tightened on her hands as he rolled off the tree trunk, taking her with him. Exton managed to land on his feet, even as the woman launched several attacks against him.

"Nice." Impressed more than annoyed, Exton attempted to block a roundhouse kick. "I guess I can rule you out as a refugee." She caught herself before she slammed into the tree trunk after he pushed her away. "They usually aren't strong enough to put up a fight."

Especially considering you had no preparation or protection during takeoff, he added silently.

"It's good to know that the ghost of Captain Chainsword has not only a body, but a brain as well," the lady snapped, pushing back her bushel of red hair as she maintained a battle stance. "Let's see if you can bleed, too."

"You're welcome to try. You certainly wouldn't be the first Osgood underling to do so."

Her eyes finally caught his. At the sight of her golden

brown eyes, he stilled.

Her eyes were familiar and foreign all at once. The color called him to the world of his home and his youth, even as the rising fear and anger lingering behind her gaze anchored him to the present moment.

A sudden, unexpected stab of compassion sank into his heart as Emery's earlier words came back to haunt him: *We are called to protect.*

It was time to change tactics, he decided grimly. Exton took a defensive stance. "Unfortunately, that would assume that I have a heart as well," he said, giving her a mocking grin. "And that's hardly likely. I am a pirate, after all."

She followed him, lashing out another kick. He easily knocked it aside, but grunted as she landed another punch to his chest.

"Are you that determined to find out?" he asked.

"You destroyed my tree," she cried. "I'll kill you for what you've done!"

She's upset about the tree? Exton frowned as he delivered a glancing blow to her shoulder. "You might be one of Osgood's pets, but you surprise me."

She stumbled momentarily. "Why would you be surprised that a student of the URS is trying to kill you?"

"Maybe I meant that you were more poorly trained than I'd expected."

Another strike lashed out at him. "You have an advantage," she accused, "of being an old man used to space travel."

Exton almost laughed, recalling he was still in his pirate costume. "Having an advantage is supposed to be the key to survival."

"There's no honor in winning a fight like that," she bit back.

"Another reason why defecting from the URS was the best decision of my life," he told her. "When survival is the only thing that matters, there is no proper place for honor—unless you consider it a victor's prize."

She fumbled for balance as he struck her at the hip and managed to get a hold of her, trapping her between the tree and his body. "There is no prize for being a monster," she objected.

Exton met her eyes with his. "If I was truly a monster," he told her slowly, softly, "I might consider *you* my prize."

She stiffened underneath him while he allowed himself a second to contemplate that exact temptation.

"Maybe I should consider you a gift instead?" He grinned humorlessly. "I'll have to thank Osgood later, when I send the URS the usual transmission following one of my victories."

"Augh!" The anger intensified as she managed to wriggle free and lash out, landing another blow to his chest.

Exton gasped in surprise and clutched at his chest. *Third time's the charm*, he thought grudgingly as his fingers brushed over the bruised area. He sucked in his breath sharply as the pain intensified.

No doubt about it. She had bruised a rib—possibly two.

Before he could rebound or retreat, he heard a distinct gasping noise. He saw the woman with the red hair and golden eyes crumple to the floor, revealing the woman behind her.

Exton nearly laughed in relief before recalling his chest pain. "Emery."

"Exton, are you okay?"

"I'll be fine," he insisted. "What did you do to her?"

Emery held up the small injection tube in her hand. "Sedative."

"Oh. Good move. Good timing, too." Exton reclined on the floor, pulling at his costume's overcoat.

"She managed to hurt you?" Emery put down the empty plunger in her hands and hurried over to her brother, skillfully skirting around the woman she'd just knocked out.

"So it seems," Exton said. He placed his hand over his ribcage again, rubbing it as the pinching pain seized him. "All this pirate padding, and none of it seems to be effective against the venom of the URS."

Emery shook her head. "I'm torn between telling you that you deserved it and wondering if I should've gotten something more powerful than a tranquilizer."

"There's no need to kill her, especially on my account."

Before Emery could respond, the medic team came up into the cargo bay of the capsule, and Exton allowed them to fuss over him. It was preferable to answering all of his sister's questions.

Exton felt his heartbeat swell into his ears as he gazed at the woman. Everything else—one medic taking off his pirate wig, another injecting serum into his bruise, Emery alternating her conversation from how this could have happened to blaming the URS for sending an assassin up to kill him—faded as he held onto his heart and watched the woman.

It wasn't until Emery asked what he wanted to do with her that he jerked himself out of his own thoughts.

"Take her to a secure medical ward," he heard himself say. "I want to ask her more questions after I chat with General St. Cloud and his fearless Daddy Dictator."

"Are you sure about that, Exton?" Emery inquired. "She could be dangerous." She nodded pointedly at the swelling bruise on the left side of his chest, as the medic finished covering it a cooling patch.

"What else would you have me do with her?" Exton asked. "Leave her here or throw her overboard, maybe? She's not a refugee, and she's not a recruit. Besides a decent fighter, I'm not really sure what she is."

"She's clearly a cadet," one of the medics said as he began taking note of her vitals. "The uniform alone stands out, as her social rank and educational achievements are displayed on her collar."

"Let me see," Emery ordered.

"I figured that much out," Exton said grudgingly. "I didn't think she was an assassin."

"She's a graduate," Emery announced, holding up the

ranking badges. "Not in university, not in military."

"It is close to graduation time for the secondary levels," the other medic spoke up in a timid voice. "That was part of the reason we picked this day to strike, wasn't it?"

Exton turned and glared at the medic, who promptly returned to her work in silence.

"It's possible," Emery admitted, drawing attention back to her. "If she's a new graduate, that would put her close to eighteen. She'd be young enough to be trained in newer combat routines. That would explain how her attack was successful."

"I'd hardly call this successful," Exton objected. "She nicked my ribs some, that's all. You know I'm a good fighter, Emery, and I keep up with the new training."

"I didn't mean to imply you are a bad fighter," Emery insisted, incensed. "But she did manage to do some damage."

"Barely," he retorted, though his fingers gripped his chest more tightly. "This guy"—he jerked his thumb in the direction of the nearest medic—"just gave me the serum for it to heal. I'll be working again in less than a rotation."

"But—"

"And I'm hardly old, even though I happen to look it at the moment," Exton added. He scowled at her as he straightened his wig.

Emery suddenly giggled, distracting him from his argument.

"What?"

"I can't tell if it was me or her," Emery said, "but I can tell your pride's been trampled a bit."

A small *mew* caught both of them off guard.

"Oh, my," Emery shrieked. "What is that thing?" She pointed toward the shadowed eyes staring down at her.

"Calm down, Em," Exton said. He placed his head in his hands as he realized he'd forgotten about the cat. "Whose pride were we just concerned about here?"

"What is it?"

"It's just a cat," Exton told her. He glanced down at the

scratches on his hand. "Although demon might be more fitting."

The cat seemed eager to agree with him. It bounced down and curled up on his knee.

"Well, look at that," Emery said. "It likes you."

Exton arched an eyebrow down at the cat, which ignored him and began bathing itself.

"A demon who likes a ghost," Exton said with a shrug. "If insulting you is all it took to get you to like me," Exton muttered to the kitten, "we'll have to see how that works on your mistress here."

"Mew," was all the response he received.

"Why don't you come with me while I go and talk to the URS?" Exton asked, petting the cat between its ears.

"Really, Exton?" Emery raised her brows in surprise.

"What?"

"You never seemed to like animals before."

"Maybe it's more that none of them have ever seemed to like me," he said, picking up the cat before turning his attention back to the woman. "Place her under guard and medic watch. Notify me when she wakes up. I'd like to talk with her some more, preferably while she's strapped down and unable to puncture my lung."

Emery frowned. "You sure she didn't get you on the head as well?"

"I'm fine," Exton insisted. "Have Tyler call the attendants into the Biovid so we can find a good grounding for the tree. Get Bruce and his lumberjack crew to get started trimming it down and drawing out its water and resources. I have some gloating to do."

Exton saw the shifting uncertainty in Emery's gaze, but his tenacity won out. "Well, if you're sure," Emery said. "I can't argue with you. Here's your hat."

"Thanks." Exton took his pirate hat and placed it back on his head, carefully readjusting the wig once more as he settled into his pirate persona. "Wouldn't want to look sloppy for His Excellency."

♦8♦

Before she even opened her eyes, Aerie could feel the chains wrapped around her wrists, trapping them beside her torso. Her bonds were strong but light, with a coarse fabric lining providing a thin layer of intended comfort. It was their restraint that provoked her to full consciousness. Aerie cursed her curiosity, even as she couldn't ignore its calling.

I just can't resist finding out what kind of trouble I'm in, can I?

Grogginess slowly left her mind as light blurred into vision and shadows transformed into shaded colors. Fear sharpened inside her as she remembered she was in enemy territory.

For a moment, Aerie squeezed her eyes shut, unsure if she wanted to recall or block out all her training on the torture practices of MENACE and the depravity of Captain Chainsword.

The number one rule: *Never get captured.* It was better to die in a fight than to be left at the mercy of the enemy.

Since she'd already broken that rule, Aerie realized, she would have to face the consequences. A new barrage of images, ranging in degree of torture and humiliation, followed either quickly or slowly by death, raced through her mind. Anxiety and fear, coupled with an adrenaline rush, caused her hands to shake as she fought against her bonds.

"Come on, come on," she muttered to herself. Moments passed before she bit her lip, trying to block out the pain in her wrists and hold back her desperation.

Long moments passed before she finally gave up, tired and sore. She slumped back against the pillow behind her.

It was then she realized the straps contained slim tubes, carefully tucked into her skin.

She glanced around and noticed she was in a room that looked more like a medical ward than a torture chamber.

Which it could be, so far as I know.

Aerie squeezed her eyes shut, trying to recall what had happened. She remembered clinging to the tree as it was knocked over and hauled … into a space shuttle.

Captain Chainsword's shuttle.

Her eyes opened as though she was seeing it, reliving it all.

She recalled the pain in her head, the roaring of both battle and blastoff, as the pressure pounded against her body; the shuttle had launched, packing her in along with the tree before it took off for the final frontier. Rage burned into her, realigning her ability to focus even as gravity's shadow had finally overwhelmed her, just in time to launch into an attack against the man responsible for her pain.

Tears flecked her eyes as her gaze finally saw past herself. She gasped in surprise. The ceiling was a crisscrossing pattern of steel-enforced windows, revealing the starry night outside the ship.

Clear of clouds and free of haze, the light dancing on the earth winked at her, as the world twirled slowly, steadily, outside her room.

Aerie did not know how long she stared, surprised at the simple beauty.

It was when the whispers reached her that she jerked her attention back to the situation at hand. Four crew members, all dressed in white coats, chatted easily together as they walked into the room. None of them seemed to notice she'd woken up. Aerie saw the insignia on their sleeves—a sharp, four-pointed star, with four smaller rays reaching out from its heart. It gleamed in the middle of an eye-shaped border.

Clearly not the URS, Aerie thought, *and not the scrawling calligraphy of MENACE.*

Confusion hit her. Dictator Osgood had been adamant that Captain Chainsword—or his ghost, anyway—had been in tight friendship with MENACE. Who were these people?

They looked like medics, but they could also be her tormentors.

The door opened again. Aerie turned to see a man walk into the room. His uniform was dark gray in color, and there was an air of authority in his movement; when the other medics nodded to him as they scurried out of his way, Aerie nearly cheered at her estimation. No doubt this man was a commander or doctor of some sort.

Probably a commander, since he was armed, she reasoned, noting the weapon in the holster at his side.

The man pulled out a screen and a stylus, and then turned his full attention on her.

Immediately, Aerie felt a rush of shyness. His eyes were the lightest blue she'd ever seen, like the sky in some of the old textbooks on display at the education center. His hair was dark and a bit longer than the General would have liked, and definitely messier than Brock would have dared.

After a moment, Aerie decided she liked it. And it seemed to suit the man in front of her. After all, what was authority but freedom with responsibility?

She almost slipped up and smiled at him before her mind screamed at her, forcing her to remember this was the enemy. An enemy who would willingly cause her great suffering. Someone who could break her, claim her, destroy her. Someone she should fight against until she was empty of all power.

"What is your name?"

It was his voice that revealed him.

His words echoed throughout the medic ward, a large room, empty of all but the two of them. Aerie felt the sound bounce off the walls and back around while it sunk in just who this man was—and how she was completely at his mercy.

Instantly, her demeanor changed, heightening her defenses and sparking outrage. "It's certainly not a matter worthy of consideration from the great Captain Chainsword," she grumbled.

His dark eyebrows arched and then he shrugged. "I was hoping you wouldn't recognize me. First impressions are so hard to shake."

When she just gaped at his irreverence, he gave her a wry grin. "Of course, I'm sure *my* first impression was a bit less exciting to you than yours was to me. It's not every day I pick up a tree and find a lady living in it."

"I wasn't living in it," Aerie asserted angrily before she could stop herself. *There's no need to give him information. Don't make his job easy!*

"Well, that's good," he said, the gentle tone somehow more scathing than his sarcasm. "I should just hate myself if I had destroyed your home."

"You should hate yourself anyway," Aerie bit back.

"Maybe I already do."

His flippancy caught her off guard as much as his admission. Aerie knew she had to be determined to keep him on the defensive. She pressed forward, forcing herself to remain focused on resisting interrogation. No matter how irresistible it was turning out to be. "Well, you should. You're the scoundrel who killed my tree!"

When he said nothing in return, she felt her heart break all over again at the loss of the Memory Tree. "You told your crew to crush its heart."

"I did," he admitted.

"You're a monster."

"You've already called me a monster."

"Just because I already said it doesn't make it any less true."

"And here I thought taking the pirate ghost costume off would help," he replied. He shifted in his seat. "I'll admit I am somewhat disappointed."

"Why would *you* be disappointed?"

"Even the devil is capable of disappointment, I'm sure," he said with a shrug. "But I was under the impression you were a trained combat soldier. I was expecting a little more creativity."

"In name-calling?" Aerie asked. "Are you crazy?"

"Crazy's not a bad attempt," he remarked, jotting down some notes on his screen. "But I'd still try for something more robust."

Aerie frowned. "It doesn't matter what I call you!"

"Of course it matters," Captain Chainsword replied. "It is your job to get under the skin of your enemy, to make his weaknesses all work against him."

"It's easier just to kill him outright," Aerie argued.

"It's easier just to kill," he agreed, "but it's the more skillful soldier who can turn the enemy's imagination against him." He glanced up at her, catching her eyes with his. "Don't you think so?"

"Why don't you take off my restraints here and we'll see about that?" Aerie asked.

To her surprise, and seemingly his as well, he smiled. "Oh, I know you'd love your fair fight, *Comrade*, but in the real world—the 'real' world, that is, not the one you pretend to exist in while you're in training—we don't fight fair."

"Is that what this is?" Aerie demanded. "You're attempting to fight me?"

"If I am, it's a poor attempt, considering you're already bound and unlikely to defeat me at this point."

Aerie tugged against her bounds again, to no avail. She glared at him. "I knew this was a prison."

"That does remind me. Welcome to the *Perdition.* I am its captain, as you know, and this room is actually a medic ward. We are on Level One of the ship. I can assure you, those are the real stars you can see out your window, though there aren't as many as you would likely expect."

"It's still a prison."

"It might surprise you to know," he said in a soft voice, "there are no prisons on the *Perdition.*"

"I don't believe you," Aerie scoffed. "Weren't you the one who just said it was the more skillful soldier who could use the enemy's imagination to win?"

At the quick frown on his face, Aerie knew she'd scored a point against him. But instead of retaliating, he simply went back to writing on his pad. "Clever girl," he commented, further frustrating her.

What kind of enemy resisted battle?

One who already had the upper hand, Aerie thought bitterly.

A few moments passed in silence as he continued to look up from his screen, then to her, and then back at the screen again.

Aerie grew uncomfortable. *Why is he here? Why can't he just leave me alone? Is this part of the torture?*

"Don't you have more important duties to take care of?" she finally asked. "Torturing me hardly seems worthy of your time. I mean, if you're *really* the captain of this starship, shouldn't you be planning your next attack on innocent people?"

"There is no one who is without sin, without iniquity," he murmured.

"I suppose I should expect such a remark from a hateful person like you."

"What do you mean by 'hateful?'"

"You know what I mean." Aerie gritted her teeth together. *This is impossible!* "Just how ignorant are you?"

"I don't know. What do you mean when you say 'hateful'? If you can't tell me, aren't you the ignorant one?"

"It means that you hate people and you don't mind hurting them," Aerie growled.

"How did you come to the conclusion I am a hateful person?"

"I would think that was obvious!" Aerie argued. "You killed the Memory Tree. You attacked my home. You're holding me prisoner and mocking me at every chance you get! How much more hateful can a person be?"

There was a long pause. "I could've been worse," he finally said.

"That's nothing to be proud of," Aerie yelled back.

"Have you considered, Comrade, that you are being just as hateful toward me? If I remember correctly, *you* were the one who attacked *me* after I freed you from the tree."

Aerie said nothing, boiling with rage and hatred for the man before her, not wanting to admit he was right. The memories of how he'd carefully untangled her hair from the new buds of the tree, and how he had safely carried her out of the tree's embrace, flooded through her. Her fists, still bound to her bed, clenched as she fought against the urge to scream.

His voice, quiet and distinct against her silence, was unnerving. "I was a bit preoccupied with the URS's retaliation when we picked up the Memory Tree," he said slowly. "I did not realize you were climbing in it. I have it on good report that the URS is keeping its civilian populations largely, if not entirely, underground. I had no reason to suspect someone was … someone would defy their orders. Especially in New Hope. I would have thought there would have been more thorough security."

He's trying to use you for information. The warning flashed through her mind.

When she said nothing, he relaxed back into his chair. "So … I will concede that it is mostly my fault you were captured."

"Mostly!?" Aerie felt her bonds strain against her blood.

"I wouldn't try too hard to break free," he told her, nodding toward the cuffs. "You were taken up into space with no preparation. It's a wonder your eardrums didn't burst and your brain isn't damaged. Or should I say more damaged, since you've grown up in the URS?"

"I suppose you think my brain is busted because I didn't burst into tears, bow down to you and your crew, and beg you to take me home?" she asked bitingly. "Maybe you're just angry and insulting me because I didn't."

While he did seem to agree with her on that point, he dismissed it. "If you weren't up in the tree in the first place, this never would have happened," he pointed out. "Seems pretty silly to me."

"It's not silly."

"Many people—many more than your beloved State will let you believe—have come to me and the crew for just such a salvation when we go down to Earth for supplies, or in this case, for battle," he told her. "You're the first one to come in a tree, and the first to resist new accommodations."

"It's not like I would have been there if I'd known you were coming."

"Agreed," the captain allowed. "Bad luck and poor timing happen to the best of us."

Aerie noticed as his left hand settled on his chest while he spoke. "Did I get you earlier?"

"Mildly," he assured her with a charming grin.

Aerie felt her face flush over as she smiled back. And then a moment later, she blanched. *Stop it!* She mentally slapped herself. *You are a prisoner. He is just teasing you. He wants information, and then he'll likely kill you. This is* not *a game.*

"I thought," he continued, "it might be easier for both of us if we could come to some agreements while you're on the ship."

"A quick death is all I ask for." She sighed and slumped forward, her resignation complete. It was too much hassle to wonder and to wait for her fate to be decided.

He seemed surprised by her request. "I'd rather not."

Her narrowed eyes shot up to his, and he clarified, "I mean kill you at all, not kill you slowly."

"Why?" Her tone was disbelieving. "You mean you want me to give you information, don't you? Why would you ever think I would do such a thing?"

"Maybe so I have something to call you other than 'Tree Girl'?" he inquired. "Or 'Silly Child,' perhaps?"

When she just looked at him quizzically, he clarified his meaning. "Tell me your name. It's a good place to start, don't you think?"

"I'll never give you any information. How could I, knowing what I know about you?"

"Perhaps there's more to me than you realize."

"You're a hateful monster! What else do I possibly need to know?"

Aerie regretted her outburst less than a second later. The captain immediately left his chair and came close to her. Instinctively, she pulled back, but the pad behind her did not allow her to go far.

As he drew near, she got a good look at his face; though no longer adorned with the pirate's wig and beard, she could see he was still masked. The apathy, the cynicism, the playful whimsy—all of it hid a deep crevice of pain inside of him.

The sudden urge to reach out and touch him shot through her. It was quickly followed by alarm and self-disgust.

"From your comments, I would assume you have yet to learn a great many things," he told her, his voice sharp.

"What do you mean by that?" she asked, boldly meeting his gaze.

"First, your name is no small matter," he said. "Destinies can be made and shaped by your name, though whether good or bad, it is up to you."

He turned away from her abruptly and began pacing by her bed. Aerie listened to his steps resonate with certainty and distinctness, like a military cadence, as she tried to breathe properly.

"Second," he continued, glancing at her from over his shoulder, "Despite what you might think, I am not a monster; merely a man."

"I hardly see the difference," she retorted, still rattled by his presence.

"I would expect that, given your education with the URS. Over the past decade, your beloved Daddy Dictator has managed to ensure your education, rigorous as it is, consists of really only following instructions, repeating the lies they prefer to the truth, and ignoring any logic that would unravel them or undermine their authority."

Aerie struggled to argue as she thought about her PAR. She thought about her final research presentation and her father's stinging rebuke.

"I'm not the one who is afraid to show my real face to my enemy," she finally replied, feeling small for such a shallow attack.

"You weren't really given much of a choice," he reminded her with a taunting look. "Hardly a matter of bravery."

"I am not afraid of anything," Aerie snapped.

"If you are not, then you are either braver than most, or you are just naïve." He placed his hand on his chest again, where she had landed her earlier blow. "While I'll give you credit for fighting well, you don't seem to realize the greatest fears we face are often inside of us."

"What's your greatest fear then?" Aerie asked.

He paused, but only momentarily. "That I have nothing left to lose." His gaze hardened. "So I won't mind making a silly, foolish girl walk the plank off my ship."

Aerie blanched. Nothing would be more torturous than a public death. The General, besides being personally mortified and disappointed in her, would likely be punished, possibly along with her siblings. The thought of an embarrassing and shameful death made survival all the more important.

It was time to redirect his attention.

She nodded toward her wrists. "With all the tubes you've hooked into me, I'm not going to be walking anywhere. Especially if the 'medicine' in these tubes is supposed to sedate me or poison me."

"It would be hard for mostly vitamins and minerals to poison you." As Aerie gawked at him, he added, "I know the tubes are an unpleasant hassle, but they'll be gone soon enough. You likely wouldn't be to walk around without it right now. Living in space is hard, even with preparation and adjustment. The medicine in those tubes will help your body recover."

Aerie glanced at the tubes in uncomfortable shock. *They're helping me? Why? Where's the torture?*

She softened her expression. "You know, I'd be less inclined to hate you if you would release me."

"I'd be more inclined to give you a proper room if you weren't so inclined to kill me."

His rebuke and reminder of her earlier attack stung. "I guess we are at an impasse then," Aerie retorted.

"I could make some concessions if you would."

"Like what?"

"Like telling me your name, for one, instead of playing games like a child."

Aerie bit her lip. "What would I get in return?" she asked, desperately irritated to find she did sound just like a child.

"This seems like a fair trade," he said. Aerie watched while he pulled something out of his pocket as he moved closer to her once more. A small *bump* tumbled across the bed, and Aerie instinctively grappled for the small, sleepy kitten. When her binding cuffs caught her, the man pressed a button and released her arms from her sides. "Be careful with the tubes," he warned. "The medic crew told me they're cleaning your blood of Earth's toxins and analyzing it for germs."

Aerie glared up at him. "Just give me the cat."

"Here. I had the vet check her, and she's surprisingly healthy." He thrust the kitten closer to her hands and then stepped back from Aerie's bed. "She seems to take after you. She managed to claw my wrist when we first met."

Aerie hugged the tiny cat to her heart, burying her face in the familiar fur. "Moona!" Aerie cried happily, feeling a sense of relief for the first time.

"Moona? Is that your name or the cat's?" the captain asked, pulling out his stylus and the medical screen once more.

"It's hers," Aerie snapped. "Of course it's hers." She reached out and stroked her cat, relieved to see there were no bumps or bruises on Moona's soft body.

"Why did you name her that?"

"I found her on a day where I could see the moon through the clouds," Aerie said, recalling that day clearly. "I saw her when I was walking around the Memory Tree, and then, all of a sudden, there she was. I couldn't resist after I saw her white face in the dim light. I couldn't decide whether 'Luna' or 'Moon' fit her better."

"So you blended it."

"Obviously." Aerie felt a flood of frustration as she

realized she was giving him more information. He had already managed to find a chip in her armor. She quickly went back to petting Moona and ignoring her captor, trying to find a way out of her situation.

It was not easy … he was waiting for her with expectancy.

Aerie wrestled with herself. The best shot she had was getting along for now, wasn't it? And as angry as it made her to give the captain credit, he *hadn't* put her in a cell, hadn't tortured her, and hadn't—she blushed—ravished her; all things he could have done easily. *Though not too easily*, she told herself.

"Fine," she acquiesced softly, giving into her desire, knowing it was against her better judgment. "My name is Aerie."

He stared at her for a long moment. "You're not lying?"

"What?" Aerie scowled. "No." She sighed. "I didn't even think about it. Maybe I should have."

The man surprised her by laughing. She stared at him; his laugh was soft and uncomfortable, almost like it had been a long time since he'd found anything funny.

Which, she reminded herself, was probably the truth. How joyous could a murderer's life be?

"You're better for it," he told her. "It's easier to keep things organized when you just tell the truth."

"If you think it's so easy to keep organized, then what's your name?" she asked, clearly surprising him with her challenge. She found it was harder to look away from him than it had been before. "I mean, I'd rather not call you 'Captain Chainsword,' if I can help it. It's a bit of a mouthful."

"I'm surprised that the URS didn't give you a full course on me, given the trouble I've caused them in the last six years."

Aerie shook her head slowly. "You know, you're right. They didn't teach us much about you, other than you've destroyed several of their bases and labs around the country."

"Well, that's true," the captain murmured.

"And how you work with the last remnants of MENACE to bring down the URS from space."

He snorted.

"And that you've been doing this for years because you want power and you want to bring the capitalists back."

He was silent for a long moment. "There's only one thing I want," he told her, and Aerie wondered, from his expression, if he was talking to her, or if he had forgotten her entirely.

She quickly interrupted him, deciding she didn't like being ignored by a stranger any more than she liked it from her own family unit. "So, no, they didn't tell us your real name." *Which is odd, come to think of it.*

Revelation hit Aerie so hard she nearly stopped breathing. The State would never conceal such important information on an enemy like that—except for one reason.

They didn't know.

Was that possible? That the State, with all its advanced technology and resources, didn't actually know who they were dealing with?

Renewed determination sparked through Aerie. She didn't have to get accepted into the Military Academy to earn her family unit's respect or her father's love. If she could give them the information on how to stop Captain Chainsword, not only would she be welcomed home, but she would be heralded as a hero.

The captain's lips pursed together. Aerie caught her breath anxiously, wondering if he suspected the nature of her treacherous thoughts.

But then, he slowly extended his hand to her. It took her a moment to recognize it as a handshake. She reached for it before she could stop herself.

Instantly, her hand disappeared inside of his as he held onto her, and she held onto him.

He was strong. She could feel small, rough patches on his palms as they rubbed against her skin. It was not an unpleasant sensation, to have his hand gripping hers, she observed, but it was still disconcerting. Her heart stilled in warning as she met his gaze, immersing herself in their daytime starlight.

"Exton," he said.

"Exton." The name felt unfamiliar, but not unwelcome, on her lips as she echoed it in her own voice. Her gaze narrowed and her tone shifted, mimicking his from earlier. "You're not lying to me, are you?"

"Not about that," he said with a smirk. "But don't worry. I'm sure I will in the very near future." He glanced down at Moona and softened his voice. "If you'll excuse me … Aerie." He dropped her hand unceremoniously and turned toward the door.

Before Aerie could stop him, he left, her hand still tingling from his touch.

♦9♦

Two days later, Exton paced throughout his room, frustrated he was unable to relish his time off-duty. Commanding the bridge and overseeing the *Perdition's* course were both necessary and routine. They demanded his full attention and he was more than happy to give it while he was working.

Since leaving Earth, he had struggled with sleep, only succeeding in getting a few hours before waking up to find just as many things on his mind as when he had gone down. He glanced down at his bed, the cushioned pallet and blankets askew from restless slumber.

For a moment, Exton wondered how his mother would react if she saw how messy he'd kept his room. His mother hadn't fought with him much when he was younger, when they lived on the outskirts of New Hope. But he could hear her chastisement clearly, telling him a messy room meant a messy mind.

Exton sighed. Maybe his mother was right. *Especially tonight.*

Everything is taken care of, he told himself for the hundredth time. The *Perdition* was on course to hide in the shadows of the moon once more. All satellite transmissions, following his traditional gloat to Dictator Osgood, had either been turned off or redirected by the Tech System for filtration. The Memory Tree had been processed for treatment. He'd managed to sidestep a few meetings with the board members of the Ecclesia.

There was nothing else on his mind. Except for her.

Aerie. His prisoner—if he decided to call her that—was fine. Hadn't he just checked on her med reports a few hours before? She was probably resting.

Probably peacefully, too, he thought bitterly. There was a strong temptation inside of him to go and wake her up.

It wasn't the first time since leaving her he'd been tempted to go see her again. She was ... *fascinating,* he decided. Her passionate defense of her tree and attachment to her cat spoke of inner strength and compassion, traits he admired. The golden amber of her eyes complemented her persistent determination, giving her a compelling face that matched her personality.

Yes, Exton decided, she was suited to her looks. The fiery hair, the piercing eyes, that expressive mouth—they all hinted at what was inside her heart and who she was. *An individualist*, he'd thought at the time, *and an idealist*, he realized later.

He rubbed his ribs, tentatively pressing the area she managed to fracture, and wondered, amused, if she had managed to break through the barrier to his heart as well.

Bitterness washed over him. *What a shame she was wasted on the URS,* he thought, not for the first time.

There was no real reason to disturb her.

For now.

That didn't mean he had to stay in his room.

As he stepped out into the hall, Exton felt the night press into him immediately. For all of Emery's insistence that the *Perdition* roamed in perpetual sunlight, he never felt its warmth; nighttime, in contrast, was compounded by an eerie feeling of quiet loneliness.

There were still crewmembers working the lighter shift at night, diligently running the ship while others slept and rested. As captain, and part-time engineer, he worked alongside both shifts when the need arose.

But, as there was not much need while his ship engineers were on top of their jobs, he was forced to find smaller projects. He smiled at the thought of the small toy truck on his desk.

Much of his childhood had been an attempt to make his father happy. He had succeeded to the point where fixing anything on the ship made him feel the warm approval of his dad.

"Things haven't changed, have they, Papa?" he muttered.

He turned down the familiar halls of his ship; Level Ten sheltered his Captain's rooms, allowing him some privacy from the rest of his crew up on Levels Two and Four. Level Three carried the sanctuary, the ship's main dining hall, and several smaller rooms designed and furnished for entertainment. Level Five was mostly for storage and supplies. Level Six was home to most of the tech systems and their many needs. Levels Seven through Nine shared classrooms, learning stations, and access to the outer plantation rooms, where the Biovid could best be seen in all its glory, with the Ark tucked below. He passed through the main body of ship, making mental notes for the coming day as he drifted through the ship.

Aerie had told him she thought him a ghost when she first encountered him. And in many ways, Exton agreed. He was just that—the living apparition of his father.

The halls and inner workings of the ship might have housed the ghost of his father, but it was his mother's spirit that had taken up residence in the Biovid.

The Biovid was a huge, oval-shaped room paneled with greenhouse windows specially designed to capture the outer light and reflect the heat inside. Located in the center of the ship's body, it stood over 100 yards tall and 400 yards wide. Soil and plants of all sorts, many of which had been pulled from Earth, resided inside the large room. More than one person remarked on how much it looked like a large rainforest had settled inside the heart of the ship.

"Eden," Exton murmured. "Biovid" was the more functional name. But "Eden" had been a popular preference for the members of the Ecclesia, and he knew many still referred to it as such.

Stepping inside the Biovid, the air instantly transformed from the cool stillness of space to the light breeziness of life. The metallic floor gave way to soil, and the efficiency of the starship's design was overwhelmed with the frivolous and the beautiful.

Plants of all kinds were organized in different pods, some for scientific observation, others for appeal. Many looked overgrown or haphazardly placed; some had vines creeping out along the Biovid's barrier, while some shot upward, reaching out to find the Suncatcher's light.

The Suncatcher was an early device he had designed for his mother and her gardens on Earth. Later on, Emery, pursuing her own horticulture studies at university, suggested some enhancements. The result was a fully functional, artificial source for light. Its beam rained down on the thousands of plants below, making the Biovid a giant womb in which plants could flourish.

Exton breathed in deeply. The scents and smells weighted down the air, making him think of home and growing up.

"Is that you, Exton?"

Exton flinched at the sound of the familiar voice. "Yes, it is, Dennis."

"You know I prefer to have others use my title," the man remarked solemnly.

Only so you can use its power if you need to. But Exton swallowed his sarcasm as his father's old mentor approached. "Reverend Thorne," he acknowledged, nodding respectfully to the older man who appeared behind him.

"I thought that was you," Reverend Thorne said.

Exton nodded. "I like to come by and visit every so often. As you know." *Which is why you are here, no doubt.*

"I'm glad I caught you. It was a pity you weren't able to make the meeting with the other board members of the Ecclesia earlier."

Exton inwardly rolled his eyes. There were several reasons he didn't mind "forgetting" the meetings with the Ecclesia, and Reverend Thorne, while he was a good man, was one of them. He always seemed … too peaceful for Exton's preference.

How did a man who helped oversee the survival of an outlawed religion sleep at night? The world was a terrible place, and Exton knew that better than most.

"Your brother's not with you, is he?" Exton asked, glancing over the reverend's shoulder.

"Don is fast asleep," Reverend Thorne assured him. "As

many of the Ecclesia are."

"I don't suppose you came here out of sheer coincidence, did you?"

"You're too efficient with your speech sometimes," Reverend Thorne said, the kind firmness in his gray eyes weakening. "But then, so was your father."

"I remember," Exton replied somberly.

"Sorry."

"It's not a problem," Exton asserted. "But I detest trickery, and wasting my time. Tell me what you want, and then be on your way."

"I know you like this place," Reverend Thorne answered. "But it is open to the Ecclesia as well as the crew."

"I came here to check on the remnants of the Memory Tree. It's finishing up with its processing soon." Exton's voice grew impatient. "Just tell me what you want."

Reverend Thorne nodded. "Very well. I can see you're in a hurry for me to go. I would like to know what you've done with the new girl on board."

"What of it?" Exton asked. "She's still in the med ward."

"She won't need to be in there for much longer," Reverend Thorne pointed out. "Decontamination doesn't last much longer than three days."

"So?"

"I thought, since word has it she has declared herself your enemy—"

"Since when do you listen to gossip?"

"Listening to it has never been the problem," the reverend told him with a small laugh. "The problem was always getting people to stop repeating it."

Exton gave a grudging smile. For all the man believed in miracles, his logic was sound. "I suppose that's true."

"I heard that she is not a refugee, and she is not a defector."

"Not a defector by choice," Exton agreed. "While she's here, she is one regardless."

"I thought perhaps it might be easier if the board took

care of her for you. We would start by selecting a guardian for her and then get her settled in."

"Like a babysitter?"

"More or less," Reverend Throne admitted. "I was thinking of a mentor, or chaperon. Someone who could show her the truth of the URS and what we're—"

"You can stop there," Exton said. "She was taken here by accident, but there's no need to try to convert her to our cause. She's young, Reverend. Barely graduated from secondary levels, and raised in the heart of New Hope to begin with. And you know better than I do that people rarely change unless they want to."

"Imagine that," the reverend muttered, before he sighed. "Youth is no reason to declare her hopeless. You were younger than her when—"

"When what?" Exton glared at him. "When my father was executed?"

Reverend Thorne went silent.

"You might have a distinct lineage of priests and traditions that embrace God and his grace," Exton continued slowly. "But around here, I am still the captain, and I am still in charge of this ship."

"But you don't know the girl any more than the rest of us do," he pointed out. "At least we would be able to get her accustomed to the community onboard better; place her with some of the younger crew and their families, that sort of thing."

"I know she's been trained for war combat," Exton told him brusquely, "and that she's a handful."

There were other things he'd learned about her in the past two days as he kept up with her reports and worked on figuring out just how much trouble she would cause them while she was onboard the *Perdition.*

Hadn't it been that strange curiosity, that surprising drive to find out more, that had prompted him to keep his distance?

"I would still recommend her to come into the Ecclesia

quarters on the other side of the ship," Reverend Thorne said. "If nothing else, I'd be happy to keep her out of your way, so you don't need to worry about her while you're running things here."

For some reason, Exton felt like punching him. "I've already decided what to do with her," he lied. "So you don't need to worry about it."

"Of course. I should have asked you first, Captain." The reverend's eyes dropped respectfully down to the ground, and Exton felt a mixed measure of shame and pride at winning the argument.

Exton didn't know why his father's community members bothered him so much. He had grown up with them in their small town, learned beside them … ate with them, prayed with them, worked with them.

Maybe it was because they had known him so well before university, Exton thought. Maybe it was because they all mourned the loss of his father, of a past he would never experience again.

Exton was willing to bet those were at least some of the bigger reasons, anyway.

"May I ask what you intend to do with the girl?" Reverend Thorne inquired.

"Huh?" Exton shook his head. "I, uh, I was going to put her in Emery's care," he said, surprised at how easily he was able to fabricate the lie. "With the harvest approaching, I'll need Tyler at the helm more often than not. She'll have the time and opportunity."

All of that was more than true, Exton realized. In fact, the more he thought about it, the more it really was the perfect solution. He could trust Emery; he'd seen her take care of other refugees, and she knew how to take command of her projects. Exton himself was proof of that.

"I'll have her move into Emery's old quarters, now that Emery's married to Tyler," he added, suddenly inspired. "And I'll keep tabs on her so I can stop her if she dares give us any troubles. Or," he added, "if we need some leverage with

Dictator Osgood."

For a moment, the reverend remained silent. "I take it from your tone your earlier conversation with the dictator did not go well?"

"No," Exton snapped. "It didn't."

"Tell me. Please." The gray eyes were tired, but they were full of patience and compassion—two things Exton never felt he completely mastered himself.

He sighed, giving in despite his reservations. "I contacted him, and I let him know about our victory."

"He would have already known."

"Yes. He wasn't happy about it. At least, I can't imagine that he was," Exton disclosed.

"What has you so worried, then?"

"He's promoted General St. Cloud. He's now second in command, after Osgood himself."

"Ah, I see. Did you get a chance to speak to St. Cloud?" Reverend Thorne asked.

"A little. He told me he was the one who was authorized to kill me now." Exton gave the reverend a small, bitter smile. "I wasn't sure if his words were intentional or not."

"Did he recognize you?"

"I have no doubt he knows who I am," Exton admitted. "Even if the people from the URS don't. Aerie more or less confirmed that they don't know much about me when I talked with her."

"Aerie?"

Exton shrugged. "The girl who arrived with the tree."

"I see." The older man reached out hesitantly, patting Exton on the arm. "You've always known St. Cloud was working under Osgood. Why is this worrying you?"

After a moment of silence, Exton sighed. "I thought this was going to be easy. All I had to do was kill the bad guy, right? But it's become much more complicated since then."

"Revenge is never an easy path," the reverend reminded him. "That's why we are called to forgive."

"There are some things that are impossible to forgive."

Exton's voice cracked angrily at the suggestion.

"You are talking to a man of God," the reverend said with a sigh. "God, who gave over his own son to die for the sins of the world. Our ideas of impossible are different."

Exton glared at him.

"But that does not mean, of course, that our idea of compassion is," Reverend Thorne continued. "You know the Ecclesia is here for you if you need it."

"I know my father wanted you to look out for me and Emery after everything that happened," Exton grumbled.

"It was almost as if he'd known."

"Let me finish," Exton snapped. "I know he wanted you to look out for me. But I do think that is where your duty ends. I am not under any obligation to follow your recommendations or counsel."

"You are a great leader, Exton," Reverend Thorne agreed. "You've been decisive and smart, and you've been kind in many ways. Your aunt's settlement is growing with the refugees you bring to her and your crew is devoted to you, the Ecclesia included. You have done much for us while you've been up here on *Perdition*." He hesitated. "And I know that it has been a lot harder to keep going, especially in light of what we've found."

"But?"

"But nothing. Your father would be proud."

No, he wouldn't. Not if he knew the truth.

Exton turned away, heading deeper into the middle of the garden. "Call up the bridge and have them schedule a new meeting with me for the Ecclesia," he called, refusing to look back. "I'll talk with you again then."

"All right," Reverend Thorne remarked, though Exton was still close enough he could hear the disappointment in his voice.

Serves him right, Exton thought. The reverend deserved to be disappointed if he thought it was so simple a thing to do, to forgive someone for killing a loved one.

Exton slowed his pace as he listened for the reverend to

exit the Biovid. When he heard the *whoosh* of the Biovid's starboard forward door shutting, he continued on.

In the center of the Biovid, there was a winding staircase leading to the other rooms below, including the Ark—and the other room, the one he'd prefer to forget. He passed by it, uneasy even as he focused on his reason for coming to the Biovid in the first place.

It wasn't as if he needed to see the Memory Tree, but Exton felt it was only right. If he was going to keep his distance from his other captive, what was the harm in checking up on this one?

At least this one couldn't talk back.

At the sight of its trunk, lounging against the softened soil, Exton wondered if "captive" was the right term to use; "casualty" might have been better.

Many years had passed since his father was executed by the URS, but Exton still recalled the day clearly in his mind. He could see his father running toward him, and hear the terror and sorrow in his voice.

Feel the warmth of his father's blood through the barrier of his university uniform.

Smell the onset of death.

Really, Exton thought a moment later, *what is a tree, or anything else, in exchange for the life of my father?*

"Nothing." He answered his own question aloud, suddenly feeling a new layer of emptiness inside the oval chamber. Exton sighed and glanced down at his hands, before turning them into fists.

He glanced up at the tree, seeing its own destroyed pride as it slumped over, the roots seeming older and gloomier than when his capsule had first uprooted it.

Part of him wanted to be fine with turning it into woodchips before blasting it toward the sun, watching the coldness of space surround it before the solar winds playfully licked at its branches. The other part of him, the part he sometimes hated, had other plans for the Memory Tree.

Exton reached up and placed a hand on the tree. He

stood there for a long time in silence. Catching sight of the small slash on his knuckles, Exton finally turned around and headed for the exit.

He needed a new distraction.

♦10♦

Aerie knew the instant she was no longer alone.

It had been only an hour since the last medic came to check her chart, vitals, etc.—anything to wake her up and make her feel uncomfortable for a few moments, before tucking her back under the covers gently and leaving the room without giving her any information.

It was comforting that they weren't torturing her. Yet.

But the medics were all similarly trained, as far as Aerie could see. Their footsteps were light and brisk as they walked in through the door, and their jackets, while clean, were full of various supplies and medicines, making them floppy and lopsided. Their movements were impersonal, regimented—but still kind enough that she was unable to escape the thought of her mother.

When Aerie heard his even footsteps, measured out with rigid certainty, she knew he had come back to see her.

Exton.

She almost shook her head. *No*, she scolded herself. *Don't think of him that way. Captain Chainsword. Or his ghost.*

Calling him by his real name proved to be a mistake. Captain Chainsword had been her adversary, the familiar, inhuman face of the ultimate enemy. Exton was an unexpected surprise—a human being with a heart full of pain and humor that might have made her laugh if she wasn't supposed to hate him.

Separating the two identities was wiser. The enemy did not deserve sympathy.

Although she had to admit, now that she'd seen his face, he didn't look a lot like the Captain Chainsword she'd seen in the capsule, or the one whose picture dominated the defector's list at the education center. Even if he were to wear all the clothes, and the wig, and the hat, she would only see past them.

She peeked at him as he grabbed her chart and began reading it while he headed toward her. She quickly squeezed her eyes shut.

Aerie instantly regretted it. There was nothing she wanted more than to see him, to watch him … to make sure he didn't smother her or inject her with poison.

Soft scuffles sounded against the floor as he pulled up a chair beside her.

For a long moment, she wondered what he was doing as he sat there. Was he watching her? Did he know she was awake?

More likely he is just reading through my chart, she realized, as the screen beeped while he made notes.

Finally, after interminable moments of waiting, he spoke. "How's my favorite patient today?"

His voice was soft and husky, both irritating and intriguing, a siren's call to pleasure despite the promised pain.

Just as she remembered it.

Against the darkness and the long hours of isolation, Aerie allowed herself to admit she'd been wondering if he would come and see her again. The medics were nice enough, even if their questions were annoying and repetitive; memories of her unit and comrades were dull or worrisome, and thoughts of escape proved to be elusive.

All proved to be poor company when compared to the pirate captain.

Frustrated, she sighed and opened her eyes. "How did you know I was awake?"

A smirk crawled up onto his face at the sight of her eyes. "I wasn't talking to you." He gestured to the small cat that had jumped up on his lap. His fingers curled around the kitten's ears as she purred in expectant appreciation.

Aerie folded her arms across her chest and narrowed her eyes at Moona. "Traitor."

Moona ignored her, as her own eyes closed with happiness. "The downfall of freedom," Exton said with a shrug, "is that people can make the wrong choices."

"Is that supposed to be some kind of insult?" Aerie asked, her temper flaring.

He raised his eyebrows. "I was only making a general observation," he told her. He leaned back in the chair, shifting Moona into his arms while he continued to pet her. "One you're no doubt familiar with, besides. But if you want to talk about something else, I'll listen."

"Ha!" Aerie wrinkled her nose at him. "Like I would tell you anything. I see your game."

"I guess you haven't missed me any since our last discussion," Exton said.

There was no way she was going to tell him the truth regarding that. "Please. It's not like you've been waltzing around thinking about me for the past two days," Aerie retorted.

"What if I have?"

She sputtered at his reply. "What?"

There was a coolness behind his blue eyes that she hated as he looked at her. "What if I have been thinking of you?"

Aerie frowned. He had to be taunting her, and deliberately, too, she decided. "It would likely only be because you don't know what do to with me yet," she wagered.

"There is that question," Exton agreed easily enough. "What will we do with you?"

"You could take me back to the States," Aerie suggested, knowing it was a gamble.

"Are you concerned about your unit missing you?"

No. "Yes."

"I find that hard to believe."

"What do you know of my unit?" Aerie snapped angrily, wondering if he was able to read her mind.

"I could take you back," Exton agreed. "But I could just as easily kill you and save myself the trouble. Or I could just kill myself, and save the URS the trouble."

"That was my next recommendation," Aerie replied in a biting tone.

"One thing you should know," he told her, "is that I am not prone to take counsel."

"And I am not prone to play the part of the invalid."

"The medics have finished checking your blood and replenishing your fluids," Exton said, glancing down at her chart. "Decontamination is complete, your vitals look good. And they even noted you seem to have a pleasant disposition." He glanced up at her with a roguish grin on his face. "I'll have to correct that, won't I?"

She only glared at him in reply. What was it about him, Aerie wondered, that made him so insufferable?

It should have been easy to hate him, but somehow she didn't—and she hated that she didn't. It made her plans to collect information for the URS more difficult.

Maybe that's his game, Aerie thought. *Befriend, and then betray.*

"So then let's talk about what to do with you," Exton offered, interrupting her thoughts.

"I'm surprised you haven't decided already." Aerie frowned. "Besides, I thought you didn't take counsel."

The smallest smile appeared on his face. "I'm not prone to take it, but I will occasionally. Making decisions about refugees and rebels is easy, but you're not really one or the other, are you?" He said it softly, purposely.

What kind of game is he playing? "No," Aerie said. "I'm not either of those."

"There are many other options I could select for you," he said, goading her. "But I find them lacking in one way or another. You're not a child, though hardly a woman. You're not an assassin, as much as you'd like to think you are."

"I'd love the chance to change your mind on that one," Aerie said, angry she was more upset by his comment on her maturity than her combat skills.

"I'm afraid we can't do that. But as for the other concern, I think we'll just have to wait and see who you are."

"I'm your enemy," Aerie told him. "There. It's that simple. Now, I'd appreciate it if you would stop with the pleasantries and start torturing me. I'll be much happier when I am dead."

"I can understand your thoughts on the matter," he said, obviously smothering a laugh, "but I'd love for you to give me the chance to change your mind."

Frustration hit her again. Was he teasing her? Or worse—was he telling the truth? "You won't make me change my mind," Aerie insisted. "I'm your enemy."

"I'm going to call your bluff."

"What? What are you talking about?"

"Here's what I think," Exton said. "I think you've had doubts about the URS before."

"Of all the presumptuous … that's not true at all! You're—" Aerie nearly choked. Her fists clenched, wanting nothing more than to fight back.

"I know you don't like hearing your loyalty questioned, but we have enough serum for your venom. I know my medics are trained better than most in the URS. They're not even trained to let you die if they think it's useless to try to save you."

Aerie winced.

He continued, "I don't care for 'captive' or 'prisoner,' because as I've told you, the *Perdition* does not have either."

"I would disagree," Aerie interrupted. "This whole ship is a prison."

"Even hell does not have captives, Aerie," he told her, shocking her as he said her name. "Everyone in hell chooses to go there."

Her brow creased. "I'm not sure I know what you mean."

"I'm sure the Ecclesia will get around to telling you all about it while you're here," Exton told her. "But the *Perdition* was not designed to be a prison, let alone hold prisoners of war. It was, ironically, designed to be a paradise of sorts."

"A paradise?" Aerie scoffed. "What kind of paradise houses nuclear weapons and threatens to use them on innocent people?"

"Would it make you feel better if I told you there were no warheads on the ship?"

"I would not believe you," Aerie said, drawing herself up proudly. "You're a known liar."

"Ah, yes," Exton replied sarcastically. "The great,

inexhaustible knowledge of the URS Education Program. How could I forget?"

Aerie bristled. "I'd rather you not talk to me, if you're just going to make fun of me."

"That's the second time you've brought that up." He leaned forward in his chair. "Do you have a problem with ridicule?"

"No," Aerie lied, her face turning a bright shade of red.

"I told you before," Exton said, "it's better to just tell the truth." He looked at her, his gaze studying her face carefully. "You'll give yourself away more than you think."

Aerie said nothing, but her fingers curled into fists.

"Let me guess. You were ridiculed by your beloved family—I mean, unit, of course."

She tightened her lips. He didn't need to know anything.

Seeing her reaction, he nodded. "Gotta admire the URS units. They tend to eat their young as though they needed fresh blood to survive. I'm glad I didn't grow up in one."

"How would you know anything about units if you've never grown up in one?" Aerie asked, anger still simmering inside of her.

"Because I grew up in a family," Exton told her. "We didn't follow the 'unit' rule. The State never had real authority over my family's household, and I had not only my family, but my community to protect me from any direct autonomy from them." He glanced out the windows above them as he leaned back in his chair. "For which I can only be grateful."

A moment passed, and Aerie couldn't squash her curiosity. *What would it have been like,* she wondered, *to live in a place that the State did not have the final say in all matters?* "I thought you said you lived near New Hope," Aerie remarked.

"I did," he agreed. "I got through their education program early, and I went on to university."

"For what degree?"

"It doesn't matter. I didn't finish." He shifted Moona onto her lap before leaning over her, drawing closer to her.

"Were you going to be a doctor?" Aerie felt her breathing

stop as she realized he was reaching for her. He ran his fingers over the bruised bump on her head where she'd been bleeding.

"No. An engineer." He touched her bump tentatively, but his kindness was unmistakable. "But I was pretty clumsy as a kid, so I know how to tend to things like this. My mom thought it was a good idea to learn."

It was strange to think of Exton as having a mother. Especially one who sounded a lot like her own.

"Stop it," Aerie muttered softly, uncomfortable with his closeness.

"It looks much better," he told her. "Only a little swelling now. The cut is scabbing over nicely, too."

She suddenly felt very conscious of her appearance. "Does it look bad?" Aerie reached her hand up to her bruise.

Exton's fingers brushed gently against her cheek, tenderly tucking her hair behind her ear. She felt her mouth go dry as she met his gaze.

"No," Exton told her. "No, it doesn't look bad at all."

He paused, and Aerie felt her face betray her once more as she blushed a deeper shade of red.

He cleared his throat and backed away. "It should be gone soon, thanks to the medicine we have available on board. You'll never know it was there in a day or two."

Aerie nodded, silent as she rubbed Moona's fur.

She watched him as he sat back down. He wasn't what she expected. He was young rather than old, an engineer rather than a pirate, solid instead of ghost, lenient instead of unforgiving, tender instead of harsh, and, she admitted uncomfortably, attractive rather than repulsive.

"I've heard the stories," she said slowly, "that Captain Chainsword was betrayed by those that were closest to him. Is that what happened to you?"

"It's certainly an understatement."

At least he confirmed it. That might be something to help the URS fight against him. Aerie felt her stomach twist at the thought.

"Let's not talk about that. Tell me about you."

"Huh?" She glanced back up at him with wide eyes.

"Humor me." He leaned back in his chair. "It's the middle of the night shift, and I have some time."

"I don't want to talk to you."

"Are you sure? Can't be that interesting here all by yourself."

She bit her lip; he had a point. It *was* boring.

"How about we make a deal?" Exton asked. "I'll tell you about me, if you tell me about you." He held out his hand, as he had before.

He has a point. And this way, I can learn more for the General. Aerie blushed, recalling it was significant no one learned whose daughter she was; it was dangerous, for her and her unit and her nation.

But surely it would be easy enough to keep that fact concealed?

She took his hand once more. "Alright," she said.

"I thought that might convince you." Exton's eyes gleamed. "So, tell me. You're clearly a new graduate. Which job were you assigned to? Or did I pick you up before you had your PAR?"

Aerie shook her head. "I was … supposed to work in the Communications Sector," she said, feeling like she was digging up a past no longer part of her life.

"You would have hated it."

Aerie was surprised when she laughed. "Yes," she agreed a moment later. "I was hoping to join the Military Academy, but I didn't impress the board during my PAR." She turned away as she recalled her father's rebuke. Tears might have come if she hadn't spent the last two days deciding she had bigger problems to worry about.

Almost as if he could read her mind, he said, "I'll bet they weren't happy with you going outside, either."

She shrugged and hugged Moona closer to her.

"So," he said, "why did you want to go to the military? It wasn't just so you could go to the Academy Ball, was it?"

"No!" Aerie insisted, even as a tiny part of her

involuntarily agreed. When he arched an eyebrow at her, she sighed. "Okay, that would have been nice, but that wasn't my primary reason for wanting to join the military."

"It's good you didn't get in. You would have hated that, too."

"I would not have," Aerie objected. "You don't know me, remember?"

"I know enough about you to know you would have hated the military." Exton nodded to the cat in her lap. "For a girl who likes her kittens and tends to a tree, you would have hated burning down homes and burying dead people."

Aerie blanched. "That's not what the military in the URS does," she argued.

"Not all of them do it," Exton agreed. "But all of them are trained to do it, and worse things besides."

He has to be lying about that, Aerie thought. "Most of my friends wanted to be pilots or work in medicine," she said, thinking of Brock and Serena, as well as her brothers.

"It doesn't matter which branch or sector you're in, Aerie," he replied. "Killing is still a required skillset, and one you do when you're ordered, no questions asked, and no hesitations allowed."

Aerie thought of her own presentation to the board, and their concerns with how she didn't follow orders. *Was that why they rejected me?* "Is that why you defected? You didn't follow orders?"

Moments passed in silence. Exton reached over and stroked Moona once more. As Aerie felt his hand brush against hers, she could not seem to breathe properly.

Finally, he spoke. "No. If anything, I followed them *too* well before I left," he told her. His eyes met hers; Aerie could see flecks of silver in his blue eyes, twinkling at her like little stars. He smiled, the small movement drawing her attention uncomfortably to his mouth. "Why did you want to join the military, when it doesn't seem like a good fit for you?"

"I wanted to go in because of my family. They've always called me weak and helpless, and I wanted nothing more than to prove them wrong."

He said nothing, so she continued, suddenly awkward at the thought of silence. "They told me I was likely destined to wind up as a breeder, or as a caretaker or cohabiter, pursuing a career in marriage." Which, she recalled, thinking of Brock, she wasn't even sure she would have attracted any interest.

"When the Board of Generals rejected my application to the military, I was upset. So I went up to the tree, and that's why I was there when you arrived," she finished, more than a little annoyed with herself for giving him the information he originally wanted.

"I'm surprised your family would call you weak," Exton told her. He put a hand on his chest. "You managed to bruise two of my ribs."

"Really?" Aerie couldn't hold back her grin. "Serves you right for killing my tree."

He gave her a mercurial smile. "What made the board reject your application to the military?"

"They told me I was too unreliable." Aerie frowned. "Not that you need to know or anything." But it felt good to tell someone what had happened, and someone besides Moona. Someone who could actually respond.

"Let me guess. You don't follow directions?"

Aerie nodded. "That, and they didn't like my final presentation."

"I'll have to hear it sometime, then," Exton said. "Anything the URS doesn't like is likely borderline seditious or treasonous, and either would greatly amuse me."

"Is that why you've come to see me?" Aerie asked, instantly riled. "To amuse yourself?"

"It's not the primary reason," he drawled. "I know there's information that we need to know while you're here—such as who you are, what kind of trouble you're going to give us, that sort of information. But … there are other reasons, too."

Other reasons he wasn't going to tell her. Aerie didn't know if the General would even figure out what had happened to her at all. Getting picked up by the ghost of

Captain Chainsword was not a likely possibility on anyone's list, including hers. Hadn't she spent the last couple of days convincing herself that was what actually happened?

"I don't think you'll have to worry too much about any of that," she told him bluntly. "If it's one thing you should know about me, it's that I'm not that important in the URS."

Exton backed away from her, running his hand through his hair. "I know enough to know you could be dangerous."

"Me?" Aerie gaped at him. "I thought you said I was not skilled enough."

"As an assassin," he corrected. "But there is something about you … something that's dangerous."

"What will you do with me then?" she asked. She watched as he put the screen down and pushed the chair back. He was leaving her, she realized, surprised to despair at the thought. Before she could stop herself, her hand reached out and grabbed his arm. "Hey! You can't leave. You didn't tell me anything about who you are."

She felt him still under her touch.

"Don't worry," he said. "I think we'll get to it. We have time."

"What do you mean?"

"If you'll accept my offer," Exton replied, "I will extend you an opportunity to join us on the *Perdition* as a temporary guest. At the moment, we are not planning to make any runs down to Earth. But after the harvest is over, we can reassess your position and consider our options."

Harvest? Aerie frowned.

She would have to return to that issue once her fate was decided; she was too concerned with another word he'd spoken.

"A guest?" Aerie repeated. "But I'm from the URS. I might sabotage your ship or spy on you." Her cheeks flushed. "Or I might cause trouble, you know, accidentally."

"Don't worry," Exton assured her. "I'll make sure you have the proper supervision and you're kept busy enough to keep from plotting against us. In the morning, you will be assigned to a mentor who will take excellent care of you."

"I can't believe you would do that," Aerie said. Suspicion, and then anger, crept through her. "What kind of game are you playing?"

"I don't play games," he told her. "But I was hoping, no doubt foolishly, that it would be enough to convince you I am not quite the monster you believe me to be." With his other hand, he reached over and patted her head gently, almost affectionately, before letting her go and heading out.

An unusual mix of shame, fear, and confusion at the seemingly innocent act forced her hand. "No doubt indeed," she murmured, watching him walk out the door.

♦11♦

Exton flexed his fingers. The memory of Aerie's hand in his burned into his mind as it warmed his flesh. A strange mix of anticipation and frustration stirred inside of him.

Hours had passed since he'd gone to see her. Exton had been unable, or unwilling, to go back to sleep since then. He chose to pass the time in the Captain's Lounge, but for the first time in a long time, the small world outside the window was unable to keep neither his interest nor his derision.

From the moment he and his crew entered space, Exton had become a ghost, unchanging against the endless tides of life and space, longing only for revenge. He knew it was no coincidence he willingly adopted the title of the ghost of Captain Chainsword.

Something about Aerie disturbed him, and he had been right to call her dangerous. For the first time in years, he felt his humanity creeping up behind him, and while he was determined to ignore it, he found that he could not ignore her.

Sighing, he looked back out the window beside him. He had a feeling he did not really *want* to ignore her, either.

The earth was far enough away that he could see the entirety of it, much like he had the night of Emery's wedding. It was strange to think that it had only been three days since he was on Earth itself, fighting and battling inside the heart of the URS.

He barely heard the door open below.

"I hope I'm not interrupting anything this time," Emery said in greeting.

"No," Exton assured her, hopping down from his perch. He landed next to her. "I've actually been waiting for you to show."

"Why?" Emery asked. "I know I'm not the only one who comes and gets you when you miss breakfast with the crew. I could have sent Mei, or Cherrie, or Alice."

"No, please don't send them, or any of the older

daughters of the crewmembers. Ever."

"Why not?" Emery teased. "They're all pretty eager to find an excuse to talk to you."

"And I'm rightfully terrified to give it to them," Exton replied. "They need jobs where they don't have to interact with me. They're barely adults."

"They're the same age as that girl we've managed to capture," Emery pointed out. "You don't seem to mind her company so much."

His eyes narrowed. "Spying on me, are you?"

"Not intentionally. But I happened to be friends with some of the medics, and one or two of them mentioned you'd visited her. And checked up on her multiple times, in one way or another."

"So?"

"You've been acting weird since we got back from Earth," Emery told him. "And then you go and see her? In the middle of the night?"

"There are any number of things that I tend to at night. I've been preoccupied," Exton replied, scratching his head nervously. "And I thought it was good to check on her, since it's my fault she's here in the first place."

Emery raised an eyebrow. "And now you're trying to explain yourself to me?"

"Ha! You wish." Exton rolled his eyes. "As it happens, Emery, I was going to talk to you about her. I think I'll let you worry about her from now on."

"What do you mean?"

"I'm putting you in charge of her. She'll be here as a temporary guest."

"A *guest?*" Emery's mouth dropped open, reminding Exton of their mother more than ever. "Exton, she's from the URS."

"So are most of us, if you recall."

"I mean, she's not a member of the Ecclesia, and she's not a refugee or a defector. Her loyalty is still to them."

"I know."

"You know," Emery replied slowly, "but you don't care?"

"Em, we're not going to make supply runs anytime soon; it's harvest time, and the water I've had collected from the Memory Tree should be enough to boost our supply," Exton reminded her. "And even while I could return her, what do you think will happen to her? She'll be in trouble with the URS, and we both know they're more merciless than me. While they don't believe in God, they certainly have used quite a few of their people as martyrs, if they don't just disappear entirely."

"That's true," Emery agreed, "but she could still turn against us."

"That's why I'm putting her under your care."

Emery wrinkled her nose. "Gee, thanks. I guess."

"It'll be easy. Or at least, as easy as she'll make it for you."

"What do you want me to do with her?"

He shrugged. "You might as well train her. Have her assigned to a job, see if she's useful in anything we need onboard."

"I don't agree with showing her the ship." Emery crossed her arms over her chest, defiant. "I'm not even sure I agree with letting her out of the med ward. She tried to hurt you, Exton."

"I survived." When she said nothing in reply, only glaring at him, he added, "I talked with her, Emery. Aerie's not going to attack me again."

"Aerie?"

"That's her name, right?"

"The medics had 'Aeris' down on their report."

"I'm guessing that she gave me her nickname, then," Exton said. A sudden thought crossed his mind. "Did she give the medics a surname?"

"Rearden, if I'm not mistaken." Emery paused. "You didn't notice that while you were with her?"

"I was making notes on her personality," Exton grumbled. "Not her name."

"Are you sure you're feeling all right?"

"What's wrong, Emery?" Exton huffed, exasperated. "I know this is a unique situation, but at most it would be three weeks we would have to deal with her."

"I'm worried."

"Then just tell me why."

"I'm worried she can hurt you."

"I just told you before she's not going to attack me. She might be a good fighter, but I can handle her."

"I didn't mean in that way," Emery said softly. "You like her."

He stiffened. If Emery could see it, he would have to face reality. A long, telling moment of silence passed between them before he finally replied, "Is there some reason I can't like her?"

"Plenty, according to your own reasons," Emery reminded him.

"Aren't you the one who was concerned I would die alone and lose my soul just a week ago?"

"So sorry for being concerned for you," Emery sneered. "But you have to agree, this isn't what I had in mind."

"Still trying to push Alice on me?" Exton teased. "Or any of the other insufferable defectors looking for a trophy for a boyfriend, or another helpless refugee only after protection?"

"No, even though Alice is a nice girl," Emery huffed. "You know what I mean, though."

"I do."

"And you still like her?"

They were both silent for a long moment. Exton knew what Emery was thinking. He had made his plans and used the *Perdition* to protect the world; if he became vulnerable, it was possible he would not be the only one to suffer the consequences.

"If Aerie does decide to turn against us, we always have the upper hand," Exton reasoned, ignoring the question.

"I'll take care to remind her of that, then," Emery said with a sigh.

"Emery."

"I know," she said. She reached out and touched his cheek. "Just be careful."

He smirked. "Duty first, Em."

"I know," she reiterated.

"I could change my mind," he continued. "Given enough time."

"I can only hope."

Before she could do anything else—beg, plead, threaten him to do just that—the bell sounding the end of the shift rang, and it was time for her to go and take care of her new charge.

Aerie was reluctant to wake up. She had grown up in New Hope, which, in being underground, felt like living in a large planetarium of sorts. Being out in the middle of the real solar system was tiring.

Tiring but beautiful.

The nature of the solar winds, the glow of the moon or Earth, both seemingly close enough to touch—all of it radiated temptation and captivated her attention through the small windows in the med ward.

She blamed that for her inability to sleep properly.

All things considered, she thought as she pulled the thin blanket over her tired face, *it's for the best.* There was no need to add a handsome space pirate captain to her list of reasons to stay awake when she would rather be dreaming.

"Miss Rearden?"

Aerie grimaced under the covers. What had possessed her to give them Brock's last name as hers?

Aerie sighed as she answered her own question. The medics, without Exton's scrutiny and suspicion, proved to be too easily misled, and General St. Cloud wasn't the greatest father in the world by far, but he was certainly the second-to-worst one to have as a father while she was on an enemy starship.

It's a good thing I wasn't raised in the Osgood unit, she thought wryly.

"Miss Rearden?" The voice was more persistent.

Aerie pulled back the sheet and sat up. "I'm up."

"Good." Tyra, one of the medics Aerie was able to recognize, smiled up at her from behind a screen. "Your assigned counselor is here to meet you. I'm just going to do one final check through your reports before discharging you to her."

"Thanks, Tyra," Aerie murmured. So, Exton had assigned her a caretaker already, just as he said. She'd been secretly hoping he would come and see her again before she had to move.

"No problem, miss," the medic replied as she squinted down at some blood samples. "It's been nice having you here with us. We always enjoy getting to know the newcomers."

"Thanks." Aerie pressed down her hair, trying to get her long locks to cooperate. "Uh, Tyra, do I have enough time before I leave? I'd like to get myself organized, if I can."

"You'll have plenty of time for that later," a new voice called from the door of the med ward. "We'll see that you're comfortable."

Tyra glanced over. "I'm almost finished with my final notes, Director. Just another few moments while I get the test results for these."

"By all means," the Director said, "take your time. We are in no rush."

Aerie studied her new counselor. Her hair was a pretty shade of brown, cut short at the chin. She was just a bit shorter than Aerie was, but Aerie could tell from just looking at her that she was older, but not by much. She was, like Exton, used to wielding authority.

Master Browning's bushy eyebrows flashed across Aerie's mind, and Master Instructor Harrick's cool gaze soon followed. Would this lady be just like them?

"Hello," Aerie said in polite greeting. She had to remind herself not to salute her. *No need to invoke any enmity for the*

URS, Aerie thought.

The Director arched an eyebrow. "You're not going to attack me first? Well, it's good to know you have some self-control."

At Tyra's surprised expression, the Director sighed. "Tyra, leave us. Check your charts in the hall."

"Yes, Director." Tyra shot an apologetic look in Aerie's direction before collecting her gear and shuffling out the door.

"I guess you heard about my, um, untraditional greeting," Aerie muttered.

"Hardly. I was the one who stopped your fight." She pointed to Aerie's neck. "I shot you with a tranquilizer, and you ended up collapsing."

"Huh." Aerie felt annoyance bubble up inside her. "That's funny. Exton never told me that part."

"Exton?"

"The captain. He, uh, told me to call him by his name." Aerie hated herself for flushing over. She was instantly reminded of being humiliated in her primary classes for daydreaming, getting caught doodling on her papers, or whispering to her friends. "I didn't realize the titles were more important here. I guess you'd rather not call me Aerie, then? I don't really want to be called 'Miss Rearden,' or 'Comrade Rearden,' if you don't mind."

The Director sighed. "Let's get a few things straight, Aerie," she said, allowing Aerie to exhale in relief, "and then we'll get started on settling you in."

"Sounds good to me," Aerie replied.

"First, I am the Coordinating Director of the *Perdition*, Emery Shep—uh, Caldwell, now." She sighed. "I have a newer last name. Sometimes I forget still."

Her stumbling made Aerie smile. *She doesn't seem as uptight as my previous instructors.* "Did you recently get assigned to be married?" Aerie asked, before she could help herself.

"Assigned to be married?" Emery frowned. "Oh, never mind. We don't marry as a career enhancement or replacement here. We marry for love."

"Love?" Aerie repeated, knowing she sounded stupid.

"Yes. And to answer your question, yes, I did get married recently," Emery continued. "My husband works on the Command Bridge."

It had been a long time since Aerie had heard the word "husband." She was, despite her better judgment, intrigued. "Love is seen as a barbaric type of response to anything but the State in the URS," Aerie mused aloud. "A genetic throwback response to emotional stimuli."

"Congratulations on your recitation of the URS Brainwashing Handbook." Emery frowned again. "I don't seem to be 'barbaric' to you, do I?"

"No, not really. But then, I don't know. I've only just met you."

"I've been assigned to be your counselor, and I don't need any more incentive to make things as difficult as I can for you," Emery told her.

"I didn't mean to insult you," Aerie promised. She sighed, and her voice dropped down to a whisper. "I tend to agree with you, even though the State doesn't allow for that." When Emery only looked at her, she added, "My mother told me she loved me very often, but it was only in secret."

"Oh." Emery cleared her throat. "Well, that's good. You might prove to be a defector yet."

Aerie felt her stomach twist with guilty sickness at the thought. As Emery began to talk about her role onboard the ship, Aerie's thoughts briefly landed on her own unit.

Was Serena back at the military academy? Was the wreckage from the battle with Captain Chainsword still present? Were her brothers working on a way to bring her home, or were they just causing Brock trouble in pilot training?

Did the General even know she was missing? What was Phoebe doing to the garden Aerie had tended with her mother?

Discomfort settled inside her.

She wasn't lying to Exton when she said she was not a top priority. Indeed, she had a feeling if it weren't for her mother, she might not have been born at all and no one would have felt a loss at the thought.

I just have to survive. She recounted her plan to herself. Get information, as much as possible, on the *Perdition* and its mysterious captain and crew, and then get home. Once there, prove idle insubordination had borne a better fruit than meaningless obedience. And then survive whatever punishment she'd earned.

Aerie couldn't say which part was going to be the hardest to accomplish.

"—and that's what I do. Any questions?"

"Uh … " Aerie just stared at her, blank-faced, angry she'd been focused on her own plans instead of the information. "No. Not now, anyway. I can always ask questions later, right?"

"Yes, of course," Emery said, giving Aerie her first glimpse of a smaller smile. "Now, let me tell you about your duties."

Good, I didn't miss this part. Aerie scooted closer.

"Exton has made it so you are a guest, but to others, we've registered you as a refugee; we don't have guests, as a general rule. We don't want people in the URS thinking of it as a travel ship."

"Believe me, we don't," Aerie assured her. "I was pretty sure you were going to kill me on sight when I got up here."

"So you wanted to take the initiative, is that it?"

"Yes." Aerie felt a spark of happiness ignite inside her. It was possible she would like Emery. "That's perfect!"

"I think I'm beginning to see why Exton thinks it'll be okay to have you as a guest," Emery said.

"Exton?" Aerie frowned. "You don't call the captain by his title, either?"

"No."

"He's not your husband, is he?" Aerie asked, suddenly alarmed at the prospect.

"Goodness, no." Emery made a face. "I told you, my husband's name is Tyler."

"Oh. Sorry. Exton's not married, is he?"

"No. He's not."

At Emery's sharp reply, Aerie's heart fluttered helplessly. "Sorry," she murmured, "but there's so much to remember."

"It's fine," Emery replied, even though her tone told Aerie a different story. "You shouldn't apologize so much."

"I've been told that by the URS, too. There's no room for apologies when it comes to survival."

"The pendulum can swing the other way just as easily," Emery told her. "Here, if you do wrong, that's when you apologize. But there's no need to keep apologizing for a wrong once you've been absolved from it."

"Sounds easy enough to remember."

"Consider it your first lesson, then. For today, we're going to get you established in your new quarters and start scheduling you for some job training."

"I would like to leave the med ward. I mean, the medics are nice and all, but … I feel trapped in here." She admitted the last part sheepishly, realizing that she *was* trapped on the ship. It wasn't like being in a different room would make any difference to that reality.

"That's a common side effect of being in space." Emery pointed to the bags of fluid and the devices behind her. "It's best to make sure you didn't have any toxins or harmful chemicals in your blood. Things happen differently in space, especially on a biological level."

"I've been wondering," Aerie muttered. "I wasn't terrible at science, but some of the more complicated astrophysics did leave me confused."

"They'll do that," Emery agreed. "That's why my studies were in horticulture."

"Really?" Aerie's eyes lit up with renewed enthusiasm. "That was what my mother pursued for a while when she was at university, before she decided to pursue a career in marriage."

Emery gave her a wry smile. "I would appreciate it if you didn't talk about marriage as a career. The URS has striven to remove all the love, it seems, and its intended meaning; we see its meaning coming from a different place than what they do."

"The love is still there," Aerie argued. "My mother loved me."

"She wasn't supposed to, at least not more than the State. And you weren't even supposed to call her 'Mother,' were you?"

Aerie bit her lip. "No, I guess not."

"You know," Emery said slowly, "there are a lot of mothers and fathers here on the *Perdition*. You might want to get used to the idea of it."

But what happens when I go back to the URS?

Aerie said nothing while Emery continued. "Exton has you registered as a refugee of the URS. You'll likely be surprised at how different things are here. You'll be assigned to work, but we can make adjustments if you are not content."

"Working is fine with me." It would give her opportunities to discover more about the *Perdition* and its crew. "I suppose I have all the time in the world to adjust."

Emery laughed. "We don't have quite that much," she amended, "but there's no sense wasting what we have."

"I suppose you are right," Aerie said. "The URS—"

"I know the stance the URS has, Aerie," Emery interrupted. "I lived in it myself, growing up. Many people here are refugees, wanderers, and rebels. It would not be a good idea to ruin your cover as a refugee. Believe me, Exton has made your life much easier, and it would do you well to embrace his gift."

Warmth settled inside her. "Exton has been … an unusual host," Aerie stated noncommittedly.

"I'm surprised to hear it as much as you," Emery admitted. "Especially after you tried to kill him."

"I know it might be a surprise to you," Aerie said, "but

I'm not surprised I failed at my attempt. If I challenged him again, I'd have better luck, I'm sure of it."

She glanced up at Emery, trying not to look as pathetically hopeful as she felt. "Will I see him around at all?"

"He has a lot of duties as captain."

"I would like to thank him for his … hospitality." Aerie decided that was the best word for it.

"I'll pass it along to him for you. Now, let's get Tyra to discharge you so we can see about getting you started on your schedule … "

As Emery rattled off a long list of things to do, Aerie stood up for the first time in days. Her hand went up to the back of her head, where Exton had touched her wound so carefully.

A sudden thought struck her. "Where's Moona?" she asked, interrupting Emery mid-lecture.

"What?"

"My cat."

"Oh, that thing," Emery said. She shrugged at Aerie's frown. "Pets are not very practical," she explained apologetically.

"Do we have time to get her?" Aerie asked.

"We'll see if the medics can have her delivered to you later."

"Are you sure she'll be all right?" Aerie thought of her kitten's tendency to wander off and bit her lip in worry.

"She should be, especially if she's been here with you all this time," Emery assured her. "The medics can see to her. There's no need to fret. You should have some time to work on getting ready for your new life, anyway. Being a space pirate is interesting, to say the least."

A space pirate. On the bright side, it did sound more exciting than working in the Comms Sec, Aerie thought. She grinned, feeling more like her regular, optimistic self. "I had a feeling it was."

♦12♦

"It's lovely." Aerie glanced around the new room, hardly daring to believe that it was now hers.

Aerie hadn't been sure of what to expect for a room. The URS was all about necessity, and from her class visits to the prisons and the camps, she was expecting a no more than a small pallet to sleep on and maybe a blanket, if she was lucky.

That was not what she found to be the case when Emery unlocked her door for her. Inside, the room was much bigger than she'd imagined, though it was only a little bigger than the room in her unit. The walls were of a sturdy black and red, giving her a small but cozy place to sleep, the pattern even reminding her of home.

There was also a closet and a bathroom, and the bed had been prepared with light gray sheets and a fluffy pillow, one much nicer than the small pad in the med ward. She pushed down the desire to pick up the pillow and bury her face in it.

A small table and two chairs were pushed up against the far wall, making a perfect alcove for reading or studying. Assuming she could find something to read or study.

Seeing the colors, Aerie had to wonder if the URS had done a paint job throughout the whole ship. Everything from the med ward to her room seemed to blend into everything else. There were gray floors, black walls, and red trim all over, with numbers posted and a sign on every corner. She wondered if it was just her room, or if the others were like it.

My room. There was no one to share it with—no Serena, no classmate, no mother, no other comrade—for the first time in her entire life.

"I'm glad you think so," Emery said behind her as she stepped inside the room and pushed some buttons, turning on more lights. "I'm sure you'll get used to it soon enough."

"When is your room check?" Aerie asked.

"We don't do room checks here."

Aerie turned to face her. "Really? You don't care if I spill things or mess things up?"

"One thing you'll find here on the *Perdition* is that you must take care of yourself for a lot of things, including making your own standards for approval. While you live here, it's up to you to decide how clean—or in the case of some people, how unclean—you want it to be."

"I'm guessing that's good as long as no one is causing a health hazard?"

Emery giggled, surprising Aerie. "Yes, that's true. We generally frown on that." She walked over to the small closet. "Your uniforms should have arrived already. Here," she said, tossing one to Aerie. "Go ahead and try it on. That one will go well with your hair."

Aerie looked down at the uniform. The light material was colored a light blue with some black trim. It reminded her of Exton's eyes.

"There are some additional items in here," Emery told her. "Boots, a belt, socks, gloves. Here's the jacket, if you're still a bit cold."

"I've seen this material before," Aerie said. "It's the same the URS uses."

"We don't spend much time searching for new resources for our crew when it comes to clothes." Emery nodded toward the uniform. "You'll find a lot of what we use here is similar to or the same as the URS."

"Why do you hate them so much?" Aerie asked. "I mean, sure, their national pride can be excessive, maybe, but everyone has a job, a unit, and a place to be in the URS, and it's all given freely."

Emery shook her head. "It's hardly free, Aerie."

"I don't understand then," Aerie replied. *What could be worth giving up fairness and a means to survival?*

"Have you ever seen anyone in the URS who didn't want to live the way they told them to?" Emery asked.

Before Aerie could reply, she thought about the homeless people cast out from the city, the ones she saw the few times she went to the surface. "A couple," she muttered.

"Then I'm surprised," Emery admitted. "Usually they kill

or imprison dissenters or insurgents. Of course, their Reeducation Program has a high success rate. We've only managed to help a couple of them after that."

Aerie thought about the Reeducation Program. *They did have a funny look on their faces when they left,* she recalled, *one that didn't seem natural.*

Feeling uncomfortable, she made her way into the bathroom and changed into her new clothes. Emery began programming her room settings.

"You'll be assigned to follow me around for the most part of this morning," Emery told her through the door. "You'll have some time, like all refugees, to get acquainted with the ship and its communities. You've been assigned to work on basic tasks first."

Aerie looked at herself in the small mirror. Her hair was still messy. Her uniform felt comfortable, even with the jacket. Three days in the med ward had left her wanting warmth. Her eyes, she noticed, were wide, but no longer with fear.

More like overwhelmed, Aerie decided.

She'd been taught that the *Perdition* was well-named, that it was the most terrible of places to wind up, that Captain Chainsword and his crew were ruthlessly unprincipled and eager to spill blood.

Maybe they were just ghost stories, Aerie thought. Designed to keep her from questioning too much.

"Don't be a fool," she whispered to herself. *These people owe you nothing. There must be a reason they are giving you this room, these nice things. They are laughing at you. They want you to believe them, and that's when they'll strike.*

"If you haven't seen it yet, there are some supplies for your hair and teeth in the drawer by the mirror," Emery called out, delighting Aerie with the discovery.

A few moments later, dressed and cleaned up, Aerie walked back into her room. Emery was standing at her kitchenette. "I'm making tea," she told her. "I hope you don't mind. I wasn't sure how long you would be."

"I don't mind," Aerie said. "I've never been in a pirate starship before. There's a lot to learn and just look at, really."

"Understandable." Emery gestured to the table, carrying over two cups. "Are you hungry? There's more in the cabinets, though not a whole lot. If you get really hungry, you'll need to go down to Level Three."

"Right now, I'm too distracted to be hungry. The medics did give me some food before I left."

"They always take good care of our patients," Emery murmured into her cup.

"I've never been treated so well," Aerie admitted. She suddenly laughed. "One time, I broke my arm when I was younger, and I had to go to the Medical Center in New Hope. I had to wait for nearly six hours with my mom while they tried to get me situated. It wasn't fun."

"I can imagine," Emery said. "Depending on what day it was, it could have been longer. Medical supplies are usually delayed in the URS, even in the capital."

"How do you know that?" Aerie asked. "It wasn't too bad. And at least I got treated. Eventually."

"Tyler, my husband, worked in computer tech. He has a sister, Meredith, who had to go to the Med Center for a blood transfusion. After nearly five hours, when it became clear she would be waiting, he hacked into the system to see if he could get her in faster. It turned out they wouldn't have been able to see her at all, until their new supplies came in three days later. She would have been dead."

"That sounds awful." Aerie remembered how nervous her mother had been in the Med Center, even though a broken arm was hardly life threatening. "Her mother must have been worried."

"It's the fact that the hospital didn't admit they couldn't treat her that bothered Tyler. They slipped out and he was able to track down a small church house, home to some members of the Ecclesia, where medical treatment was possible."

"So the medics, then, are they from the Ecclesia? I saw

their insignia. I know they're not from MENACE."

"No, they're not from MENACE." Emery's brusque response made Aerie flinch.

"Just wondering. I've never seen it before."

"Many of them are student apprentices here," Emery explained. "They are part of the Ecclesia. As are most people aboard the ship."

"I've never heard of that nation before I came here."

"They are more than a nation. They share something deeper than culture and rules, and even a leader."

"Isn't Exton their leader?"

"No, Exton is the captain of the ship. It's different."

"Oh." Aerie frowned. "That's unusual."

"It's more of a religion," Emery explained. "I'm sure that the URS has not told you anything about religion, since it is forbidden by the State, and anything forbidden by the State is evil."

"I see," she murmured, disturbed at how much that made sense. *Maybe a little too much sense.* Aerie looked down. She tried some of the tea, surprised at the sweet taste. "So, how long will I be here?"

"We don't know yet."

"What if my unit is looking for me?"

"They won't find you." Emery set down her cup. "It's pretty simple. The ship is currently out of range for most messages. We're currently headed back around the moon once more, and then we'll head back toward Earth since it is the end of our growing season. We don't have much longer before the harvest."

Before Aerie could ask about the harvest, Emery added, "Right now, only Dictator Osgood and General St. Cloud, and possibly a few others, would have access to the satellite feeds they would need in order to be able to reach us."

Aerie felt her breath leave her. She knew the General would not be happy to discover his daughter had been taken as a prisoner—*guest*—aboard an enemy ship. And she didn't think she would be safe letting Emery know she was the daughter of the highest-ranking general in the enemy state. They'd been nice enough to her as an accidental refugee. As a political piece, she would surely suffer.

"What if I wanted to send a message?"

"You're not allowed." Emery sat back in her chair. "Right now, we're not enemies, Aerie, unless you insist on it."

"I already told Exton I was the enemy," Aerie grumbled. "For all the good it did."

Emery frowned. "You're our guest, by our mistake, and we want to do what we can to make you feel welcome here. But we can't have you threaten the rest of the ship. I assume from what he's told me that Exton thought you would cooperate."

Aerie flinched. "I will," she said, her voice barely audible as she thought about her self-assigned reconnaissance mission.

"It's better for your family, too, if you refrain from contacting them, despite what you might think. The URS might see your family as a threat to the State," Emery went on, ignoring Aerie's sudden apprehension. "They could see you reaching out to them from the *Perdition* as an anti-establishment movement, a resistance of sorts."

Aerie was about to object, when she realized Emery had the right of it. Thinking about her PAR, Aerie knew the URS didn't take well to non-conformity, political or otherwise. "I guess with my mother dead, there's no reason anyone would miss me."

"Your mother's gone?" Emery's eyes softened, and Aerie was surprised by the genuine empathy she saw in her eyes. "I'm sorry to hear that. My mother has passed on, too."

"My mom was a great lady," Aerie said quietly. "I miss her so much it hurts to think of her. It's been close to five years now. She died just after my birthday."

"My mom died about ten years ago, a few months after my father. For a long time, I cried when I thought about her."

Aerie nodded, unable to say anything. *I should be used to*

being shocked by now, she thought. Having something in common with her enemy surprised her, especially something as deep and painful and true as missing a mother.

"I felt better after Exton told me it hurt more *not* to think of her," Emery said. "I always liked that. He's really clever like that sometimes, but you can't let him get a big head over it or he'll just be insufferable."

"He knew your mother?"

"Oh. I'm his sister."

Aerie gaped. "You are?"

Emery smiled, and Aerie could see a small dimple appear, just like the one Exton had over the left corner of his mouth. "Yes, I don't mention it too often," she said. "We don't look much alike. We both help run the ship and keep our parents' legacies alive."

Aerie just continued to watch her, mentally berating herself as she blushed.

"There's no need to be embarrassed," Emery told her.

Embarrassment quickly transformed to anger. "I just didn't realize he'd be sending you to spy on me for him."

"He's not like that." Emery sighed. "You don't need to be so paranoid."

"I'm paranoid?"

"Seems like it," Emery muttered as she picked up her cup and headed toward the compact dishwasher. "I don't know why he likes you. That would get on my nerves after a while."

Aerie felt her blush go from red to purple. *Exton likes me?*

"Maybe he feels sorry for you," Emery continued, talking more to herself than Aerie, making Aerie's stomach tumble once more, despite the tea. "That would explain why he's been so nice."

"You'll have to ask him about it," Aerie muttered. "I certainly gave him no reason to like me."

"There's no point in asking him to explain himself," Emery told her, stating it with such a resigned quality Aerie knew she was familiar with it. "Let's just get to business, shall we?"

She nodded, trying her best not to show her irritation. *Let's get this over with. I can start collecting information on the* Perdition *faster if we can get out of here.*

"Here is where your schedule is posted," Emery said, pointing to the screen placed beside the door. "You can change it between daily and weekly settings. Today, you're going to follow me around the ship for the morning and you'll be working on Level Five. At the end of this shift, you'll be free to congregate with the other families and crewmembers on Level Three."

"Oh? I'll have free time?" Aerie had to stop herself from wriggling her butt in excitement. That would give her time to go investigating, she thought.

"Yes," Emery told her. She pressed another button on the screen. "Here's a map of the ship here. Your room is on this level, in the centerfold region of the ship. We are on Level Two"—she pointed to the different floors—"and this here, Level Five, is where you'll start working later. The med ward is on Level One. Other floors are off-limits to you at this time, such as where our researchers and our students are working."

"What's this?" Aerie asked, pointing to the large oval-shaped room on the screen's diagram. "Is that where the engine is?"

"No." Emery paused. "That's the Biovid." Before Aerie could ask more about it, she continued, "Here's where your room is. We'll start familiarizing you with the ship from here."

Aerie nodded. "I think I'll be able to handle the screen. It's similar to the URS tech, too." *Although not the new NETech,* she thought with a small smile.

"Good. It also acts as an intercom and public announcement device. You can get news from its different channels, though we really only have the station that's run by our students and a couple from Earth that are filtered through the ship." She smiled wistfully. "The Ecclesia are very fond of music, you know."

"That's nice." *Even if it seems a bit frivolous.* Aerie had only heard music at ceremonies and graduations, and she could understand the appeal of it to some people. Brock had mentioned once how music didn't seem to encourage the proper, pious attitude most befitting the State, and ever since then Aerie had found his remark to be true.

She decided not to mention it to Emery. Aerie turned her attention to the bit of information she could use to help herself. "You get Earth news up here?"

"We're very aware of what happens on Earth, Aerie," Emery said. "It's part of our survival to know. You'll be able to see some of the reports on Levels Three and Four when you head down for your meals and entertainment."

Aerie hoped fervently that there were not any broadcasts about General St. Cloud's missing unit member. She sidestepped Emery and picked up the boots she'd seen earlier. "Well, let's get moving. After all that time in the med ward, I'm ready to stretch my legs a bit more."

♦13♦

The beeping noise was bothersome, Exton decided as he stepped onto the Command Bridge, but it was well worth its trouble to hear it. The notification system only beeped when he had messages, and he only had messages when he managed to anger the right people in the URS.

Specifically, Dictator Osgood.

Although it could be General St. Cloud as well now. He weighed his options of erasing the messages or answering them.

He pressed down on the "Delete" button. There was no need to answer if he had the upper hand.

"Thanks, Cap," Jared replied from behind the control monitor. "That was getting annoying."

"I agree," Exton remarked. "It is much less irritating in here without the constant reminder of the URS."

"It wasn't anything important, was it?"

"I doubt it. More bluster and pomp, probably. Or maybe the bounty on our heads got bigger."

"They're going to run out of credit and gold at this rate," Jared said with a laugh.

Exton nodded. "Give me the reports."

"We're back to the usual path, Cap. The ship is circling around the earth again, following its path with the moon. Currently, we're … "

As Jared began his daily chore of updating him on the condition of the ship, the solar winds, the monitors, and various other atmospheric considerations, Exton noticed another blinking light.

"Tyler," he called, interrupting Jared's exposition. "Get Emery up here. Aunt Patty's got a message for us."

"Okay, Captain," Tyler responded from the forward main control.

"Sorry, Jared," Exton apologized. "Continue, please."

"That's all I had, Cap."

"Oh. Well, good job. Keep me updated on any navigation

concerns."

"Will do." Jared cleared his throat. "The only other thing I thought I'd bring to your attention is from one of the Tech System managers, Greer. She says there's been some unusual activity near the Old Nova Scotian shores."

"What kind of activity?"

"A lot of movement," he said. "She's working night shift, but I read her report from last night. She said several vehicles, military grade, were driving up from New Hope over the past two days."

"Could it be training for the newbies, since that just graduated?" Exton thought about Aerie. He didn't need to look further than her to recall how he had interrupted the URS's graduation day.

"It's possible," Jared said. "But unusual."

Unusual was never an always or never situation, Exton knew. Still, he thought it best to check it out. "Have the report sent down to me. See if the day shift can track any other activity in the area to get a better idea of what we're dealing with here."

"Yes, sir," Jared replied. "I'll get that to you right away, sir."

Tyler came up behind him. "He's eager to please."

"You have him well-trained, that's for sure."

"Being a people-pleaser has its advantages. I would know."

"Not always," Exton replied with a smirk. "I can name a few times for you when it was not only *not* an advantage, but an inconvenient and dangerous one."

Tyler shrugged. "Sometimes fun and standing your moral ground are the same thing."

"Agreed. Is Emery coming?"

"She's on her way. She's got your new recruit in tow."

Exton felt a rush of satisfaction. "Good. She'll get to see the Command Bridge while she's here then. That'll take care of some of Emery's tasks. I like getting on Em's good side."

"It's good to do it while you can," Tyler said, "especially

if you're determined to get on her bad side so frequently. She told me you have a crush."

"I should have known she would tell you," Exton muttered with a grimace.

"You have to admit, it's a fitting punishment for all the teasing you gave us while we were dating," Tyler replied.

"Poetic justice has never been my strong suit."

"I know. You prefer revenge."

Exton shot him a glare, but before he could respond further to his best friend's teasing, the door behind him opened. "Get ready," Exton muttered to Tyler. "I'm going to have you talk to her. And Tyler, I'll need you to keep it light. She doesn't know the truth about the *Perdition*, or the URS or any of that."

"From what I've heard, she should be interesting."

"She is."

Exton turned just as Emery came up to him, Aerie following behind her. In her new uniform and freshened up, Aerie radiated vitality. She was clearly enjoying her newfound freedom aboard, no longer confined to the med ward. Her eyes were round and large, trying to mask her curiosity.

He knew the moment she saw him; he was gratified to see a slight flush appear over her cheeks as she met his gaze for the shortest second of his life.

"What did you need, Exton?"

Exton didn't have to exude any effort in ignoring Aerie while Emery demanded his attention. He gave Emery a welcoming smile before drawing her aside. "Something has come up. Follow me. Tyler, please watch our guest here for a moment."

Exton glanced behind him enough to see Aerie frown a bit at his abruptness, but he knew Tyler could smooth things over easily.

"What's happened?" Emery asked as they headed over to a small room off the Bridge.

"Aunt Patty's sent us another message," he told her. "I thought you'd like to be here when I played it."

"There's no other reason you could possibly want me here, is there?" Emery's brow arched suspiciously.

"I'll admit it's nice to have your charge join us here on the Command Bridge," Exton replied, "but family is family."

"I guess it has been a few weeks since we last heard from her," Emery admitted. "Play the message."

Exton pressed down on the blinking button, and a moment later a voice that reminded him so much of his mother's filled the small room.

"Hi, kids. Wanted to give you a call. I know it's close to the anniversary. Also wanted to give my best blessing to Emery and her new husband … "

"That's all?" Exton muttered in a blistered tone. "Sheesh. She could have waited. We'll see her soon enough, won't we?"

"Stop talking," Emery hissed, punching him on the shoulder. "There's more."

"The settlement is growing in number, but we've been careful to screen everyone as they come in. We have enough people to get much of the work done … "

"It's just an update," Exton grumbled.

"Shut up."

" … a new refugee from the Old West is here now. He says there are only a few pockets of resistance left up north now. He worked in the Comms Sec; he says that the URS has a new tool for their communications. I wanted to warn you … "

"They're changing their communication method?" Emery repeated. "That's not good."

"I knew something was wrong." Exton shook his head as he paused the message. "And no, Em, it wasn't guilt."

"What are you talking about?"

"When we attacked, Osgood sent out a bunch of fighter jets and began launching a lot of attacks."

"I know," Emery said. "You mentioned that it was out of character for him."

"And it was. And this is why. He's mobilizing his forces. He's planning something."

"So?"

"So, more people are in danger."

"They've always been in danger with him in charge."

"They're using us as an excuse for battle now."

"Which is what they've been doing since we've been here," Emery reminded him.

"We've managed to derail their space program, and to keep them at an impasse for the past six years," Exton continued. "They must have something that's a game changer."

Emery started to look worried. "I see."

Exton's face was grim. "We need to know what they're planning."

"I'll send Aunt Patty a message back and let her know we're on it."

"Good. Once you're done, have the Tech Systems recheck their satellite monitoring. There's no use worrying about new communications if we can find a different frequency or see if there's a missed code somewhere in what we do have."

"Okay," Emery approved. "Anything else you want me to do that will keep me preoccupied long enough for you to get some time in with Aerie?"

"Aerie?" he repeated. "You're calling her that, too, are you?"

Emery frowned. "She asked me to."

Regardless of her curt reply, Exton smiled. "You can see why I like her."

"She's silly enough with some of her ideas and her questions," Emery said slowly, "but she's fairly easy to like." At Exton's grin, she wrinkled her nose and added, "Or at least easy enough to get along with."

"That's the sister I know," Exton replied with a laugh. "What else did you learn about her?"

"She doesn't trust us, but she likes us," Emery said. "She was impressed with the med care."

"Most refugees are."

"Her mother died when she was younger."

"No wonder you've taken a liking to her. You like having people to mother."

Emery frowned. "She's interested in plants."

"Keep her out of the Biovid for a few more days, then. I have the Memory Tree being processed in there. There's no need to make her hate me more."

"I don't think she hates you, although she might wish it." Emery smiled. "You're a puzzle to her."

"And she's curious."

"Yes."

"I noticed that pretty quickly, myself." Exton grinned. "Are you relatively certain she won't try to kill us now?"

"Relatively." She sighed. "But I'm not sure she would join us. There's something holding her back, and it's strong."

"What do you think it is?"

"Not a boyfriend, if you're worried about that," Emery teased. "I'd guess pride, but I'm not sure."

"Good to know." He was almost out the door when he turned back to her. "One more thing, Em. This message is confidential. I don't mind if you tell Tyler, but keep it quiet. We still don't have specifics."

"Will do."

The thought of the URS doing anything was rightfully terrifying, but it could be a sign of desperation. Maybe the end was coming for the URS.

Exton almost groaned to himself. He had just decided it was okay to let his heart breathe a little. Was it possible he was buying into the idea of optimism already?

As if in answer to his question, Exton heard Aerie laugh. Turning to see her, to look at her, to watch her hair catch the light as it fell in soft waves down her back … he decided he couldn't help it, any more than he could stop himself from liking her in the first place.

"What's so amusing?" he asked, coming up to Tyler.

"I was just telling Aerie how I met Emery for the first time." Tyler straightened his posture at Exton's approach.

"You have to admit, Exton, it was kind of funny. I mean, you hadn't even mentioned you had a sister while we at university together. I was just getting to the part where Emery came around asking for you, Exton, and I'd been talking to her about 'my roommate' and his irritating, antisocial habits."

"Never say so." Aerie smiled as she turned to face Exton, who only shrugged in response. "He didn't tell me she was his sister either," Aerie told Tyler, "so I can sympathize with you."

"For what?" Exton asked. "Looking like an idiot, or just feeling like one?"

"Maybe a bit of both," Aerie snapped, turning her full attention to him. "Seems inconsiderate, really."

"You should be flattered I have a habit of neglecting to inform others of my family," Exton told her. "It would really only be inconsiderate if I lied to you about it."

"You lied about her spying on me."

"She's the best we have, and more compassionate than me by half." Exton rolled his eyes. "I'm not interested in spying on you. If I was, I'd be able to set up a cam in the med ward much more easily than lose my Coordinating Director to be your personal escort around the ship."

"I should have had my cam to record you saying that," Tyler remarked. "She would have loved hearing it."

"Well, don't tell her about it. She doesn't need the praise."

"She said the same thing about you," Aerie recalled. "It seems you have a lot in common."

"Then in that case, I would say it was the poor observational training the URS gave you, rather than my lapse in manners," Exton said. "That makes sense, given the other areas in which the URS has been lacking in preparing their students."

"Hey," Aerie objected. "I'll gladly show you just how 'lacking' they were in preparing me for battle. Just tell me where to meet you, and we'll have a rematch."

"I won the *original* match. There's no need for me to agree to a rematch."

"Only because you had help." Aerie smirked. "Emery told me she was the one who had to sedate me after I attacked you."

"She didn't apologize for that, did she?" Exton shook his head. "My goodness, lady, what are you doing to my crew?"

Aerie laughed again, and Exton smiled. When he saw the amused expression on Tyler's face, he quickly hid it. "There's no need for you to stain my honor over a technicality."

"Getting tranquilized is hardly a technicality."

"You were almost done fighting anyway," Exton insisted. "Emery just helped put you over the edge. I still would have won, and it would have been a lot more painful for you."

"I disagree. I could have had you knocked out before she stepped in and you stepped up." Aerie brushed back a lock of her hair from her face. "Come on. Just agree to a rematch. Deal?"

She held out her hand, and Exton only paused for a moment before taking it. "Fine," he agreed. "Just let me know when you're free, and we'll schedule it."

"I'd bet anything the crew would love to watch. Maybe we could set up a cam in the gymnasium?" Tyler suggested.

Exton glared at him. "I don't think so."

"Scared?" Aerie asked, the grin on her face glowing with anticipation.

"No," Exton told her. "Just irritated I have to attend to a childish need for attention."

"I am *not* a child." She frowned. "You're such a—"

"All right, Exton," Emery spoke up, interrupting Aerie's argument. "I got those tasks finished up. Now, please excuse me and my charge. We were headed down to Level Five, where Aerie's scheduled for some basic work training." Glancing at Aerie's face, she frowned. "Exton, you really need to stop provoking her, you know."

"I didn't say anything," Exton assured her, making Aerie scowl. He squeezed her hand gently, enough to make her blush, before letting go. "Excuse me. Duty first."

Exton could hear Emery's sigh as he walked away.

♦14♦

When they arrived on Level Five, Aerie felt her face finally return to its normal temperature.

"I'd just let it go," Emery told her. "Exton has a strange sense of humor."

"I didn't think he was joking about the child remark," Aerie muttered.

"Then stop acting like one," Emery said.

"I'm not acting like one."

"I'm sure that's just what a child would say, too."

Aerie was about to respond when she saw Emery had a kind smile on her face. *I'll show them*, she thought, *when I beat him in battle.*

"For the next part of your shift," Emery said, "you're going to be working on Level Five with some of our other crewmembers. I will pick you up here, by the elevator, when the shift is over."

Aerie looked up and down the endless halls. "Which elevator is this?"

"This is the forward port elevator," Emery replied. "It's one of the few elevators that can go to all levels of the ship."

"When will I get to see the other levels?"

"Some you won't. Others you'll get to see as you work through basic training and move onto more advanced jobs."

Aerie smiled. "So what is basic?" she asked. "I know that the URS has basic training for combatants. Is that similar?"

Emery gave her a reluctant laugh. "Goodness, no. Not at all."

"What is it then?"

"Basic starts with basic duties. Cleaning and repairs top the list."

"Cleaning?" Aerie repeated.

"Yep. Cleaning. Here comes your instructor now," Emery said, nodding toward a tall shadow making its way down the hall.

Aerie straightened her posture as an older lady

approached, followed by a girl Aerie thought seemed close to her own age. *There's no harm in making a good impression*, Aerie told herself, *even though I know I'm not obligated to.*

"Aerie, this is Olga, our Level Five Manager, and one of her assistants, Alice." Emery gestured to the long halls. "Olga runs this level and sees to the cleaning of the entire ship."

Aerie gave a small smile to Alice, who seemed to be studying her. At the strange look on Alice's face, Aerie took an uncomfortable step back.

She decided to focus her attention on her instructor instead. Olga's dark eyes and bushy hair made Aerie wonder if she could have been Master Browning's mother, had she been born in an earlier time.

"It's no easy task, neither," Olga remarked. She inclined her head in greeting. "So we got a new recruit, do we? Another refugee?"

"Yes," Aerie spoke up. "Please call me Aerie. I'm here to learn how to clean today."

"Cleaning is secondary," Olga told her. "Caring for yourself and others is primary."

While Aerie was momentarily confused at the lady's comment, Emery stepped forward and instructed Olga on the timeline and other matters; Aerie barely listened, already figuring that Emery was warning Olga in some kind of manner or code what to expect from her as a former URS member.

Not even former, Aerie corrected herself. She was a reluctant recruit to the *Perdition* and her crew at best. An enemy, at worst.

An outsider, no question.

Alice sighed, nearly making Aerie glance over at her. There was a hardened gleam in her eyes, one that surprised Aerie.

Was it possible Alice didn't like her?

Aerie wasn't sure why Alice would have a problem with her; glancing at her, she was sure she'd never even seen Alice before.

It's not like I am not used to it. Recalling how she would feel once other students found out she was St. Cloud's charge, Aerie gave up.

She surveyed the surroundings; much of it seemed like an endless hallway, the same as the level where her room was located. But she had a feeling that these rooms were made for storage, more than people. Cleaning meant supplies, and sometimes machines, even in the URS.

Surely this can't be that *different from home*, she thought.

"Don't worry, Director, I'll see to her care," Olga said, jerking Aerie back to the situation at hand. "So, Aerie, was it? A bit of an unusual name."

"My mother's choice," Aerie murmured.

Olga's eyes twinkled in appreciation. "I can see why you joined with us. You've figured out there's no one to love you down there, huh?"

"What?" Aerie sputtered. "Of course—" She put her hand over her mouth, hurriedly glancing at Alice. *As far as she knows, I'm* supposed *to be here*. "I mean, of course."

Olga laughed, her broad figure radiating warmth. "You remind me a bit of my eldest daughter, Misha. She had some trouble adjusting after we defected too, even though her heart had defected before her brain realized it."

"I'm not stupid," Aerie objected.

Alice giggled from behind, making Aerie wish she'd been better about controlling herself.

"I didn't mean it as an insult, hun. I was just saying that you'll grow into this place just fine, even though it might take some time," the lady replied. "Come, follow me and we'll get you started, won't we, Alice?"

Alice nodded dutifully. "Yes, Madame."

"There's a reason they start the other new refugees down here, you know."

"What? Why is that?" Aerie asked, using two steps for each one Olga took.

"Well, me, for one." Olga smiled. "I was born in the URS, up in the northern part of the UNA before it changed its name. My mama had come from the Old Federation, and we knew the signs quite well when it came to revolution."

"Revolution is not always a bad thing," Alice said from behind them.

"Yes, that is true, Alice," Olga said as she pulled out a large key ring.

Aerie stared; she'd never seen so many keys at once. She was further surprised to see they were not digital keys, but keys that looked like museum relics from the Old Republic.

"But you have to agree revolution is not always good, either, because it usually means there are such polarized opponents that there is no way to handle conversations without violence or extreme measures." After jiggling the lock, Olga opened the first door. "Let's get a smock to cover your uniform before we begin, Aerie. It'd be a shame to get a pretty thing like you all messy."

Shameful at how happy the woman's compliment made her feel, Aerie took the coverlets Olga held out to her and handed one to Alice. It was followed by several other tools, including a few Aerie couldn't identify. As she studied them in a state of half-dread and half-intrigue, she turned her attention to Olga. "How long have you been on the *Perdition*?"

"I was picked up shortly after they launched the ship," Olga said, stacking up more items on a nearby cart. "Captain Chainsword used many of the trees from the mountains near my home."

"Used?"

"Trees can carry large supplies of water," Olga told her. "Some of the Redwoods were able to hold more than eleven hundred gallons at a time."

Aerie thought of the Memory Tree. It had been close to eighty feet tall. *Was water what Exton had been after, in addition to revenge?*

"It doesn't hurt that the ones we have here can be used in the air filtration systems aboard, too, so there's always a pretty good supply of oxygen."

"So … trees have their uses here in space?"

"Yes, indeed," Olga told her. "Now, since you're from the URS, tell me what experience you have."

"I was a new grad," Aerie murmured. "I didn't have any work experience."

"I know they always make you do something," Olga said. "What did you do in your free time?"

"Uh … "

"Did you train with the combat groups? Research studies?"

"If I wasn't training, I mostly daydreamed. Sometimes I would sneak out," Aerie admitted, her face turning red. *I need to stop blushing so much. These people are obviously different from the URS. There's no need to make them think I am lying.*

"Frequently?"

If she had been home in the URS, she would have lied. But here, she decided to take Exton's advice to heart, as much as she could; she didn't see any point in making who she was into something else. It helped that the crew seemed to appreciate her faults on more than one occasion.

"Sometimes," Aerie admitted. "I liked going outside, even though it wasn't really allowed."

"Then you should have some good cleaning experience," Olga said. "You would have had to, or you would have been punished for disobeying orders."

Aerie thought about the mud and the dirt she would have tracked home. *Maybe that was how the General found out about my trips to the Memory Tree*, she thought bitterly. *I didn't clean well enough.* "I've cleaned my rooms before."

"We're not talking about organizing things in a certain way. We're talking about making sure things are in the best condition possible for the people we love and watch out for."

"What's the difference?" Aerie snorted.

"The URS just wanted you to do things a certain way. Anyone can follow orders."

She was surprised by how Olga seemed to echo her own thoughts.

"Aren't Alice and I just following orders by getting training done?" Aerie glanced over at Alice, who had just come in from the opposite end of the hall. There was a surprised look on Alice's face that made Aerie almost laugh. *Has she really never challenged anything that Olga's told her to do?*

"I didn't order you to do nothing yet, hun." Olga grinned.

Alice spoke up as she finished tying her own cleaning smock. "Blind obedience and purposeful work are two different things."

An unsettling feeling crept down Aerie's back as her own arguments to the General popped into her mind. She suddenly wondered if Exton had managed to let his crew know of her uncertainties regarding the URS. She stiffened, taking another step away from Olga.

"We're going to start with this level," Olga told her, ignoring her sudden aversion. "We have ten levels on the ship to clean, and several hallways inside each; of course, we don't often clean the Captains' rooms or the hangar. He told us not to worry about his own hellish chambers." She laughed.

"He said that?" Aerie asked.

"He's a good boy," Olga said, almost as if she could read Aerie's mind. "And a better captain. But I think he's lonely."

That surprised Aerie—the idea that the space pirate captain, the one she'd been taught to fear and hate, was lonely. "So you like him?"

"Well enough. I don't see much of him during the day to day, of course. The Ecclesia is who's really in charge, but the captain is still the leader. He gives us orders to protect us, and we well know it. He's risked so much for us."

"He has you on a ship floating around the earth," Aerie pointed out. "I would say you've risked more."

Alice cleared her throat. "Some of us," she said, "would risk even more for him, too, for all he's done for us."

Aerie turned to face the girl. Alice's bright blonde hair was long enough to cover her eyes as she turned away, but Aerie was sure, from the inflection in her voice, Alice had a great admiration for her captain.

Olga squinted at her cleaning, aging her ten years. "I would have nothing to risk my life on, if it weren't for Captain and the Ecclesia."

Aerie turned her attention back to Olga. "You're part of the Ecclesia?"

"Have you heard of it?" Olga asked. She nodded to the last door at the end of the hall. "Here's where we'll start today."

"The URS outlaws religion," Aerie reminded her. "So, not really."

"The Ecclesia was an underground movement at one time. They worship God as the Creator of all things, and perfect in love, power, and goodness. They didn't believe government should tell people how or what to worship."

"So they have a council that tells you what to believe and how to act?"

"You can't order someone to love you," Olga said, pulling out a cleaning tool. "But if you do love someone, there are good ways to demonstrate your love. The Ecclesia have kept their beliefs regarding that since the Old Republic fell, and their ancestors, even before that, for thousands of years."

"Thousands of years?" It was hard for Aerie to imagine such a great expanse of time. The URS was not even a hundred years old.

"I'm sure that one of the elders would be happy to tell you the history if you're interested. Father Dennis, the Reverend Thorne, and Brother Donald are the main leaders. They're brothers, close to my husband's age. We attend their services every week, if you'd like to join me."

"Oh. Well, I'll think about it," Aerie said noncommittedly. She was already doubtful. How could a good god's religion be in charge of holding the world hostage with nuclear arms?

Besides, sometimes there was danger in knowing the answers to questions. *And not just danger*, Aerie thought. *There was also suffering, confusion, hatred, and fear.*

That was part of the reason the State took care of things like that, Aerie recalled, feeling a sudden sense of appreciation.

"The best thing to do when it comes to cleaning is to start at the top. I work my way left to right, like I'm reading a book. Old language habit, but it works for cleaning. You start with the ceiling. Any stains, discoloration, or any damage has to be checked. Proper diagnosis matters. If you don't know the cause of something, it's unlikely you know the cure."

Aerie nodded as Olga continued. Alice took to cleaning in different rooms. Aerie was glad for a small reprieve from her company; while Alice seemed agreeable enough, there was something disquieting about her presence.

"From the ceiling, check all devices; if you end up cleaning the bottom only to find a problem at the top, you'll have to clean everything again. No sense in wasting time and energy on inefficiency."

Aerie scanned the hallway. "I don't see any marks."

"You got to look closer," Olga insisted. "Imperfections will try to hide, and not just in people. Behind fixtures, under shadows, even in plain sight. Check again. And then check again. Be sure before you move onto the walls. There's nothing inefficient about using time to check to make sure you're right."

Aerie had a feeling Olga was going to be just as demanding as Master Browning had been.

Aerie soon realized that while she was every bit as demanding as she'd feared, Olga was still enjoyable. She liked to talk more than Master Browning did (unless he was shouting). As Aerie listened to Olga's stories, she found the time slipping by quickly, with little effort.

Olga told her about growing up in the Western URS after the time of the Old Republic, and how she had found about the *Perdition.* Aerie could barely hear Olga tell her story over the loud vibrating of her Sprayvac, but she heard enough to giggle at the right time and ask questions.

She flicked the switch off and felt her ears tingle. "So, Olga," she asked, "why did you think life up here was better?"

"Life up here *is* better," Olga insisted. "We are here by choice and blessed opportunity, Aerie. You should know that."

"I do," she said, "but there's just such a difference. It seems like a hard jump to make."

"It's hard for some people," Olga agreed. "It's hard to be open to trust people, and work with people, even those who are not at their best and a long time from it, if you know what I mean. But you can either have faith, or you can live in fear. And, hun, I was done living in fear." Olga stopped and put her hands on her hips. "Wasn't there something you were afraid of, that, in being here, you don't feel a little silly about?"

"Like what?"

"Like the URS's expectations, for one." Olga threw her head back and laughed. "I used to be so afraid of not passing my physical courses that they would punish me by limiting my time with the younger kids." Seeing Aerie's confused look, she explained, "I always liked kids, wanted my own. But no one wanted me for a cohabiter, and a career in marriage without desire robbed me of all my dignity." She made a face. "What little I had left at the time."

"So you came here?"

"Yes, I did come here, and here's where I met my husband. He works up in the bakery. You'll probably meet him soon, as you go through the rest of your training. His name's Sean."

"And you're happy?"

"Of course. I have six kids and a loving husband." She laughed. "Working is the only way to get peace apart from them sometimes, but God knows I love them more than life itself."

"So the Ecclesia are better masters than the State?" Aerie asked. "Because they believe in love, and they can get people to listen that way, rather than using fear?"

"It's not so simple," Olga said. "But you'll see what I

mean." She took Aerie's hand, rubbing her arm in a soothing manner, reminding Aerie of her own mother. "True love both casts out fear while still fearing the right things."

"I don't understand."

"You'll see. If you're looking," Olga said, pointing to the ceiling. "If you're paying attention, you'll see what I mean."

Aerie glanced up and grinned. "I suppose I should've guessed your instruction would work on more than one level."

"Hun, if you can clean, you can do anything. Cleaning means exposing yourself to a problem, examining it, taking time with it, and working on it. Finding the best way to make things right. If cleaning isn't a grand metaphor for love, I don't know what is. Now, let me show you how to change the linens."

♦15♦

Cleaning might have been a grand metaphor for love in Olga's eyes, Aerie thought, but it was a lot of painstaking work. She felt her back aching as she made her way to her bed. After the ceilings had been scrubbed, the walls washed and sanitized, the beddings changed, the laundry collected, and the floor washed for one part of one level of the ship, she was surprised at how glad she was to see Emery.

Her fingers were raw and slightly red, her nose numb, and Aerie was pretty sure wearing her hair down had been a mistake.

I'll ask for a tie and pull it back tomorrow. The loose hair had fallen in her face several times while she was scrubbing, vacuuming, and changing out laundry.

But the cumbersome quality of her hair was nothing compared to the uncertainty of her observations. She'd been given enough glimpses around the *Perdition* to know some of its architecture, but it wasn't just the ship that was turning out to be full of twists and turns, uncertainties and questions.

It was the people.

At one spot, a bunch of small children, no more than four years old, came rushing in, yelling and screaming and laughing at each other. Aerie stared at them, both appalled and envious at their disregard for proper decorum and etiquette.

All the way from Exton to Olga, to the children she'd passed in the hallways, from Tyler to Emery, from Olga's other charges to the engineers and repairmen, and even the students she saw in the gymnasium—they were all so different, and they didn't seem to mind.

They were alike in some areas, Aerie knew, but they didn't let the differences bother them. They all agreed on the idea of survival, but that wasn't their defining reason for living life. In fact, many of them seemed poised to give their lives over to death, in order to protect their way of life.

All my life the State had been the reason behind our survival. Our survival depended on the State, and the State made sure we survived.

How was it that the people on the *Perdition* had separated themselves and found something just as functional, if not better, than that?

This is not a game. The voice inside her head argued with her. *Your father would be upset with you.*

If he didn't even want her to call him that, though, did it mean he could he really be a father?

Stop questioning these things.

Why? Because they don't hold up to scrutiny?

They are still threatening the URS. They are still carrying nuclear weapons. These people have a good life, at the expense of others. And Captain Chainsword, no matter what you call him or how much you may think you like him, still killed your tree. He works with MENACE. He wants to destroy your way of life, and everything you've ever known and loved.

Aerie breathed in deeply and clutched at her forehead, trying to relax against her pillow. Arguing with herself after a long day of work proved to be too exhausting.

"I guess I don't know what to think," Aerie muttered.

"Don't tell me I've succeeded in brainwashing you already."

Exton's voice hit Aerie hard. She nearly fell off her bed as she shot up. She glared at him as he causally stood in her doorway.

He was just … maddening, she thought.

"Hey," she exclaimed. "You're not supposed to be in here."

Exton grinned at her, and she hated that she liked it. "Come on, Aerie. You know I can charm you when it suits me."

"So I guess earlier on the Command Bridge, that was not a good time?"

"I agreed to your fight," Exton reminded her. "It was your idea. I don't see how that could be anything less than what you wanted."

"Is that why you're here?" Aerie demanded. "Are you

here to see about our rematch?"

"No." He reached into his pocket and pulled out a familiar ball of fur.

"Moona!" Aerie hurried forward and grabbed her. "There you are."

"Tyra came off-duty and mentioned you were worried about her," Exton told her. "So I thought I'd bring her down to you."

Aerie ignored him while she set Moona down on her bed and hurried to get her some water. She could feel his eyes on her as he continued talking.

"Seems she's pretty small still, so you might need some extra pillows or blankets to keep her warm. I thought you could use another dish for her, too, since personal rooms don't usually have that many, so another one will be here with the mail later on."

Aerie watched as Moona kneaded her claws into her space blanket; she cringed, hoping the fabric was sturdy enough to withstand her cat's claws. "Maybe an extra blanket for her wouldn't be a bad idea," she conceded.

As she turned around, she almost collided with Exton.

He didn't just move quickly, he changed quickly, too. He had somehow managed to change from enemy captain to cat caretaker.

As he closed the space between them, Aerie felt her breathing falter. He was close enough that she caught his scent, an intoxicating blend of menthol and musk. "What are you doing?" she asked, her voice sounding weak to her own ears.

"Checking your head," he told her, as his hands came up and felt the scrape on her scalp. A moment passed before he threaded his fingers through the rest of her locks. "Touching your hair."

Heat pooled in her stomach as his touch went from coolly impersonal to tenderly coy. "Why?"

"If you don't want me to," he said deliberately, "you can tell me to stop, and I'll stop."

She felt like she was screaming at herself, telling her body to move. But she wasn't listening. "No," Aerie whispered. "It's okay. I just don't usually let people … touch my hair."

Her eyes met his, and Aerie felt the last ounce of any front she could have mustered against her feelings fall away.

She liked him. Against her better judgment, her father's wishes, and her nation's orders, she liked him.

Aerie thought back to the moment at graduation, where she'd looked up at his portrait as Captain Chainsword. I was right about him, she thought ruefully. He *was* dangerous, in all the wrong ways.

His hands fell away from her wound, falling down to caress her face. Her breath stopped, her eyes widened; she saw the challenge in him, along with the hesitations, the questions. Before she could decide on her answer, Moona interrupted them.

"Mew."

Aerie nearly jumped at the sound of her kitten's call, and even Exton seemed surprised at the disruption.

"That reminds me," he said, withdrawing from her, "I have her food here, too." He walked over to the door and pulled in a bag that had been sitting outside. "Here."

"Thanks," Aerie said, blushing. "I appreciate it." She took the bag and put it on the small table behind them. "So, um, you're off duty now?" she asked. *Way to go. You sound like a moron.*

Exton nodded. "For a while. It's enough time to get something to eat and relax a bit." He grinned at her again. "I don't suppose you're up for that rematch, now that we both have a full day of work behind us?"

"No thanks," Aerie replied breezily. If he could tease her, she would more than return the favor. "I'd like to catch you when you have a clear disadvantage."

"That's hardly fair."

"Well, we're not equal anyway," Aerie told him. "So if we're going to be on unfair footing anyway, I might as well try to make it as good for me as possible."

"When you use the words 'fair' and 'equal,' they are not actually talking about the same things. You realize this, right?"

"Yes," Aerie admitted with a sigh. "But I was hoping you wouldn't notice."

"It's part of my job to notice things like that. Once you realize how much the URS uses language to confuse people, it's impossible *not* to notice."

Aerie frowned. "I don't intentionally do it," she objected.

"You just did it."

"Okay, not a lot."

"You still did it." When she looked down at the ground, feeling angry and guilty, he reached for her.

She flinched.

He faltered. "You're allowed to argue with me, Aerie, but that doesn't mean you'll win."

The tension in her shoulders relaxed slightly. Her arms crossed her chest in defiance. "So good to know I have your permission, *Captain.*"

"That's another thing they do. They allow their emotions to get in the way of discussion."

"No they don't."

"If disagreements come up, they always bring up the issue of survival," Exton reminded her. "What does it mean 'to survive,' according to them? It changes, constantly; not that change is bad in itself. But there are a lot of things you can make a person do to survive. You can easily make a person lose his humanity in the name of survival."

"What do you mean?"

Exton arched an eyebrow. "It's a shame when people lose their humanity, even for survival. Morality's usually among the first to go. Truth is redefined over and over again, until there's nothing left—or just enough left to allow someone to control the chaos. Love is as a liability before eventually becoming unlike itself. Acceptance means agreement. Dissent means hatred and defiance."

"Death means death," Aerie countered. "You can't do

anything if you're dead."

"There are much worse things than death."

"I find that hard to believe."

"Then I'll bet anything you've never wished you were dead."

Aerie thought about how terrible she'd felt, unable to gain her acceptance into the military. She had thought about dying. But Exton was right. She had never *wished* to be dead. "Have you?" she asked.

"Have I what?"

"Have you ever wished you were dead?" Aerie wasn't sure he would even answer, but she couldn't regret asking the question. She wanted to get to know him better. He'd been kind to her—much kinder than she deserved as a prisoner of war, and much kinder than she knew the URS would have treated him. If truth was such a big deal to him, she would force him to give her his.

Exton moved, shifting his weight in discomfort. "When the URS killed my father, for one," he finally replied.

Whatever else Aerie had been expecting, that was not it. She felt her lips part in shock, with silence as her only reply.

"Yes, death is death," Exton said, repeating her earlier arguments and making her recoil. "That's why what we do with life matters infinitely more."

There was such conviction in his words. The two ideologies—the URS and Exton's—clashed inside of her mind. While she did not disbelieve Exton, it was hard to dismiss the question of whether or not the State acted rightfully.

Emery's earlier words on how the State dealt with those who rebelled echoed inside her mind.

"Emery told me," Aerie said quietly, her voice close to a whisper, "that your mother died a few months after your dad. Did the URS kill her, too?"

"No." Exton shook his head. "But they might as well have. She loved my father more than anything. Without him, she wasted away. In some ways, they would have been doing her a favor by killing her."

His fists clenched as he turned away from her. "But I suppose it's a long history, and one I don't have time to tell you today."

"Exton." As he looked back at her, Aerie found it hard to keep her eyes from watering. "I'm sorry."

"I don't want your pity," he scoffed.

"Then what do you want? Tell me," Aerie demanded. "Tell me the truth."

"There's no point in telling you the truth," Exton told her, "if you don't trust me."

She felt trapped. "I might trust you if you tell me the truth."

"More likely you'll decide if the truth is something you want to trust or not." He shook his head. "Maybe we'll have this discussion another time, later on. I have a meeting with the Ecclesia to attend in a few moments, and I wouldn't want to keep them waiting. I just came to drop off your cat."

"That's not fair," Aerie insisted.

"You're right, but not in the way that you think."

"What do you mean?"

"Aerie," Exton began, "the URS has only guaranteed you survival. You've survived, and you've been doing it for what, seventeen years or so?"

"Almost eighteen. My birthday's next month." She frowned. "I don't see how that matters, though."

"I've been against them for more than ten years," Exton replied. "I've been on this ship for six years. I know my place. You," he told her as he turned away from her again, "have been on this ship, an *enemy* ship, for less than a week. I've guaranteed you nothing."

"You've given me some things," Aerie said.

"Yes, but I've also taken quite a few things away. Your freedom, your 'unit,' because I would never call it 'family,' and your future with the URS as a normal cog in their machine. And you can't forget what I did to your precious Memory Tree."

"Yes, but—"

"How could you trust someone like me? Take my word as truth?"

She said nothing. Her own logical arguments, her own barriers to trusting him, agreed with his reasoning wholeheartedly.

"And that's just the beginning," Exton told her. "How could you forgive me for the trespasses I would commit on your home in the future?"

"You're going to attack the URS?" Aerie asked, taken aback. She felt her legs go limp at the thought. She felt around for the chair behind her and slumped down.

"What if I do?" He shook his head. "You might be in my world," he told her, "but you still live in theirs."

Aerie watched as Exton walked over to her bed. He reached down and patted Moona on the head. "I've got to go," he said. "If you're determined to stay an enemy, Aerie, you'll stay away from me."

"Exton, wait." Aerie pushed herself up and hurried after him. *I don't want you to leave.* She reached out and grabbed his arm, just as she had before in the med ward.

"I told you before I'd most likely lie to you at some point," Exton replied. "This is one thing I won't lie about. I don't trust you, Aerie."

Stinging pain tugged at her heart, sending a surprising rush of tears to her eyes. Before Aerie responded in equal ire and inflicted reciprocating wounds with her words, his hands took hold of her shoulders.

"But," he continued, "I'm more than tempted to."

Aerie saw the icy hardness of his eyes melt—felt herself fall, sinking into him as he pulled her in close. Her eyes closed as he pressed his lips against hers.

His kiss, quick and even chaste, boiled up a storm of fire inside her. Nervous anticipation blossomed into shy curiosity.

Aerie felt her fingers reflexively reach for him, wanting to keep him close even as she knew it was better to push him away. A shiver went down her spine as she braced her hands against his chest.

Before she could stop him, Exton let go and backed away from her. Aerie swallowed a moan of protest, wanting nothing more than to pull him back.

As if he knew her dilemma, he headed toward her door. "I've got to go. I'll see you again soon." He waved and gave her a quick smirk before he disappeared from view.

She felt like she watched the door for a long time after he left, feeling more witless than ever.

The *Perdition* might have just descended once more behind the moon, but Exton no longer felt the pressure of surrounding darkness; he'd savored his taste of sunlight, one that would burn inside of him, keeping him warm throughout the long night.

He glanced out the window in the Captain's Lounge, the small room more freeing and suffocating than ever.

A small part of his mind—the sensible part, he decided—cringed in fear over what he had done.

He ran his finger over his bottom lip, reliving the moment when he pressed his mouth against Aerie's, giving in to his desire to steal a taste of her. He once more felt the wild rush of longing, the rising satisfaction as his curiosity had been gratified, even as a growing, possessive hunger ignited inside of him.

Exton sighed. He leaned against the coolness of the windowpane as he remembered how, at their second meeting, he'd assured her he was only a man after she called him a monster.

Kissing Aerie had unleashed a vulnerability from deep inside him, one he never thought he would experience again. The threat of humanity, once more swept up in the tides of time, terrified him—even as it exhilarated him.

He knew better than most the truth of human nature, how deeply in the dark the beast inside the human heart could reside.

I will have to be careful, he thought.

Frustration bit at him as he felt the line between man and monster begin to blur.

♦16♦

It was several days later when Aerie woke up, instantly plagued by guilt. Catching sight of the clock in her room, it confirmed what she feared to be true.

She'd overslept. Significantly.

"I can't believe I didn't hear the alarm," she moaned to herself as she reached for her uniform and tripped over her blankets. "I'm late for work!"

Aerie watched herself in her mirror, her eyes wide with impending shame and punishment. As she finished brushing her teeth, she tried to reassure herself she would be fine.

"It shouldn't be too bad," she murmured to herself. "I mean, I've been pretty good, right? Olga says my cleaning skills have improved greatly since I started, and Exton, while I haven't seen him since he kissed me, I'm sure he wouldn't punish me over this. At least, I don't think so … "

An odd mix of elation and depression swept over her.

She knew it was best not to read too much into a kiss, no matter how warm it made her feel. After all, Serena was living proof boys could kiss you and it meant nothing to them in the end. And if the rumors about her older sister's reputation were true, they could do a lot more, too, and still leave you wondering.

Aerie bit her lip as a new fear took hold of her. What if Exton hadn't been as affected by their kiss as she was? It wasn't like he had come see her or anything since then.

"Ugh, I've got to stop this," she muttered, pulling out the small dish Sean, Olga's husband, had given to her. He'd made a recipe especially for Moona after meeting Aerie a few days before, and chatting with her just as freely and openly as Olga had.

Moona twisted around her legs, seeming to agree, though Aerie was hard pressed to wonder if it was at the food or her inner turmoil. "You're certainly not helping," Aerie told her.

"Mew."

The small kitten's reply made Aerie smile, even as she

rolled her eyes. She glanced over at the desk behind her, where she'd stored her small collection of shorthand notes detailing what she'd learned about the *Perdition* and its crew.

She ran her hands through her hair impatiently as she scurried around her room.

They shouldn't really worry too much, even if I am late. I mean, they should be working to make me *happy, if anything. Right? I could go back to the URS and give up a lot of information on them …*

She sighed.

Each day since she'd started working, she woke up sternly lecturing herself on how to behave, how she needed to do more investigation into the *Perdition* and its insufferably kind crew, and how to find a way to salvage her loyalty to the URS.

But as soon as work ended, she somehow forgot the demands she placed on herself.

After work, she would meet with Emery, who was increasingly open and friendly as they wandered through the different parts of the ship. Children would dart past her in play. She would find herself daydreaming of a pirate's stolen kiss.

It wasn't until the end of the day that Aerie's concerns about the State, along with her initiative to collect information for the URS, seemed to reappear.

There was a knock at the door. The sound jolted her out of her thoughts.

"I'm coming," Aerie called. "I know I'm late for work, but I can stay late. There's no reason to—" She stopped mid-sentence when she saw Emery in the doorway, wearing a blue dress.

"To what? Punish you?" Emery finished.

Aerie shifted her feet uncomfortably, knowing Emery was right. "Um … well, yeah, I guess."

Aerie felt her guilt dissolve as Emery smiled. "There's no need for that. Today's your day off," Emery told her. Seeing her reaction, Emery added, "I guess you were too tired when I mentioned it yesterday?"

"Most likely." But then, she knew she didn't deserve a day off. *With all my mistakes on the job, the URS would have demoted me or placed me in Reeducation by now.*

Aerie stepped back from the doorway. "Please, come in. I was just making breakfast. Or maybe lunch by now, looking at the time."

"You don't come down to the dining hall much."

"This is easier."

Emery wrinkled her nose. "Easier? How is cooking your own food easier?" She gestured toward the door. "Come on. We've got some work to do. We'll get lunch on the way."

"The way to what?"

"Since we have some time, and you've been here long enough, I thought I would run through emergency drill procedures with you. It won't take long. And there's better food down in the dining hall."

Aerie flustered. "I don't know if I want to eat with everyone else."

"Why?" Emery narrowed her gaze at her.

"I just … "

I just don't want to make friends or enemies of you and your crew.

Aerie nodded toward Emery's dress in an effort to stall. "I don't have anything nice to wear."

"Then wear a uniform. Not too many people dress up on Sundays. I did today, but I'm one of the few people who dress up. I like to, and this was actually my wedding dress. I sent it out to have it dyed a week ago, and I just got it back."

Aerie fought off the impulse to ask Emery what her wedding was like; she'd never been to one before, but she knew there was never much to it. "It's lovely."

Aerie thought of her attempts at fixing her clothes; cleaning was easy compared to sewing up some of the tears and holes she'd gotten over the years. "I've never been good at stuff like that."

"Do you want to learn? If you're interested in working with the clothes, I can see about switching your job assignment."

"No, that's okay," Aerie quickly assured her. "Olga and her assistants are warming up to me nicely."

"Even Alice?" Emery laughed.

"A little." *A very little.*

"You shouldn't take it personally. She has a crush on Exton, and there was a rumor at your arrival that might have something to do with her resentment."

"Rumor?"

Emery waved it away. "That you'd attacked him."

"Well, I did, technically."

"Aerie," Emery said, "Exton listed you as a refugee so there wouldn't be any worry among our shipmates. Alice would see an attack on Exton as sign of war."

"She does seem to really like him," she agreed. "She has been less aloof these last few days, anyway." Aerie thought about how kind Alice had been when she'd showed her how to braid back her hair.

"Well, then don't worry about it. You'll likely win her over yet. But for now, get dressed and come with me." Emery planted her hands on her hips. "You're not afraid of getting to know more people, are you?"

"The URS let us have friends." Aerie sniffed indignantly, grabbing a new set of clothes and hurrying into the bathroom to change.

"Yes, but I'm willing to bet you didn't have many."

"Hey!"

"It's true, isn't it?"

Aerie finished getting ready as she thought about the safest answer to that question. She sighed to herself. It wasn't easy to explain she'd been driven by near-desperation to get into the military, eliminating a lot of time she could have reserved for making friends.

The only close friend she had was Brock, and that was most likely because her father seemed to approve of him, and he was able to help her train.

She walked out of the bathroom to find Emery waiting patiently for her response. "My father didn't encourage friendships. And neither did my training regimen," she said, deciding that was the safest answer she could give.

"That's the beauty of being here," Emery insisted. "You have more time to make friends. And you can meet people while you work."

"I've met a lot of nice people." She glanced back over at her desk, where her papers still sat, taunting her with their brevity. Part of her wanted to remain in solitude; if she kept to herself, she wouldn't run the risk of liking her captivity.

Even if she was attracted to her captor and thought about his kiss more than she should.

It was that stinging reminder that compelled her to go out more than anything. If Exton could ignore her, Aerie decided, it wasn't going to be because she made it easy for him. "All right," she agreed. "I'm ready to go."

"Most of the time you won't work the weekend," Emery assured her, leading her out of the room. "We'll let you know. Different shifts will take different weeks and work the extra day. Some volunteer, but in the next few days we'll have plenty of work open for the harvest." She flashed Aerie a grin as they walked down the hall. "So you better watch out for the order."

"What is the harvest?" Aerie asked. "I've been wondering."

After a moment of consideration, Emery nodded. "I suppose I can tell you. You might have figured it out some already, but we don't just work on the ship up here."

"I know you told me before that the Ecclesia, that religious group, has some students up here." Aerie slowed as she saw a child, no more than three years old, run to a woman who was clearly his mother. "And there are families here."

"Yes. Well, it's part of what we do besides education and provide for families. We grow crops up here, in the ship's classrooms and outer regions."

"You do? Like a greenhouse from the Old Republic?"

"Exactly." Emery nodded.

"That's amazing!"

"That's not the reaction we get from most refugees," Emery admitted with a rueful smile. "There's been a large decrease in animal and plant populations throughout much of Earth. Toward the end of the Old Republic, many people wanted to get rid of its institutions and start their own. A lot of them had forgotten that just because something is old and traditional, it does not mean it is useless or meaningless."

"But it's perfect." Aerie clapped her hands in happiness. "The *Perdition* is out in space, so you always have a good amount of sunshine available. You can easily grow plants up here."

"Not quite as easily as it seems," Emery said. "But for the most part, yes, that's about how it works."

"I'd love to see it." Aerie smiled. "My mother had a small garden where we lived. She wasn't allowed to grow a lot, but I've been working with it for the past couple of years to keep her plants alive. New Hope didn't have a lot of natural light, and the artificial light was unreliable. You probably get a lot more of a crop here than I did there."

"Yes. Once a year, we work for several shifts to get all the food harvested and stored. Out of tradition, we feast for a day, and then we replant seeds afterward. It's a big job, added into the regular routines here on the ship."

"And that provides enough food for the whole ship, for the whole year?"

Emery shook her head. "We have other sources of food, but the harvest is a good portion of it. Every year, we get a bigger crop."

"You said it's coming up soon?"

"This week."

Aerie bounced with pleasure, thinking of her mother and the simple joy she'd always had around her garden back home. "I'm excited for it."

"You did mention you had an interest in horticulture," Emery said. "I guess if you'd like to see our plantation section, we can go on the way back from the hangar."

"That would be wonderful!" Aerie wiggled her butt in excitement.

"I'm glad you're energetic. You'll need it for the emergency drills," Emery told her. "No one would call them fun."

Aerie felt her mood deflate, but despite herself, she laughed. "I grew up in the URS," she said. "I'm used to being disappointed."

Emery giggled. "Careful. You're starting to sound more and more like one of us."

"I was just joking," Aerie quickly apologized, horrified she'd so easily made light of her disappointment with the State. "I didn't mean it."

"It's okay, you know, if you want to join us," Emery told her quietly. "We'll protect you."

"My unit has some terrifying connections," Aerie murmured. "I wouldn't want to harm—"

"Connections? I thought you said you were of little importance."

The concerned look on Emery's face made Aerie fluster. "The Rearden unit," she forced herself to say, "includes some friends with General St. Cloud's family. That's all. But I'm definitely not important."

Emery stopped. "You know St. Cloud?"

The condemnation in her voice was sharp; it cut straight into Aerie's heart.

"Uh, not very well, of course," Aerie insisted as she began to fidget uncontrollably. "I'm not sure how my unit would get him to act for them, anyway; it probably doesn't matter. Like I said, I'm not important enough."

After a long moment, Emery sighed. "If you say so," she said. Her blue-green eyes softened. "I know it seems like we're all just worried about ourselves and our business here on the ship. But Olga told me that she and several of the others have enjoyed your company as well. You would be missed."

An old pain twisted inside her heart. "Oh, really?"

Emery nodded. "I can attest myself, it's nice having you around. It would be nice to have you stay … if you decide you want to, of course."

Guilt and fear festered together in Aerie's stomach alongside joy. "I've liked it, too," Aerie said, her voice soft and slow as the truth both freed and condemned her. "I have an older sister, and she's nothing like you. I mean, *I wish* she was more like you, not that you're not a good—"

"I know what you meant." Emery's kind smile disappeared. "Which makes me worried, now that I know you've met General St. Cloud."

"Wouldn't Osgood be worse?"

"You might think so, but actually he's not." Emery shook her head. "Osgood is just a politician. To maintain its grip on the State, St. Cloud is the force. Without Osgood, St. Cloud could be the next dictator. Without St. Cloud, Osgood would easily lose control of the URS."

"So, St. Cloud is the one you guys want to take down?" Aerie asked, surprised her father was more critical to the State than she had estimated. She always knew he was important, as the Lieutenant Commander-in-Chief, but she never would have suspected he was higher on the enemy's list than Osgood.

Emery, lost in her own thoughts, ignored her question. "If the Rearden unit contacts St. Cloud, we might be in trouble."

"I won't say anything." Aerie promised, suddenly terrified. "If it helps, I don't think they can do anything this far out. The URS doesn't have much of a space program, since the *Perdition* has been taking out satellites."

"We're heading closer to Earth for the harvest," Emery reminded her.

"I still doubt they would attack." Aerie thought about her father's career. "They generally don't attack unless they know for sure they would win. And you do have the upper hand out here in space, since their space program was delayed several years ago."

When Emery raised her brows, Aerie blushed. "I'm sure you knew that already," she murmured.

"It's good to have you confirm it."

"You won't tell anyone, will you?" Aerie's nerves continued to jumble around inside of her. "That I know St. Cloud?"

"I've met the man myself," Emery told her. "And so has my brother, of course. Exton hates him." She sighed. "I'd hate to make it into more of something than it's not."

Fear, silent and crippling, raged through Aerie. She struggled to control it, but the pulsating power of adrenaline screamed through her blood. She wanted to confess she'd lied, that she was not who they thought, that she was the enemy, just as she'd asserted she was all along.

But she couldn't. There was some part of her that wanted to stay, to really be the person they thought she was—to hide Aerie St. Cloud underneath a new name and a new life, until she disappeared forever.

Traitor! The voice reared by the State drummed its disappointment into her.

Emery nodded toward the elevator ahead. "Either way, I'm not going to do it now. But from the sound of it, it's a good thing that we're going to go over the emergency exits."

Aerie just nodded, still fighting with herself as she wordlessly followed.

♦17♦

"Wow." Aerie stared down the hangar, amazed. "That's a lot of ships."

"We do have quite a collection here," Emery said, allowing her gaze to follow Aerie's down along row after row of shuttles and cargo shippers. "There are others, more like specialty ships, in the rear cargo hold, but these are the ones we use most often for supply runs."

Aerie couldn't stop the rush of excitement. As much as she felt guilty and terrified, she was happy to be back in a familiar setting. The *Perdition's* hangar, full of its variety of ships and bustling activity, reminded her of the Military Academy.

The hangar doors were closed. From her position on the second level staircase, she couldn't make out the details of the far end, but from the forward port side she could see several rows of supplies and ships being unloaded, and the ships personnel running through checks and making repairs.

"I heard the rumors that Captain Chainsword had a collection of MENACE fighters," Aerie recalled. "Is that true?"

Emery coughed back a laugh. "I'm sure Exton would be amused to hear that," she replied. "You should ask him about that later. Right now, we're here to focus on the emergency escape pods."

Emery pointed to the emergency escape pods lining the *Perdition's* haul at different points. "They are the 'lifeboats' of our pirate ship here."

The pods were slim and narrow, placed perfectly inside the hollows in the ship's sides. "I almost didn't see them," Aerie admitted with a small laugh. "A lot's going on down here."

"We're approximately two days from Earth, heading toward the southern hemisphere." Emery indicated a ship at the far end. "That's the shuttle you came on, right there."

"The one with the chainsword on it?"

"Yes, that's the one."

"I imagine that's Exton's favorite," Aerie said.

"I imagine it is, too." Emery smiled. She glanced at Aerie. "But I think for different reasons than you do."

Aerie said nothing as her face flushed over in embarrassment and, despite her better judgment, pleasure.

"Come on. I'll show you how to use the pods."

"How likely is it that you'll ever need to?" Aerie asked as she followed Emery down the walkway. "I mean, I know that the URS is against you guys in principle, but I've never been sure of how they're fighting you."

"Their methods of fighting are quieter," Emery admitted. "Most of the incidents would be classified as a military matter by the State. Civilians have to rely on different sources to learn the truth."

"Is that part of the reason the Ecclesia and other religions were outlawed?"

"Outlawed," Emery agreed, "but not obliterated."

"Obviously." Aerie gestured around the hangar. "You have a large amount of people here."

"Not everyone here is a member of the Ecclesia," Emery reminded her. "And this is a skeleton crew at best. If our students were not on board, we would be pressed for service."

"Why are they here?" Aerie asked. "Doesn't the Ecclesia have anywhere else to go?"

"This ship is the best place to study for certain subjects, for now. We have a network of cities and people that have circled through here in the last several of years; we have to keep changing things up when the URS starts cracking down on us."

"I wonder why they would be against the Ecclesia," Aerie admitted. "I mean, I get that the State would be upset at having a person's loyalty divided—"

"Loyalty is *everything*, Aerie." Emery shook her head. "Loyalty is the first step toward love. Allegiance leads to obedience. To have someone's full trust is a powerful gift.

Think about how much you feel you owe to the State. What would happen if it asked you to do something you would never do otherwise? Lose your home? Leave your family? Move to a faraway place?"

Aerie turned away, looking back toward the people around her who were running around and continuing their orders. "I'm in somewhat of that situation now," she said.

"But not by your choice or conviction."

"It's still the same ending."

"The lesson you've learned is different than the one I am trying to convey to you." Emery came up and paused beside her. "Could you willingly give your life for the State if they asked it of you?"

When Aerie started to respond, Emery shook her head. "I don't want you to answer," she said. "Not now. I know from my own experience that you've been trained to do just that."

Frustrated, Aerie frowned. "Then why did you ask?"

"I'm trying to show you what real devotion looks like. Many people think it is happy or joyful. It can be, but more often than not devotion looks like sacrifice, discomfort, humiliation, and pain."

"I've done that for the URS," Aerie insisted. "Training was hard, you know. And learning was not always easy. I gave up many things trying to make them happy."

And I still didn't get what I wanted.

"So you know something of devotion and obedience. But what if they took advantage of your trust?"

Aerie huffed. "They haven't," she insisted. But she felt a twinge of regret as she recalled her father's remarks following her PAR, and how even though she had given her trust over to the State—along with its leaders and teachers, and even His Excellency himself—they had never trusted her with the freedom to make her own decisions.

"Then you're one of the fortunate few who have never experienced that feeling," Emery remarked. "Trust me, it is awful."

Aerie believed her but felt as though she was betraying

her home to admit it. "Surely even the Ecclesia has used people for their gain before," she said.

"You're right." Emery nodded somberly. "It has happened in the past. As a group we regret that and take measures to prevent it from happening again; we don't justify it in the name of 'survival.'"

"How do you know it's not happening now?" Aerie asked.

"How do you know the URS isn't using you?" Emery smirked.

"I didn't mean any disrespect," Aerie murmured. "I was just wondering."

"The long answer is complicated. The short answer is that something greater than religion has my trust." Emery pursed her lips. "There is a difference between religion and God himself."

"It sounds interesting," Aerie replied, her own curiosity piqued, even if she was reluctant to voice it.

"Interesting enough that they are outlawed. You can imagine how the URS would feel about someone else determining what you believed to be right and wrong."

"The URS teaches right and wrong are relative terms," Aerie said, "since survival is all that matters in the end."

"It's the same thing as earlier," Emery countered. "The destination is the same, but the journey is much different."

"I think I'm beginning to see why the URS wouldn't allow religion." The URS already had enough rules and requirements of its own; not to mention, they wouldn't like a god to have the first and final say in any matter.

"That does make it hard on us. It is hard to hide something as personal as faith." Emery smiled. "You've probably seen some of the key differences here in how people live and act."

Aerie nodded, thinking about the how willing people were to help out—even people like Alice, who seemed unsure of her, or Sean, who had just met her.

But that's not exclusive to here, Aerie reminded herself. She thought about the times Brock had stayed late after school or visited her unit to help her with her training. She owed him much for his patience with her and his kindness. Aerie knew she was fooling herself if she thought lending him her father's accounts of his battles against MENACE or inviting him to stay for dinner somehow made up for everything he had given her.

Of course, he was more of the exception to the rule. Aerie remembered one time when Serena had laughed in her face when Aerie had asked for help on a finishing a biology assignment early. "Just do it yourself," she'd snapped. "Or do it along with your class. There's no need to teach you to expect help when you ask for it."

That is a dangerous assumption, no matter if I am here on the Perdition *or not.*

"Aerie?"

"Huh?" Aerie jolted, stepping out of the memory. "Sorry. What were you saying?"

"I'll need to show you how to operate the escape pod, and then we can go see the plantation section."

"Great." Aerie turned and followed Emery down to the nearest set of escape pods.

The escape pods were long and rounded at the ends, providing enough space for up to three people in each. Like the rest of the ship, they were painted dark, with red trim. There were numbers on the side labeling the small capsules. She knew enough of fighter technology to recognize a homing beacon signal attached to the different ends.

All in all, they were very similar to some of the ones she'd seen in the education center's simulator training sector.

"If you step inside, I can show you how to operate it." Emery suddenly stopped and pursed her lips. "I hope you don't take this the wrong way, but I should tell you now there's no point in trying to escape using these. The coordinates for landing are pre-programmed by the Command Bridge."

Aerie grinned. "I won't try," she promised. "Assuming I

haven't worn out my welcome."

Emery giggled. "You haven't." She opened the capsule door and stepped inside ahead of Aerie. "The door can be opened from the outside, until you lock it from the inside. This is good, too, if you end up in enemy territory and need to hold up in here until we can send a rescue crew."

Aerie nodded as she stepped inside. "This is pretty similar to the URS space pod models," she said, running her hand over the control console. "I got to tour them with my brothers once."

Emery was silent for a moment. Then she asked, "Do you recognize anything else?"

Her suddenly stilted tone made Aerie curious as she glanced around. The URS had extremely similar tech. The model was not quite the same, but then it had been over five years since the *Perdition* launched. "Plenty, actually. Did Exton have contractors from the URS build these?" she asked. "Because they seem to have—"

Her voice trailed off as realization struck. The moment she said it, all of it came together in her mind. The ship, the pods, the uniforms, all of it …

"Exton stole this ship, didn't he?" Aerie asked. "He stole the ship from the URS." More pieces fell into place. "That's why they haven't been able to develop their space program. This ship *was* their space program."

Emery seemed to smother a sigh. "It's not quite as simple as that, Aerie."

"But it's true, isn't it? Tell me," Aerie demanded. "I know these pods are straight from the URS. They're built with standard life support and reentrance capabilities, secure harnesses and trackers, and an emergency stasis option."

"If you recognize all the different controls, I guess we can finish up here," Emery remarked hesitantly.

"That's why the State didn't tell us much about Exton and the crew on the *Perdition*," Aerie continued. "Because they didn't want us to know about their loss."

"They do have a lot more losses than most hear about,"

Emery replied.

Aerie turned to face her. "Do they know who you are? Who Exton is?"

When she hesitated, Aerie pushed forward. "Come on, Emery. Just tell me the truth."

Emery sighed. "There is little doubt they know who we are."

Aerie felt the breath rush out of her. *There goes my attempt to gather information to stay out of trouble.* "So Exton did steal the ship?"

"Ha!" Emery snorted disdainfully. "It's impossible to steal what is rightfully yours."

It took a long moment for the weight of her statement to sink in; once it fell into place, there was no going back.

Aerie felt her mind racing with questions—and doubt and fear and anger. "What do you mean it's rightfully his?" she asked. "He had to have stolen it. I know my tech, and this is all URS tech!"

"Who do you think designs URS tech?" Emery gestured around her. "These are all designed by engineers."

"This ship has an older model of tech; it's at least three years old, and the newest NETech hasn't been installed. Exton can't be *that* old," Aerie argued. "He told me that he didn't even finish his time at university, even if he was studying how to be an engineer. Surely you don't expect me to believe—"

"Our father was the best aeronautic engineer the URS had before they killed him ten years ago." Emery shook her head. "He was the designer of this ship, and many others, for the URS forces."

Aerie felt her arguments clog her throat as Emery continued. "He was killed when he found out *Paradise* was going to be used for battle, rather than what the URS had told him originally."

Long seconds of silence passed before Aerie dared to ask a question. "*Paradise*?" Aerie asked quietly.

"The original name of the *Perdition*."

"What is—why that name?"

"Part of the Ecclesial teaching is on the idea of Heaven," she explained. "The URS, when they came to my father with their proposal, wanted a starship that could provide a means of comfortable living in space while conducting experiments. He agreed. When he found out they were planning on using a good deal of the storage for nuclear and fission bombs, and using it to engage in warfare, he objected." Emery's eyes glittered with fierce pride and harrowing sadness. "Strongly."

"And you're sure of this?" Aerie asked.

"I am."

"Oh."

Emery raised an eyebrow. "That's all you have to say about the matter?"

"It's a lot to take in," Aerie murmured apologetically. "I'm sorry."

Emery's eyes narrowed in angry sadness. "I suppose it is hard for you to accept it," she said slowly.

"This is a pretty big claim to make," Aerie argued. *How does someone just steal a ship like this? Especially from the URS?* Aerie wondered if it was possible Emery had been misinformed. Or if she was lying. "I don't want to talk about this anymore," Aerie mumbled.

"That's fine." Emery straightened, masking her anger with professionalism. "Then let's get through the procedures—"

"I have to go," Aerie announced. At Emery's stricken look, Aerie added, "I'm sorry, Emery."

"Aerie—"

Before she could change her mind or let Emery stop her, Aerie raced out of the hangar and down the hall, then ducked into the elevator. She almost crumbled to the floor as the she pushed the button for her floor and the doors shut.

♦18♦

"Don't look at me like that," Emery grumbled as she glared at her brother. "I hate that expression."

"What expression?" Exton replied with a smirk. "The one that tells you that I told you so?"

"Duh." She stuck her tongue out at him. "Enjoy your triumphant arrogance while you can."

"I'd think you would be happy that she ran away after you told her the truth," Exton replied. "Maybe you should even pity me. After all, if she can't trust us, then I am a fool to like her."

Emery paused for a moment before she shrugged. "I don't think giving you sympathy would work," she replied. "In fact, I think that would just make you all the more unbearable."

"Maybe I wouldn't be quite so unbearable if you hadn't lost her after she ran out of the hangar."

"You need to—"

"You guys *both* need to relax," Tyler said from the far end of the Records Room. "I'm pulling the cam shots now so we can find her."

"Speaking of which, did you find anything else out from the satellite feeds?" Emery asked. "I know she's assured us she is of no importance, but it's always nice to know for sure."

Tyler glanced up. "I have had the team filtering through a bunch of news feeds, and I didn't hear anything on a missing persons case that would match, or any news that we had taken an accidental hostage when we attacked."

"Have you heard anything about St. Cloud?" Emery asked. "Has he looked into her disappearance at all?"

"Why would he care?" Exton rolled his eyes. "The man has no conscience, just like his boss. Osgood didn't seem to mind attacking in full force. I doubt they would be concerned with any missing people or causalities."

"I was just asking," Emery snapped. "It's good to keep track of these things."

"It is strange," Tyler said, "she doesn't seem to have a public file."

"Most students don't," Emery said. "Not until they are placed in work assignments. That's part of the reason Exton and I didn't have them, either."

"Aerie told me she'd been assigned to the Communication Sector," Exton offered.

"But she never started," Tyler reminded him. "She might have been pulled once she didn't show up for work."

"You could try hacking into the school records," Emery suggested.

"I can definitely try," Tyler said. "And it really shouldn't make much difference to them. They probably know we're able to do it already."

"There's no use speculating," Exton asked. "We all know the URS doesn't tend to publish its reports accurately."

"You would have thought that they would have reported something about the Memory Tree besides its capture," Emery said. "I mean, if nothing else, it would have made the tree's destruction more memorable, to have a victim in there, even if it was an unidentified one."

"Aerie wasn't supposed to be there, though. Maybe they disregarded it because they don't know."

"It's possible." Exton shrugged. "Maybe I should have taken some of those calls from Osgood, if that was the case."

"Well, we all know you're obviously not worried about it." Emery crossed her arms.

"There *is* nothing to worry about right now."

"I'm not as sure as you are on that."

"I can tell." Exton sighed. He had been off-duty for only a few moments when Emery came around and ordered him into the Records Room with Tyler. "But I have a feeling since it's your fault that she ran away, you're more inclined to find a way to blame in on me."

"Hey," Emery said. "I'm not the one who missed the fact

that there was a person in the tree to begin with. And then decided against all reason to actually *like* her."

"You like her, too," Exton argued. "You're her friend."

"I've known her for more than a week. You liked her after less than ten minutes."

"Maybe my instincts are better than yours."

"Can you guys please calm down?" Tyler said, drawing angry glares from both parties. "Look, Em, Exton's right for now. There's no way the URS can attack us right now. So there's no use worrying about it on our end. And as for her, Exton, you might want to go and talk with her."

"You think?" Emery sneered.

Exton grinned. "As a matter of fact," he said, "I had a few matters I was going to take care of. I'll add tracking down Aerie to my list."

"Ha." Emery glared at him. She put her head in her hands and slumped over beside Tyler.

Exton knew his sister well enough to know she was genuinely concerned for Aerie. She was probably also having a hard time realizing Aerie, even though she'd been friendly, was not ready to consider staying on the *Perdition.*

Such a judgment miscalculation would bother him, too.

It must be a family legacy, Exton thought, recalling their father's faith in friendship.

Emery glanced up at him. "I know what you're thinking, Exton, and it would be better to stop before I hurt you."

"If you can," Exton scoffed.

Before he could taunt her further, she put a hand on Tyler's shoulders. "You can try searching the Medical Center records," she said. "Aerie told me when she was younger she'd broken her arm. She went there with her mother for treatment."

"That's a good idea," Exton agreed.

"I'll get on it. I just found her," Tyler said. "She's up on Level Three, rear starboard side, near the sanctuary."

"Good." Exton exited the room, grabbing a small bag hanging near the Command Bridge. "Keep me informed of her positions if you see her move."

Emery had to be lying. She *had* to be.

But as much as she might have wanted that to be true, that explanation didn't quite fit, Aerie realized bitterly.

"I don't even know why it matters to me so much," Aerie grumbled, her voice weak and pathetic to her own ears.

That's not true.

"It matters," she muttered to herself, "I don't know what to do. I'm not sure what to believe. Something is wrong, and I want the truth."

It was astounding to realize that the truth mattered.

Aerie allowed her thoughts to simmer inside her mind as she speculated. *Why did it matter if Exton stole the ship or not? He's the enemy. He's supposed to do bad things. It shouldn't matter at all.*

She thought about how he had gently pulled her free of the Memory Tree. How he took care of Moona for her. How he checked the gash on her head.

Just because he's kind to me and my cat, doesn't mean he's capable of being treacherous in other areas.

Aerie thought about his warning to her, and about how she had to stay away from him if she wanted to remain his enemy. She thought about the pain she'd seen in his eyes when he told her his father had been killed.

And, she reasoned, if he had stolen the ship, he stole it for his father. Misguided honor, maybe?

Or, Aerie realized, if he had stolen it from the URS after learning it was going to house weapons of worldly destruction, then he'd actually *saved* people from dying.

Would the URS arm their starship? With weapons? To kill people?

It's not like the URS wouldn't do something if they needed to survive, including executions. Or go to war.

But should it really surprise her that they would do things

in a less than savory manner to protect their laws?

If Exton and Emery's father had been part of a religion, and he was against the use of his ship, then wouldn't the State's actions, as unpleasant as they were, be fully justified?

Could they be justified, if the State *had* lied to Exton and Emery's father?

They wouldn't have needed to do that, Aerie thought. Surely not. If they wanted his unwilling cooperation, all they had to do was order him. Or, she admitted reluctantly, they could have threatened him.

But …

Her own thoughts, so long ago and far away, echoed through her mind mockingly. *Would the State lie to people? If it was for their own good.*

Aerie felt the solid foundation of her life suddenly disappear. Her whole life she had listened to the URS. She knew on some level that they had lied before.

Emery's question came back to haunt her. *"What if they took advantage of your trust?"*

Could the State have been lying about *everything*?

No, Aerie thought, *they wouldn't lie about everything. Just enough to keep people believing what they wanted. For the good of the State. At the expense of the individual.*

Emery could lie as well, of course. *She just admitted earlier that she likes having you around. Would it be such a stretch to believe she would lie about this to you, to get you to stay on her side? Especially if Exton does like you?*

She was surprised by the vitriolic tone she heard in her own thoughts.

How do I know who is telling me the truth?

Aerie knew the URS would lie to her, but they were also the ones who had trained her in logic and learning.

They were the ones who told her Captain Chainsword was a ghost, working with MENACE, determined to destroy their nation; they were the ones who told her the crew of the *Perdition* would torture her.

And they were wrong about all of it! She was accepted

here, appreciated here. In only a matter of days, Emery had become a welcome presence, more than Serena had ever been. Olga and Sean, along with her other new friends, made cleaning tolerable and work less like work than she'd ever known. Even dealing with children seemed to be less of a chore here! And Exton …

She thought about the moment she'd first seen him, beside her in the medical ward, about how warm and wary he made her feel. He'd told her plainly the *Perdition* had enough power to overcome her venom.

Aerie decided it was time to make him prove it.

As she made her decision, her mind seemed to step out of its fog. She blinked, surprised to realize she was mindlessly waltzing around the *Perdition* with no idea where she was going.

"Stupid, stupid … " Aerie shook her head at herself. "Pay attention to what you're doing. You need to watch where you're going. This is how the URS managed to lie to you so well … " She flustered over as she heard herself.

I need answers, not assumptions.

Thinking of her home made her heart ache. She wondered how Brock was doing with his military training, if he wondered about her, if her brothers were treating him nice in the training program they were in together. Aerie wondered if they thought of her at all.

She doubted it.

Another part of her, the angry side, wanted to go and march up to her father, then shake him as she demanded the truth from his own lips about Captain Chainsword, and why the State was so intent on hiding the truth from its people.

A familiar shadow at the far right side of the corridor caught her eye. She felt her heart stop, along with her stride.

Exton was standing near the wall at the far end of atrium, talking with a woman with curly brown hair. Aerie felt a surprising rush of nerves as she watched Exton nod to the lady beside him. The lady, with her long hair, was certainly pretty. Aerie subconsciously ran her hand through her own red hair.

Just who is that?

Obviously, Exton had a lot of admirers. Hadn't she talked with some of them herself this past week? Even Alice had considerably warmed to the topic of the mysterious captain.

Exton was certainly handsome, but he wasn't married. *Of course, that doesn't always matter, does it?* Aerie thought. She knew a number of men and women from the URS had only seen marriage as an obligation to survive. Pleasure came from other places.

I have to stop this. Aerie felt her face flush over red again, which she knew only made things worse. How attractive could she be with her ruddy face and bright ginger hair?

Before Aerie could decide what to do, a man came out and put his arm around the lady. A small boy was on his shoulders. Aerie watched with surprise when the lady kissed the man, clearly genuinely happy to see him.

Are they married? Aerie wondered. She couldn't imagine the General and her mother doing that.

Exton pulled out a small object from behind his back. Aerie saw it was a small vehicle of some kind. Upon further examination, she realized it was a toy.

Exton held it out to the small child, who gleefully cheered at the sight of it.

Aerie melted. "That's so sweet," she murmured, unable to help herself.

Another reason to like Exton, she thought reluctantly, watching him as he gave the child a high-five and a smile before the family took off into the sanctuary. He was good with kids.

Exton turned. Aerie knew he saw her; the cool iciness of his gaze melted as she stared back determinedly. Inwardly, she resolved not to allow him to gain the upper hand.

At least, not any more than he already had.

"I thought I'd see you here," Exton said as he came to stand beside her.

"Why did you give that child a toy?" Aerie almost slapped

herself for sounding so angry.

"That was Judith and Aidan, and their son is Timothy," Exton told her calmly, ignoring her frosty tone. "They've been part of the *Perdition* with me since the beginning. Timothy's only four, and he's got a sibling on the way. He's good at breaking toys, which won't help much when it comes to sharing with his new sibling." He shrugged. "So after he breaks them, I fix them."

"The engineering background helps with that, I guess."

"Yes." He glanced down at her. "You weren't jealous, were you?"

"No!"

He grinned. "I was wondering if you had missed me."

"The only time I missed you," Aerie told him, "was when I was fighting you by the tree."

He ignored her taunting. "Emery told me she was going to take you through the emergency drills today."

Aerie was caught off guard. She'd forgotten about the reason she even saw the fighters in the first place. "I, uh, finished them. And then forgot them."

He sighed. "I talked with Emery some just a few moments ago. She said you might be angry."

"I'm not." *Liar.*

Exton took her arm. "Liar. I *know* you're angry. I can tell by the look on your face. Why don't you tell me what's wrong?"

"I want answers," Aerie insisted, pulling back from him. "I want to know the truth."

"You'll get it. But not here. Come with me." He dropped his voice. "I'd hate for even more rumors about you to get around the ship."

"Fine." Aerie squared her shoulders and followed after him. "Where are we going, *Captain*?"

"Somewhere we can talk and not worry about interruptions," Exton assured her. "If you want answers, I'll give them to you. But what you decide to do with them is up to you."

Because she couldn't think of anything clever to say in return, Aerie remained silent as she marched on behind him.

♦19♦

Exton felt his blood pump with anticipation. He was not excited to see that Aerie was in a bad mood, but he was excited to be with her again.

The past week, he'd tried to ignore her, to prove to himself he could survive without her—as if spending six years in space, having no idea of her existence, and focusing on his plans for revenge against the URS were somehow not proof enough.

But as he opened up the door to the Captain's Lounge and pushed her in, ignoring her muffled protests, he knew he'd been foolish—foolish to think he could forget about her, foolish to think he would let himself, foolish to think he even wanted to try.

"What is this place?" Aerie's voice momentarily lost its edge as she glanced around the small room.

"This is the Captain's Lounge," he told her. "I adopted it as my own a few days after the *Perdition* took off from Earth."

"It seems a little small."

"When you leave the whole world behind, every room is a small room," Exton replied. "But this is *my* room. I don't have a lot of people come here. Emery will pop in, and Tyler will, too, on occasion."

"Don't you have a real room?"

He grinned at her sudden blush. "I do. It's down next to the hangar on Level Ten, actually. You might have passed by it while you were in the hangar."

"I didn't pay much attention to the hangar after I talked to Emery."

"I had an inkling."

"You don't need to mock me."

"I know you have a problem with it," Exton remarked, watching her temper flare at his flippancy. "I'm not trying to provoke you."

"You're *supposed* to provoke me," she argued. "You're supposed to be the enemy!"

Exton was glad to hear her define him on those terms. She had insisted she was his enemy when they'd first met; she wasn't so certain of that anymore.

It was a nice feeling.

"Do you want me to be the enemy?" he asked.

"Yes. No. I mean, I don't know." Aerie huffed. "I want the truth. Tell me the truth."

"You won't believe me." He crossed his arms and leaned back against the wall. "You don't trust me."

"We've had this conversation before." Aerie shook her head. "I don't care."

"I do."

"How do we trust each other, then?" Aerie asked, her voice full of nervous desperation. "How do I know this is not a game?"

"I don't play games, remember? I told you that before."

"You also told me you would lie to me," she countered.

"I wasn't playing a game when I kissed you before," he promised, "and I'm not lying about it now."

She took an uneasy step back from him. "So how can I trust you?"

"Let's make another deal." Exton extended his hand to her, offering her a truce. "We have a good record with deals."

"*I* do. You don't." Aerie crossed her arms. "You said you would tell me more about yourself that first time, but you left before you did."

"I'll tell you that stuff now, along with the rest of it."

"And we haven't had our rematch yet."

"Do you want to take care of that now?" he asked. "Neither of us scheduled it. And you were the one who was going to make the call on when, as I recall, so you could have a 'fair, unfair' advantage."

Aerie frowned. "We don't have to do that now."

"Here's the new deal: I won't lie to you, and you don't lie to me. What do you think?"

"That won't work." She brushed a wayward lock of hair out of her eyes. "We have no way to know if we're really telling each other the truth."

"We can try."

She hesitated for a moment, but then she took his hand. "Fine," she agreed. "I accept."

He surprised her by drawing her hand up to his lips and kissing her knuckles in a gallant manner. The surprising caress managed to render her silent.

Exton almost laughed at her response. To know he'd driven his bubbly, spirited Aerie to a standstill overwhelmed him. "The first thing I'm going to not lie to you about," he said, "is that I'm going to kiss you right now."

"You want to kiss me? But why—*umph*."

Her words, along with her questions, faded as he leaned in and pressed his mouth against hers. Exton knew her uncertainty was gone a second later when her hands clutched at him and held him close.

She might not have trusted him entirely, but she was curious about him. That was enough for him.

For the moment.

"The second thing I'm not going to lie to you about," he told her, his breath warm against her mouth, "is that I've wanted to do that since the last time I kissed you."

She trembled. "Me, too," Aerie admitted, her voice barely a whisper. "But I'm not sure why."

"I'm sure we'll figure it out," he murmured, pulling her closer.

He closed his eyes as the taste of her washed over him, beckoning him to kiss her, imploring him to lose himself in her essence.

His body seemed to move of its own accord. He could feel his fingers twisting in her fiery tresses, his hands moving down the curves of her body, his arms tightening around her—the cool air of the small room whisked away as the warmth of desire sparked.

"Aerie." Her name was a whisper against her lips.

"What?" She eased away from him. "Am I doing it wrong?"

"Huh?" Dazed, he opened his eyes. At the sight of hers, wide-eyed with wonder and hesitation, he shook his head. "No. No, you're doing fine." He kissed her again, as if to prove it.

"That's good," she murmured. "I've never kissed anyone before."

Her statement caught him by surprise, enough to pull back. "Never?" he asked.

She blushed. "There's no need to make me feel stupid about it," Aerie insisted. "I just never—" She stopped as he began laughing. "It's not funny, Exton."

"I know," he said. "I'm just ridiculously happy you've never kissed anyone else. It'll save me some trouble hunting them down and killing them."

Aerie frowned and pushed back against him, freeing herself from his grasp. He smiled, even as she shoved past him.

"I'm not making fun of you," he told her. "I'm serious." He took her arm. "I'm glad you're mine, and only mine."

Aerie felt her face fluster. "I'm not yours," she insisted. "How can I be, when I'm not sure about so many other things?"

Of all things, this is one thing you don't have to be unsure of, Aerie.

His thought hung silently in the air, as if his mind expected him to say it. But Exton conceded Aerie had a point, and it was that point that stopped him.

"If you want more time," he told her, "you have it. You don't have to make any life-altering decisions tonight."

"I don't?"

The genuine surprise in her voice, mixed with wary suspicion, made him curse the URS and their fear mongering all over again. "Of course not. You're free to make your own decisions while you're here."

"I'm not free while I'm here," Aerie corrected him. "Remember? You won't take me back home."

There was an abrupt moment of silence as Exton frowned. "Clever girl," he muttered. "I can't take you home right now. We're both trapped here, Aerie, by things bigger than both of us."

She didn't seem to agree with his argument, but a moment later she spoke again.

"What if I don't want to kiss you anymore?" Aerie asked. "Are you still okay with my choice?"

"I'll make another deal with you." Exton smirked as he leaned closer to her, only a breath away. He felt her tremble saw her eyes look to his mouth. Her lips parted and her eyes fluttered shut as their breath mingled together.

"I'll only kiss you if you promise to kiss me back." He reached over and tenderly ruffled her hair as he pulled back. "But in the meantime, you're not allowed to kiss anyone else."

"How are you going to enforce that?" Aerie asked, a small pout on her face, clearly disappointed he hadn't kissed her again.

"I'm Captain Chainsword," Exton reminded her in a playful tone. "If anyone else tries to take what is mine, he'll walk the plank."

Before she could reply, he took her hand in his. "I know you have questions about other things, things that are just as important."

"Yes," Aerie agreed, sounding as though she was trying to recall just what those things were.

"Truth matters. What we believe matters." He met her gaze, just as he had the first time he met her. "I'm going to tell you the truth about the *Perdition*. Can you trust me?"

Aerie slowly nodded. "Okay."

"It might take a while," he added, "because it doesn't actually start with me. Like all history, it builds on the past."

"From the Old Republic?"

"I can start there," he remarked with a grin. "But I can go back further if you want an excuse to hang around longer."

She smiled at his teasing. "I think starting at the Old Republic sounds good."

"Going to cripple my ego, are you?"

"It's such a large target," Aerie replied, laughing this time. "How can I resist?"

Exton looked at her, watching her until she blushed. "How can you resist, indeed."

"Enough teasing. Tell me about the Old Republic."

"You likely know that a few years after the United Nations broke apart, war broke out."

"That was when nuclear war devastated the planet," Aerie recited. "The URS told us that the resulting ash and debris covered most of the world and toxic rain became commonplace, eating up food resources, slowly killing off populations."

"That's true," Exton replied. "What they usually leave out at this point is that the United States of America was just the USA at the time, not the UNA. It declared a state of emergency and the presidency turned into a self-appointed dictatorship."

"You know, you're right," Aerie replied. "I'd never thought of that. They don't dwell long on that particular topic." She giggled. "Can you imagine trying to convince the URS that they are still under the USA government's emergency powers?"

"It doesn't sound like a bad idea to me, honestly," Exton said. "The United States was ill-equipped to handle a large-scale disaster, but it was a fairly stable government system where the people were able to hold its elected officials accountable, most of the time." He shrugged. "At least, more than the URS is able to now."

"I know it's a complicated problem." Aerie sighed. "I'm sorry I interrupted. Please, go on."

"Soon after, the USA joined with the northern country, Canada, to help with the ecological backlash," Exton continued. "They became UNA, the United Nations of America. And the war, made increasingly difficult by food and communication issues, was largely postponed." Exton shifted against the wall. "That's another part they usually forget to mention."

"So we're still at war with the Middle East?"

"Technically. But not quite."

"Why would we even bother fighting a war like that? With the world this way?" Aerie hopped up to the window seat. She glanced out the window, looking down at the earth. It was too far away to make out any clear land divisions or see the dark oceans underneath the swirling clouds.

Exton came up beside her. "Some people will have power at any price."

Aerie frowned. "That's what they say."

"And that's what they do," Exton said. "The loudest people in the room are the ones who are usually trying to hide their own hypocrisy."

"It still seems wrong."

"To you, and me, maybe." Exton shrugged. "It's been hard since the fall of the Old Republic to convince people that all of humanity is broken."

"It's like that thing you said before," Aerie recalled. "Iniquity."

"Yes." Exton nodded toward the earth. "All the religions in the world, before this time, agreed that there was something just not right within the heart of humanity."

"So that brokenness led to war?"

"It always does, Aerie. That hasn't changed in thousands of years. Once the Old Republic dissolved into a dictatorship, new alliances formed. You've heard of MENACE."

"I've heard of them," Aerie agreed, thinking of the General's accounts in his books. "They have been the arch enemy of the URS for decades now."

"The URS doesn't tell you, but it wasn't always that way. They were allies once."

"No, that's not possible." Aerie recalled the stories from the General's reports. "They never shared the same values."

"That's the part where, in some cases, it makes sense," Exton explained. "It was the perfect way to partner up and then have no qualms about destroying an ally.

"The UNA secretly partnered with MENACE to take

over the rest of the northern hemisphere; the Southern Hemisphere had largely been lost, except for the most remote of locations, and they didn't see the need to care much about it."

Aerie shook her head. "I don't know if I can believe it."

"Why not?" he asked. "The URS hates capitalism, right?"

"Yes."

"Think about capitalism in terms of war. War is a form of competition, just like capitalism, so—"

"So it would make sense to get rid of the competition," Aerie finished. The wonder of new discovery darkened with the destructive reality it left behind. "You're right. That does make sense."

"That's how the Old Republic did it. Convince the private sector to work for the public, and then they betrayed them."

"It's an idea with applicable merit," Aerie agreed slowly. "You're right. They didn't teach us this history in the URS." She frowned. "How did you learn it?"

"The Ecclesia, among its virtues, keeps records of the world history. It has, since its creation at the turn of the Common Era, written and recorded many historical accounts as well as religious ones. Context," he explained, "is critical to understanding truth."

"Can I see some of their records?" Aerie asked.

"Sure." Exton smiled. "Tyler is my Commander, but he is also an avid reader. He can let you into the Records Room anytime you're free."

"I hope I'll have some time this week. Emery said I could help with the harvest."

"You want to help with the harvest?" Exton asked, surprised. "Did she actually tell you what it is?"

"It's harvesting crops."

"And you still *want* to help? It's dirty work."

"Cleaning with Olga and Alice has been dirty work at times," Aerie bantered back. "I would love to see how your plants are growing up here." She blushed. "My mother was a horticulture student before she was assigned to marry the—I mean, my father."

"Sounds like she would have gotten along with my mother." Exton considered mentioning the Biovid, before he shoved the thought of it aside. He'd show it to her later. It wasn't ready yet, he reminded himself.

He glanced over at her as she continued to watch the endlessly expanding frontier outside the window. "Hey," he said.

She glanced at him.

"I know it's a bit off topic, but have you heard if there has been talk in the biochemistry and horticulture fields to wipe out the rest of earth's populations?"

Aerie's eyes widened. "Why would they do that?"

"It was something my parents heard when I was younger." Exton turned and faced out the window again. "I was wondering if they'd made any progress on it."

"You think the URS would continue that kind of research after they've won all the wars?" Aerie asked. "I mean," she added with a blush, "besides the war you have with them?"

"My father was an engineer who started out by working with the horticulture and biochemists, developing machinery for them and the forestry department. It was how he met my mother, and many of our family's friends. Mom loved her flowers and plants and worked diligently on the URS gardens. But she decided to raise me and Emery once we came along. General St. Cloud was not happy about this."

Aerie flinched. "I can imagine," she mumbled.

"Before that, my mother and a team of others were given the task of weaponizing plant DNA. I'm waiting to hear of the day they perfect it." He shrugged. "I know they've made advancements in plenty of other areas." He gave her a playful smirk. "Including some of their more recent fighting techniques, thanks to you."

Aerie smiled but said nothing.

She wanted to, though. He could tell, the way she was carefully thinking things through. Her eyes were her downfall. With those all-too-expressive amber eyes, she would never be a good liar.

Exton leaned back and looked at her. And waited. *She hates to wait.*

Finally, Aerie spoke. "I know about their experiments to weaponize pollen seeds," she said quietly.

"It doesn't surprise me," Exton said. "I've been waiting for it, to be honest."

"Why?" Aerie lowered her gaze from his again. "Why were you waiting for that particular information?"

"Because of the old 'take-over-the-world' ploy. My father started this project—the *Perdition*—when I was young, as a way to help people live comfortably in space for a long period of time. There aren't many reasons why any nation would need that, let alone moral reasons to have it. It seemed reasonable to assume that it could be used as a lifeboat of sorts."

"You do have a point," Aerie remarked, her voice soft.

"My family grew up along with the ship. I watched him work on it, and when I could walk and use his tools, I helped him build it."

"You did?"

"Yes." Exton smiled. "I'm not lying to you, Aerie."

Her eyes were still wary, while her voice was still a whisper. But Exton could hear the certainty in it. "I know."

"Papa had a lot of friends who also worked on it. They were members of the Ecclesia. Most of them up here are also people I grew up with and their kids, and some grandkids now, too.

"My parents converted when I was young. Emery has also made much study of it since then. I think that's part of the reason she fell in love with Tyler."

"You weren't a member of the Ecclesia?" Aerie asked.

Exton cringed at the surprise in her voice. "I mostly ignored it, to be honest. I was young. I wanted to be famous. So when General St. Cloud took notice of my skills, I was thrilled. Both Emery and I managed to impress a lot of our superiors with our skills and training, thanks to our parents."

"Your mother was a horticulturalist?"

"Close. She studied as a botanist."

"Emery learned from her."

"Yes."

Aerie's eyes were sad as she turned to him. "And your dad taught you about engineering."

"Yes."

"So you did steal this ship from the URS?" Aerie asked.

He sighed. "I wouldn't call it stealing, per say."

Aerie gave him a tiny smile. "Emery said about the same thing."

"I was only fourteen when my father was killed by the URS. Emery and I were lined up for early entrance into different universities. I'd talked with St. Cloud about working for the military."

"He would have liked that." Aerie cleared her throat. "I imagine."

"He did." Exton clenched his fists. "I think it was part of the reason they were not willing to give my father another punishment."

"Exton." She put her hand on his, and he mindlessly stared at it for a long moment, before grasping onto her.

"After my father was killed, I felt guilty for weeks. It was only later that I began to feel angry. My father was a good man. Idealistic, but he wanted to make the world a better place for the people, not for the State. I could no longer agree with the State. Tyler was my best friend at the time. We were at university when I told him what happened. He was there for the military, studying aeronautics and astrophysics for their new space fighter program. We decided to find a way to commit treason and honor my father's memory."

"So you decided to steal back his ship."

"Yes. It took months of planning, but I still can't believe somedays how we managed to pull it off. The URS was using my father's ship as a prototype at the time, at New Hope's Military Academy. But we got it; many members of the Ecclesia helped us launch it, as you might have figured. It was a miracle, but we got it."

He relaxed against the window, feeling the cool of the steel-enforced glass behind him. "So that's the story."

"I see." Aerie nervously laced her fingers together in her lap. "So you took the ship out of revenge for your father's death. And you managed to stop them from using their weapons on other nations from space?"

"I wouldn't say 'managed.'" He turned away. "They've still attacked different countries, and we've been unable to do much about it. The nice thing about the Ecclesia is that they have a reliable network of informants. We are sometimes able to get people out, if they believe us, but we are unable to save everyone or the places."

"If that's the truth," Aerie said slowly, "then you are a hero."

Exton shook his head. "No, I'm not. I am the reason my father died. Anything I can do to stop the URS from destroying the world is still not enough to absolve me of that sin."

"And you're sure that the URS is lying to its people?"

He frowned at her. "Even you know that, Aerie."

"They have good intentions. Sometimes."

"That doesn't mean that it's not harmful. Surely you can think of some instances where they do cause problems for their populations."

He watched her face, her expression changing slowly from concentration to disbelief, to uncertainty to despair. Exton nodded as her eyes met his once more. "There are others here, others who are older than me, and they can tell you more. Several refugees can also attest to contrary reports from the URS history record."

"Like what?"

Exton rubbed his chin thoughtfully. "There are a few bigger ones that come to mind. MENACE, for example, never poisoned the Hudson River eight years ago; I knew a water systems specialist who confided in me that the water had been polluted from a mutated bacterium growth."

Aerie nodded. "I wondered about that myself a few years ago," she admitted quietly. "I took samples one day and examined them. The bacteria wasn't mutated, but it was a specialized culture which only grows in certain conditions. MENACE would not have had the resources for it, most likely." Her lip trembled. "My mom knew a lot about things like that, so she helped with the cultures."

Exton said nothing for several moments. He glanced at the earth through the window overhead, allowing her time to digest all the new—readjusted—information.

"Is that why you rescue people?" Aerie finally asked. "To save them from the URS?"

"Sometimes," he admitted. "Many of them want to be here, with the Ecclesia. They think it's safe."

"Is it?"

Exton sighed. "It's safer than a lot of other places, especially for people who believe in something greater that the URS."

"Something greater?"

"When your beliefs fail you, you need to look to something greater," he told her. "The Ecclesia have God."

"What do you have?" Aerie asked quietly.

"Right now? Revenge."

At her shocked expression, he laughed coldly. "I wasn't playing a game," he said, "when I told you my greatest fear was that I have nothing else to lose."

"But you're a good person." Aerie blushed. "At least, I think so. I mean, you help people."

"I didn't set out to help people when I stole this ship."

"But you did."

"Is there such a thing as being accidentally good?"

Aerie frowned at his teasing tone. "You're not giving yourself enough credit."

"I doubt it."

"I know you better than I did before," she said, taking a step closer to him. "From being around here, listening to people tell me about you and their lives. I know you've been a good leader."

"All it takes to mess it up is one bad decision."

"That doesn't make you a monster," Aerie whispered.

"That doesn't mean that you believe it," he countered.

Aerie sighed. "I think I need some time to think it over still." She tightened her grip on his hand. "I don't *disbelieve* you, though."

Small steps. "I understand." Exton checked the time. "It's getting late," he said. "If you want to help with the harvest tomorrow, you'd better get back to your room."

"Exton." She blushed as she said his name. "Can we stay here for a bit longer?"

"Sure, if you want." He grinned. "The privacy is nice, isn't it?"

"Yes." She nodded toward the window. "The view is, too."

"It's definitely different from the one in New Hope. Assuming it hasn't drastically changed in the last six years."

"It hasn't," Aerie assured him. "Sometimes I have trouble when I am working, when I see windows here, because I start staring out into space," she admitted. "Olga's told me it's natural, and that once I get used to it it'll be easier to focus on work. I hope I don't get used to it."

"I don't blame you." He followed her gaze. "Once you lose something like that, it's really hard to get it back."

She slumped back against the wall, letting herself fall into a sitting position. "Come and sit with me."

Exton moved to sit next to her. He was surprised when she took his arm and wrapped it around her shoulders.

"It's a little cold in here," she murmured inconspicuously, snuggling into the small niche of his shoulder.

"I never notice anymore," he admitted, drawing her closer. "You're warm to me."

"Is this where I hit you?" she asked, reaching out and gently touching the left side of his chest.

"Yes. It's better now."

"That's good." She smiled up at him. "I'm not lying to

you when I say I'm happy that it's better."

"I'm glad you're not lying."

"Let's not lie to each other about other stuff."

"Like what?"

"Just other stuff, not related to war or politics or anything." Aerie shrugged. "What's your favorite color? That seems pretty basic."

"You always start with the basics?"

"When it comes to you? Hardly."

He laughed. "That's true. I like blue best. It's the only primary color that stays blue, no matter how light or dark you make it."

"That's neat. I never thought of that," Aerie said. "My favorite color is—"

"Wait," he interrupted. "Let me guess. It is red?"

"Yeah. How did you know?" Aerie asked.

He grinned. "Just had a feeling."

As they continued, as best as they could, to have a normal conversation, Exton felt her relax against him, her warmth gradually pulling him into quiet contentment. He didn't know if she was doing it out of sympathy at hearing his story, or if she was slowly leaving her shyness and hesitancy behind. Either way, he admired her bravery and compassion.

And even though he was paying attention to all her questions and answers, all he really wanted to ask her was if he could kiss her again. Despite his feelings on the matter, he decided against it.

There is no rushing this, he thought. He had time, as little as it might have been, and if she was going to trust him, he knew he had to give it to her.

♦20♦

With a hulking basket full of crops on her back, Aerie felt a momentary sense of satisfaction stem from her efforts as she deftly climbed down into one of the *Perdition's* storage pantries.

She knew of the gymnasium on Level Four, and she had attempted to get a workout in just once before. But the stares and whispers that seemed to follow her drove her out of the room.

That was the least of her worries for the moment. There was a war to consider, sinister intentions to weigh, and her own hesitations to condemn.

And on top of that, as of this morning there were at least a hundred rooms of crops that needed harvested, collected, and stored.

"Looks great, Aerie," Alice said. "How's the rest of your room coming?"

Aerie smiled as she handed her basket off to Alice. "It's almost done," she answered. "Naomi and Orla, the other girls working with me, will be down in a few moments."

"You guys are sure going fast." Alice gestured toward the storage shelves. "Kyo and I will find a way to make room for more."

Aerie grinned.

"I like how your hair is styled today," Alice said. "It looks like you're getting better about braiding it."

"Yes," Aerie agreed with a small laugh. "I appreciate you showing me how to do it."

Alice tweaked one of her short curls. "I almost wish I had longer hair still. It's just easier."

"My mother liked my hair long," Aerie recalled. "She died a few years ago."

"Did she have long hair like yours, too?"

"Yes." Aerie grinned. "And I like it this way, too, of course."

"That's why you keep it like that?"

"My mother's hair was a darker shade of red than mine. But she liked to keep it longer, too. Why do you ask?"

Alice shrugged. "You remind me of one of the ladies I used to know in the Chaya settlement, where I used to live, before I applied to come and work on the *Perdition*. I thought you might be related."

"Chaya settlement?"

"It's a small place close to the fertile crescent area, where the Mediterranean Sea used to be. It's one of the Ecclesia's camping grounds."

Aerie frowned. "My mother's name was Merra."

"That was her name, too."

That's … weird.

"I'll have to ask Exton about that," Aerie decided. "That's strange. Maybe she is related to me. I don't have any relatives on my mother's side that I know about."

"Exton?" Alice repeated. "You mean the Captain?"

"Yes." Aerie immediately felt her face turning red. "Yes, that's who I meant. The Captain. Sorry."

"Does he talk to you?" Alice asked. "I've heard he lets people call him by his name that he's close to."

"We haven't talked that much." Aerie tried to shrug it off. "I mean, I've talked way more with Emery."

"I've heard he's taken a liking to one of the new refugees," Alice said. "I was wondering if it was you. You're so pretty."

Aerie felt her mouth drop open in surprise. "Well, thank you, but—"

"Do you have a crush on him, too?"

"I've heard that the Ecclesia teaches that gossiping is—"

"Gossip and staying informed are different things," Alice interrupted. "But I was right. It is you, isn't it?"

"I—"

"Are you almost done up there, Aerie?" Orla called down from below. "I've got my batch ready."

"Coming." Aerie smiled back at Alice, trying not to feel like it was forced all of a sudden. "I'll see you in a bit. Excuse me."

She breathed a sigh of relief as she passed Orla. The small, graceful woman didn't seem to sense her distress.

No wonder there are so many whispers around, if they think Exton is attracted to me.

Well, he is, Aerie thought, correcting herself. But it wasn't like that was anyone's business but his, and hers, too.

Aerie smiled, thinking of how they spent a good hour together in the Captain's Lounge, just talking and sitting in the small room, watching the celestial bodies shift through the high window.

He walked her to her room, said good night, and left her wondering if she hated or admired his fortitude in keeping his promise not to kiss her unless she wanted him to.

Aerie realized, somewhere in the middle of her restless night of half-sleep, confusing dreams, and discomforting darkness, that it wasn't Exton she was angry with, but herself.

She was lying to others, and she been lied to; maybe she was even lying to herself.

Aerie woke up to Emery at the door, letting her know she'd been excused from working with Olga that day so she could help with the harvest.

The work was pleasant, if hard, but Aerie was unable to find peace. The work was absorbing enough that the dull hum of disappointment and confusion were able to be held at bay, but only just so.

Aerie passed by a window. Awe struck her all over again as she gazed out to see the small, growing shadow of Earth against the darkness of space. The sun shone brightly on its cloud cover, illuminating the soft tapestry of wind patterns flowing over the world. She could see faint traces of green and orange glow at the northern pole, where the gray waters of the ocean faded to blue.

"It really is an ugly sort of beautiful," Aerie murmured to herself.

Just like me.

It was an unfortunate mess she was in, and Aerie felt the

anger creeping into her heart again.

The truth *mattered.* Why did this surprise her?

Aerie sighed. She thought about her notes on the crew and the *Perdition. It was a stupid idea to begin with*, she thought. The URS didn't need to know about the *Perdition.* Of course, that was no reason to stop asking questions. She wanted to find things out for herself while she was onboard. And she would.

As for the URS … Aerie decided her father was going to have a lot of questions to answer when she got back.

If she went back.

If only it could be so easy to stay.

It was hard to imagine a world where she did not go to class, or work, where she did not get to talk with people she had grown up with, where she did not see the same things outside her window she'd always seen. Brock, Serena, her brothers, and her father. Even her stepmother, Phoebe, and her class of peers.

But in the past week, it had become increasingly difficult to imagine going to a job where there was none of Olga's kindness, living in a place without a friendship like Emery's, and leaving behind a world with Exton's kisses.

Her guilt prompted her to ignore her thoughts on the matter before she examined them too closely.

Instead, she wondered what it would have been like to meet Exton before his heart had been crushed.

"Daydreaming again?"

"Exton." Aerie jumped at his voice. It was as if she'd summoned him. "What are you doing here?"

He grinned at her. "Maybe I came to work."

"Really?" Aerie arched her brow. "You're not here to spend time with me?"

"I can be, if you want." He gave her a smug look. "But for that to happen, you'd have to tell me first, and I don't think you want to sacrifice your pride."

"It can't just happen?" Aerie asked. "I have to ask for it?"

"Like forgiveness for a most egregious sin," he

confirmed.

Aerie laughed. "I'll take the penance for my pride," she said, "because I don't want to impose on your hospitality too much."

"You're not. Didn't Emery explain how the work system goes here?" Exton asked. "You'll get credits for working, and you can spend them on what you want."

Aerie recalled Emery mentioning something like that as they walked around the *Perdition.* "I guess I didn't understand," she admitted.

"You can use them for classes, with the Ecclesia, if you'd like. Emery mentioned you like botany and plants."

"That would be wonderful," Aerie agreed, excitement starting to bubble up inside of her. "What kind of classes can I afford?"

"You can look it up once you get to your room to know for sure, but there are plenty of classes. I'm sure you could find at least one to interest you."

"Are classes the only things I could buy?" Aerie asked. "What do other people use their money for?"

"Room, board, and food, some entertainment—"

"Wait," Aerie interrupted. "It costs something to live and eat here?"

"Yes, but you don't need to worry about it. You're my guest," Exton reminded her softly. "You don't pay for that."

"Who pays for it then?" Aerie asked.

"I do."

She paused, startled. "You're paying for me to be here?"

"I have enough credits, if that's what you're worried about."

"I didn't know."

"It's fine." He took her hand. "I wanted to."

"I'll pay you back," she promised.

"No. I don't want you to." Exton shook his head. "It's a gift, Aerie."

"Then I should give you something to make it equal."

"Equal and fair again, huh?" Exton sighed. "It's not like

that here, Aerie. When you're given a gift, you don't try to pay for it. You just take care of it."

As she stared at him, he began to laugh. "You should see your face right now. Has no one ever given you anything, without any expectation of repayment or thanks before?"

"I … I don't know."

"Well, then consider this time onboard with us a first, from me to you." He took her hand and tugged. "You've been working on the harvest long enough today. Come and see everything that the Ecclesia has set up in the gym."

Aerie saw Orla coming down from the storage pantry and Naomi making her way over, a speculative gleam in the older woman's eye. "I don't know. I still have a lot of work to do."

"You'll get it done," he told her. "I've been watching you work."

"You have?" Aerie's question was soft and full of awe.

He smiled. "Yes. It's very relaxing for me. You seem to take it pretty seriously most of the time. You about had a fit when those kids two rooms over ran through here. But you didn't scold them. You laughed and redirected them, and then when they were gone you grumbled while you picked up all the fallen sprouts off the floors."

"I would have scolded them if they weren't so … so … "

"Young?" he offered.

"Maybe."

"Aerie, the harvest is going to last all week," Exton reminded her. "Come and see the traditional first day festivities with me, and then you can come back and work." Exton reached over and brushed her bangs out of her eyes, marveling at the uncertainty and relentless curiosity he saw in their amber-colored seas.

"Are you sure?" she asked. "What will people say?"

"Who cares?" Exton scowled. "Everyone talks about me, Aerie. There's very little stopping it. Even God, who, I will be the first to admit, has infinitely more power and influence in such matters than I do, can't get all his followers to stop the gossip on this ship."

She giggled. "If you're sure … "

"I'm sure."

"I don't want to ruin you."

"If you ruin me, I'll ruin you."

"Is that another deal?" Aerie asked. She saw the playful smile on his face as she grasped his hand in hers.

"Yes."

"I'm beginning to like our deals."

His hand tightened around hers. "Me, too."

Exton couldn't recall the last time he'd enjoyed dancing.

The last time he danced was Emery's wedding, and he had loathed it. Of course, it was not for a lack of skill or partner; Emery was beautiful and wistful and awing, her movements graceful and precise despite his rusty skills.

But that was Emery, through and through. Exton knew his sister was a romantic at heart, and a practical woman at will.

In contrast, Aerie was an unexpected adventure. She was hesitant but brave, curious but polite—and she always looked to him to catch her if she fell.

Aerie laughed and smiled as he twirled her around, pulled her in close, and led her into turns.

"You're having fun," she said. From her tone, Exton knew it wasn't a question.

"It seems I am," he said. "Are you?"

Not that Emery's wedding wasn't as cheerful and happy as the Harvest, he thought. *It was just different with Aerie.*

So much is different with Aerie.

"I don't think I've ever danced like this before," she confided, giving him another one of her guilty smiles, the kind Exton both loved and hated.

He hated she was still wired to side with the URS more often than not, but he knew she was coming around. And he knew what it was like. Hadn't he experienced the same thing ten years ago, before he cut ties with them and committed treason?

Maybe a few more weeks here will help her.

"You mean you've never danced just to have a good time, rather than for ceremony or matters of State?"

Exton might have been teasing her, but her eyes were somber as she nodded. "You're right," she replied.

Those eyes, he thought. So big and bright, even when they were sad. There was something about them that tugged at his heart.

With his attention focused on her, Exton suddenly stumbled. He felt her crash into him, her arms pull him close, and instant concern cross her features.

Exton fell back into his memory of the moment where he picked her up out of the tree and held onto her. His chest ached in that moment, weakened by the desire to respond to her vulnerability.

All over again, he felt the thick, hardened barrier around his heart crack in triumphant rebellion. This time there was no fear, only falling—and then he was free.

"Are you okay?" Aerie asked, as other people laughed and danced around the room as though the floor hadn't slipped out from under his feet, as though nothing out of the ordinary had occurred in the last, longest second of his life. "You have a strange look on your face."

A pair of dancers bounced against him, but he only clung more tightly to her.

How could life change so much, in less than a twinkling of an eye?

"I do believe," Exton told her quietly, "that you've ruined me."

He couldn't tell if she fully understood what he meant, but her eyes twinkled with joy. A second later, she wrapped her arms around his neck, and, standing up on tiptoes, she gently pressed her lips against his.

The shock of her shy kiss sent lightning dashing across his senses. If his heart hadn't already insisted on loving her, his soul would have demanded it. The room, with all its stares and whispers, whisked away into nothingness as his arms tightened around her. He closed his eyes as his hands ran up her body to cradle her face and keep her close.

She drew back a moment later. "Exton," Aerie muttered, glancing around uneasily. There was a red tint to her cheeks. "People are looking at us."

"That's your fault," he murmured, "for breaking our deal."

"The deal was that you wouldn't kiss me unless I wanted you to," Aerie replied with a renewed sense of a challenge. "It said nothing about me kissing you."

"You are too clever at all the wrong times," he teased. "If you're uncomfortable with people watching, we can go somewhere else."

"I'm enjoying the dance," Aerie said, some embarrassment still evident as she pulled him back into the rhythm of the song. "Emery told me she loves music, and this makes me see why. It goes from reverent to joyful to sorrowful, and then to resolved. It's very nice."

"I agree with you. Music is much better outside the URS."

"Most things are, don't you think?" Aerie asked teasingly, before she turned her attention back to dancing. "I can't imagine this won't last for much longer."

"It'll go long into the night," Exton promised. "This is one of our traditions here."

"Why? Won't the people get tired?"

"It started as we began to harvest the crops from the first year of being in space," Exton explained. "The Ecclesia have a history of celebrations like this, where different events and foods mean different things." He nodded to the other side of the room, where Emery was dancing with Tyler. "You can ask either of them for more details if you're interested."

"You didn't study that part, then?" Aerie asked.

"No." Exton gave her a smirk. "I don't usually even show up for this celebration; if I do, it's only for a few moments. Long enough to be seen."

"Long enough to be seen but quick enough not to be missed?"

"That sounds about right."

"Do you have a lot of secrets?"

"What?" He frowned down at her. "What do you mean by that?"

"I was just wondering," she said with a shrug. "People who carry a lot of secrets tend to avoid people. Or so I've noticed, anyway."

"You have some secrets too, then?" Exton asked.

"I asked you first," she insisted.

He looked beyond her, to where Reverend Thorne and Brother Don were chatting with some of the Command Bridge crewmembers. "Every captain has some secrets," he said. "All leaders do."

Aerie followed his gaze, before glancing over at Emery. "Do you really have a collection of MENACE fighters onboard?" she asked. When he looked down at her in surprise, she explained, "Emery said I should ask you about it."

"Curious, are you?"

"On a regular basis," Aerie said with a sigh. "Or so I've been told."

"Curiosity is not a virtue of the State," Exton recalled. "But I would consider it one here."

"So you'll tell me about the MENACE fighters?" Aerie grinned.

"Relentlessly curious." He slowed to a stop and pulled her back from the dancing area. "It's probably better if I show you."

Her eyes went wide with a mix of suspicion and pleasure. "Show me? You mean the rumor was true?"

"Sort of. It's complicated."

"But you can show me? And you would do that?" Aerie asked. "Can we go right now?"

Exton watched as she wiggled her bottom and laced her fingers together, clearly trying to contain her excitement. "If you want." He considered the matter more closely as he saw more people duck their eyes from his gaze. He didn't need to subject Aerie to their probing looks, he thought.

"Then let's go." Aerie started tugging him behind her. "I want answers, Exton."

"I'm glad to hear that," he said, slowing her down. "But there's no need to gallop out of here. And I have to warn you, Aerie, while the truth is important, it's not always pleasant."

"Well, you've already managed to teach me that," Aerie grumbled, "and I don't seem to have suffered anything lethal."

He smirked. "Suffering is still suffering, even if it's temporary."

"I can handle it."

"I envy your confidence," Exton replied. "You make me wish I had more of it myself."

Loving her is not going to be easy, he thought.

♦21♦

Aerie glanced around the rear hangar full of enemy star fighters, all of them gleaming. Her excitement suddenly tempered with caution. "They seem like they're in working order."

"They are. We only used some of our larger shuttles, including the one you came in on, for supply runs and transports. We don't use these for much." Exton glanced over to see a frown on Aerie's face. "What is it?"

Aerie stepped back as her frown deepened. Something uneasy had settled into her mind while she stood there overlooking the hangar.

Something was wrong.

Stupid, stop thinking something is wrong just because you're enjoying yourself. You're allowed *to be here, and if the General was here, he would likely encourage you to get a good look at their available forces …*

Aerie frowned. *A good look …*

Exton indicated the far end. "There's a smaller airstrip down here that opens up near the orbital thrusters; it's actually a smart design. The rear of the ship has to be protected, because if we lose flight power we're not able to do much to resist against an attack, let alone fight back."

"I studied warfare," Aerie reminded him. "Not a lot of specific air battle maneuvers, but I like to think it wouldn't be that hard to fight in the air and space."

"Everyone likes to think it would be easy." Exton shrugged before Aerie recalled he'd battled it out against her father's forces several times over the last six years.

"You don't use these on your missions when you go down to Earth?" Aerie asked.

"No. We don't use these fighters, or at least we haven't used them for battle. Sometimes we take them out to use for scouting missions." He grinned. "Or military feints. We don't do it too often, because the URS can use those as propaganda."

"I have seen some of the news reels," Aerie admitted. "These do look like the same ships." She tried to recall the footage.

"What's wrong?"

"And these are all you have?" Aerie frowned as she looked down at the smaller hangar located in the rear of the *Perdition.* "Just the twelve?"

"Yes. The *Perdition* had a hard enough time taking off with these in it," Exton assured her. She watched as he visibly winced. "It was one of the many reasons I thought our attempt to recapture the ship from the URS would fail."

"You'll have to tell me about it sometime." Aerie laughed. "I'd love to hear how you managed to defeat my father."

The instant the words were out of her mouth, she blanched. "Sorry," she muttered, avoiding Exton's suddenly suspicious eyes, "I mean, the URS."

Her nerves screamed at her as she hurried over to the nearest ship. "Right now, I'd really love to see what it feels like to sit in one of these."

Exton hesitated for just a moment—long enough for Aerie to fear being caught, and therefore forced to prepare for their battle rematch—before he seemed to push past his doubt. But once he came over and unlatched the hatch, Aerie felt a small rush of relief.

"I'm curious about something," Exton said, making Aerie's stress reignite.

"What?" Aerie asked, avoiding his gaze as she scooted into the cockpit of the one-man star fighter.

Not now, she thought. Not now that they had made a deal not to lie to each other. *Please, please, please don't ask about my family.*

She glanced around and frowned. "Hang on," she interrupted. "There's something wrong here."

Exton glanced over at her. "What is it?"

"This is … I wonder … "Aerie ignored his question as she pushed in a code for ignition.

"Hey, come on, Aerie," Exton called over the roar of the

engine and the *whir* of power the small fighter emitted. "It's one thing to see it, it's another to try to turn it on and take it for a test drive."

She pushed his voice out of her head while she glanced at the monitors. Familiar patterns, signals, and symbols blazed throughout the small cockpit.

"Aerie!"

"Huh?" Aerie glanced back at him, just as he began to reach for her. "Oh, sorry." She turned off the engine.

"What was that about?" Exton asked. "I mean, I know you're curious, but—"

Aerie was surprised to find that her hands were shaking. "This is a URS ship," she said, her voice full of incredulous shock. "The console, the codes, everything. It's all the same tech."

She glanced down at the starboard and port consoles, further surprised to see what looked like an early version of NETech implanted into the pilot controls. "This is … "

"It was confusing for me at first, too," Exton remarked, clearly aware of her discomfort, "if that helps you some."

"I don't understand," Aerie whispered. "What would MENACE be doing with all this tech? I mean, they've been largely disbanded since … " She swiveled around to face Exton.

She thought about the General's memoirs of battles with MENACE, about all the documentation and history lectures she had endured at her school.

"Was MENACE forming an alliance with the URS, right before you stole the ship?" Aerie asked.

"No." He shook his head.

"But then how did they get all this military tech from the URS?"

"There are only a couple of situations that would explain it," Exton said. "I can assure you, it's the one you least want to be true."

When she just frowned, Exton shrugged. "Didn't you think it would be strange for me to take off with a bunch of so-called enemy ships inside of it?"

Aerie frowned. "I didn't think of it," she muttered apologetically. *I was too worried about my earlier slip up about the General.* "But now that you've said it, you're right."

"Taking over a starship is not an easy business," Exton told her, as he pulled her down out of the cockpit. "I can fully assure you that smuggling a dozen enemy fighter ships onboard would have made it impossible." He looked past her, toward the rest of the collection.

Aerie slumped over. "The URS was setting up to go to war with MENACE when you stole the ship, weren't they? But the URS wouldn't capture a bunch of enemy ships just to put them into space, would they?"

"Not quite," Exton said. "But close. MENACE has been an empty and largely imaginary threat for the last two decades." He scowled. "Grant Osgood is no saint, but when he took over, he did manage to swiftly destroy most of what remained of them."

Aerie fought against the idea. "That's impossible!"

"Is it?"

The gentle question angered her more than any derision.

"That's not easy to accept," Aerie said. "I mean, you're more or less telling me that MENACE is not real. Not anymore."

"There will always be people who long for war," Exton replied. "But since the times of the Old Republic, and the execution of the capitalists, there hasn't been a lot of resources."

"What's that got to do with anything?"

"War is not just a military concern. It's often a political, economic, and personal one." Exton leaned against the hatch. "Either way, people like that—people with political, economic, or personal agendas—will go to war once the resources to do so are available. When capitalism was outlawed, the governments were able to take control of that."

"Wouldn't that make people stop going to war, then?" Aerie asked, thinking of the long wait times at the medical centers and the long wait times for certain resources. It was hard to go to war when basic living took up so much time and required so much waiting.

"It's easy to plan smaller, guerilla warfare tactics. One person is only so capable," he explained. "And it is hard to get a hold of weapons to fight an entire nation. But once a larger body of people come together, such as the URS, it becomes a means to control its people and its resources."

"I thought you said that UNA worked with MENACE once."

"It did. MENACE *was* real, once. They were an unreliable ally of UNA. They tried to work together, but it turned ugly quick. MENACE destroyed the energy grids across North America in the last wars of the Old Republic, but they forgot that in killing off a large population of the world, they lost their markets. They collapsed economically, and civil war devastated them, ruining their access to resources."

"Their markets?"

"Economic markets. The world will be run as a business from here on out, till the end of the world, including societies. That means war, in the traditional sense, has to be profitable. And the 'business,' which in the case of the URS has to be the government, is the one who decides if it is or not."

He crossed his arms over his chest as she stared at him. "Think about it. Essentialism is at the core of many businesses who want profit. Focusing on survival, obedience, and placement—it makes sense, both in business and in social engineering. They can't exactly 'fire' you when you live under their control. So they have to sell ideas; mainly obedience to the State, above all else. If you don't conform, you die or you cease to live free."

"I don't know if I believe you." Aerie shook her head. "This is too much."

"The proof is right here, Aerie," he told her. "You said it yourself. This is URS tech. They were setting the nation up for a new war."

"But you just said MENACE had been defeated by Osgood when he took over."

"It was. The URS has just been using their name as a scapegoat. It's a false enemy now."

Aerie felt her mouth drop open. She'd suspected—no, she *knew* on some level that they had lied before. But …

Exton continued. "That's part of the reason that Captain Chainsword's ghost has no qualms about working with MENACE. It makes a good story, doesn't it?" He grimaced.

"So does the one where it turns out you're just a rebel against a nation of only death, disaster, and dictatorship," Aerie pointed out.

"I know it's hard to accept," Exton said. "I was surprised to find them here, too. But once I examined them, I wasn't that surprised anymore."

"Congratulations," Aerie grumbled angrily. "I suppose you saw the NETech, too?"

"NETech?" Exton frowned. "No, my father worked on some of the ship's design. They were modified for weaponry, but I'd recognize his work anywhere."

Her anger disappeared as surprise replaced it. "Your dad designed these ships?"

You have to be careful here. Aerie knew that she couldn't completely rely on Exton. But …

But I'm more than tempted to.

She felt her palms begin to sweat.

"I don't think he knew they were being used for a power play," Exton said, interrupting her internal rebuke. "But he was a master engineer, Aerie. He designed the *Perdition.* You know he was talented."

"Did he have a hand in designing the NET, too?" Aerie asked. "They just started adding it into the Air Force."

"What's NET?"

"NET, or NETech, is the name for Neuro-Enzyme Transmission Technology." Aerie pointed to the small panels along the pilot seat. "It's similar to the way that plants communicate with their synapses. A transmission device connects with the engine and feeds into the right enzymes to create a certain response. In this case, a pilot would be able to skip hearing his instructions while flying; it would feel as though his instincts had taken over."

"Wouldn't that be dangerous?"

"No; enzymes and chemicals and synapses are all natural forms of communication inside the body. Injecting it directly from an outside source is only a matter of translation. It wouldn't be hard to rewire someone's mind with that kind of interference."

Aerie glanced down at the system and its connections. For the first time, she felt a little afraid of it. If that was possible for the battlefield, it could also work in other places. She wasn't sure how she felt about that.

"Even in battle?" Exton asked, drawing her out of her inner speculation as she climbed out of the ship.

She nodded. "Especially if they were briefed on an objective beforehand," Aerie informed him. "Since the satellites are being watched, this program is not very well known outside the military. It is, actually, classified information."

"How do you know about it?"

Aerie hesitated. "I heard about it from General St. Cloud," she answered carefully. "I wasn't supposed to. He mentioned it after my PAR."

She watched as his fists clenched and his frowned deepened. "I suppose if anyone would know about it, *he* would," Exton growled.

Inside of her, worry started to stir. She knew her father was a sore point with Exton. Aerie cleared her throat. "So, the URS was going to send out a fleet of MENACE ships to down the space program?"

"I'm not sure of all the specifics," Exton admitted. "But when I communicate with Osgood or St. Cloud, I know I messed up their plans to go to war once more."

"And as long as you remain out here," Aerie mused, "you are further delaying their plans. Because they can't control you."

"Maybe." He sighed. "There are other reasons we stayed, too. After my father's death, my aunt started a new colony down in the southern ocean isles, far enough away from the URS and its influence. That's the other part of the reason for the harvest, too. We celebrate with them, provide for them, watch out for them. We want to make sure the refugees down there and their families are safe."

"You should have seen some of the hatred Captain Chainsword inspired at my graduation ceremony. They hate you. And they've managed to turn the whole generation against you," Aerie said. "But you're still here, likely saving them from pointless death."

"I never set out to save anyone." He shrugged. "I might just be making it worse for them in the end, anyway."

"You were just going to take the ship, but you have been up here in order to keep the world at peace."

"The world's not at peace, Aerie," he retorted.

"But it's not *in* pieces, either," she argued. "As long as you're here, you're keeping the world in a stasis of sorts."

When he said nothing, she took hold of his arm. "Why did you tell me these things?"

"The world's not the only thing that has been in stasis," Exton told her. "Do you know how hard and painful it is to bring a heart back to life?"

"No, I don't," Aerie told him quietly. "But I will do everything I can to make it better."

He drew her closer, embracing her. "You already have."

"You just said you had pain because of me."

"Not all pain is bad, Aerie. Sometimes pain just means that there is something greater worth suffering for."

She smiled. "Are you going to kiss me again?"

"Man is a fallen creature, Aerie; the first man was said to have fallen into sin, away from all that was bright and beautiful and good, just so he could stay at the side of his true love," Exton said, leaning his forehead against hers. "But I won't kiss you if you don't want me to."

"I want you to," Aerie murmured. Her eyes fluttered shut as he smiled and drew even closer to her.

The first touch of his lips on hers sent a deep yearning through her soul, waking the warmth all through her body. She was surprised at the fervency she felt, the sudden desperation to respond to him.

Was this what Serena spent her life chasing after? Aerie wondered. To feel this beautiful and treasured, to know that someone knew her and still wanted to be with her?

A soft moan escaped her unexpectedly. "Exton," she muttered. "I want you." She flushed red, her face full of heat.

He stopped kissing her and moved back from her. "I've wanted you since I first saw you."

"Really?" Aerie laughed. "When I attacked you?"

"Before that." He ran his hands through her hair, fiddling with her braid. "I was the one who found you in the tree, remember? You were just like a fairy or sprite, sleeping in the hollow of your home. In hindsight, I should have known you would have had some fight in you, after I killed the Memory Tree."

He looked into her eyes intently. "Can you forgive me for that, Aerie? For destroying your tree?"

Aerie shifted in his arms, suddenly uncomfortable. "I think I can forgive you for that," she said. "I was always different from the URS, you know."

"I know. That's why I want you to stay."

"You want me to stay?" Aerie asked, hope and excitement bubbling up inside of her.

"Yes."

She giggled happily. "I think I want to, too." She sighed, before frowning.

"What's wrong?"

"I always thought I had to change to be accepted. But I guess there are some things you just can't change."

"People can change, Aerie. But more often than not, people change us. If we want them to, or if we allow them to." He smiled at her. "So I guess you didn't really want to change, then."

"Not until recently," she admitted.

"I'm glad." Exton grinned. "Especially since you'll forgive me for ruining your tree?"

Aerie sighed. "I'm not happy about it, but I can forgive you."

Exton grinned, then grabbed her arms and planted a kiss on her forehead. "Thank you."

She felt an indignant spark of anger at his response, like he'd just been trying to placate a small child. "I'm not weak for agreeing to forgive you," Aerie insisted.

"I know." He took her hands in his and squeezed them. "Of all people, Aerie, I know how hard it is to forgive someone. I know it very well—so well I have still refused to do it. But I had a feeling you would. You were right, you know. That day in the med ward. You are braver than most."

She blushed at his words. "There are still some things I'm scared of," she admitted quietly. *Such as telling you who my real father is.*

"Bravery doesn't mean you're not scared." He pulled her close again. "There are some things I'm scared of, too."

Then he kissed her again, softly and lightly. Aerie smiled, recalling their first kiss. She had to smother a chuckle at the memory.

"What's so funny?" he asked.

"It's nothing. It's just, well, my first kiss was supposed to be at the military ball." She wrapped her arms around him, laying her head on his chest. "I thought it had to be with at the right time and place to be magical and memorable. I never thought that it only needed the right person."

"Aerie."

Her name was barely above a whisper as he bent down to kiss her again, but Aerie could hear the longing in his voice.

His lips were an inch away from hers when the alarm started going off.

♦22♦

It took Exton several more seconds than he would have liked to admit for him to make sense of the sudden flashing lights and blaring alarm.

Aerie recoiled at the noise, grimacing as she covered her ears. "What is that?!" she yelled.

He tucked his hands over his own ears. "Come this way." He motioned as he turned and started toward the elevator.

This better be important.

Not just anything was allowed to interrupt his time with Aerie. Especially when she'd just admitted she wanted to be with him.

He hit the button with more force than needed, but he felt it was justified.

"What is happening?" Aerie asked.

"Hang on."

The elevator came a moment later. Once the doors shut, the noise was instantly dimmed.

"Whew," Aerie said. "That was loud."

"Things are always louder in the hangar," Exton said. "Something about the echoes." He ran his fingers through his hair.

"Is everything okay?"

"I don't know. It's late. We don't have drills this late." He shook his head. "We only have a few moments of warning if the URS is going to attack."

"But why would they attack now?" Aerie asked. "I know we're getting closer to Earth, but at this location we're in more of their blind spot, since we're coming in closer to the southern pole."

"That's exactly what has me worried," Exton said as they stepped up to Level One on the Command Bridge.

"Sir," Jared called. "It's a Redbird, Foxtrot-Tango-Kilo, approaching from over the Old Fed airspace."

It was funny how, even after years of stagnancy, it was second nature to jump in on a battle call. *Even one with the worst timing possible.*

He glanced over at Aerie, allowing himself one last moment to enjoy her closeness. He would have to call Tyler to get Emery to come and take her down level.

"Call our Vet Quarters, see about getting Rhodey or Felix down in the XCR," Exton ordered. "Tell them it's a Code AAB, no drill, and we need a four-oh response. That should get them moving quickly enough."

"Yes, Captain." Jared saluted and hurried away.

"See if you can get Miguel, too," he called. "We might need more than two at the controls down there."

"On it!" Jared replied.

Aerie reached over and put her hand on his arm. "What is it?"

There was something in him that was wired for weakness at the sight of her eyes. "We're under attack, by all indicators."

"By the URS? Osgood's attacking us?"

"I'm going to find out," he promised. "Just hang out here for a moment. I've got to take care of a few things."

"Okay." Aerie nodded as she moved off to the side of the Bridge. "Please be careful, Exton."

He heard the worry in her voice but was at a loss as far as comforting her. He hurried over to the ship console and motioned several of his crewmembers to move over to his side.

"Thora," he called, turning to the woman with the raven-colored locks. She'd been a dependable situation analyst for years. "Give me the details. Atmospheric conditions?"

"Pressure rising with the Redbird."

"Good," he said. "Maybe that'll give us an advantage. Greer? What information do you have on the PO?"

"It's greetings from home," she said, confusing him for a moment before he recalled Greer was from an outpost of the URS, near the old Canadian-United States border. "Point of origin is estimated near forty-four degrees north, sixty-three degrees west."

"Nova Scotia." He rubbed his temples. "I should have guessed." He recalled the reports of the extra activity around the area. *It looks like they're finally ready to strike,* he thought. *Bring it on, Osgood.*

Retaliation would be swift, Exton decided. Especially if anyone got hurt. He glanced over at Aerie again. She gave him a resolute look, proud and humble all at once, as she watched him command the flurry of activity.

Her approval and admiration settled some of his nerves, even as it stirred a new fear inside of him.

I need to get her out of here. She's not safe here.

"Sir?" Greer came up behind him with a readout in her hand. "What is it?"

He reluctantly turned his attention away from Aerie. "Nothing. Get me a transmission line down to the URS Military Headquarters. No, wait …" Exton paused as an unsettling began to churn in his stomach. "Never mind. Just have a transmission line cleared and secure waiting for me. I'll log in the location as needed."

Something about this is off again, he thought. He'd had this feeling when he'd accidentally picked up Aerie along with the Memory Tree.

"Right away, Captain."

Why only one? Why only one missile? And why an FTK-Redbird?

It was a smaller missile, Exton knew. One that might have escaped the URS's own missile systems on Earth, even if it was no match for the sensitivity of the *Perdition's* monitoring systems.

"Thora," he called. "Can you confirm there is only one Redbird approaching from Earth?"

"Give me one moment, Captain," Thora replied. "Let me check through the other systems of the URS and see if the Tech Filters caught anything from the satellite feeds."

"Thanks. Let me know." He turned to another cadet. "Name?" he asked.

"Ali," the cadet responded with a salute. "I'm working on giving you an ETA on the Redbird, Captain."

"Good. Give it to me ASAP. And page the Commander. We're going to need him."

"Yes, Captain," Ali said with a grin.

"Thanks." *He's new to the* Perdition, Exton recalled. *This must be his first battle onboard.*

Looking at how young he seemed, Exton was suddenly willing to bet it was his first official battle, period.

"Shields are at max power," Greer called. "Ready for impact if needed."

"Engines are on standby," Thora called. "Redbird staying course."

We need to get out of here.

Where is Tyler? Exton wondered as he headed toward the helm. It took him a moment to remember he'd just seen him down at the harvest, dancing with Emery.

It seems impossible, Exton thought, *that this would happen on the day of the harvest celebration.*

Tyler arrived less than a moment later, with Emery in tow. Exton felt a rush of relief to see his friend and sister. "We're here."

"Good. I have need of your services," he said. "Emery, take Aerie down level, somewhere safe and away from the ship's gravity center—away from all major turbine clusters."

Emery nodded. She turned to Aerie. "Let's go, Aerie. It'll be alright."

Exton couldn't stop the small smile from escaping. *Emery sounded just like Mom there,* he thought. "Take care," he called. "I'll see you in a bit."

Aerie made no attempt at objection, surprising him just in the slightest. She nodded somberly, the light in her eyes seeming to dim as she departed. Emery tugged her along behind her, and then when the door shut, she disappeared.

I have to protect her.

Adrenaline rushed and his focus sharpened. Exton cleared his throat. "Thora? How are the reports?"

"Got them. The Redbird's a loner, but it's being followed by several Heatseekers, coming up from New Hope itself."

"Heatseekers?" Exton ignored the dread he felt at the edge of his mind. "Which model? Can you tell?"

"Sierra-Bravo-Deltas."

"The SBD Heat Bombers? The ones with the disguised radar signals?" Exton frowned. "What was the point of sending up a screaming Redbird if they were going to … " His voice trailed off as a new idea formed in his mind.

The Redbird was a small missile. Through the large shields of the URS, it would go largely undetected until it reached past the atmosphere, when the beta-thrusters would kick in. No one would send it, except as a warning shot.

Was someone warning them an attack was on the way?

Is it possible? Exton wondered.

"Who do we have on the ground in Nova Scotia?" he called. "Any allies? Friends? Defectors?"

"I'll check the roster, sir," Thora replied.

"Good. See what you can find out." He paused. "See if you can get Dennis up here."

It was too much to hope for, Exton chided himself. But if the *Perdition* had an ally on the ground in the URS, Reverend Thorne would be the one to know.

The Ecclesia has their moments, Exton thought with a grim look.

"I'll relay the question to the Rev," Thora informed him as she saluted him and went back to work.

"Exton," Tyler called. "The Heatseekers are locked on us."

"Evasive maneuvers," Exton ordered. "See if you can shake them."

"Cap," a new voice called from behind him.

Exton glanced over to see his Veteran Control Officer walk through the door. The older man, with fuzzy, graying hair and a perpetually stern countenance, saluted him as he made strides across the Command Bridge.

"Rhodey," he greeted. "We have a situation."

"Masters and our crew are down at the ready," the officer replied gruffly. "We're on standby, running through the final check."

"How long till you're ready for retaliation?"

"Ready to what?" Tyler came up beside them. "Exton, you're not going to bomb the URS now, are you?"

"Tyler," Exton snapped, "this is not the time or the place to challenge me. We have Heatseekers locked onto us. I'm going to deploy a decoy of my own."

"We've been attacked," Jared spoke up. "Retaliation is a perfectly expected response."

"We don't do the expected," Exton argued. "Officer Rhodey, when your men are ready, signal the Bridge. Tack on a tracker, and once it's loose we're going to go full throttle."

"Captain," Ali interrupted. "ETA is ninety-three seconds. Estimated POI is going to be mid-ship."

"Commander," Exton called. "Send out the alert to the crewmembers on duty to prepare for lockdown."

"Already done," Tyler called back.

"Thora? Where are the Heatseekers?"

"Approaching on the port side. There's eight of them."

The Heatseekers are going to be trickier, Exton thought. With the heat-seeking technology packed in with its shielded core, they were a persistent piece of weaponry. It would be harder to throw them off. Especially in space, where they were the only clear target for miles.

He briefly recalled Heatseekers had been forbidden by the Geneva Accords before the United Nations fell. The law wouldn't apply, Exton knew, because it was being used in space.

Rhodey spoke up. "We have a go on retaliation. The lamb is ready," he called.

"That's one of the smaller nuclear bombs?" Exton asked.

"Yep."

He hated that he felt he had no choice. "Dispatch the lamb. Lock on to it, and once we're two minutes out, shoot it down."

"Yes, Captain." Rhodey nodded, already heading off the Command Bridge.

Exton turned to Tyler. "Commander, cloak the ship and then blast us out of here. Head toward the oh-six-four-two mark. Get us out of here."

"Got it." Tyler push the ship full throttle, keying in the coordinates.

"Prepare for impact in sixty," Exton called. "Send out notices over the intercom. Be on standby to for the Redbird."

Tyler came up beside him. "You're going to let a nuke explode?" he asked.

"Yes. It'll create enough heat that the seekers should get pulled in."

"You're sure it will work?"

Exton glanced at the control board listlessly. "If it doesn't, we'll have to see about sending out a team separately to destroy them individually."

"Jared would love the combat run." Tyler tried to muster up a smile.

Exton only nodded; for the first time in a long time, he prayed everything would work out.

"The lamb's been hit. It's away!" Thora called. "Prepare for backlash."

A rush of power propelled past the *Perdition*, brushing up and pushing against it. Exton could hear the ship groaning in the aftermath's flames.

The monitors flared and the lights momentarily dimmed, before turning on once more.

"Power regulating," Ali called.

Tyler groaned. "We've been knocked off course," he called, hurrying over to correct the flightpath.

"Give it another ten seconds," Ali told him. "The nuclear core's explosion will return after the radioactive stats return to normal levels."

Greer spoke up. "Captain," she called, her voice laced with hidden worry. "We have a confirmed hit from the Redbird."

"Where did it hit?" Exton asked.

"Close to the Biovid," Greer told him, pointing to the

screen. "Indicators show it did not explode, but it still breached the panels."

Exton felt a rush of anger and despair. "Send someone down there to check on it, immediately. We can't risk the Biovid."

"Right away."

"Back on course," Tyler exclaimed happily. "We're back on target for the rendezvous point."

"Good work." Exton relaxed some at the news. *Even if the Biovid is hit,* he thought, *we'll be able to drift easily and out of sight while we get it fixed.* "I guess Aunt Patty's going to get to see you again sooner than you'd thought, Tyler."

Tyler grinned. "She's a nice lady, despite your attempts to convince me that she has it out for me."

"You keep thinking that," Exton said with a small grin. "I'm not giving up."

The crew relaxed, even as the readouts kept pouring in. Everything seemed to return to normal too quickly, Exton noticed. *But then, after six years of normal, it was the default anymore.*

"Why do you think they attacked now?" Tyler asked. "It's a strange time to attack."

"They've had plenty of time to work with my father's designs," Exton muttered thoughtfully.

"Captain," Thora called. "Reverend Thorne is unable to come up to the bridge right now. He is preoccupied with helping with the children." She smiled. "My own included."

"I can imagine they were pretty frightened," Exton said.

"He did tell me that we don't have any known active connections in that region," she informed him. "But he did say that it could be a new follower or a hidden agent."

"Thanks," he replied. "Order up a more thorough investigation. I want to be aware of any new developments." He turned to Tyler. "What's our ETA for the rendezvous point?"

"Twenty-three hours and change."

He nodded. "You have command of the bridge," he said.

"I've got some gloating to do. Place a shuffler on my outgoing message, would you?"

"Same as always," Tyler promised. "Tell Osgood we all said hi."

Exton nodded grimly. "I'm sure he'll be just delighted to hear from us, especially after he just tried to kill us."

♦23♦

Emery had just entered into the Ecclesia's sanctuary—their safe space destination—when Aerie felt the blast of the nuclear bomb explode all around her. She was thrown forward onto the floor.

Heat's fiery shadow seemed to pour through the haul as the power flickered and the lights died out, causing many people, including children and babies, to cry out.

"What's going on?" Aerie pushed herself up some, but couldn't see anyone else.

"Aerie," Emery called. "Where are you?"

"Right here." Aerie reached out and felt Emery's arm. "I'm right beside you. I've got you."

"That's not me."

"Oh."

A laugh, deep and almost gruff in tone, resounded from the body attached to the arm.

Aerie gasped and dropped it. "Sorry, sir," she said.

"It's no problem. Is that Miss Rearden, by any chance?" the man asked.

"Er, yeah," Aerie answered. "It's me."

"Nice to meet you. I'm Brother Don, one of the elders of the Ecclesia."

"Oh." Aerie nodded, chastising herself a moment later when she realized no one could see her. "Nice to meet you too," she replied.

The lights turned on, and Aerie found herself on the floor next to an older man with gray-flecked hair. He was wearing loose clothes, a trait Aerie had come to associate with the Ecclesia.

"Are you okay?" she asked, standing up and hurrying over to help him up. "I didn't hurt you, did I?"

"No, you didn't." He grabbed onto her hand as she pulled him up to his feet. "Thank you."

"Brother, what just happened?" Aerie asked.

"A nuke went off, that's all."

Aerie's gaze darkened. "I thought Exton said there were no nukes onboard," she said.

"They're attached to the outside of the ship, in special compartments, technically," he told her. "But that was definitely an explosion."

Aerie frowned as she recalled Exton's words: *Would it make you feel better if I told you there were no nukes onboard?*

Saved by a technicality! Aerie thought angrily, remembering his other claim, that he'd defeated her in battle. *I'll have to remember this for our rematch.*

Emery stepped forward. "Aerie. You know the URS wanted the *Perdition* to be equipped with weapons, and that includes bombs and nuclear warheads."

She sighed. "I suppose it's pointless to argue about it right now," she said, "considering it just helped save us."

There was a small *beep!* coming from Emery's pocket. She pulled out her intercom. "Yes?"

Aerie turned back to Don, while Emery tried to go somewhere where she could hear. "You're a member of the Ecclesia. I've heard them say they value life. Don't you think it's a little hypocritical to have bombs onboard this ship?"

"We value all life," he told her, "and that includes our own. We are allowed to protect ourselves from attack and protect those we love."

"Even if it means killing other people?"

"We live in a fallen world," Don said. "We protect others we love, often risking our own lives in the process."

"So, yes, then."

"Sometimes," he corrected gently. "But that is not a flat response across the board, nor ongoing approval to do so when I say it. It is a call to careful consideration, including understanding the responsibility we have for our choices, difficult as they may be."

"I see," Aerie said.

"All responsibilities have limitations in this world. All labels have their limits, and all causes have an end."

Aerie contemplated his response for a moment. "That

would mean other decisions, too. Like hiding the truth from people. Or joining a revolution."

"Yes," he said. "Legality can change and laws are subject to the constraints of human activity. Morality is, by very definition, universal."

"Aerie."

Aerie turned to see Emery had rejoined her. "Come on with me," Emery said, pulling Aerie's arm. "I have an assignment for us."

Aerie turned back to Don. "Thank you for your time. I'll remember what you said." She reached out and shook his hand.

"You're welcome." He gestured to the crowd behind him. "I've got to help the others now myself. Go with God, Miss Rearden."

"Aerie," she called back, correcting him as she followed in step behind Emery. "Please, just call me Aerie."

"What is this place?" Aerie asked, stepping into the Biovid.

"Some of the Ecclesia call it 'Eden,'" Emery replied with a smile, barely visible with her oxygen mask on. "But the technical name for it now is the Biovid."

"Eden?"

"It's from the Bible, an old collection of books known as the Word of God." Emery glanced around. "God created the world and Eden was the special place, the paradise garden in which he placed man and woman."

"It sounds familiar," Aerie said. "I've heard of it before." She thought back to her childhood, when her mother would plant new seeds in her own small garden. *She had called her garden Eden, too!*

"There are many theologians and philosophers who say that deep in the heart of mankind, we are all still searching for Eden," Emery told her, interrupting Aerie's reminiscence. "I have no qualms in agreeing with them."

Emery gestured toward the far end. "There's something coming up from the starboard midsection," she said. "Let's head in that direction."

"Right." Aerie adjusted her own mask, frowning as she tugged back some stray strands of hair stuck to the visor. "What are we doing in here again?"

"We're looking for a missile that might have breached the ship."

"Isn't that dangerous?" Aerie asked.

"That's why we have the oxygen masks, and I have the emergency kit with me," Emery said, indicating a small pack she wore on her back. "And that's also why I didn't ask for Exton's permission for you to come in here."

"He wouldn't like it?" Aerie asked. "But he knows I love plants and gardening."

"He told me not to let you come in here for a bit yet. Something to do with your tree, if I understood him correctly."

"Oh."

Emery stopped and turned back to Aerie. "Stay close to me. Believe me, I'm sure Exton would be furious with me for allowing you in here. But the Biovid was especially designed for my mother, and since she is no longer here—"

"It's rightfully yours?" Aerie finished with a grin. "Just like the ship is Exton's?"

"That's right."

The loving pride on Emery's face said it all. She was this place's rightful mother, Aerie thought.

"I'm surprised you don't have a permanent job working in here," Aerie said. "If it was me, I don't think I would ever leave this place. This is the most wonderful place in the whole ship."

"I love this place," Emery admitted. "But most of the care it is given is automated. I can't say the same for my brother or Tyler. Being the Coordinating Director allowed me to have more oversight where they're concerned."

Aerie nodded in agreement. "And it gives you permission to do what you want in here, I imagine."

"Of course. I assign myself a lot of inspections here, even though it technically wouldn't be needed otherwise." Emery's eye gleamed. "That's part of the reason why, if it's been breached, we're going to have a serious issue."

"What happened?"

"According to the notes I got from one of the analysts, the sensor went off signaling a breach. It was a smaller missile, so we should have enough time to prevent any major damage."

"What kind of missile was it?" Aerie asked.

"An FTK-Redbird."

"A Redbird?" Aerie repeated. She faltered behind Emery.

"What is it?"

She hesitated for a moment. *Should I even say it?* Aerie wondered. *They might want to know more, and I … I can't deal with the possibility of Exton rejecting me.*

Aerie sighed. Realizing Emery was looking at her with concern, she gave in. "That was my father's nickname for my mother," Aerie said. "That's all."

"Is the Rearden family active in the military?" Emery asked. "I saw some reports when we looked up your unit, but I don't recall any military record."

Brock's father was … a dentist? Doctor? I can't remember.

Aerie shrugged. "It probably doesn't matter. I just … you know, miss her. I miss her more being here than I ever have when I was in New Hope."

"From the sound of it, she would have liked this place," Emery said. "You said she liked plants and animals."

"She did," Aerie said. "Maybe that's why."

Emery came up beside her and put her hand on her shoulder. "Here's what I think. I think you miss her more now because you're all alone here, but you've always had her in your heart. And here, you're allowed to become more like her without getting ridiculed or stigmatized for it."

Aerie felt her nose prickle with unshed tears. "I won't

argue with that," she finally replied a moment later.

"Exton said that you wanted to go into the military. Is that true?"

"I *did*," Aerie told her. "Now I know I would have made a bad soldier. Maybe if I was in the Air Force. My brothers are pilots."

"It does seem like it would be easier to kill someone if you don't actually have to aim and shoot," Emery said. "And you do seem to know your tech."

"I do," Aerie said. "But Exton was right about me. I'm not cut out for military service." She grinned. "Don't worry though; I haven't admitted that to him."

"I love my brother," Emery said. "But he has his flaws." She studied Aerie for a moment. "You don't seem to mind them so much."

"It makes it easier that I enjoy his company," Aerie admitted as they continued forward.

"You care for him." Her words were succinct, but the tone carried a great deal of understanding and acceptance.

"Yes, I do." Aerie blushed, thinking of the time she spent with Exton in the hangar earlier. "I really do. I've never felt this way about anyone before."

Emery raised her eyebrows. "Never?"

"Well, there was a boy I had a crush on," she admitted, thinking of Brock, "but what I felt for him was nothing compared to how I feel now."

Since she had been gone, she was better able to see that Brock had been too bound by duty and expectations of others, including her father's. She would never be able to tell if he liked her because of her, or because of her father. Aerie shuddered at the thought.

"You know," Emery said slowly, "when Exton first told me about you, I was hesitant. I was still hopeful, but I was more hesitant. It hasn't been long since you met him, but I do believe love happens in a timeline all its own." She smiled over at Aerie. "I'm glad I can stop worrying so much."

Instant guilt and shame sent turmoil running through

Aerie.

"Of course, I still have to worry some," Emery continued, oblivious to Aerie's discomfort. "Once Papa was killed, Exton changed drastically. It was almost like he woke up the next morning and he was a new person."

"I know he was deeply affected by his loss," Aerie agreed.

"Traumatized doesn't begin to cover it," Emery said, shaking her head. "He saw it happen. He went home unexpectedly and found Papa arguing with St. Cloud over the *Paradise*—"

"St. Cloud?" Aerie asked. "General St. Cloud?" *My father was there?*

"Yes." Emery frowned. "He was the one who killed Papa when he refused to give him the *Paradise*."

Aerie stopped and stumbled. She let herself fumble with her mask as she tried to absorb the new information.

My father killed Exton and Emery's father? What?!

"I wasn't there, but Exton saw the whole thing," Emery said. "He only told me about it once, but I'll never forget the look on his face when he talked about it."

Aerie crumbled inside her mask, pressing her hands into her head as it began to ache along with her heart. She felt almost like she had trouble breathing.

It is possible, Aerie admitted to herself. Her father wasn't Osgood's Lieutenant Commander-in-Chief for nothing, after all.

Ten years ago, he would have been a rising General in position for a Command, she thought. Aerie could easily see him taking on an execution for a promotion.

This is awful, Aerie thought. She'd never imagined her father actually killing someone until that moment. Maybe because it was such a personal, calculated action, to take the life of a person looking you in the eye and measuring you up. She shuddered again, thinking of what Don had told her earlier.

Was Exton and Emery's father worth killing?

She hesitated. The General did take his work seriously.

He would have done it under orders.

Was it possible there was a mistake?

"Are you okay?" Emery asked.

"Yes. Just tripped," Aerie murmured distractedly. "Trying to fix the mask."

"Oh, okay. Let me know if you need help," Emery said.

"It's fine." Aerie stood up. "So that's why you guys hate St. Cloud more than Osgood?"

"It is on a more personal level when it comes to St. Cloud," Emery admitted. "It's easy to think the URS is just an evil nation or an enemy that needs to be destroyed and wiped out. But the truth is, a lot of them are just misguided and brainwashed people, with cares and concerns of their own. I actually have a lot of compassion for them, sometimes. I was so close to being among them."

Emery's compassion for her enemy was what finally made Aerie shake her head. "Why are you telling me all this?"

"It's the truth."

"I suppose." Aerie sighed. "I don't always see why it matters."

"You don't believe me about my father and Exton stealing the ship, do you?"

"I've seen the MENACE ships," Aerie told her. "And, while it is still a lot to take in, I have to wonder if there was a misunderstanding or something."

"My father is still dead," she told her flatly. "That is a truth that you cannot deny."

Aerie flinched. "But what if his killer didn't mean to do it?"

"Exton saw the exchange, Aerie. He was only fourteen, but he knew what was happening. Our mother explained to us what happened. We didn't know that the URS had ordered a starship, and that our father was the lead engineer. You remember what life is like at that age."

"There's a lot of career orientation and basic training to complete." Aerie nodded.

There was an inescapable sadness in Emery's voice as she

added, "I feel sorry for my peers, Aerie. But I do not waste my compassion on St. Cloud and his ilk."

"What if he was pressured to do it? Or if he was ordered to do it? There are problems with society still, even though the state has worked to end its problems. And you hate the URS, but you don't hate the individual people in it. If the individual does not take responsibility for himself, why would the rest of society?" Aerie paused. "You don't hate me, do you?"

"Of course not." Emery sighed. "But it is different."

"How so?"

She thought about it a moment. "Let me show you," she said.

Emery turned and came over to her. She put her pack on the ground and unzipped it. Aerie peeked over, trying to see what she had. But she knew she never expected to be handed a small gun.

"Here," Emery said. "Shoot me."

She took a step back, as though the shock of Emery's statement had physically hit her. "What?" Aerie looked at her incredulously.

"Shoot me." Emery watched her. "You're from the URS. You're a guest here, not a refugee, and you haven't committed yourself to the Ecclesia. You're still an active comrade from the URS."

"So?" Aerie shook her head. "That doesn't have to do with anything."

"Sure it does. If you shoot me, right now, you'll be taking down one of Captain Chainsword's highest-ranking associates." Emery held steady. "You'd be commended, publicly, since it's the first time someone from the URS has managed to get onboard—believe me, they've tried from time to time—and the first one to make a significant kill.

"If you shoot me now," Emery said, "you'll also be able to use my clearance card"—she waved it around in front of Aerie's gaze—"to hack an escape pod and land down on Earth somewhere, though it would still take a while to get there. We're more than a day out from Earth."

Emery crossed her arms over her chest. "You might even be able to shoot Exton while you're at it. He'd never suspect you now."

Aerie continued to stare mindlessly at the gun in her hand. It had been awhile since she'd held a weapon. Long enough that it felt strange and unusual, like it didn't belong in her life anymore.

She fit the gun in her hand, thinking through what Emery was saying.

Emery is right. I would be commended, publically. I would be honored—maybe even accepted by my unit!

At her thoughts, Aerie shook her head. It was the first time in several days she had even thought about how much she had wanted the acceptance of her unit.

It means nothing to me now, she realized. *If they can't accept me the way Exton and Emery have—even provisionally—then they likely never wanted to in the first place.*

Maybe that was why my mother tried so hard to love me, Aerie thought. *She knew no one else in the unit would.*

Her eyes watered as she handed Emery back the gun. "No."

Emery smirked. "I didn't think you would do it," she said.

"I am not weak," Aerie snapped, watching as Emery placed the gun back in her pack.

"You're not weak for valuing life," Emery told her softly. She reached out and gave her a warm hug. "You couldn't be weak, besides. Not if you're going to marry my brother one day."

"Huh?" Aerie jumped and turned red.

"Sorry." Emery laughed. "I couldn't resist," she said. "He teased me and Tyler relentlessly when we were dating."

"Oh." Aerie shrugged and tried to laugh. Then she thought about what Emery had told her. "I don't think he'll want to marry me," Aerie muttered.

"What?" Emery frowned. "That's not like you, to think like that."

Enough is enough, Aerie thought. *I have to tell them.*

"The truth is," Aerie said, "I've been lying."

It was Emery's turn to stare at her, mindlessly horrified. "What?"

"I've been lying," Aerie choked, "about who I am." She shook her head. "My last name isn't Rearden. It's St. Cloud." She glanced up at Emery tentatively. "I'm General St. Cloud's youngest charge."

For the longest, quietest moment of Aerie's life, Emery just stared at her.

She couldn't stand it. She had to explain.

"I'm so sorry I had to lie," Aerie told her. "When I woke up onboard the ship, I didn't know about the Ecclesia or this place, or you or Exton. I thought you would torture me or kill me. I didn't want to add incentive by telling you I was St. Cloud's daughter."

Emery slumped onto her knees. "I need a moment," she said.

Aerie didn't hear her. "I didn't know I would love you and Exton more than my own unit. You're like my older sister, only my older sister is terrible—"

"You're really St. Cloud's daughter?" Emery shook her head. "I should have known!" She stood up. "I should have known. I *knew* from the start there was something off about you and your records and your stories." She threw up her hands. "And you lied to me, directly, about having ties to the St. Cloud family."

"I misled you," Aerie corrected automatically, before she realized that made it sound worse.

If that is even possible.

"I can't believe this," Emery hissed. "You lied to me, and you lied to my brother!"

"Everything else was real," Aerie insisted. "I just lied about my name."

"You let us think you were unimportant to the URS," Emery snapped. "Don't you think that maybe, just maybe, one of the reasons we were attacked today was because you're here?!"

Aerie stilled. "No, I hadn't thought of that."

"I have to tell Exton," Emery said. "He's going to be devastated."

"I'm sorry," Aerie cried. "I'm so sorry. If I could change it, I would. I don't even like being his daughter! He doesn't even call me that, you know. He hasn't really spent any time with me or my family since my mother died."

"Well, I'm so sorry for you!" Emery yelled angrily. "It must be just absolutely terrible to be you right now."

Aerie stepped back, holding up her hands in bitter defeat. "I'm sorry," she reiterated.

"We trusted you, Aerie!" Emery shook her head. "Even if not completely, we *liked* you."

"I'm sorry. I know I've messed this up." She shook her head. "I gotta go." She turned around and fled, moving deeper into the heart of the Biovid.

"Hey, come back! You're not allowed in here," Emery called after her.

But the more Emery called, the faster Aerie ran. She barely paid attention to where she was going, until her eyes were so watery she gave up entirely.

She ran for several moments before she tripped over a discarded tree limb, hiding in a patch of tall grass.

"Oof!" Aerie grumbled as her hands smeared across the ground. "What in the—?" She broke off in a gasp as she examined the tree branch she'd fallen over.

And then she slowly looked up.

The Memory Tree, still weathered looking, with its top branches severely trimmed back, waved at her.

"My tree," she gasped. "It's here." She hurried to get up, wiping her muddy hands over her eyes. Aerie went over to the tree and pressed against it, running her hands all over it.

The familiar patterns of lichens were damaged, but the main branches were still sturdy. *Perhaps even stronger than they were before.*

Aerie felt a wave of awe and reignited joy. "It really is

you, isn't it?" she asked. A small smile blossomed up onto her face. "I almost want to see if Moona's up there, nestled inside one of your nooks."

"I take it Exton didn't tell you about saving your tree, did he?"

"Emery." Aerie whirled around, terrified and scared. In her amazement, she'd failed to hear Emery's approaching steps. She stammered for a moment, before Emery took off her oxygen mask and shook her head.

"I'm not going to hurt you," Emery told her. "I'm angry at you, but I won't hurt you."

"I'm sorry," Aerie whispered, looking down at the ground. She pressed against the tree.

"Answer my question. Exton didn't tell you that he was going to save your tree, did he?"

"No." Aerie shook her head. "In fact"—she snorted—"he asked me to forgive him for destroying it before the attack."

Emery sighed. "That is just like him to do that. He doesn't allow people to suffer illusions very often, least of all himself. He wanted to see if you would forgive him without knowing the tree was still alive."

"That's why he saved it?" Aerie asked. "Because of me?"

"I'm not entirely sure. Exton has been growing a large variety of plants in here. Some for their food, others for their rarity. I can see why he would save it for that reason alone."

Aerie thought about how much he had tried to save, to protect. He followed in his father's footsteps to please a ghost who could never be satisfied. *He wants something greater than revenge.*

She turned back to Emery. "I'm sorry," she said. "I really have ruined him, haven't I?"

Emery sighed. "We'll have to see. That's his call. Not ours."

"Emery—"

"Until then, Aerie, we need to leave. The haul wasn't breached in here," Emery said. "But the Suncatcher has been damaged. Part of it is outside. I'll need to file a report and have Exton fix it."

Aerie hesitated. "Will he be able to fix it?" she asked.

"He should be able to." Emery sighed. "He's good at fixing things." She shook her head. "Hopefully, he'll be able to fix this situation between the two of you, too, without breaking anything else."

"You're going to make me go talk to him, aren't you?" Aerie asked.

"I can't make you," Emery told her bitterly. "But either you're going to tell him, or I'm going to tell him, and if I have to tell him, it's going to be after I've stuffed you in an escape pod and sent you back to the URS where you belong."

♦24♦

Exton adjusted the pirate hat on his head as he stood in the Captain's private Comms Sec.

Something is wrong again, he thought, once more tugging the wig and beard into place.

The coat was too warm. When had he ever had that issue? And why did he feel no rush of pleasure as he thought about rubbing in the news he'd survived another attempt on his life?

For the first time in a long time, he actually hated dressing the part of the ghost of his father.

Exton felt the smooth edge of his jacket, before running his hand over where Aerie had bruised his ribs.

"This is Aerie's fault." As soon as he said it, he knew it was true.

The last time he had worn the coat was when he met her. And he couldn't explain it. He couldn't explain how she'd changed his life. Or why.

The screen buzzed to life as it picked up a signal. Exton pushed the matter to the back of his mind. He had a dictator to reprimand.

Glancing down at the console, Exton was impressed by the readings. "A fully secured line?" he muttered. "That's unusual for the leader of the 'fair' world."

"I'm sure that you'll understand why I don't want to share this conversation with the rest of the world," the voice said on the other end. "Including Dictator Osgood."

Exton nearly jumped at General St. Cloud's voice. He caught himself just in time, only frowning at the sudden appearance of his nemesis on the screen. Though the connection sparkled with static at points, Exton did not need a clear reception to see General St. Cloud's eyes narrow in determination.

"General," Exton said, just barely inclining his head in greeting.

"You can take off the pirate costume, Exton." The

General shook his head. "I'll give you the necessary points for creativity, but this is not official URS business that I have with you."

Exton stilled. In all the times that General St. Cloud had communicated with the *Perdition*, he'd never indicated that he knew who Exton really was. He had always addressed him as "Captain Chainsword."

"I suppose I shouldn't be surprised that you figured out my disguise." He reached up and took off the hat and wig, revealing his face fully to his enemy. "Is that better, *Master?*"

"You always had a stubborn streak of defiance, even in class," the general retorted. "I had a feeling you would insist on being difficult tonight."

"That was part of the reason you wanted to mentor me, if I remember correctly," Exton sneered. "Admit it. Military Tactics and History would have been a lot more boring if I hadn't been there."

"Believe it or not, I didn't come to remember better times. Or to expose myself to your childishness."

"You said it's not official business from the URS," Exton pointed out. "If it's not, then I want to know why my crew had to defend itself against a batch of Heatseekers recently."

"It was a cover," St. Cloud said. "We have things to discuss, you and I, and you were obstinate enough to leave your transmission line shut. I had to get your attention somehow."

"There's nothing we have to discuss," Exton insisted. "I was expecting Osgood, not you."

"You have always maintained, along with the rest of the Ecclesia, that family is important."

"You don't know anything about me anymore," Exton snapped. "Just because you were my recruiter, doesn't mean that you know everything about me."

"I know enough to make some good guesses," St. Cloud replied, visibly struggling to control his tone.

"That information meant nothing the moment you killed my father."

St. Cloud sighed. "We don't have much time, Exton," he said. "Silas was a good man, but—"

"Obviously that didn't help my father at all in the end." Exton frowned. "You won't have to worry about that issue with me."

"Enough." St. Cloud straightened. "I'm calling to see if you've kidnapped my daughter."

Exton laughed. "I've never kidnapped anyone, no matter what falsehoods Osgood mandated," he said. "You know as well as I do that the *Perdition* is not designed to be a prison. Captives are more trouble than they're worth."

"I've looked all over for her as quietly as I could. I am not reaching you under Osgood's orders. My conclusions have led me to believe she might be with you on the *Perdition,* or among one of your ally's camps."

"I wasn't aware you even had a *family,*" Exton replied, recalling the dedication St. Cloud espoused when he'd trained under him. "What makes you think she's here with us?"

"My daughter has been missing since the day after you attacked New Hope," St. Cloud said. "I found her uniform hat at the sight where the Memory Tree was planted."

"It is possible she left you on her own, isn't it?"

"You don't know my daughter the way I do. As much as she thinks she's capable of surviving the real world, she's much too soft-hearted."

A lightheaded sense of panic took over Exton. He gripped the console, trying to project strength when all he could do was hold on. "When we attacked, we only picked up a defector named Rearden—"

"That has to be Aerie," St. Cloud said. "Her boyfriend's last name was Rearden."

"Aerie?" Exton whispered.

"You do have her then?" The look of tender relief on St. Cloud's face alarmed Exton as never before. "That's her. That's her name, Aeris St. Clo—"

Exton reached over and shut off his receiver, cutting St. Cloud off in mid-sentence.

Then he punched the console hard enough to send sparks flying out of the screen. He squeezed his eyes shut against the pain in his fist.

Aerie.

Her face swam in his mind's eye, and it was only then that he was able to see it: The same shape of the eyes, a shade lighter than St. Cloud's.

"She lied to me."

The words echoed around him as the anger and pain inside of him finally overwhelmed him.

"Augh!" He tore off his pirate jacket and threw it into the corner of his private Comms Sec. And then Exton marched out the door, a dangerous and desperate expression on his face.

He could feel the stunned expressions of his crew as he headed toward the Bridge. "Where is she?" he called. "Where is Aerie?"

The crewmembers lowered their gazes or turned away, a thick layer of unease settling in around them.

"I want her location, and I want it now."

Exton glanced over as Tyler came in the door. "You. Come with me."

"What's wrong?" Tyler asked. "What did Osgood say?"

"Come with me," Exton repeated, dragging him to the Records Room. "Now."

Once they were inside, he turned to him. "Where are Aerie's records?"

"We didn't find much," Tyler said. "Remember? You were with me and Emery while we looked."

"You didn't look hard enough." Exton grabbed him by his jacket and shook him. "You should have looked harder!"

"Calm down, Exton," Tyler snapped. "What's wrong? Tell me what Osgood said."

"Osgood didn't say anything," Exton shouted. "I just got off the line with St. Cloud."

A look of understanding appeared in Tyler's gaze. "Well, that explains why you're so angry. I know you can't stand the man."

"He's her father."

The whole room went silent. Tyler said nothing, only looked confused.

"St. Cloud is Aerie's father," Exton clarified. "She's his charge. His *daughter*. He actually called her that, too!"

"Why—"

"*He* is the second in command of the URS. Our sworn enemy. My father's killer. And he just broke their stupid code by calling her his 'daughter.'"

"Maybe he loves her?"

"Exactly!" Exton dropped Tyler's jacket and turned away. "He loves her. What kind of person would a monster like him love?"

"Are you worried about Aerie?"

"Don't say her name!" Exton grumbled. "She *lied* to me. She tricked all of us. Brilliantly, too. St. Cloud probably sent her here as a spy."

"I don't know, Exton—"

"That was smart of him. I was expecting he would send someone to try and kill me, not someone—" He stopped himself before he admitted it aloud. *Not someone who would love me.*

He sighed. "Where is she?"

Tyler faltered. "She was with Emery last I spoke with her. But, Exton, it is possible she's not a spy. You should hear her out."

Exton glared at him. "Why should I?"

"Because," his friend told him, "she loves you."

"She's pretending to love me. St. Cloud told me himself she has a boyfriend down there."

Tyler's mouth dropped open. "Are you sure?" he asked a moment later. "You know as well as I do that your judgment when it comes to St. Cloud is—"

"Is what?" Exton barked.

"Is compromised at best." Tyler snorted. "Fundamentally off, at worst."

"He killed my father."

"I know. That's why you stole the ship. That's why we were going to destroy the URS." Tyler shook his head. "And when you saw what the URS was planning, that's why you decided to stay up here instead, barricading the ship between them and the rest of the world."

Exton slouched against the wall. "What am I going to do?" he asked.

"Talk to her."

"I don't know if I can," Exton admitted, clenching his fists. *I don't know if I could talk to her without hurting her.*

After a long moment, he finally turned to Tyler. "I need to think about it first. Cover for me."

"Take your time," Tyler said. "I'll alert you if there's any other activity. Thora cleared us before she went off-shift."

"Thanks."

Exton headed out the door, unsure of where to go or what to do.

Only to find Aerie standing before him, a sad wariness in her eyes as she stood beside a diffident Emery.

As he watched, she opened her mouth and began to speak. "Exton—"

"Captain, please," he corrected, his tone bitter, tasting of bile as he talked. "Comrade St. Cloud."

Her face flushed over red, a reaction that might have made him smile not even ten minutes before.

Emery stepped forward. "Exton … "

But he waved her off. "Not now, Emery," he said. "Comrade St. Cloud and I are having a discussion."

"I'd hardly call snapping orders at me a discussion," Aerie said. "I can explain."

"I'd hardly call lying the same thing an explanation," Exton said, stepping forward and taking her by the arm. "But I'll humor you, on the way down to the hangar."

"Exton, let me explain," Aerie started as he jerked her out of the Command Bridge and led her down the hall. "I—"

"*Captain*," he interrupted. "All subordinates should

address the captain by his title."

"I was never your subordinate," Aerie argued. "I was your *guest.*"

"And you've clearly overstayed your welcome," Exton shot back. "It's time for you to go back home."

"What are you going to do with me?" Aerie asked, this time visibly afraid.

"I'm going to order an escape pod for you," he said as he pushed the elevator button for Level Ten. "And then send you back."

"I don't want to leave!" The elevator doors shut as she grasped his hand on her arm. "Please, Exton, please don't send me away. I wanted to tell you the truth but—"

"But what?" His gaze burned through her. "Your father wouldn't have approved? Or were you more concerned with your boyfriend?"

"Boyfriend?" Aerie frowned. "I don't have a—"

Exton shook her hand off of his. "*Your father* was pretty clear on the matter."

"*He* liked Brock! He approved of Brock," Aerie nearly shouted. "It doesn't mean that I was his girlfriend!"

She grabbed his jacket this time. "I swear to you, I just borrowed his name. He wasn't—isn't—my boyfriend."

He felt a twinge as the smallest crack in his defenses rattled through him. "And St. Cloud?" Exton asked. "Am I supposed to believe that he's not your father, either?"

Defeated, Aerie shook her head. "He is," she confessed, her voice nearly a whisper. "But he doesn't love me. He doesn't care about me."

"He loves you enough that he nearly blew up this ship trying to get my attention," Exton yelled back. "There are over a thousand people on this ship, and your father nearly killed them because of you!"

"And he almost killed me, too, right along with them," Aerie pointed out. "That should tell you all you need to know."

"That's hardly all I needed to know," Exton bit back.

The elevator stopped and he grabbed her arm again, pulling her toward the nearest collection of escape pods.

"No!" Aerie fought back, gripping onto the elevator doors. "No, don't make me go. Exton, please!"

He was done hearing her pleas. He picked her up, surprising her with the force of his power and strength. She scrambled and squirmed, trying to free herself.

Exton groaned as she managed to kick him in the side. With the pain, his grip on her loosened enough that she was able to escape.

"Oh, my." She gasped. "Are you alright?" Aerie came back over and reached for him.

He swatted her away. "This is what you wanted, isn't it?" Exton scowled down at her. "You wanted to be free. To go home. I'm granting you your wish."

"I know about the tree," she shouted. "I know you didn't kill the Memory Tree."

Her words made him stumble. "So what?" he asked.

"Please, Exton," she said. "I know you're angry with me for lying about who I was, and I know that there is no escaping my heritage." Aerie hung her head. "I didn't want to tell you my real name any more than you wanted to tell me about the tree."

"I was going to tell you about the tree," Exton argued. "Eventually. It was supposed to be a surprise."

"Well"—Aerie tried to smile—"I was going to tell you the truth, too." Her small smile disappeared as he angrily stared down at her. "You could say it was like a surprise."

"This surprise is *terrible*," he snapped.

"I know." She ducked her head. "After Emery told me about how my father—"

"Don't say it," he yelled. "You don't get to talk about it. You lied to me! You broke our deal."

"I lied about who I was before we made the deal," Aerie countered. "I haven't lied to you about anything else, I promise."

"You let me believe it was the truth," he said. "You let

me—" Exton stopped, inwardly fighting himself and fighting her, and unable to move as the war inside him raged. When she glanced up at him, he could only glare down at her.

She tentatively reached for him. "Exton," she murmured, "I know you wanted me to love you at your worst. And I do. I love you."

Her words hit him with more force than her kick, sending startling pain through his whole body. He clutched at his chest as Aerie's eyes met his.

"Can't you do the same for me?" she asked.

Those eyes! The lighting in the hanger made the amber sparkle with golden dust, sparking like a light in a safe harbor; the tenderness inside beckoned to him.

Before he could stop himself, he was reaching for her. Exton grabbed her and kissed her, pressing into her with punishing kisses, hard and hot in a heady mix.

Aerie gripped onto him, meeting his pain with her passion. He could feel her tremble against him, even as she pushed into him; he could taste of the scent of her as it enveloped him, wrapping around his mind until he ceased to think at all.

He broke away from her, leaving her breathless. "Say it again," he demanded.

Her breath was uneven and her eyes were clouded with passion, but her resolve was unmistakable. "I love you."

Exton silently cursed himself and his weakness; he caught her close, in a rigid, impersonal grasp, and dragged her along with him to a small alcove where his room was located. He barely managed to open the door as she began to fight back.

"What are you doing?" Aerie asked. "Where are we going? Come on, Exton, tell me!"

He said nothing, silencing her questions with another kiss. She melted against him as he held her against tightly the wall.

He tore his mouth away from her and pushed her.

"Hey," Aerie grumbled as she fell back onto the floor of the room.

"Stay here," Exton ordered, his voice dark and dangerous as he slammed the door shut.

As Aerie banged on the door from the other side, he locked it securely and slumped against it.

What have I done? Exton could only wonder how more complicated he'd made his life by keeping her on the *Perdition.*

He closed his eyes and let his head fall into his hands, grimacing while Aerie called out for him.

Exton thought bitterly of the night when Emery had come looking for him, wanting a dance for her wedding. He believed back then that revenge was a serious business, and there was no room in his life for a silly thing like love.

He had been right.

Exhaustion, uncertainty, and emotional turmoil swept over him.

♦25♦

After several minutes of hitting and kicking the door, and then a few attempts at charging the door, Aerie finally gave up on getting out.

She knew it was pointless, as surely as she knew the moment Exton left. The comfort of his presence vanished, along with the occasional, ragged breath. It took him several moments, but when he did go, the rhythm of his steps, the same as they had been the day she met him, echoed softly down the hall.

Aerie sighed. "At least he didn't put me on an emergency pod."

But, she admitted silently, she wasn't sure where she was, let alone whether or not it was a better place to be.

And she had no idea of how long she would be in there, either.

It was dark in the room, with a few floor lights giving off a soft beam. She fumbled around, finally finding the switch and flicking it on.

"Wow. This place is a mess," Aerie said as she saw the room.

Clothes, papers, and collections of things that looked like either tools or toys nearly covered the desk. There were some tool kits shoved under his table, and the kitchenette was full of empty and half-empty cups.

She was startled to see stacks of old books scattered about on different surfaces—chairs, the counter, and the bookshelf; there were even a couple sticking out from under the bed. Curious, she picked one up: *The Hobbit,* by J. R. R. Tolkien.

"This is the strangest book I've ever seen," she murmured, flipping through some of the pages. There were no military ranks or strategies, no recognizable names, and nothing about the URS at all.

She carefully placed it on the edge of the bed before she did another double-take.

A bed.

She was in someone's room.

Frowning, Aerie recalled what Exton had told her before. His room was on Level Ten, along with the escape pods and the hangar full of ships.

His room.

Aerie suddenly faltered as the realization struck, and she nearly tripped over a wrinkled jacket. Her steps became more careful as she headed for the kitchenette space.

She picked up one of the cups; at the smell of old coffee coming from it, she almost laughed. "No wonder he complains about not sleeping well," she muttered. "There have to be at least thirty cups here."

Aerie glanced around the room. "Well," she said, "I can see why he told Olga to forget about cleaning it up."

Thinking of Olga sent a wave of pain through Aerie. She missed the older woman who'd taken her under her wing.

Caring for others is primary; cleaning is secondary.

A new determination set in as Aerie recalled her mentor's words. She tightened the band around her hair, carefully took off her uniform jacket, and got to work.

The room was dark without the brightness of the Suncatcher, but it was nothing compared to the darkness inside his heart.

The ridges of the tree trunk were rough against his back, but Exton had another type of pain on his mind as he sat beneath the tree.

Slouching forward, he was unable to recall what exactly had possessed him to come to the Memory Tree.

Madness, most likely, he thought as he silently groaned to himself.

Where else could he go? The Captain's Lounge was home to memories of his time spent with Aerie, memories that made the small room seem even smaller, and its view rendered dull and uninteresting.

Everything was much less interesting when he had Aerie to consider. Between his desire for revenge and his feelings for her, he wondered if he would be able to think of anything else while she was still with him on the *Perdition.*

His fists clenched; he was upset at the sudden urge of temptation to use Aerie against the URS.

"Why, God?" he nearly shouted. "Why give me someone I want but I would never be sure of?"

"That's probably the exact reason," a voice said from behind him.

Exton groaned. "Not now, Dennis!" He jumped to his feet and swiveled around to see the Reverend looking down at him with pity and compassion.

The old man had never made Exton more angry. "This is none of your business!"

"I'm making it my business," Reverend Thorne said. "I won't sit by while you are in pain. Your father wanted me to look after you. And he would come back to haunt me if I didn't say something now."

"If he does come, tell him to come and talk to me directly," Exton snapped. "I don't like the idea of you as an intercessor."

The Reverend gave him a kind smile. "Exton, you have been despondent since your father's death. You tried revenge, but upon finding out that MENACE is a façade from the URS, you have used your anger to leverage our safety and the world's survival. Not too many people know how close you and the URS were to being allies."

"I don't want to talk about this with you," Exton grumbled.

"No, you'd rather lick your wounded pride and hide behind your pain," Reverend Thorne accused.

"How would you feel if you couldn't trust someone you loved?" Exton rounded on him.

"Tell me what happened, and I'll tell you what I think."

"She lied to me." Exton grimaced as he gave in to the

Reverend's challenge, angry he'd been pushed into giving away the truth. But his grief lightened, ever so slightly, that he couldn't make himself stop. "She wasn't who she said she was."

"Aerie?" Reverend Thorne asked. "You found out she is St. Cloud's daughter?"

Exton reached out and grabbed his shoulders. "You knew she was St. Cloud's daughter?"

"Of course. I haven't seen her in many years, but her mother was a member of the Ecclesia. When I heard her name, I had a feeling it was her. When I saw her with you outside the sanctuary one day, I knew for certain it was her; she is unmistakably Merra's daughter."

"And you didn't tell me?!" Exton roared.

"We are called to protect, Exton." He shrugged. "I think it was a good thing, to protect her from the poison of your vengeance as much as it was to protect you from her."

"You didn't protect me."

"I *tried* to protect you from her," the Reverend said. "Back in the beginning, when she first came here, remember?"

"You should have told me the truth!"

"And what would you have done if you knew who she was in the beginning?"

"I don't know, but I sure wouldn't have fallen in love with her," Exton shot back. He felt his inside crumble again. He placed his face in his hands as he relived his first moments with Aerie.

Watching her struggle to fight him for killing her tree.

Sleeping peacefully in the med ward.

Watching her eyes alternate between wonder and wariness.

"There is a bigger picture here, Exton. You need to step back and see it. Yes, she is St. Cloud's daughter," the Reverend said, interrupting his thoughts. "But she is also Merra's daughter. That makes her one of ours. If you had known who she was, what would you have done with her?"

Exton thought about that moment—the moment he first saw her, tucked into the tree like a fairy sprite.

"I would have returned her," Exton finally responded. *Because I wouldn't have been able to bear the sight of her.*

"And that's the problem," he continued. "I don't want her to leave now, but it's too painful to see her." *It's too tempting to hurt her, to ruin her. To take her and keep her for the rest of my life.*

Reverend Thorne nodded. "No one escapes suffering in this life, Exton; for even our Lord suffered. You have managed to stave off the pain of your father's death all these years with revenge."

"I don't want to talk about this with you."

"I know we are at an impasse," Reverend Thorne said, "as the *Perdition* is keeping the URS from doing more substantial damage to the world. But I do not think you need to keep punishing yourself for your father's death."

"I said I didn't want to talk about this with you."

"I'm just pointing out that you needn't suffer as much as you think you should."

"You know nothing of my suffering," Exton shouted, before turning on his heel and marching away.

"If that's really how you feel," Reverend Thorne called out, "maybe you should just marry her, so she can make you suffer for the rest of your life."

"I'm not talking about this with you anymore, Dennis," he said. "I'm leaving."

"Settle your mind with prayer," the Reverend called out to him. "Don't dismiss your heart."

Exton refused to acknowledge he had heard him, but he found it impossible to ignore the Reverend's words.

Aerie tried to smile as she observed her work. The countertops were clear, the bed was made, and all the clothes were picked up and tucked away. *I won't be able to wash them,*

she thought as she finished putting the last of the uniform shirts carefully in his closet, but it was hard for her to completely regret it. As strong as it was, Exton's scent comforted her.

Even though he likely hates me now, Aerie thought.

"But not enough to get rid of me," she reminded herself, trying to push past her sadness. Crippling despair didn't seem to be very helpful, she thought.

Her fingers tingled from rubbing off stains, and her knees were sore from kneeling as she cleared out the items from under the bed.

"Oh well," she murmured. "At least I have something to do to pass the time that is constructive."

More than once, she had been tempted to put down her work and pick up one of the many books Exton had collected. But she was reluctant to do so, for fear of messing them up more than they already were. Several books were stained, folded over, and well-lived in. There were heat stains on some, making her wonder if he had been reading after hours while living at the university, or even at his home in the URS.

She ran her fingers over the binding on the latest one she'd found. "*Fahrenheit 451*," she read aloud. *Why does that title seem familiar?*

She pulled out the book and recognized the cover. She thought of the collection of books the General kept in his small room. She'd only ever seen it a few times, when she was younger.

Aerie suddenly remembered her mother sitting in a chair once, reading it. In her mind's eye, she saw her mother look up at her and then shut the book forcefully and slide it out of view as she reached out for her youngest daughter.

"Mom read this," Aerie realized. She flipped through the first couple of pages, surprised to find it wasn't a book about military tactics or the environment.

Have I never seen a novel before? Aerie wondered. She flipped through the last pages and sighed.

A page fell out a second later, making her jolt. *That's just what I need right now—another reason for Exton to hate me.*

She hurried to pick it up, and then faltered at the sight of it.

It wasn't a page that had fallen out; it was a picture.

One of those old photographs, she realized, recognizing the old digital camera filter. She picked it up and pulled it closer to the bedside lamp.

Looking at it, she was able to see it was a picture of Exton and some people. *I would recognize him anywhere,* Aerie thought wistfully, but the photograph almost managed to prove her wrong.

He was clearly younger in the picture, and happier, too; his eyes were still clear; even while they were more innocent, they were no less shrewd.

The lines of his face were rounder, less sharp than they were now, Aerie noticed. She traced the wide smile on his face, not surprised to see the small dimple on his left cheek.

She stared at his picture for a long time, before she recalled she still had more to clean up.

Aerie briefly glanced at the other two figures in the picture. One was wearing a priestly frock, and the woman was wearing a crimson dress. She started to place the picture on Exton's bedside table when she gasped, nearly dropping the photograph, as she suddenly recognized the woman.

It was her mother. Beautiful, elusive, and bubbly, Merra St. Cloud was clearly enjoying herself in the picture as she looked off to the edge of the photo.

Aerie frowned. What was her mother looking at?

She examined the photo more clearly and noticed part of it was folded over, cutting off the picture. She unfolded it to see her father standing there, a large, red "X" drawn over his face.

"That's not a surprise," Aerie said. She folded the picture back into place, deciding that, even if her mother was looking at her father with an adoring look, it was better to leave him out of it.

She turned it over, looking for a date, something to give her an idea of when it had been taken.

Instead, there was a small message:

To Exton, my most accomplished student in many ways.

St. Cloud.

Aerie put the picture down on the table, confused. Her father had taught Exton?

She stood up, starting to lecture herself on getting caught up in her daydreams, before she stopped. Aerie turned around and grabbed the picture, and then tucked it carefully into the hidden pocket in her own uniform jacket.

Aerie knew it was wrong to steal, but she didn't think it was wrong to take something away from Exton that clearly reminded him of his pain. It wasn't like she had any reminder of her mother.

And, Aerie rationalized further, the picture did technically have both of her parents. Surely that made her a better owner than Exton.

She put the picture away, but she still felt awed by the expression her mother wore, by the happiness she exuded as she glanced at Aerie's father.

Mom must have really loved the General.

Aerie went back to work cleaning, finding comfort knowing if someone as wonderful as her mother could love someone as terrible as her father, there might be hope that Exton could love her one day, too.

Hours passed before Exton finally decided he should go and see her.

The pressing quality of the night shift finally hit a point where he couldn't stand it; whether it was more depressive or oppressive, he couldn't say.

But he knew he wanted the light again.

He wanted to be with her. Aerie, for better or worse, carried sunshine in her soul and cast back the shadows residing in his heart.

But there is an appointed time for even daybreak, he told himself as he wandered through the ship, off-duty but still running through the checkoffs at different levels.

Most of the crew, shaken by the attack the previous night, went about their business as usual; he was polite, succinct, and focused while he interacted with them—nothing out of the ordinary—though it felt like his body had become a puppet of sorts, and routine was acting as his puppet master.

He passed the elevator on Level Nine and paused.

Man was given free will, he knew. Beliefs mattered. Truth mattered. Choices mattered, actions had consequences.

So why is it so hard to know which ones were the right ones?

His finger hovered over the "down" button.

"Exton!"

He jerked around, awkwardly shuffling his feet to keep his balance. "Tyler," he grumbled. "What is it?"

"Emery wants you to come back up to the Bridge."

"Why?" He scratched his head, exasperated. "Is my grieving time over?"

Tyler held up his hands defensively. "I'm sorry, Exton. General St. Cloud is back on the line."

"I turned it off."

"Emery told me the console had been damaged. When she attempted to repair it, the reception resumed. He was waiting on the other end."

"It's been hours since I left."

"At least a full day." Tyler nodded. "His resolve seems sincere."

"St. Cloud has never done anything with less," Exton retorted. "That's why he's Osgood's right-hand man."

"He's threatening more missiles if he doesn't get Aerie back. I think he really does love her."

"If he's threatening war against the whole *Perdition*, he's going to end up killing her, Tyler. It seems like an empty threat."

"He's not talking about war with us, exactly. He said the

next target is going to be Petra."

"What?" Shock slammed into him. "How does he even know about Aunt Patty's settlement?"

"I was hoping that you would go and ask him that yourself," Tyler admitted. "Emery sent for me to find you immediately."

"I should have just killed them all," Exton said. "I should have just destroyed them back at the beginning."

"You know why we didn't, and why we couldn't—and why we still can't. The Ark and the Biovid are still not complete."

"I know," Exton exclaimed. "I know. I thought we would be able to outlast them, to run away and start over. I know it's not possible now. Not if he knows about Petra."

"But if St. Cloud really does love Aerie, he'll keep his word after we—"

"I don't care if he loves her."

"I'm also guessing you don't know how he can," Tyler snapped.

Exton's anger disappeared as confusion replaced it.

Tyler's voice softened. "You don't know the length a father will go to protect his child."

"My father—"

"Even a child who hasn't been born yet."

Exton finally stopped and stared at his friend.

Tyler met his gaze steadily. "Emery's pregnant."

Exton looked away. A rush of emotion, happiness and joy for his friend and sister, tackled him, conflicting with the grievances in his heart.

He was going to be an uncle.

He attempted a smile. "You guys sure didn't waste any time, did you?"

Tyler smiled back. "We've wasted a lot of time already, Exton."

"What do you mean by that? You both came up here with me of your own choice."

"I'm not talking about that, Exton. I've known you for

nearly eight years. It took me a long time to admit to myself I loved Emery, and that things would settle down and then I could tell her."

"You just started dating last year."

"So? I've known her long enough to know she's the one person who I want to be by my side the rest of my life." He grinned sheepishly. "And it took her some convincing, too, of course."

"To fall in love with you?"

"No. To love me more than she feared the future." Tyler shrugged. "I know what it is to be afraid. I know what it is like to wonder if loving someone is worth the risk of losing your life.

"But it's too painful to wonder." Tyler came up beside him. "And I see the same thing going on with you. It's too painful for you *not* to see Aerie."

"What do you mean?" Exton asked.

"If she's causing you pain, it's because she gives you so much pleasure. Go and talk with her. I know she cares for you."

"She said she loved me." The words barely sounded out of his mouth.

"Then give her the chance to live up to it. Denying her now is just denying your own heart."

"Tyler," Exton said. He gripped his friend's arm. "What if I use her against the URS? Or the general?"

"The URS doesn't hold the same value on families that we do," Tyler reminded him. "I don't think you could find a way to use her against them. And you wouldn't anyway, if you love her back, because her pain would be your pain."

"What about her father?"

"Is there anything a father dreads more than having their daughter fall in love with the enemy? She's already a pawn. You might as well make her your queen."

Exton was surprised to hear himself laugh, bitter and hopeful all at once. "Chess is for a civilized fight," he said.

"Well, it's your move," Tyler said.

"I don't know what to do. I can't trust her."

"Trust is not inherently given," Tyler reminded him. "It is something that must be earned."

"That's not very helpful."

Tyler gave him a contrite look. "I'm running out of ideas, because I need you to come with me to the Bridge."

"Come on then," Exton said, gripping his friend's shoulder in comradery. "I don't want to make Emery upset. Especially if she's pregnant now."

Tyler laughed. "We just found out a few days ago. We were going to say something at the Harvest."

"We'll plan a celebration later," Exton promised. "No niece or nephew of mine is going to be neglected because of a little thing like war."

♦26♦

"I want her back."

"Well, it is nice to see you again, too, St. Cloud," Exton muttered disdainfully. He'd barely managed to get into the room before the screen was lit up with St. Cloud's stern face.

"You did find her, though, didn't you?" St. Cloud asked. "Aeris is there with you?"

"Having doubts about my abilities, are you?" Exton knew he was only human, so it was only right that he indulged in making the older man squirm in anger. Especially if St. Cloud was going to be forced to cooperate with him.

"She is my youngest daughter," the general said. "I need to have her back."

Exton sighed. "Yes, she's here. What would you do for her?"

"There's going to be a price on this?" St. Cloud frowned. "I would have thought that the Ecclesia would be against that."

"They probably are, but you're dealing with me, not them," Exton replied, grimacing as he thought about his conversation with Dennis. *Reverend Thorne might be willing to act as a messenger, on the bright side.*

"If you require a price," St. Cloud finally remarked, "I would trade myself for her. If that is what you want."

Exton sighed. "No, I mean, what would the URS do for her? Will she be safe if I return her?"

"I am not acting under Osgood's orders by reaching out to you," St. Cloud reminded him.

"Yes, I know."

"I am not saying this lightly, Exton." St. Cloud's brow furrowed. "This is treason for me. But I want my daughter back. I have her placed under medical leave here; no one but me knows the truth."

"No one knows that she's been missing at all?" Exton was surprised. "It must be nice to have the military clearance to do that."

"Aerie is my youngest daughter."

"Daughter?" Exton repeated.

"Some might call her a charge," St. Cloud amended.

But he did not correct himself in the use of the term, Exton noted. Inwardly, he groaned. Was it possible Tyler was right about him?

He cleared his throat. "You willingly called her your daughter. Do you love her then? Even more than the State?"

"Of course I do. That is treason, too, as you well know."

Exton felt hate boil up inside of him. "I know. I loved my father."

The general said nothing, only closing his eyes. Whether in sorrow, submission, or new understanding, Exton couldn't say.

"I hear you're threatening to bomb Petra if we don't give her back to you," Exton said. "Is that true?"

"I will do what it takes to get her back. Even bombing the last sustainable remnant of your resistance movement and the last giant hub of the Ecclesia." He glared at Exton through the screen. "It would be a shame if you lost the rest of your family and your father's hopes."

Exton tried to ignore his baiting. "How do you even know about Petra?"

"*I* know about Petra. Osgood does not. Yet."

Exton was taken aback by that admission. "Will you tell him right before you order the air strikes against us?" he asked.

"He doesn't need to know," St. Cloud said, "unless there is a need to bomb them."

"Such as the failure to return Aerie to you."

"Yes."

Time to go back to the situation at hand. "What would the URS do to her if she was returned?" Exton asked. "It might surprise you to know—or maybe it won't—that she has many friends up here, and many people who have befriended her, freely, and without compulsion."

"That's Aerie." St. Cloud snorted. "She wanted to go into

the military, but she has no mindset for it."

Exton agreed, but said nothing. "You seem to have a similar weakness at the moment."

A frown appeared on St. Cloud's face. "Just tell me what you want, and I'll give it to you. Anything for her, anything at all." He ducked his head down. "She's the last of her mother that I have with me."

St. Cloud knew who he was, he knew about Petra, and he was committing treason against the URS to get his daughter back. Exton knew he would need time to analyze everything.

"I'll have to think about it," Exton said. "And I have to ask her, too, of course."

"Fine. Can I see her?"

Exton turned away. "We'll make arrangements soon. How long is this line secure?"

"This line will be secure for another day, before the URS technical moderators recognize that I've had it altered."

"I'll talk with you again before the end of tomorrow, then." Exton paused. "And you should know, as her father, Aerie is up here with us. She's actually enjoying her time here, from what I've heard from others who are working with her."

"She's happy? And safe?"

"For the moment."

And isn't that the truth of it?

St. Cloud nodded. "Thank you."

Exton narrowed his gaze as he looked at the older man on the screen. Relief barely touched on his features, but he'd never known St. Cloud to let his emotions interfere with his judgments.

It was, Exton recalled, one of the things he had trouble with himself. St. Cloud had called it weakness before.

He probably would say the same thing now, except he is the one benefiting from it.

"If you really love her," Exton asked before he turned off the screen, "would you be willing to let her go?"

The general sighed. "It's complicated," he said. "She has a duty to the State here. While I am willing to negotiate her release, I need her back before they realize her records have been falsified. She will be branded a traitor. And then there will be no mercy for her."

"Well," Exton said after a moment of thought, "you would be the one to know the extent of the URS's mercy."

At the sight of St. Cloud's stricken expression, Exton signed off, too overwhelmed to continue sparring.

Exton breathed in deeply, trying to steady himself. He was getting tired, he noticed. He needed rest.

Probably a whole week of rest. Or two weeks.

He turned around and headed out, immediately coming face-to-face with Emery's blue-green eyes.

"Well?" she asked. "What did he say?"

"He said he'd rather not blow up Petra, for one," Exton assured her. "And two, he wants Aerie back."

"You didn't send her back."

He knew from her tone she disapproved, even if she understood. "No." He sighed. "I locked her in my room."

"You don't want to send her away."

"What I want doesn't matter," he insisted.

"That's a lie," Emery argued. "You can't keep lying to yourself, Exton."

"I'm not lying to myself," he insisted. "I *know*, for example, that Aerie lied to us—all of us—about who she is. I know that I can't trust her."

"I know you're tempted to."

Exton flinched, feeling the sting of her words. "More tempted than I've ever been in my life," Exton agreed quietly. "But I can't risk Petra. Not even for her."

"I understand," Emery said, putting her hand on his shoulder. "But I also know that sending her back is the last thing you want to do."

He shrugged.

"Because you love her."

"Of course I do," Exton snapped. "But it's not enough. It's not enough to save people, Emery. It's not enough to help us now, here, right in this place."

"We need to find another way."

"There is no other way." He glanced around. "St. Cloud said she's been put on medical leave, under his orders. All she needs to do is to get back there, and she can resume her life. It'll be easy for her. She has her boyfriend or whatever waiting for her, and her father, and her whole life."

"She loves you."

"Then she'll make it easier for us to get rid of her."

"St. Cloud knows about Petra. We could still be in danger."

"I'm not using her as a political card," Exton snapped.

Emery gave him a warm smile. "No, you wouldn't do that, would you? You never even thought of it."

"Oh, I've thought of it," he assured her. "But I'm not going to do it just because it would feel good."

"Not paying for your pleasures?" Emery asked, and the small, half-hesitant note in her voice irritated him.

"Not this time," Exton snarled, before he walked away. He stopped and then added, "By the way, congratulations on the baby. I'm happy for you."

Emery came up beside him. "Thank you," she said, wrapping her arms around him and hugging him from behind. "I love you, Exton. You've always been a good brother to me."

"No, I haven't." He patted her hand. "But I'll try hard to be a better one."

"Then give Aerie a chance," Emery said. "She told me the truth, you know. Before you found out. We were on our way up to see you when … "

"I don't care," he lied.

"Go and see her."

"I might hurt her," he said softly.

"No more than she's hurting now, I'll bet."

Exton shrugged. "I can think of worse ways to suffer."

"Do you want me to go with you?" Emery teased. "Hold your hand, like Mom used to when we were scared?"

He frowned at her, which only made her smile grow.

"Keep it up and I'll convince the medics to put you on medical leave," he warned.

Emery giggled as he headed out of the Command Bridge.

♦♦♦♦

She was asleep.

Exton had been reluctant to believe it at first, but after hearing her quiet breathing, he was sure of it. Just as sure as he was that he wasn't dreaming or disoriented, even if the clean room gave him pause when he first walked in.

Especially when he didn't trip over anything.

The small lamp by his bedside was on, casting a small light on her as she slept, curled up on his neatly made bed.

He couldn't stop the smile when he saw his old copy of *The Hobbit* open and partially peeking out from under a pillow. Her uniform jacket covered her upper body, while her boots hung over the bed.

Exton sat down at his desk, trying to relax in his chair. He watched her, his eyes never leaving her face.

We have time. Not much, but we have some time.

He walked over to the closet and pulled a spare blanket out from the top shelf. He spread it over her, tucking her feet under the cover. After a moment of consideration, he decided to leave the light on.

And then he carefully, so as not to disturb her, slid down and lay next to her. He closed his eyes and allowed sleep to settle into him, figuring that if she tried to kill him the door was locked, and he would choose death at her hands over life without love.

Sleep seemed to only last for a moment, before the waking world called to him again.

"Exton."

"What?" he muttered, his voice heavy with sleep while his eyes were still closed. He curled into the warmth beside him and tried to block out the light.

"I love you."

Exton stilled. *Aerie.*

Long, silent moments passed as he gradually realized she was lying against him, her body pressed into his, her face buried in his shoulder.

As he woke up, he realized his arm was wrapped around her protectively, possessively.

He remembered the day in the Captain's Lounge, where he told her, foolishly and naively, that she was his.

"Do you mean it?" Exton murmured down into her hair.

"Yes, I do."

He jolted at her response. He hadn't been expecting an answer.

"I'll make a deal with you," Aerie whispered. "I'll love you if you love me."

Her voice was playful and hopeful, and it was all too easy to agree to that.

But he knew better.

He sighed and moved away from her, sitting up in the bed. Exton opened his eyes and blinked, allowing the rest of the room to come into focus.

"What? What is it?" Aerie asked. The hope had disappeared from her voice. "Did I say something wrong?"

"I'm the one who usually sets the terms for the deals," Exton said.

"That's not enough of a reason to say no," Aerie objected.

"Love isn't like that, Aerie. Real love does not use conditions and stipulations. Relationships do, but not love."

"Why did you come back here at all then?" She sat up on her knees. "You could have just left me alone here to rot away in your room."

"I thought about it." He smirked. "It would have been easier."

He regretted his teasing when he saw the shimmer of tears in her eyes. "But your father wants you back. He's threatened to destroy Petra if we don't take you back down to him."

"Petra?"

"My aunt's settlement, in the Antarctic zone." Exton stood up and straightened out his uniform. "He's not even supposed to know about it. No one does, outside the Ecclesia, really."

"Maybe someone told him."

"Yes," Exton looked at her pointedly. "Maybe someone did."

"I'm not his spy."

"I'm just saying someone like you could easily have done so."

"I'm *not* a spy."

"Regardless, I can't let him attack them. They're not shielded well enough to survive."

"So you're just going to send me away?" Aerie got up and stormed over to him, vehemence in her voice. "You'll stick me in an escape pod, toss me down to Earth, and forget I was ever here?"

"I will take you back, Aerie."

"Nothing will stop me from staying with you," Aerie insisted. "I'll go to the Ecclesia. I'll talk to Emery or Olga or someone. *Anyone.* I don't want to go. I don't want to leave you."

"I don't want you anymore," Exton told her, deliberately making her flinch. She stepped back from him, and he hated himself for it. *Don't make this harder on yourself, Aerie. Or me.*

"You're lying," she shot back. "I know you're lying."

"You're a danger to us here. You've lied to us, and you've brought this mess on yourself," he told her. "Do you have any idea how much harder you've made our lives?"

"I made it better," Aerie argued. "You wouldn't have even known the General knew about your aunt's settlement. Now you do. You can fight him better now that he's shown his hand."

"You can't stay here. You don't even pay for yourself here."

"I've worked. I can handle my credit on my own, so you

don't have to worry about it anymore."

"You don't belong here."

"This is the only place where I have ever belonged!"

"I don't want you here anymore."

"Yes, you do!" She stepped forward again, her resolve returning as he was running out of arguments.

He threw up his hands in exasperation. "What about Petra? Would you have an entire settlement wiped out so you could stay with me?"

"We can find a way to protect them." Aerie gestured toward his desk. "I know you have nuclear weapons here. We can bluff until we can convince the General to let me go."

"You'd be a traitor to the URS."

"I already am!"

"No, you're not. He's protecting you, Aerie. He's put you on medical leave. No one other than your father knows you're missing."

"No one?" She stopped for a moment, surprised at the new information.

"No." Exton snorted. "Not even your boyfriend, from the sound of it."

"He was never my boyfriend. I told you that," Aerie snarled.

"Regardless, you'll be able to return to your life."

"I don't want to."

"You've always wanted this, Aerie," Exton told her. He sighed. "Your father is fighting for your return."

"And I'm fighting you for the right to stay." Aerie's eyes lit up. "I want our rematch now."

"Not now, Aerie."

"If I win," she barreled onward, "I get to stay."

"If you lose?" Exton asked.

"I won't lose." She adjusted her feet into a fighting stance.

"Aerie, stop." He came up to her and placed his hands on her shoulder. "There's too much on the line for you to—ah, ha!"

He reached around her and grasped her, getting her into a tight hold. "I got you."

"Hey!" Her arms went flailing, but Exton had the advantage. He tightened his hold on her arms with one arm and lifted her off the ground with his other.

He swiveled around and tossed her down onto the bed, before securing her with his body on hers. His legs wrapped around hers, while his arms held hers down.

Aerie flailed against him. "You cheated!" She kicked at him unsuccessfully, trying to break free.

"I told you when we first met that we don't fight fair here, Aerie. I've got you. Yield."

"Never!" Aerie frowned up at him. She butted her head into his chin.

"I said I would fight you in a rematch. You've had your fight, Aerie, and you lost."

"You need to lose the smirk."

Exton was surprised to find that he was smiling. "Submit, Aerie." He lowered his voice. "If you love me, you'll relent."

"I might love you, but I don't trust you."

"Welcome to my world."

"It must be your world, because it's much more convenient for you than it is for me."

"Believe me, there's nothing convenient about this for me." He met her gaze, allowing her to feel the weight of his body on her. She slowly stopped fighting as the color in her cheeks heightened.

"I ... yield." The tears in her eyes mixed with shame as he reached for her.

"Thank you." Exton leaned down to place a kiss on her brow. *That had to be extremely difficult for her,* he thought affectionately.

But when she raised her lips up to meet his, and like an instinct in his soul, implanted before time began, he kissed her.

Passion and desperation instantly threatened his self-control, momentarily overbidding his senses. Aerie responded to him, linking her arms around him and pulling him closer to her.

As the warmth between them exploded into searing heat, Exton pulled back from her.

"Don't," Aerie moaned. "Don't stop."

Anger—at himself, at her, at their whole situation—finally allowed him to break away completely, against the raging tide of temptation as she held onto him. He stepped back from her swiftly.

"You shouldn't tempt me, Aerie." He began pacing away from her, anything to relieve the pain. "I'm already tempted to use you against the URS. Don't tempt me to hurt you more than I already have."

"You're killing me," Aerie cried.

"I am already dead!" Exton reminded her. *I was foolish to think a ghost could be brought back to life.* "I need you to go back to the URS. To your father."

Pain poured out of her gaze. "You're doing this just to hurt me."

"Then we are even," he shot back. "I can't let everyone else suffer for my mistake. You need to go back, for your own good as much as anyone's."

"How can you say that?" Aerie sat up slowly.

"Because you're getting what you've always wanted—your freedom."

"I don't—"

He turned toward her. "If you trust me," he said, "you'll agree with me in this matter. Petra is the main reason we believe we can win against the URS. It's one thing to destroy, Aerie. It's another to protect. Petra is the hope of the world right now, as a place that can handle refugees and establish a sound government—one that doesn't take advantage of its people. If we lose Petra—"

"I know." Aerie slumped over, defeated. "I know."

He was crushed to see her spirit extinguished. *I can't do this anymore.*

"I have to go prepare for your transport," he muttered.

He hesitated. "I'm sorry."

He hurried out the door and locked it behind him. But he faltered for a few moments, scarcely able to believe he managed not to condemn his soul in the process of breaking her heart.

It was only as he heard her soft weeping that he realized he was condemned already, and the price of redemption was too steep.

♦27♦

Aerie wasn't sure how long it was she remained there, curled up on Exton's bed, alone, with only the darkness for comfort. She only knew that each second seemed to stretch out painfully, as it pulled her further away from Exton's comfort, and it pushed her toward a future without him entirely.

She wrapped her arms around a pillow drenched in her shed tears. There was nothing left to do but go back now, Aerie thought bitterly.

A knock at the door sounded softly. "Aerie?"

Aerie jolted, and strained her ears. "Emery?" she answered. "Emery, is that you?"

"Yes," she replied.

"Can you get me out of here? Exton's trying to take me back to the URS—"

"I know," Emery interrupted. "I've come to say goodbye. I can't help you. The door is locked and secured, Aerie. Even if I wanted to help, I couldn't."

"Because he's your brother, I know," Aerie said with a sign.

"No, because he's the captain." Aerie could almost see the wistful smile on Emery's face. "He's my brother, and I love him. But I think he's wrong in this matter. Once I heard he didn't send you away earlier, I knew."

"Knew what?"

"I knew that you matter to him."

"I don't know about that," Aerie admitted, defeated. She walked over to the door and stood next to it. "He has a strange way of showing it."

"It's not quite as difficult for me to see it as it might be for you." Emery's back pressed against the door. "But I know he's in pain."

"Because of me?"

"Yes."

"I didn't mean for things to go this way," Aerie squirmed.

"I'm not talking about your deception, or even because of Petra. I'm trying to tell you, I'm happy that he's found something—someone—worth coming back to life for."

"I don't think he sees it that way."

"Even if he did, he wouldn't know what to do with it, likely," Emery snorted.

Aerie managed a small smile. "You know, Emery, I was just thinking about how much my mom would have liked you."

"My mother would have liked you, too." Emery sighed. "I don't have much more time. I have to get back to the Bridge. But I wanted to tell you that I will miss you. And I'm sorry you can't stay."

"Oh, Emery," Aerie felt tears swell up behind her eyes again. "You're my best friend, you know that? And I love you."

"I love you too," Emery replied.

"I wish I could hug you."

Emery laughed, her voice cracking slightly, making Aerie wondering if she was having trouble holding back tears, too.

"Emery?" she called. "Can you do me a favor?"

"What is it?"

"Can you take care of Moona for me?" Aerie bit her lip. "I don't know how long I've been here."

"You've been in here for about a day and a half. We're coming up on Earth now. Exton and St. Cloud have made arrangements to meet in a few hours." Emery paused. "I'll see to it that Moona is well taken care of."

Aerie sniffed. "Tell her I'll miss her and I love her, too. But I'll be happy knowing she's in your care."

Emery sighed. "I'm not particularly fond of cats," she admitted, "but if nothing else, I'll keep her until Exton returns, so *he* can take care of her."

"That's perfect," Aerie murmured. "Thank you."

"Exton's coming out of the elevator," Emery said. "I'm going to sneak off in the opposite direction." She paused. "Hopefully, I'll see you soon. Don't give up, Aerie. God is a god of miracles."

Aerie sighed. *God, if you are there, help me find a way to stay with these people I've come to love so much.*

She wasn't sure if he heard her or not. But when the door finally opened, she felt more steady, and ready to face her fate.

♦♦♦♦

"Move out," Exton commanded the guards. They left, their movements regimented like seconds on a clock, counting down to her demise.

He turned to her. "Aerie," he said. "It's time."

She lowered her gaze. "I know."

"Your father's ship just landed."

"Where are we, anyway?" Aerie asked.

"Outside of Nova Scotia," he said. "There's a special medical ward here that will claim you as a victim of an attack and have you admitted. General St. Cloud told me he would see to it that you would be back at work within the week."

"I'm sure he'd love that." She sighed. "I already know you can't forgive me and you won't forgive my father. I love you anyway. You were the one who said that real love doesn't come with conditions. I understand that."

Exton came over and released her seatbelt. "You'll need to unbuckle," he told her, trying to smile kindly at her.

"I'm not fighting you," Aerie promised. "I … I know you need to protect the others. I know you need to take me back." She met his gaze. "I do trust you, Exton, and if this is really what you think is best, I'll follow you."

He ran his hand over her hair softly, pleasing her and paining her at the movement. When the last of her tresses fell free from him, she sighed.

"I do want you to know, however," she said, as he began to lead her out of the ship, "that even though you've returned me, I'll never be free of you."

When he paused, she added, "You told me once that

everyone has to have something greater in their lives. You said it was God for the Ecclesia, and revenge for you. For me, I thought I needed my family's love and acceptance. I was wrong. I just needed you."

"Find something greater than me, Aerie," he told her. "I'm hurting you. I'm letting you down already."

"What's greater than love?" Aerie asked.

"Truth."

"Well, the truth is I love you." She lowered her eyes again. "Whether you love me or not."

He was silent for a long moment. Aerie peeked up just in time to see him reach for her.

"Oh, Aerie," he murmured, before he kissed her. His arms wrapped around her, cradling her in the nook of his shoulder. "I do love you."

Aerie felt his kiss, gentle and slow, reveling in his embrace. She struggled to relax against him, confused even as she felt torn apart.

He pulled back from her once more, this time achingly slow. "Your father is waiting to see you."

The words flattened her.

She nodded and eased out of his grip, even though he seemed reluctant to let her go. *I could fight here.* And, she realized, she would likely win.

But it wouldn't be successful in the long-term, she thought bitterly. She would show Exton she could trust him, and she had to show him that he could trust her to follow orders.

Following orders. Aerie shook her head to herself as she stepped down off the shuttle behind Exton. No wonder he had trouble trusting her. *Apparently,* she thought, chagrined, *it has been a lifelong problem.*

Aerie squinted her eyes against the dying light of day. The world beneath her feet was soft, the muddy molding already encasing her boots. She glanced ahead, and there he was.

The General was walking up from the small plane he'd no doubt piloted to the site himself. Aerie was surprised to see she no longer recognized him as a daughter would, but as an enemy. She saw his right foot limping slightly, and his body seemed more tired than she'd noticed before.

She walked out to greet him. She glanced over at Exton and his guards. "Please wait till we leave before you go."

It was a small request, one Aerie had a feeling Exton had meant to fulfill on his own. When she saw his curt nod, she rejoiced inwardly.

At least she'd get to see him until the very end.

"General," Aerie said. She held out her hand to shake his.

He sighed. "Two weeks in enemy territory and you've already forgotten proper procedures, Aerie?"

"I don't want to bow to you here," Aerie told him, her voice hardened with anger. "Especially since I heard you threatened several hundred people's lives to get me back."

"I would have threatened more," he told her, "if it would have gotten you home."

"I *was* home," Aerie told him. She glanced back at Exton. "I love him, Daddy."

She was as surprised as he was to hear her say "Daddy," but she pushed forward. "I want to stay with him."

"You can't." The General shook his head. "You're in danger as it is."

"But—"

"You're also endangering them, Aerie. Their survival, along with the Ecclesia, depends on our cunning. You can't just disappear."

"Help me, then," she said.

"It would be too suspicious," he argued. "I can't. I have to cause you more trouble as it is."

"Why?" Aerie suddenly heard the wind rushing through the trees. She turned back to see the General pull out his gun. "What are you doing?"

Before he could answer, Aerie knew. She turned back to Exton.

"Exton, it's a setup!" Aerie called. "Go!"

The instant her cry hit the wind, a team of fighter jets came rushing over the skyline.

She turned back to her father. "You tricked us!"

"Aerie!" Exton called from behind her.

"I had to," he said, sadly. "There is much you don't know about me, or my mission, Aerie." He lifted his gun and took aim for Exton.

"No!" Before Aerie could think, she grabbed his arm and twisted it back. Her other arm lashed out and punched him, hitting him square in the nose.

Aerie gasped in horror, before she heard Exton calling her again. "Come back, Aerie," he called. "We're leaving."

She lost her fear and grinned. "Coming!" Aerie turned back to her father as his nose ran with a thick trail of blood. "I'm sorry, sir."

And then she took off. "Exton."

The jets screamed as they dove and shot past them, and missiles exploded all around her. But when she found Exton's arms again, she knew nothing but joy.

"Aerie." He picked her up and swung her around once. "Let's go home."

She kissed him, hugging him as he held her, while he carried her toward the ship.

She barely noticed the glint of sunlight in the distance—and then it was all she could see.

"Exton, look out!" She pushed him aside.

Blood splurged from her shoulder less than a second later.

"Aeris!" the General's voice echoed in the distance.

"Aerie," Exton grabbed her as she tripped. Both of them fell to the ground as strong, burning pain ran down the length of her arm and across her chest.

She cried out in pain as she gripped onto Exton. "Ouch!"

A missile exploded into Exton's shuttle. She heard the crew crying out orders, trying to get it to fly, all while Exton tore his jacket to try making a bandage for her wound.

Aerie studied him, watching in quiet wonder. He was in shock as he held her, clearly uncertain of what to do. "It'll be okay, it'll be okay," he gasped.

She felt her grip on reality lessen as the pain overflowed her mind and senses. "That's what you said last time." Aerie laughed quietly.

"Stay with me, Aerie," Exton ordered. "Please, don't leave me." He hugged her close as he pushed down on the blood. "I was wrong," he croaked. "I was wrong. God did just dump someone into the ship just for me, didn't he?"

He kissed her forehead. "Please forgive me."

Aerie thought she managed to smile at his words before she lost consciousness.

"Get away from her, or the next bullet will go through you."

Exton glared up at St. Cloud, his eyes blurred over. "I'm not letting you take her."

"I'm her father. If anything, I'm not letting you *keep* her." St. Cloud lounged at him, landing a forceful kick on Exton's chest.

Exton, still tangled up in Aerie's legs, struggled to move as his opponent attacked again.

This time he tasted blood. He wiped his face off with his hands. "Why do you always do this to me!?"

St. Cloud ignored him, reaching down and hoisting Aerie up. She began to struggle as the pain woke her up.

Exton fought against his pain. "Aerie!"

"Stand down, St. Cloud!" A pair of Exton's guards came down the ship's ramp. "We have you locked on target."

St. Cloud held Aerie firmly against his chest. He glared at Exton. "Here's a promise I'll keep: Leave my family alone, and I'll leave yours alone."

Before Exton could respond, St. Cloud fired on the guards. The two dropped to the ground. He then turned the gun on Exton.

"No," Exton gasped. He scrambled back.

He was surprised when St. Cloud holstered his weapon.

"Contrary to what Osgood thinks," he said, "I do believe there are worse things than death."

He pulled out a syringe and pushed the plunger into Aerie's arm.

"What are you doing?" Exton yelled, watching in horror as Aerie flinched and then collapsed. "What did you do?"

"One of the better technologies that the URS has developed," St. Cloud said, "is the use of Memory Serum. A thousand NanoTech robots all programed to flood the synapses in the mind."

"I don't understand."

"This will block out her memories of the past six weeks."

Angry shock poured through him. "You monster!" he cried. "Aerie!"

"There's no use in calling for her now. Once she's awake and her wound is healed, she'll never remember you." He glanced around, seeming to search the horizon.

Before Exton could turn completely around, he heard them. A team of helicopters, flying low, appeared out of the clouds.

Pain slashed through him, while blood, warm and sticky, oozed out of his head. He felt dazed as he gripped his head, where St. Cloud had bashed him with his weapon.

"Remember my warning, Exton," St. Cloud said. "You've ruined my plans before, but I won't let you ruin them again. You've returned Aerie to me, so for that I'll forget about Petra. But mark my words, you must never see her again."

The helicopters began firing, and Exton watched as St. Cloud, surprisingly agile for a man in his forties, disappeared into his plane.

"No."

He fell back against the brown, muddy grass, watching as the clouds fell into darkness.

It was moments later, after St. Cloud had taken off and the crew finally managed to account for its losses, that Exton felt a hand on his forehead.

"He always did have a very good aim." A woman's voice

washed over him. "Here, drink this. He's gone now."

After dutifully sipping on a warm drink that tasted like bile, Exton opened his eyes. A woman with dark hair loomed over him. She had a pilot's uniform on, but the insignia was not from the URS. She had the mark of the Ecclesia on her shoulder.

"Who are you?" he asked.

The woman removed the better portion of her fighter goggles. Even in the moonlight, he could see her eyes were green, dappled with golden flecks. "My name is Merra," she said. "And considering what I've heard about you concerning my daughter, Exton Shepherd, it's about time we met again."

The beeping sounds of a med ward were familiar, but her mind refused to put a name to the place. She almost smiled.

Aerie sighed and opened her eyes, immediately flinching from the bright lights. All of them artificial, she noticed, her mouth twisting into a frown. *It's not supposed to be like that … is it?*

"Aerie. You're awake, at last."

Aerie turned toward the sound of her name. She blinked a few times, clearing her vision. The shadowed figure of a man, close to her own age, came into focus, and she grinned. "Brock."

His hazel eyes lit up with happiness. "I was worried about you."

"Where am I?" Aerie asked.

"You're in the New Hope Hospital, the critical care wing. You've been in here for over two weeks. This is the first day that I've been allowed to come in and sit with you." He smiled. "I'm honored you decided to wake up for me."

"Two weeks? What happened?" Aerie asked. She frowned.

"You were finishing up a course test on combat training," Brock said. "They called you in after your PAR. They said that you'd taken the wrong test and wanted to correct it."

"So what happened?" Aerie tried to give him a smile, but it hurt. She tentatively touched her face. She had a bloody lip still, she noticed. That was weird. *If I have been in here for two weeks, why am I still bleeding?*

"You were climbing up the ropes course and you fell."

"That doesn't sound like me." Aerie frowned. "I'm a good climber. People would notice if I just fell."

"They think you might have had a seizure," Brock told her. "Or so General St. Cloud told me. Apparently, it can be a genetic trait. Your mother—er, former unit director—had a history of it."

"My mother?" *There was something about my mother,* she remembered.

He reached over and took her hand. "Aerie, we've been worried about you."

"There's no need to worry," Aerie assured him. "Now that I'm awake, I'm sure I'll be back to normal before too much longer."

"You've got some work to catch up on."

"Oh, no!" Aerie shot up into a sitting position. "I've missed my first few weeks of work!" Then she frowned. "Did I get into the military?" she asked. "This won't disqualify me, will it?"

"I guess you don't remember." Brock sighed. "They said you might have some issues with your memory for the next couple of months. You hit your head pretty hard."

He reached over and touched the small bump on her head.

Instantly, Aerie felt a rush of shyness. "Were you assigned to be a doctor?" she asked. Then she frowned. "No, you were an engineer. You told me."

"Huh?" Brock's eyes raised in surprise. "No, I got into the pilot program at the New Hope Military Academy."

"Oh." Aerie frowned. "I thought … " She closed her eyes and pressed her palms against them. Eyes the color of the lightest blue fluttered into her vision. "I thought … "

"The medics here are getting the paperwork together to clear you," Brock said. "Once you're settled in at home again, would you want to come over and meet my parents?"

"Parents?"

"Yes. I've met yours," Brock said with a smile. "I thought it would be okay to introduce you to mine."

"Why?"

"Because. We like each other."

"I might have borrowed your name," Aerie snapped, "but you're not my boyfriend." Instantly, she felt a rush of pain and tiredness, while Brock only looked stricken.

She glanced over at her shoulder. "What happened to my shoulder?"

"When you fell, you landed on some equipment that was lying around." Brock frowned. "You really don't remember anything?"

"I'm … I'm trying to," Aerie said. "I'd like to rest for a bit, if you don't mind, Brock."

"I can imagine this is overwhelming," Brock said. "I'll come back tomorrow. Your father said he would come and see you later."

"Oh, okay." Aerie curled into a sleeping position, facing away from the door. "Thanks. Thanks for letting me know."

"Sure." He squeezed her hand gently and then left.

Aerie waited until he left the room before allowing herself to cry. Her hands covered her face. *Something is wrong,* she thought. *Something is wrong, and I have to figure it out.*

She pulled the sheet over her head, blocking out the lights, and struggled to find sleep.

THE BREADTH OF CREATION

BOOK TWO OF *THE DIVINE SPACE PIRATES*

♦♦♦♦

C. S. Johnson

For Sam, an old friend, and for Tyler, a new one. As always, words and stories fail me when I think of how much you mean to me.

This is also for Julia, my favorite new cousin, whose enthusiasm has been a lifesaver more often than I can remember, and Dakota, who reminds me all over again that despite differences in time, space, and life, friendships can be made through the magic of books.

♦1♦

There was a chill in the air that had little to do with the weather or the ever-sinking sun setting on the brink of the horizon. The undeniable bitterness near the bottom of the world clawed at him, along with the pain in his heart, while the breeze tauntingly brushed against the lingering bump on his head. For the moment, he ignored it, content to stare up at the branches of the tree before him, as he ran fingers ran down its trunk.

The wind pushed harder into him, finally breaking him of his cool reserve. As his fingers curled into an angry fist, Exton Shepherd once more felt the temptation to give in to his vengeful desires.

"Aerie." Defeat settled into him as he stared up at the Memory Tree.

Exton and his crew had finished replanting it only hours earlier. Afterward, the others slowly filtered away from the scene, leaving Exton behind.

He glanced behind him, where Petra's campus lights began to shine as the end of the western Antarctic peninsula finally turned away from the sun.

Petra, while far from plenteous in its crops, would provide a steady stream of care and nutrients for the Memory Tree. It would grow to be a part of the land as much as it was already a part of Petra's history.

Exton didn't care about that. He missed Aerie.

How has she only been gone for just over a week?

She would've been pleased at his decision to plant the Memory Tree in his family's new home.

If she had been with him, she likely would be buzzing all around the place, making sure that the tree could get the right amount of sunlight and that the soil had been dug deeply enough. Without her, it fell to Emery, his younger sister, to do just that. And Emery had reveled in it, giving them twice the amount of nagging needed.

But Exton knew it was not even close to being the same.

Maybe, he thought, on some level, the Memory Tree was having its own form of revenge on him. Wasn't he the one to haul it out of its original home back in New Hope? Wasn't he the one who ordered it ripped from the earth, only saving the slightest bit of it, before setting it down in the middle of the *Perdition*?

Now, as he studied its staggering, uneven branches, it was the tree's turn to rip his heart out of his chest and replant it in an empty shell of his former life.

It was, he supposed, a possibility. But as he patted down the last of the earth around the roots, his heart ached with bitterness at the certainty of the truth.

This is all St. Cloud's fault.

When his lumberjack crew accidentally captured Aerie at New Hope, he had only meant to steal the Memory Tree. He wanted to crush the heart of the URS, and stealing the tree that had survived through so much in its life, so much that it had become a symbol of their city, and by extension, the whole of the nation, seemed too easy a target to pass up.

He and his crew had attacked the city and stolen the tree, roots and all, burning the remaining seedlings, and retreated to the coldness of space.

Only to find Aerie curled up inside the tree.

He struggled to breathe normally as he thought about the moment he'd first seen her. His life had changed, even if he hadn't known it.

But Aerie had not only changed his life—she'd brought his heart back to life. Her passion, her fire, her trust, her eagerness—all of it had called to him, crying out to him as he walked in the valley of shadow and death, beckoning him back into the sweet sunlight. Not even finding out she was the daughter of his father's executioner caused his steps to falter as he came home to her.

It had been a miracle, an undeniable act of divine intervention.

Now, he was just a man with a crushed heart and a weakened tree for his trouble.

He smirked disdainfully. "Emery always warned me I loved irony too much," he said, as the pain twisted deeply into his heart.

A beeping noise coming from his coat interrupted his thoughts. Seeing it was his comm device, he groaned, but he quickly freed it from his pocket, knowing it was the wiser course of action.

The voice on the other end greeted him in familiar, jovial tones. "Come in, Cap. Are you there?"

"Affirmative," Exton answered. "How's the weather up there, Jared?"

Exton could almost see the smile on Jared's face. His copilot had always been eager to prove himself. He had embraced the opportunity to pilot the *Perdition* while Exton and his family remained in Petra.

"Definitely not as wet as Petra is looking. You've got a warm front moving in from the transantarctic mountains."

"How long until it hits the settlement?"

"About twenty minutes."

"I better head inside then," he said. "Did you alert Aunt Patty?"

"You mean Director Ward?"

Exton ran a hand over his face in silent self-disgust. *Just how tired am I?* His aunt was a proud, stubborn lady, and she would bristle at his mistake. She was the one, he recalled, who insisted on keeping her title after fleeing the URS. Patricia Ward, his mother's sister, did not believe in much, but for her, formality was a kind of comfort, one that was only put aside for family.

Since Exton tended to agree with her, he immediately rectified his lapse. "Yes, that's who I meant," he said. "Did you alert Director Ward?"

"I sent a message down to Director Caldwell, but I'll forward it on to Director Ward as well."

He had a feeling Tyler would have told Jared to inform Emery.

"Excellent." Exton clicked off his device. *Better get back before Emery gets worried.*

Not that there was much to worry about. From where he stood, he could see Petra's settlement clearly. Since they first established it, it had only grown. More defectors came to seek refuge from the URS and its oppressive government each year.

On some level, I suppose we should thank the URS, Exton thought. The United Revolutionary States, the former regions of UNA, the alliance between Canada and the United States, had prompted a lot of people to leave with their extreme censorship after MENACE, the Middle Eastern Nuclear Arms Coalition and Enterprise, had officially been destroyed. To maintain power, the ghost of the former enemy was resurrected; few knew the flesh and bones of the organization had permanently fallen.

The result was largely a war of the imagination, where the enemies had a façade and allies had a front. Exton knew this for certain, just as he knew that, as the ghost of Captain Chainsword, piloting the pirated starship *Perdition*, he filled a vital role in the reality of the URS's imaginary war.

Exton walked down the path toward the settlement shields, picking up his pace. He knew that the rain was coming now, and not just from Jared's warning.

"If you go in now, you'll miss the storm entirely, Exton."

Exton felt his feet stumble as he turned to face Merra St. Cloud.

She leaned against one of the many supply sheds outside the main campus, looking like a combat queen ready to face any battle that came her way. Her arms were folded across her chest, and her hair, a dark red streaked with muted shades of gray, was loose. "You enjoyed the rain when you were younger."

Aerie's mother is a lot different from what I expected.

When she showed up at Nova Scotia after Aerie had been lost to him, Exton was even more flabbergasted and flustered. Discovering Merra was alive had only been slightly less shocking than finding out she was the leader and coordinator of his rescue.

When he was younger, he barely paid any attention to General St. Cloud's wife, often following the General's own lead. She was a beauty, for sure, with her wild hair and glowing green eyes.

Seeing her now in her aviator's uniform, with her goggles always either around her neck or up on her head as she waltzed around in full confidence, Exton had a feeling she had been purposeful in making herself known but easily forgotten.

Every day he spent in her company since the struggle with St. Cloud only made that instinct more pronounced.

"Being in space for so long has lessened my affection for the weather," he told her.

"No wonder you fell for my daughter then," Merra said with a smirk. "Predictability gets old."

Exton said nothing as Merra came up to him. She was only a few inches taller than Aerie, he noticed. There were other, more subtle similarities between the two, but Merra's presence only seemed to sharpen Aerie's absence. Unlike Aerie's open wonder and her curious energy, Merra's gaze was full of shrewdness; her eyes were quick to spot weakness and her mind was always alert, working on a plan to exploit it.

"Why are you still here?" Exton asked, giving up on any pretense of patience. "Emery gave you and your ship clearance to leave once we arrived here. I already told you I'm not taking on additional passengers once I go back to the *Perdition.*"

"Why else would I be here?" Merra asked. "I'm here to help you, of course."

He snorted. "Forgive me for my skepticism, but I know how much Aerie missed you when you supposedly 'died.' Why should I believe you are telling me the truth now?"

"Because now we can defeat the URS," Merra said.

"So you need my help more than you want to help me?" he asked.

She frowned. "If we join forces, we can fight the URS

and destroy them."

"I doubt it," Exton replied. "Grant Osgood is an evil man, to be sure, but he's smart. We would need a lot more people to defeat him."

"What about the Ecclesia?"

"You know as well as I do that many, while they do oppose the government, have no alternatives, or too many alternatives, to survive on their own. Not all of them will want to go to war, but all of them will hate us if we make them."

"That does tend to be the drawback of supporting individualism," Merra agreed. "But you can unite them, Exton. They know of what good you have done on the *Perdition*."

"We're pirates more than soldiers," Exton told her.

"But you *want* to go to war, don't you? You've always wanted this, ever since St. Cloud killed your father. That's why you stole the *Perdition* in the first place."

Discomfort settled into Exton. *Is that what I was really after?*

He thought back to his time onboard the *Perdition*. He knew it had been only a matter of time before the URS managed to find a way to reclaim or destroy the *Perdition* and its pirate crew. But he always assumed they would make the first step.

"The Ecclesia is smart to try to stay out of it as much as they can. Besides, religious dictatorships have a way of going bad, and fast, and they've known this. That's part of the reason I'm the Captain of the *Perdition*, not one of their puppets or pastors or whatever."

"I'm not talking about setting up a religious dictatorship. You can lead us back to what we once had—a free people, under a constitutional, democratic republic."

Added into the seductive call of vengeance, the thought nearly consumed him.

But he shook his head. "No. I've already lost my father, and now I've lost Aerie. The cost is too high."

Merra gave him a hollow laugh. "You think you've lost

things?" She gestured around to the settlement and all the grounds surrounding it. "Some people have lost more. Some people have even less."

"I can't speak for them—"

"You could, though."

"I don't want to."

"You're scared to."

"And rightfully so," Exton snapped.

At his tone, she just arched a brow, acting as if he was a child throwing a tantrum. Exton glanced down to see that his hands were shaking. He tried to slow his breathing down and relax; he had to remain calm.

He had to remain calm or he would do something he would really regret.

"Look," he said carefully, "I know the *Perdition* was meant to be a warship retreat of sorts. My father died protesting that. We keep it to protect people more than anything else. I won't turn into what I despise to defeat my enemy."

"That's a shame," Merra remarked.

"It's a shame I know what power is, and that it has to be handled carefully?" he retorted.

"Carefully, yes. But you *do* have to use it where you can. Wasn't the Memory Tree proof of that?"

Exton gritted his teeth. "Our retaliations were small," he said. "We upset labs where illegal and immoral experiments go on. We've had to fight for supplies. We protect populations from needless violence when we can. We keep track of what they're doing so we can put a stop to it quickly. It's not the same as an open war."

"Isn't it, though?" Merra gestured toward Palmer Bay, where the water would lead to the open ocean. "Your attacks might have been small, but they succeeded. And you can't discount Petra itself. Now the people have a nation that is a viable alternative. The URS is on the brink of being finished, but it only works if we are all in this fight together."

"So you say," Exton said as he rolled his eyes. "I know you've been in exile all these years."

Merra frowned. "Just because I haven't been there, doesn't mean I don't know what's going on. I have my contacts, Exton, just as the Ecclesia and Victor have theirs. I knew enough to come and get you from Nova Scotia, didn't I?"

It took Exton a moment to recall General St. Cloud's given name, but less than a second to glare at her. "I'm not discussing this, Merra."

"Pity," she said. "Or maybe not, because this means I'll get to talk to you about it, uninterrupted."

"You know, you're nothing like Aerie," Exton told her.

Merra smiled. "And it's to your advantage that I'm not. I'm actually comfortable with fighting for what I believe in, even if it costs me something."

"I gave Aerie over to St. Cloud so he *wouldn't* destroy Petra. You wouldn't be here if I hadn't done that."

"But he can destroy Petra anyway," Merra pointed out. "You're on the defensive, Exton. It's only a matter of time before he tries to use the leverage you've given him to get the *Perdition* back in the hands of the URS, or worse."

He hated that she had a point.

"You can't win a defensive war," she said. "At least, not effectively. You have less land, less access to resources, and less manpower. Petra doesn't have the capabilities at this point to withstand one attack, let alone years of attacks. The only way you'll win—the only way you can protect your friends and family, *and* get Aerie back—is to take the war to the rest of the world first."

"Are you trying to frighten me now?" Exton asked. "Guilt didn't work, so now you're moving on to threats?"

"Logic isn't a threat," Merra insisted. "Besides, you know Osgood has been moving toward open war with you anyway. He has years of propaganda to use against you. And you know he has been planning something. His new communication system, his push for more recruits, and mobilization of his forces around different parts of the world—everything is in place for him to prop up a centralized government, one that would oppress people as much as it already does in New Hope."

He *really* hated that she had a point. But war was still war. Lives would be lost, and forever changed. The cost was high—even if he wanted revenge against St. Cloud for all his cruelty.

He sighed. "Why do you want war so openly? What do you have to gain from it but trouble?"

"Because I want my family back!" Merra yelled. When he just stared at her, she continued. "I want my children and my husband, all of us, together, once more. That's something worth fighting for."

Exton could understand. His father had been killed by the URS. His mother died of grief. Their dreams had rotted away like the forbidden fruit of the Tree of Knowledge of Good and Evil, leaving a bad taste throughout the rest of the world.

Exton knew he had Emery, but she had Tyler, and now they had a baby on the way. Emery had a family now. He didn't.

If only St. Cloud hadn't destroyed Aerie's memories of him when he used the Memory Serum, he might've had a family, too.

"Even if we went to war," he said carefully, "the Aerie I knew is gone."

"No she's not," Merra scoffed. "Just her memory of you is gone."

"Her memory of me and everything the *Perdition* stood for."

"If you don't want to fight her for her," Merra said, "I can see why you won't fight for the rest of the world."

He narrowed his gaze angrily.

She sneered back. "I suppose you think it would be best for her to continue her life in the URS? Maybe she'll go back to that Rearden boy. He's been very diligent about seeing to her care since she was returned."

Exton felt a rush of unpleasantness pool inside of him.

"He has Victor's approval, you know," Merra continued.

"He'll be allowed to apply for cohabitation, see about getting them set up in a unit of their own."

Exton struggled to push away the thought of some other boy kissing Aerie, holding her, keeping her for himself.

She's mine.

Was it really such a risk to get her back? Even if it meant war? What if Merra was right, and they could win?

Merra's just using you. She has her own agenda.

He finally managed to find some clarity at that thought. He couldn't trust Merra St. Cloud any more than he was able to trust Aerie when he first met her. "Playing on my pride now?"

She smirked. "It's working."

The pounding in his head came as the rain started to fall. For a long moment, as the storm settled inside the Antarctic circle, Exton met Merra's gaze coldly. "What makes you think we can really win?"

"First of all, you already have a large number of people who want to go to war on your side." Merra gestured behind him, where Exton could see more men and women as they hurried into the shelter of Petra's settlement.

"Not all of them do."

"The URS has been vulnerable for some time now," she continued, ignoring his small protest. "Like any good totalitarian regime, it's sowing the seeds of its own destruction. They've been cracking down on dissenters and defectors precisely because they know there's an alternative now. The Ecclesia has managed to spread the word around. More people are asking for Petra's aid."

Exton knew all too well of the power news and gossip had in the Ecclesia. He often relied on its accuracy, even though the leaders bemoaned its frequency. He sighed. "What else?"

"Osgood has largely finished consolidating his power," she said. "Victor has been promoted to his Lieutenant Commander-in-Chief. Given his background in military leadership, his replacement would be easy to disregard, along with the rest of his inner circle."

"Who replaced St. Cloud in the role of Chief Military Strategist?" Exton hadn't thought about the general's replacement.

Merra laughed. "It's Gerard Dubois. He's one of Osgood's 'yes men,' all the way through. Victor hated teaching him while he was in school."

Exton felt a warning shot burn through him. Before he could ask further questions about Gerard's appointment, Merra once more continued on with her planning.

"It'll be simple to take them down. We can use the ships you have in the *Perdition*, along with the forces I've accumulated from Chaya, and then … "

As Merra droned on, Exton made a mental note to tell Tyler about Gerard before allowing himself to focus once more on Merra. Given the option, he knew Merra would try to overrun him, and while he hated to admit it, she was already starting to make him reconsider his position.

He'd seen the end of the resistance, but he never thought it would be as volatile as it was shaping up to be. He knew the risks of going to war, and that had kept him from targeting larger camps or disrupting warfare with greater collateral risks.

But as Merra's words washed over him, he recognized he had been far too quick to say Merra was nothing like Aerie.

Aerie had brought his heart back to life. Now, Merra was pushing for his hope.

He stood there, watching the Memory Tree as it weathered its first storm.

What could really go wrong if we went on the offensive? Exton wondered. The URS was already killing people. St. Cloud had Aerie tucked away, back under his watchful eye, and he knew about Petra.

What could they really do to him to make his life worse?

As if to answer his question, Exton felt pain rushing from the remnant of the bump on the back of his head, his souvenir from the battle with St. Cloud, as the rain began to fall.

♦2♦

The headache was back.

Aeris St. Cloud mindlessly watched the monitor before her, trying hard not to show any outward signs of the turmoil going on inside of her.

Aerie quietly squirmed in her chair. She'd already been reprimanded three times this morning, and if Director Anand had his way, he'd make her work late—*again.*

Her head suddenly pulsed with another layer of irritation at the thought of her boss, but Aerie knew it had nothing to do with the reoccurring bouts of pain she'd been experiencing for the last week. The distinctive throbbing in the back of her head always seemed to accompany an unexplainable pain in her heart.

And it was very, very safe to say Director Anand would never find his way into her heart.

The doctors at the med center said that her headaches would be a side effect from her injuries, but they would eventually wear off—if she didn't stress herself or wear herself down. They told her to focus on the future and going through physical therapy, that her memory would likely come back when she least expected it, blah-blah-blah-blah-blah.

Aerie rolled her eyes at the thought of stress. That was all her work was, really, especially since her boss had already held her overtime for being late or slow or disobedient, and she'd only been out of the hospital and on her feet for three days.

She supposed the doctors were all well and good about giving their useless advice, but they didn't seem to understand how stressful it was for her to be unable to recall anything about her injuries. She repeatedly tried recall the moment she fell from her climbing assessment, much to dismay of her doctors, and even her father.

You mean the General, she mentally corrected herself.

But, Aerie thought, it was hard to think of him as just the

General. Since she'd been hospitalized, he had taken the time to come and check in with her and see how she was doing. For the first time since her mother died, Aerie felt like he was more of the father she remembered from her childhood. She was shocked when he told her, in no uncertain terms, that she had "been through hell" and should only focus on the future.

"Remembering what happened won't help you, Aeris," he'd said. "Getting better is more important."

Aerie almost smiled at the memory.

It was nice to see that he cared, but she was determined to right her wrong from her climbing assessment, no matter what he told her. That included being aware of what went wrong. Once her shoulder was better, she would show them, she decided.

Her head ached again, making her sigh in dismay. Going through hell was a lot easier than climbing out of it, apparently.

"Aerie."

Aerie glanced over to see Claire, one of her graduating class members who also had been assigned to Comms Sec. She was nice enough to Aerie, and Aerie was glad she had someone familiar by her side, especially since she was struggling with her memory.

"What?" Aerie whispered back, giving her a small smile even though it felt like her head was splitting open.

"Pay attention," Claire said. "You've had a comm waiting for three minutes now." She gestured toward the blinking light on Aerie's control board, before turning her attention back to her own station.

Aerie had to wonder if Claire actually cared about her or if she was looking for a promotion. Or maybe, Aerie recalled, she was just slipping back into her usual self. Claire liked to boss people around. That was part of the reason that she was selected as a coordinator for their graduation ceremony.

Her headache spiked as she tried to recall the ceremony. Brock Rearden, her best friend, had been there. He hadn't told her much about it. He mentioned that Dictator Osgood showed up, but she couldn't remember why.

Why had he been there? Why *would* he be there?

She thought about asking Claire when the pain in the back of her head intensified drastically. She struggled to order herself to work.

Claire glanced her way again. "Aerie," she hissed. Her voice was more insistent this time.

"I'll get to it," Aerie muttered. "Just give me a moment, would you?"

Claire nodded, and then went back to ignoring her.

Aerie closed her eyes for another long moment. Between answering the comms, learning how the systems were set up, and rerouting different signals, she was kept perpetually busy. But she was able to keep up when she felt like it. Even with the addition of the new protocols on counteracting any signal jamming and integrating the new NETech into the comms system, it should've been no surprise she was getting headaches more frequently.

Finally, seeing no other choice, she flicked on her comm line. "Comms sec," Aerie said, careful to enunciate every word.

It was true her boss had reproached her for her sloppiness and apathetic disdain for her job, but there was nothing bad he could say about her performance otherwise.

As the caller informed her of another malfunctioning pipe in one of the student commissaries, and went on about how it was causing all sorts of smelly problems in the mess hall, aerie let out a soft, barely perceivable sigh.

Is this it? Aerie wondered. *Is this all I will do until I grow old and die? Answer other people's problems and connect them with plumbers?*

She wished she could remember more of her PAR. Surely, she didn't receive this as some sort of punishment?

Pain exploded around her head. Aerie gasped at the sudden outpouring. She finally clutched at her headset and tore it off, barely negating the temptation to toss it into her monitor.

"What's wrong?" Claire asked.

"My head still hurts," Aerie told her. She rubbed the spot on the back of her head, the point where the pain seemed to be permanently housed.

"Let me get Director Anand," Claire said, and before Aerie could tell her very emphatically not to, she was out of her seat and through the nearby exit.

Aerie slumped over. "Great." *I already have one headache. I don't need another one.*

Alone for the moment, she leaned back in her seat and closed her eyes, allowing herself a moment to relax; after all, she was going to get in trouble either way.

The instant she closed her eyes, she felt the world as she knew it sweep away. Nondescript clouds gave way to the darkest night, where stars glimmered in the distance while the sun burned brightly.

She felt like she was standing right in the middle of it, looking through a window at the top of a small room, with someone … someone holding her.

Aerie opened her eyes. The vision faded away, but the feeling of warmth and excitement stayed behind.

Suspicion and fear crept into her. This wasn't the first time she had a daydream that felt much more real than any daydream she'd had before. And according to her school records, she had a *lot* of daydreams.

Am I going crazy? Or is it possible—

"What do you think you're doing, Comrade St. Cloud?"

Aerie jumped as Director Anand came into the room. She quickly reached for her headset. "Nothing," she tried to assure him, but his beady eyes bore into her.

"Comrade Luceno here tells me that you are not working consistently through your tasks," he said, nodding toward Claire as she sat down, her back straight, a new sense of superiority clouding around her.

Aerie bit her lip. "Well, I am still recovering—"

He waved his hand, brushing her concerns aside. "Look, Comrade, you're putting me in a very difficult situation here.

I will need to contact your unit leader—"

"No!" Aerie objected. "No, there's no need, sir."

The worst part, Aerie decided, was that if Director Anand actually contacted her unit, it was likely the General would be the one to take his call, since he was finding more excuses to come home and see her. She knew no matter how much the General had been careful to oversee her recuperation, he would not be happy to hear she was holding up operations at her job.

If I knew it was only Phoebe who would hear his complaint, I wouldn't care quite so much.

Aerie knew she could withstand her stepmother's disappointment; she'd done it before, several times. But Aerie wasn't sure if she could deal with her father's, especially when, for the first time since her mom died, he was paying attention to her.

"I'm sorry to say, Comrade St. Cloud, you are not leaving me much choice," Anand continued. "Protocol clearly states that this is what I must do in such instances as this."

Before Aerie could argue with him further, a bell rang, signaling the end of the shift. She looked up at Anand eagerly.

Anand sighed. "Alright, I will let it go this time. Stay here and finish up your reports. But tomorrow, I want no mistakes."

Aerie beamed. "Thank you, Director," she said as she saluted him.

His dark brows furrowed. "There is nothing to thank me for, Comrade St. Cloud. I am only doing my duty to the URS. You would be wise to do the same."

"I should be done in no time," Aerie assured him.

Anand shook his head. "All our time goes to serving the URS. It is the quality of your work you need to perfect, not the quantity. Thinking anything less was dangerously close to being traitorous."

He turned on his heel and walked out the door, clearly angry he'd failed to give her a proper reprimand and punishment.

Beside her, Aerie heard Claire sigh.

Aerie gave her a quick, mischievous grin. "Dangerously close is still not technically traitorous, so I should be in the clear, right?"

Claire shook her head. "Aerie, you've been clear to work for a week now. If you're still not feeling well, then you need to go back to the med center."

"I'm fine," Aerie lied, thinking of how much she hated the med center. *I don't want to go back there ever again if I can help it.*

Thinking of how lost and empty she felt when she woke up from her coma strengthened her. She reached for her keyboard and began typing in her notes.

Aerie was surprised when Claire continued talking to her. "If you're really fine, then you need to do a better job. I don't want Comrade Anand thinking all the first year recruits are as bad as you."

Aerie stopped typing.

"I didn't mean it that way," Claire quickly insisted. "It's just … you've always had people protect you. I think it's about time you stepped up."

Aerie stiffened. "If you're sorry, you can just say so," she replied. "There's no need to insult me after you apologize."

Claire hardened her expression. "Sorry then. See you tomorrow."

"Okay." As she typed, slower this time, Aerie watched Claire walk away. She was surprised when Claire actually apologized; it was never something the state encouraged.

And no wonder. It wasn't like she managed to help me feel better.

She was about to pull her headset back on when there was a knock at the door. Aerie glanced up to see a woman standing there.

She had a pretty shade of blonde hair, and it was long enough to pull back into a bun; there was a small braid in her hair at the side, similar to the one Aerie had carefully crafted in her own hair. From where she was sitting, Aerie could tell the woman was close to her age, but from her medical uniform, she was likely a year or two older.

"Can I help you?" Aerie asked.

"I'm looking for comrade St. Cloud," she said.

"That's me." Aerie bristled, just waiting for more disappointment.

Instead, the woman smiled. "Oh, good. I wasn't sure I'd catch you before the shift ended," she said. "I have a message for you from the med center. They'd like you to come back again."

Aerie frowned. "But I was cleared to work."

The woman shrugged. "I'm not a doctor," she said. "I just do what they tell me."

Aerie snorted disdainfully. "Isn't that what we all do?" she muttered.

Aerie was surprised to hear the woman giggle. The moment Aerie's eyes caught hers, her hands flew over her mouth and her eyes went wide, allowing Aerie to see the sparkle in a sea of chestnut.

Suddenly, she seemed much more familiar.

The woman cleared her throat delicately, but Aerie knew she was just covering up her laughter. "There's a sickness going around, I guess," she said.

Aerie knew the woman was amending her statements. They were, like her own earlier comments, dangerously close to being traitorous.

But not technically, Aerie thought with a smile. She came up to the woman. "I'll have to make sure I don't get it from you then, Comrade, uh … what's your name?"

"Oh! Oh, well, you can just call me Meredith, if you'd like."

"I'm Aerie," Aerie said as she extended her hand out to the woman in a handshake.

Before Aerie could properly examine why she even reached out a hand to Meredith at all, Meredith shook it. Aerie felt a whisper of a memory run through her—the feel of her hand in another's strong grasp, one with a gentle roughness, one that grabbed her heart as well as her hand.

"Are you alright?" Meredith asked, concerned lines etching into her young face.

Aerie shrugged. "I guess I'll go and find out. Don't want to keep the med center waiting."

"Yes," Meredith agreed. "They're the ones who like to keep people waiting."

"Exactly!" Aerie giggled, more delighted by Meredith's slight to the government-run system than the joke itself. "Are you headed back there too?"

"I'll take you back. I've got a few more hours on my shift," she said. "I work as a nursing assistant."

"Oh. That sounds interesting."

Meredith wrinkled her nose. "Interesting, maybe. I have to put in another couple of years before I get promoted," she said. "As an assistant, I have to do a lot of the dirty work."

"Such as delivering messages to wayward patients?" Aerie asked.

"Not quite," Meredith said with a small laugh. "More like cleaning up after wounds and other bodily liquids."

"Ew!" Aerie shuddered. "Gross."

"It is," she agreed. "This is actually my favorite part of my job. Even if this is technically my lunch break."

"Well, my brain might be damaged, and my shoulder might be strained, but my legs are fully functional," Aerie told her. "I can speed up some."

She took Meredith's arm and hauled her through the Comms Sec building, feeling better for the first time in a long, long time. It was nice to feel like she'd found a friend.

♦3♦

"Here we are," Meredith said, as she led Aerie down the hall of the New Hope Hospital.

Aerie winced at the crowded waiting rooms as she passed by. There always seemed to be a shortage of medical supplies.

I wonder why I never get calls about this down in the Comms Sec? Aerie shook her head sadly as she watched a little boy sit next to his unit director. He kept trying to hold her hand, but she wouldn't let him. Aerie had a feeling Phoebe would do the same thing to her, so she smiled kindly at the little boy before Meredith pulled her toward the stairs.

"If there are other people around who need care more, I can wait," Aerie said. "I mean, it's no problem to skip dinner with my unit tonight."

Meredith shook her head. "We have your room ready," she said. "It's up a few floors, so I'll need you to stay close to me. I also need you to make sure you don't talk to anyone, alright?" She gave her a tepid smile. "The patients and staff are very preoccupied. Don't try to draw attention to yourself."

Weird, but understandable. Aerie nodded. "Okay."

They ascended to the top floor, and Aerie recognized it at once. "This is where I was brought to recover when I fell," she said.

"Shh!" Meredith reminded her, putting a finger to her lips.

Aerie grimaced apologetically, before turning her attention to her surroundings. Her mind began to feel the familiar drizzle of pain.

"Here's your room," Meredith said, opening the door. "Please wait here. The doctor will be along soon."

"Thanks." Aerie smiled. "I hope you can get your lunch finished."

"Don't count on it," Meredith said, but she smiled. "I'll see you around."

"Bye." Aerie watched as the door closed. She decided she would do something nice for Meredith soon. *Maybe I can bring her lunch one day, to thank her for her kindness.*

"It's not like I have a lot of friends, especially ones I trust," she muttered to herself. "Why not try to make one?"

She turned and glanced around the room, not surprised to find it was still as eerie and uncomfortable as the last time she was there.

Aerie sat down on the bed and looked at the clock. Meredith had joked before about the slow waiting times, but once she had a room, it surely wouldn't be so bad?

What did it matter if did take a long time? I'd only be missing out on dinner with my unit, and with Serena and the twins home, I'd rather not be there anyway.

Ever since she was twelve and their mother died, Aerie had been determined to get into the military. Since then, her siblings had derided her or ignored her at every turn. Aerie never felt welcome at home. It was as if her mother's absence had not only left a hole in her heart, but one in her family.

Unit, she mentally corrected herself.

Aerie sighed as she glanced at the time. As she was just about to go and look for someone, something caught her eye on the bedside table. She saw a folded jacket lying there. Just underneath it, there was a file with her name on it.

Curiosity had always been a calling. Aerie reached over and took the jacket.

As the smooth fabric touched her fingers, she realized the jacket was hers.

It was hers, even though it wasn't in the usual style for the URS. It was the same color, but the cut was slightly older, she realized. *How is this mine?*

But she remembered putting it on, tucking it around her as she stepped out of a dark room.

"When did I get this?" Aerie wondered aloud as she put the jacket on. It warmed her instantly. But she frowned as she couldn't recall having it issued to her or picking it out among her selection of clothes.

Pain followed instantly, and she gasped. Her hands flew up to her forehead, and she tried to block out the pain, to no avail.

"Huh?" Aerie's nose tickled as it caught the scent carried on the jacket. It was a warm and musky scent, one that was strangely and painfully familiar to her.

She gripped her arms around her, holding herself as the pain in her head pulsated through the rest of her body.

That was when she realized the jacket had a small hole near the left shoulder. There were dark stains around the hole, and Aerie remembered pain, excruciating pain.

"Something's wrong here," she said. She reached over and grabbed the folder with her name on it.

Sure enough, there was an X-ray with her name on it, with several spots of shrapnel dotting her shoulder.

"I was shot."

Aerie heard herself say the words, but she wasn't sure if she believed them.

Her body's memory of the situation swept through her, and Aerie could see it; she could see her tears, and feel the blood as it seeped out of her arm. She could feel the panic as it swelled up inside of her.

She could also hear the sounds coming back to her. A helicopter—or maybe several—were flying overhead. A man was holding her, pleading with her to stay with him.

The information in her file slowly slipped onto the floor. Aerie just stared at it, even though her mind was reeling.

The last week or so had been hard on her. She had instances where whole scenes would floor her mind, and Aerie, knowing herself, had squashed them down, thinking they were just daydreams.

But now, the daydreams morphed into memories.

The pain in her head roared.

"Augh!" Aerie grabbed at the back of her head and rubbed it, trying to massage away the mass of agony that had settled inside.

The door opened, and Aerie looked up to see a doctor,

one she was not familiar with, standing in the entrance. "What are you doing in here?" he asked.

"I … I have a terrible headache," she said. "Can you help me?"

He glanced down at the screen in his hand. "You're not on my chart," he said. "How did you get in here?"

Aerie felt her suspicion turn into fear. She didn't have an appointment here.

Someone was trying to tell her something.

And other someones—namely, Brock and her father—had lied to her.

"I'm sorry," she said, "I just didn't know where else to go."

The doctor's lips tightened. He was clearly annoyed. "We can get you into the system downstairs in the med center," he said. "The hospital is really only for admitted patients."

"I'm sorry," Aerie muttered again. She ducked her head.

"Come along," he said. "I'll take you back down there. I need this room, so you'll have to hurry up."

"I can find it on my own," Aerie replied, pushing past him.

She faltered only when he grabbed the file out of her hand. "This is for our records," he said. "I don't know how you got them, but these files stay here."

"Oh. I brought it from home," Aerie lied. She had to keep those files. If she ever wanted to figure out the truth, she needed to know what happened. The file was her first major clue, and she couldn't lose it.

He tightened his hand around the file. "I'm sorry, Comrade," he said. "These are clearly hospital files," he said, pointing to the watermark on the back. "When you get your appointment set up, we can see about sending you home with a declassified file."

"But—"

"Now, I need you to leave. I have another patient coming," the doctor snapped.

The file disappeared along with the doctor, as he hurried

down the hallway. Aerie stared at him, mindlessly, as he headed toward a patient in a wheelchair.

Rage bit at her as she realized she'd lost her only real clue.

Inspiration struck. *Meredith!*

All she had to do was find Meredith again. Then Meredith would be able to help her find out the truth. Aerie wandered through the hospital, keeping her eyes open for any medical assistant who looked like Meredith.

"Excuse me," Aerie said, as she came up to an information station. She smiled brightly at the man behind the desk. "I'm looking for a med assistant named Meredith."

After some blatant lies and unsuccessful attempts at flirting to get her way, the man agreed to look up Meredith.

Aerie cheered silently as she waited. *This is going to work. This has to work. I need to know what's going on.*

The man was quiet, but cordial, as he informed her there was no one on staff as a medical assistant named Meredith.

Aerie heard the signal call for shift change a moment later.

"I can't help you, Comrade," the man said. "And my shift is over. It's time for me to leave, and you probably should too."

"But I need to find—"

"This is a hospital," he reminded her. "You're not the only person who needs something."

Aerie shut her mouth. *At least the headaches have gone away some,* she thought appreciatively. She walked through the hospital halls, still carefully looking for the woman who had come to see her earlier.

I have to find her.

Aerie stepped outside of the med center, bitterness metastasizing inside of her.

What am I supposed to do now?

Aerie wrinkled her nose. She knew what she was *supposed* to do. It was nearly dinnertime.

She didn't want to go to dinner with her unit, even if it was required. Earlier, when she was hopelessly bored by her work, she thought about going to the arena instead, where her so-called accident happened, to try to finish the climbing course again.

That was out of the question now. Aerie mentally berated herself. She was one of the best climbers in her class. Short of the building collapsing, she should've been able to hold on.

"Aerie!"

Anger further sparked inside of her at the sound of Brock Rearden's voice. She glanced over to see him as he came up to her.

"What?" she asked, barely containing her vitriol.

"I was wondering where you were," he said. "Your unit is looking for you."

"I don't want to go to dinner," she said. "I had a bad day at work and I have a headache."

"But it's your eighteenth birthday," he said. "Your unit had a special dinner planned for you, under the General's orders."

Aerie was briefly diverted from her newest mission. "My birthday?" she repeated. "That's today?"

"Yes. You didn't remember?" Brock laughed. He put a hand on her shoulder as he steered her toward her housing unit.

Aerie said nothing. She couldn't believe that she'd forgotten her birthday.

Of course, I can't believe I forgot I was shot, either.

Her attention snapped back to Brock. He'd been her friend throughout their education. He helped her train, showing her advanced techniques and offering her alternative moves when it would benefit her. She had invited him over to dinner in exchange for his tutelage, and she'd given him some of her father's memoirs on his battle with MENACE to read. They were close. Or as close as they were allowed to be, anyway.

Now, he was in the military, training to be a fighter pilot. With only a few weeks of training in, he was already one of the rising stars of the new grads.

Aerie was slightly jealous. She wanted to go into the military, too.

Or did she?

If nothing else, after her injury, she was more than reluctant to admit to herself she was glad she hadn't been assigned to the military.

Of course, Aerie told herself, sitting around and hearing complaints from all over the city was far from what she wanted to do with the rest of her life.

"You really should stand up straight," Brock said, interrupting her thoughts.

"Huh?"

"I said, you really should stand up straight," he repeated. "We're new grads and now full citizens of the URS. We have a reputation to uphold."

Despite her anger and frustration, Aerie gave him a small smile. "You do, maybe," she said. "But I'm not military. You can stand straight enough for the both of us if you'd like."

"Come on, Aerie. It wouldn't hurt to go in to see your unit with your head up." His hazel eyes, speckled with green and brown, softened as he held her gaze. "I know they bother you."

"Well," Aerie replied, "you should know why, considering you see them more often than I do."

"Cal and Dorian are pretty cool," he remarked. "We do hang out in class and after training. But I know they think you're … young yet, and don't have much experience in the world."

"Young" must mean "weak" in their eyes. Aerie grinned. "I take it Serena's already hit on you?"

"What? Oh, uh, no, of course not."

Aerie laughed at the obvious lie. "I *knew* she would. She goes after all the best-looking guys, no matter how much younger they are."

Brock smiled. "So, you think I'm good-looking?"

Aerie flinched. *Did I really just say that?*

It was her turn to struggle with her words. Finally, she

just shrugged. "I guess so."

He reached over and took her hand.

Instantly, she pulled away. "We're almost at my housing unit," Aerie said.

"We have a little bit of time to ourselves," Brock said. He looked at her for a long moment, and Aerie knew he wanted to spend the time with her. Because he liked her, and because he wanted to be with her.

Aerie sighed. "All of our time is for the URS," she said, repeating the words Director Anand had been so self-righteous in declaring earlier.

Brock didn't seem to recognize the scorn in her voice. "Yeah, I guess you're right," he agreed, and then he straightened his shoulders even more. "I should remember that. After all, the General said he would be at your dinner tonight as well. I better make sure he knows his colleagues are doing a good job instructing me."

Aerie only sighed and snuggled into her jacket, letting the scent of it soothe her as they continued to walk in silence.

♦4♦

Exton struggled to find peace inside of him, even though he knew it wasn't there. He had a duty toward others, and he knew the full weight of that responsibility. He had to be careful, objective, and sure.

None of that ever seemed to matter when it came to convincing Emery.

"I fail to see why we allow her to stay here," Emery muttered as she moved around the small cabin Aunt Patty had prepared for them. "Aerie's mother or not, I say we kick her out tomorrow."

"She did save me," Exton reminded her.

"Mew."

Emery was briefly distracted as Aerie's cat, Moona, jumped up onto the desk she was attempting to straighten up. "I'm beginning to think she did that on purpose, to ingratiate herself to us," Emery said darkly, as Exton reached out to pet the white-faced kitten. "Or, more likely, to just convince you to launch into a full-scale war against the URS."

"We've technically been at war with them for years now, Em." He shrugged. "Ever since we stole the ship out of their military base."

"We've been *against* them," Emery said. "We've never tried to *conquer* them."

"Which is where Merra makes a good point. How are we ever going to win a war when we don't have anything to offer besides our opponent's destruction?"

Emery grabbed another pile of Tyler's papers and stacked them neatly on his desk. "We have plenty to offer," she said. "Faith, freedom, liberty, the right to choose your own life. We have dreamers, they have workers."

"But no way of ensuring it, which means at worst we're making an empty offer."

Emery frowned. "The URS can't guarantee a good life, either. At least our community gets the chance to choose."

"The URS can enforce it."

"Well, no one would want that sort of life."

"I don't know, plenty of people seem content with it. Or at least, enough to go along with it."

"Well, then, why would you want to go to war with them, if you're worried about people being content?"

Exton sighed. "You're making this difficult."

"No, I'm not," Emery told him as she sat down in the desk chair. Moona jumped into her lap, and Emery, while she had initially been wary of cats, smiled down at her. "Sweet kitty," she murmured.

"What are you doing then?" Exton asked.

"I'm pointing out that you wanted to steal the *Perdition.* I understand that. It was Papa's ship, and the URS sent out St. Cloud, and he killed him for the ship. Now it's fallen into our hands, to protect his legacy and his property."

"Which we can use to make the world a better place."

"By destroying it first?" Emery shook her head. "With all the Old Republic's wars, they've already managed to send the world into some kind of shock, I'm sure. We can't do that and expect to have a world left when we're done. If we survive."

"We don't have to destroy the whole world to make it a better place," he told her.

"I love you, Exton. You are my brother, and I will stand with you as long as I can. But I can't stand for this." Emery gazed up at him with their mother's blue-green eyes. "I'm going to have a baby in another eight months. I don't want a world at war."

"It already is at war. And we can win it."

"If we step up our attacks, according to you." Emery sighed. "I can't believe Merra's arguments are working."

"She has some good points."

"*Some* good points does not mean she has it *all* right, and that's enough ambiguity to send people chasing pipe dreams."

The door opened, making the two of them jump. Moona skirted off Emery's lap and headed to greet the newcomer, as

Emery and Exton recovered at the same time.

Both of them sent narrowed gazes at Tyler Caldwell as he walked into the room and scooped up the cat.

Tyler grimaced at the sight of his wife and brother-in-law. "I see I'm interrupting," he said. "Maybe I should just go back out … ?" He made his way back to the door.

"Wait," Emery and Exton both called.

Tyler groaned. "I don't want to have to take sides," he insisted.

"Exton wants to attack the URS."

"Again?" Tyler looked over at him and grinned. "What did you have in mind this time, Captain?"

"Tyler!" Emery admonished.

"What?" Tyler frowned. "We usually go along with his ideas when it comes to this sort of stuff. I've been waiting for this since Aerie was taken."

Exton felt all the warmth in his body leave him at the reminder.

"Maybe you should just go," Emery muttered, "if you're going to take his side."

"Come on, don't be like that," Tyler came around the desk and gave her an affectionate kiss on the forehead.

"Merra's trying to get Exton to agree to join with her and take the war to the URS," Emery said, ignoring Tyler's plea.

"Merra said we can win." Exton paused, before he added, "We can stop them. If we do that, maybe we can even get Aerie back." Seeing the quiet tenderness in Tyler's eyes as he gazed down at Emery, Exton decided not to mention the other reason he was convinced it was time to act; he made a mental note to bring it up later.

"It wouldn't be the first time a man went to war for a woman he loved," Tyler said, only to have Emery glare at him again, while Exton frowned.

"I'm not going to war just for her."

"But you do admit this is, at least in part, to get Aerie?" Emery jumped up, nearly knocking into Tyler as he stood over her. "Come on, Exton. Tyler and I have a better plan for getting her back."

"If she comes here, St. Cloud was adamant about destroying Petra." Exton shook his head. "I can't just take her back. We'll need to have enough of threat to keep him at bay. And I can't just wait around until St. Cloud decides to threaten Petra with something else."

Tyler rubbed his chin thoughtfully. "That's true," he said. "St. Cloud is second in command now. He can order things to be done at any time. To be honest, I'm surprised we haven't been attacked here yet. Since he got Aerie back, what's keeping him from breaking his word?"

"Honor." A new voice spoke up from the doorway.

They all turned to see Exton and Emery's aunt. Her arms were folded defiantly against her chest, while her close-cropped hair was ruffled, as if she'd just come down out of a flight check.

Which, Exton thought, was probably what had happened. Aunt Patty loved tinkering with the ships in the hangar when she had the chance, the very opposite of her sister in skills and interest. Emery and Exton's mother, Evelyn, was always more likely to be found in the fields or working in her private gardens.

"St. Cloud was always one to take his word seriously," Patty said. "That's part of the reason Osgood made him his right-hand man. If he makes a promise, there's little that will stand in the way of him fulfilling it."

"Talk to Merra about that," Exton grumbled. "He married someone else after her 'death,' didn't he?"

"She's dead by the States' registers," Patty replied. "You know the URS has a strong position on how to run units and their households. His second wife is little more than his employee."

"Especially since St. Cloud has four charges," Tyler put in. "That's the highest amount of charges a unit can have. In that big of a unit, there would have to be more than one unit overseer."

Back when he had known General St. Cloud as one of his

instructors, Exton had barely realized he had a unit. Other than Merra, St. Cloud had never mentioned his charges. After St. Cloud had killed Exton's father and delivered the *Paradise*, *Perdition*'s former title, to the URS and their space program, Exton had set out to destroy him.

But it had never crossed his mind to examine the St. Cloud family. That was a mistake that caught up with him when Aerie had managed to get herself tangled up in the Memory Tree.

A mistake that turned out to be a miracle, Exton thought ruefully.

Still, he turned his attention to the St. Cloud unit as soon as he'd been able to sit up in the hospital bed in the back of Merra's shuttle. He knew now that Aerie had a sister, Serena, who worked in military medical services, and two twin brothers, who were fighter pilots in their last year of schooling. Merra had "died" close to the time he had taken off in the *Perdition*, which might have explained why he didn't know much about her, or Aerie's stepmother, Phoebe.

"I'm not worried about St. Cloud's unit. I'm more worried about how Merra's talking Exton into blowing up the URS than about the drama surrounding the St. Cloud unit right now," Emery snapped, bringing Exton's attention back to the problems at hand.

Patty raised her eyebrows in surprise. "Well, it would be about time we started fighting more," she said.

"Aunt Patty!" Emery looked at her incredulously. "Are you saying we should attack the URS, too?"

"I know you don't like the thought of it, Emery," Patty said. "But the URS has been asking for it for a long time. The Ecclesia have tried staying, and tried running away. This is the last place on Earth they can run to. And others are starting to wake up and see it. Between that and Exton's smaller attacks, and the other camps of resistance starting to rise up, we're headed for a confrontation whether we like it or not."

"That's no reason to throw the first punch."

"It's better to throw the punch if it's going to knock them

out," Exton said. "Can't we agree on that much, Em?"

Emery sighed.

Moona meowed, as if she was in agreement with Emery's thoughts on the matter.

"The alternative is not going to get us anywhere," Tyler said. "We can wait forever, but you know they're not going to give up their power. They'll be coming for us anyway, considering how many refugees and dissenters we've taken in lately."

"And in the meantime, people suffer," Patty said. "I can't tell you how many of the people here are good folks who got tangled up in the wrong situation. They wanted to be free. That's why they're here, and that's why they will want to help, too."

"But this works," Emery said. "Your leadership and the board of directors are all good at establishing accountability and keeping it."

"Yes," Patty agreed. "We have an advantage in that, and that will hold when we go into battle. We have been here long enough, and we've taken in enough people, that we know how to govern effectively, even if we have to ruffle a few feathers every now and then."

"Merra said that the URS government is tightening controls and regulations," Exton said. "All the power is concentrated to an inner circle."

Patty nodded. "That'll happen after too many calls for censorship," she said. "Too many people have said the wrong things for them to get very far up the power chain."

"So we only need to take out the inner circle, and then subdue the remaining powers," Exton said. "We don't need to burn everything to the ground—just everything that stands in the way of building a better nation."

"We can strengthen the good in the meantime," Tyler added. "Several I know of have already started stepping up to work in different organizations, so they can be ready to help when the time is right, including my sister and our parents."

Exton turned to Emery. "See, Em? We don't need to

destroy the URS to win. They've been destroying themselves for some time now. All we have to do is take out a few of their bigger support beams, and then have a system in place to keep all of the good from falling."

Emery sighed. "I'm not sure that's what Merra wants."

"I know you don't like her much," Tyler said.

"Who here really does?" Emery wrinkled her nose. "She walks around like she's in charge here, even ordering some of our workers around."

"Moving in on your turf, is she?" Exton couldn't help but grin.

Emery shot him a hard look. "It's true I don't like her," she admitted, "but I'm more upset at what she's doing to you, Exton. I know you want Aerie back, and she's using that to get what she wants."

"Aerie's gone for now," Exton said quietly. "I told you, St. Cloud injected her with Memory Serum. She's not going to remember me. Or any of us. Any plan we have to get her back will have to come after we free the rest of the world."

"So all you really want is revenge," Emery said.

"Revenge is all I have, as usual," Exton shot back. "It's fitting."

"Personal revenge is one thing," Emery said. "Going to war in revenge is thoughtless and reckless, especially when we are called to protect."

"The *Perdition* has been a shield, a refuge for many," Patty said. "Petra was started because of this. But if we want to make the world a better place, it is time to be a sword. How many more people will the URS put through their labor programs, valuing them only as workers? How many more will be like this Aerie, that suffer for their dissent?"

Emery said nothing, while Exton clenched his fists.

"You know, Aerie might be able to break through it yet," Tyler said softly. "It's not a high chance, but it's still there. And you've got to believe it's possible."

Exton shook his head. "The stats you're thinking of are for the Reeducation Program in the URS," he said. "This is different."

"Surely not much different though," Patty said. "The URS is not terribly creative. There's no need to have variety when variety can easily become competition."

"We're all very aware of how the URS views competition," Exton murmured.

Emery reached out and took his hand. "Exton … "

He pulled back from her grasp, reaching down to pet Moona again. He was grateful for the cat, and the distraction she provided. "If we're going to try to fight them," he said, changing the subject, "I'll need to talk to Dennis and Don about this. I'll need to make it clear the Ecclesia does not need to join me in our offensives."

Emery sighed. "I guess I'm overruled in this," she said. "If this is what you really want."

"Even if you weren't overruled by us, you would be by the URS itself," Patty said. "Less than two months ago, Kamalo came here, right out of New Hope's Comms Sec department. He knows they've been ramping up their comm tech, likely for war."

Exton paused. *Aerie was supposed to work in the Comms Sec,* he recalled. *Are they putting her in danger now?*

Emery sniffed.

"This isn't what I would choose if there were better options," Exton told her. "But it's the only way to protect what we have, while bringing a new vision to the people—a world where freedom will be respected, and the responsibilities with it will be understood and supported."

"I'll still want to help you, too."

"I'll need people to analyze the incoming intelligence," Exton told her. "I'll have you help with that. Sorting through information should be easy enough for you and the baby."

"Don't use my baby as an excuse to shuffle me to the sidelines," Emery said.

"I'm not doing that at all," he insisted. "That will keep you in the central hub of everything. You'll be in constant communication and you'll be able to protect and inform us."

Emery sighed. "Sorry. I should've known better than to think you would be able to get rid of me."

"After all these years, it's still an impossible feat, I assure you." He came over beside her and gave her a hug.

"Go on," Emery said, shooing him away. "Go start getting everyone ready. If we're going to take the war to the URS, let's make sure it's a good one."

"A real knockout," Patty said with a smirk. "As always, you have my support, Exton. I'll see to strengthening up our defenses. If the *Perdition* can help cover us, we should be able to hold off any retaliatory attack from St. Cloud."

"And I'll help, too," Tyler offered. "This is a moral issue. Good people have to stand up and do something. War is messy, but if we can strategize and pool our resources, we can mess up only what needs messed up."

"And in the meantime, we can work to get Aerie back," Emery said, her optimism returning briefly. "No matter what you've told yourself, Exton, I know you believe there's hope."

"Mew."

Humbled, Exton felt a rush of pride and love as he looked at the people (and the cat) beside him. He had been in many places alone, but he knew that he'd never really been alone. "Thank you."

"You're welcome," Emery replied. "Now, seriously, go. We'll need to finalize our plans before we actually do something."

Exton nodded and hurried out. While he was not happy about the risk involved for others, there was a surge of satisfaction inside of him at the thought of beating the URS, and St. Cloud, at their own game.

Exton slowed his steps as he glanced out the window. In the pool of moonlight across the nearby water, he saw the reflection of the Memory Tree. He remembered how it felt, pressing his fingers against its brittle bark as he silently vowed to let it live and flourish as his heart never would.

He had no peace earlier, and now he only had it at the

prospect of ridding the world of the rest of its peace.

Aerie had called him a monster when she first met him. Maybe she was right all along.

♦5♦

Aerie looked out at the night sky projections from the top of her unit housing. She was still huddled up in the jacket she'd been given at the hospital. It was the only comfort she had that night.

She saw the projection of the moon on the underground sky of New Hope and instantly bristled.

That's not what the moon looks like.

The memories inside of her from before her injury pounded themselves into her mind's eye, even as the pain accompanied it. There was a picture of the moon, so bright and full of light, with its pockmarked face calling out in perpetual delight.

Or maybe agony, now that she thought of it.

Another memory came to the surface; this one was easier to recall. It was from several weeks ago, not long after the mid-quarter break.

The moon was there, in her mind, only much smaller, though somehow brighter. She was watching it from the top of her tree, the Memory Tree, after she'd sneaked away from one of her class trips to journey to the city's surface.

"Moona," she murmured, and she suddenly wondered what had become of her kitten. *Was she still up there, curling up in the branches of the Memory Tree?*

She sighed as the pain in her head once more increased, and the hole in her heart seemed more pronounced than ever.

"Hey."

Aerie glanced over to see Brock come up onto the roof beside her. "Hey," she murmured. She was not up for another attempt at conversation. All throughout dinner, it had been hard enough to smile through all the snips and jokes at her expense from her siblings, and Serena's relentless flirting with Brock was no better.

Even when the General came and stepped in, Aerie somehow felt more awful. Claire's earlier comments about people needing to protect her stirred continuously inside her mind.

"Are you okay?" Brock asked. "I was just talking to the General, and I noticed you were gone. He said you might be out here."

"I'm okay," Aerie said. She shrugged her shoulders. "Just another headache."

"Oh." He scooted closer to her. "I'm sorry."

Aerie was surprised. "No one in the URS apologizes."

He grinned. "Well, sometimes you have to," he said. "It's just not generally a good thing. In this case, though, I am genuinely sorry you're not feeling well."

"Thanks." Aerie patted his hand.

"Are you cold?" Brock asked. He put his arm around her shoulders. "Here, let me help you warm up."

"No," Aerie said, drawing back from him.

"What's wrong? Are you afraid of me?" Brock asked. His tone was hard, and Aerie knew he was struggling not to let his emotions get the better of him.

"No," Aerie replied. "I'm not."

"Then what's wrong?" he asked. "Before we graduated, you were always willing to talk to me. Ever since I got accepted into the military and you didn't, I feel like there's this barrier between us. I mean, I know you're probably jealous, but I still want you to come with me to the Military Academy Ball."

"I'm not afraid of you," Aerie grumbled. "I'm angry at you."

"What?" He was clearly upset. "Why are you mad at me? I haven't done anything wrong. It's not my fault that I got into the military and you didn't. I told you that it would've been better if you'd just followed instructions and did the report you were assigned."

Aerie felt her mind slosh around inside as she tried to keep up with his pace. There were so many things she wanted to address about how wrong he was.

"Okay, first, let me start with this. I just want to be left alone for a little while, okay?" Aerie said. "Since I've been back, everything seems to move so slowly, and so quickly. I mean, I forgot it was my birthday!"

"You're angry at me for wanting to spend time with you?" Brock asked.

"You're just too persistent about it," Aerie told him. She sighed. He'd always been her friend. Before her injury, she knew she'd liked him. It was just … now, she didn't know what, but she just knew something about her life was missing. Something more than just two or three weeks.

She hugged herself into the jacket, and, swamped by the scent of it, she also knew something wasn't just missing. Something was *wrong*—seriously and sinisterly wrong.

"Okay," Brock said. "I'll try to give you some more space."

"Thank you," Aerie muttered.

"I hope you feel better soon," he said. "If there's something I can do to help, please let me know, alright?"

"Alright," she said. Aerie fully expected him to leave at that, so she was surprised when he just relaxed and looked up at the fake moon with her.

A few moments passed between them in silence, and Aerie allowed herself to relax a little bit, too.

She tensed up immediately when Brock began to talk again.

"You know, I'm glad you told me that I've been too pushy lately," Brock said. He gave her a sheepish smile, which, on him, looked distinctively out of character. "I was sort of going to ask you if you wanted to start seeing each other more."

She frowned at him.

"I guess that's a bad idea," he said, immediately retreating back into silence.

"We already do spend time together," Aerie told him.

"I meant … I meant in a different way." Brock looked over at her. "I wanted to see if you would agree to apply for cohabitation."

"With you?" Aerie's cheeks flushed over. Cohabitation was usually the first major step in getting a private unit. Cohabiters could apply for a small apartment where they would live together for a contracted amount of time, and, at the end of it, if they wanted to continue the relationship, they could apply for a full union. From there, children—charges—were either planned or adopted in order to create a unit.

"Of course, with me." Brock's tone was more straggled as he said, "I've known you for a long time, and I think we would be good together. I know you've been injured lately and things feel a little strange, but they won't always be like that."

"Hopefully."

Brock hesitated. "Well, I've been waiting to ask you for a long time. I know the General has high standards for who is interested in you."

Aerie let that sink in as Brock waited. *I wonder why the General doesn't seem to have the same sense of responsibility when it comes to Serena and my brothers?*

"I've never noticed it," Aerie admitted. "He always seems to be … not here."

"He's here now," Brock pointed out. "Which is why I know our time is limited."

Aerie grinned. "Did he really give you a time limit?"

"More or less." He smiled back at her. "But he knows you're a full citizen now. You can make your own decisions."

"Not the important ones," Aerie said, before she could stop herself.

Brock flinched, and she instantly regretted it.

"I didn't mean you," she amended quickly. "I just had another bad day at work. I'd love to transfer."

"You can always reapply for the military next year," he said. "Or you can go to university. I think you'd like that better."

"You mean *you* would like it better if I went on to higher learning, don't you?" Aerie teased.

"You'd be safer," Brock said, giving her a sheepish grin.

"Dictator Osgood has told me that MENACE is once more on the move. He's been ordering more troops to attack some of the places where resistance camps have managed to get a foothold. They've been getting bolder lately."

"That doesn't sound good for you."

He shook his head. "I wouldn't worry about it. I'm stationed here, where they have all the latest advancements in flight tech and piloting available. They want to keep me here. I'm almost disappointed by it, to be honest."

"You want to fight MENACE?"

"Of course. They are a disease on this earth," Brock insisted, his tone edged with bitterness. "They've caused all sorts of problems for people, breaking up units and devastating those who are left behind. And did you know that they support religion? It's disgusting. How could they support something that's utterly harmful to the world? It's only right that they get their due."

Aerie was surprised by how personal his speech seemed to be. She had to wonder if MENACE had done something specific to Brock or his unit. He seemed too angry to simply want to defeat them for personal glory.

The more she thought about it, the more that theory made sense. She'd let him borrow the books with the General's accounts in them. With the battle details and the analysis of MENACE as a tribal group, they were the perfect source to learn about the nation's enemy.

She watched as he ran a hand through his short brown hair and grumbled, clearly struggling to get his thoughts back under control.

Time to change the subject, Aerie decided. "So, you think I would be good at university?"

"Absolutely," Brock said, clearly relieved at the new direction of the conversation. "I know you aced your environmental education. I heard General Lowell talking about your final presentation the other day."

"My final presentation?" Aerie was surprised to see she'd forgotten about that as well. She couldn't remember the presentation itself, but she was able to remember the research.

That was how I found Moona, she recalled. The kitten had been aboveground, scrounging around for food, when Aerie found her. She smiled, thinking of her dirty face.

"Yeah, I think you really impressed them. Master Harrick even sealed the presentation. She said she would put it through to the university counsel for further study."

"Really?" Aerie's eyes lit up. "Maybe I should go back to school after all."

"You would have access to a lot more resources," Brock said.

"I'll have to think about it some more."

"Well, you would have to finish up your year of service in Comms Sec. And I would want to be finished up with my basic training before we did anything."

"We?"

"Yeah," Brock said. "To apply for our own unit."

"Brock—" Aerie felt discomfort choke her once more.

"Come on, Aerie. I know you. I know you would be happy going back to school and working through the research sector. I can make you happy. Who else knows you so well?" Brock took her hand gently. "We could make a good unit."

Aerie felt her body stiffen. "I don't want a unit," she said slowly. "I want a family."

"It's the same thing," Brock said, after he swallowed his surprise.

"No, it's not." Aerie shook her head. "If it was the same, we could call it 'family,' without fear."

"Well, the term is limited."

"I would argue the term 'unit,' is far more limited." She glanced down at Brock. He was afraid, she realized. He didn't want the URS to change. He was well on his way to a good position within the system, and he didn't want to do anything that would jeopardize that.

On some level, she felt sorry for him. On the upside, she knew how to handle this discussion now.

"Something is wrong here, Brock," she said. "As my comrade, as my friend, I am telling you something is wrong." She pulled her hand out of his and pressed it to her forehead.

"You're just a little confused," Brock said. "Getting a concussion and going into a coma for a few weeks can have that effect."

"It's more than that, Brock." She was just about to tell some of what she'd found earlier when he continued.

"I know you're not feeling at your best, but we have always been close. You can move in with me and maybe that will help you move on from what happened."

Aerie was suddenly very tired of their conversation.

"Move on?" She shook her head. "I don't want to move on. I want to go back, if anything!"

"Go back to where?" Brock asked, his exasperation creeping into his tone. "The hospital?"

"Don't you think living here is just weird, Brock? Like something is missing? That there's something greater out there and we just can't see it or say it or ask about it for some reason?"

"No." His answer was as quick as it was blunt.

"Well, you're lucky then," Aerie said, disappointed. "I look around and see how there are so few people who seem present. They have a job to do."

"We need to have a job to do, to survive. And it's our orders."

"Anyone can follow orders," Aerie argued. "Don't you see? Jobs are supposed to be secondary. Caring for others is supposed to be primary. Or at least, don't you think so?"

"Well, I would care for you if you let me," Brock said. "I did care for you. I visited you in the hospital, remember?"

"Do you love me?" Aerie asked, as she was suddenly caught off guard.

He blushed. "Love is a barbaric response to emotion stimuli," he said, which only made her head ache more. "But I will take care of you. I'll help you do your best for the state, so we can ensure survival."

"Survival. Ha." Aerie stood up and stepped away. "What's the point of living if you're just going to survive?"

"Once you're dead, you don't matter."

"Only if my life doesn't matter," Aerie argued back, surprised at herself. *Do I really think these things?*

"I know you're still not completely well," Brock said, his voice hardened, "but you're starting to sound like a defector."

"Well, maybe I am one," she whispered. There was a small thrill about openly saying it.

"What would the General say about that?"

Aerie thought about it. Now that she knew she had been lied to about her injuries, the General's concern was reframed in her mind. Rather than seeing it as a concerned father looking in on his daughter, Aerie now saw it more like a warden checking in on his prisoner. "He'd probably agree. I'm treated like a defector, and by my own father, too."

"General St. Cloud is concerned for your health. Which he should be, if these are the thoughts you're thinking."

"What happens to defectors?" Aerie asked, suddenly intrigued at the thought. "You're in the military now. Tell me."

"Reeducation and reassignment," Brock said, clearly frustrated by the change in subject as well as the turn of the conversation. "There are not a lot of people who fail reeducation."

"What happens to them?" Aerie asked, thinking of the Reeducation Center. It was located near the med center, and for all the time she had been living in New Hope, she had only ever seen a few people go in and out.

"I don't know, exactly," Brock said. "It's classified, and it can vary depending on the subject in question."

"I wonder if I can find out," Aerie said, more to herself than to Brock.

"I don't know why you care so much."

"Come on, Brock," Aerie said. "Don't you want to do something greater than just survive?"

"Well, I just spent the evening trying to, but you don't

want to accept my offer," he shot back, making her flinch.

He got up and brushed past her, heading for the door. "I have to go now. If you really believe something is wrong here, Aerie, I can't help you. If anything, I believe that if something is wrong, it's only because you're making it that way."

He turned and gave her a salute, properly, and then momentarily faltered. "Here," he said, reaching into his pocket. "I brought a gift for you. I thought it might help you remember some."

He pushed the small item into Aerie's hand and then walked away.

Aerie looked down the crisp envelope in her hand. While she was still upset about Brock, she couldn't blame him for leaving.

I guess I wasn't being very nice, Aerie thought, suddenly regretting how much strain she was putting on Brock. After all, she didn't know for sure if he had lied to her. It didn't seem like he knew the truth about her injuries.

And if he really did care about her, it couldn't have been easy for him to hear her disparage the URS. He had always been good about following the rules and living up to the expectations placed on him. That was part of the reason she had been comfortable liking him in the beginning.

She glanced down at the envelope in her hand. Curious, she peeled it open and pulled out the small item inside.

It was a photo slide of her, with Brock and some of their peers from graduation. Aerie glanced at her face in the photo and sighed. She didn't have to recall the pain of all the pins in her hair to know she'd been uncomfortable at the ceremony.

Her eyes moved over to Brock, and she was surprised to see a gentle look on his face as he looked at her. Another stab of guilt went through her. She resolved to apologize to Brock in the morning as she tucked the slide into her jacket pocket.

"Aeris."

Aerie jolted as the General appeared in the door. "Yes, sir?"

"It's late. You'd better go inside. I heard from Director Anand today. You have an early start at work tomorrow."

Aerie nodded, trying to hide her anger. She didn't know enough to confront her father over the issue of his lies, and with the long day at work, the disappointing dinner, and her string of headaches, all she wanted to do was go to bed. "I'll be down soon," she promised, keeping her voice level.

"Good." He paused for a moment. "Did Brock ask you anything important?"

Aerie dug her hands into her pockets and looked away.

"You did respond, did you?" The vexation in his voice was unmistakable. "When he asked you to cohabitate?"

"No," Aerie said. "I … I need time to think about it."

"It would be good for you to say yes."

"Why?" Aerie snapped. "So I can leave you and this unit forever? So you'll never have to worry about me again?"

"I'll always worry about you," the General said, surprising her. "But Brock is a good man, and a good solider. He can protect you. He's well-liked by the board of generals, and even Dictator Osgood has spoken well of him."

"Good to know." Aerie scowled.

He crossed his arms. "I know that's not what *you* want, but he would be good for you."

She was tempted to ask if he'd handpicked Brock himself, considering how Brock mentioned the General had requirements. "And it would be good for you, as well, if I said yes?" Aerie asked. "I'd hate to make you look bad before the Dictator."

"You've already made yourself look bad," the General told her, his voice impatient and brusque. "You've been injured in a very routine way. You've been unable to focus on your work. From the reports I've read, I know you're not taking all the doctor's advice. Believe me, you've done plenty to disappoint your leaders. Entering into a cohabitation agreement with Brock Rearden would be a step in the right direction."

Aerie felt her shoulders slump just slightly at her father's words. But she also felt resolve harden inside of her.

"You just don't understand, Aerie," he said with a sigh, before he turned and headed back down the stairs. The General paused for a moment, before he glanced back at her. "I would worry less for you and more for the man you marry, should you accept an offer."

For a moment, Aerie almost believed he was kidding with her. Before she could say anything else, he turned and left her alone. Again.

Aerie felt another twinge of pain as she pulled her jacket around herself more tightly. The comfort it had given her earlier betrayed her, making her long for something she couldn't name and a place she couldn't remember.

♦6♦

Exton had never enjoyed meeting with the Ecclesia, especially when he knew he was going to oppose their position directly. That was why he'd prepared for the worst when it came to meeting with the leaders to tell them about his plans.

With Merra at his side, and Aunt Patty at his back, he fully expected the meeting to drag on for hours as disappointments, disagreements, and endless caveats and stipulations were debated.

So he was surprised, and somewhat suspicious, when Dennis, Reverend Thorne, one of the most persistent, perpetual thorns in his side, merely called for a majority vote and pushed it through.

Out of the nine leaders of the Ecclesia, six voted to approve his decision.

"Well, Exton," Reverend Thorne said, "there you go."

"You really approve of us going to war?" Exton asked, stunned by the ease of the result.

"We have approved that *you* go to war," Reverend Thorne said. "You have that right, and I suspect you well know it."

"Why vote on it then?"

"We feel, on some level, we must insert our voice into this situation," Brother Don, Dennis' brother, said. "This is a precarious situation, and we must not back down from clarifying our role."

Yes, and you wouldn't feel right unless you were given adequate time to get all your opinions out.

Sister Katalina, one of the younger leaders, also spoke up. "It is not our wish to discourage you, Exton," she said. "We know that war is unpleasant and counterintuitive to the mission of the Ecclesia, but we also know it is a reality we cannot escape, especially in a fallen world. If it must be done, let it be done well, and honorably."

"That sums up the quandary nicely," Exton murmured.

She ignored him, but gave him a prudent look. "We recognize that you have provided a voice for the rebels and dissenters, just as you have provided the Ecclesia a home on your starship, as well as accommodations here at Petra."

"We suffer no illusions. We know we are the greater beneficiary of our relationship," Reverend Thorne said. "And we know that we do not influence your decisions in a great way."

Patty stepped forward. "We welcome the opportunity to serve Silas' cause. We are also grateful for the help we have received from the Ecclesia."

Exton was momentarily distracted at hearing his father's name. For a moment, he longed for the days of his childhood, where life seemed easier and his father's friends seemed more like his family.

But the moment passed, and Exton knew there was no room for heady nostalgia when it came to repairing the world.

"We do not wish to strain our partnership," another leader, Brother Amos, said, his voice gravelly and grim. "We see great opportunity in providing service to those who have found their way to Petra, even if they are not members of the Ecclesia. It is our way of strengthening ourselves as well as honoring our commitment to the Creator."

"But?" Exton asked.

"But nothing," Reverend Thorne told him. "Individually, we stand with you. The URS has silenced us and outlawed us, and we are welcome to support you as much as we see fit, individually."

"So this is not a group endorsement," Exton said, as he realized what was going on.

"We wish to maintain a strong presence, particularly serving as medics and caretakers. We will continue to help supervise the harvest and Petra's protection," Don said. "But the Ecclesia is not a military force, and we ask that you recognize we may differ from person to person on how to support you, even if we withhold support."

"I can grant you that," Exton said. "That's how it has

always been on the *Perdition.*"

"We know," Reverend Thorne said. "But war is not just a strain on the body and mind. We ask that you continue to honor our request, to keep this in mind as the war continues on." He held his palms out. "There will be times when you cannot order us to act. You may ask, of course, but we may say no. And you might get a different answer, depending on who you ask."

Exton nodded. "I understand."

"The Ecclesia is like a body," Sister Katalina said. "We are connected by physical means, but no matter how much you want it to, an ear will not see and a hand will not hear. But there will likely be instances where you will ask of the hand to reach out and take something, and you will only get silence."

"I understand," Exton repeated, starting to get frustrated. They were treating him like a child. "Thank you for your—"

"We understand," Merra said, stepping in front of him. "We respect the rule of individual conscience. We do ask for the right to change your mind when we disagree. Often in life, and especially in wartime, we must make difficult choices."

Reverend Thorne considered her words. "I suppose there are instances that are unique and deserve deeper reflection." He looked to the other members, most of whom nodded in return.

Exton noticed that among the curt nods, there were several that held wary glances as they looked at Merra.

Merra held a unique reputation among the Ecclesia; she'd been at one of their bigger settlements for several years, helping out and quietly assembling a fighter squad. She was respected, but Exton began to wonder if she was more feared than admired.

He could understand their hesitancy when it came to working with someone as shrewd as Merra. They didn't want to be taken advantage of.

It was after several more rounds of the usual objections

that the meeting was finally adjourned, and Exton walked out of the room to find Emery pacing the hallway.

"What's wrong?" he asked.

"Nothing." She narrowed her gaze as she watched the others, including Merra and Reverend Thorne, head out of the small council room. "I wanted to see how the meeting turned out."

"Business as usual," he assured her. "I got my way, and it took twice as long as it needed to."

"But half the time it usually takes."

"The only bright side to this, I realize."

"Look," Emery said, "I know you want to fight St. Cloud. I know the war has escalated. But do you know you're doing the right thing, Exton?"

"Not entirely," he admitted quietly. "But I will never be a hundred percent sure about something like this. There are too many factors involved for it to go as planned."

"This reminds me of how things were during the first year on *Perdition*," Emery said. "I know you had a plan, but you didn't follow through."

Exton nodded. After finding out the *Perdition* was carrying MENACE fighters, Exton had proof that the URS was using their old enemy as a way to justify taking over other countries and their resources. He had initially wanted to bomb New Hope in revenge for his father's death. After seeing the full scale of the treachery of the URS, he paused.

At least he paused long enough to find a way to salvage what little good was left in the world.

Now, he thought, it was time to go after what was bad.

"I'm glad I didn't follow through in that case," Exton said. "Everything turned out for the better that we didn't use the nukes to bomb the URS then."

"The Ark is still on the ship," Emery reminded him. "But I hope you'll think long and hard before you get to that point."

"I hope so, too."

"I was almost hoping the Ecclesia would say something

to change your mind."

"That's never managed stop me before."

She crossed her arms. "I figured they wouldn't be able to do that," she huffed. "I'm familiar with their positions and yours enough to know it was a foolish gamble."

"If you're familiar with their stances," Merra said as she came between them, "then you know we've been given a great gift, even if we're going to have to treat it with kid gloves."

Emery narrowed her eyes. "What do you mean?"

"I was fully expecting the Ecclesia to rebuke our stance, frankly," Merra said. "They've never been keen on war, especially given their history with it."

"The fact that they didn't makes you happy?"

"Of course." She met Emery's gaze without a qualm. "They'll be more than happy to help where they can, but they can't fully endorse it. That's good. It'll keep their influence down, for one thing, and it'll give us an advantage, with all their medical resources and their information channels."

"From the sound of it, you've had this experience before," Exton said. "Is that how you managed to fake your death and escape St. Cloud?"

Merra shot him an angry look for the first time. But she blinked, and it disappeared instantly. Despite her quickness, Exton knew he'd scored a point against her.

"Well," she said with a forced smile, "I guess you could say that. But I was thinking more along the lines of how I established my fighter squadron at Chaya, and at several of the other resistance-led city-states I've been to."

"I guess that means you have a target in mind already?" Emery asked. "Since you have some experience with this."

"Of course."

"What?" Exton rounded on her. "You have a plan?"

"I always have a plan," Merra told him. "And contingency ones, too, so shut your mouth and stop looking so surprised. It's not an attractive look, especially since you're now officially on the offensive. Now, we have to get ready for our first strike. We'll be ready to leave by the end of the week."

"We just got started!"

She arched a brow. "So? We can handle a small strike together, Exton. Consider it a training exercise in teamwork."

"We just got the approval from the Ecclesia," Exton said. "We'll have to do some scouting for volunteers and fighters and—"

"Your aunt and I have a list of suggestions for leadership," Merra replied. "We've already regulated who needs to stay at Petra to keep its level of production steady and lend support in case of a retaliatory strike—"

"You've started recruiting people already?" Exton was bewildered. He'd only just agreed to this a day ago, and already he had forces being mobilized. Without his supervision, no less.

His distrust of Merra deepened as her smile widened.

"No," Merra said. "We've been scouting. We don't recruit until the people in question agree to come with us. Which they are free to refuse," she added, seeing Emery's angry expression.

"If you're scouting, you have a plan. And a target."

"I already told you I did."

"Where, then?" Exton asked.

Merra shifted her weight and put her hands on her hips determinedly. "We strike at Chaya first."

"Chaya?" Exton repeated. "Why? I thought you had a force there."

"I do," Merra said. "But we've been attacked, recently, and our water was poisoned with a new bacterium. Several were too weak to take on the URS without aid."

"What happened?" Emery asked. "We didn't hear about this."

Patty came up behind them. "The URS has been using new technology to communicate," she said. "Kamalo, one of our newer refugees, says they have perfected something called NETech, and they're using it in more of their flight programs now."

"Aerie told me about NETech," Exton recalled. "She saw it in the MENACE ships we have on the *Perdition*."

"It's been around for a while. It was largely experimental." Merra frowned. "If that's the case, I can see why we didn't pick it up on our frequencies."

"What is it?" Emery asked.

"NETech is the shorthand name of Neuro-Enzyme Transmission. It's a special kind of technology that's supposed to work similar to plant synapses," Merra said.

"Aerie told me that, too. It's a way to translate electrical impulses, or frequencies, into enzyme catalysts. The pilot of a ship would receive it, his mind would interpret the message instantly, and he would know what to do."

"No more verbal orders, then," Emery said. "Nothing would be needed to communicate over the airwaves."

"Exactly," Merra said. "So you can understand, how in a water shortage, we were too distracted to realize the extent of what was going on when Chaya was retaken."

Patty nodded. "I'll have Kamalo come and brief you on their new tech, Exton," she said. "He'll be able to tell you all about it."

"Good." Exton sighed silently to himself. War was a consuming path.

He turned to Merra. "How small of a strike force will you need?"

"Not too many. Ten, at the most. We have to free my forces at Chaya before we can get the aid to the prisoners there," Merra said. "There were a lot of children there."

"Children?" Emery glanced at Exton, more worry on her face.

He watched as her hand moved down to her belly, where her own child was growing inside of her.

"War is not easy on anyone," Merra said grimly. "Especially children. We will need to hurry."

"Agreed," Exton said, stepping in front of Emery. He didn't like the way Merra was looking at Emery. It was one thing to trample all over his authority and influence his decisions; it was another to try to manipulate Emery's.

Merra's eyes gleamed. "This is already turning out better than I could've hoped," she said, her voice clearly anticipating the upcoming clash.

Exton glared at her. "There's no need to be excited about it," he told her, his tone harder than he expected it to be.

"You're a new player in this game, Exton. But I'm not. I know what I want, and I am not afraid to take it, especially now that I have the resources to do so," Merra replied.

"I can understand vengeance, Merra."

"It's not vengeance we have in common, believe it or not." She gave him a cryptic smile and then said, "I am more concerned with what makes us different anyway."

"What would that be?"

"You don't know how far you're willing to go get what you want. I know that perfectly." She smiled, her bright eyes making her seem younger and more bubbly than before. "Now, go and get your task force assembled. I'll pass along the plan of attack. When it comes time, I'll contact my forces and get them ready to strike once you give the signal."

Exton watched as she left, struggling to hold his temper. He wouldn't miss her, he decided.

"Between Merra and St. Cloud, you'd almost think Aerie was adopted," Emery said.

Despite everything, Exton was surprised to hear himself laugh. "That's true."

"We still have to hurry though. Merra's right about that, especially if there are children in danger," Emery said. She turned to Patty. "Take me to the hangar where our ships are. I'll start an inspection so we can leave ASAP. Maybe Patty and some of her people here can get care packages together for the kids."

"Call up Greer for me, too," Exton called after them as Patty led Emery down the hall. "She's one of the best analysts we have. She'll be able to get the MENACE fighters ready. Those are our best bet for attacking."

Exton rubbed at the back of his head as he stood in the

hallway, watching his friends and allies hurry off. The bump, where St. Cloud had bludgeoned him, was finally vanishing. Only a little lump remained.

"Did the meeting go as you expected?" Reverend Thorne's voice was soft and unexpected as he sauntered up beside him, but it still managed to make Exton feel guilty.

"About," he said instead, hoping his demeanor would show the reverend that he was capable of standing up to him.

"Good." Reverend Thorne nodded. "I will leave you to it and attend to my own duties."

"What're your duties?" Exton asked. "I didn't ask anything of you yet."

"I have to go and pray," Reverend Thorne said. "There is a great deal to pray about here."

After disagreeing with his father's old friend and mentor for so long, Exton felt a strange mix of emotions as he watched him walk away. It was never easy finding common ground with people when they insisted on making his life more difficult.

♦7♦

"But Director Anand," Aerie said, clasping her hands together and putting on her best humble beggar face, "I *really* have an appointment today. I was mistaken before, but today I really do have to go to the med center—"

"We have to finish up the NETech training today, Comrade—"

"I already know about it," Aerie insisted. "*I* finished my training with it."

"You finished your training with it, but it was far from perfect."

"I did better than anyone else."

"You need to work on the basics still," Anand argued, his tan face beginning to flush over with an angry red. "It is inconceivable you did as well as you did on the NETech training when your comms are regularly reported for failures or your incompetency."

Aerie blushed, but she pushed it back. She knew that she did any number of things to slow down the system. She just didn't care enough to try anymore.

"But, sir, I have to leave. I have my physical—"

"Stop." Anand frowned at her, his tan face wrinkled in displeasure. "You have been lying to get out of working late all week, Comrade St. Cloud."

"I'm not lying now," Aerie insisted, even though she knew he had a point. She had lied to him. At this point, she could only hope to avoid that particularly grueling conversation.

The good news, Aerie thought, was she had plenty of practice this week avoiding conversations. She had managed to sidestep Brock more than once, and, while she had never been particularly chatty with Serena or her brothers, she had taken on a new project to divert their attentions.

They thought she was going down to the rec center to swim so she could work on her injured shoulder. It was a nice cover, and they all believed her.

And why wouldn't they? From what Aerie could tell, all of them believed the story that she'd fallen from the ropes course. No one knew she'd gotten shot, and no one suspected she thought otherwise.

"Comrade St. Cloud," Anand said, "you cannot expect me to believe you after all the—"

"You can't expect me to work my hardest if I'm not feeling my best," Aerie interrupted. "I've been trying to work with my physical therapist all week, getting in extra hours, just so I can do a better job."

"I also find that hard to believe."

"I *need* to go," Aerie insisted. "I can bring in a note from my doctor tomorrow, if you'd like, but I absolutely need to go."

Anand hesitated, and Aerie glanced worriedly at the clock.

She rejoiced a second later when he sighed. She knew that sigh, even though she'd only been working for two weeks now.

"Fine. But this is the last time, do you hear me?"

"Oh, thank you!" Aerie bowed, saluting him formally as she grabbed her jacket off the back of her chair.

"Wait," Anand called. "I'm not finished. You will have to come early tomorrow to make up for today. The whole department has to have full mastery of the NETech by the end of next month."

"Why?" Aerie asked. "Why is it suddenly being pushed?"

She recalled some of the lectures she'd attended on it with Master Harrick and her classmates only a few months ago. It seemed strange that the URS was determined to roll it out so quickly. They usually took years to develop and test new equipment.

"That is not any of your business," Anand told her in his usual, disappointed tone. "You need to be here tomorrow at 400 hours, Comrade."

Aerie faltered as the excitement rushed out of her. *Great. Just great.*

Anand continued, "You owe a debt to the state for all the things that it has given you over the years. It is only fair."

"Alright," Aerie agreed, trying not to sound completely defeated as she left the room. She waved good-bye to Claire, who was still packing up her things.

Claire didn't notice.

Either that, or she doesn't care.

Aerie decided *she* didn't care if Claire responded or not. In the last week, she'd largely ignored or overlooked Aerie's attempts at conversation.

On the bright side, she'd given up on telling Aerie to answer her comms, so Aerie didn't feel quite as pressured if she slumped down in her chair and took a break several times an hour.

She bounded down the stairs of Comms Sec, and then she headed off toward the med center. Aerie grinned to herself when she was sure no one was looking.

She had an appointment alright—just not one with her doctor. Aerie had "scheduled" an appointment with herself, to go and look for Meredith.

Aerie knew her only remaining clue to finding the truth was to find the girl who had led her to the hospital.

Every day after work for the past several days, when she was able to get out of it, she'd taken care to find a place to watch the med center. She was lucky to find an old library, where she would go and pretend to read for several hours before she had to go home for the night, all while keeping an eye out for the girl who called herself Meredith.

Aerie was surprised, and disappointed, she hadn't seen Meredith around.

She tried to come at the time when Meredith had come for her before, thinking it wasn't too much to hope that she would go out for lunch, or even take on an extra assignment to go and fetch someone else.

If she worked at the med center at all.

"Stupid! Stupid, stupid, stupid," she muttered to herself. *Why hadn't I thought of that before? If Meredith had only been sent to find me, it's possible she was only used to come and get me.*

Aerie sighed as her stomach rumbled.

Speaking of a lunch break, she thought. Anand was a raging beast at her today, making her work through lunch, after he discovered—by pure coincidence—that she hadn't gone to her physical therapist's office yesterday. One of his unit members saw her at the library.

Which, she thought, was probably being watched now. Anand and her father made no secret that they were in contact.

She steered away from the library at the last moment. Aerie was about to head into the med center to pretend she had a real appointment, when she saw her.

Meredith.

Aerie squinted. From where she was, she could see Meredith—or a girl who looked like her—as she hurried down the street. She was still wearing her medical assistant robes, by the look of it; it was hard to tell completely, because she was wearing a large coat overtop, one of the ones that were more appropriate for when the winter would settle in.

Aerie didn't hesitate. She took off after her.

"Meredith," she called, and the girl faltered enough that Aerie was sure she heard her.

That was why, when she sped up, Aerie only felt the fury she knew she reserved for the worst sorts of people.

She knew I was calling her! Why is she trying to lose me? Aerie wondered as she ran, struggling to keep Meredith in sight as she wove her way through the crowds.

"Come back," Aerie called.

When others started looking at her, Aerie stopped calling and slowed down a little. She didn't need *another* source for the General to use to spy on her.

It was only when Meredith disappeared down an alleyway that Aerie let out a loud groan. "Ugh! This is so unfair."

She glanced down at the ground. Lying at her feet was a small roll of bandages, the kind that they used in the hospital to treat wounds.

Did she drop this? Aerie frowned.

In the end, she pocketed the bandages in her own jacket and turned around, looking to see where she was. Aerie hadn't paid too much attention to where she was going while she was trying to keep track of Meredith's movements.

She was relieved to find she was close to her old school, the New Hope Education Center 616.

"I haven't been here … since graduation, I guess," Aerie said, as her head prickled with pain.

A sudden burst of inspiration unleashed itself through her mind.

"I can go and see Master Harrick," she said aloud as she made her way toward the building.

She dreaded school while she was in it. As Aerie passed through the familiar halls, grateful no one thought to pay her any attention, for once, she easily recalled several memories.

Laughing with Brock and some of her other friends, the few that there were, as they headed toward the commissary.

Talking about homework with some of her kinder teachers, the ones that didn't seem to notice when she daydreamed in their class—or at least, the ones who were kind enough to repeat the information.

Waiting. Endlessly waiting for some big moment to come, always on edge because it was never certain that it would come.

Aerie stopped short as she tried to put a name to her silent expectation. *What had I been waiting for?* she wondered. *Probably acceptance. Or love.*

Her heart beat faster at the thought, and she had to grip it to get herself to keep moving. Flashes of a fragment of her memory appeared before her: Eyes colored blue, as hard as ice, full of sadness as much as sureness; they softened, melting into joy as she watched them.

Before she could cry out the unknown name inside of her heart, her head screeched with a new surge of soreness. She whimpered at her discomfort.

"At least it's only my head," she murmured. Aerie was

grateful she'd found the empty hallway where she remembered the broken air duct was. Otherwise, it would have been even more awkward to explain herself to someone else.

After the pain dissipated to a manageable level, Aerie hurriedly climbed up to the surface.

She breathed in the fresh air on top of the underground city. There was a spiked quality to it, one that prickled her nose, as the unfiltered air carried the natural bit of nature; Aerie breathed in deeply, intoxicated as much as she was repelled.

Once she regained her resolve, Aerie didn't stop. She set out for the Memory Tree, a new hope rising within her.

Only to be crushed as she reached the place where the Memory Tree once stood.

There was only a mess of ash and soot around her, all gathering around a huge hole in the ground. Scorch marks clawed through the area; rainwater had puddled into the new scratches on the surface of the earth.

"It's not here," she said.

More images flashed across her mind. Her head burned in pain as she recalled bruising it when she was captured, picked up with the tree.

Aerie slumped over to her knees. "I … I can't believe it."

Thinking of something, she hurriedly stood up. "Moona!" she cried. "Moona! Where are you?"

There was no answer. Aerie noticed that there were no other people here this time. She thought about trying to find one of the homeless or crippled people she would see sometimes, to try to figure out what had happened.

"Moona!" she tried again.

Aerie turned around, taking in the new landscape. There were broken buildings, burned down, and twisted beams of metal laying alongside blackened shards of glass.

She gasped at every turn, and even more at the memories flooding over the tidal wave of pain in her mind.

"I should've known you would find your way here before

too long."

Aerie nearly screamed. She whirled around to find her father glaring at her. "What are you doing here?" she asked.

"What am *I* doing here?" the General asked. "What are *you* doing here? You know coming to the surface is forbidden."

"*You're* up here," Aerie said, knowing her argument was weak.

"I make the rules," he said. "I can bend them as often as you break them."

"I guess Anand told you I was skipping out of work early?" Aerie asked, changing the subject. She didn't want to know if she would be punished for this or not—or what the punishment was likely going to be, since she didn't think there was a way her father *wouldn't* punish her for this.

"Yes," the General said. "Not that you need to know. And it's Director Anand to you. You are a full citizen, but you are still a worker."

"Yes, sorry. So *Director Anand* was the one who told you about me leaving," Aerie corrected herself. She was momentarily sidetracked from the loss of the Memory Tree at the thought of grabbing her boss and folding him up into one of her file boxes. Considering how much he loved his dull, immaculately starched uniforms, she knew that would be enough to send his system into shock.

"He told me that you seemed to be going to physical therapy a whole lot than what could be beneficial for your health." The General eyed her, clearly angry.

"I thought the fresh air would be good," she said.

"Don't lie to me, Aeris," he snapped. "I knew of your visits here before you graduated, as does the URS. That's part of the reason they didn't want you in the military, remember?" He smiled disdainfully. "No, I guess you wouldn't remember."

"I remember that I got shot," Aerie told him, deciding the bluff was well worth the risk just to see the shock and horror on his face.

She was easily disappointed; while he narrowed his eyes, her words had no other apparent effect on him.

Aerie took her chance. "I want to know the truth." Her words were soft, but her heart cried out for the truth, desperate to know it above everything else.

"How much do you remember?"

"I remember I was captured." Aerie glanced back at the Memory Tree.

The General's eyes closed for a long moment, as if he needed to steady himself. When he opened them again, he took a step closer to her and put his hand on her good shoulder. "I can't tell you how proud I am of you," he said. "I am sorry that I underestimated your strength."

It was Aerie's turn to be shocked and horrified. Her father? Apologizing?

Terror swept through her. "What did you do?" she whispered. "You did something, didn't you?"

"Look, Aerie," he said softly. "I know there are likely some empty spaces still. You were captured by MENACE and its allies. You were tortured and shot. If I did anything horrible to you, it was to protect you from the memories of what you went through."

"MENACE captured me … and destroyed the Memory Tree?" Aerie recalled the feeling, knowing it was gone to her.

"Yes. And you can't tell anyone about this. You can't," the General said. "I knew at once what happened when I found your hat at the scene."

"You knew I was up here at the time," Aerie said, putting it all together. "And you got me back."

He nodded somberly. "It took me several days to get a hold of your captor," he said. "When you were returned, you were in pain. So I changed your files. I put you on approved medical leave in the system. Osgood doesn't know what happened."

"No one else knows … no one knows I was captured?" Aerie repeated.

"No. That's why I was hoping the concussion would take

care of your memory, alright? There is nothing good that can come from you remembering. I would be reprimanded at best. You could be taken into the States' custody, where they might make you relive all the awful things you went through."

She wanted to yell that nothing horrible had happened to her. But she wasn't sure. "MENACE does have a horrible human rights record," Aerie remarked, her voice listless against the stillness of her surroundings. She felt lost again.

The General nodded. He dropped down to one knee and looked at her. "You are my daughter," he said quietly. "I would do anything to keep you safe. Anything. That is the truth."

Aerie looked into his eyes and felt the tears well up in her own. She reached out and launched herself into his arms. "I'm sorry I doubted you, Daddy."

"I'm sorry too," he said, squeezing her back.

Aerie allowed herself a long moment to revel in his embrace. Ever since her mother died, she had wondered if her father was lost, too. But in that moment, Aerie wondered if he'd always been there, trapped within his own grief.

He pulled away from her gently. "That's why I need you to stay away from here, Aerie. I need you to stay safe. The URS suspects something; I have Osgood's trust, but I have a lot of enemies. Any man would, in my position. There are some who would do anything to get to me, and that includes using you."

Aerie glanced over his shoulder toward the swirling mass of crusted earth, where her favorite place had once been. "Okay," she said. "I'll stay away from here. And I can play the game when it comes to the URS, too."

"We do not win against death, Aerie. Survival is not a game. And even if it is, it is not one we will ever win against."

♦8♦

"Are you crazy? This is not a game, Exton," Emery said, berating her brother as he packed up his supplies. "You're playing with your life."

Exton ignored her as he grabbed his survival pack off the floor of his room. "I have a duty to the people I'm going to be leading," he told her calmly.

"Yes, you do." Emery grabbed his arm. "You have a duty to stay alive."

"This is the first time in weeks I've felt truly alive," he said. At her scowl, he sighed. "Besides, I won't ask the people that follow orders to do anything less than I'm willing to do. That's a mark of a good leader."

"Did Merra tell you that?"

Exton gave her a rueful smile. "No, actually that was something I learned from St. Cloud."

Emery groaned. "That man is right about all the worst things, isn't he?"

"No." Exton shook his head. "He was wrong to kill our father. I won't change my mind there."

Emery said nothing, but Exton knew she agreed with him.

"I don't know why you're so angry with me," Exton said a moment later as he continued to pack up his things. "Tyler offered to come, too."

"Tyler has always gone running after you," Emery argued. "I figure if I can get you to step down, he'll be more manageable."

"Marriage suits you, I see," he teased.

"As ever, your cynicism suits you."

He stilled and sat down on the cot. Exton took one last look around the room he'd been using while at Petra. There was nothing there of familiarity or comfort. Emery leaned against the door, still simmering.

"Em, I thought all the labs we destroyed and outposts we

dismantled were small game. And they were. But the way I was going about getting vengeance was all over the place. Imagine how we can make the world a better place now that we have a plan and we have hope."

Emery snorted. "I take back my comment about your cynicism," she said dryly. "Now you're sounding like an optimist."

He grinned. "After the past six years in space, don't you think it's about time I found something realistic to hope for?"

"I don't like this."

"You never liked my previous attacks, either."

"I don't trust Merra. She's the one with the plan, from my point of view."

"Neither do I," he told her. "That's all the more reason that I go with her now. I want to see what she's capable of, and why."

"Being married to St. Cloud, I'm sure anything is possible," Emery said.

"You have to give her credit. She managed to leave him."

"She broke Aerie's heart in the process," Emery pointed out. "I can't imagine our mother doing that."

He stood up. "All the more reason to watch her."

Emery only nodded, as worry etched further into her face.

"We'll be okay, Em. If it'll make you feel better, I'll tell Tyler to stay here. Or better yet, I'll tell him to stay and monitor the situation from the *Perdition* when we get up there. That's one place where Merra won't be able to manipulate us." Exton came up and wrapped his arm around her, drawing her close so he could ruffle her hair.

"So you think." But Emery smiled. "I do miss being in space. Isn't that something?"

"Go and rest for a bit," he said. "I know you haven't been sleeping well."

"Can you blame me?" she asked.

"Yes," he replied easily, making her flash him a quick sneer. "But I haven't been sleeping well, either."

Emery met his eyes. "I wanted to tell you, before you leave, that Tyler and I have been working on a plan to get Aerie back."

Exton forced himself to remain calm, even as his heart threatened to choke him. "I know you're worried for me—"

"She was my friend, too, Exton."

"I know, but—"

"But nothing." She sent him a smirk. "If you're going to go to war against my wishes, I can surely do this against yours."

He bristled. "Just don't hope for a miracle," he finally said. "We both know St. Cloud has access to resources we could never dream of."

"Tyler knows that better than most," Emery reminded him. "And he still has hope."

Exton looked away. "I know," he said. "That should prove my point."

"If anything, it proves *my* point. You can't give up hope. God is still a god of miracles."

Exton frowned. God might've brought Aerie to him, but he was still the one who took her away, too.

"Besides," Emery added, "St. Cloud might have advanced resources, but we still have something he doesn't."

"What's that?" Exton asked, his voice bitter.

"Her love."

Exton nearly laughed, but, in seeing his sister's persistence and determination, he only shrugged. "It's a nice sentiment, Emery, but it's hollow. She's always wanted his love. Even if she has ours, she'll still want his."

Before Emery could argue with him further, his comm device beeped again.

"That's got to be Merra," he said as he picked up his pack. "I've got to go. I've got a long flight and a long day ahead of me."

"When will you be back?" Emery asked.

"If we win, we'll stay a while to reestablish the community to safe levels," Exton said. "Merra's force is still stationed there. I know she wants to go after other imprisoned towns and URS supply lines under the cloud cover."

"Ecological disaster has done quite a bit of damage," Emery said. "But at least we can use it to our advantage."

"While I'm gone," he said, "try to stay out of trouble." He pointed to her belly. "And take care of your baby. That's my niece or nephew in there."

Emery pushed him out the door. "I can take care of myself and my baby just fine," she said. "It's you I'm worried about."

"With good reason," Exton agreed.

With his pack in his hand, he hurried off toward the hangar. He walked down the hall with certain steps, knowing he was hours away from fighting the enemy from a cramped fighter cockpit.

As he turned into the hangar, he saw that the doors were open and the rest of his combat squad—all his friends and coworkers from *Perdition*—were rushing around as Merra called out orders from her forward position.

Outside the hangar, he could see the clear blue of the sea and sky, the green of Antarctica's once-hidden hills, as the sun shone brightly in its mid-morning ascent. Cutting through the light was the shadow of the Memory Tree.

In the morning light, the tree seemed to be a shade all its own. As Exton glanced at its stark lines, it conjured up the haunted feeling of his father's memory.

He shook his head to clear his vision. He knew his father would be disappointed in his choices. But he also knew his father had died because he refused to see the failure of his ideas.

Exton settled down deeper into the cockpit of his chosen MENACE fighter as he listened to the radio chatter between his squad members. There was a current of excitement running through the conversations as they headed closer to their target.

Almost as if they knew this day would come. Exton closed his eyes for a moment, allowing the full weight of that responsibility to fall into his full consideration.

The memory of St. Cloud standing over him at the Nova Scotian base came to his mind.

"You've ruined my plans before, but I won't let you ruin them again."

What plans? What plans had he ruined for St. Cloud?

Before he could find an answer, another memory fell into his mind's eye. St. Cloud, standing over his father's slumped body, the gun in his hand still smoking.

"Are you doing alright there, Captain?"

Ali's voice came over his intercom from the ship beside him, dragging him out of his reminiscence.

"I'm fine," Exton responded, even though his frown deepened. Ali sounded so young—of course, compared to his age, eighteen or nineteen *was* young.

"Just checking in, sir. Your flanking's getting too close for comfort."

"Adjusting now," Exton said, as he shifted his plane a few degrees to the right. "Thanks."

"Roger that, sir." Ali's response contained a barely smothered laugh.

"Ninety-nine, approaching target," Merra called through the intercom, prompting Exton push his concerns away.

"Roger," Exton replied automatically, echoing the responses of his team. His eyes glazed over the control panel before him, only focusing again when he turned and glanced out his portside window. There wasn't much he could see, other than the vertical stabilizer of Ali's fighter.

They'd entered Earth's atmosphere not even an hour before. They came in near the equator, heading east, chasing after the sunlight.

"Okay, crew," Merra called. "Chaya's on lockdown; comms are being rerouted through *Perdition*'s filter. Once we're over the land, drop down and cut off their power supply. Campus generators are located at the four corners of the campus. Use small missiles."

"X-ray missiles should do the trick," Ali said.

"Roger that," Jared called. "I had a lot of those stocked in our arsenals specifically at Merra's recommendation."

Exton brooded over Jared's excitement. This was probably the first time he'd been out of the *Perdition* since he came onboard, Exton realized. He hoped Jared, like Ali, would be able to keep his enthusiasm under control.

"The NETech can still get through," another pilot called.

Exton wasn't surprised to hear Greer. She was one of the *Perdition*'s tech analysts and had been one of the first to join them. Out of all the others Merra had listed for him to check, Exton knew she was quite good with strategy.

"Yes, but it will have its limitations." Kamalo, whom Exton had only briefly met in the hangar down in Petra, chimed in over the intercom. "The way the NETech works is to stir the impulse and lead it toward action. We will be able to do much damage before backup can be deployed."

"Roger," everyone called.

The settlement of Chaya was located near the eastern shore near the old Mediterranean seashore. While the URS had several navy ships at their disposal, Exton knew from his time under St. Cloud's tutelage that the real threat came from their Craftcarriers, large flying ships capable of providing intense air support and reinforcements. Fortunately, the URS had only commissioned a few of them, before they turned their interest toward his father's work on the *Perdition.*

Of course, Exton thought, that was six years ago. He was unsure of how many more might have been finished since then.

In the dense clouds surrounding the middle of the world, there were lots of places to hide, and lots of places to place radio scramblers. There were any number of other concerns, too, from storms that could gather at a moment's notice or toxic cloud formations.

"Tyler," Exton called, pressing in the comm for the *Perdition.*

"Here."

Exton almost smiled. Tyler's voice was compliant, but full of disappointment. Exton had kept his word to Emery; he'd ordered Tyler to remain on the *Perdition* to keep track of their progress and reroute all URS communications from the surrounding areas.

"Chaya's coming up. What's the weather report?"

"Thora's given me the data," Tyler said. "No problems ahead. Despite the clouds, you're in the clear."

"Thanks."

"You got it, Captain."

Exton nearly rolled his eyes. "You can come next time," he said. "I wouldn't mope around if I were you."

"You'll have to run it by Emery first," Tyler replied.

Exton laughed. "Speaking of my beloved sister, how is the Biovid doing?"

"I just got that report from her. All's well. The Suncatcher's running at max power."

"Tell the engineers I said thanks," Exton said. "I didn't think St. Cloud's Redbird would leave us any permanent damage."

"The missile, no. But I'd watch the other one you've got on your squad," Tyler said.

"What do you mean?"

"Oh. Emery said that St. Cloud used to call Merra 'Redbird,' as an affectionate nickname of sorts."

"I can see where that one would give us more trouble," Exton replied quietly.

"You're coming up on the target," Tyler said. "Watch yourself, Captain. We'll be here when you get back."

"You got it," Exton said, before turning his attention forward. Chaya came into sight a moment later.

The Ecclesia had a long history with the settlement of Chaya; the fact that the small outpost had fallen while he was recuperating surprised him.

Maybe that was part of the plans that I ruined for St. Cloud; URS aggressions have increased over the years, despite the Perdition *working to curb their international appetites.*

"Chaya in sight," Merra said.

"Roger," everyone called.

Exton frowned. There were seven of them, he recalled. There was Jared, and Ali, Greer, Merra, and Kamalo. Who was the last pilot?

"Alice," Merra called. "You're to maintain your position above the settlement to help guide the care package delivery once it arrives."

Alice? Exton recalled the young woman with short blond hair. More than once, Emery had hinted at what a nice girl she was in hopes he would take notice of her. And in some ways he had—he saw right away she was besotted with him and the romantic, idealized version of himself he'd created in order to oppose the URS. Alice would never accept him for who he truly was.

Hearing she was accompanying them, he was suddenly wary.

What's she doing with a fighter?

"Copy, Merra." Alice's voice was strong, even though he knew she was nervous.

He paged her over the intercom. She answered him quickly.

"Alice," Exton said, "if you fear you are in danger, do not hesitate to leave and find cover. You can help us from a distance. That's a direct order."

"Yes, Captain," she replied.

Her tone made him wonder if she would actually follow through on her instructions. She was Aerie's friend, after all, he recalled, amused as he remembered Aerie's own self-admitted failing when it came to disregarding instructions.

I miss you, Aerie.

Seeing no other alternative, Exton tucked her into his heart as the battle began. Enemy fire, sporadic and random, began to burst upward from the ground.

"Keep your flanking until oh-four-six," Merra called. "Then split off to tackle the generators. Alice, hold your position center."

"Roger," Alice replied.

"Exton," Merra called. "My forces are being held captive in the center, in the holding cells below the campus."

A warning popped up on his screen. "We have Kazuz's, rocket launchers, coming up from center right," he said. "We're close enough the rockets could do serious damage."

"*Ag man*," Kamalo grunted as he swiveled and shot upward. "Avoid them."

"I'll take them out," Merra called. "Alice, provide flank cover to Ali and Greer."

Exton hurried to take out one of the rocket launchers as they sped forward. He was surprised when they didn't aim at his ship, but instead aligned their targeting sensors at Alice's ship.

"Why are they after Alice?" Exton wondered, as he realized they were all aiming for her.

They must assume she's the leader. As the shots began to fire, Exton used his own missiles to cover Alice. His aim was true, and his attack met theirs with fire in midair. As Exton ran through the explosion, he radioed Alice.

"Alice, you're vulnerable," he said. "See if you can go up higher."

"Roger, Captain." She dutifully shot up and began to hover a few more hundred yards up, keeping herself in the middle of the campus.

"Well, that'll help with her positioning some," he grumbled to himself, knowing it was only a matter of time before more powerful weapons were called in.

"We have a takeoff at the far airstrip," Jared called.

"I'll take care of it," Exton offered.

"Watch your back, Cap," Jared said. "You've got a shadow."

He glanced at his rear receptor readings and saw he did have an enemy fighter tailing him. "I'll keep it guessing."

Exton hurried toward the airstrip on the south end of the campus, keeping low enough to tempt more of the Kazuz squad but high enough to anticipate their moves.

Another explosion rocked his airwaves as Greer let out a victory whoop. "Got the tower," she called.

"Minimal damage," Merra reported. "Swing around and hit it from the other side."

"Roger."

Exton saw the smoke tower rising from the far end of his visual. He saw the flames coming up from the base a second later. "Watch for the fire; some of those flames are pretty high," he warned.

After another round of affirmative replies, he turned back to the airplane taking off.

It was an older plane, he noticed. With the comms jammed, it was stalled on the runway.

"Target locked," he called. A missile in the middle of the airstrip would be enough, he decided. He didn't need to hit the ship itself. "I'm going to stall its takeoff."

He just pressed the button when Merra cried out. "No, wait, Exton!" she called.

His missile shot out and struck into the magnetic shield around the plane. Exton realized too late that it was a proton shield.

The missile exploded against the shield. The shock sent Exton's plane whirling haphazardly. His wing clipped against the outer wall of the camp, sending him further spiraling out of control.

"Mayday, mayday," Exton grumbled, leaning into the quick turns to try to stabilize his engines. He was relieved to see he had some control still. He would be able to land with minimal damage.

"Pull up, *boet*," Kamalo called.

"I'll be fine," Exton replied, still processing his shock and responding to the damage to his ship. "Just keep on firing at those towers."

"Shadow's back," Jared warned. "I'm coming to cover

you. See if you can hold on."

"Roger," Exton replied.

Before he could process it, the fighter was bouncing onto the ground, grappling with his harness as the plane crashed into the settlement wall. He felt his knee bash painfully into his ship's dashboard.

For the longest moment of his life, Exton went through a shock test to make sure he was okay. He then unbuckled himself and picked up his comm.

"What was that, Merra?" he yelled. "Why does that plane have a magnetic proton shield?"

There was a tense silence coming from the other end.

"Merra!" he repeated. "Answer me."

While he was waiting, Alice managed to shoot the ship out of the sky with larger missiles; the explosion swept over the campus, sending an even more dense haboob through the region.

After that, everything stilled for a long moment while the fighting stalled.

Exton picked up his comm again. "Tell me what was in the plane, Merra. You must have some idea."

"It was taking off with a weapon," Merra said. "Chaya is not only a settlement. It's a research lab. That weapon is one of its deadliest inventions."

"What is it?" Exton asked. "A nuke? A hydrogen bomb?"

"No. It's an ecobomb," she said. "A team of our eco-scientists used genetic engineering to grow a strain of algae that can poison seawater."

"No wonder Chaya had its water poisoned, then," he snapped. "You were going to use it."

"Of course," Merra told him sharply. "We don't apologize for overthrowing tyrants, Exton. We know when to lay down our arms. Osgood doesn't. Who do you think ordered it in the first place? We defected, leaving behind all our coded research."

Exton was about to reprimand her for keeping vital information from him when he was interrupted by Ali.

"Captain," Ali called. "You have approaching guards. Watch yourself."

"We're still taking out the towers," Greer said. "We'll cover where we can."

"Negative," Exton said with a sigh. He was going to have a talk with Merra later, and he was going to try not to strangle her. "I'll take care of them. Stay on course."

He grabbed his laser gun and pulled himself out of the cockpit.

Using the ship for cover, Exton tried to get a better assessment of the damage done to his ship.

Before he could more closely examine his fighter's crushed wing, he was grabbed by one of the guards.

Exton nearly dropped his weapon in surprise, but turned around to fight.

A few punches later, along with some serious pain in his knuckles, he was able to get the man into a chokehold.

"Stand down, or we'll shoot!" another guard called.

Exton glanced over to see the guard had a nervous look on his face. It was clear he didn't want to shoot with his superior in Exton's grip.

"You'll likely shoot anyway," Exton told him. He moved forward suddenly, pulling his captive with him.

"Augh!" the other guard shrieked and fired.

Exton felt the body in his hands fall as the bullet struck him. Caught off balance, he barely managed to swing himself free before hitting the ground.

The other guard ran away as one of Exton's friends came over and started firing.

From his position, Exton could see Kamalo's dark face break into a grin as he passed by. He waved his thanks.

Exton glanced down at the guard who had tried to capture him. He was dead.

As a sigh escaped him, Exton leaned over and began to rifle through his pockets for anything that could help their cause. He paused when he felt the guard's radio going off.

Didn't Tyler jam their comms?

He picked it up to hear a woman calling for survivors.

"Come in. This is the Capital Command calling in. Emergency response, come in."

"Capital Command?" Exton frowned. "Why is New Hope calling in this early? It's hardly three o'clock in the morning there."

Surely some other base would have answered.

"We have received your signal over the NET. Are there any survivors? Hello?"

Exton held the radio up and pressed the response button. "None worth saving," he said. "My crew and I are taking over."

"No." The responder's voice was hushed and quiet, and suddenly Exton felt bewildered. He had a terrible feeling inside of him, one that almost didn't want it to be true—

"You're a monster," the voice snapped at him, angry and defiant to the last, in a tone which was all too familiar to him.

"Aerie?" Exton asked in disbelief.

♦9♦

"Aerie?"

Aerie felt her world turn upside down and inside out all at the same time at the sound of her name coming from the other side of the comm, half a world away.

Her breath sucked in sharply. *I know that voice.*

"Aerie, is that really you?" The voice spoke to her again, this time calling to her heart.

It was as irresistible as ever.

"Who … who are you?" she whispered, unable to say anything else. She felt as though she'd been slapped, and by her own self, no less. One moment she was furious, and the next she was pained beyond feeling. How could she respond to someone like this, without knowing who he was?

No, she mentally corrected herself. She knew who he was. She knew his voice. He was the one who she'd been missing these past weeks, the man with blue eyes who kept swimming to the surface of her mind before her headaches rushed in to ruin it.

"Please," she whispered. "Tell me—"

The comm system flickered off and then died.

"No!" she protested. "No, no." Her head raged in pain while her arms hit the panel. She slumped into her chair and tried not to yell.

That was all she wanted to do. Yell and scream and rage, until the agony in her head was gone and the ache in her heart was satisfied.

Her head fell into her hands as more memories started to come rushing.

"Crush its heart!"

"No," she whispered, just as she had that day. That face, the face of her enemy became clear.

Captain Chainsword's ghost.

But he wasn't a ghost, Aerie remembered. Her hands dug into the back of her head as she dived into the darkness inside of her.

She'd fought him. Finding herself out of options, she fought off Captain Chainsword as soon as he freed her from the tree.

His eyes.

Aerie's eyes started to water. She remembered. His eyes were blue, like ice, full of pain and loneliness. The smell of him, that lingered on the jacket she wore …

I remember him. I …

She saw his hand reaching out for hers. She felt the memory of it as it held hers, startling her, shaking up everything she thought she knew about him and herself, too.

"Exton."

His name filled the empty hole inside, the one she carried with her for the past several weeks. Not only did she suddenly know who she was and what had happened to her, she knew what she had to do.

She had to get back to him.

Aerie stood up and took off her headset, emboldened by the rush of pain in her head. She didn't care anymore. After weeks of whispers and digging for the deep secrets inside of her, she had broken free. She finally had something greater than pain to sustain her.

The door banged open. "What on earth is going on?" Anand asked as he scurried over to her.

"Why are you here?" Aerie asked, shocked at his arrival. She'd come in early as he asked, but she never expected to see Director Anand until his shift began.

"The office alarm went off," he said. "Did you come in here without punching the code?"

"Oh. I forgot," Aerie replied sheepishly. There was a code she had to type in when she entered the room and booted up the monitors. She'd forgotten about it, so Anand was alerted.

He must have been the one who turned off the power, Aerie realized, upset at her own foolishness. It was included as part of the system to stop hackers or information leaks.

"Why are you here? It's not time for your shift."

"There was an attack, sir," Aerie said. "I … I got here early, because you said yesterday that I needed to come in early if I wasn't going to stay late. You remember that?"

Aerie felt too clumsy with her words. She was grateful for the moment when Anand rubbed his tired eyes and blinked, as though he was having a hard time putting everything together, too.

"I … I got here and went right to work practicing with the NETech protocol," she admitted, hoping that she wouldn't be punished for that. No one had ever said she *couldn't* use it, even though she knew someone as uptight as Anand would be against it. "I picked it up and saw there was trouble. No one else was here, so I sent out a query. I had to reroute the regular comms, since they were jammed, or I would've called sooner."

Aerie was glad to see he was more interested in pulling up the information on the monitor than paying attention to her. She was still reeling from the shock of hearing Exton's voice calling her name again.

She rubbed her shoulder, still not completely sure how she wound up back in the URS.

"Oh, no." Anand gasped. "The settlement at Chaya is being attacked."

"Yes," Aerie said, not sure of anything else to say. "Their regular comms are not responding. I managed to reroute and widen our comm frequencies, sending the jamming signal scrambling."

If that's one good thing I've learned since working here, she thought, unable to stop a spurt of pride. This was something that would have made her father proud of her.

"What did you do after answering the alert?" Anand asked. "Did you call for a status report?"

"I immediately sent out a signal, calling on all frequencies for survivors." She tried to look innocent. "I didn't know how bad the attack was."

"Did you inform anyone?"

"What? No, of course not. I just found out what was happening, sir."

Anand shook his head. "We need to inform General St. Cloud immediately, so he can respond."

"Do you think he'll send military relief?" Aerie asked. She suddenly wondered if her brothers or Brock would be sent out to help the fighting.

Maybe I can hop along for a ride …

Aerie's heart soared. She knew where Exton was. She could get to him while he was still there, if she hurried.

Anand began typing a message. "I don't know what Dictator Osgood will order," he admitted. "Chaya is a smaller settlement. We have only had control over it for a couple of weeks."

"Why would it be attacked then?" Aerie asked.

"This is not the first time we have had our smaller advances attacked and rebuffed," Anand snapped. "And it will likely not be the last."

Aerie shrunk back and continued to monitor the screen. The satellite images coming through were coarse and blurry, but it was enough to make out several smoking pillars.

"Stay here," Anand ordered as he headed back out of the room. "I have to notify our superiors."

The minute he walked out of the room, Aerie grabbed her headset and put it back on. She tried to call in again, but it was no use.

Aerie glanced over at the monitor and pulled up the frequency readings. She tried to scramble them to get around the jamming signal once more, but it was useless.

I guess I got lucky the first time. Or they fixed it so I couldn't hack their hacking, Aerie thought bitterly.

When Anand came back and told her to forward the readouts to the New Hope military base, Aerie found herself further frustrated.

Nothing was working. She was no longer able to get through. She was just a civilian now, and one who just had her access to communicating with the nation's enemy cut off.

There has to be some way to get there, Aerie thought, weighing her options.

There was no way the General would let her go. At the thought of her father, Aerie was instantly caught up in the memory of how it felt to have him hold her up on the surface of the world.

He'd been lying, she realized. Her hands suddenly clenched into fists as she tasted a bitter mix of blood and bile. Her father hadn't done anything to protect her—he'd done everything he could to protect himself!

That is just like him, too, Aerie thought.

For a long, awful moment, she simmered in her fury and stewed in her resentment.

But then she smiled.

I'm going to disappoint him. And that is just like me.

Aerie stood up. She tore off her headset and slammed it down on her consol. Then she grabbed her jacket off her chair and hurried out the door, brushing past Claire as she headed in for her shift.

"Aerie, where are you going?" Claire called after her. "Director Anand will be upset."

Aerie didn't reply. She couldn't tell Claire that she was finally on a mission, and one that had no place for Anand's orders.

She didn't stop to reply, and she didn't stop running until she was outside of the Comms Sec building. Once she was free, she turned in the direction of the military base.

It wouldn't take long before the General called for her. He would know from her skipping out on work that she suspected something at minimum.

"I can't stay here any longer," Aerie whispered as she ducked through the city alleyways. Even though the lights were on the daytime setting, it was harder to see everything in the alley shadows. That was fine with her. She just wanted to get where she needed to be, and she wasn't going to stop for anything.

Aerie revised that decision as she passed the education

center.

Brock was there, heading inside.

"Brock!" she called. She easily cut through the steady stream of students and faculty to catch up with him.

"Aerie." Brock's eyes lit up as he caught sight of her. "I was just thinking about you." He cleared his throat as some of his peers looked at him. "I mean, Comrade."

Aerie faltered for a moment. She hadn't spoken much to Brock since her birthday, and most of their conversation had been in terse and guarded tones.

She almost groaned; she didn't want to have to turn this conversation into an argument over cohabitation options.

Hoping she could steer clear of that topic, she reached out and tugged at his arm. "I need to talk with you, now," she said.

"I have to get to my class—"

"Now." Aerie gave him a pleading look. "Please, Brock."

He stilled, and for a long moment Aerie was sure he was going to say no. But when he finally spoke, he said, "Alright."

That was enough for her, she decided. She could ignore the uncertain sigh that escaped him.

They ducked into a room beside the atrium. Aerie blinked in surprise as she recognized the dark room they stepped into was the auditorium. It had been several weeks since her graduation ceremony, but everything was as she remembered it, even the stillness.

"What is it?" Brock asked. "I hope this is worth it, because I'm going to get—"

"There's been an attack," Aerie said. "I need you to go to the military base with me." That was about as vague as she could state her case, and she was going to use it to her advantage.

"What?" Brock asked.

Aerie tried not to grumble, just as she tried not to show how impatient she was getting. "I said, there's been an attack," she repeated.

"Why haven't we been alerted?" Brock asked. He pulled

out his military comm and glanced at it. "I don't have any messages."

Before Aerie could reply, the comm started beeping.

"There you go," she murmured.

"General St. Cloud calling," the voice barked from the other line. "All senior pilots must report to the base for emergency training. Repeat, all senior—"

Brock clicked the comm off. "It's not an attack," he said. "They're just doing training this morning."

"You need to go," Aerie insisted. "And you need to take me with you. Trust me, it's an attack."

"Why should I trust you?" he asked. "You don't trust me. You won't even go to the Military Ball with me."

Aerie tried not to sigh. What was a little social gathering compared to this?

"I was the one who answered the distress signal," she told him. Aerie took his hand and tugged him toward the door. "Come on."

His eyes narrowed at her. "Aerie," he said, "I know you wanted to be part of the military, but I thought you were past that. For now, anyway."

Aerie wanted nothing more than to punch him. *What is wrong with him? Why is he not listening to me? Didn't I just tell him that there was an attack going on?!*

There was nothing left to do. She had to tell him the truth. "Brock, I wasn't injured in a climbing accident," she said. "I wasn't in a medical facility for two weeks. I was captured by Captain Chainsword and shot."

He stared at her.

"I'm not lying," Aerie said. "That's the reason I have been unable to move on." She put her hand on her shoulder, the dull ache of her wound nothing compared to the damage to her pride.

"So … Captain Chainsword captured you after graduation?" Brock asked.

"It was after my PAR," Aerie murmured, hoping that he wouldn't ask for details. She didn't want Brock to know about her trips to the Memory Tree any more than the General wanted anyone else to know. "I was up on the surface when he attacked, and I wound up in his custody on the *Perdition.*"

Aerie felt her eyes moisten. As she said the words aloud, she thought of the quiet rhythms of the starship—the playful children, roaming freely; the efficiency of the design, packed with pleasures; the people, kind and generous and loving; the captain, mysterious and honorable and trusting.

"And … he hurt you?" Brock asked.

Aerie laughed. "Not as much as I hurt him, probably," she said, grimacing as the discomfort in her head began to pool at the back. She reached up and pressed into her head, and the pain lessened somewhat.

"What did he do to you?" Brock's voice was quiet but angry.

He loved me.

Aerie shook her head. "I don't want to talk about it," she told him. "But I want to go and see him. He's the one who's behind the attack at Chaya."

She was surprised to see Brock shaking. He turned from her to glare up at the picture of Captain Chainsword on the wall, where his picture was surrounded by other enemies of the URS.

"I can understand that you want revenge," Brock said, looking up at the picture.

Aerie didn't say anything. She was surprised by the venom in Brock's voice. "Why do you hate him so much?" she asked, suddenly curious. Brock had always been upset by the mention of the enemy pirate captain, but the more she thought about it, the more she realized he had a special hatred for the face posted on the auditorium wall.

"He's everything the URS hates, Aerie." Brock turned to her. "I know plenty of the people he's hurt. And now he's hurt you."

She was stunned to see how upset he was, and hurried to comfort him.

"It wasn't your fault I was captured," Aerie told him. She reached up and patted his cheek. "And I survived. There's no need to worry about it now."

"I've always tried to watch out for you, you know," Brock told her. His voice was soft. "That's why I offered to help you train, the first day of our secondary classes."

Aerie blushed and took a step back from him. "It's been a long time since I thought about that," she admitted.

Several years before, when she fell during a training course, the first one after their return from a campus retreat, Aerie was berated and humiliated by one of their instructors. It didn't help that her mother had recently died and her siblings were still in school. They laughed along with everyone else, at her.

Only Brock had stepped forward and offered to help her afterward.

She glanced back at Brock uneasily now, as he continued to stare angrily at the picture on the wall.

Aerie knew she couldn't share in his vision. When she looked up at the captain, she would never see an enemy. Not anymore. She looked up at him and felt the call more than ever to return to Exton.

"I forgot you were the one who talked to me first," Aerie said, returning her attention to Brock. "I always thought I was tagging along after you."

No, Aerie realized, instead, Brock was chasing her. And if what he said before was true, he was smart enough to see the General could easily pose a threat to his future. Especially if he made the wrong move.

Brock took her hand. "I've always had a soft spot for you, Aerie."

It was awkward, but it was the opening she needed.

"Then will you help me get to Chaya?" she asked.

Brock sighed. "I don't know if I'll even be going to Chaya," he said. "I haven't been summoned for training or anything. Only the seniors have been called. There is also the possibility that you've been misinformed."

"I heard the distress call myself!" Aerie nearly shouted, her words echoing in the empty hallows of the large room.

"Maybe your information was mixed up."

"Why don't you just tell me you think I'm being stupid?" Aerie snapped. She pulled her hand out of his. "I should've known better than to ask you to help me break the rules."

"Rules matter, Aerie," Brock told her, in a tone that made her think of the General.

"Truth matters more, Brock," Aerie shot back, as she headed out of the auditorium.

"What is truth?" Brock scoffed. "The truth is what the URS says, and it is all to help keep us alive."

Aerie shook her head. "*Exactly!*" she said. "The URS just wants to control us, Brock. To control *you*."

"That's insane, Aerie."

"Do you know that the General actually told me that it would make me look good if I accepted your cohabitation proposal?"

"Well, he's got a point," Brock said.

"Ugh! And you wonder why I don't want to," Aerie replied. "Do you honestly want me to enter into a cohabitation agreement with you because the government would want me to?"

"It's not like you wouldn't be able to—"

"Answer me!" Aerie crossed her arms over her chest. "Answer the question. Do you want me to live with you just because the state thinks I should?"

She paused for a moment, before she looked back up at the picture of Captain Chainsword. "Don't you want me to want to be with you, of my own choosing?"

Brock said nothing for a long time. Aerie waited, her ears perked so much she was sure she could hear the angry humming of his heart.

Finally, he spoke. "You're sounding more and more like a defector every time I talk to you."

Aerie frowned. "Then maybe I shouldn't talk to you anymore," she said. She didn't wait for him to respond this time. She turned on her heel and headed out of the room.

She slammed the door behind her, upset Brock had been a lost cause after all, despite everything they had shared over the years.

Before she could make it out of the school, Aerie felt a hand grab her. "Hey!"

"Comrade St. Cloud, you will remain still."

Aerie glanced up, surprised to see a number of guards had suddenly assembled around her. "What's going on?" she asked. Was it possible she was in trouble for hearing the distress call this morning?

"Comrade St. Cloud." A man with a shadow of a beard on his face stepped forward. "You must come with us."

Aerie glanced nervously at the badges on his uniform and recognized the rank; it was the same as the General had worn when she was younger. The man had to be from among the most elite circles of governmental control, but he couldn't be much younger than thirty.

That doesn't bode well, Aerie thought nervously. Aggressive and relentless workers were the ones who rose to the top first.

"Comrade." The man took another step forward.

"Who are you?" Aerie asked.

"My name is Lieutenant Dubois," he said. "I have been authorized to place you under arrest."

"Why?" Aerie asked.

He frowned, his dark eyebrows coming together as he met her gaze intently. Aerie involuntarily flinched as he spoke. "You have failed at your assigned work. We are taking you to the Reeducation Center for processing."

"No," Aerie argued, fighting against them. Her arms were trapped as she was dragged away. "No, stop! This isn't fair," she insisted. "I want to see my father."

Lieutenant Dubois let out a dry laugh. "Who do you think authorized your arrest?"

"What?" Aerie gasped in disbelief. She felt her last chance slip away from her. She took a long step back and tried to bolt for the nearest exit.

"Aerie?" Brock called from behind her. "What's going on?"

"Brock!" she called. "Brock, help—"

There was only a thick pounding sound as someone knocked her over the head. Her vision slid away as her eyes closed, her consciousness following immediately after.

♦10♦

I can't believe she didn't know who I was.

Despite the urgency around him, Exton felt his movements stiffen as he relived that moment all over again—as he had for the last several hours—that moment Aerie yelled at him, then asked him who he was. He heard the confusion and the conviction in her voice, all at the same time, as she was unable to come up with the answer to her question on her own.

Aerie was alive, but she was no longer his.

He'd been prepared for that. Ever since he woke up in Merra's care outside of Halifax, he knew that the Memory Serum would rob him of the best of her.

He told himself that he was prepared for that. *Maybe just not quite so soon.*

That probably accounted for most of the reasons he hadn't been able to get much sleep since the attack. Soon after his ship crashed, Merra and the others were able to knock out the power generators, leaving most of the URS guards in lockdown inside.

After that, it was easy enough to convince them to surrender.

Most of them, anyway, Exton thought with a wry grin as he picked up another bandage.

"How are you feeling, sir?" he asked, turning to the defiant man sitting on the ground in front of him.

"I feel like beating you to a pulp," the man replied. "And the name is Abbas. There is no need to pretend you respect me."

"I'm not inclined to let you beat me up," Exton said calmly. "Which is fortunate for you, really. You've already lost enough blood with the cut down your arm, and your broken leg will give you a disadvantage."

Abbas grunted, but allowed Exton to continue binding up his wound.

"Despite what your beloved dictator might say, we don't actually torture people."

"Then why am I bleeding?" the man retorted.

Exton sighed silently to himself. He hated that he'd volunteered to help aid the med crew. There were not a lot of complicated medical issues, but providing care was the first goal they had after they secured the base—and that included providing care to their enemy as well as the innocent.

From his grumpiness as much as his uniform, Exton knew Abbas was one of the many guards who had been wounded in the attack on Chaya.

"I never said we don't fight," Exton replied as he finished tightening the bandage around the man's arm. "There, that should help. If you need anything else for it, you can let one of us know, sir."

"Abbas," the man corrected him. "And I will never come to you for help. You work for the Redbird, don't you?"

Exton frowned. Abbas was looking off into the distance. Exton followed his gaze and watched as Merra came out of the camp, carrying a small boy in her arms. "You mean her?"

"We know her as Redbird. That witch has been around here for years," he said. "She's known for her trickery. Once she was gone, we easily took down Chaya's defenses. She's ruthless." Abbas glanced at his wound disdainfully as an aid worker came to take him back to the prison cell. "You'd better be careful to stay out of her way, or she'll sacrifice you, too."

"If she's as ruthless as you say, you should've known she would've come back," Exton muttered, even though Abbas was already out of earshot.

Exton packed up his supplies. He was done helping for now, he decided. He'd wanted to talk to Merra about her intentions and her plans, and it seemed like a good time to force her to explain herself.

"Merra," he called. She turned to face him as he approached. Her aviation goggles, covered in mud, were pushed back comfortably into her hair, and she still wore her uniform from yesterday's battle.

Exton couldn't help but feel another rush of surprise. From what he remembered, and from what Aerie had told him about her mother, Exton thought Merra would be such a gentle creature, full of love and patience and otherworldly wonder.

He could not have been more wrong. She was full of grit and shrewdness so sharp it was a wonder he was able to stand before her, even after the battle had long been decided.

"What is it?" Merra asked. "Is Tyler going to be late with the new aid shipment?"

"No. That's not what I wanted to discuss with you," Exton said.

Her eyes gleamed. "I thought that might be the case, but I was hoping otherwise," she said. She gave the boy in her arms a tight hug before setting him down on the ground.

Exton looked down at the little boy, surprised to see such a mature look in such a young child. He had dark circles under his eyes, which quickly narrowed as he looked up at Exton.

"Go see Joya and Alice, Marcus," Merra said. "She'll have something for you, I'm sure, while Mommy talks business."

As the child toddled off, Exton just stared. Shock raced through him at her words. "He's your son?"

"Of course," Merra said with a measured grin. "Couldn't you tell?"

Exton watched as the small child, with his brown hair, headed back toward the camp. Alice came running up with one of the settlers, and they both tended to the boy.

"Alice knew you from before," Exton said, as it all came together. "That's why she's here. Her loyalty is to you."

"To our cause," Merra insisted, even as her smile suggested otherwise. She laughed a moment later. "But maybe more so toward my son. She always loved caring for him while she was here before."

Exton watched as Marcus grabbed onto Alice and hugged her affectionately.

Another realization struck him. "That's why you wanted us to attack Chaya. They had your son and you wanted to free him."

"While you were recovering from Aerie's loss," Merra said, "I got the word about the attack. With Chaya's recent trouble, and the bomb finally ready for use, I had a feeling leaving with some of our better troops was a risk. I was right."

He noticed she did not apologize for holding back, either in keeping the information to herself or for the ferocity of her attack. Again.

"Why did you come to Halifax if you knew it would be a risk, then?"

Merra shook her head. "You wouldn't understand."

"I wouldn't understand what?" Exton clenched his fists as he tried to restrain himself. "Revenge? War? Hate? What wouldn't I understand?"

"Sacrifice is necessary," Merra said. "I don't think you would understand. I have been fighting the URS for a long time—much longer than you have."

"My father died at his hands!" Exton roared. "Don't you dare tell me I don't know about sacrifice."

"Sacrifice and loss are different things," Merra pointed out calmly. "You *lost* your father. I had to sacrifice my family."

"Your family is still alive at least."

"Sometimes death is kinder." Merra arched her brow. "Don't you feel that way about Aerie?"

Exton thought about hearing her voice, about how she sounded so unsure. Would her death be easier on him? Was endless vengeance preferable to hope repeatedly deferred?

All he wanted to do now was go get her, and then kiss her until she was so senseless she couldn't help but remember him.

Merra continued, "It would've been easier for you if she had died. I know it's hard for you to believe, but it's better she is with Victor. He can protect her. If I hadn't thought that, I wouldn't have left her there myself."

Exton felt himself snap back into the present moment. "You don't speak for me. I'm nothing like you," he said. "I won't leave Aerie behind the way you did."

"She was a necessary loss, Exton, even if it was a regrettable one." Merra shook her head. "You don't speak for me, either. If you really want to know, I had to leave all those years ago because of Marcus. If Marcus was going to survive, I had to give up my life in the URS. Faking my death was the only possible solution at the time."

She folded her arms defiantly. "Aerie will forgive me, once she realizes the truth about what has happened, and what is happening now."

"Well, I'm glad you're not losing sleep over it," Exton grumbled. "What is the truth?"

"The truth is that we need to overthrow the URS," Merra said. "And I've known that since even before I found out about Marcus."

Exton turned back to see Alice and his nanny had taken him into the shade and given him something to snack on.

Merra followed his gaze. "After four kids, you know the State takes measures to make sure a woman has no more children."

Exton slowly nodded. He knew the requirements for sterilization that came with population control, and despite her position as St. Cloud's wife, Merra would have had to get the required surgery. "I've heard."

"Aerie was supposed to be my last child. When I came to Chaya, I found out tubal litigations can grow back, though it doesn't happen very often, especially to women my age. It was a miracle, you know."

Exton once more turned toward the little boy as Alice, alongside another woman, chased him around in circles. Exton noticed for the first time how he shared some distinctive traits with Aerie—the light amber eyes, the copper undertones in his brown hair that spoke of the St. Cloud bloodline. As the little boy looked back at him, Exton wondered if an inherent suspicion of him was also a hereditary trait.

"They would've killed Marcus if they found out." Merra shook her head. "They're the ones who really killed your father, too. Victor was just following their orders."

He bristled. "Orders can be disobeyed."

"Even if Victor had, do you think the URS wouldn't have still managed to get the ship from Silas?" Merra scoffed. "I've been watching them since I left, Exton. It's not hard to see you messed up their plans, big time, and I congratulate you on your efforts. But they will find a way to get what they want if we give them the chance."

"Well, thanks," Exton muttered sarcastically. "I was aiming for your approval all along, too."

"No need to be nasty about it."

"No need to be so blasé about it."

"It's been over five years since I died to the URS," Merra snapped, momentarily losing her cool façade. "My son lives. You will not shame me for making a necessary choice."

He stepped back. "I didn't mean that. I apologize if that is what you thought I meant. It wasn't."

Merra's eyes softened. "It's alright. I know you were likely thinking of Aerie and how hurt she was."

Exton said nothing. He had a new appreciation for Merra's strength, even if he still disagreed with her on several other points. She was, as she had declared before, willing to do what it took to gain what she wanted. He could only hope her efforts would help others as well, and that Aerie would be able to forgive her for her decisions.

"I know you miss her," Merra said as she watched him. "I do, too. Once the URS is defeated, we will be able to see her again. I will have my family back together, and the world will be in better hands."

"She won't know me." Exton heard the tired, ragged quality of his voice.

"She won't know me, either. But have a little faith," Merra said with a shrug. "Can't hurt, in times like these, when there it just seems like there is too much to do."

Before he could reply, his comm went off. Exton flicked the switch and was not surprised to hear Tyler on the other end. He was surprised, however, at the urgency in his voice.

"Exton," Tyler called. "Emery's landing at Chaya with the other aid shipments. I need you to go and see her."

"Hang on." Exton glanced at Merra. "Excuse me."

She nodded. "I can hold down the fort, now that I'm back. Take some time to see to your business. Whatever you need."

Exton narrowed his eyes at Merra's back as she headed back toward the camp, already barking out orders. He watched, frustrated, as Merra took out her own comm device while it blinked.

Who is calling her? Exton wondered.

"Exton?" Tyler's voice called.

"Headed over now. Sorry," Exton replied. "Is Emery okay?"

"She's fine," Tyler said. "It's Aerie who's in trouble."

"What?" Exton felt his heart constrict. "What are you talking about?"

"We didn't want to tell you until we had a more definite plan in place," Tyler explained. "But Emery and I managed to find a way to contact Aerie through the Ecclesia remnant in New Hope."

"That's dangerous," Exton muttered. "St. Cloud is not stupid. He'll be watching her."

"We've been doing this sort of thing for years, remember? We know how to play the game."

"This isn't a game." Exton shook his head. Emery would bash him for the irony, especially since she knew how to use his own methods against him. "What's wrong with Aerie?"

"She managed to get herself assigned to the Reeducation program. She's been taken into custody."

Exton felt the world sink away from him.

"She's an official enemy of the state," Tyler said. There was almost a smile in his voice. "Seems like she didn't have to remember us to get arrested, either. She was one of us all along."

Exton's hands started shaking. He knew only some of what went on inside the Reeducation Center, but what he knew was enough to make him tremble.

He picked up his pace, heading toward the small airstrip, where he could see his trademark shuttle, the one with the Chainsword painted in bright colors along its side, had landed. As he hurried, all he could think of was hearing Aerie's voice earlier.

St. Cloud must have found out about it.

He squeezed his hand around his comm painfully. "This is my fault."

"How is this your fault?" Tyler asked. "You didn't do anything to her. St. Cloud still approved her arrest."

"I didn't—what? St. Cloud gave his approval to label her a traitor himself?" Exton recalled the conversation he had with General St. Cloud the day before he returned Aerie to him.

He'd said he loved her, and he knew it was treason.

That monster. He lied to me. No father would do this to his own daughter.

"I have to get her," he said. "St. Cloud's already damaged her enough."

"Yes," Tyler said. "Meredith's promised to keep me updated. But you have to hurry. We all know what they do to dissenters in Reeducation."

"Exton," Merra called out to him as she came running up beside him.

"Not now," he yelled back.

"Are you going to get Aerie now?"

Exton stopped, suddenly suspicious. He narrowed his eyes at her. "What have you heard?"

Merra blinked too innocently at him. "Heard what?"

She knows already. But who is telling her?

Exton shook his head. He would have to worry about it later. "Aerie's in trouble. But you know that already, don't you?"

"Oh, please. Why else would your shuttle be here with the aid shipments?" Merra asked, gesturing toward the airstrip. "I figured something was up. We've freed my forces, Exton. You might as well go and get Aerie. We can protect her with the resources we have here."

From her tone alone, Exton knew Merra had already been briefed on Aerie's situation.

Why won't she just admit it? Why is she doing this? Who is she protecting this time?

Was it possible the rest of the Ecclesia knew of Aerie's fate as well as Tyler? He could see the Reverend Thorne or Brother Don telling Merra. He knew they were close and they had a shared history.

Exton continued to study Merra's face, but there was nothing but a guileless look in her expression as she pressured him onward. "Well? What are you waiting for? Get in the ship and go."

Deep unease settled inside of him. He didn't trust Merra. He knew she withheld information more than once from him and others. It was a risk, leaving her here without supervision.

But Aerie needed him, whether she remembered him or not. And he needed her, whether he admitted it or not.

"What?" Merra huffed indignantly. "What is it? You're not having doubts about her, are you?"

Not about Aerie.

"Exton, you have to hurry," Tyler repeated. "Emery's onboard, waiting to take you to New Hope. The Ecclesia have a small window for us to move in. We have to take it."

"I know," he snapped. He glanced over at the ship, still unsure of how he felt about this. He saw Emery wave at him from the cockpit. He waved back, but he did not move forward.

"Then what are you waiting for?" Merra shot back. "If you really love my daughter, you will go and rescue her. This isn't the time to hesitate, if she's really what you want."

He really did want her back. More than anything. And

that was enough to allow Merra to take over at Chaya while he went off to infiltrate the URS.

"Okay," Exton finally replied. "I'm going."

"Good." Tyler sighed with relief. "I'll be in contact with you soon."

"Tyler?" Despite the upcoming battle, and the trouble it would likely bring, Exton smiled. "Thank you."

"No thanks needed," Tyler said. "Now, go and get Aerie."

♦11♦

Drip.
Drip.
Drip.

The dripping noise was discomforting at best, and irritating at worst, Aerie decided as she started to climb out of her mindless stupor once more. She blinked her eyes open, only to find herself lying down on an uncomfortable pallet.

She didn't know how much time had passed since she'd been placed in the cell. Aerie knew it had to be at least a full day, since her stomach was grumbling with growing hunger, but there was no way to be entirely sure of the passage of time.

At least the pain was no longer at the back of her head. Now, it was at the front, as she tried to open her eyes. At first, she wasn't sure if something was wrong with her eyes. The room she was in was dark, with the lights only letting a dim spark escape them.

Her vision sharpened as her eyes adapted to the darkened atmosphere. She peered more intently at the light fixtures. One of the lights at the top of the prison cell had blown out.

Probably some time ago, too, by the look of it.

She struggled to sit up, rubbing her shoulders and her arms, trying to get warm. When she'd first woken up, she tried to keep moving around the cell, but it was a mindless activity, one that made her even more anxious than sitting around waiting for something to happen—waiting for some sign to be given, some event to be hinted at. Moving around proved to be a mistake, too, as she depleted her energy and her hunger increased.

Aerie pulled her jacket more tightly across herself, trying to huddle into the small warmth it gave her.

Something stuck into her chest as she snuggled deeper.

"What was that?" Aerie reached into the small, secret pocket and pulled out an object. A small piece of paper fluttered out along with it, twirling onto the ground.

Aerie recognized the photo slide; it was the one Brock had given her for her birthday.

"I'd forgotten about that," she murmured, before setting it down on the pallet beside her. Aerie turned her attention to the paper.

She picked it up and glanced down. It was an old photograph, from the days of digital cameras, that featured a young boy, standing with her mother and father, and another man.

Another hidden memory slipped out—this time of the man that boy became, as he lost his father and his faith, even as he kept his fire and his honor.

Aerie felt her fingers tingle as her nose prickled. "I know you," she whispered, running her fingers over his face.

Exton, where are you?

She tried to recall the last time she'd seen him. What had happened?

"Well, I got shot," she murmured to herself, wincing at her shoulder's stiffness. The cold and the dark added much to its discomfort. She looked at the picture again, forcing herself to move beyond the instant pain in her head, pushing onward toward the memories she knew were inside her heart.

She remembered the grim determination on Exton's face. She felt the warmth of his body on hers. She heard the sadness of a woman's voice …

Emery.

Emery had been her friend. She was Exton's sister. She hadn't wanted Aerie to leave.

But I had to go. Because …

The General … her father managed to get Exton to release her to him.

So he knew. He knew the truth about what happened. I fought with him. I wanted to stay with Exton.

Aerie sighed. She wanted to be with him now.

Glancing around, Aerie doubted she was in any position to do anything more than wish for that possibility. The room she was being held in was small and dark, with no windows. She was freezing and starving and alone. The perpetual night was beginning to wear on her nerves.

Which was probably what they wanted, Aerie recalled. She hadn't learned much about the Reeducation Center when she was in school. Most instructors did not talk about it, only saying that it was for incorrigible students. From others, she heard the whispers that warned of the place, saying it was a place that was specifically designed to break the human will.

She gulped. She didn't want to think about that.

Doing nothing had to be better than that, she thought grimly.

There was still the slim chance that the General would step in and stop her admittance into the Reeducation Center.

"Ha." Aerie shook her head. Looking down at the younger portrait of her father in her hand, with the bright red "X" marked over his face, she knew it was a likely hopeless cause.

The lock on the door clicked.

Aerie jumped and quickly stuffed the picture back into the depths of her pocket. She grabbed the photo slide of Brock at graduation and thrust it on top of it, desperate to keep the photo from the URS.

They've already taken everything I love away from me—my mother died, my father has abandoned and condemned me, and Exton is halfway around the world. I won't let them take anything else.

She dropped her head onto her chest. How did one person manage to hold onto such sadness?

"Comrade St. Cloud?"

Aerie jolted. *I know that voice.*

Meredith was at her door.

"You!" Aerie hissed. "What are you doing here?"

Meredith shook her head ever so slightly. "I need to change your sheets," she said crisply. "It should only take a few moments. If you try to interfere, you will be subdued."

As the door shut behind her, Meredith began moving swiftly. "I can't be here long," she whispered to Aerie. "And

I'm sorry you're here. I can't do anything to help right now, or it would be too suspicious. They're already watching me."

"Who? The URS?" Aerie asked.

"Shh … we can whisper in here, but that's all," Meredith told her as she stripped the pallet of its thin sheet cover. "But yes. The URS is very careful about who has access to enemies of the State."

That's what I am now, Aerie reminded herself. *An enemy. Or at least, an acknowledged one.*

"Do they know about … about how we met?" Aerie asked softly.

Meredith shook her head. "I've been put in charge of your care," she said. "But I can't make it easy on you, especially if we're going to try to rescue you. I hope you can understand."

Aerie nodded, before the full meaning of her words hit her. "Who's going to rescue me?"

"The Ecclesia," Meredith said. Her dark eyes glittered in the small light. "Do you remember them? I know you've been able to remember some things."

Aerie frowned, digging around inside her memory. "I remember the *Perdition*," she said.

"I was hoping you would be able to remember more."

"That's why you showed me my med file," Aerie realized.

"Yes." Meredith nodded. "I saved your jacket for you when you first came to the hospital. I know the *Perdition*'s clothing when I see it."

"You saved me," Aerie whispered. "I can't thank you enough."

Meredith grimaced. "I haven't saved you yet. The Ecclesia and I are working to help get you free."

"The Ecclesia?"

"Some of them are on the crew of the *Perdition*," Meredith said as she put a new cover on the small bed, tucking the sheet under in a brisk, practiced movement. "I have special contacts there that are very interested in getting you back home."

"Home?" Aerie felt herself fall against the hard, stone walls. Home with Exton, and Emery, and all the other people her mind could not remember but her heart could not forget.

She felt a rush of excitement. Her butt involuntarily wriggled in anticipation.

"We have to time it just right," Meredith said. "I have some contacts and we're all working on a plan. Most of the dissenters who are sent here are sent to the southern region. The URS has an older facility there. We can intercept once we know for sure."

Aerie reached out and took her arm. "Thank you for this."

"It wasn't our intention to get you sent here." Meredith looked at her apologetically. "You will still have to be processed here. It is not going to be pleasant. You might not be so thankful by the time the doctors come to get you."

Aerie shook her head. "I'll survive," she said. "And it'll help knowing that it's not for a long time."

"'Long time' is still a relative term," Meredith said. She suddenly looked sad. "I have been here for five years, and every day still feels like an eternity to me."

"Come with me, then," Aerie said. "Surely we can both escape."

Meredith shook her head. "I have something greater than my comfort," she whispered.

Something greater. Aerie remembered Exton talking about that.

Before she could ask about it, Meredith cleared her throat pointedly. "I have other duties to attend to," she said, her brusque tone returning as she gathered up the old set of sheets.

Aerie watched as she walked stiffly out the door. The lock jiggled closed once more.

With nothing more to do but hope, Aerie sat back down on her pallet. The new sheets felt the same as the old ones, but the comfort that they brought her was undeniably new.

Hours passed as Aerie sat in silence, trying to remember

more. She fought off the accompanying headaches, knowing that the pain of *not* knowing was worse than the pain any pounding headache could bring.

Another medical assistant, one Aerie didn't recognize, brought some weak tea and hard bread for her to eat. This one said nothing to her, just threw it down on the floor and headed back out of the room.

I guess I'm not the only one who hates their job, Aerie thought. Her stomach rumbled as she contemplated the meal. She picked up the bread and sniffed at it, surprised to find that she had no desire to eat it. She put the tea and bread aside, determined to save it for later.

"After all my headaches today," Aerie murmured, "I just want to take a nap."

She struggled to fall asleep, unable to get comfortable.

Before she could doze off into deeper sleep, her door opened and a team of medics came in.

"Is she asleep?" Aerie heard one of them ask.

"Barely," another one answered.

"Let's just get this part done and over with," the last one said. She held up a needle.

Aerie nearly jolted upright, but she tightened. She didn't want them to know she wasn't asleep—she wanted to know what they were up to, and she didn't want them to punish her further.

"Injecting local anesthesia," the lady medic said as she thrust the needle into Aerie's shoulder. She instantly jerked in response, but the other medics held her down.

"She's strong," one of them said, as Aerie's legs flailed against him.

"She'll be broken soon enough," the other one said as he pressed down on her arms. "Here, give me the chip."

Aerie squeezed her eyes shut as she felt a burning strip of metal press against the underside her wrist. She heard the sizzle of her flesh and struggled not to let her anguish slip free. She tasted blood on the inside of her cheek as tears slipped quietly from her eyes.

"Good job. Let's get the rest of her vitals," the lady medic said, "and then we'll move onto stage three."

"She's not scheduled for deportation?"

"No." The lady shook her head as she turned toward the small cart behind her. She took out a blood vial. "Osgood wants her here, under close supervision. Says she's his new favorite patient."

That's surprising, Aerie thought as she continued to bite back her objections. She wasn't aware she'd ever caused anyone from the higher levels of the URS to take notice of her.

"He knows it's better having an upper hand when it comes to dealing with St. Cloud," the other tech said.

Aerie sucked in her breath as another needle pricked her skin. She felt her energy slide out of her as several vials were filled with her blood.

It seemed like hours had passed before the lady stripped off her gloves. "Alright. We're finished here. For now. Let's get these back to the lab for testing and process her records."

"Next time, we'll have to give her more sleeping potion," one of the medics said. "She's barely asleep." He pinched her leg, in a playful, sadistic manner, and Aerie jolted at the discomfort. He laughed.

"Don't make it worse," the other man said.

"She's still down at least. At worst, she'll just think this was a bad dream."

"You really should control yourself. Even if General St. Cloud reported her, he'll still be upset with you if you break protocol," the lady replied. "But I'll mark your suggestion down in her file. I thought the tea was enough considering her height and weight, but upping the dosage can't hurt. Or at least, it can't hurt her."

The tea! Aerie was suddenly grateful she had been unwilling to eat or drink much of the meal she was given. She was determined to keep her wits about her, even if she had to suffer from the pain of being awake.

She knew that it was more important for her to know

what was going on.

The medics packed up and left her, leaving her eternally grateful to be alone once more.

Long moments passed before she allowed herself—forced herself—to move. Her arms ached from being poked with all the needles. The cold settled into a deeper level, and her shoulder still pinched in discomfort.

She glanced down at her wrist. There was a small band of metal burned into her skin, formed into numbers. Aerie could see her blood vessels underneath, inflamed from the unwelcome contact.

An enemy of the State, Aerie reminded herself. The numbers had been branded into her, marking her for life. Awkwardly, she rubbed her fingertips over the raised digits. It would take some getting used to, she decided, but the worst part of the pain seemed to be over.

If this is the worst they do, I'll be alright.

Aerie was determined to be alright anyway. Even if Grant Osgood was excited to have her enrolled in the program.

She considered the man who was her father's boss and her nation's leader. Osgood had always been a cunning figure, even if he seemed affable at first. She had never really liked him, and hesitated to call him handsome as many other students and workers did. Experiencing firsthand how the people were treated and branded at the Reeducation Center, she decided she liked him even less.

Why is he so happy to have me here? Aerie wondered. Was it just to get to the General?

Aerie sighed as she pulled out the picture from her pocket again. She could only hope that Meredith would come back with news soon. With the tea outed as a sleeping draught, she knew she couldn't hold on much longer. She was already starting to drift off to sleep against her will.

Aerie didn't know time had passed at all, until the door suddenly burst open, jolting her from an uneasy sleep.

"What is it?" Aerie murmured, rubbing her eyes. She looked up to see a man standing in the doorway, shadows cloaking him. *Am I about to be rescued?*

"It's time you and I had a chat," the man said. He stepped up closer to her face, and Aerie could see it was the man who had arrested her, Lieutenant Dubois.

♦12♦

Aerie hated that her vision swam in and out as she was hauled off her pallet and dragged into the hallway. She stumbled and fell, scraping her knee against the floor. Even though she grunted at the pain, she was relieved it helped to wake her up more. She was still tired.

"Come," the lieutenant snapped. "I have been looking forward to this ever since I delivered you to the Reeducation Center."

"Why?" Aerie mumbled.

"Speak up, Comrade," Lieutenant Dubois called out to her as he led her to a new room.

Aerie had to blink several times as her eyes slowly and unwillingly adjusted to the bright light. There was a hospital bed in the middle of the room, surrounded by a few techs and several large machines.

"Why are you so interested in talking with me, Lieutenant?" she asked, this time nearly shouting as he pushed her into the room.

"You'll find out soon enough," he told her. A beeping sound went off on the comm attached to his uniform. He groaned, before he reached into a drawer and pulled out a garment. "Here. The medics will get you ready while I answer this."

The medical gown, thin and cool, hit her squarely in the chest. Her shoulder ached as she reached up to grasp it, and then she felt the first inkling of fear strong enough to put her body on full alert.

A woman clothed with a pair of scrubs and a facemask came up to her. "Let me take your jacket."

Aerie was relieved to recognize Meredith at the sound of her voice, but she quickly caught the warning in the woman's eye.

She clamped her mouth shut, clenched her fists, and slowly began to take off her jacket in the freezing room. Aerie took one last chance to cling to it, trying desperately to memorize the scent that had mixed with her own over the last week. Her standard uniform, with its short sleeves and flexible material, would not keep her from the cold.

When Lieutenant Dubois came back into the room, an angry look on his face, she knew it was the only comfort she would be allowed.

Behind her, Meredith gasped. "Gerard? What are you doing here? I thought you were promoted."

Aerie swiveled at Meredith's outburst, turning just in time to see a small device fall out of her hands.

"Pick that up, you clumsy fool," the lieutenant snapped.

Meredith instantly dropped down and hurriedly picked up the item that fell. Aerie noticed her hands were shaking.

Lieutenant Dubois must've noticed it too, because he kicked her hand before she could stand up and laughed.

"It's no business of yours at all if I've been asked to see to Comrade St. Cloud's introduction to the Reeducation Program," he growled. "Now, pick up your tools and get back to work."

Aerie felt a rush of pity for Meredith as she scurried around, hiding her face in shame.

"Now, Comrade, on to you."

Aerie's eyes flashed back to the lieutenant's as he began speaking to her. She knew from Meredith's experience, she would likely be punished for making him angry.

"First of all, please call me Gerard," he began, his mood already shifting back from impatient irritation to one of vicious pleasure. "We're going to become close, you and I, and I wouldn't want you to feel any excess need to please simply because I am third in command."

Aerie said nothing. She was too nervous and too disgusted at the thought of even talking to him. To add to the chaos, she was held down by other members of the med team as small patches and strange devices were placed on her arms, neck, and forehead.

She considered herself fortunate that he seemed to enjoy

hearing himself talk. He often answered for her, as he went through the list of several defects in her character and some of the charges listed against her. It was only when he told her how this was all just for her own good that Aerie finally found the fortitude to respond.

"My own good?" Aerie shook her head. "You mean for the good of the URS."

"It is the same," Gerard assured her as he pushed a button.

A million or more spikes of lightning shot through her, entering in through the patches plastered on her upper body. Her mind raged, suddenly a beacon of horrific pain. She felt the scream rise in her throat even as she doubled down on her private resolve to be silent. Her body convulsed at the electroshock treatment; Aerie felt the straps around her legs and wrists tighten.

It was over seemingly long moments later, even though she knew it had only been seconds. Aerie felt tears drip down from her eyes, but she was proud that she'd remained silent.

"Please, call me Gerard," Lieutenant Dubois said. "And there's really no need to interrupt me, especially when it's my job to be asking the questions rather than answering them."

Aerie gaped at him, but still said nothing.

I can do this. I can survive this.

Her fingers shook and her body felt slack, but her mind was clear.

In fact, Aerie noticed, it was much more clear than it had been in weeks. For the first time, she could picture meeting Exton clearly in her head.

She could remember the fear and the uncertainty, as she was trapped on his ship, and then the anger and determination eating away at her patience as she fought with him. Aerie could remember the warmth he surrounded her with, as she slumped out of the tree, no stronger than she was now, strapped down to a medical bed, with electrodes placed on her skin.

"You're the enemy," she muttered, thinking of how she'd

seen Exton at the time, still dressed up in his pirate outfit.

"Oh, I'm far from your enemy," Gerard told her.

No. No, this time Gerard is the enemy. Exton never treated you this way.

She was about to ask him what he wanted from her when he pushed down on the button again.

Searing pain clung to her nerves, sending the burning fire all through her body.

This time, she screamed, the lightning pulsing through her even more perversely.

"Stop!" she hollered. "Stop it. I didn't even ask you a question."

"Ah, but you wanted to, didn't you, Aeris?" Gerard asked. "Or should I call you Aerie? It seems to be what so many of your unit members call you."

Aerie said nothing. She was determined to keep her focus on him. She might have screamed, but there was no reason to think he had power over her mind the same way he had the advantage over controlling her pain.

"Tell me," he ordered.

"Aerie's fine," she said, barely able to choke out the words.

"There now, that wasn't so hard. I assume." He held his hand over the button. "Now, say my name."

Aerie glared at him. "Gerard." She felt sick at saying it, as though she was going to vomit.

"There. We're almost friends now."

"I'd never be your friend," Aerie spat. "We're not supposed to have friends in the URS, remember?"

"Is that why you became a defector?"

Aerie's thoughts swept her away momentarily. Inside her mind, she recalled feeling the cool metal of the gun in her hand as Emery handed it to her.

"Shoot me," Emery said.

"No." Aerie gasped. That was the moment she realized it: She *was* a defector. She wanted to be there, on the *Perdition*, with all her new friends—people who cared about her, and people she genuinely cared about in return. People who didn't hold it over her that she disagreed with them on things. People who could accept her for who she was. People who could teach her how to be a better person while inspiring her to learn how to do just that on her own.

Another memory came rushing into her mind.

"Caring for others is primary, while cleaning is secondary." Aerie nearly laughed. Even cleaning the hallways with Olga, that jovial but demanding tutor of hers, was better than working under a snooty dictator like Director Anand.

"No?" Gerard's voice brought her back to the small room, where she was cold and hurting and trapped. "Then, enlighten me. Why do you want to defect from the URS?"

Aerie didn't know what to say. She fumbled around, searching for an answer. Before she could respond, there was a knock at the door.

"Just a few moments," Gerard called, before he turned back to her. "I've had a special request, straight down from the dictator himself, to break you. He's concerned how his second-in-command could have raised such an incorrigible charge."

So, this is about my father.

"Osgood is more than willing to blame your original unit director for this malfeasance," Gerard continued.

Mom. Aerie felt her heart skip a beat.

"She grew feckless in her last days, too," Gerard said. "We were relieved when she died, to be honest. Never thought we would thank MENACE, but the poison they dumped into the Hudson River actually managed to benefit us when it started giving her seizures from exposure."

Aerie struggled to hide her surprise. She remembered that. It had been several years ago, but she'd gone with her mom down to the Hudson. She had created cultures and examined them. She knew that it was just mutated bacteria, not a biological weapon.

But the URS didn't know that. Or at least, they didn't broadcast it as such.

She seethed, remembering all over again how much the URS couldn't be trusted. Even if they were to tell the truth, it would be diminished by the multitude of their lies.

And next to the mention of her mother, it was enough to anger her enough to keep fighting.

"The URS and its famous fairness," Aerie muttered.

Gerard pushed the button again, unleashing another round of torturous pain on her. Aerie felt the straps at her hands dig into her skin enough to make blood seep out in strips. "I'm beginning to think you enjoy the electroshocks, Aerie."

Aerie only grunted in response, unable to find a fitting reply.

"Is that why you decided to try to leave the URS so many times?" Gerard asked. "We're too fair here, for wanting people to be equal, to have everyone exactly the same?"

"No," Aerie muttered. "I didn't … "

She stopped.

"Didn't what?" Gerard bellowed in her ear. He took her face in his hands roughly. "At the heart of every traitor, there is a reason why. I want to know why."

"Why what?"

Pain washed over her again, while Gerard turned away in a huff.

He's growing impatient, she realized as she caught her breath.

"What do you want me to tell you?" Aerie yelled, before Gerard pushed down on the button again.

"If this is not going to work for us," Gerard told her, "I can always turn up the power."

Her heart ached as she remembered Exton, and how he managed to get her to cooperate with him. Gerard, in contrast, was the true bully.

"I'd rather you turn up the charm," Aerie replied before she could stop herself.

"You don't find me charming?" Gerard's eyebrows raised, as though he was insulted.

Sensing she'd found a weakness, Aerie barely gave him a

shrug.

She was relieved when he laughed a moment later. "You'll have to excuse me," he said through the last of his laughs. "I don't get many defectors as young as yourself to work with. But then, I've only been working here in the Reeducation program for seven years now."

Aerie watched him carefully. "If you've only been here for seven years, you must have started just before Captain Chainsword stole his starship from the URS."

Aerie was too tired to tell if he was taken aback or angry at her remark. But when he spoke, there was a heady vehemence in his voice.

"Captain Chainsword is nothing more than a silly myth," he said. "He's just a boy playing a dangerous game, and hardly a threatening one at that."

Aerie was surprised. "So you know him then."

He sneered. "Of course I know him. I'm the third-highest ranking leader of this nation. But I also went to school with him. I was in his class when we both studied under your unit leader. General St. Cloud favored him, even though I was clearly the better student. Biggest mistake of his life, especially when that traitor went off and joined MENACE."

Aerie blinked in surprise. "You knew Exton when he was younger?"

Rage burned into Gerard's vision. "How do you know his name?" he yelled, already pushing down on the button. "Tell me!"

The shockwave of pain demanded her full attention. Aerie cried out, even as her mind felt strangely free, the rest of her body wracked in excruciating misery.

When the sparks had stopped, she slumped forward, no longer worried about the blood around her wrists. Her body continued to scream in pain, as breathing became a terrible chore and her eyes, already tired from the sleep deprivation, couldn't seem to focus.

"Tell me how you know about him," Gerard bellowed once more. His words seemed to reverberate against the walls, echoing agonizingly back into her ears. "Did you learn about him from your unit director? Does General St. Cloud know about Exton, too?"

Before Aerie could reply, there was another knock at the door, this time louder—loud enough that it didn't sound like a knock at all.

Gerard spun toward the door. "Not yet!" he yelled. He turned back to Aerie. "No one else is supposed to know about Exton's true identity as Captain Chainsword. I thought I was the only one. Tell me, does St. Cloud know about him or not?"

"Doesn't Osgood know?" Aerie asked. She instantly regretted it, as she was dosed with another round of shocks. Under the patches on her arms, she could feel the hardened blistering of her skin as it burned.

"No," Gerard snapped. "And it is going to stay that way, until I can take Exton down. He always got what I wanted, and he didn't mind injuring me in the process. I will kill him one day, even if I have to kill you first."

Aerie mustered up what strength she could. "You won't break me," she vowed.

"We'll see about that," Gerard told her.

As he came up so close to her, she could see the hatred in his gaze. She shuddered and slinked back, pushing herself further into the uncomfortable bed behind her. "If you know Exton Shepherd at all, then you're no longer just an enemy—you're a threat. And I take threats very seriously."

Before he could make another move, the door slammed open. Aerie could barely raise her head to see what was going on, but she heard Meredith scream and knew it couldn't be anything good.

Gerard shouted out orders and the other medics went running, but they weren't able to get out beyond the man in the doorway. Aerie saw him go down a second later, taking a direct hit to the jaw.

Aerie felt her heart surge in hope and panic as sirens began to go off in the distance.

Meredith, somewhat recovered, hurried to release her from her bonds while the fighting continued. "Can you stand?" she asked, raising her voice loud enough to be heard over the alarms. "I'm sorry for all of that."

"I'll live," Aerie replied, extremely relieved to be freed. "Are you okay? I saw him hurt you earlier."

She gave Aerie a shaky smile. "He was promoted recently, but he worked here for several years. I just wasn't expecting to see him again, here, like this."

Aerie wondered if she was telling the whole truth, but she was too exhausted to do much more than wonder as Meredith carefully pulled out the last of her IVs.

"We need to get you out of here."

Aerie barely shook her head. "I can't move," she mumbled. She gripped her shaking hands, feeling the stickiness of dried blood.

"Aerie."

A man's voice called to her, and Aerie forced herself to try to move, for all the good it did. Her body was still reeling from its pain.

"I'm here to rescue you."

Her energy levels were low, but Aerie cheered at his muffled words.

Exton. He's finally come for me!

"Is that really you?" Aerie reached up clumsily, and felt a hand wrap around her arm.

He steadied her and pulled her up to her feet.

She stumbled, relieved, as he leaned forward and caught her. She held onto him tightly, pressing her face into his shoulder. "I've been waiting for you. I've missed you so much."

"Come on," he said. "We need to move quickly if we're going to get to the Military Academy before they realize what I've done and they shut me out."

Aerie frowned. Exton hadn't been a student in the military. He told her that he had been studying to be an engineer.

She gazed up at the man who held her, and she did a double-take. "Brock?"

"Who did you think it was?"

Aerie almost snapped at him, but she saw that his eyes were soft. He was trying to add levity to the situation, she realized, as his grip tightened around her.

"Never mind, just hang on. This might be uncomfortable."

"Wait."

"We've got to go," he said. "What is it?"

"I … I need my jacket," she said. "I'm cold."

"I'll get you another one at the base—" Brock's words were cut off as Meredith stepped forward.

"Here." Meredith gave her a kind smile as she handed her the jacket. "Be careful." She leaned forward and gave Aerie a hug, one Aerie could barely feel from being shocked so much.

But as she held onto Meredith, Aerie heard her whisper, "Please say hello to my brother for me when you get back to the *Perdition.*"

A memory floated to the surface of her mind, one of a young man with similar blond hair and brown eyes as Meredith—Tyler, Emery's husband, and a close friend of Exton's. Aerie recalled how he'd been kind to her, and supportive of Exton, everything Aerie had ever wanted in a friend herself.

Aerie grinned. "I will," she promised. "Thank you. And please be careful, too."

Meredith nodded, before heading out of the room, screaming in terror as she played the role she'd assigned for herself.

"Are you ready now?" Brock asked as he turned to Aerie.

"Yes," Aerie said as she nodded. "Let's go."

♦14♦

Aerie had been to the New Hope Military Academy several times throughout her school career. She remembered walking around the building in awe, trying to take everything in and memorize it, preparing herself for the day when she would be accepted into its hallowed halls. She recalled feeling strong and powerful, able to move the destiny of the world by just being there.

Now, as she tucked her face down even more into Brock's shoulder, trying to find warmth as they approached the hangar, she felt nothing but winded contempt for the place and, she admitted silently, for herself at her earlier naiveté.

"Just hold on, Aerie," Brock told her. "It'll be alright. I'll make sure you're okay."

"You have a plan?" she asked, surprised. She wasn't sure what had caused Brock to break the rules he revered, but she was even more surprised he seemed so confident about being able to do it successfully.

He surprised her by giving her a small smile. "Just trust me."

Aerie balked and tightened her grip around him, despite the uncomfortable feeling of swaying back and forth in his arms. Around them, more alarms were going off, and she knew this could end very badly. She prayed they would be able to escape.

"I don't want to go back to the center," she said quietly. She squeezed her eyes shut in shame, reliving the seconds of torture and recalling Gerard's gleeful face.

She scowled. Between Gerard's sick pleasure and the agony shooting through her body, she didn't know which was worse to remember.

I'll have to ask Exton about him. Aerie wondered why Gerard hated him so much.

Thinking of Exton made her heart soar. Maybe Brock

would take her to the Chaya settlement after all, now that they were officially URS dissenters.

Before she could ask Brock about heading for Chaya, she heard a voice call out to him from behind them.

"Brock!"

Aerie stiffened at her sister's call. *What is Serena doing here?* She turned to see her older sister was in her work uniform, hurrying down the hall with a med pack strapped on her back. Belatedly, Aerie recalled she worked at the base as a combat med.

"Serena," Brock called back.

Aerie felt even more uncomfortable as she heard him use Serena's first name.

"What are you—?" Serena's voice faltered and the charismatic lilt disappeared. "Aerie."

"Serena." Aerie bit her lip before she raised her chin, trying to look brave, even though she knew she was a mess. She was still dressed in her uniform, with the hospital gown over her shirt, and she was barefoot. Her hair was loose, and she didn't want to know what her face looked like after hours of sleep deprivation and torture.

"What happened to you?" Serena asked, not out of concern but contempt. "Why are you here like that? You didn't make Brock do something, did you?"

As Brock explained their situation to Serena, Aerie sighed. Despite Serena's aloofness, Aerie had never felt she lived up to her sister's legacy. Serena was smart and sharp, and everyone knew her for one reason or another. With their mother's green eyes and reddish-brown hair, Serena easily had her pick of admirers. She was tall and toned, and more than once she had been hailed as the beauty of the family.

"Well, whatever she did to twist you up in her mess, you can't go into the hangar with her," Serena said angrily, jolting Aerie back to the present. "There's a battle going on. A couple of fighters have been stolen and several workers have been injured."

The hallway shook as explosions started to cry out from

the hangar. Angry shouts and frightened screams accompanied the roaring sound of crumbling structures.

Aerie felt Brock's grip tighten around her, but this time it seemed to be more because of irritation rather than desperation. "We've got to leave, Serena. I'm sorry."

He turned away for a moment, before glancing back at her. "Why don't you come with us? Aerie could use the medical support."

Aerie felt her mouth drop open. Serena looked equally appalled by the situation.

"Come on. I know you're the best we have on the military med services," Brock said.

Serena shot Aerie a smug smile at the compliment, but she still hesitated. "I don't know. Cal and Dorian are taking off. If we head out, we might get caught in the battle."

"It's a risk we'll have to take," Brock said. "Aerie and I need to get out of here."

Serena narrowed her eyes. "I know *she* has to leave, especially if she doesn't want to end up in Reeducation again."

Aerie stuck her tongue out at her. Before Serena could retaliate, Brock stepped forward.

"I'm helping Aerie," he declared. "I'm *not* leaving her behind."

"Well, she's not well," Serena said with a groan. "And really, Brock, she's a *traitor.* Who cares about her?"

Aerie winced at Serena's accusation and shrunk back from her glare.

"I do."

Aerie felt a rush of warmth toward Brock. *What do you know?* Aerie wondered. *Brock is capable of being loyal to me, even over the State.*

She was just beginning to believe she had underestimated Brock when he ruined the moment by asking Serena to come with them.

"Come with us, Serena, please," Brock said. "I'll need you to help take care of her while we get out of here. And I'll need a copilot for the cargo ship, anyway."

Serena chewed on her lip thoughtfully. "I don't want to be responsible when the URS captures us and hauls us back here for punishment."

"You don't have to come if you don't think you can survive," Aerie retorted.

"Aerie," Brock muttered.

Serena ignored him. "So, the little mother is challenging me? That's amusing, because I always won our games when we were kids."

"We're not kids anymore, and this is not a game," Aerie said. "So if you don't think you have it in you, don't bother. I might be the one who needs medical help, but at least I know I can survive this better than you."

"I was trained to survive the worst parts of war long before you were even in combat class," Serena snapped. "What do you know about that? You spent all your free time at the housing unit with our mother, helping her weed out her garden, before she managed to get herself killed."

"I learned plenty," Aerie shot back. "I'll bet anything you're just scared."

"Scared?" Serena huffed. "You're the one who should be scared. You're the one who's bleeding and can't even walk." She nodded to the small trail of blood following from Aerie's leg as it dripped down onto the legs of Brock's pants.

Aerie blushed before turning to Brock. "I can take care of my own medical needs while you get us out of here."

There was another explosion that blasted through the corridor, and Aerie felt herself sway dangerously as Brock staggered under the blast.

"Come on," Brock ordered. "We need to get to a transport."

He hurried off, and Aerie was able to glance over his shoulder just enough to see Serena scowl as she started to follow them.

"Wait! I'm coming."

Great. I don't need her along for the ride.

"Can I put you down for a bit, Aerie?" Brock asked. "Are you feeling well enough to walk?"

She nodded and blushed. "Yes, please."

"Here, put your arm around my shoulder," Brock said as he shifted her.

Aerie felt her legs buckle as she straightened, but with Brock's support she knew she could make it to a ship.

"Now, let's head for that cargo carrier right there. It'll be big enough for all of us, and it should be stocked with enough supplies."

"Where are we going?" Aerie asked.

Brock didn't appear to hear her as he hurried her forward. Several people called out to him, but he waved them off with his free arm. Serena raced up behind them, easily matching Brock's uneven pace.

Others were hurrying around, trying to get to their different positions while the hangar was under attack. As Brock pulled her out of the hallway and into the hangar, Aerie was able to see more of the damage that had been caused.

There were some people who were injured, but it looked like the loss was minimal. She could hear pilots being called to their fighters over the announcement system, and she could hear other warnings as the newly minted URS fighters were cleared for takeoff.

"This is incredible," Aerie said, her voice hushed. *What was going on?*

"Seems like two traitors stole two of our new ships," Serena said. "I wonder where the twins are."

"They could've taken off already," Brock said.

"No, Cal and Dorian are sequenced for launch behind their squad commander, Drex. He's over there, that big guy by the fuel center, but his ship is gone," Serena replied.

"Cal and Dorian are here?" Aerie asked.

"Somewhere," Serena said with a shrug. "They were called."

Brock turned his attention to the cargo ship's docking

bay. "Here," he said, thrusting Aerie over to Serena. "Let me see if I can hack the code for this shuttle."

Serena shoved Aerie away from her, sending her flying to the ground. "Here," she said, stepping up next to Brock. "There's an emergency med code we can use to break in."

"Oh, cool." Brock's eyes lit up.

Aerie frowned, but she hurried to get up off the floor again. *Just keep going,* she thought. *You'll be able to find Exton soon, even if you have to deal with Serena for the next several hours … or days.*

Realizing the uncertainty of their situation, Aerie lost her balance again. She fell to the floor, hard, hitting her hip against the cement flooring. She scrambled to move, but this time she forced herself to move slowly.

As she gradually got back on her feet, she did have to wonder what Brock had in mind.

Before she could ask him, the docking doors opened. Serena made her way inside as another blast ricocheted off the outer hangar walls. A large explosion went off in the background, making Aerie wonder if a ship had been shot down.

Are we even going to be able to get out of here?

Brock grabbed her once more, picking her up into his arms. "Come on, Aerie," he said. He smiled down at her, kindly. "I'm sorry that you fell. I thought Serena would hold you while I waited."

"Well, we know not to expect that again," Aerie grumbled.

"At least she got us into the ship," Brock said as he followed Serena down toward the cockpit.

As they came out of the galley, Brock led her into the small infirmary. Inside were only a couple of stations, with only one examination bed. Aerie was about to ask if she could join him in the cockpit until Serena was ready to fix her up, when he interrupted her.

"Here," Brock said as he set her down onto the medic chair. He buckled her in, careful not to hurt her. Aerie was grateful, especially when he took the time to loop the straps around her injured shoulder, even though she knew they were pressed for time.

Aerie reached out and took Brock's arm. "Wait."

"What is it?" Brock looked down at her, and for a moment, Aerie saw his gaze soften. Even as the world was at war, the hangar was attacked, and Serena was cursing loudly in the cockpit next door, she felt herself taken aback by Brock's concern.

She had wanted to ask him to turn on the monitors in the infirmary so she could monitor their flight from where she was. But Aerie faltered, and instead only said, "Thank you. I know this wasn't an easy thing for you to do."

He nodded.

"I didn't like it when you seemed to side with them on so much," Aerie admitted. "I wasn't sure you were my friend." She was going to ask him if he had help from the Ecclesia when another bomb exploded outside the hangar.

"Sometimes friendship means looking out for each other's better interests," Brock told her. He reached down and ruffled her hair some, before leaning down.

Aerie was surprised to feel the quick warmth of his lips on hers.

She jolted back in surprise, her head digging into the cushion of the chair.

He backed away and grinned. Before she could tell him she wasn't interested in him that way, he turned his gaze back to the helm. "I gotta head up there and help Serena take off. I'll send her back here once we're clear."

Aerie watched as Brock headed out to leave, feeling awkward.

"Brock!" Serena called. "Get out here. One of those fighters just took out the signal tower!"

Brock turned to Aerie. "I'm going to have to take off manually," he said. "Don't move from the chair. It'll be a bumpy enough ride."

"Okay," Aerie said.

As she settled into her chair, she felt the ship begin to move.

Aerie began to try to clean up the blood seeping from her cuts and scrapes, and where the IV needles had been inserted. She tenderly ran her fingers over the small blackened bumps where the electrode patches had been placed on her arms, and she hoped Serena had some burn cream in her med pack.

She wasn't concerned as she felt the ship swerve and drop and accelerate; she knew Brock was a good pilot, and Serena had enough sense to know how to follow directions on a plane. It was only when Brock hollered that she leaned forward.

The monitor was beeping loudly. There was another ship coming their way.

"It's Captain Chainsword's shuttle," Brock called out. "Hold on, Aerie. This is too good of an opportunity to miss. We're going to attack."

Exton!

"No." She gasped. As the ship sailed out of the hangar, she began to fumble with her seatbelt.

♦15♦

Exton jolted awake suddenly, as his body jostled around with the turbulence. He reached out in front of him as he blinked open his eyes, surprised to find there was no control console in front of him.

"You okay?" Emery's voice was stark against the quietness filling the rest of the ship. He glanced over at his sister, watching her for a long moment as she sat calmly in the copilot's seat.

"Yeah," he murmured, rubbing his eyes.

"We're passing through the last little bit of a storm."

"Where are we?" He glanced outside the window. All he could see from the ship was a grim, gray line of clouds, fighting the sea every inch of the horizon.

"I was just about to wake you up," Emery told him. "We have about ten minutes until we arrive in New Hope airspace, and twelve from the rendezvous point."

He nodded, taking in the ship's readings. He was surprised to see he had slept as long as he had. He was confident that Emery, along with the five other crew members, would cover for him, and he had been exhausted. The weariness of the battle at Chaya and its aftermath had settled into him and finally lulled him into an uneasy sleep.

Despite everything working in his favor, he still had trouble convincing himself to rest. Exton had been waiting for the moment he could act, and he was energized at the thought.

He sat up in his chair. Excitement at seeing Aerie again, even knowing she wouldn't remember him, gave him the power to fight off his fatigue.

He glanced over at his sister, who was calmly piloting the ship, as they prepared to attack.

"You didn't have to come, you know."

Emery flinched; Exton knew his remark caught Emery off guard, but not enough that she'd let it slide. "I didn't want to stay on the *Perdition.* You always get to have all the fun," she replied.

"I know you worry."

"I also happen to be your best pilot." Emery's hands tightened around the controls as she shot him a sneer.

Exton knew she had a point, but he was certain that wasn't the reason she had shown up aboard his favorite ship, the one in which he met Aerie for the first time.

"Still," he said, "you have to watch yourself with the baby, don't you?"

"As I've told you before, you can't use my baby to get rid of me."

"I'll have to find some other excuse then."

She glared at him, briefly, before turning her attention back to the screen in front of her. "I'll keep finding ways around them, Exton, and you're lucky I do. I'm the one who managed to get in contact with Aerie through the Ecclesia, didn't I?"

"You have a point," Exton said. "By the way, who did you get to go behind my back to do it? Was it Dennis or Don? I know they know pretty much all the remnant leaders."

"It wasn't either of them, actually, nor any of the others. Tyler contacted Meredith."

Recalling the relentless cheerfulness of Tyler's sister, Exton scowled. "She's already in enough danger, especially because of what happened when we took back the *Perdition.* You shouldn't have done that."

"Well, you shouldn't have returned Aerie in the first place," Emery shot back. "You should've threatened St. Cloud with a nuke to New Hope or something like that."

"He knows who we are, Emery. He would still have plenty to hold against us."

"If you're worried about the people who trade with us or the people who get stuff from the black markets—"

"That's only part of it, but what I meant was more along the line of what he knows about our family and the Ecclesia.

St. Cloud's smart, and he's known our family for a long time."

"I know that. He's probably watching for you at this point."

Exton smiled at her. Despite his teasing, he was glad to have her by his side. "Roger that."

Exton looked down as they headed in toward the lands of their childhood home. He could see the rolling hills just beyond New Hope, where he and his father started construction of the *Perdition* together. It was tempting to slide back into the memories of his childhood. But the moment passed, and the horizon shifted. The New Hope Military Academy, the shining bright spot among the ruins of New York from which New Hope was born, came into view.

"I miss our home," Exton admitted quietly, more to himself than anyone else.

"I know. I do, too." Emery gave him a sad smile. "You know, I was wondering something."

Exton sighed. He knew an inquisition in the making when he heard it from his sister.

"I know Merra's convincing, but you don't do anything you don't want to do, unless you feel you have to." She glanced over at him. "Was there another reason you decided war was the best response to the URS?"

"I started changing my mind once Merra told me that Gerard was the one who was promoted to St. Cloud's old position as chief military strategist," he said quietly.

"Gerard?" Emery balked. "He's been promoted?" she asked, her voice incredulous.

"Yes," Exton said quietly. "I felt the same way."

Emery closed her eyes briefly. "Do you think Osgood is intentionally doing this to us?"

"I wouldn't put it past him, if we were better acquainted. So far, St. Cloud seems to be the one who is calling the shots when it comes to us." Exton thought of Osgood, the man who had ordered his father's execution and the man who was behind the URS's many woes. His fingers dug into his palms as he clenched his fists. "But St. Cloud hated dealing with Gerard when we were in class together, and he made no secret of it."

"I know Meredith's been watching him," Emery said. "It's been close to seven years since everything happened. Do you think we'll have to … ?"

"I don't know," Exton replied glumly. He didn't want to think about it, especially after Meredith's role in helping Aerie. "I know we promised Meredith we would do everything we could, though. And now that Gerard has been promoted, going on the offensive seemed like a good way to draw him out."

Before either of them could speculate further, a beeping noise sounded out from the control console. Emery frowned. "Something's wrong."

There was something in her tone which made Exton pause. "What is it?"

"The military academy. It seems to be in the middle of a battle already."

Exton turned to face Thora, who had arrived with Emery as part of a new attack crew. "What does the data show?"

"Two ships are attacking the base," Thora said as she studied the incoming figures. "Two URS fighter-class. It looks like there's another one about to launch, but it's a cargo carrier."

The feeling that something was off came rushing at him once more. Before, when he attacked the Memory Tree, he felt the force of Osgood's attack was too strong. This time, it was the timing. The timing was off.

"See if you can link up to the attacking fighters' comms," he ordered. "Maybe we can help them."

"Exton, we need to get Aerie first. If anything, this is the perfect distraction. We can slip in, slip out, and no one will be the wiser."

"The Ecclesia said they were going to get Aerie to us," Exton reminded her. "I need to know the specs."

"I guess it is true they haven't contacted Tyler," Emery

said. "They were supposed to call him when they had her."

Exton turned to his other side, where another one of his aids stood at the ready. "Sir. What's your name?"

The man turned and eyed him. "I know it's been awhile, Captain, but I'm Phil."

"Sorry," Exton muttered. There were over a thousand workers on the *Perdition* and several more thousand people down at Petra. He couldn't remember them all, and he had no idea why people expected him to. "Phil, get me the *Perdition.* See if Jared or Tyler is at the helm. Thora, can you link up the comms to the fighters?"

"Rerouting comm signals," Thora replied with a press of a button. "We'll know in a moment."

"*Perdition* on the comm, sir," Phil replied.

"Tyler, can you hear me?" Exton called. "What's going on at the military academy?"

"The Ecclesia have staged an attack," Tyler responded. "I was just about to call you."

"Did you hear anything?"

"Meredith said Aerie's been picked up, but she wasn't delivered to the team. Our contacts in New Hope had a way to slip her out to the old building site."

Exton felt his heart stop. "She didn't make it?"

"Not to the team. One of them saw her taken into another ship, with two other people."

"Can you hack the surveillance feed?" Exton asked.

Before Tyler could answer, a new alarm went off.

"Cargo ship approaching, with locked targets," Emery called. "Buckle up, it's time for evasive maneuvers."

Two blazes of fire streamed through the sky toward them. The missiles barely passed them, as Emery rolled the ship to the side. Exton hurried to strap himself in, certain that the missiles had only missed by the slimmest of chances.

Either that, or I've just witnessed another miracle.

"Exton, are you there?" Tyler's voice came in over the comm once more.

"What is it?"

"We have two more fighters launching behind the approaching ship," Emery said. "Sensors on alert, shields up to maximum power."

"We have a bit of a problem," Tyler said.

"What is it?"

"St. Cloud is on the line here. He says he wants to talk to you."

"St. Cloud?" Exton snarled. "Put him on."

"Are you sure?"

"I'm sure I'll regret this, but I want to know how he managed to get through our jamming signals."

"Can't argue with you there," Tyler muttered. "At this rate, I'm going to have to go back to school and learn some more tricks myself."

"Just put him on."

"Rerouting now."

St. Cloud's voice came over the line a second later. "Exton, I didn't think I would get the chance to make your acquaintance again so soon."

"Worried for the bump on my head, were you?" Exton gritted his teeth. "You already knew you would have to hit harder if you wanted to stop me."

"I happen to know how sturdy your head is," the general bit back. "You're lucky I didn't straight up kill you."

"You're lucky Aerie was there to protect you," Exton said, his voice rising in anger. "I could have just killed you there and taken care of it."

"This is a very lovely chat," St. Cloud said, "but I have a more pressing issue I want to discuss. If you think you're really going to be able to attack the entire New Hope Military Base with just your shuttle, then perhaps you should be more worried about it."

Exton struggled not to yell any amount of obscenities in response. He wasn't about to admit that they were there to pick up Aerie.

"If you're here for Aerie," St. Cloud said, "you just missed her. She's on the cargo ship with my other daughter."

Exton's rage turned into bewilderment. "Why are you telling me this?" he yelled. "What makes you think I believe you, after everything you've done to me and my family? And what makes you think I'm here for Aerie to begin with?"

"You should recall I know you better than even you know yourself. I trained you to be who you are, Exton, as a fighter and as a leader."

Exton felt a rush of rage that nearly blinded him. "You're wrong," he said, thinking of nothing else he could say to derail him.

"We'll have to revisit the argument later. For now, I'd rather you didn't blow up the cargo transport ship," St. Cloud said. "And I thought I'd give you the proper incentive to avoid doing just that."

"Why should I believe you?" Exton yelled again.

"You can't," St. Cloud replied easily enough. "But are you willing to bet your rage on Aerie's life?" With that, the image of his enemy faded away.

Emery reached over and took his arm, offering her support as she signaled to him to calm down. It was a small comfort, one that didn't go far as Exton watched the cargo ship cruise by, heading off into the cloudy horizon.

"Follow that ship," he muttered to Emery. "If Aerie's on it, we'll get her."

"What if St. Cloud is lying?" Emery asked.

"Aerie's still supposed to be transferred to the old site," Exton said. "The Ecclesia can keep her there safely until we get back."

"Captain," Phil called. "There are two new fighters coming at us."

"Prepare to engage," Exton said. "If we're able to take them out while we're here, all the better. That'll save our allies and our people from some attacks, at least."

"Sir," Thora said. "The new pair of fighters are fighting with the others. Should we move to assist?"

Exton grimaced as one fighter jet exploded. "Not yet," he said. "We can't be sure we won't hit one of our guys. Thora, were you able to find a way to open the comms?"

"No, Captain," Thora called. She brushed her long hair out of her face. "Still working on getting an open line. There's more interference as we move away from the base."

Static came over the monitor as Thora tried to reach out to the different fighters. Exton looked off into the distance as the cargo ship disappeared into the cloudy horizon.

We have to hurry.

"Emery," he called, "can you—"

Boom!

Beside them, another fighter burst into a ball of flames, before the burning twisted metal fell out of the sky.

"No survivors from that one," Phil murmured. "A direct hit."

Exton watched as the two remaining ships, instead of fighting with each other or heading back to the base, took off in the direction of the cargo ship. He gripped the console controls, wondering if they would attack Aerie's ship before he could get to them.

But when the fighters flanked the cargo ship, taking on a protective role a moment later, Exton felt a mix of suspicion and relief.

"They must not be from the Ecclesia," Emery said.

"No, not likely. Our team members were the ones they blew up," Phil concluded. "Tyler was able to hack the feeds. Those fighters aren't on our side."

"What are they doing?" Exton asked. "Why aren't they attacking the cargo ship? Even if they're not our allies, why are they protecting Aerie? She's an enemy of the URS now."

"It's entirely possible they are working with the Ecclesia, even if they aren't members," Emery said, uncertainty still overshadowing the hope in her voice. "We do harbor our share of dissenters, and they don't seem to be concerned with us. Should we follow them?"

"Captain," Thora called. "The cloud cover is getting thicker the further away from New Hope we get. We're having trouble with our comms. If we do follow them into the thick cloud covering, we might not be able to reach the *Perdition.*"

Exton grimaced. He hated to shut out Tyler and the rest of his allies, even if he knew it would only take a couple of hours. The cloud cover posed other threats, too; there were traces of toxins and ash, left over from the nuclear radiation, and it was entirely possible that the cargo ship could disappear without a moment's notice. *Especially,* he thought, *if they are only headed this way with the hope of losing us.*

He hesitated for the longest moment he could. Emery looked back at him, and Exton had no answer. But he made his choice, praying that it was the right one.

"See if you can track the cargo ship directly," Exton ordered. "I know it'll be hard with all the cloud cover, but it's more important that we follow that one than the others. We don't know enough about them. Their orders might be to act as decoys now."

"Roger," Emery answered. "Thora, can you help me with the tracker?"

Exton sat back in his chair, trying to calm his nerves and release the tension in his body. He'd been *so close* to getting Aerie back.

I hope you're okay, Aerie.

Exton knew he was going to get back to her. He knew it, just as surely as he knew it was only a matter of time now.

Emery had insisted before that God was still a god of miracles, and if there was ever a time for miracles, it was now.

♦16♦

"What do you think you're doing?!" Brock yelled, as Aerie launched herself over the control console.

"Stop it," Aerie shouted back. "You can't attack him! He's … he's … " She blushed furiously as she faltered.

Serena scowled at her. "We're focusing on saving you," she reminded Aerie. "Did you ever stop to think that if we managed to take down the number one enemy of our nation, you'd be given some slack?"

"I don't need you to protect me," Aerie snapped.

"Yes, you do. And you're getting blood all over the control board."

Aerie glanced down to see the little lines of blood dripping out of her arms. "I'll clean it up," she muttered apologetically.

"Aerie, please, just go sit down," Brock ordered. He sighed indignantly as he straightened in his seat. "You got your wish, apparently. You managed to move my missile target. He's still out there."

Relief and gratitude sunk into her, even as she realized there was still danger—danger for Exton, if Brock or the URS continued to fight him, and danger for herself, if she revealed to Serena or Brock her exact feelings about the space pirate captain.

She knew she had to convince them to refrain from attacking Exton again.

"Look," she said slowly, "we can't attack him."

"Why not?" Brock frowned at her.

"Because," Aerie said slowly. *Come on, think, think, think! This is no time to be stupid about this.*

An idea hit her, full force.

"Because he's the perfect scapegoat," Aerie explained. "With him out there, the other fighters will be less worried about following and attacking us."

When they both refrained from responding right away,

Aerie knew she'd said the right thing. Now she just had to make sure she didn't overplay her hand.

"I mean, really, Brock," she said, turning to him. Aerie knew if she could win him over, it would be easier to get Serena to go along with her plan. "You saw what they were doing to me in the med ward of the Reeducation Center. Do you think they'll let a little thing like killing one of our enemies stop them from sending me back there?"

"No," he said. He turned back to the console and sighed. "Fine. You were probably right. But Serena's right about the blood. You need her help."

Serena unbuckled and stood up. "I'll take care of her wounds," she said, her voice full of reluctance. "You just find a place we can land."

"It's going to be a while," Brock said. "We're pretty far away from our destination."

"Where are we headed?" Aerie asked, suddenly curious. Where was it possible to go and hide from the URS?

"Let's just hope we have some insulated jackets in this ship somewhere," Brock said. "We're going south."

"Are you going to Petra?" Aerie asked, before recalling she wasn't supposed to know about Petra in the first place.

Brock gave her a quizzical look, but before Aerie could get more details, Serena jumped up. "Come on, Aerie! Watch it," she yelled. "Now you're dripping on my uniform, and thanks to you, this is the only one I have."

Serena stood up angrily. "Brock, can you take care of the helm by yourself?"

"Sure," Brock said. "I've plugged in the coordinates. We should be fine."

Aerie glanced out the front window, surprised to see they were surrounded by thick, gray clouds.

At least I have some of idea of where we're going, Aerie thought.

"If you're sure." Serena pursed her lips together.

A second later, Aerie jumped as a pair of URS fighters came up beside the ship. She gasped. "Look out!"

"Don't worry about it," Brock said. "That's just Cal and

Dorian."

Even Serena seemed surprised. "What are they doing here?"

"They're following us," Brock said.

"I can see that much," Serena muttered as she rolled her eyes. "*Why* are they here?"

"They agreed to come with me." Brock shifted uncomfortably in his seat.

"Why?" Aerie asked. She glared out the window, as one of her twin brothers—Cal, most likely, since he was more of the show-off—twirled his ship around. "Was it just to protect me?"

"I know you might not like it, but it's helpful," Brock told her. "And they are my friends, Aerie, even if you don't like them."

"But—"

"Aerie, watch it! You're still getting blood everywhere. Come on," Serena interjected, grabbing Aerie by the shoulders and pushing her out of the cockpit and toward the infirmary. "I'd better clean you up now, before you make an even bigger mess."

"But I want—"

"Come with me, now!" Serena's voice carried enough authority to make Aerie comply. She didn't have the strength to resist much anyway. Nor did she really want to. Knowing she was safe from the URS was enough for her, for the moment.

She barely watched as Serena cleaned off her wounds, even chiseling off some of the burnt skin on her upper forearms.

"Well," Serena huffed indignantly. "It seems you've finally improved some when it comes to following directions."

Aerie's face burned. Serena didn't know it, but she had hit a particularly sore point.

"You know, Cal and Dorian and I don't protect you of our own choosing," Serena told her. "Before Mom died, she told us if anything ever happened to you, we would have to take care of you."

Aerie stiffened as Serena talked about their mother—and in such familiar terms. Aerie realized she'd never known that Serena referred to their mother as "Mom."

"So if you're wondering why the twins are out there in their fighters following us, it's probably because of that."

Aerie softened. "I'm sorry I never realized how much Mom meant to you," she said softly.

Serena flinched. "Don't worry about it. And don't apologize. It's a sign of weakness."

"The URS says that," Aerie replied. "I don't believe them about that. And I don't believe that about love anymore, either."

"Oh, great," Serena scoffed. "So I suppose you're one of those people who are convinced that there's some person out there who will complete your life, and they'll love you forever and all that garbage now?"

"Why do you say that?" Aerie asked. "Is it wrong to believe love is not just a response to stimuli?"

"Here," Serena said, throwing her a food pack. "Eat this. You need to eat."

Aerie complied, but repeated her question. "Why do you think love is nothing special?"

"It's a subjective feeling," Serena said.

"That doesn't mean it's wrong."

"It doesn't mean that it's right." Serena shook her head. "Objectivity is better."

"But what about marriage? What if it's more—"

"Don't be silly, Aerie. Marriages were thought to be for love once, but it didn't work out. That's part of the reason the URS scrapped the idea and they went with units. It's much better for everyone if no one can really get hurt."

"That's just silly," Aerie said. "They threw out something good because part of it was bad?"

"Pain *is* bad, Aerie." Serena rolled her eyes. "I shouldn't have to tell you that. And anyway, weddings were just ceremonies to show off wealth, and marriages were hardly harmonious. The divorce rate was just deplorable before the Union of North America was reformed into the URS."

"But some people still made it," Aerie insisted.

"Yeah, likely people who didn't know their full options or what they were really doing. You're young yet," Serena said. "You don't know what you're talking about. Love still boils down to science. Circumstances, sex, age, attraction, and the advantage of being in a relationship. Those things change with time."

"What about the relationships you can't choose?"

Serena shook her head. "Those doesn't matter. If you're stuck, you're stuck."

"It has to matter some, or I doubt you and our brothers would be here," Aerie pointed out.

"Well, I was talking more about the idealistic, romantic idiots who believe in marriage for love instead of material advantage." Serena's jaw tightened in irritation. "I wasn't talking about family."

"But you were just talking about Mom."

"So?"

"So you didn't just like her because of a response to stimuli?"

Serena laughed. "I barely liked her at all. She was always causing trouble for us." When Aerie frowned, Serena shrugged. "I guess you don't remember as much of it as I do. She allowed us to read books, you know—not the textbook kind, but novels, the kind with frivolous stories and imaginary people and places."

"She got in trouble for that?" Aerie asked. She thought of Exton's collection of books, the ones she'd found in his room.

"Of course. *I* got in trouble for it, too. The URS is dedicated to survival. There's hardly any value in novels when it comes to survival."

"If there's no value, why did she get in trouble for it?"

"Because, Aerie, *time* is valuable. You could learn several more useful things in the amount of time it took to read a novel."

"The General is the one who had the books," Aerie said, remembering.

"For collector's items." Serena sighed. "Look, I don't want to talk about it. Mom made our lives harder by her insistence on silly things. You did the same thing a lot, too, come to think of it. No matter what you say, there's no novel we ever had that could tell you how to properly bandage a wound and interpret blood composition readings." She gestured to the monitor at the side of the room, where her blood samples were going through several testing protocols.

Aerie glanced over at the monitor, her gaze listless. She wondered if part of the reason Serena didn't seem to like her that much was because she reminded her of their mother.

"If I cause you so many problems, why are you here then?" Aerie asked. "Mom's gone. What she said before shouldn't sway you any."

Serena frowned. "Brock asked for help. That's why I'm here. You think I enjoy tagging after my little sister, particularly one who's already cost our family so much?"

"I don't see why my actions should bother you."

"I don't either." Serena's frown deepened.

"But they do."

"They would bother anyone," Serena snapped. "You're an enemy of the United Revolutionary States, the most fair and equal country that's left in the world."

"Fair and equal aren't the same things."

"Doesn't matter, as long as it's the same results."

Aerie said nothing as Serena continued to wipe off the bloodstains and bandage up her wounds. She had never been close with her sister. Serena was a few years older than her, and even though they came from the same unit, it was more like they came from different worlds. They never agreed much before their mother died, and it seemed that chasm had only grown as they got older.

Her brothers had teased her, but they never seemed to be

malicious about it the way Serena had. Aerie saw that now, even if they'd hurt her with their taunting more than she would've admitted at the time.

Aerie thought about Exton and Emery, glad she was finally able to recall them without the headache. She remembered how at ease they were with each other, still able to disagree and fight, yet walk away friends. They looked out for each other.

Different worlds indeed, Aerie thought as she studied Serena's face while she finished tying off the last of her bandages.

"There," Serena said. "Now, *stay here*. You need to rest. Even though the electroshock was on a lower setting—"

"You've got to be kidding me," Aerie grumbled.

"You'll be fine. There aren't likely to be any long-term effects, given your age and general health," Serena told her. "I'm checking some of your blood for infections and the like, but I don't expect to see anything out of the ordinary."

"Thank you," Aerie said quietly.

"It's standard procedure."

"It still kind of you."

Serena bristled. "Fine," she said. "I'm going to go back up to help Brock at the helm. You stay here and rest. I'll be back in a bit."

"Okay."

Aerie watched as Serena disappeared out the door. She sighed as she closed her eyes and leaned back, her body finally at its final limits.

Aerie didn't know how long she slept, only that when she awoke from her dreams, it was to the explosive fire and alarms blaring.

"What in the world is *that*?!"

Aerie smiled at the surprise in Serena's voice. It was not very often that she was caught off guard. Her smile disappeared a moment later when the ship rocked, hit by a blast from the side.

"We're hit!" Brock's voice was infinitely more terrifying.

Aerie glanced around. She saw the blood composition monitor blinking, and her body was stiff and sore from sleeping in the medic chair. But her bandages were holding up, and the burned areas of her skin had dulled from a charred black to a smoky gray.

She made her choice and unbuckled herself. She stretched quickly, trying to ignore the queasiness of her stomach. The ship shuddered around her, as the battle continued around them.

Finally, Aerie made her way back to the cockpit. "What's going on?" she asked, as she glanced out the front window. She gaped at the sight before her.

Directly in front of them was a large, gray ship. It was so large, it disappeared into the cloud cover and appeared to be almost a wall in the middle of the sky.

"What is that?" Aerie felt a new wave of fear as it crested inside of her.

"It's got to be one of the Craftcarriers from the URS," Brock said. "They don't have a lot in commission, but they still use them."

"What are they used for?" Aerie asked.

"They mostly monitor the lands around and outside of URS control," Brock said. "They can also provide fuel for planes and other vehicles in mid-flight, even allowing them to land on it if there's a need for repairs."

"I'm guessing they can also attack," Serena said grimly as she pulled up the comm station. "They're not responding to our frequency."

"They've already tried to shoot us down," Brock said. "I doubt they're worried about telling us what they're going to do."

Another shot fired out from the top of the carrier. Brock swerved to miss, but the lasers managed to cut across the bottom hull.

"Watch it," Serena muttered.

"This ship is bigger than the fighters I've trained on," Brock reminded her.

Static came pouring over the comm.

"Hey, are you guys alright?"

Aerie was relieved to hear Cal's voice over the comm. "Cal," she called, before either Brock or Serena could answer him. "We're fine. How are you?"

"Good to hear you're alright, Aerie," Cal called back. "No doubt a bit worse for the wear, though, right?"

"No time to tease," Brock interrupted, for which Aerie was glad. She gave him a warm smile as he asked Cal for updates.

"We've been followed," Cal said. "Captain Chainsword's ghost is right behind us."

"Don't worry about him!" Aerie insisted. "What about the Craftcarrier?"

"Well, as you can see," Cal said as he grunted, no doubt dodging another blast, "they're not happy to see us."

Another line beeped in, increasing the stream of static.

"Understatement of the year, Cal," Dorian chimed in, his voice more serious. "They must've been notified we're on the run."

"Not to mention we're in stolen fighters," Cal said cheerfully.

"I wonder what kind of comm tech they're using," Aerie said. She glanced at the readout. "The interference is terrible."

"If it makes you feel better, I've dismantled my NETech," Cal told her. "That seems to have helped."

"Let me see if I can make the connection stronger," she said. Aerie reached out and tried to widen the frequencies, trying to bypass some of the cloud interference. The cloud cover made it difficult; the air seemed to crackle with energy the more she tried to reroute the system.

"Just be careful," Brock told her. "I don't want you overexerting yourself."

"If there's ever been a time to work through

overexertion, it's now," Aerie retorted. She took over the controls as Brock managed to dodge another round of attacks.

Serena settled into the small gunnery. "Let's see if we can take out some of their towers," she said as she began working with the targeting display.

Brock grimaced. "I think I can fly well enough to get past them," he said as he shot upward. "There's no need to make the URS even more angry at us."

"It's not like we're going to get caught," Aerie said. "Go ahead and take them out, Serena."

"*I'm* in charge, Aerie," Brock said as he began to spiral, turning the ship over to avoid the remaining fire. "Not you."

Aerie heard a small beeping noise coming up from the console. "You just keep flying," Aerie told Brock. "Serena can handle the weapons. I'll take care of the comms."

"I said I'm the one in charge," Brock said.

Aerie smiled coyishly. "Then do your job," she said, already expanding the comm frequencies.

She felt her heart jump as she was able to catch Exton's frequency. As the ship lurched to the left, she was able to key in a response request.

Static came in reply, and she was just about to transmit a message when a large explosion rocked their ship, blowing it off course and sending it into an unexpected course.

"What was that?" Aerie yelled, gripping onto the console as the turbulence sent them reeling around the cockpit.

Aerie turned to face Serena, whose face was suddenly white with fear. "What happened?" Aerie asked again. She felt her own hands go numb as she realized she wasn't able to hear the static from Exton's ship anymore.

"They got a direct hit on his ship," Serena said slowly. "I can't believe it … "

"Who?" Aerie demanded to know. *Exton!*

"I see him!" Brock cheered a second later. "Cal managed to eject himself."

"That's a relief," Serena murmured.

Aerie glanced over at the screen. She saw Cal's fighter as its fiery remnants fell into the clouds below. She could just make out a small pilot with his parachute as he flew up from the heart of the explosion.

She heaved a sigh of relief.

"Why isn't he signaling us?" Brock asked.

Aerie glanced down at the comms. "We're flying silent," she realized. "The comms must have been compromised in the blast."

"Great," Brock muttered. "Now how will we know when he lands?"

"I'll try to fix it."

"Go low, Brock," Serena said. "I can hold them off from here. We can track him with the monitor."

"We'll be sitting ducks to the Craftcarrier."

"Go down steep then, and use what you have of those flying skills to get us fully past the ship."

Brock said nothing but angled the ship downward as he avoided fire. Serena shot several rounds at the craft as Brock headed down after Cal, while Aerie tried to open the comm frequencies again.

She sighed, angry with herself as she hailed Dorian's fighter. There was no way to send a message, and she wasn't receiving any either.

"Captain Chainsword's below," Serena called out. "Huh. That's weird."

"What's going on?" Brock asked.

"It looks like he's got Cal."

"What?" Brock and Aerie turned to see Serena was right. Cal's parachute blossomed out from behind Exton's shuttle as the side door closed.

"He managed to pull him into his shuttle," Serena said, a hint of reluctant admiration in her voice.

"He has him," Aerie said excitedly. "He saved him!"

"That's not good news," Brock asserted. "He's our enemy."

"No he's not," Aerie insisted. "I mean, we're all

technically the enemies of the URS now."

"That doesn't make him our friend," Brock argued. "The enemy of my enemy is still my enemy, no matter what people say. That's how some of the greatest betrayals in history have happened—false assumptions."

"Brock," Serena called, "pay attention!"

Another blast rocked the ship. Aerie could feel the heat of the flames.

"We've been hit!" Brock yelled, as smoke began to fill the cabin.

"Can you stabilize it?" Serena asked as she shuffled out of the gunnery. She pushed Aerie out of the way as she hurried over to the copilot chair.

"I think so," he said. "But we're going to need to get out of here, and fast."

"I'm putting on the boosters," Serena said.

"Aerie, buckle up." Brock reached up and clicked on several notches. "We're about to go up a few G's, and the ship's stasis shielding might not protect us."

Aerie fumbled her way into a seat and strapped herself down, as Brock maneuvered the ship through an opening underneath the Craftcarrier's main hull.

"What … about … Cal?" Serena asked, her voice reverberating as she tried managed to force the words out of her mouth.

"We'll have to get him and Dorian later," Brock replied, grunting at the pressure.

Aerie heard the pulsating power of her blood as it throbbed through her body. She felt her whole body push into her chair, while a wave of nausea churned up inside of her.

She focused her gaze on the window, watching as the gray cloud cover gradually dissipated, allowing the world and all its color to come through. The ship began to slow down, but there was no way for Aerie to tell how far they'd flown.

"We're going to burn out the last of our fuel, and the landing will be a little bumpy," Brock said. He cracked his knuckles loudly. “But we’re safe for now.”

Serena groaned. “I knew I shouldn’t have come.”

Aerie said nothing. She watched as the mountains and hills seemed to rise out of the ground, with ice at the top, and waterfalls crying down their depths. There were areas of rugged terrain patchworked together with trees and hills. Aerie noticed the sunlight was shining through in a way she’d never seen before, giving a brightness to the area clouds had robbed other places of.

“It’s beautiful here,” Aerie said.

“Hold on,” Brock called. “We’re about to land.”

The ship scraped against the rocky ground. Aerie squeezed her eyes as the metal scratched open. She could feel the heat from the compartment below, as she collapsed.

A moment later, it was over. The ship bounced and jostled and twisted into the ground, finally coming to stop.

She opened her eyes tentatively. “Thank God. We’re okay.”

“We’ll have to go out the back,” Brock said as he glanced over at the readings from the main console. “This isn’t good.”

“It’ll be alright,” Aerie said as she unbuckled and stood up, carefully finding her balance. She held still while the last of her nausea left her, and then proceeded to make her way out of the ship.

She coughed as she came to the cargo bay; there were several small fires still burning as she made her way through the room.

“Aerie, wait for us,” Serena yelled. “I need help with the med tech and my supplies. And we could use another hand with raiding the weapons closet. We don’t know who’s going to come and get us while we’re here. Hello? Did you hear me?”

Aerie didn’t listen. As she stepped outside, a twinkle of light caught her attention from the sky. She recognized the shuttle, and the signature weapon painted on its side, as it swept past her and began to land.

"Aerie, get back here!" Brock yelled. "It's dangerous!"

Aerie jumped down the walkway and started running over, barely noticing the chill in the air. "Exton!" she cried.

♦17♦

"So, you're Captain Chainsword, then?"

Exton grumbled an inaudible response back, choosing to mostly ignore the pilot he'd barely managed to pluck out of the sky.

Emery shot him a sympathetic smirk, and he almost hated her for it. She had warned him of the risk in rescuing the pilot who came dangerously close to dying, even though she moved quickly in agreement.

The Craftcarrier, rising up out of the cloud cover, was the first surprise they came across in hours, but it was far from the most shocking. Between the unexpected prompt to save the pilot parachuting to what could only be loosely termed safety, and finding out the pilot in question was clearly another one of St. Cloud's offspring, Exton was getting tired of being surprised. He was just glad Emery had managed to expertly pilot the ship at a steep enough angle to catch him.

At the sharp display of her skill, Exton was more than willing to admit she was the better pilot between them.

"You don't seem so tough to me," the pilot called out again.

"You're awfully confident for someone who's strapped down to a chair," Exton pointed out.

The pilot frowned at him, twisting the bruise on his face, one he said he received as he pulled out of his fighter jet. "I'll get out of here soon enough, or I'll die here with the rest of you. I'm not afraid of death."

"By the sound of it, you seem to be afraid to stop talking," Exton said. "It was a miracle we were able to catch you from your plane without damaging our own shuttle. The least you could do is let us concentrate on getting out of here."

"You'll never escape the URS," the pilot retorted.

"I've managed to avoid them so far."

"You'll be sorry for all the trouble you've caused."

As Emery whipped the ship around, dodging fire, Exton shot the pilot a grim look. "You'll be sorry, too, if you keep bothering us, especially if we end up dying due to your distracting comments."

"We won't end up dying," Emery said coolly. "*I'm* the one who's flying this ship."

"Your skills are nothing comparing to the power of the Craftcarrier," the pilot asserted.

"Well," Exton said, finally standing up, "we have an advantage in dealing with them." He glanced over at Emery, who pushed a few buttons and pulled on a few switches, getting ready to target the Craftcarrier's stabilizers.

Just one hit, and then we'll have the upper hand.

Exton nodded approvingly, and missiles were loaded.

With the shuttle's tracking and navigation equipment, they'd picked up on the Craftcarrier easily, even if it had been a surprise.

"We're losing Aerie's ship," Emery said. "It looks like they just took a hit."

"Is she okay?" Exton faltered and headed over to see the monitor. "Phil, see if you can aim for the reverse stabilizers of the Craftcarrier. Once your shot's clear, let's head out."

"Why do you care so much about my sister?" the pilot called, obviously disturbed by the information. "Are you trying to kill her yourself? She's not worth it. She's an enemy of the State now."

Exton ignored him. Aerie had been more than willing to leave her world behind and stay with him. From what little she had said about her siblings, and what he had been able to deduce, she didn't fit in with her unit at all, and they didn't seem to care much. In fact, he had the direct impression that they were eager to keep her that way. Her brother, whatever his name was, lived up to that expectation.

A burst of power let out from the forward portside. "Missile's away, Captain," Phil called.

As the missile hit its mark, Exton felt a surge of satisfaction, despite the gasp of surprise on the pilot's face.

"How?" he asked. "How did you do that? That was only one shot, and you disabled it … how?"

Phil spoke up. "I can take our new guest into the back if he's upsetting you."

"He's fine," Exton muttered darkly. "For now." As much as he hated dealing with him, he wanted the pilot to see with his own eyes that they weren't trying to kill Aerie. And it was nice to hear it confirmed that Aerie *was* on the cargo ship.

"The cargo ship is headed down," Phil called. "Seems it had its main thruster taken out. It won't last in the air."

"Follow it," Exton ordered.

"What about the other fighter?" Thora said. "It seems to be attacking the carrier still."

"Leave it. We're more concerned about the other ship." He came up beside Emery. "See if you can catch up. I don't want to lose sight of it."

"We're coming up on the southern bend of Argentina's old borders," Emery said, glancing at the coordinates. "There should be plenty of open space for them to land."

Exton nodded. He turned his attention back to the pilot. "We're headed for landing," he said. "We should be able to locate your sister's ship."

When the pilot just stared back at him, angry and silent, Exton was strongly reminded of Aerie's own defenses when he first met her. *What is Osgood teaching these people?*

"You might as well kill me now," the pilot said. "I'll tell you nothing."

"I didn't save you just so I could kill you," Exton told him. "And I don't want any information you're not willing to give. I have other ways of getting what I need concerning the States. If there is something I'd like to know, it's only your name, so I can call the other ships and let them know we have you."

The pilot considered this for a moment before he resisted. "I won't have you use me as bait."

"They already know you're here, most likely. We were able to get a partial signal from them a few moments ago."

Exton gripped his hands together. He'd been hoping to hear something from them, but just as he'd answered it, the signal died.

Probably cut off from all the fighting and interference.

"Landing in three, Exton," Emery called back. "Buckle up."

Exton hurried and took the seat in front of the pilot. As the shuttle landed, Exton felt a wave of nervous energy wash through him. He could see the cargo ship less than a hundred yards away.

He turned back to the pilot. "Want to go over to their ship with me?"

The pilot scoffed, but said nothing.

Emery smiled at him. "Maybe I can get him to talk, Exton. Thora can help me while Phil does the after-flight inspection."

"I'd rather help interrogate," the older man muttered as Exton passed him.

Exton grinned. "Maybe next time, Phil." He clapped a hand on his shoulder, and then headed out of the ship, barely pausing to zip up his warmer jacket.

The moment he stepped out of the ship, he saw someone running toward them. His heart lurched; he would recognize those golden ginger locks anywhere.

"Exton!"

Disbelief struck him, but dispersed a second later, as the shock of hearing her say his name dissolved into pure joy.

Once more, he had his miracle.

"Thank you, Lord," he whispered, overcome.

He shook it off a second later. Exton took off, heading for her. "Aerie!"

Every step over the rocky dirt and the stilted grass brought him closer to her seemed too surreal. After the weeks of missing her, it seemed more like a lifetime had passed, yet nothing had changed. The wave of pleasure, the surge of protectiveness—all of it rushed out of him, as he finally reached out and took hold of her again.

Exton crashed into Aerie, already grasping for her as the force of their collision nearly toppled them over. Exton wrapped his arms around her and crushed her against him, reveling as the wave of warmth passed between them. He felt her stumble and he moved to catch her, keeping her close.

The rest of the world around him seemed bitter and cold, but he had his sunlight back.

"I can't believe it's you," she said, her breath warm against his neck.

"I can't believe you remember me," he said, allowing his hands to get lost in her hair. He smiled at the small braid, recalling how proudly she'd worn them in her hair on the *Perdition.*

It was too perfect, he thought, to have her in his arms once again.

"I can't believe it," he said, hugging her again, overjoyed and overwhelmed to have his Aerie back—*all* back.

She gave him a small grin. "I remembered you after I heard your voice again, when you were at Chaya."

Exton felt a rush of gratitude for Merra's decision to fight for the first time, finally glad he had been insistent enough to go.

Anything, he thought. Anything was worth it, for this moment.

"I've traveled and fought all around the world," he told her. "And all of it was worth it, just to get back to you."

"I know how you feel," Aerie said. "I'm so happy my coma and my amnesia wore off."

"Coma?" Exton stepped back from her. "Is that what they told you?"

She frowned, but after seeing his expression, Aerie sighed. "I should've known *that* was a lie," she said. "My father told me some of it after I began to remember on my own."

"He injected you with Memory Serum at Nova Scotia," Exton told her quietly. "He was hoping you would forget everything entirely."

Aerie's eyes glittered as she reached for him. "I couldn't forget you. I swear, even if it took me some time to remember your name and your face, you haunted me."

Exton laughed. "That's a switch. You haunted me from the moment we first met." He glanced down at her lips, watching as they trembled. He cradled her face in his hands as he drew her mouth to his, giving her the kiss he had been contemplating since he'd lost her.

Aerie responded to him at once, pushing up onto her tiptoes to meet his kiss with her own. Her hands tugged at his shoulders as she relaxed into him.

How did sunlight have such a potent taste? Exton wondered as he held onto her and the warmth between them exploded, encompassing them, allowing the dark of the night and the chill of loneliness to be vanquished by their age-old nemeses of light and love.

"God, I've missed you," he whispered.

"I'm missed you so much, too." Aerie's fingers tightened, burrowing into his jacket as he held her. "This feels like coming home after a long trip."

"You are my home," Exton told her, kissing her once more. He felt her shiver, but he knew it wasn't from the cold.

Voices from the cargo ship called out, interrupting their reunion.

"Aerie!"

"Aerie, what do you think you're doing?"

Exton barely heard them at first, but when they grew louder and more insistent, he reluctantly pulled away and glanced over Aerie's shoulder to see two other people headed toward them.

"Sorry." Aerie flinched. "That's my friend Brock, and my older sister, Serena."

"Brock Rearden, by any chance?" Exton asked, arching his brow down at her.

"Yes," she admitted. "I didn't tell them the truth about us. They're probably wondering who you are and—"

"And why I'm kissing you?" he asked, giving her another

quick kiss before more than reluctantly pulling back.

Aerie smiled and flushed red, while Exton felt a rush of pleasure. "I'd almost forgotten how fun it is to make you blush," he told her.

"Don't tease me in front of my family," Aerie said. "They tease me enough."

"Don't worry." Exton kept his arm around her protectively as the two others from her ship approached. "I'm very happy you're here, but I know we have to take care of other things."

"I know."

There were legitimately several other things he had to tell her. With his decision to take on the URS directly, aided by loyal dissenters and volunteers from the Ecclesia, war waged across the world. Aerie's mother, who was not only not dead, was leading a league of troops. And he would have to tell her about his old friend, too, Exton recalled.

As if she knew of all the trouble he had to report, Aerie nodded. "It's not going to be pleasant."

"Duty first," he told her. "We can revisit this conversation later, when we're alone."

Her face burned red, all over again.

"Speaking of unpleasantness," Exton said, "I have one of your brothers in my shuttle. He's not talking to me, so I might have to get you to get him to disembark."

"How did you know he's my brother, if he's not talking to you?"

"He looks too much like St. Cloud," Exton admitted with a grimace. "And he wanted to know why I was so concerned about your ship. Emery's in there with him now, trying to get him to open up some."

"Emery's here?" Aerie's eyes lit up with happiness. "I've missed her, too. Serena—"

"—wants some answers," Serena said as she came up and stood behind Aerie, her free hand planted firmly on her hip as her med pack sat squarely on her shoulders. "What in the world do you think you're doing, Aerie?"

Exton almost laughed at her irritated expression. "Well, you're definitely Merra's daughter."

Aerie and Serena looked shocked, before Exton realized neither of them likely knew the truth about their mother, or how he knew her.

He glanced over at Aerie apologetically. He didn't want to be the one to tell them about Merra's choices. He also had to tell Aerie about his past—all of it, including the parts he didn't like to think about.

Before he could explain, Brock stepped forward. "Take your hands off Aerie," he snarled.

Exton instinctively and intentionally tightened his grip around Aerie. "I don't believe we have been formally introduced."

"I don't care who you are," Brock snapped, stepping forward angrily. "I know you're the enemy."

"Brock, I told you before, he's not our enemy," Aerie said. "Please."

"Well, he's clearly not *your* enemy," Brock grumbled. He glared at Exton.

Beside him, Exton could feel Aerie stiffen.

"Brock, Serena, this is Exton," Aerie said, her voice clearly strained as the tension around them increased.

"And he works with MENACE," Brock said.

"No." Aerie shook her head. "No, he doesn't. Please—"

A beeping noise came from Exton's pocket. As Aerie tried to assure Brock and Serena he could be trusted, Exton slowly backed away from the ensuing argument and turned his attention to his comm.

"Exton, we have a ship approaching," Emery said. "It seems to be the other fighter from before."

"Can you establish a hailing frequency?"

"No, he's flying silent."

Exton frowned. "Keep the shuttle's shields up to maximum," he said. "I'll see if we can't contact him from Aerie's ship."

"I've already sent a message to Tyler updating him,"

Emery said. "Now that we're out of the cloud cover, interference is minimal."

"Good."

"Roger that," Emery said.

"Is that Emery?" Aerie asked, as she turned her attention to him.

"I'll check in with you again in a bit, Em," Exton said, before he turned off the comm.

"I can't wait to see her again." Aerie clapped her hands together happily before she turned to the others.

Exton saw Brock and Serena still looked angry and doubtful, but he knew he had to find a way to work with them. He had a feeling it was going to be significantly harder to convince them he could be trusted than it had been to convince Aerie.

"There's another fighter headed this way," he told them. "It's your other escort."

"Dorian," Serena murmured. "He followed us, but our comms are down. Our ship will need some significant repairs."

"We can try to communicate with him from my shuttle," Exton offered.

"No thanks." Serena gave him a sneer. "We don't want your help."

"If you're going to get the ship fixed, you'll need his help," Aerie told her, surprising Exton with her sharp tone. "We don't have any support this far out. We need to work together right now. The least we could do is try to contact Dorian."

"We just need to make sure he's not hostile," Exton said. "We don't want him blowing up either of our ships."

"He should blow up your shuttle, after all the trouble you've caused," Brock said.

"Brock!" Aerie admonished him. "He picked up Cal for us, remember? And he's still on the ship right now."

"That's the angry pilot I caught earlier, I presume?" Exton asked.

"That's not the point, Aerie," Brock said, charging onward, ignoring Exton. "Cal knows it is better to die in the line of duty than to live through the torture of captivity."

"There is no torture on the *Perdition*," Aerie shot back.

"I suppose you're going to tell me now that no one ever died from fighting MENACE, either?"

"I can promise you that my team doesn't cooperate with MENACE," Exton said, stepping forward. He didn't know much about Brock, but it was clear he was fixated on MENACE, and he had a temper.

"I don't trust you," Brock yelled.

Exton frowned. "The feeling is mutual," he said. "But that's not going to get us anywhere right now. Can we at least agree to a temporary truce for now?"

"Yes," Aerie insisted. "We can."

Serena rolled her eyes. Brock grumbled, but said nothing. He glared at Aerie bitterly. Exton knew he was as upset as he was confused by everything.

It was, he decided, best to keep Brock preoccupied with other matters. Exton didn't want Aerie to worry about Brock causing further issues.

"In the meantime, how is your ship? Can you fly at all?" Exton asked.

"Not at the moment," Serena said. "We have severe damage to the lower compartments, and our fuel has been depleted from the last burn. Fighting the Craftcarrier was—"

She was interrupted as Dorian's fighter came rushing past them, sending up a large dustbowl of wind and dirt before landing about a hundred yards away.

Great, Exton thought, as he and the others started coughing and covering their faces.

He had Aerie back, but there were still plenty of problems, and more were steadily approaching.

♦18♦

The world had never seemed to be more filled with possibilities, Aerie thought. With a content smile on her face, she snuggled further into Exton's embrace. His arm tightened around her in response. It was harder to walk, but Aerie didn't mind.

"This is a miracle," Aerie said, as they continued to head over to his shuttle. The chainsword décor winked at her playfully in the light of the setting sun. She turned back to see Serena and Brock were clearly arguing as they walked several steps behind them.

"I never really believed in miracles until you came into my life," Exton told her. "I always thought that was something more for Emery than for me."

"You just needed a different kind of miracle," Aerie told him. "I did, too."

He shrugged. "We might need a couple more if we're going to get to Petra in one piece."

"Is that where you're going to take us?" Aerie grinned. "I can't wait."

She'd wanted to see Petra before, and she thought she would never get the chance. But now, here in this place, she was safe from the General. Or at least, she could believe it.

"We're not too far from Petra," Exton told her. "I'm not sure what we'll do. Your family members pose a threat to us, as does your bodyguard friend."

"They can't be any worse than I was at first, can they?"

Exton chuckled. "Hard to believe it, but yes, they can."

"Why?" Aerie asked, slowing down her pace some.

"You were always a bigger threat to my heart, and by extension, the crew onboard the *Perdition*," Exton said. "Down here, it's Petra that's more vulnerable."

"Oh. That makes sense."

He gave her a charming grin. "You weren't worried I thought you were weak, were you?"

"No," she said.

"I know you're lying," he told her, before he leaned down.

Aerie sighed as she reached up to meet his lips with hers again. He was a head taller than her, but he still made her feel comfortable in his arms as he held her.

There is just no one like him, she thought, before she allowed herself to be swept away, if only for the moment.

"That does remind me," Exton said as he pulled away, "why was Brock with you to begin with? I know you've trained to be decent pilot. What did you bring him for?"

"Huh?" Aerie blinked, upset that her brain was full of mush already.

"Why did Brock come with you?" Exton repeated.

Aerie felt the heat rise in her cheeks again. "I actually didn't come on my own because I could barely make it out of the Reeducation Center," she admitted. "In fact, if he hadn't rescued me, I would probably still be there."

"No, you wouldn't." Exton looked toward the shuttle. "I would've rescued you."

Aerie saw the grim shadow on his face and said nothing. She didn't want to tell him about her time at the Reeducation Center. He would blame himself for not being there sooner. *He already feels terrible about that*, she realized.

Skipping over several details, Aerie told Exton how Brock had broken into the Reeducation Center and carried her to the hangar, where he had a ship set up and ready to go.

"The Ecclesia were also working to get you free," Exton told her.

"Meredith told me about that," Aerie said. "She's Tyler's sister, isn't she?"

"Yes." Exton nodded. "She's a few years older than me."

"She was very kind. I didn't realize the connection between Meredith and Tyler until we were leaving her there." Aerie frowned. "I wish my memory had come back sooner. I might've been able to convince her to come with us."

"She wouldn't have come, if it makes you feel better. She

didn't want to escape before, after we managed to get the *Perdition* into space," Exton said.

Curiosity sparked inside of her. "Why?" Aerie thought of all the horrible things she'd experienced in the center. "Why would she want to stay in such an awful place?"

"I'll tell you a bit about it later," Exton said as they came up next to the shuttle entrance ramp. "Right now, Emery and I are going to need your help to calm the others down and cooperate with us."

"I don't know how successful I'll be," Aerie admitted. "Cal and Dorian have never taken me seriously, and Serena doesn't seem to like me. I don't know what to expect from Brock. I was surprised he even came to rescue me at all."

Exton nodded. "I don't want to leave them here," Exton said. "But Petra is too important, Aerie. If they can't agree to come to terms with me and my crew, we're not going to be able to take them there. We'll have to take them back to another URS hub."

Aerie glanced back at the setting sun and sighed happily. "I wouldn't think it would be hard to just stay here," she said. "It's lovely, and the URS wouldn't see this area as a priority."

"You don't know that for sure," Exton reminded her. "With the Craftcarrier momentarily crippled, the fleet could decide to send out drones or smaller ships to see if there are any nearby threats."

"You don't think they would attack us, do you?"

"I wouldn't put it past them. I know, from the scouting we did when we set up Petra, that this part of the world is largely ignored, but that's only because it is considered either easy to control or easy to ignore. If Osgood or your father see this place as a potential threat, I wouldn't put it past them to come and attack."

"Great." Aerie sighed.

Exton hesitated slightly, and Aerie caught him. "What?" she asked. "What else?"

"There is also reason to believe that the URS would try to track us down and attack because of the battle at Chaya," he said.

"That's true." Aerie frowned. "Why did you attack Chaya?"

"It's another long story," Exton said. He unlatched the entrance to the shuttle and stepped inside. "You'll learn more about it once we get to Petra."

Instantly, Aerie could hear her brother's voice, as he yelled several threats and vulgarities from another room.

"If we get to Petra," Exton murmured. He held back as Brock and Serena walked into the shuttle, before he shut them in.

Aerie gave Exton a quick smile as Cal continued to argue. "I guess you were right. It does seem like I was easier to deal with."

She saw Brock glance at her quizzically once more, and Aerie knew she had a few stories of her own to explain to him. Serena, she noticed, was her usual surly self.

"Let me go!" Cal shouted. "I want to see my family!"

"We're here," Aerie said.

"Aerie." Cal struggled to sit up straight in his chair. "You made it."

"You should know by now that Brock's a good pilot." Aerie gave Brock a small smile over her shoulder, one that he willfully ignored.

Aerie groaned to herself. *Please don't let this mean he's going to be a problem,* she thought. She could only hope that Exton wasn't going to cause her any additional problems. She thought of the surprise kiss Brock had given her on the cargo ship, and her worry only doubled.

"Dorian's here," Serena said, forcing Aerie's attention back to the moment. "He just landed."

"Can you help us contact him?" Exton asked.

"I don't want to help you," Cal said. "I might be stuck here, outside of the URS, but I'm not a traitor." He stood his ground. "I won't work with Captain Chainsword."

"Not even after he saved your life?" Aerie asked, incredulously. "We saw him pull your parachute into the shuttle."

"It's not my fault he decided to save me," Cal snapped.

"*You're* Captain Chainsword?" Brock said.

Aerie and Exton swiveled around, just in time to see Brock launch himself at Exton.

"No!" Aerie cried, as Brock lashed out a punch.

Exton managed to sidestep its full impact, the hit grazing his shoulder. His retaliation was swift, as he caught Brock in the stomach with his elbow.

"Stop," Aerie yelled again, as Brock tumbled to the floor. Exton stepped back, and Brock tried to recover from getting the wind knocked out of him.

"He's a killer, Aerie," Brock told her. "Don't you care?"

"Brock, please," Aerie said. "I'll explain everything later, but now, you have to trust me. We can trust him. Nothing is as it seems."

"I don't think I can trust you, then," Brock replied.

"He's a good man," Aerie insisted. "Exton saved my life."

Exton raised his eyebrows at her statement, but he decided not to argue with her.

Aerie met his icy gaze and felt her heart melt all over again.

Behind her, Serena scoffed. "He's already a legendary pirate. I suppose it's not so much of a jump to assume he's a legendary lover, too."

Aerie felt another rush of embarrassment. "Shut up, Serena."

"So it's true." Brock picked himself up off the shuttle floor. "You love him."

The words came out of his mouth full of bitterness and bile, but Aerie nodded. "Yes, I do."

"That's why you wanted to go see him," Brock said accusingly.

Aerie nodded. "Yes," she said. "We'll discuss everything later. Right now, we need to find a way to work with each other."

She turned her attention back to Cal. Clearing her throat,

she continued, "So, Cal, I need you to help us. We need to contact Dorian, get him over here, and then we can start moving again, before the Craftcarrier comes after us or the URS sends more people looking for us."

"You're going to take us as prisoners?" Serena asked.

"No," Aerie insisted, before Exton could say anything. "And I'd rather not just leave you here, especially since the cargo ship is going to need some bigger repairs."

Brock scowled. "I don't want to go with you."

"Me, neither," Cal said.

"Come on," Aerie said. "All of you worked hard to save me. Offering you a safe place to stay is the least I can do." She looked at each one of them intently, silently pleading with them to accept her deal.

Cal glanced over at Brock, and then back to Aerie. She waited, pretending not to notice Exton was no longer smiling. She knew he wasn't happy about extending an invitation, especially since he had just told her, not even ten minutes before, that Petra was too important to risk on their possible rage.

But Aerie was sure, if they were able to come and see the Ecclesia, and the many good people she'd met, there would be nothing to worry about. Surely her family would be able to see why she loved Exton and his community after seeing it for themselves.

I'll explain that to him once we're on our way to Petra, she decided.

"Okay, fine," Cal said. "I'll help. But get me out of this chair."

"You have to promise not to hurt anyone," Aerie said quickly. "I don't want you hurting my friends."

"Fine," he repeated.

She turned to Exton. "There you go," she said, trying to ignore his hardened gaze.

"I've got the key," a familiar voice called over from the doorway.

Aerie glanced over to see Emery as she came in, her blue-green eyes sparkling with joy. "Emery!" Aerie called, rushing over to see her friend.

Emery seemed surprised as she embraced her.

"What's wrong?" Aerie asked.

"I didn't expect you to remember us," Emery admitted to her quietly. "Exton told me what happened with the Memory Serum."

Aerie grinned. "I'm surprised you didn't hear from Meredith. She helped me jog my memory."

"I'm glad it worked," Emery said with a smile. "We'll have to discuss more later. Right now, we have other things to worry about."

"No kidding." Aerie nodded.

Emery released Cal from his chair, and together they were able to contact Dorian.

As Cal and Dorian talked over the comm, Exton came up beside Aerie. "Are you happy?" he asked.

"I'm happy to see you," Aerie replied innocently.

He didn't let her get away with it. "I don't like this, Aerie." He glanced over at Brock, who was still simmering with anger, and Serena, who was looking around the shuttle, clearly stuck between indulging in her disdain and scouting for weaknesses.

Aerie folded her arms across her chest. "Come on, Exton. Please give them a chance. Petra will be fine, even with my family inside. You have defenses ready, don't you?"

"We have protocols in place," Exton replied. "But you do realize that you're risking their fate as well as ours, right?"

"What do you mean?" Aerie asked.

"We work through a system of secrets," Exton replied. "Petra will only survive if it's a secret. We have strengthened our defenses since the encounter with St. Cloud, but it's a slow process. If your family and friend can't keep our trust or their word, we will have to take care of them."

"By punishing them?"

"More or less."

Aerie knew what he was implying. If Serena, Brock, and

her brothers posed a threat to Petra, there would be no hesitation.

But, she thought, surely it was going to be okay. "You'll let them come, then?" she asked.

"I don't have much of a choice, since you've decided for me," he told her.

"I won't do it again," Aerie said.

He frowned. "I hope not, Aerie. I love you, I really do, but this is not something you should make a habit of doing."

A new memory stirred inside of her mind. She recalled Exton as he pushed her away from him, as he kept himself back from her, as he decided he would return her to the General, rather than risking Petra.

Aerie gripped her arm in frustration, feeling the small bumps of the metal tag that had been branded into her skin. "You're not always right about everything," she said.

"It's not up to you to try to make the adjustment without me."

"I should still have a say."

He sighed. "I don't want to have this discussion with you right now, Aerie."

"Why?" she demanded to know. "Because I'm right?"

"No, because even if you're right, the decisions are still mine to make when it comes to Petra and the *Perdition.* It is a useless argument and you'll only be mad at me at the end of it."

"You told me before I could argue with you."

He smirked. "I also told you that it didn't mean you would win."

Before she could respond, he pulled her close, giving her a gentle kiss on her forehead.

Aerie softened, leaning into him. He'd told her that he had traveled all over the world in pursuit of her; she had gone through various levels of suffering to meet him. He wasn't going to go against her in letting her family and Brock come to Petra. The least she could do was work with him.

A few moments passed. While Dorian and Cal talked

between themselves, Brock and Serena exchanged irritated glances, and Emery and other members of the shuttle crew organized their plans.

As Exton held her against him, Aerie allowed herself to enjoy the moment. She could see the sun setting outside of the shuttle's window, and she knew it was the beginning of a new chapter of her life.

♦19♦

Several hours and several arguments later, Exton reached over and took hold of Aerie's hand as the shuttle settled into its landing strip. Aerie smiled over at him and squeezed his hand in return.

He still felt a wave of disbelief that she was here with him, and she was safe. She seemed to be in a similar state, with her eyes wide as she watched the darkened snow-capped mountains in the distance. The sun was just beginning to rise at the bottom of the world, and already he could make out the walls of Petra's fortress and its surrounding territory.

"Can we get off yet?" Exton could hear Serena's question from the other side of the cabin, and he had to wonder if she was intentionally trying to be disruptive.

Cal started asking questions about what was going to happen to them and where they were.

Exton was about to call back and assure them they were more than fortunate to be where they were when Brock answered them in a surly tone. "We're at Petra. You can calm down. This is where the defectors go."

He was surprised at Brock's information, if not his attitude. Before Exton could ask Aerie if she'd mentioned Petra to Brock, Emery began powering down the shuttle.

"Touchdown," Emery called. "Beginning post-flight check."

"Roger," Thora replied.

Exton tugged on Aerie's hand. "Welcome to Petra," he said, watching in wonder as her eyes shimmered with pleasure.

"I'm so happy to be here with you," she told him.

"I'd love to show you around."

"Will we ever go back to the *Perdition*?" Aerie asked. "I'd love to see it again."

"In a few weeks, perhaps," he said. "Or even sooner, depending on what we need for battle. We had to make a stop at the *Perdition* for some med supplies when we attacked Chaya."

"Battle?" Aerie frowned.

He hesitated. "I told you there were a lot of things we had to catch up on."

Before he could elaborate, Emery came up to them. "Post-flight check complete, Exton."

"Thanks."

Emery glanced back at the cabin, full of Aerie's family. "What are we going to do about them?"

"Get Aunt Patty," Exton said. "I'm sure she can take care of them."

"I'll have them go to the med check then, and I'll have her meet us there," Emery said.

"Med check?" Aerie asked, her face suddenly pale.

"It's standard procedure," Emery told her. She smiled. "Although this one won't take two or three days to finish. Part of the benefit of being on Earth is that biological elements are more predictable."

Aerie nodded but looked unsure.

Exton ran a hand through her hair, for both his pleasure and her comfort. "I guess you're tired of being stuck in medical wards," he said. "After your shoulder and everything."

Aerie nodded. "My shoulder's doing better, even if it gets a little stiff every now and then."

"The Ecclesia has sent some of their doctors down here," Exton told her. "We can get better care for you here, more than likely. Even for shoulder injuries."

"Thanks."

He tugged at her hand. "Come on," he said. "Let's disembark. We're just in time to see the sunrise."

Aerie followed him out, and Exton was not disappointed by her wonder when she finally had her first, unfiltered look at Petra.

"It's beautiful," she said.

Exton grinned as he followed her gaze. The snowy

mountains loomed in the distance, reflecting the approaching sunlight off their pointed tips. From the top of the mountains, the snow gradually faded to brown and gray rock, while up from the ground green grass grew. This time of year, during the longer daylight hours, it was even possible to see some flowers from the settlement.

Petra's fortress was simple, cutting into its surroundings bluntly. Exton surveyed the buildings, the simple but sturdy structures where he and his community lived and worked.

Behind them, Exton heard Cal's arguments fall silent, while Serena and Brock both faltered in their steps.

"This is Petra?" Brock finally asked. "Doesn't look as big as I thought it would."

"There's more than you'd think," Exton told him, unable to stop himself from objecting to Brock's comment.

"Be nice, Brock," Aerie hissed. "You're a guest here."

"I didn't ask to be," Brock muttered back.

Why were you flying down here in the first place then? Aerie suddenly wondered if Brock had meant to come to Petra or if he'd had somewhere else in mind. She didn't remember him saying anything about their destination.

"Just stop it," Serena said to Brock. "It's better we're here than stuck back in the middle of nowhere. At least this place should have some decent food."

"We'll get to that," Emery said as she came up beside them. "I just reached out to Aunt Patty. She's coming up from the med checkpoint now."

Exton glanced over at the small building beside the hangar as his aunt stepped out into the sunlight. "My mother's sister," he explained to Aerie. "She runs Petra as the community organizer and leader."

Emery nudged him. "Thora and I can take the rest of these guys to the checkpoint. You and Aerie might as well get some time together. Go show her around. We can get her checked later."

"And here I thought you were going to make my life more difficult, for all I teased you and Tyler," Exton said.

"I think life has been hard enough on Aerie," Emery told him quietly. She gave him a smirk. "Besides, you'll still have to deal with Tyler."

"That's true. Are you sure you can handle them without Aerie?" Exton asked. He glanced over at Aerie, as she still stood taking in the sight before her.

"Yeah." Emery nodded. "Tyler wanted to schedule a meeting with us later. He has updates on Chaya and some other things. You and Aerie might as well make up for some lost time before we have to take care of that."

"Thank you." His voice was quiet, but his sister would still be able to hear his gratitude.

"No problem." She winked and then turned to Aerie. "It's wonderful to have you here, Aerie. We're glad to have you back."

"I missed you, too, Emery," Aerie said.

"We'll have some time later to catch up," Emery told her. "But I know my brother has been pining for you. It's better if I let him have you while we can."

"Contact me if anything changes," Exton replied, grinning at Emery's teasing. He had to admit she was right, and he was thankful for her offer.

"What about the checkpoint?" Aerie asked.

"We'll get to it later," Exton said, as he watched Emery hurry to catch up with Thora and the others. He turned just in time to see Brock send another glare at him. "Come on. There's something I want to show you."

Aerie felt tired as she headed up into the hills above the settlement, but she was invigorated by Exton's presence. He still held tightly onto her hand, as if he was afraid he would lose her again if he let her go.

"We're almost there," Exton told her.

"Where are we going?" Aerie asked.

"Not far."

"That's not really an—" Aerie stopped talking as she stepped up next to Exton and saw the familiar sight before her. Her mouth dropped open in surprise.

It was her tree—the Memory Tree.

Memories flicked through her mind once more. She remembered the gashes in the ground in New Hope, where the Memory Tree once stood, where she was uprooted along with it, and how it brought her to Exton.

She walked up beside it, felt the familiar bumps of the trunk, then glanced up and saw the welcoming patterns of lichens and moss. Aerie had felt a kinship with the tree, living in a lonely world—and once more, they shared such a bond, as she realized she was no longer alone.

"This is where we first met," Exton said behind her.

"I remember," Aerie said.

"I like the tree better, now that it's here at Petra."

"Well, you would." Aerie laughed.

"It suits this place better, too." Exton looked out across the landscape. "We didn't think we could survive the first winter we were here. The tree has always been a testament to survival. I'm hoping that in giving it another chance to prove itself, it'll inspire others who come here."

"I can't imagine why they would object." Aerie gestured toward the mountains. "It's beautiful here."

"The weather is probably the hardest part," Exton said. "We don't have the same resources as New Hope or other parts of the URS, so it's chillier here than most people would like."

"It is kind of cold," Aerie said. She toyed with the idea of trying to climb up to her favorite branches, but she was still tired. Instead, she sat down at the base of the trunk, drawing Exton down beside her, like the day he had in the Captain's Lounge.

"It doesn't change much throughout the year," Exton said as he put his arm around her. "It's really only because of the war that the glaciers melted enough to let people come here and live year-round."

"Is that why you decided to build Petra here?" Aerie asked.

"Some of the reason," he said. "The Old Palmer Bay area is the most northern part of Antarctica, and some of the continent was never even claimed, so it was a solid political move. We wouldn't disturb anyone's land."

"That had to make it hard, though, with not having a place to start."

"It was." He nodded, thinking about the first couple of years he helped shepherd people and supplies to Petra with the help of the *Perdition* and his friends and family.

"It was worth it, though, wasn't it?" Aerie asked.

"Definitely." Exton glanced back at the settlement, a distinct sense of pride swelling up inside his heart. "It's a grand thing to be able to make the life you want for yourself—to be able to dream freely, and make those dreams come true. That's a right not given to us by government—that's a right inherent inside of us, inalienable, given by our Creator."

Aerie nodded. "The more it's taken away, the more people seem like robots, and less human." She thought about Brock. He embraced the rule of government much more than she did. What was the dream in his heart that he longed for, one that he might not even dare to admit to himself? she wondered.

"When the war broke out between UNA and MENACE, things changed too rapidly," Exton said. "The government faced a lot of issues. To survive, people had to give up what the government deemed 'unnecessary.' That's why religion was outlawed and eventually demonized, along with the arts and certain books and other things. The Ecclesia, most of them, decided to leave, especially when the dictatorship began and UNA became the Revolutionary States."

"But they couldn't leave," Aerie said. "No one leaves the URS."

"Not that they would let you know about it."

"I guess that's true. I guess I did hear stories from time to time," Aerie said. "My mom would tell me stories. I would also hear them from different places around the city, and in school. It was hard to resist."

"For you, I'm sure," Exton said, pulling her closer. "You and that curiosity."

"It's a good thing I have it," Aerie told him. "That's why I was able to remember as much as I did about meeting you."

"I've always loved that about you. Which is why I know you want to know the rest of the story."

She stuck her tongue out at him playfully.

"Petra is more than just part of our history here," Exton said. "Petra was the name of a place of protection in the Ecclesia's teachings, and some think it will be again when the end of time comes."

Aerie shivered at the thought. "Do you think we'll live to see that?"

"I don't know," Exton said. "But no one is supposed to know when it'll be, so that's the good and bad part I guess. You only have to take a risk with what you think is likely, not with what actually happens.

"Right now, the URS seems to be moving toward further advancement," he added. "They've conquered or subdued a good amount of the world, so it makes me wonder if they're after us now."

"Without you and the *Perdition*," Aerie said, "I'm sure they would've taken over the world by now." She stared at Exton with new admiration, realizing all over again how much he had worked to protect people he didn't know, even though he lost so many people he loved.

He shrugged. "It's not enough."

"No one can do it alone," Aerie told him, reaching out her other hand in comfort.

Exton took her hand. "Now that you're free from St. Cloud's charge, I'm glad you're here with me," he said. "I'm hoping you'll stay here."

"I want to stay with *you*," Aerie said. "No matter if it's here or not." She leaned over and pressed herself into his chest.

"Aerie."

She felt him tremble underneath her, and she looked up, momentarily distracted. "I didn't hurt you, did I?"

"No."

"That's where I hurt you before," she said.

"It's healed," Exton assured her. "In fact, I don't think I've ever felt better." He cupped her cheek in his hand as he leaned down and kissed her.

Aerie moaned softly, already moving to meet him. Her eyes closed, shutting out everything as she tasted him once more. She couldn't agree more, she decided, before wrapping her arms around him.

All her senses were sent blazing as he held her. His hands were in her hair, running over her shoulders, pressing into her back.

She shuddered, surprised by the heavy wave of desire.

"Are you cold?" he asked.

"No," she managed, barely registering the question before finding his lips again.

She forgot about the cold completely as she lost herself in his kiss. Aerie couldn't tell if Exton pulled her into his lap or if her body acted of its own accord. All she knew was her body was suddenly plunged into an intoxicating warmth, and she had no objection to drowning in the sensation.

"Aerie." He pulled away briefly as he whispered her name. Before she could protest, Aerie felt the wind rush out of her in pure pleasure as his mouth found her throat.

Aerie was struggling to breathe properly when he suddenly stopped.

"What? What is it?" she asked, blinking the passion out of her eyes.

"What's this?" he asked, placing his fingers gently on her neck.

Aerie reached up, felt the roughened patch of skin, and faltered.

"What is it?" he asked, already frowning.

"It's fine," Aerie said. She laced her fingers through his hair and pressed her lips against his once more.

"That's where they hurt you, isn't it?" Exton asked, rubbing his fingers over where the electrode patch had been.

"It doesn't hurt anymore," Aerie said.

Exton met her gaze. "It might not hurt you, but it hurts me." He kissed the mark lovingly, and Aerie felt her heart skip a beat at his gentleness.

"The whole thing almost feels like a dream now that I'm here," she said.

"I'm sorry." He brushed her bangs out of her face. "I shouldn't have let you go."

"You didn't have a choice," Aerie said. "I know my father. He can be absolutely ruthless."

"I know him pretty well, too," Exton said. "I should have been able to anticipate everything. When I heard he was the one who signed your arrest warrant, I knew he had lied to me."

Aerie frowned. "I heard Osgood was the one who was really excited about it."

"He would be," Exton said. "He loves to make examples of people. It wouldn't shock me to know he suspects St. Cloud. And I suppose he has good reason. He was the one who told me you were already gone when we arrived at New Hope."

"Who? My father?" Aerie was surprised.

"Yes."

She frowned. She couldn't imagine her father calling Exton to save him the trouble. If anything, calling Exton only helped prevent him from getting into any trouble with St. Cloud's forces. "I wonder why."

"I don't know what he wants," Exton said. "He seems to be playing a deep game. But if he's willing to put you through torture, I know it can't be good."

"I don't want to talk about that," Aerie told him. "Meredith was there to protect me some."

"Not enough." Exton placed a kiss on her temple,

another sore spot from her time at the Reeducation Center. "Especially if Osgood was happy about it. I've heard stories and seen some of what he can do to people he captures. He's a sadistic man."

Aerie felt his fingers tighten against her, and she suddenly wondered if Exton had any personal connection to anyone else Osgood had tortured.

"I heard he was glad it would affect the General," Aerie said. "One of the techs said Osgood liked having an advantage when it came to dealing with my father."

"I can't blame him there." Exton ran his hand down her neck, before placing a tender kiss on her other wound. He grimaced a moment later. "I admired St. Cloud for a long time, before he betrayed my family. I know he is a formidable opponent, and Osgood is right to distrust him."

"That reminds me. I have something of yours," she said. Aerie pulled back, swinging her legs out to the side, as she reached for the photo in her pocket. She took it out and handed it to him. "I hope you won't be upset with me for taking it."

Exton took the picture and stilled. "Where did you get this?"

"You had it in your room on the *Perdition*," Aerie admitted sheepishly. "I took it, figuring you wouldn't miss it. And that is my mother in the picture. I recognized her when I saw her. Of course, I know my father, too, even with the red 'X' drawn over his face."

She gave him a smile as he looked it over. When he crumpled it up in his fist a moment later, she was appalled. "Hey!"

"What?" he asked as he tossed the photo away.

"That was a picture of my mother," Aerie said. "Even if you don't like my father, you can at least let me keep it. I don't have any pictures of her."

He sighed, moving her off his lap before he stood up. "I wouldn't worry about that," Exton told her, his voice surprisingly harsh. "Did anyone else know you had the picture?"

"No," Aerie said. "At least, I don't think so." She frowned, wondering if Meredith or any of her coworkers had seen it.

"I'm not entirely sure what the URS knows about me and my family," Exton said. "But I don't want them drawing too many connections between me and my past. I really should burn this, actually."

He picked up the wrinkled photo and tucked it into his pocket.

"Why does it matter down here?" Aerie asked. "You could still keep it."

"I don't *want* to keep it."

She stepped back at his sharp tone. "Why?" she asked, knowing she was coming precariously close to the edge of his patience.

He looked as though he wanted to say something. She waited for a long moment expectantly, but she'd known him long enough to know he did not explain himself very often.

"Come on," he said. "I'll explain it to you as we head back. Others are waiting for us."

♦20♦

Exton led Aerie back down the hill toward the settlement. He thought of the photo she'd shown him and grimaced. Exton didn't want to think about those days—those days when he knew who his family could trust and how to protect the people who meant the most to him.

Maybe that's all the more reason to tell her.

"I'm really glad you're here," Exton began, as he held her hand tightly in his own. "It feels like forever since you were taken away."

Aerie nodded. "When I think of all the hours I was stuck at work or in the med ward, I'm tempted to ask for some more Memory Serum," she said. "It almost seems as bad as the Reeducation Center."

Exton smiled. "I take it you hated your job? Or," he teased, "did you just hate following orders?"

"Both!" Aerie declared with a small laugh. "Director Anand was a nightmare to deal with. And I didn't have any friends."

"Well, you'll have friends here," Exton said. "But the nightmares might continue."

"What do you mean?"

"We're officially at war." There was just no other way to tell her. "We went on the offensive at Chaya. That was why I was there."

Aerie's eyes darkened, making him think of St. Cloud. "You didn't go to war just to get me back, did you?"

"No. I didn't want to do that," he said. He drew her close to him, never taking his eyes off her face. "Believe me, I love you. I would've done anything to get you back. When I was saved at Halifax, after losing you—both to your father and likely to the Memory Serum—I was devastated and injured. War did not seem like a wise move."

"What changed your mind?" Aerie asked. "You didn't know about me until you saw me."

He hesitated. "There were … other complications, mainly that there was nothing stopping St. Cloud from destroying Petra now that he had you, anyway."

"I doubt he would do it."

"Maybe," Exton said. "He has always been a man of his word." *Another reason I did not want to risk Petra when he demanded Aerie back in the first place.*

"Was there something else?"

"You could say that."

"What was it?" Aerie asked.

Exton sighed. "I found out who Osgood promoted to your father's old position." With his free hand, he reached into his pocket and pulled out the photo again. "He promoted a man named Gerard Dubois to his third in command."

"We've met," Aerie muttered dryly.

Exton scowled. "How?"

"He was the one who carried out the arrest," Aerie told him. "And he was the one who … who was in charge of my reeducation."

The chill in the air disappeared as he felt his heart ice over. "He was the one who tortured you?"

"It was his old job, I guess." Aerie looked away. "Meredith was surprised to see him—"

"I can't believe it," Exton muttered. "He's gone too far, and he's too far gone. I'll have to kill him for sure now."

"What are you talking about?" Aerie asked.

Exton held out the photograph to her. "This man in the picture here is his father," he said. "Gerard's dad was a member of the Ecclesia, same as me. He was also in your father's class, the one he used to teach in New Hope. Gerard was older than me, like most of the students, but we were good friends."

Aerie gazed at the photo with renewed concern. "I didn't think about the man," she said, her fingers gently touching the photograph's edges.

"Gerard was the one who actually took this photo,"

Exton told her. "He was always interested in the arts. To this day, I'm convinced that he was only let into the class because of St. Cloud. Not that Gerard wasn't smart, but he never managed to keep up. I think he made St. Cloud look bad. I know St. Cloud hated him for that, even though Gerard was always very agreeable."

"What happened to him?" Aerie's voice was soft and quiet. "He definitely doesn't seem to be the same person anymore."

Exton felt the sting of Gerard's fate, even as he wanted to hurt him for what he'd done to Aerie.

He stopped walking and strengthened his grip on Aerie's hand. He didn't want to tell her the story, but he had to. *Especially since it's clear Gerard is completely gone now.*

"When me and the others went in to steal the *Perdition* from the URS," he began, "we had to time everything perfectly. It was one of the most terrifying experiences of my life, trying to infiltrate New Hope's military base. We had plenty of first-hand insider reports, since most of the people who were defecting with me worked there at one point or another."

He turned and looked over at Petra, his gaze glossing over as he relived it. "I was eighteen years old at the time. Gerard was in his early twenties then. I was in university, and he was one of my main contacts at the base. He worked as a sentry."

"He helped you steal the *Perdition*."

He nodded. "Yes. He provided the codes for us to break in and steal it, and with his help we coordinated a diversion."

"I'm guessing that he didn't make it onboard?"

Exton shook his head. "No. There was an issue, and he stayed behind to save me. He was captured and assigned to the Reeducation Center."

Aerie flinched. "I was only there for a couple days," she said, "and that was long enough. If it's been more than six years, then … "

Exton nodded glumly. He didn't have to tell her that the

Reeducation Center had dehumanized Gerard before remaking him into the hardened, hollow man he was now.

"He still knows you," Aerie told him. "He told me that you had run off to join MENACE, even though you were just a kid from his class."

"I imagine the Reeducation Center did a thorough job of reorienting his memories and his desires," Exton said. "I couldn't save him. Once we were up in space, some of the med students tried to find a way to undo the damage done by the Reeducation program. We never had much luck."

"That's why you were so certain I was done for."

He nodded. Exton began walking again, more stiffly this time. "When I heard Gerard had been released, I didn't think he would ever be anything but a cog in the State's system. But when he was promoted, to third in command no less, I knew it was much worse than I could have ever imagined."

"He told me he hasn't told Osgood about you," Aerie said.

Exton was surprised. *Or maybe I'm not. What better way of proving himself to the URS than by taking me down?*

"He was my friend, and I failed him. If he hasn't said anything to Osgood, it's more likely because he wants revenge himself rather than any latent feeling of loyalty. When Gerard was captured, Tyler and I promised we would do everything we could to find a way to reverse the reeducation process, but success has been extremely limited. We have only had a few people, yourself included, be able to overcome the effects of the treatments. And most of them, also like you, were not under their influence for very long."

Aerie said nothing, but Exton had a feeling he'd guessed the truth. She slowed her pace down as they drew closer to the settlement.

"So you heard he'd been promoted and you wanted to go to war for that?" she asked.

"There are other reasons, too," Exton said. "The URS has been unable to stop the dissenters from leaving—part of the reason their work force is always lacking, even if their military recruits keep increasing—and a number of other things that all suggest they're ready to go on more of an offensive role."

"So you're trying to go on the offensive before they do?"

"If we can stop them, we should."

"I know you've been angry with the URS for some time," Aerie said. "But this is taking it to a new level."

"A level where we can win," Exton said. He was discouraged to see the doubt in her expression. "A level where we can save people, not just separate ourselves from the status quo."

"Who told you that?"

Exton almost told her the truth about her mother, but he decided to give Merra a chance to do that herself. He made a mental note to mention it to her when he called in for a report on Chaya. "We're fighting for the things worth fighting for, Aerie."

"The URS has been fighting, too," Aerie said. "Don't you think it's the same thing?"

"Not at all," he said. "The Founding Fighters of the last two generations fought for the people to conform to their image of fairness. That's not how life works—that's tyranny. People are intrinsically different, and we need a system that rewards that, not punishes it."

"But you could lose," Aerie said.

"War is always a gamble."

"It could be the end of us."

"It could be the beginning of something greater than just us." Exton felt a rush of anger as his intentions were questioned, and by Aerie of all people. *How can she still defend the URS enough to let it stand as it is?*

He softened a moment when she thrust herself back into his arms. "You could get hurt," she said. "I could lose you."

"It was not an easy choice," Exton told her softly, running his hands down her back as he tried to comfort her. "But plenty of good has already come from fighting the URS. And more will follow."

For a long moment, he just held her. "War was not an easy choice, Aerie. But this—what we have, you and me—it's the easiest thing in the world."

He could feel her body mold against his. Finally, he heard her whisper, "I know."

Before he could move to kiss her again, she stepped back. "The General will not be happy about this. Promise me you will *not* underestimate my father."

"I'm not worried about him," Exton told her.

"I read his accounts with the real MENACE," Aerie said. "If anyone can win a war, it's the General."

"I know him well, too, Aerie. I studied under him for years. I thought he was my family's friend. He and Merra both came to my community in friendship and in faith."

"And he still caught you off guard," Aerie pointed out apologetically. "I'm sorry. I just don't want you to get hurt."

"I don't want you to get hurt either." He sighed. "I'm confident it was the right decision after speaking with a variety of people on the matter," he told her. Remembering Marcus at Chaya, he knew he had made the right choice, even if it hadn't been easy.

Apprehension came over him swiftly, like a shadow. Aerie might have wanted to join the military before, but Exton knew—as did St. Cloud—that she did not have the temperament for it. Would Aerie still want to stay with him if he was leading the small nation of the Ecclesia remnant and their allies into war?

Glancing over at her now, seeing her worried, doubtful expression, he did not know how she would answer that.

Maybe she will change her mind once she settles in.

"Well," he said as he pulled her into the entrance of the settlement's hangar. "We need to get you checked in and registered, but it shouldn't take—"

Exton faltered as he saw an all-too familiar ship docking in one of the open landing sites.

"What is it?" Aerie asked him.

Before he could reach for his comm, the ship's entrance

opened up and Merra St. Cloud came walking down the gangway.

"Aerie." Merra's voice called out as she turned to face them.

Even from where he was standing, Exton could see she was full of the same self-assurance she'd always worn as she strutted around Petra's settlement.

He felt Aerie's hand go limp.

"I might as well tell you now," Exton said. "Your mother's alive."

♦21♦

Aerie felt her heart stop as she heard her mother's voice call her name. It was a sound she never expected to hear again, and hearing it in the small airbase of a defector's camp dazzled her as much as it disturbed her.

"Aerie!" Merra's voice rang out across the large room.

She glanced over at Exton as he frowned. *He knew the truth*, she realized. He just didn't know how to break it to her.

"Your mother was the one who saved me from St. Cloud when we went to Nova Scotia," he told her quietly, as if to answer her silent question. "I didn't know about her before then."

Aerie said nothing for a long moment, before she tugged her hand free from Exton and rubbed her eyes. She was still tired, and even though time with Exton, along with the walk around the campus, had invigorated her, Aerie was hesitant to believe her eyes.

"Aerie." Merra came up to her.

In the twinkling of an eye, Aerie found herself once more wrapped up in the embrace of someone she loved.

"Mom?" she finally managed.

It took her a moment for the reality to sink in. As Aerie held onto her mother, she tried to figure out what was different and what was the same. In growing over the last five years—nearly six—Aerie was surprised to see how close she was to her mother's height.

"I've missed you so much, my darling," Merra whispered into her ear, still holding onto her tightly.

In the end, Aerie decided *she* was the one who had changed the most between them. Her mother's free-spiritedness had always been there, just restrained.

"I can't believe it's you," Aerie croaked, as her eyes began to fill a wet mixture of shock and joy.

Merra pulled back from her. "I can't tell you how much I've been longing for this day."

Aerie stepped back. Suddenly, she didn't want to discuss any part of her life for the last several years with her mother. Her loneliness began to shift from feeling like emptiness inside of her to one of rejection.

She abandoned me. She's alive, but she left me, all alone, to fend for myself with the General and the others.

"What's wrong?" Merra asked.

"Exton said you saved him," she said, unable to think of anything else.

"Oh, that's right." Merra grinned as she glanced over at Exton, who, Aerie saw, was still frowning.

"What were you doing at Halifax?" Aerie asked.

"What I'm doing everywhere I go," Merra answered. "I was fighting the URS. When I heard about the situation, I wanted to make sure nothing went wrong. So I took up a small squadron of my forces and headed over."

Aerie glanced back at Exton, still unsure of how to respond. He remained silent this time, as if to tell her he had no answers for her.

"There's so much information," Aerie finally muttered. "I think I need to lie down for a while."

Before anyone said anything else, Exton's comm beeped. He glanced apologetically at Aerie, before stepping back. "I have to get this," he said. "I'll be only a few moments. Excuse me."

She gave him a tight smile, but she knew from his expression there was nothing he could do about it.

And, Aerie knew, it was possible he was leaving her with her mother because he thought it might be good for her.

Merra certainly didn't seem to mind. She folded her arms across her chest and gave Aerie a grin. "Well, that was good timing. Now we can talk and we don't have to worry about him getting upset."

"Why would he get upset?" Aerie asked.

Merra waved the issue away. "I'm going to have to ask him to get more aid to Chaya," she said. "The *Perdition* has already sent quite a bit, so I'm sure he'll be suspicious."

"You were at Chaya, too?"

"Of course. That's where I've been for the last several years, with some glaring exceptions."

Aerie recalled the day Alice had been helping her in the plantation rooms on the *Perdition*. "Alice knows you," she muttered.

Merra nodded. "She does. She's a good kid, just like you. I've enjoyed her company, even if she made me miss you."

"You missed me?" Aerie felt her voice start to tremble. "Then why did you leave me?"

"I'd rather have the rest of the family with me while I explain," Merra replied. "It'll be easier to only have to explain it once. I'll make the arrangements after I meet with Exton and Director Ward, and check in with my forces."

"Your forces?"

"Of course," Merra said. "Who do you think twisted Exton into fighting in the first place? I didn't just spend all those years at your father's side worrying about my plants and my kids."

Aerie felt the room began to spin. "Why are you doing this?" she asked. "Why couldn't you just stay with me at New Hope? You had to go and ruin everything like this?"

Merra frowned. "You should be grateful," she said. "You wouldn't be here otherwise."

"Exton wouldn't be risking his life if it weren't for you."

Merra's green eyes gleamed. "I'm glad to see the rumors are true. You really do love him."

"Of course I do." Aerie frowned. "Why else would I be so upset at the idea that he's in danger, particularly if I'm the reason behind it?"

"You're not the reason behind it," Merra said. "You're just part of the collateral. And anyway, it matters little, now that you're an enemy of the State."

"He's still risking his life to join the war."

"He was already risking it," Merra replied. "He's been a risk for the URS ever since he stole back the *Perdition*. I wouldn't worry about him, though. I know he's smart, Aerie.

He's seen the signs. He knows that time is running out."

"Running out?"

"The URS was bound to attack the *Perdition* sooner or later. They already did. Do you really think that it'll be the last of the attacks once the URS manages to break through the *Perdition*'s communications jamming?"

Aerie faltered. She knew firsthand they were already being taught how to reroute the comm systems, and how the NETech was going to give them a new advantage in battle strategy.

As if she could read her mind, Merra said, "They've been making plans for years, Aerie, to take the *Perdition* down. Exton's just taking the path that will save the most lives."

"You don't know that."

"The odds are on my side." Merra softened. "But I can see, if you really do love him, why it hurts you so. I was worried for Victor, too. I'm still worried for him."

"But you left him, too," Aerie nearly yelled, surprised at the venom in her voice.

"We'll discuss that later," Merra remarked easily. "Now, why don't you go and take a nap? You're clearly exhausted."

"Don't tell me what I am," Aerie snapped.

"You always had a temper when you were tired."

"You don't know me anymore."

"No," Merra said. "You don't know me anymore, Aerie, if you ever did at all. You were only allowed glimpses back in the URS."

"I liked that mother better," Aerie replied bitingly.

Merra smiled. "Cute."

Aerie turned on her heels and headed away. She didn't know where she was going, but she just wanted to get away.

Mom is alive. I can't believe it.

Aerie almost laughed, thinking how this was how Exton had to have felt earlier when he'd met her outside his ship.

Aerie thought about the day when she, that morning so close to her twelfth birthday, had woken up to find her mother was gone. She'd had a seizure, suspected to be the result of a deadly bacterial reaction, while she was piloting a vehicle on the way back from the outer regions of New Hope. The General quietly informed her and the rest of the unit of her mother's death, before telling her she had to report to the Central District for a full counseling check-up.

She blinked, realizing she had no idea where she was going.

"Aerie."

Aerie felt a wave of relief hit her as she heard Emery call out to her. She turned to see her friend hurrying toward her. "Emery," she said, trying to smile.

Emery came up and hugged her. "I know you're upset," Emery said. "I saw Merra's ship register for landing at the checkpoint."

"I can't believe she … " Aerie struggled to find the right words.

"We were surprised she was alive, too. She came with some of her forces to save Exton at Halifax, once he took you down to General St. Cloud."

Aerie shook her head. "No. I think I was going to say I can't believe she left me. It's like I didn't even know her at all."

Emery patted her shoulder comfortingly. "My father worked on his ships quite a bit when he was alive. I barely saw him. I know Exton is more the engineer than I am, so I imagine he misses him more than I do."

"You don't miss your father?" Aerie asked.

"No, of course not. I miss Papa every day, and my mom, too," Emery assured her. "I just don't think I knew him very well."

"Oh."

"I guess it's not very reassuring to hear that children are surprised at who their parents are, outside of being parents."

Aerie snorted. "I know the General less as a father than anything else. I thought I knew my mother."

"You might just be seeing a different side of her," Emery said. "Give it time."

"You'll be here to help me, won't you?" Aerie asked.

"Of course." Emery smiled. "I've missed you terribly, too, you know. Somehow you managed to get under my skin."

Aerie giggled, already feeling better. "Speaking of getting under your skin," she said, "how did the rest of my family fair?"

Emery rolled her eyes. "Ungrateful, to the last," she said. "Brock is still at the med center. He had a few bruises we wanted to take care of. Serena and your brothers are getting their quarters assigned."

"I guess I have to get that taken care of, too." Aerie yawned. "Hopefully it won't take long."

"It shouldn't." Emery smiled. "Especially if you decide to get married to my brother."

"Married?" Aerie blushed.

"You love him, don't you?" Emery asked.

"Of course I do." Aerie looked down at the floor. "But, it's, well, so sudden. In the URS, you can apply for cohabitation and there's a waiting period to see if you want it to last enough to where you can adopt or have kids, and even then there are restrictions."

Emery nodded sympathetically, even though Aerie thought she could see some sadness in her gaze. "I'd forgotten about that," she said. "We definitely don't see marriage the same way the URS does."

"I mean, they want things to work out, and the units to stay together," Aerie said. "It's better that way, you know. Better to be too careful than too reckless with things like that."

"We all have to take risks sometimes, I guess," Emery said. "But if you're not ready, it's okay. Committing to something that big does deserve a lot of consideration. Tyler and I waited a long time."

"Really?" Aerie was surprised.

Emery gave her a small smile. "I'm practical by nature and necessity, Aerie. I don't like to take risks. Tyler and I had always been good friends, and, being up here, it seemed like it was only a matter of time before we would face destruction. But six years passed, and I finally realized I wasn't really living."

"Exton felt that way, too," Aerie said.

"He didn't feel it the same way I did. He was—is—angry. He can't forgive the URS for taking away Papa. And I struggle with this too, sometimes. But I was afraid. I am afraid. With Exton's decision to involve us in an offensive war, I am still afraid for the future. Some days, the only thing that keeps me going is knowing that I would still be afraid, even if I didn't have Tyler, and now, our baby."

"Baby?" Aerie blinked. "You're going to have a baby?"

Emery's smile was all the confirmation Aerie needed; it was perfect blend of fear and joy, hesitancy and constancy. "Yes," she said.

"Wow." Aerie glanced down at Emery's belly, trying to recall the last time she'd seen a pregnant woman.

"So, yes," Emery said, "I have a lot of reasons to be afraid."

"I feel the same way," Aerie admitted. "I don't think I've processed everything yet."

"Well, you are tired. Come with me," Emery said, taking her hand. "I'll take you to the med center here. While you're there you can sleep, and by the time you're finished, we should have some accommodations prepared."

"Okay." Aerie sighed. "Thank you, Emery."

"What are friends for?" Emery grinned. "Besides, I'm sure I'll need your help, too, one of these days."

"I can't imagine you needing help," Aerie said. "You're always so calm and in control."

"It's carefully managed on the outside," Emery said. "On the inside, it's a real mess."

"Good to know. I don't feel quite as intimidated now."

"You shouldn't," Emery said with a grin. "I happen to like you."

"I'm glad."

"I'm sure Exton is, too. I know he considers you a miracle, but you've always been more of a gift to me. And when you're given a gift, you should just try to take care of it."

"You do a good job of that," Aerie assured her. "And I'm grateful for that."

"I'm sure you'll be even more grateful after you sleep some," Emery told her. "That is something to keep in mind as you go through the check-up."

Aerie tried to keep her groan to herself.

♦22♦

While Aerie dealt with the medical team at Petra, Exton was once more caught up in the routines the *Perdition* demanded of him.

Although, he thought, *this isn't exactly routine.*

When Tyler had contacted him with the news that they'd been able to build a program to detect the Craftcarriers, Exton hurried off to one of the nearby transmission offices, where he would be able to talk with his friend and Commander in peace. He felt bad about leaving Aerie behind with her mother, but he had been understandably distracted. More than one of *Perdition*'s market suppliers had complained about the Craftcarriers in the past, and now, having fought with one, he was better prepared to conquer that problem.

"That'll really help us out, Tyler," Exton said to his friend, as he gave the last few lines of coding for the program. It began installing onto Petra's monitor as he turned back to the video screen. "Thanks."

"You'll need to give a lot of the credit to Thora," Tyler said. "She sent up all the reports to me after you landed in Petra. We've managed to get a reading on the one that you hobbled."

"I'll see to it that she's commended."

"She'd probably appreciate some time off so she can take a vacation or something with her kids."

"I'll keep that in mind." Exton grinned back at his profile on the screen. "How is everything else onboard?"

"We're still well out of sight. Hiding under the world has always been easy for us, even on the *Perdition*," Tyler said. "Routines are normal here, although we're going to need more med supplies. Merra's taken full advantage, and she'll probably ask for more."

"I had a feeling she would," Exton muttered glumly.

"She's an able leader, though," Tyler said. "Some of the crew have mentioned she's pretty thrifty with what we give her, so you know it's not being wasted or hoarded."

"Aerie met with her earlier."

Tyler was silent for a long moment. "Dare I ask how it went?"

"Aerie stormed off. Emery found her."

"That's something to be thankful for—that Emery found her, I mean, not that she's upset."

"I knew what you meant. And at least it gives Em a chance to practice her mothering skills," Exton said. "And on someone other than me."

Tyler laughed. "True enough."

"I'm worried about her."

"Aerie, or Emery?"

"Both, but Aerie more." Exton sighed. "Among other things, she told me that our old friend Gerard was the one who was assigned to 'reeducate' her."

"Does Meredith know?" Tyler asked quietly.

"Aerie said she was there with her." Exton waited for Tyler to respond. When he said nothing, he pushed forward. "Have you heard from her at all?"

"Meredith? Yes, she contacted us after Aerie was able to escape, though it was well after you were already chasing down her ship," Tyler replied. "She wanted me to let you know we lost two members when the other URS fighters shot them down."

Exton felt his heart grow heavy at the sad news. "I'm sorry to hear that."

He almost expected Tyler to say something about how they were no longer in the world, but they were in a better place, or how they lived their lives sacrificially for others. But he said nothing, and Exton had to wonder if this was how it was going to be for the remainder of the war.

Exton finally shook his head, as if he had to snap himself out of it.

"I know Aerie's upset at the thought of war," Exton said. "I can't blame her for feeling that way."

"Hopefully it will be a quick war."

"War is never quick unless a lot of people die quickly."

"Or the right people die quickly," Tyler said dolefully. "Well, the light shift is nearly over. We'll be able to get more people to check on the new program in a few hours. Predicting the anomalies in the atmosphere will be the hardest part, since Thora focused mainly on weather patterns, rather than the Craftcarrier's movements. It might be trickier, too, depending on how many are gathered in a particular area."

"We know the URS didn't commission any in recent years," Exton said. "In fact, they haven't built anything significant for several years. Not since … "

"Not since we took the *Perdition* back from them," Tyler finished.

Exton felt the reality of that moment all over again—the one where his father was still alive, and then the next second, he was gone. His breath caught in his throat at the clarity of the memory, and he felt his heart harden over once more.

"They were probably worried we'd steal that one, too," Tyler said, breaking the spell despair had cast on him.

"Probably," Exton said.

"I wonder why we haven't seen them up to more tricks. I'll have to check on that."

Exton watched as Tyler yawned, and he suddenly smiled.

"I trust your skills," Exton replied, still struggling to recover from reliving his father's death. "But it couldn't hurt to have a few more coders check for you. Especially if you have been working for the last several shifts."

"You used to make it look easy," Tyler said.

"You should've thought of that before Jared left."

"He'll be coming back once Merra's given him the okay."

"I'll assume that's part of the reason she's here, too," Exton muttered. "I guess I better go see exactly what she wants."

"There's no need to hurry to get Jared back," Tyler said. "His replacement, Henry, is doing a good job."

"As much as I agree with you," Exton said, "I'm more

terrified of *not* knowing what Merra wants. I have a feeling if she wants something badly enough, she'll find a way to get it, no matter what I say."

"That is pretty terrifying," Tyler said. "I hope she doesn't decide she wants to come up here."

"I'm about to go find out." Exton waved to his friend as he cut the video feed. "Wish me luck."

He heard Tyler's garbled, "Good luck," before the transmission cut out completely.

The weariness of the world seemed to settle onto him as he stood up. It was closing in on midday, but there were signs rain would be moving in again. Exton wondered, as he headed out to the hangar once more, if he wasn't the only one to feel it. The people he passed were diligent in going about their duties, but there was a slight sluggishness to their work that was hardly perceivable. He might have thought he was imagining it if he didn't seem to struggle with it himself.

The thought of finding Aerie and getting some rest sorely tempted him.

The temptation was blown away a second later as the door to one of the many shipping offices bounced open and Merra walked out.

"Thank you for your cooperation," she called back to the office manager. "I'll expect the shipment to be deployed before too long."

"I'll still need the Captain's approval, or Director Ward's signature."

"You'll get it." Merra's eyes narrowed at the older man.

Exton was glad to see he had the fortitude not to flinch. He cleared his throat. "Merra, I've been looking for you," he called, inciting a look of gratitude from the man in the office standing behind her.

"What is it?" Merra asked, her eyes quickly losing their ruthless expression.

"We have business to discuss," he said. "Follow me."

He led them back toward the office, seeing no better alternative. He knew from his instruction from St. Cloud that with instances like this, it was always better to be able to determine the field of battle. But he also knew in dealing with Merra, that wasn't likely to give him any edge.

Finally, he turned to face her. "Why are you here?"

Seamlessly, Merra's willing compliance transformed into staunch authority as she arched her brow. "I came to see my kids, of course," she said. "Once I heard they were on their way here, I decided to head out from Chaya. I also have full notes for further aid if you can spare it, Exton."

"So I've figured, from what I overheard you say to the office manager at the hangar."

"If you're worried about the amount, don't be. Chaya has excellent connections with several of the Middle East traders and other settlements. We've managed to make our position clear, now that you and the Ecclesia are backing us."

"The Ecclesia have no official position," Exton reminded her. "But speaking of them, I want to know how you found out about Aerie and the others."

"I have my sources," Merra answered coyly.

"Was it someone from the Ecclesia?"

"Ha! The Ecclesia are made of naive and gullible leaders, too beholden to God to understand the wars of men," Merra said. "While they have good gossip lines, I have better places to go for military intel."

Exton was surprised at the derision in her tone. "I thought you liked the Ecclesia."

"Of course. I love them, Exton, I really do." She smiled. "But we all have weaknesses, Exton, and there are some days I can't tell if theirs is too little spine or too much holy fear. It's too much for some of them to recognize the right times to stand up and take a difficult stance."

"Sometimes we are not sure of what is right," Exton muttered, angry to hear his defense of the Ecclesia. He was irritated to find himself agreeing with Merra's assessment.

"Compassion has to be tempered by competency," Merra said, "but so does faith with fact, and justice with mercy. We might attack, but we make sure to minimize damage."

But we still have to attack. Exton sighed. "I don't have time to argue philosophy."

"Practical philosophy is always up for debate," Merra said. "But you're right. There's a time for everything under the sun. And when it comes to time, we never have enough of it."

Exton nodded. "How did things go with Aerie?"

"Predictably." Merra gave him a forced smile. "She's upset."

"She'll need some time to adjust."

"Certainly."

"Did the others see you yet?"

"No," Merra said. "I've been arranging meetings, and I fully intend to be back en route to Chaya soon enough."

"You are going to see them, though?"

"Of course," she said. "I came here to see them. Getting more supplies and informing you of warfront developments while I'm here is just being efficient."

"I'm going to request, formally as a leader in this community, that you do not seek them out until tomorrow."

A door opened up, and Exton saw Aunt Patty as she came inside.

Merra sniffed haughtily. "I will agree, formally, to your request. But if I see them of their own accord, it's not for you to call."

"Fine." He agreed, only because he knew it would be pointless to argue with her, and he had other things that required his attention.

Merra walked out of the room, giving Patty a courteous nod as she passed her in the doorway.

Patty glanced at Exton. "If you want me to send someone to tail her, I can do that. There are plenty of people who can spare an hour or two."

"She was St. Cloud's wife," Exton said. "I wouldn't put it past her to murder someone if she thought they gave her enough reason to."

Patty smirked. "Maybe I should see if some of our more

anxious defectors are up for such a task. She'll give them some exercise."

"I don't think it's the kind you'd want to encourage," Exton replied.

"We'll see," Patty said. She pushed some of her wayward white bangs out of her eyes. "I have been in contact with some of our other brothers and sisters around the world. You were right about the URS and their forces."

"They're mobilizing. Do we know where?"

"They've been sent all over the world," Patty said. "Rumors say they're building something big."

"Not another Craftcarrier, I hope." Exton leaned back against the console. "We don't have the forces to successfully take care of them."

"You did pretty well with the one hanging out over South America."

"We immobilized it," Exton said. "And it'll likely be on the ground for a couple days at least. But destroying it will take a lot of firepower."

"I'll keep an ear to the ground," Patty said. "In the meantime, things here are going well. Your girlfriend and her family unit are all getting situated. The Rearden boy is still in the med ward, but the others have been assigned rooms and bunks."

"They didn't give you any trouble, did they?" Exton asked. "I know they weren't happy about being here."

"We can take what chaos they'll cause, if they cause any at all. The young lady was poking around our med supplies, but that was the most disruptive thing they've done so far. Unless," she said with a disapproving look, "you count their appetites. The twins alone ate enough for five people."

"I'm glad to hear that's the worst of it." He rubbed his forehead. "It seems we have enough to worry about."

"You've had a long night, Exton." Patty reached out and put a hand on his shoulder. "Go get some rest."

"Soon enough," Exton said.

"The best of us still need rest," Patty insisted. "We're all in this together. Emery and I can keep watch for now. She's already taken over the counsel room.."

"I know she misses Tyler."

"Work has always been an escape for our family," Patty said with a sigh. "Even your mother obsessed with her plants, and your father with his inventions and his machines."

"What do you obsess over?" Exton asked.

"Now?" Patty's eyes gleamed, reminding him of his mother's cheerfulness. "Justice. Law and order is my calling."

"Fitting."

"I know yours is revenge," Patty said. She glanced over at him, eying him carefully. "I would encourage you to forgo it."

"I will," Exton said. "Eventually."

Patty nodded. "Eventually is good enough for me. You know better than most that some people will always want war. I hope you're aware of the same influence that revenge can bring."

"I am." Exton thought about Aerie. "But it helps that I do have something else to care for these days."

"Go and tend to her, then," Patty said, surprising him with her perceptiveness. "I'm sure she'll be happy to see you, too."

Exton smiled. "Thanks."

♦23♦

Aerie felt the tenderness of sleep start to peel away from her as a strange awareness took over. She sighed, peacefully and ruefully, before she turned over onto her side.

"Can't sleep?"

Aerie didn't even have to open her eyes to know why she'd woken up. "Exton." Her hand reached out for his expectantly.

She was surprised when her fingers brushed up against a warm pluff of fur. "Huh?" Aerie opened her eyes to see Exton sitting next to her bed with Moona in his arms.

Aerie instantly felt a rush of happiness as it consumed her. "Moona."

"I thought you would like some company." Exton gave her a charming smirk, and instantly Aerie was reminded all over again of their time together on the *Perdition.*

She pushed herself upright in the small cot she'd been assigned earlier. Exton waited for her to settle in before he passed the cat onto her lap.

Aerie cuddled with Moona, laughing as the cat sniffed her carefully. "I guess it's been a while since I've seen you, Moona," she whispered. "I barely recognize you!"

"She's definitely gotten fatter," Exton said, as he reached over and ruffled the feline's fur.

Moona meowed at him, before scuttling away from him.

"Guess I lost her esteem," he murmured playfully as Aerie laughed.

"Thank you for taking care of her while I was … " Her eyes fell to the ground, humbled and touched.

He brushed off her thanks. "Emery's the one who deserves more of your thanks. Besides, Moona is good company down here. The adults as well as the kids are charmed by her."

"It still means a lot to me." Aerie tightened her grip on Moona and settled the finicky cat down on her lap. "And it is nice to see her again, especially after going through the med screening."

"You survived."

"Not unscathed," Aerie murmured. She rubbed the sore area around her left wrist, where she had been branded by the med tech team at the Reeducation Center. There were some anomalies in her reports and they were double-checking the results. She was about to show it to Exton when he stood up.

Aerie reached for him before he could get far. "Where are you going?"

"I'm just getting your chart," he said, glancing over toward the row of scanners behind him.

"Oh." She gave him a sheepish grin and let his arm go.

"Don't worry," he said, as he ran his fingers through her hair affectionately. "I'll be back in a moment."

Aerie contented herself with Moona as she watched Exton. She had slept for several hours, and she was surprised she wasn't disturbed by the others.

But then, she reasoned, there had to be plenty to do around Petra, just the same as there had been a plethora of activity around the *Perdition.* And at least she had a little more privacy, even if it was a small room in the medical ward.

Exton sat by her with a med tablet and began reading through her notes. "Looks like your shoulder's going to need some physical therapy yet."

Aerie made a face. "Great. I suppose your med students can't do much else for it?"

"Not that I know of," he said, "but we can ask. It also looks like you had some wounds that were rebandaged."

"From the IV and the injections," Aerie explained. "Serena tidied me up on the way here."

"She did a good job, by the looks of it. One of your nurses made a comment about it."

"Serena's been trained in military medicine."

Aerie could've sworn she saw him hesitate.

"She'd make a good addition to our team," he said.

She nearly laughed at the thought of Serena being willing

to help Petra, but she knew Exton would try to find common ground with Serena and the others. He had enemies, but that didn't mean he set out to make them, Aerie knew. "I'll let her know."

Exton didn't seem to hear her, as his face contorted into an angry frown.

"What is it?" Aerie asked.

"They gave you the electroshock treatment," he said. "Those monsters."

Aerie felt her grip tighten around Moona's fur. "Gerard told me it was on a lower setting."

"He was probably telling the truth. The doctors here didn't see much internal tissue damage," Exton growled as he looked further down through the reports. "That's good at least."

Aerie set Moona down and pulled off her jacket. "You can see if you want. It doesn't hurt anymore." She pushed back her uniform sleeves to show him where the other sets of electroshock patches had been placed.

Exton put the notes aside and ran his hands over the small, rough patches. "I'm sorry," he said. "I'll make sure Gerard pays for this."

"If he was brainwashed by the URS, you shouldn't blame him," Aerie told him softly.

"He hurt you."

"He's been hurt, too."

Exton stood up, and for a moment Aerie thought she had angered him enough to leave. She was about to say something, anything to keep him close to her, when he reached for her.

"Aerie." He sat down on the bed beside her, and Aerie immediately scooted over, making more room for him on the narrow cot. His hands caught her face, and he looked down at her, the intensity of his blue eyes mesmerizing her.

"What?" she uttered, already anticipating his kiss.

"You are extraordinary, you know that?" he whispered. He shook his head, and Aerie was confused before he said, "I told you before I've never been very good at forgiving people."

"You forgave me," Aerie pointed out. "For lying about who I was."

"I suppose I did forgive you for that," Exton said. "Forgiveness is always hard, but I love you, and that makes it an infinitely easier chore. Forgiving someone I hate, or someone I barely know, seems impossible. Especially with the charges against them."

"I know." Aerie reached over and placed her hands on his chest. "You've had terrible things happen in your life."

"You have, too." He caressed her cheek. "But you still forgive people."

"Well, maybe my mother will prove to be the real test of that ability," Aerie replied, recalling her earlier sense of betrayal.

"I was shocked to see her, too, if it makes you feel better."

"It doesn't." Her voice was flat. "I can't believe it. She left me, and the others, too. It hurts. I was sad when she died, but now I feel angry."

"I know it can't be easy," he said, "but I have a feeling you'll forgive her, too."

"I don't want to talk about it now," Aerie whispered.

"What do you want to talk about?"

"Nothing." Aerie couldn't wait any longer; she felt the wall of her patience fall, and she knew there was no going back the moment her mouth met his.

Exton responded at once. His arm wrapped around her, careful to avoid her injured shoulder, as he drew her closer to him. Aerie fumbled with the thin sheet, tugging it out from between them, allowing him to slide down next to her.

She felt her body shiver as she could feel the full length of his body next to hers.

"*Mew.*" Moona seemed indignant, as she was crowded between them. She slinked out, tickling Aerie with her tail as she jumped down from the bed.

Aerie glanced at Exton and they both laughed. “Sorry, Moona,” Aerie said, already reaching for Exton again. *I’ll make it up to her later.*

Before she could think another thought, she was consumed with passion. Exton held her close, his hand running down her back, pressing into her hips as he kissed her.

Aerie stifled a moan. His kisses were hot and demanding, the taste of him intoxicating her, drugging her senses while warming her body.

“Exton,” she murmured, as his lips found her throat again. She felt a whisper of shock move through her, rippling pleasure all across her senses.

She was surprised when he pulled away. “What?” she asked. “What’s wrong?”

He sighed. “I know you didn’t want to talk,” he began, “but I think we need to.”

“What is it?” she asked, sitting up. “You still want me, don’t you?”

“More than anything,” Exton told her, sending a rush of relief through her. “And that’s why we need to talk.” He paused before adding, “About marriage.”

She blushed. “I don’t know how I feel about a career in marriage.”

“Just marriage, Aerie.” He gave her a quick grin. “I’ve never wanted anyone the way I want you. But I don’t just want you, or your body. I want more.”

“What more can I give you?” Aerie asked. “I know Emery said that the URS and the Ecclesia view marriage differently.”

“We do,” he said, nodding. “Marriage is more than just a relationship and sex to us. It is not just about pleasure, but about personal sacrifice and shared obligations. It’s the highest level of commitment, which is why, on some level, the URS probably made it into a form of career for society. I want a bond with you that I have with no one else—where you and I give ourselves to each other completely in love and trust."

Aerie felt the warmth he'd removed between them a moment earlier start to reemerge, even though he hadn't moved. "You trust me?" she asked.

He nodded. "I do. I love you, too, of course. And I love you so much I want all our friends, our family, and our children to know it and hold me accountable to your care and comfort, for all the days of my life, to the cost of my life, if need be. To me, it is the most honorable way I can love you—even if it might not seem like the most pleasurable."

"You would really do that for me?" Aerie felt her nose prickle in response.

He grinned in reply. "All I need to know, Aerie, is if you can commit to me in the same way, and come walk with me through the rest of our lives."

Aerie trembled at the thought. She had never known someone that loved her enough to die for her; her parents seemed too aloof, her family never seemed to understand, and her friendships—even her close one with Brock—had limits. The thought of Exton's love and his passion for her was dizzying as much as it was irresistible.

"I … I don't know," she answered honestly.

"Why not?" There was a surprising amount of irritation in his voice. "You never complained about my deals before."

She smiled at the memory of all his deals; they had been the cornerstone of their relationship. "It's been awhile since we made one," Aerie said carefully.

"So?"

Aerie knew he was frustrated. She had been so willing to stay with him on the *Perdition.* Why did she feel such apprehension now?

Because! Aerie cried to herself. *Because there's a war and my mother and all sorts of other complications!*

"Tell me what you're thinking," he said, this time more kindly. "I can tell something's bothering you."

"What if we … what if we end up like my parents?" Aerie asked. She hoped he didn't hear the small undertone of fear in her voice. "My mother left me. And my father. And the rest of us. I don't understand why, but I know the pain that I felt when it happened."

"I'm sorry you're in pain," he told her. Exton's eyes held hers, full of sincerity and kindness. "But we are not your parents. I can promise you that you're nothing like your mother, and I'm nothing like your father."

"That's true enough," Aerie said.

"It's highly unlikely you would be able to fake your own death for another." He smiled. "Should I be on the lookout for that?"

"No," Aerie said with a huff. "Of course not. That's not what I meant. Not entirely, anyway."

"My mother loved my father so much she died of grief a few months after he did," Exton said. "It's always a risk, and I would never want that for you. But, if we can be together in the meantime, I would still have a hard time letting you go." As he said it, he tightened his hold on her.

Aerie reached over and kissed him again, reveling in the rapture rushing through her. "I know if you want to try, then I want to try. I love you, and I want to be with you, too."

"You have some time to make sure. You have my word on it."

"Thank you." Aerie gave him a quizzical look. "You know, for a space pirate, you sure do care a lot about honor."

"Maybe it's an older notion of honor among thieves," he said.

"I'm not a thief."

"You were the one who stole my heart," he said, giving her another quick, soft kiss.

Aerie laughed. "I'm going to keep it, too," she declared.

"See? What we have works. Even if it's terribly inconvenient for me some of the time," he said, pulling her down next to him on the bed.

"What are you doing?" she asked, as he settled her into the crook of his shoulder.

"Going to sleep."

When he yawned a moment later, she laughed. "I guess you've had a pretty tiring day."

"I've been up for a very long time, going through reports and talking with different people," he said. He tucked her into the heat of his body and curled his arm possessively around her. "And tomorrow's going to prove equally busy, I'm sure. But I don't want to leave you."

"It's okay," Aerie whispered back. "We never seem to have enough time together."

"That's true," he said disdainfully.

Aerie pressed against him, placing a loving kiss onto his shoulder as she allowed herself to get comfortable. She didn't want him to leave, either. "I guess if I've stolen your heart, it's nothing for you to steal some room on my mattress."

He gave her only a small, husky laugh in reply. Aerie knew he was sleeping a few moments later by the rhythm of his breathing. Moona came back up onto the bed and curled at their feet.

"I guess you've forgiven us, then?" Aerie asked.

Moona just ignored her.

Aerie stared out into the darkness, trying to fall back into sleep, still able to taste the sweetness of Exton's kisses as his words of love and devotion, of sharing a life of work and play and family, circled joyfully around inside her mind.

♦24♦

There was something miraculous, Exton decided, about watching Aerie sleep.

His comm had beeped a few times, waking him, but after checking the time, he ignored the messages for a few moments of peace with the woman he loved, and the one who loved him back.

She hadn't slept well, obviously disturbed by nightmares, but when he curled her against him during the night, she calmed down. It reminded him of the night they shared on the *Perdition*, and he wasn't surprised to wake up with her bedcover on the floor. The warmth between them was more than enough to shutter out the cold.

Exton looked down at her now, the soft glow of the early morning hours lending a gentle light to her features. Her golden red hair was loose, splayed out across the pillows, her breathing was gentle and easy, and her mouth had fallen open during the night.

The comm beeped again, and Exton knew he didn't have much longer before the rest of the world demanded that his attention be torn from her.

How can she not know she is mine? Exton wondered. *She belongs to me.*

Knowing the truth about her parents was no small matter, but Exton had a feeling Aerie was still unable to admit she wanted her parents' love and acceptance as much as she wanted his. Suddenly finding out the truth about her mother leaving them, and her father, would have shocked her. He'd known previously of her devotion to her mother, and, having grown up watching Emery toddle after their own mother, he even understood it.

And for all the evil St. Cloud had done in the name of the URS, Exton knew he was a man who kept his word, and that someone like Aerie would want his esteem.

He'd wanted that himself, not too many years before.

Exton sighed ruefully as he carefully untangled himself from her, before he stumbled out of the small bed. He tucked in the fallen cover around her, to keep in the warmth. He brushed a couple tresses back from her face, placing them behind her ear.

"Exton?" she murmured, and he paused.

"Wait for me, my love," he whispered beside her, giving her a kiss on the forehead before he left the room and headed down the hall.

Exton was just about to respond to his comm when he stopped. Standing before him, glaring down at him, was Brock.

"What are you doing here?" Exton asked. He suddenly felt a lot better about setting the lock on Aerie's door. He didn't want her to be subjected to Brock's surly attitude this early in the morning.

"I could ask you the same question," Brock bit back.

Good to know where I stand with him, at least. Exton crossed his arms over his chest. "I know my way around Petra," he said. "I was just checking to see if you were lost or not. Nothing else."

Brock's hands clenched into fists. "You were with Aerie, weren't you?"

Exton felt the heat rise from around his collar, but he said nothing.

"If you really love her, you should let her go," Brock told him.

"If I said that to you, you would be ready to punch me." Exton glanced down at Brock's fists. "Not that you're not ready now."

Brock gave him a reluctant smirk. "You think you're so smart, don't you? It's such a shame you can't see what's right in front of your face."

"If that's a threat—"

Brock grunted. "It doesn't have to come from me," he said. "The whole nation of the URS wants you dead. You think you're smart enough to outrun them forever?"

"I just have to outrun them longer than they outrun me," Exton replied. "That's the way the game is played, isn't it? Anything for survival."

"You're going to get her killed," Brock said, pushing on, ignoring the attempts that challenged his reasoning.

Exton refused to let Brock make him doubt he was doing the right thing, but he had to admit he had already caused Aerie a great amount of pain.

An amount of pain, he thought bitterly, that Brock had been able to save her from. In the end, Exton knew Brock was his rival for Aerie's affections, but their goal was the same. They both wanted her to be safe. And if that was the only common ground they had between them, he could find a way to respect Brock.

Of course, respecting someone doesn't mean I have to like *him.*

"What would you have me do?" Exton asked.

"You should let her go somewhere else."

"Aerie has been able to walk away from me for some time," Exton said evenly. "She has a right to refuse me, too. But she doesn't. She wants to stay with me, and I want to be with her."

"She's not yours," Brock hissed. He crossed his arms over his chest. "I'll bet anything she didn't tell you about our kiss on the cargo ship."

Surprise briefly fluttered through him, but Exton remained calm. *No, she didn't,* Exton thought, *but she didn't tell you about me, either.*

If Brock thought he would get away with creating division between him and Aerie, he was a fool.

"You should give her the choice."

"You don't really mean that." Exton frowned. "What you really mean is that you want her to choose you."

Brock's eyes darkened as he scowled.

Exton stood his ground. "Like it or not, she *is* mine, and she has been mine since she was captured and brought onto the *Perdition.*"

"She was supposed to be mine!" Brock yelled. "I was the

one who rescued her from the Reeducation Center. I was the one who took care of her after she was injured."

"You mean after St. Cloud injected her with Memory Serum?" Exton asked. "So she'd forget all about me and the *Perdition*?"

"I didn't know about that." Brock faltered only slightly. "But I still looked after her. When we were in school, I helped her train and made sure I earned her unit director's respect so he would approve of me."

"I know she considers you a friend."

"I was her *only* friend in the URS."

"If you are her friend, then you should be glad she's here," Exton pointed out. "She's been named an enemy of the State. I might be on their enemy list, but now she is, too. She might be in enemy territory, but they don't know about Petra."

Outside of St. Cloud, he added silently to himself.

"If you don't think they know about this place, you're crazy. They will find you, eventually," Brock said. "And then Aerie will die if you don't let her go." He turned on his heel and stormed away.

Exton felt his suspicion deepen as he considered Brock's warning. Did Osgood know about Petra? Exton wasn't sure, but there was the question of where Brock had been planning on taking Aerie once he'd freed her. Where else would he go, but Petra, especially with a cargo ship like the one he'd taken?

But then, how did Brock know about Petra anyway?

Either way, he did save Aerie, and I owe him for that.

"Brock," Exton called out to him. "You are welcome here, since you have no other place to go, and because even though you hate me, I am grateful for how you helped Aerie escape the URS."

Brock whirled around. "I can go anywhere I want," he said. "But I'm not leaving without Aerie."

"She's staying here."

"We'll see about that," Brock snapped.

"I suppose you can think that you can leave at any time,"

Exton remarked, "but I know the punishment for betraying the URS, and even you don't deserve to pay that price."

Brock fumed even more, but he said nothing as he stared murderously at Exton.

"I think it's fair to give you a warning," Exton said. "I'll be monitoring you. I won't have you hurting my community, Aerie included."

"How is this place any different from the URS then, if that is the case?" Brock grumbled.

Exton didn't get a chance to answer as Brock walked away.

He felt a hand on his shoulder and he turned to see Emery. "If you want, I can get see about arranging that transport for him."

"I'm tempted to let you," Exton muttered. "But I don't want to risk Aerie's wrath. And I don't think you should, either."

"Not yet, anyway," Emery said with a small smile.

"What are you doing up?" he asked. "Did your comm go off, too?"

"I was the one who contacted you," Emery said. "When you didn't answer, I thought I would come get you."

"Something wrong?"

"Henry's got an update for us," she said. "The *Perdition* has been working to find and locate the different Craftcarriers, now that we have some more intel on them. One of them just went off course."

"Headed toward Petra?"

She grimaced. "It looks like its headed for the area where the cargo ship crashed," she said, "but we're not sure."

Exton felt a familiar, unwelcome feeling. "What else is happening?"

"What do you mean?"

"What else is happening around the URS capital and their bases? If we can check their movements, we might be able to get a better idea of what they're planning."

"I don't know," Emery admitted. "But I'll have Henry

and the others check."

"*We'll* have them check," Exton said, as he headed down the hall with her.

"Henry said that there are a few shuttles from the *Perdition* that will be making rounds to Chaya and here."

"Delay their arrival here," Exton ordered. "I don't want anything coming here until we see what the Craftcarrier is up to."

"You think an attack is coming, then?" Emery asked. Her eyes were worried.

Exton knew it was not the time to lie to her. "There's a good chance," he said. "St. Cloud told me that he wouldn't tell Osgood about Petra if we returned Aerie. He could still attack us, but now we have the added pleasure of her brothers and her sister here. It can't be a coincidence."

"I can't believe he would really attack with all of them here."

"Loyalty to the State is everything, Em," Exton reminded her. "St. Cloud shot up a Redbird at the *Perdition.* He allowed the SBD Heatseekers to launch, while Aerie was onboard, no less. He signed the arrest warrant for Aerie to be assigned to the Reeducation Center. Merra faked her own death to escape him. What further proof do you need to know he's a ruthless, sociopathic monster only loyal to the URS?"

"I guess you have a point," Emery said with a sigh.

"There's also the not-so-small matter of how he killed our father," Exton continued, barely registering that Emery had agreed with him. "And now, our brainwashed friend Gerard is in third command of the entire country, and he was responsible for Aerie's torture—"

Emery's gasp pulled Exton out of his tirade. He took one look at her face and realized he was losing control of himself. He cleared his throat as he mentally berated himself.

I'll have to work on that. I can't let St. Cloud get to me. That's how Aerie got into trouble the first time.

"Sorry, Em," he muttered.

"Meredith will be so sad."

"She saw it, apparently."

"I didn't know that." Emery's face crumbled. "She must know that we'll likely have to kill him. I was worried about that."

"I don't want to think about it," Exton said. "I know she was in love with him before, and they were going to get married, but she has to see that the man she loved is gone."

"She'll be devastated, but she'll understand. In time." Emery glanced up at him. "What are the chances we can capture him and bring him here?"

"I thought about that. I'm not sure we would be able to cure him at all," Exton said. "Just having him here could be dangerous to others."

"I guess so. Maybe there's a chance he'll remember who he is, especially if he's away from the URS."

"I hope so." Exton sighed. "I'd hate to hurt Meredith, especially after Tyler and I promised her we would try to save him. If she's been content to work at the Reeducation Center just to be near him all these years, she'll probably need a lot more time to recover than we have."

"We'll have to give her all we can," Emery said. "She's Tyler's sister."

Exton nodded. *We'll find a way to make it work out.*

They entered into a command hub, and Patty glanced up from over a console. "Hey, kids," she called. "Early day?"

"Henry just contacted me," Emery said. "We've got a problem."

"And possibly a big one, too, by the looks of it," Exton said.

Patty picked up her large container. "Thank God we have coffee then. Tell me what's wrong."

♦25♦

Of all the things that Aerie thought were impossible, sitting around the breakfast table with her mother and her siblings seemed to be one of the most impossible.

Exton said that I was his miracle, and Emery said their god was a god of miracles. Maybe this is one for me? Aerie wondered humorlessly, as Merra finished reintroducing herself to the others.

She sighed as she barely looked at her food. Since she had intercepted that call from Chaya, her life, and her appetite, had never been the same.

Or at least, she decided, her appetite for food had diminished. She thought about Exton, and how she woke up to find he had taken the time to tuck her into the covers before he left earlier. A small smile came to her lips at the memory; while Aerie had woken up from a disconcerting sleep after he left, the knowledge he had seen to her care before he was, she assumed, called away, was touching.

A loud *bang* on the table jerked her attention away from her thoughts. She glanced up to see Serena had slammed her cup onto the table.

"What are you smiling about?" Serena asked, glaring at her from across the table.

"Nothing," Aerie muttered, blushing, embarrassed she had been caught daydreaming, and further embarrassed because she had been caught daydreaming about Exton.

"I guess you think this is amusing?" Serena asked. "That having our *mother* show up out of nowhere after all this time, in the enemy's base no less, is funny?"

"Why would I think it's funny?" Aerie asked. "I was just as surprised when I saw her yesterday."

"You saw her yesterday?" Serena fumed. "You always were her favorite."

"You know, girls, I'm right here," Merra said. "And since I'm the adult here—"

"We're *all* adults now," Serena snapped.

"I'm still your mother," Merra reminded her with a scowl.

"Well, technically, you haven't been for the last six years," Cal said, as he continued to wolf down his breakfast. Aerie could tell the shock of seeing his mother again was over, as his hunger returned.

"I have always been your mother," Merra insisted. "Whether I've been around or not."

"Phoebe is supposed to be our unit director now," Serena said.

Aerie was surprised to see Merra's lips tighten bitterly at her statement. "Let's not talk about her," she said. "I would rather discuss other things."

"I guess you can ask Serena why she hasn't gotten any offers to cohabitate," Dorian said with a laugh.

"Hey! I've gotten plenty of offers," Serena said back. "I just don't accept any of them."

"And they're all secretly relieved," Cal said. "They know you'd never make a good unit director."

"At least I wasn't breeding material, like Aerie."

"Maybe it would make you a more pleasant person to deal with," Dorian said.

"Says the person who can't even get a girl to look at him, let alone cohabitate."

Merra glanced over at Aerie as the others continued arguing with each other. "I always wondered why you wanted them to accept you so badly."

Aerie was suddenly torn between laughing and crying, but she settled for remaining stoic.

When her mother left her as a little girl at the budding age of twelve, Aerie had felt lost. There was some part of her that was glad to have Merra back, especially since she did have a way of helping her see things in a new light. But there was so much more to settle still.

Aerie glanced back at Serena and her brothers, as they continued to give each other dirty looks and make even worse comments.

When she turned back to Merra, she felt an overwhelming amount of warmth in her gaze.

If Aerie had been younger, she might have grinned. Now that she was older, she just stood up and frowned down at her siblings. "Stop it!" she shouted, making the other people sitting at nearby tables glance over. She fought hard not to feel embarrassed, and not to let them see she was uncomfortable.

Aerie lowered her voice. "You guys have to stop it," she said. "As much you might not like it, you are *guests* here. Exton can throw you out at any point."

Serena leaned back. "Great. She's bringing her boy-toy into this."

Cal and Dorian laughed.

Aerie frowned. "He *is* in charge here," she shot back. "And you're only here in the first place because I insisted on it. Otherwise, you would still be stuck out in the middle of nowhere with a busted ship."

"Bravo, my girl," Merra murmured, as Serena, Cal, and Dorian all glanced away uneasily.

"And you!" Aerie turned on her. "I don't know what you've been doing, or what you think you're doing, but calling us for breakfast like we're all still children is wrong. You stepped out of our lives, and we have the right to choose to let you back in. Or not," she added, lowering her voice some.

Unlike her siblings, Merra didn't even flinch. She smiled. "That's fair," she said.

"Fine." Aerie felt her face flush over. "Fine. Now, what did you want from us? Director Ward was going to give us work assignments today."

"I'm okay with skipping that," Cal muttered.

"You're lazy," Dorian said.

"Hey, you can't blame me for not being excited," Cal said as he leaned back in his chair. "I didn't even want to come. I only came because the General told me to follow Brock."

Aerie turned her full focus on him. "What do you mean, the General told you to follow Brock?"

"I don't know. I figured the General was probably watching him since he was trying to get you to cohabitate with him," Cal said, shrugging his shoulders

"That's why we both came," Dorian said. "Didn't you know that?"

Serena huffed. "She wouldn't. She's always had us looking out for her, even when she had no idea of what was going on."

Aerie felt her earlier embarrassment morph into anger. "I don't need your protection," she snapped.

"Well, you obviously needed someone to rescue you," Serena said. "Brock wouldn't be here otherwise, and neither would any of us."

"Brock *asked* you to come!"

"And you know, a long time ago, I was told by *our mother*—that lady right there, in addition to our father—to watch out for you!" Serena frowned. "You've always been protected, and you've always been the one stupid enough to get into trouble anyway."

Aerie thought about how she'd been accidentally captured by Exon's shuttle the first time, and how she was arrested later on. "I can fight my own battles," she insisted, pushing past her doubt. "I was trained the same as you were, and I tested higher in combat than anyone else in the family. It's not my fault that I didn't make it to military—"

"If you really need to place the blame for that," Merra said, "you should blame Victor. He didn't think you would be happy in the military, and he didn't think you would do well there, either. That's why he wanted you in Comms Sec."

"What?!" Aerie swiveled on her. "He did that on purpose?"

"Of course." Merra sat back and sipped at her tea, smiling over the rim of her cup. "He really does love you, even if you don't believe it."

Aerie felt her mouth drop open, as Serena huffed. "It's not his love we're here to question. It's yours."

Merra nodded, still unfazed by the attacks and

accusations leveraged against her. "As Aerie stated, you have the right to believe what you want."

She's been expecting this, Aerie realized.

Merra leaned forward. "Let me start by apologizing for deceiving you," she said. "I know this is a shock, and I know this is not the best time for this, with the world at war and everything."

"You think?" Serena scoffed.

"My reason, not defense, for such a move has a lot to do with the situation the world is in," Merra said. "I have been working to undermine the URS for many years now."

Aerie felt another rush of shock at the revelation; the identical look of shock on her twin brothers' faces seemed to indicate they were experiencing a similar reaction.

Serena, on the other hand, stood up. "I knew it!"

"You always were the most intuitive," Merra said with a glowing smile. "I wasn't surprised to hear you were put in the medical field. You'll make a good doctor one day."

It was Serena's turn to blush, but she held still. "I won't be flattered into doing what you want me to."

Aerie was about to say that their mother had only wanted to meet them for breakfast when Merra interrupted her.

"You don't even know what it is that I want," Merra said. "You might be interested. Fighting along with the defectors and the resistance movement would be good for you. And you, too, boys," she said, turning her attention to the twins. "I have a few fighters that you could easily pilot."

Cal and Dorian exchanged glances. Aerie knew they were both disconcerted with the idea, even if they both loved to fly.

"What about Brock?" she asked, trying to buy them time.

Merra shrugged. "I haven't met with him yet," she said, dismissing the concern. "I'd like to, frankly, since I have a few questions for him, especially where it concerns you, Aerie."

"Shouldn't you be more worried about Captain Chainsword?" Serena growled.

"No, I like him." Merra gave Aerie a wink. "And I think he's well suited for her."

Aerie frowned, fighting off another round of embarrassment. "I don't want to talk about him with you," she snapped. "I don't want to talk about him with any of you. I've told you the truth, and that's all you need to know about him."

"I disagree," Serena said.

"What, are you jealous?" Dorian asked. He shrugged. "Aerie's in love with a terrorist, let her be in love with a terrorist."

"He's not the bad guy!" Aerie said. "He's trying to protect the world."

"Aerie's right," Merra asserted. "Do you think in the last eighty or so years of the URS rule, they've really made life better for their people? They've really only found an effective means of controlling them, and their overconfidence has finally shown their weakness."

"The URS isn't perfect," Serena said through clenched teeth. "But this idea that overthrowing them is somehow a better option is just illogical."

"That's why Petra is here," Merra said. "You haven't been here long, but surely you can see that the system they have in place here works."

"They're buying goods on a black market," Serena said. "And they're using people inside the URS to betray their nation."

"People don't work in collectives very well," Merra said. "It's been a downside to the URS tribal conditioning for years."

"Their system might work for a population this small, maybe," Dorian said. "But for the world? I doubt it would work."

"The URS hasn't even conquered the world, despite their attempts," Merra said. "If it weren't for all the nuclear fallout from before the creation of the Revolutionary States, they wouldn't even have what they do."

"Well, what does work?" Cal asked. "So far, the rest of the world has some catching up to do. Like it or not, the URS is still the best place in the world to be."

"That's propaganda at its finest," Merra said, rolling her eyes. "We can go back to a republic system."

"Republics don't work." Serena leaned over the table. "They've only worked for a couple of times, and then, for only a few hundred years at a time."

"The URS has only been in power for about eighty," Merra argued back. "And it's already breaking down."

"That's because of people like you," Serena insisted. "People who want to do their own thing and won't listen to rational arguments."

"First, people are able to rationalize just about anything, including the brainwashing of populations. Second, there's more to life than reason," Merra said. "Call it luck or fate or miracles, there's more than enough evidence to suggest that being completely rational doesn't work, either."

"Human beings are rationale creatures. We seek out order."

"Human beings are also irrational creatures," Merra argued back. "We are also incapable of keeping order."

"Forcing order is better."

"Better than what? Acknowledging our shortcomings and finding a system that will check individual as well as group influence?"

"Stop," Aerie cried, interrupting. "That's enough. We're not getting anywhere." She turned to face her mother. "We're here because you wanted to see us. I've made up my mind. I'm leaving, and the others need to come with me. Director Ward will be looking for us soon."

"Wait." Merra stood up. "Just give me another few moments."

"To say what?" Aerie asked. "You've already told us you were working against the URS. That's enough of a reason to fake your death and leave us behind, isn't it?"

Her tone was scathing, and Aerie was satisfied to see

Merra wince.

"I know that's what it seems like," Merra said. "But I'm telling you the truth. I worked to shuffle a lot of the research in the horticulture department out to Chaya, where we have continued research. You want to know why Exton started fighting with us? Because I convinced him we could finally win if we supported each other."

"You?" Aerie felt the breath rush out of her.

"You're the leader of the defectors?" Cal asked, while Dorian's hand flew up to cover his dropped jaw.

"There are several leaders, and several different factions around the world that are defectors," Merra said. "But I'm one of them. I lead Chaya's forces."

"Can you dimwits see it? She's always been the enemy," Serena said darkly. "Phoebe told me that she was under a lot of scrutiny, so that's why it was better she died."

"What?" Aerie frowned. "Phoebe never said that."

"She never said it to *you*," Serena said. "She knew you were the one who was most like Mom. Phoebe doesn't tell you anything, or even do anything for you, unless she has to because of that. And that's also why when the General warned us not to let anything happen to you, we figured it was a smart move to protect our unit."

"And even then, you managed to go and ruin everything, dragging Brock and then us into it," Dorian added. Aerie was about to round on him when he smiled. "I guess we should've been watching you more closely. You're more of a force to be reckoned with than I imagined."

Cal huffed. "Yeah, really."

Their admiration, even if it was reluctantly given, left Aerie even more speechless.

She was saved from responding when she heard a familiar voice behind her.

"I'm here, Merra."

Aerie glanced up, surprised to see Alice suddenly standing next to Merra. "Alice!" she cried happily, jumping up out of her seat at the sight of her coworker and her friend. "You're here."

"Hi Aerie," Alice replied. She gave her a polite nod. "I heard that you'd arrived here. I'm glad to see the rumors were true."

Aerie grinned, but before she could ask Alice about anything else, she noticed Alice was holding the hand of a small boy.

"Who's that?" Aerie asked. "Your little brother or something?"

"No," Alice said. "He's *your* little brother."

Aerie felt her legs back into the table, and she scrambled to sit down. She glanced over at Merra. "Mom?" she asked.

Merra nodded. "This is Marcus," she said. "When I left you, I was close to a month pregnant."

"But … you already have four kids," Serena said, her voice full of confusion.

Merra nodded. "I know. Turns out, sometimes the body can heal from the URS's sterilization methods."

"So *that's* the real reason you left," Aerie said. "You didn't want to give Marcus up."

"It would have been impossible to hide him," Merra said quietly. "And you know how much the government is willing to allow for mistakes."

"The downfall of freedom is that people can make bad choices," Aerie murmured.

Merra took Marcus into her arms. "He's four years old right now," she said, as Cal and Dorian came over to get a closer look. "But I've told him stories about you all his life. He's been looking forward to meeting you."

Aerie saw even Serena was curiously staring at the surprise addition to their family.

"Hi," the small boy said, looking just as intrigued by the people around the table as they were about him.

"Hi," Aerie replied, automatically smiling. *So that was why Mom left us. To fight the URS and save her baby.*

She knew enough about the sterilization laws to know Merra was right; there would have been no way to save

Marcus had she tried to stay. He would have been terminated as soon as they found out about him.

But why didn't she tell me? Aerie wondered. *Didn't she trust me?*

That seemed to be the running theme throughout her life. Her unit had worked to protect her, from her father and her mother all the way down to her siblings. Even Claire had mentioned that they needed to watch her because she didn't seem capable of taking care of herself. And then there was Exton, who told her on the *Perdition* he didn't want to trust her, even if he was tempted to.

But he trusts me now, Aerie recalled. Maybe that was something—a sign that things were going to change.

She smiled as Marcus reached out for her, and she realized that things were already changing.

As she held her brother for the first time, Aerie decided that she could understand her mother's actions, even if she wasn't ready to forgive her completely. *But Exton is right,* she thought. *I probably will forgive her.*

"Aerie," Marcus said.

"What is it?" she asked.

"That's you."

Aerie giggled. "Yep, that's me."

Marcus backed away from her. "I want our mommy back now."

"Alright." Aerie gave him a smile as she handed him back to Merra, who looked at her with pride.

"I might not have been the best mother to you, Aerie," Merra told her quietly, "but I think you'll make a good one yourself." She grinned. "If that's what Exton wants, too, of course. A strong marriage helps make a strong family."

"Mom." Aerie flushed over again, but this time she felt less embarrassed and more emboldened.

Before she could further respond, a siren started going off.

Instantly, the other residents started to move, many of them standing up and leaving their food behind.

Aerie flinched at the high-pitched sound, wishing it was as acceptable for her to place her hands over her ears as it was for Marcus.

Before she could ask what was happening, Merra took charge. "We have to get to the shelter, now."

When they all failed to move, she glowered down at them, reminding Aerie of the few times she'd seen her mother get angry when they were younger.

"I said, now!" she yelled, already turning toward the exit. "Move!"

Aerie snapped to attention and hurried after her.

The instant she was out of the commissary, she felt a hand grab her.

It was Brock. "Come with me," he said.

Aerie glanced back to see Merra and the others were still headed down the hall. No one noticed Brock had begun to pull her toward the hangar. "What's going on?"

"We're leaving."

Aerie struggled to break free. "I'm supposed to follow them."

"I know you don't want to lose them. But if you really want to save them, you'll come with me."

"What are you talking about?" Aerie asked, taking another step back from him.

Brock's hazel eyes, once so kind and capable, turned dark. "The URS is on their way here."

Aerie narrowed her eyes. "How do you know?"

"Why else would alarms be going off?" Brock asked, gesturing to the flood of people running around them.

"It could be a drill." Aerie felt like kicking herself for how weak her argument sounded.

"No." Brock shook his head. "I was worried about this. The URS has picked up on your signal."

"Signal?"

Brock lowered his gaze. "Serena told me while you were asleep in the ship," he said, "that you had something strange in your blood. I remembered later that all those who are admitted for reeducation are tagged and a tracer is placed inside of them. I didn't get a chance to tell you before … before we were distracted by everything, with the Craftcarriers and then with Captain Chainsword."

Aerie felt the blood drain out of her face as Brock reached out and took her hand. Turning it over, he ran his fingers over the small, rubber bumps on her wrist, the ones that were branded into her skin. "There," he said. "There's a tracker underneath this that's welded into your skin and bloodstream."

Aerie felt her knees buckle. "I did this," she whimpered, looking around as the sirens continued to flash. Outside, she could hear activity in the hangar as ships were getting readied. "They're going to kill everyone here. And it'll be all my fault."

"Come with me," Brock said. He tugged her to her feet. "You know I'm a good pilot. I can take you out of this place, and then the URS will follow. Come on."

He started to lead her toward the hangar, and Aerie stumbled along behind him.

What should I do? What's going to happen?

Suddenly, she stopped.

"What's wrong?" Brock asked.

"I don't know," Aerie said slowly. She looked back in the direction where her family had gone. "I think we should tell the others first."

"You'll only waste time," Brock warned her.

"I'm not sure this will work."

"Yes, it will," he insisted. "Please, Aerie. It's me, Brock. We've been friends for years. You know you can trust me. I know you're not in love with me, but I've known you for a long time, and you've only known this Exton guy for what? Three weeks? A month? Are you really going to believe him over everything you've known and lived for since you were born?"

Aerie looked up at Brock, feeling helpless. She had no way of explaining to him just how much Exton had changed her life without hurting him.

"He told me the *truth*," Aerie finally said. "It doesn't matter what I knew before if it wasn't the truth."

Brock tightened his grip on her. "Aerie, I feel like I've lost you."

"I don't feel like I'm lost," Aerie replied. "I feel … I feel almost like I've been *found*." Something had changed, she realized. Something had changed since she found herself on the *Perdition*, and even though she couldn't fully explain it, she knew it was a change in the right direction. It wasn't just Exton, or his family, or even his cause. It was something else, something more, and she could not explain that to Brock.

"If I can't change your mind about this," Brock said, "I have no other choice."

Aerie gave him a tentative smile. "Thank you for letting me make my own decision about this, Brock. I know it has to be hard for—"

Her words were cut off when Brock's fist shot out as he began attacking her.

♦26♦

Exton watched, momentarily transfixed, as Patty put down her empty mug on a nearby countertop, while activity continued to bustle all around them. Time had passed both quickly and slowly, and he'd forgotten his own coffee cup in the wake of oncoming battle.

Emery was sitting down at a desk, finally, as she was searching through some of their older records.

"We have a legion of URS forces in Panama," she said, pulling a map up onto her screen. "There are some scattered forces in other South American principalities, but Panama has the highest soldier count."

"That's got to be one of their loading sites." Exton centered himself in the middle of the room, watching as Patty sent the evacuation codes, while he talked with Henry Carville, Tyler's primary copilot now that Jared was grounded.

"Okay, Captain," Henry said, "we're sending the latest imaging. It looks like you're right. There's been some massive damage to the area where you landed."

"Great." His sarcasm was sharp enough to draw blood. Exton tapped his foot impatiently, watching for updated satellite feeds to come in. "Let's get a good look at it. We need to know what kind of fire power they have onboard. There's got to be more than what we saw while we were in the air."

"Affirmative," Henry said. "I'll send these down to Rhodey, too, to see if he can't help us identify any."

"Thanks. Tell Rhodey he has my thanks, too." Exton sighed.

From the information that the *Perdition* had been able to pick up from their location, there were only three major Craftcarriers currently in movement, as they slowly circled the world, hidden by the dense cloud cover.

The Craftcarrier they ran into earlier was still afloat, running on standby power, but its movements, especially toward the clear skies of the Antarctic Ocean, had finally allowed for it to reveal itself.

"Did Tyler and his crew find any additional leads from Panama?" Exton asked. "IP addresses, coding signals, hidden frequencies, anything?"

"Not sure. I'll have an analyst look at the information we pulled up, so we can anticipate them in the future," Henry said. "For right now, there's only one carrier coming your way."

Exton had to bite back his sarcasm. "Good."

"Exton," Emery called. "I found them."

"You found the blueprints?" Exton stepped over to see Emery's progress.

"Yep. Here they are—Papa's old Craftcarrier schematics." Emery frowned. "We won't know how much they were modified by the final team of engineers."

Exton glanced down at the files, dismayed to find Emery had a point. "Em, see if you can pull up the log from my Chainsword shuttle. We can try to compare and see if they made any significant modifications on the outside."

"Good idea."

Exton glanced over at the time. He was tempted to ask Henry if Tyler was awake yet. The early morning hours had passed, but he knew day shift wouldn't be up for another hour onboard the *Perdition.*

"These files are scattered everywhere," Emery said. "Look, there's an old blueprint of the *Perdition* in here, too."

"Silas was commissioned to work on the *Paradise*—I mean the *Perdition*—before the Craftcarriers were finished," Patty said. "The URS had to coordinate it between several different building sites. Silas hated moving from site to site. That was part of the reason he was very adamant about keeping the *Perdition* close by and in one primary location."

"I do remember visiting one of the sites for the carriers when we were younger," Emery said. "When was that, Exton? When I was six?"

"If you're thinking of the one in the Canadian West, even

younger than that, I think," Exton said. "Papa began working on the *Perdition* when I was seven. I got to help him with some of the construction."

They glanced down at the scanned prints. Exton recognized several examples of his father's trademark style—the efficient spacing, the security designs, and the centric clusters of living and command centers.

Exton shuffled through the different drawings, looking for any signs of weaknesses he'd missed before. He knew they had been lucky in the shuttle. There was too much at risk for them to depend on luck this time.

"I miss him," Emery murmured softly.

Exton nodded. "I do, too." He smiled down at the blueprints of the *Perdition.* "I don't think I've seen this since we were barely teenagers."

"The *Perdition* is almost ten years old," Emery reminded him. "We were able to steal it only after the URS put all the finishing touches on the inside."

"I'll be twenty-five in a few months. No need to make me feel older than I need to."

"You grew up quick," Patty said, putting a comforting hand on his shoulder. "My sister would be proud of you."

Exton only nodded.

"Look at this." She pointed to a side note on the screen. "It's one of Papa's notes. '212528—see Lu for details, tell Exton about Ark.'"

"Who's Lu?" Exton asked. "I don't remember anyone with that name."

"Papa did have a system all his own," Emery reminded him with a sad smile. "Remember? Even his friends called him 'Boötes.'"

"Aunt Patty," Exton called. "Do you know who Lu is, the one Papa is talking about here?"

Patty frowned as she glanced at the blueprints. "Let me think it over," she said. "We have to take care of this mess first."

"True." Exton turned back to the main screen where the

satellite imaging was coming in. He saw the first picture, and saw that only the Craftcarrier was blurry.

He had been on the *Perdition* for the majority of the past six years. Exton knew that there was a lot of technological advancement being made. *It wouldn't be hard to make an image scrambler to help camouflage vehicles*, he thought. Most of the technology before the URS was created had been lost, supposedly, but even the *Perdition* had been outfitted with a missile scrambler capable of messing with smaller missiles.

"Blow up that image," he called to one of the techs behind him, pointing at the newest image. There was a large, black mass on the picture, and he had a sinking feeling he knew what it was.

"Yes, sir."

Exton watched as the black hole on the photo was enlarged.

The remnants of a cargo ship were blasted into dust, with only random scraps of twisted, burning metal sticking out of the darkened earth every few feet.

"Well, we don't have to worry about going to pick up Brock's ship now," Emery said with a sigh. "That might make it harder to get rid of him."

"We still have that fighter one of Aerie's brothers came in on," Exton said.

"I guess that's true. Maybe that's what Brock was doing in the hangar earlier this morning."

Exton frowned. "Why was he in the hangar? I thought he was in the med ward for his injury."

"He was. But I saw him coming out of the hangar and heading back that way a few hours after midnight."

"Where is he now?" Exton asked.

"He should be heading down to the mountain shelters with the others," Emery said. "If you're worried about him, I'll see if I can find him on the cams."

"Do it."

"Exton, the Craftcarrier is hovering around the area surrounding the ship," Patty said. "It looks like it's waiting for orders."

"Henry," Exton called. "Can you have a tech check the comm feeds for any filtration?"

"Will do, Captain."

"Let me know what they pick up."

"Exton," Emery said, interrupting. "Brock's down by the hangar. He's got Aerie with him."

"He told me that he didn't want to leave without Aerie, and if he thinks he can take her away from me again, he's crazy."

"He might be crazier than you think," Emery said. "Look."

Exton glanced down at the monitor where Emery was looking. Rage and fear collided into him, as he saw Aerie struggling against Brock in the commissary hallway.

"What are you waiting for?" Emery asked. "Go and help her."

Exton hesitated, looking around. The room took on a strange, surreal quality. They were trying to prepare for a possible battle. He had a responsibility to his community.

"Go," Emery urged him again. "We can take care of things here."

"Thank you," he murmured. "I'll be back in a few moments. Ground all flights in the meantime. Once I have Aerie, clear them. If we need to send ships out, we will."

Emery nodded. "You got it."

"Don't forget, I'm here, too," Patty called as she leaned over another data screen with an analyst. "I'll look for more weaknesses in the carrier design and compare the blueprints while you're gone."

Exton barely heard them. His anger was already simmering around inside him, his heartbeat pounding between his ears as he headed off to find Brock.

♦27♦

Aerie gasped as she barely managed to slip under Brock's advance. "Brock, what do you think you're doing?" she asked, outraged. "Stop it!"

"I might not be able to convince you to come with my words," he said, "but I know I can still win in a fight against you."

"This is not who you are," Aerie yelled back as she dodged another punch.

"Well, we're even then," Brock said. "You haven't been yourself either, not since graduation."

"If you think this will make me love you, you're wrong," Aerie told him as she slipped down into a slide tackle. She was relieved to see it work, as Brock stumbled and had to brace himself against the wall.

"I still want to protect you, Aerie. Even if you don't love me, even if you've been brainwashed," Brock said as he reached for her again.

"If I have been brainwashed, it was by the State," Aerie insisted. She gasped in pain as he caught her by twisting her injured shoulder.

Aerie elbowed him in the gut and slammed her foot on his instep to break his hold. When he loosened his grip, she wiggled free.

Before he could say another word, she turned and fled, holding her shoulder as it pulsed with pain. Aerie bit her lip, wanting nothing more than to find her mother, or Exton, or anyone who could help her find a way to destroy the tracer on her wrist.

Fear laced through her while her shoulder hummed in flinching pain. While Brock's methods were appalling, Aerie knew he was likely right: She would have to leave, especially if there was no way to neutralize the tracker.

I don't want to leave. It feels wrong to leave.

She just turned the corner when she ran right into Exton.

"Exton, thank goodness you found me." Despite the pain her shoulder, she wrapped her arms around him tightly, hiding her face in his chest.

His arms embraced her easily. "Aerie," he said. "I was just coming to find you. Where's Brock?"

"Back there," she managed, grimacing in pain.

"If he hurt you, I swear to God I'll—"

"There's no time right now," Aerie said. "The URS is heading here, to attack."

He frowned. "How do you know?" he asked. "We only sent the signal for an evac drill. An attack has not been verified."

"Brock told me," Aerie said. "He told me I was branded with a tracer at the Reeducation Center. Serena found it while she was taking care of me during our escape."

"What are you—"

Aerie was about to show him the tracer when Brock came running around the corner. He halted as he saw Aerie holding onto Exton, an angry blush crossing his cheeks.

Exton tightened his grip on Aerie. "What do you think you're doing?"

"I *was* trying to protect her, and Petra," Brock insisted. "She's got a tracer in her blood. It's standard procedure at the Reeducation Center."

"And you would know this because … ?"

"Because I am a high-ranking officer in the military," Brock said. "Or I was, before I gave it all up to get Aerie." He glared at her once more, and Aerie, despite the pain in her shoulder, softened.

He shifted his feet, clearly uncomfortable. "I forgot about it until Serena was running diagnostics on her before we came here. And when the Craftcarrier showed up, I forgot it entirely."

Aerie could feel the tension thicken between them.

"There you are!"

They all turned to see Serena as she charged down the hall. "Come on, Aerie," she said, clearly disgruntled. "Our *mother* asked me to go and find you so we can head to the mountains."

"Serena," Brock said. "You can tell them I'm not lying."

She sighed. "Oh, great," she grumbled. "Is this some kind of weird fight over my sister?"

"Not at the moment," Exton said, as he shot a look of warning over at Brock. "He says Aerie has a tracker on her."

Serena nodded. "That's standard URS procedure," she said.

"Why didn't you tell me?" Aerie demanded. She pulled back from Exton, ready to argue as menacingly as she could. "I put everyone here in danger."

"Relax," Serena said. "The tracer has a relatively weak signal. It would be highly unlikely if they did find you, especially this far out from their other bases."

"Well, the Craftcarrier we ran into is off-course," Aerie said. "What do you think about that?"

A look of genuine surprise settled onto Serena's face. "That's unfortunate," she muttered.

"Unfortunate?" Aerie roared. "I could be putting everyone in danger! We have to get rid of it, now." She glanced up at Exton. "Please, don't make me leave."

He shook his head. "No, we can fix this. Right?" He glanced over at Serena for an answer.

"It'll be hard to get rid of it," Serena said. She reached forward and pulled back Aerie's jacket sleeve, revealing the small line of numbers surrounding the burned skin. "This is a special kind of synthetic material. It's burned into the body and the blood system. If you try to cut it out, you risk cutting down to the bone."

Exton ran his hand over the small bumps. "What else can we do?"

"I'd talk to the med team," Serena said. "They might be able to do something with it. Haven't you dealt with this before?"

"We have tried to find a way to undo the damage of the Reeducation Center," Exton admitted. "Only a few people have managed to overcome its programming, but this must be part of a newer protocol system. We've never seen this before that I know of."

Serena smirked. "The URS was trying to stop you," she said. "That's why they began marking them, I'll bet."

"And you don't see anything wrong with tagging people like cattle?" Exton said.

"Not if they're a danger to themselves or society," Serena said, easily dismissing the question.

Before he could argue with her further, Aerie tugged on his arm. "Do you think Meredith would know about it?" she asked him quietly.

"I don't know," he whispered back.

"From what I know, it's a two-part signal tracer," Brock said. "There's a part in the blood system, and then there's a biometric signifier in the strip. You would need to remove the band and give her a full transfusion to get rid of the tracker."

Aerie jolted as Exton's comm beeped again. "We don't have time for that," she said.

"I will make time for you," Exton said. He turned to Brock and Serena. "Follow me. We're going to head back to the med ward. First, we need to find out what is going on. And then, we'll work to make things right."

Aerie latched onto his hand as he led the way. "I could be putting everyone in danger again," she said.

"Or Brock could be lying," Exton told her, so quietly only she could hear. "Either way, you're right. We don't have the time for this. If you are sending out a signal, we can find another way to stop it."

"You can?" Aerie asked.

"The emergency shelters were carved out of the mountain," Exton said. "It's deep and insulated enough it would be unlikely that the signal would go through."

"Why are we going to the med ward then?"

"I'll set you up with a tech," he said. "We need to see for ourselves what's going on. I don't trust either of them, Aerie, and I don't want to put Petra or you in any additional danger."

The crippling sensation of fear and devastation that had settled into her upon learning of her tracker receded ever so slightly. "I love you," Aerie whispered.

He smiled at her, bringing her hand up to his lips, never breaking the cadence of his pace.

Exton waited until Tyra, one of the medics Aerie remembered from the *Perdition,* had settled her into a small room with Serena and Brock before turning to his comm.

He allowed himself a moment to breathe, trying to relax. Exton had known that taking his crew and his community to the frontlines of a war they had been eager to ignore was bound to be exhausting.

It's one thing to anticipate it, and another to live through it.

The comm beeped again, and this time he responded. "Yes?"

"The Craftcarrier is moving toward Petra," Emery said. Her tone was dark and sad. "Merra's here, and starting to call her forces for takeoff."

"How did she get in the control room?" Exton grumbled.

"Patty let her in. Like it or not, Merra is the leader of Chaya's forces."

"Like it? I hate it." He let his head fall into his hand at the thought. "She's not waiting for any plan?"

"That's the good news," Emery said. "Patty's found a few areas on the Craftcarrier where, if we can hit them, it'll stop them."

"If that's the case, taking them out over the water would be our best bet for a short battle." Exton's hope renewed. "How many fighters do we have ready?"

"Merra has four of her fighters present," Emery said, "including her own."

"How many do we have?"

"We have your shuttle and Dorian's fighter, as well as another MENANCE fighter." Emery paused. "Tyler has relieved Henry from his shift and wants to know if you want backup."

"We have a small op ready," Exton said. "Tell him to have them on standby. Did Rhodey report in?"

"He did." Emery paused. "He said from what he could see, it looked just like fission missiles and some lasers that destroyed the cargo ship."

"Good to know they're not packing anything else," Exton said.

"Speaking of which, Rhodey wanted me to tell you that it would have to be an absolute last resort to drop one of the *Perdition*'s nuclear bombs on the Craftcarrier, especially over the sea. The radiation could get into Petra's water system and cause a lot of other problems for us."

"He's never been one to work when he didn't want to," Exton muttered.

"I happen to agree with him, as a student of horticulture."

"I agree with him, too," Exton assured her. "I just wish he would've given me more options."

"I know. I know you want to protect Petra as much as I do."

He nodded. "I'll be there shortly. Have what fighters we have get ready to follow Merra. I'm sure she'll love having more power."

"Roger that."

Exton glanced back to see Tyra and Serena were discussing different medical techniques, Brock was sitting in the corner, and Aerie was watching him. Exton gave her a small smile, and when her eyes filled with worry, he knew she had seen through its illusion.

He walked over to her, careful to avoid the IV Tyra had recently stuck in her hand. "The Craftcarrier is heading this way," he told her.

"If you need to go, then go," Aerie told him.

He could tell she was trying to be brave.

"Tyra said this shouldn't take long, since she knows what to look for, but I know you're needed in other places," she said.

"I have some time," he said, hoping he was telling her the truth. "And I want to stay with you for now. I don't want you trying to leave Petra or sneak out of this medic ward. If you were the one who tipped off the URS to our location, it doesn't matter now. They know we're here."

"I'm so sorry." The defeat and anguish in her voice crushed him.

"We knew it was only a matter of time," Exton said. "There was no point in hoping we could evade them for the rest of our lives. This just moves up the schedule some."

"It also put you in the position of fighting a full-blown war."

"I have always wondered if it would come to this," Exton told her quietly. "I have been wondering it since long before I met you."

"I wish we hadn't met," Aerie said. "Then you would be safe."

"Safe but still alone," he told her. "And still facing this reality. It's better this way."

"Not in every way," Aerie insisted.

He sighed. "There are few things in this life that are perfect. But," he said, reaching over and threading his fingers through her hair, "this is one of them."

She gave him a small, grateful smile.

"We still have a little time," Exton told her. "Merra's leading a small coalition of our air forces against the carrier."

Aerie wrinkled her nose. "I can't believe you agreed to that."

"I didn't. She and my aunt are becoming fast friends, apparently. But she is a good pilot. I saw her in action at Chaya."

Aerie nodded slowly. "I remember one of my instructors once told me she had scored high in combat training, too."

They sat in silence for several moments, while Tyra and

Serena continued to discuss the different machines and medical practice, and Brock continued to sulk in his seat.

Tyra finally turned to Aerie. "You do have liquid transmitted in your blood," she said. "And the strip here does contain a biometric chip."

"See?" Brock stood up and looked haughtily at Exton. "I wasn't lying."

"You said I'd need a transfusion to get it out of my system," Aerie said. She glanced back to Tyra. "Is that true?"

"Yes, it is," Tyra confirmed. "But—"

"I'd be happy to do it," Brock said. "I have Type O blood."

Serena smirked. "Good to know you're a universal donor," she said. "I'll have to keep that in mind for the future."

Brock smiled. "Go ahead, Serena," he said. "I don't mind. If it'll help Aerie, I'm ready."

"It's very kind of you," Tyra said, "but—"

"It really is," Aerie agreed.

Exton could tell by looking at her, Aerie was happy that Brock was still trying to be friendly. He sighed to himself. *Doesn't she remember that she was just fighting with him by the mess hall?*

"It is very kind of him, but there's no need," Tyra said.

Everyone turned to look at her with similar confused expressions.

"What do you mean?" Exton finally asked.

"Her tracer and her chip have gone silent," Tyra said. "There's no signal going out from it anymore."

"Do you think the electric shock managed to disable it?" Aerie asked. "I think that's what happened to my Memory Serum."

"I found traces of that, too," Tyra said. "But it's a different composition—a synthetic metalloid nanobot. It was fried. The tracer is able to withstand a much higher rate of electric shock."

"So what killed it?" Brock asked.

"It could have been deactivated," Tyra said. "That would be my first guess."

"That's impossible," Brock said. "It would have had to have been shut off by Grant Osgood himself."

"Or maybe … General St. Cloud?" Exton asked.

Brock turned on him. "That's an accusation of treason. General St. Cloud was the one who had her arrested," he said, pointing to Aerie. "Dictator Osgood would only trust someone so willing to sacrifice everything for the State, and St. Cloud proved it by arresting her."

"You're technically a traitor yourself," Serena reminded him. "There's no reason to defend him."

Brock looked ready to attack her next, but Tyra interrupted him. "It's possible something else happened," she said. "Deactivation was just a first guess. We might never know."

"But I'm safe?" Aerie asked.

"Yes. We might be able to remove the strip at another time," she said. "Right now, our medical services are spread a little thinner than we'd like. Several of the Ecclesia's students have gone to Chaya at Merra's command."

"They'll be called back soon," Exton said. "We'll likely need them here."

Before anyone could agree or disagree with him, several loud shrieks rumbled throughout the community.

Exton glanced out the window. "There goes the reason why, too."

"Mom just took off?" Aerie guessed.

"Yep." Exton turned to Tyra. "Can you discharge Aerie? We need to go."

♦28♦

Aerie felt lightheaded as she entered the control room with Exton.

Serena had decided to stay with Tyra, and after convincing Exton that Tyra and the other medics could use a hand, and they could take care of Serena if she got tough, he let her.

Aerie was glad to see her sister was starting to see how Petra was a good place to stay. Or at least, it was a safe place to stay.

And let's hope it stays that way. She glanced down at her wrist, where the strip still prodded out from her skin. She was glad she wasn't giving away the location of Petra.

Anymore, at least, she thought to herself. Aerie knew it was still likely that she had given away the location.

And Exton still loved her, despite all the trouble she caused him. A dizzying sense of rightness took hold of her, as she realized that, if they survived this, she never wanted to be parted from him again.

"Exton," Emery called from her seat. "Tyler's on the line."

"Commander," Exton said in greeting.

"I was just asking for you," Tyler said. "The Craftcarrier's still moving toward Petra, but some riots have broken out at New Hope."

"Any of ours?" Exton asked.

"Not that I can tell," Tyler said. "I was wondering if Merra would know. She has several of her forces at Chaya holding the ground, but I caught some of her fighters leaving the camp a few days ago."

Aerie felt her eyes widen. "Mom," she whispered.

"Is there any other movement?" Exton asked.

"That was it. The URS forces at Halifax are silent, and their other command centers around America are running through their routines."

"Aunt Patty mentioned Panama earlier. What's the news from them?"

"The cloud cover makes it hard to pull out any information from them," Tyler said. "But the Craftcarrier's movement toward Petra demonstrates they are significantly adding to its thickness."

"We'll have to notify the environmental protestors," Exton replied.

"I take it you've heard back from Rhodey, too?"

"Yes. No nukes."

"I'm still in position," Tyler said. "I'm just behind the South Pole if you need me to send out more shuttles."

"Hopefully, it won't come to that," Exton said. "Can you send me a feed from your monitoring cam?"

"Roger."

Exton glanced over at Emery. "Have you been able to pick up anything on the—"

The monitor blinked, and Emery smiled. "Yes," she said. "The Craftcarrier is just over the horizon. They're still running more slowly than expected, even with Merra's forces out there, but it is approaching steadily."

A small *boom* echoed back, and Patty cheered. "We got a hit on one of the reverse stabilizers!"

Aerie glanced over at Brock nervously. "I guess this makes you miss the URS some, huh?"

He shook his head. "Not really. The URS had more organization and more people. And the NETech really helped. There was no discussion of plans."

"My mother is a skilled pilot," Aerie said. "And she's used to getting her way. I'm hoping she'll be able to stop the carrier before it arrives here, and that she'll do it without losing any of our troops."

"What about the other side?" Brock asked. "You know that there are a lot of people on the Craftcarriers. Over a hundred, easy, and possibly up to six hundred. What about them?"

"I … guess they'll die or they'll surrender," Aerie said.

She brightened. "They might turn back," she said. "They could go back to their regular position, and then they wouldn't lose anyone."

Brock gave her a reluctant smile. "You always were too idealistic," he said. "That's not how the URS works. Or really any good defense."

Aerie slumped over. "It's better than thinking of what's really going to happen," she said.

"I agree," Brock told her quietly. "But it doesn't help in the long run. Still, it's something I admired about you."

"Why?" Aerie asked. "If it's no help in the long run?"

"Long-term goals are met by short-term battles," Brock told her. "And it was … nice to see someone with a different vision for the future of the URS, if you want to know the truth. You seemed to think everything would be alright in the end."

"I still believe that," Aerie said.

"You changed sides."

"I was always on the wrong side," she said. "The URS has no need for dreamers, for people like me. They had a vision. I didn't want to conform to it willingly, or at least without a fight."

"This is still a dangerous fight."

"I still believe that it's worth it," Aerie told him. "If Exton has taught me anything, it's that there is a price we pay for what we believe, no matter what it is."

Brock hardened. "I don't like him."

"You don't know him the way I do," Aerie said. "I've watched him suffer so much, just because he loves me."

"I guess I didn't suffer enough then?" Brock asked.

Aerie blushed. "Brock, I—"

"No, don't say it. I don't want to hear it," he said. "I know there's nothing I can do."

Aerie felt the sting of his remark, but, as he leaned back against the wall, she had hope that they would be able to be friends again, even if it was not going to happen right away.

"Exton, do you copy? Command, do you copy?"

Aerie glanced up, surprised to hear her mother's voice coming over the comms.

"We read you, Merra," he replied.

"We seem to be experiencing a problem," Merra said. "Our comms are jammed."

"How are you broadcasting to us?" Exton asked.

"I have no idea," Merra admitted. "I'm further out from the carrier than the others are. I started getting static as they approached the craft."

"It's possible that they have a scrambler onboard," Aerie said. "It can be used to break into the enemy's comms as well as cut them off—"

A new voice came over the comm, as Merra's line became full of static. "Is that you, Aerie, my dear friend?"

Aerie went speechless with fear and shame as she recognized Gerard's voice. Her gaze met Exton's, and she watched as he froze, torn between running over to her or replying.

She was glad when he decided to answer the call.

"That's none of your concern, Gerard," Exton replied.

"Oh, it's the great Exton Shepherd, now, is it?" Gerard asked. "What happened to playing Captain Chainsword?"

"I came down from the *Perdition* specifically to ruin your day." Exton crossed his arms as he turned toward the monitor.

"It's a lost cause," Gerard assured him. "I'm here on the URSS *Rothsburton*," he said, "and I'm the one who is leading the charge against you."

"What charge would that be?"

"You're harboring dissenters and refugees from the URS," Gerard replied. "You are breaking our law, so we will engage."

"If you were smart, you would go back to poisoning the atmosphere around the equator," Exton said. "If you come any closer, we will shoot you down."

"I've already broken through your comm lines."

"And we've already broken through your carrier's

defense."

Gerard paused. "It doesn't mean you'll win."

"And turning around now doesn't mean you'll never get your chance to battle me," Exton replied. "But I'd still prefer less causalities."

"There's a reason we don't call them formalities," Gerard said. "I look forward to destroying you."

The line went dead.

Aerie felt her knees go weak, as the voice of her torturer left the room full of an uncomfortable silence.

Patty broke the silence. "Are we able to reestablish communications with Merra and her forces?"

Emery shook her head. "No, but give me a moment. Maybe I can try to hack into their system and disrupt it from here."

As the other techs resumed their work, and Patty and Emery focused on the comms, Exton made his way down to Aerie.

"Are you okay?" he asked.

Aerie gave him a shaky smile. "Yes," she said. Hearing herself say it aloud gave her more courage. She clenched her hands into fists. "And I can help you fight them."

"I'm not letting you go into battle," Exton warned.

"No, it's not that. I can help with the comms," she said. "I actually did go to work in the Comms Sec, remember? I know how to reroute their signals."

Exton put his hand to his chin. "I suppose we could give it a try. It just might work."

"Great." Aerie glanced over at Brock. "Are you going to be okay here?"

"Exton, come here," Emery said. "Tyler's on the line."

As Exton hurried back over to the main console, Brock gave Aerie a reluctant smile. "I'll be fine. Eventually," he said.

Aerie took his arm, briefly. "I know it's hard for you to believe, but I know exactly how you feel." She ignored the surprised look on his face and hurried to catch up to Exton.

Tyler was talking to him as she approached.

"—so I can't connect with the fighters, either, or we'll risk the integrity of the comms on the *Perdition*."

Aerie stepped up. "Tyler," she said. "It's me."

"Welcome back, Aerie," he said, greeting her kindly. "It's nice to hear your voice again."

"You can thank Meredith for that."

"I already have," he assured her. "It's nice to see Exton getting back to his usual, surly self. His extra-surly attitude was getting to be too much."

Aerie laughed, before getting back to the business at hand. "I'm going to try to rework the comm signals," she said. "I'll need you to keep an eye out on the battle up there."

"No problem."

Aerie hurriedly glanced at the monitor. Emery skirted out from behind her.

"Can I help?" Emery asked.

"This console is similar to a URS design," Aerie said. "Only there's no NETech input. That's probably how Gerard is connected to the main URS base from the Craftcarrier."

"Probably?"

Aerie shrugged. "I'm familiar with the system," she said. "But I'm not sure what they're doing with the NETech right now. The regular comms, I can reroute in a few moments."

She keyed in the familiar codes, hoping to get a response. As she began typing and looking for the backdoors to the carrier, Exton kept watch on the screens.

"How much longer do you need, Aerie?" he asked. "The Craftcarrier might be miles out from the shore, but Merra's forces still need to hit the port and starboard stabilizers before it'll go down."

"I'm hurrying," Aerie said. "I finished rebooting the signal reader. It's widening its frame; that should make it capable of maneuvering around the URS jamming frequency."

"How long?" Exton asked.

"A few moments," Aerie called back.

"That's not enough time."

She gave him her best grin. "We'll make it enough," she said. She turned to Emery. "Can I get more power?"

Emery paused for only the slightest second. "Rerouting power," she said. Emery looked back. "I'm diverting it from the main power source here at Petra. We only have a few moments before the cold will settle in."

Another blast resounded over the screen.

"Merra's team hit another stabilizer," Emery informed them. "We just need two more."

"Two more to stop it, and then we'll see what we end up with," Exton said.

"Close enough," Emery said, sticking her tongue at him.

He only briefly smiled back. "If we can't get this up, I'm going to go out and fly myself," he said.

"What? No," Aerie said. "No, we need you here, Exton."

"They need me out there, too, if we're going to stop that carrier."

"I'll bet that's just what Gerard wants, too," Aerie snapped. "I know he hates you, Exton. You can't let him do this to Petra."

"I'm not letting him," Exton argued back. "That's the point. I'm not going to sit here when I can go help out there."

"Just wait," Aerie said. "I've got this."

"Aerie's good at not listening," Brock said, making her face burn. "She did this in the cargo ship, too."

Before Aerie could turn her ire on him, the comm signal began to hum.

Aerie cheered a moment later, as static came over the line and began to clear. "Got it," she said. "Mom, can you hear me? It's Aerie."

"Aerie," Merra replied. "I can hear you loud and clear."

"Turns out the General was right," Aerie said. "I got the jamming signal to stop."

"That's my girl."

"Exton and Director Ward are here," Aerie said. She gave Exton a smug, triumphant look as she added, "And they have some directions for you."

"Merra," Exton said, smoothly inserting himself into the conversation. "We need you to speed up the attack run. It's still advancing."

"I know. We're trying to outrun some of the carrier's battlements," she replied. "Several of their ships have deployed, but not to attack."

Exton blanched. "They're not attacking you?"

"No. Looks like a suicide run," Merra said. "Let me circle around and see what we can do."

"Exton," Tyler said, interrupting. "Gerard's just made his exit."

"That coward," Exton grumbled to himself. "Are you sure, Tyler?"

"Yes. I was able to watch him take off using the monitoring system. It's definitely him in the transporter shuttle. He's headed north."

"Can we stop him?"

Before Tyler could reply, Merra came through the comm once more. "I've got a good visual on the Craftcarrier's position. We're going to have to stop it now, completely, if we're going to protect Petra."

Aerie saw the tension in Exton's face as he asked, "Is there any way you can—"

Merra interrupted him. "We're going to have to aim for the main power core if we want to stop it now."

"What? No," Exton said. "The main power core will—"

"Missile's away!" Merra cried.

Less than a second later, a sonic *boom* ripped through the room, causing Aerie to stumble. She gripped the console, but the room rocked as the nuclear engine of the Craftcarrier exploded. Several of the others yelled and shouted as they were thrown backward by the power of the explosion.

Exton crawled over to Aerie. "Are you alright?" he asked, as he hurried to pull her upright once more.

"I'm fine," Aerie said. She glanced up at the monitor to see the carrier blow up in a bright light, before it flickered into static.

"I'm glad I was sitting," Emery murmured, rubbing her temples. "That was some whiplash."

"Are you okay?" Aerie asked her. "And the baby?"

Emery nodded, patting her stomach. "We're fine, but I'm going to need to lie down after that one."

"I'm surprised the building didn't break," Aerie admitted, as Exton focused on the flickering console display.

Emery smiled. "We knew we had to build Petra to last. Even though this sort of thing wasn't what we were expecting, necessarily."

"I can't believe she did that," Exton growled. "Blowing the main engine on a Craftcarrier that size will send the engine's radiation leaking. It could damage our water supply and harm the crops."

Aerie came up beside him as the monitor returned to normal. She heard the static from the comms, but there was no need to contact the others now.

Several fighters were flying back toward the campus, as the Craftcarrier, now in several large pieces, fell into the ocean water. Huge waves rose high into the air, as if to embrace the fiery remnants pouring down from the sky.

"Shut the hangar doors," Exton called. "We're going to have a small tsunami on our hands."

"Hang on, I'll be there in a sec," Merra said, her voice breaking through the silence on the other side of the comm line, just as Patty pressed the button.

"No, Mom, don't!" Aerie called, watching in horror as the large hangar doors began to close.

The doors shut, and Aerie saw Merra's fighter slip inside, but her other forces swung around and headed toward the distant mountains, and the base was swept up in the displaced seawater.

"She doesn't listen at all, does she?" Aerie asked through gritted teeth.

"Well, what do you know," Exton said. "Maybe you're more like her than I thought."

♦29♦

Over the next several hours, Petra worked hard to return to normal as much as it could. Despite the capsized Craftcarrier pieces piercing the horizon, there was a cloud of excitement in the air all around the camp, one that had nothing to do with burning debris or steam pouring up from the murky bay waters.

They had won. It was not an easy victory, or an expected victory, or a clean victory, but Petra had endured.

Many attributed this to divine providence, while others were content to celebrate their good luck and skillful leaders.

Exton hated them all for it.

They didn't know how much damage the Craftcarrier, blown apart, would do to Petra's crops or water, and they didn't know how much the Palmer Bay area would need to recover from the shock of the attack. They didn't know how many people died, how many people Gerard had selfishly risked for his own ambition.

"Are you doing okay?"

Exton jolted at Aerie's voice. He didn't know how long he had been standing outside the camp, watching as the sun fell back over the edge of the world once more, but as Aerie came up beside him, he knew it had been longer than he'd originally planned.

"I'll be fine," he said.

"Cal and Dorian are signed up to take shifts, watching for survivors," Aerie informed him. "I think they're just eager to fly again, but Mom is watching them. I think they'll be okay. They might even be okay with staying here soon."

"I'm not surprised," he said. "They'll want to watch out for you."

Aerie grinned. "I think they'll be happier than you think to turn that responsibility over to you." Her smile disappeared. "Especially if I am as bad as my mother when it comes to following directions."

"I didn't mean it as an insult," Exton replied. "If that's the deciding factor on whether or not they'll relinquish you to me, then by all means, you don't need to follow instructions ever again."

"I'm not a prize," Aerie said.

"I know." He gave her a small smile, running his hands through her hair. "I'm not a monster."

Aerie blushed at his tender touch. "I'll make sure to remind you of that."

"I'll likely need it as war continues on. And maybe even after we win." He sighed, seeing the worrisome expression on her face. He wasn't surprised; she knew as well as he did that there was a price to pay for their pursuits.

"What else is happening?" he asked.

"Emery's off-duty. And I made her sit down and eat. I know she had a long day."

"She did. I'm glad to hear it's over for her."

"But not for you?" Aerie asked as she slipped her hand inside of his.

"Not for us," he said, correcting her. "We have some unfinished business to take care of, if you're ready." He squeezed her hand in his, and it was enough, after the long day of fighting, and before the long night of planning, to make his heart burn with a renewed fervor.

"I don't think there's a way to get ready for everything," Aerie admitted quietly.

"We'll learn as we go," Exton said "You have my word."

Aerie's eyes glimmered in the setting sun. "Then that's enough for me."

Their wedding was going to be small and quiet, a private affair held under the Memory Tree. Very few people were invited, and Aerie had a feeling Exton preferred it that way.

She didn't dress up in anything special; she wore a new uniform. It was a new one, one that marked her as a member of Petra. On some level, Aerie felt it was symbolic of her future, even as it paid homage to her past, and that was more than fitting for the occasion. At least, she remembered with a small smile, in her opinion. Emery had been less than thrilled at her choice, bemoaning the fact she'd left her wedding dress on the *Perdition.*

With the new uniform's longer sleeves and matching gloves, Aerie decided to leave her jacket behind, the one she had worn since Meredith had returned it to her. As she put it down, Aerie heard something break.

"What was that?" she wondered aloud.

Aerie saw something shiny sticking out of the jacket pocket. It was the photo slide, the one where she was standing with Brock and some of their comrades at graduation. As she watched, it fizzled and cracked down the middle, blurring the image.

At once, Aerie felt discomforted at the damage her carelessness had caused. She was secretly glad that Brock was nowhere to be found as she walked out of the campus to find Exton.

Once she found him, she smiled. "You're in a new uniform, too," she said in greeting.

"I know this is quick," he said. "But I did want you to be pleased by it."

"I told you before," Aerie said as she took his hand, "that I was expecting my first kiss at the Military Ball."

"Which you're not going to with Brock, by the way."

"I know." Aerie rolled her eyes. "But after everything, my first kiss was magical because it was with the right person."

"And that's enough to convince you marriage will be magical, too?"

"I'm fine with the logic of it," Aerie said with a laugh. "It's not like I'm going to run a science experiment to see if I get any other answers."

"That's good. Because I wouldn't let you."

"I'm bad at following directions."

"Directions, maybe, but you don't seem to mind

following my lead when it comes to this sort of thing."

"What sort of—"

Exton interrupted her, kissing her into silence. He pressed against her, his mouth moving on her hungrily.

She forgot about their discussion as she sought to meet his passion with her own.

When he broke away a moment later, Aerie had already forgotten what they'd been talking about. All that was left, running through her mind, was how much she wanted more.

"Come on." Exton tugged at her arm, while she steadied her mind's focus.

They made their way to the Memory Tree, where Reverend Thorne was waiting for them. Tyler was standing there too.

Aerie gave him a hug in greeting. "How is Meredith?" she asked quietly. "Is she … okay, at all?"

"She's taken the news of Gerard's involvement in stride," Tyler said. "My parents are there to help her through it. She is keeping an ear out to let us know if he arrives in New Hope."

"Do you think he will?"

"After that escape? It's possible, but he'll likely want to come and fight with reinforcements first. The Gerard Exton and I knew was never so proud," Tyler said. "But since his reeducation, he has become unrecognizable to us. He has a reputation for cruelty that never would have happened otherwise."

"I know," Aerie muttered.

Tyler nodded sadly. "If he does go back to New Hope, he'll have to answer to Osgood. Gerard knows that the Daddy Dictator doesn't put up with failure very well."

Aerie recalled hearing how happy Osgood was to have her arrested. She shook her head. It was too hard, she decided, to try to understand evil and imagine how people became willing participants in it.

But then, she realized, *I had almost been a contributor myself.*

"I'm glad someone is there for Meredith," Aerie finally said. "I owe her a great deal for what she did for me."

"We all owe her a lot for what she does. She also sneaks extra supplies out to one of our churches in New Hope. She's saved a lot of people by being willing to be placed in such a horrible job," Tyler told her.

Aerie thought about the day she'd followed Meredith on the street. *Was that what she was doing?* Aerie wondered.

Reverend Thorne stepped up. "Shall I begin?"

"Not everyone is here," Aerie said.

"You can start with the opening," Exton said. He looked at Aerie. "I'm sure the others will get here before the important part."

"I thought it was all an important part?" Aerie muttered, as she stepped forward.

They began listening to the reverend discuss how he was working on a special festival to remind them in the future of the great miracle of the battle.

Seeing Exton's irritated expression, as he looked back at the water-logged carrier still bobbing in the sea uncomfortably, Aerie frowned. "Are you okay?" she murmured softly, trying hard not to interrupt the reverend's speech.

"I'm fine," he told her. "I was just wondering where your mother was."

"That's right. Where is she?" Aerie asked.

Tyler scooted forward at her question. "Merra's coming with Emery," he said. "I just talked to her. They'll be here soon. They're picking up your sister, too."

"Serena and Tyra have been working in the med ward together nearly all day," Aerie said. "I almost forgot about her. I hope she doesn't ruin this for me."

"She could never ruin it for me," Exton told her, reaching over to caress her cheek.

Aerie couldn't resist; she leaned in and kissed him gently.

Reverend Thorne cleared his throat. "You should just wait," he said. "We'll get to that part in a few moments."

"Give it a rest, Dennis," Exton replied. He brought Aerie closer to him, pressing into her even harder.

Aerie had a feeling that he was doing it just to irritate the reverend, but she was too enthralled to care much for his reasoning.

"The reverend's objection is not unreasonable," Emery called from behind them, winded from her run. "I thought the ceremony was over."

Aerie grinned as she looked at her. "We wouldn't start without you," she said.

It was then that Aerie noticed Emery was carrying Moona. She instantly hurried past Exton and reached for her cat. "You brought Moona!"

"I didn't exactly have enough time to think of a better gift," Emery said, as Aerie huddled the white cat against her. "So I thought she would do the trick."

"What's my present going to be then?" Exton asked.

Emery folded her arms across her chest. "No dancing," she said.

He laughed, for the first time in a long time it seemed. "You really do know me well," he said.

"Of course I do." Emery stepped up and took her position next to Tyler. "And I love you anyway."

"The feeling is mutual," Aerie replied as she reached out and hugged her soon-to-be sister-in-law. "Where's my mom?"

"She received a message and was delayed," Emery said. "But she said she would be there in a few moments."

"Leave it to Merra," Exton muttered.

"Serena's coming with her," Emery added. "So it shouldn't be too much of a wait. Your sister seems eager to get this over with."

"I know how she feels," Exton said, grinning as he looked over at Aerie. "But I have a much different reason for wishing it so."

Aerie blushed.

"Enough," Reverend Thorne said. "If all of you are in such a hurry, I can get right to the point."

"That's fine," Exton said.

"Just a few more moments, please?"

"It'll be okay, Aerie."

Aerie felt uneasy, but one look into Exton's eyes and she couldn't stop herself from agreeing. There was some part of her, she felt, that was just daring her to hope for the best, and she couldn't resist it. Not when she knew Exton was waiting for her.

The ceremony continued, with Reverend Thorne calling attention to the permanent things about life and love, the necessity of the simple things, which were never easy but came in steps. Aerie felt bad for daydreaming. She felt like she and Exton were surrounded by love, as though it was a physical, manifest presence between them.

And when they both agreed to take each other in love, all the days of their lives, and sealed the promise with a kiss, Aerie could have sworn the earth moved, crying out in pure joy.

It was only when she looked up, the passion in her eyes clouding her vision, and the love in her heart full to bursting, that she realized it wasn't shaking or screeching because of her love.

While Moona meowed angrily and darted up the Memory Tree, Aerie watched through her windblown hair as a URS shuttle streaked toward the camp, whipping past them at high velocity, only to land less than a hundred yards away.

"Who is that?" Aerie instantly regretted yelling so loudly, as she accidentally sucked in a lungful of dirt.

Exton coughed and glanced over through the kicked-up dust storm. "I'm not sure who it is," he answered, "but I'm guessing it's trouble."

Before anyone could say anything else, Aerie heard her mother's voice cry out.

"Victor!"

Aerie, along with everyone else, turned to see Merra running toward the ship. The excitement on Merra's face, along with the unbridled joy, confused her.

She turned back toward the ship, to see the General

coming down the shuttle entrance.

Aerie nearly choked. "What's my father doing here? Any why is my mom so happy?"

There was a look of stunned horror on Exton's face, one she was sure that matched her own, as Merra jumped up and grabbed the man, who barely managed to stay standing under the impact.

Aerie was terrified her mother would attack, and she hurried over. But she faltered when it was clear Merra wasn't interested in attacking.

Aerie watched, dumbstruck, as her mother embraced her father, kissing him passionately as he held onto her.

♦30♦

Exton felt just as bewildered, watching the scene unfolding before him.

"Well," Tyler said, "I guess you two will have more empathy now for Reverend Thorne, and how he was trying to stop you from kissing so much earlier."

"I don't appreciate the attempts at levity," Exton yelled. He didn't think Aerie did, either, as he saw the bewilderment on her face.

"I now pronounce you husband and wife," Reverend Thorne said hurriedly, shutting his book and picking up his long robes. "Well, I must be going now."

The Reverend's not-so-subtle desperation was the first thing that made Exton grab his arm.

"No!" Exton said as he stopped him. "No, you stay here. You knew about this, didn't you?"

"You'd be shocked to know what I know," Reverend Thorne snapped back. "And it is part of my duty not to repeat it."

"We both know you've already broken that rule."

"I aim to break it no further, for my transgressions are great enough."

"You should still stay," Aerie said. "In case we need to bury someone."

Exton was surprised to hear the amount of anger in her voice. He was further surprised to see her stomp off, heading for her parents.

Emery sighed. "I was worried about this."

Exton felt another round of surprise. "What do you know about it?" he asked.

"I've been monitoring for signs of Gerard," Emery said. "Meredith is off duty for a few days, but I did hear that there was an attempt on Osgood's life, following the news that Petra was under attack."

"How long have you known?"

"Just a few hours." Emery glanced over to where St. Cloud and Merra were still locked in each other's arms. "There was only a rumor, and it was an unsuccessful attempt anyway. Dictator Osgood is still alive."

"So you think St. Cloud did it?"

"The thought crossed my mind," she admitted.

"Why?"

"Because of Marcus," Emery said. "I never felt right about how Merra managed to leave, and I never understood why St. Cloud would do all those things, but still contact you to let you know where Aerie was when we had gone to get her."

"You can't understand evil," Exton insisted, before he turned and headed to catch up to Aerie.

"What is this?" Aerie was demanding to know. "What you are doing here?"

Exton arrived just in time to see St. Cloud frown. "I guess a father can't come to his daughter's wedding without being interrogated like a criminal?"

"You are a criminal," Exton insisted. "You killed my father, don't you remember?"

St. Cloud sighed. "Nice to see you again, Exton."

"You're too late to stop the wedding," Aerie told him. "If that's why you're here."

"He's here because he tried to kill Osgood," Exton said. "Aren't you?"

St. Cloud's eyes darkened. "Word gets around fast, doesn't it?"

Aerie looked horrified. "What are you talking about?"

Merra stepped up. "I think it's time we told them the truth, Victor."

"I don't think they'll believe us," he replied, keeping his focus on Exton. "We'll have to earn their trust first."

"Do you have something in mind?" Merra asked. "I've already done that."

Aerie and Exton exchanged a knowing glance. From her expression, Exton knew that Aerie was skeptical of her mother; Merra was overplaying her confidence.

St. Cloud turned his attention to Exton. "I am asking for your protection," he said.

"No."

St. Cloud cocked an eyebrow at him. "I guess you're smart not to trust me right away, but there are things you don't know, and there are things you must be told. If we are going to protect this world from the URS, we're going to have to work together."

"No," Exton repeated.

"Aerie," St. Cloud said, "don't you think Exton should at least listen to what your mother and I have to say?"

Aerie bit her lip, and Exton mentally cursed him. St. Cloud knew Aerie's weakness, just as he did—she was already wondering what it was that they had to say.

"Aerie, go inside Petra," Exton said. "You don't need to be a part of this."

"No," Aerie said softly. "I stand with you, Exton. I won't leave you with my parents." She narrowed her eyes at the two of them. "For all of our sakes."

Merra came up beside Exton. "Exton, you know me well enough. You know I wouldn't jeopardize Petra for anything less than winning the war."

But you would still put it in danger—if you could risk it and win.

"I need you to listen to Victor."

"Why should I care about him?" Exton asked, the old, angry rage bursting out inside of him once more. "He killed my father!"

"Because he's the only hope for freeing the world from the URS."

"What are you talking about?"

"Victor and I are members of the Ecclesia. We are not exactly the peacemakers that Dennis would've liked, but there you have it. He was not happy when I decided to pursue this course, but he understood it."

"What course?"

"Victor is a prestigious figure in the government. He's

been on the fast track to his position for years," Merra continued. "When he and I met, we were both ambitious, and we wanted a real family. We thought we could get away with it because Osgood and St. Cloud were friends, and I had a good reputation in the horticulture industry."

Aerie stepped up beside him, taking his hand. "What does this have to do with anything?"

"We're double agents," St. Cloud said. "We have been for years, since long before you were born."

"I had my children, and I tried to raise them and keep my career," Merra explained. "But it's very hard to teach your children your values when the State is in charge of their education."

"They would have had access to the earliest education resources," Exton said. He knew what she was talking about. With St. Cloud and Merra both in top positions, they would have been in school from the very beginning.

"Yes. I met your mother through the gardening circle," she said. "And she invited me into the Ecclesia, eventually, while I was pregnant with Aerie."

"Dennis said you were one of theirs," he said, glancing over to see the reverend had taken the opportunity to flee back to the campus.

"I am." Merra smiled. "As much as Dennis would like to disown me for it, given all the trouble Victor and I have caused over the years."

"The Ecclesia wants to be free, too," Exton said.

Merra shook her head. "They can't. They cannot be entirely free of this world, and it is sad that they are content to let it fall apart in the meantime," she said. "They suffer, for what little they do, yes, but that is the calling we all embrace."

"You suffer more than they do."

Merra drew herself up proudly. "Of course. Victor and I began to work to overthrow the URS shortly before Aerie was born. I stepped down from my position to raise my children. But I remained involved in side projects."

Exton recalled the battle at Chaya. "Such as the ecobomb?"

"That's just a new one. Years ago, I was also working on the Biovid with your mother. Victor and I both knew about *Paradise*. Everything was going well for a few years. But then, the previous dictator, under Osgood's suggestion, began curving the birthrate by force. Each unit was given a limit, and measures were made to ensure those limits were kept."

"But you got pregnant."

"Do you know what it is like to worry about the safety of your child, even before it is born?"

Merra's self-righteous indignation was wearying, but Exton knew she saw herself as doing what was right. And he couldn't blame her for that. He thought of Emery's child, and how he might have a family with Aerie one day, too. Exton commended Merra for her bravery in taking the risk she did to protect her child.

But even though he could understand her, he still wished she was more open to telling him the whole truth, not just bits and pieces when it suited her.

And that's probably exactly why she does it in the first place.

"So you faked your own death," Exton said. "To protect Marcus. And St. Cloud knew about everything." He saw Aerie's eyes widen.

"Yes." Merra folded her arms across her chest.

"And you've been planning this war for many years now." Exton said it, and he knew it was true. St. Cloud's comments about his plans seemed more logical now.

"I had been planning to destroy *Paradise*, so the URS would be significantly set back."

"Especially with Silas dead," St. Cloud said.

Aerie gasped. "Stop it," she shouted. "Stop talking about that. Exton already hates you enough."

"And you, Aerie?" St. Cloud asked. "Do you hate me?"

Aerie clenched her fists, clearly shocked and torn apart by the question. "I'm tempted to! Especially when you don't want to listen to me!"

"I'm going to make this easy on you," St. Cloud said. He

held out his wrists to Exton. "If you can't take me as a dissenter or a political refugee, take me as a prisoner."

Exton hardened his gaze. "We don't take prisoners."

"You're at war now. You have to."

"I could just kill you," he said softly.

While Aerie's eyes widened in fear, and Merra scowled at him disapprovingly, St. Cloud laughed.

"What's so funny?" Exton growled.

"I doubt you'll do that," St. Cloud said.

"Why?"

"Because if you do, you'll never know the *real* reason I killed your father."

At his words, Exton felt his body act of its own accord, as he lunged forward and punched St. Cloud, his fist landing square across the General's face.

"Exton," Aerie muttered.

Merra came forward and stepped between them. "That's enough," she commanded, as blood began to spurt from St. Cloud's nose.

"It is," Exton said, trying to breathe properly. He hated how terrible he felt. He had been hoping that in striking the man who took his father away, he would have gained a sense of satisfaction, or even a feeling of peace.

But St. Cloud was smart, Exton realized. He didn't just want him to pay for his crimes now. Exton wanted an explanation for them.

He flexed his fingers, trying to stimulate relief in his fist. It ached from hitting the General's face. Exton turned away and headed back toward Petra. "Fine. Have it your way. I will accept your deal. For now."

"You will?" St. Cloud asked.

"You will?" Aerie echoed.

"Yes. You can be our prisoner. But it will be on my terms," Exton said, continuing to walk away. "Now, I'm going to go make the arrangements for your incarceration."

St. Cloud sniffed. "I hope you're satisfied, Aerie. It doesn't look like your marriage is getting off to a good start."

Exton gritted his teeth, determined to keep moving forward. He didn't want to see Aerie's crestfallen face, he didn't want to wonder if she was already regretting the promises she'd made to him, and he didn't want to look back at the Memory Tree as it stood proud and tall against the smoking horizon. Seeing it now, planted firmly in the ground, able to withstand so much trouble, would only convict him, as his thoughts turned away from wedded bliss, back to the familiar darkness of revenge.

THE PRICE OF PARADISE

BOOK THREE OF *THE DIVINE SPACE PIRATES*

♦♦♦♦

C. S. Johnson

For Sam. Of all things I have learned, the things you have taught me remain among my favorites. I am so grateful for you.

This is also for Tyler, a good student and friend, and fellow coffee shop patron. That is no small added blessing to my life.

And finally, some of this is for Ryan. I know you'll likely never read it, but that's okay—I know you've lived it. I used a lot of what you taught me about marriage, with all its pains and pleasures in this one. Your love is literally inspiring!

♦1♦

A muted amount of simulated sunlight sprinkled down from the ceiling lights softly as the beginning of the night's end arrived. The room was peaceful and quiet, warm and comforting. All of it was calling her back to coveted sleep, almost tempting her to fall away from the real world for a few more moments.

Almost, Aerie thought groggily, turning over in her half-slumber. She reached out and felt the coldness of the empty sheets beside her. Instantly, the silence of the room, the one she now shared with Exton, suddenly seemed heavy with his brooding.

Her eyes blinked open, and she looked over to find Exton in the dim light. He was on the other side of the room, sitting at his desk. There was a book open in front of him, but he was clearly preoccupied with his own enigmatic thoughts rather than lost in the world of his novel.

Aerie felt a sense of helplessness settle over her. With the war going on around the world, there was always plenty to mull over, and there was very little she felt she could do to make it better for either of them.

It didn't help that in the last weeks since they had returned to the *Perdition,* Aerie knew both she and Exton had trouble sleeping for more than a few hours at a time.

The sense of helplessness increased.

Her husband was still much of a stranger to her, even if she did claim his heart and his body as her own. *And now his name, too*, she reminded herself, allowing that sense of complete belonging to wash over her once more. The warmth of that confidence allowed her a moment of reprieve from the chilly reality before her.

Aerie continued to watch Exton silently as he leaned over the book on his desktop. He was partially turned away from her, his face hidden, even as it allowed her a clear view of his broad shoulders and muscled back. If his mood was less forlorn, Aerie might have allowed herself the time to remember the strength of his back under her hands, the tautness of his body as it moved along hers, and the desperate eagerness of their passion as it overcame and consumed them.

As if he sensed her gaze, he sat up straighter. "Are you awake, Aerie?" Exton asked, his voice heavy, weighted with concern.

While she heard no irritation in his tone, she fleetingly wondered if he missed the isolation of his room before they'd been married. Aerie was glad he still had access to the Captain's Lounge, where he could think in peace, alone with the comfort of being above the world's problems, protected from the world of problems he faced as captain of the *Perdition.*

"I am," she admitted. She pushed herself up into a sitting position, pulling the sheet up against her skin more tightly as the coldness crept closer.

"Did you sleep well?"

"Well enough," she said, giving him a small smile as he finally turned around to see her.

He returned the smile, and Aerie was pleased to see his eyes light up in hope. "Good. I'm glad to see your nightmares have gone away some."

Aerie winced. She didn't like to be reminded of her time being tortured by the URS, but there were some moments in her sleep where she slipped back into that world unwillingly. More than once since they were married, Exton had woken her up to get her to stop shaking, only to have to lull her back to sleep.

"What about your nightmares?" Aerie asked.

"My nightmares begin when I wake up and I have to leave you," Exton told her as he came and sat down beside her. He reached over and ran his hand through her golden red hair affectionately.

Aerie arched against his hand, contented by his touch.

"I'm going to have an especially hard time today, since your mother's coming."

"Oh, really?" Aerie's eyes widened. "I'm surprised."

"She wants something. Promise me you'll be careful if you see her. She's good at getting what she wants."

"I guess I do have issues where my family is concerned," Aerie said lightly.

"Then you know I have good cause for being worried."

Aerie rolled her eyes. She thought about arguing back, but she knew it wasn't just her mother that made him uneasy.

Ever since Exton had gone and talked with her father, General St. Cloud, about the death of his father, Exton had struggled with sleep as much as she did. Now that they were married—and in more than one way, stuck together—Aerie didn't want to fight with him, especially over family matters. *It's … complicated,* she decided silently to herself.

She looked up as Exton wrapped his arm around her, pulling her into a tight embrace.

"I wish we had more time," he said with a sigh.

"Me, too," Aerie murmured, relaxing against him.

"I guess honeymoons don't last long when there's a war going on," Exton said.

Aerie laughed. "They don't even have honeymoons in the URS, if it makes you feel better."

"I'd forgotten about that. I suppose as much as we try to preserve the things we'd like to keep, change is inevitable." He sighed. "Even Emery and Tyler didn't have much of a honeymoon. We attacked the Memory Tree only a few days after their wedding. It seems like we haven't had a lot of downtime since then."

"I hope you're not blaming me," Aerie said.

"Oh, I wouldn't blame you … entirely."

She sneered at him, while he gave her a charming grin in return. As much as she knew he was teasing her, she knew he had a point. The reality they faced, and what was at stake, was a risk that seemed too large to even properly contemplate, and she was caught in the middle of it. "I suppose our problems are small compared to the rest of the world's," Aerie mused aloud.

"Loving you is not a problem," Exton assured her with a quick kiss.

"You have a lot more problems because you do love me," Aerie pointed out somberly, thinking of all she had put him through in the last several weeks.

She tried not to grimace at the thought of her rescue from the URS, and the fact that the rest of her difficult, semi-dysfunctional family was under Petra's protection.

And then there's Brock, too, Aerie recalled, thinking of how withdrawn and upset he had been prior to her departure. She could only hope he was starting to see he could fit in, easily, especially with Petra's fighter pilot squad. Her older twin brothers, Caledon and Dorian, had jumped at the chance to fly when Director Ward, Exton's aunt, offered them positions.

Of course, the offer was only extended once Merra approved, and even then the boys had several stern warnings from both their mother and father. Even after years of separation, it seemed Victor and Merra St. Cloud were in perfect sync when it came to ordering their children around and warning them to behave.

Well, not all the children, Aerie thought dejectedly. Her older sister, Serena, was the only one of all four—*no, now it's five*—of the St. Cloud siblings that stumped her parents. Serena had shrugged off both the General's comments and her mother's appeals, taking on a role in the medical division at Petra's medical ward.

Aerie knew her sister was proficient as a combat med, but with her attitude and general personality, Serena was bound to cause problems no matter where she was. Aerie just hoped she wouldn't be the one who had to answer for Serena's disparities.

"Loving you is something that might bring me trouble," Exton said, interrupting Aerie as she silently listed her family's sins. "But it is also one of the only reasons I work to find solutions."

"So the world is better off because you love me?" Aerie

asked.

"My world certainly is." His icy blue eyes softened as they looked into hers. In their half-lit room, as they faced each other, Aerie felt as though they were surrounded by a cloud of invisible fire and softness, almost as if their love was made manifest between them. The extra-sensory sensation spirited around them, and she felt it bond them together all over again.

Aerie's heart swelled. The uncertainty she'd felt earlier faded as a rush of hope and determination rekindled inside of her.

Exton glanced toward the door. "I know the war makes the world's future seem even more uncertain than it already is, Aerie. That's what makes what we do all the more precious."

At the sudden look of frustration on his face, Aerie hesitated. She felt him distancing himself from her, and in her disappointment, her curiosity pushed back. "Are you still upset about what my father told you?"

"No," he snapped, his response stinging as it cut through the air. He withdrew even further from her, as if he'd been scorched, and the warmth between them flickered away with it.

"I know you're lying when you say it like that." Aerie shifted, reaching for her uniform as she stepped out of bed. Disappointment metamorphized into defiance, and she struggled to keep her temper in check.

"I don't like to be reminded of his lies about my father."

"You have a rough history with the General," Aerie said quietly, "but he's never lied to you."

"He *has* lied to me, plenty of times."

"About what?" Aerie glanced over her shoulder. "I don't remember any time when he did."

"When you first came onboard and he found out you were here, he said that he would trade you for himself, and that he would do anything to keep you safe."

"Well, that is a tall order, according to Serena and my

brothers," Aerie said. "That doesn't mean he was lying."

"He signed the warrant for your arrest less than a month later."

"He *had* to, or Osgood would've suspected him of being a traitor. He didn't have to tell you that Brock had already managed to get me away from New Hope's Reeducation Center."

"Are you actually defending him?" Exton stood up and crossed his arms over his chest. "After all the pain he's caused you?"

"It's complicated," Aerie insisted. "I know you didn't like it, but he has no reason to lie to us now that's he's one of us."

"That didn't stop your mother from lying to us about getting information from him."

"My mother's a different person than my father," Aerie argued.

"Where do you think she learned it from?" Exton retorted.

Aerie pursed her lips, already regretting that she'd brought it up in the first place.

They'd arrived on the *Perdition* with General St. Cloud two weeks before. Once the General was cleared for admittance, he was placed in a special room and not allowed to leave. Aerie was saddened that Exton had indeed taken the General's request to be his prisoner at his word; she was hoping he'd at least allow him to be a guest onboard the *Perdition* as she had been.

It's complicated.

She frowned. That was beginning to be a reoccurring theme, she noticed.

To make things worse, ever since the General had met with him to discuss the death of Exton's father, Aerie had sensed a change in Exton, one that was far from healing, forgiveness, or reconciliation.

If anything, Aerie thought, Exton's pain, the pain she'd seen inside of him when he first came to visit her as himself, rather than the notorious Captain Chainsword, the pain she wanted nothing more than to soothe over and respond to, had exponentially increased; it had been drilled even further into the recesses of his heart.

Aerie watched him now as he shuffled around the room, with seemingly no specific goal in mind.

"I'm going to get ready," she said, refraining from engaging in their fight—*discussion*—further, heading into the bathroom instead. She quietly shut the door behind her as she tried to hold back the growing anger and frustration inside of her.

Aerie was not entirely sure of exactly what her father had told Exton, and she had no way of imagining how terrible it was, especially as she saw how it made Exton as upset as he was.

Since the meeting, Aerie waited and welcomed his body with her own, telling him in her own way she would be ready for him when he was ready to share. There had been plenty to do, settling into her new job in the Biovid and helping around the starship.

Maybe that was the most irritating part, Aerie thought. She knew from her own experiences on the *Perdition* before that there was a time for everything. Exton had mourned his father's death for over ten years. He wasn't likely going to have peace at any new information overnight. But Aerie had been hoping Exton would've confided in her more by now, especially since she had tried so hard to be a good wife and worker.

Maybe he doubted her loyalty? After all, Aerie knew he hated it when she defended her father.

But it wasn't like she agreed with all of his decisions, either. Aerie wasn't happy that Exton had agreed to make her father the first prisoner of war.

On the other hand, it wasn't like she was happy with her father, either.

Her head fell into her hands as a bitter resentment washed through her. *This is such a mess. I never should've agreed to this. We got married too quickly.*

The sudden thought of losing all the good things she'd experienced—all the joy they'd shared, all the comfort he'd given her while she fought off her nightmares, all the laughter and kisses and closeness—left her short of breath.

"Calm down," she whispered to herself. Taking a deep breath, and then six more, Aerie forced herself to relax.

There was no point in getting hysterical. They had time. She didn't know how much or how little, but they had time. Aerie knew she loved Exton, and because of that she would give him time, as long as she could.

As she finished dressing, Aerie was relieved to hear Exton moving on the other side of the door. When she came out of the bathroom, he was nearly ready for the day.

He glanced over at her as she stood in the doorway. His eyes met hers, and he stopped buttoning up his uniform jacket. Unspoken and unformed words passed between them, and there was a distinct change in the room's atmosphere.

Aerie watched as he walked over to her. He reached out and cupped her cheek, and she leaned into it. "I'm sorry," he said. "I don't want to hurt you."

She put her hand over his. "I know."

Exton drew her closer and kissed her temple, before allowing her to rest her head on his chest.

Aerie wrapped her arms around him tightly, holding him for a long moment. There was nothing like holding him, she thought. "I forgive you, of course," she murmured a moment later. "But I suppose you already know that."

"If there's one person between us who can be counted on to forgive egregious behavior, it's you," he murmured, playfully nuzzling her shoulder.

"You forgave me, too, you know," Aerie reminded him. "I did lie to you about who I was when I first came here. Don't be so hard on yourself. And have a little faith in me."

"What do you mean?"

She steadied herself against him carefully. "I want you to tell me what my father said to you."

For a long moment, he was quiet, and Aerie wondered if

he was going to respond at all.

But then he nodded. "Okay. But not right now, with your mom coming today. We can talk about it later, after she's gone."

While it was irritating for Aerie to know she would have to wait, she was glad. *It is enough. For now.*

"Okay." She stood up on her tiptoes to press her lips against his softly. He kissed her back, the gentle spark igniting into a full flame.

Exton reached down, running his hands down the curves of her body. Before Aerie knew it, her mind was clouded with desire; she barely noticed when he picked her up.

"We don't have much time," Aerie whispered as he laid her down on the bed, even as she was already reaching for him.

"We'll make it enough," he promised her.

Aerie knew she should try to fight harder, but Exton seemed to prefer kissing her into silence, and she preferred to let him. There was nothing she wanted more than to know that their love would be enough to bridge the gaps between them.

♦2♦

It took Exton a moment to realize that the usual rhythm of his steps carried a new beat as he made his way through the *Perdition*'s familiar hallways. It took him another few moments to decide he liked it.

After more than six years in space, it was a nice change, he decided. Even if it was impractical.

There is nothing wrong with having hope.

It was having false or foolish hope that was risky, and he knew the difference between the two.

There was a good chance that he, along with the other forces of the defectors, could topple the URS and its oppressive regime. With the small collection of forces fighting them, and the added arsenal of the *Perdition*, Merra St. Cloud, for all her trouble, had been proven right over the past several weeks—the URS stronghold had sown its own seeds of destruction as they fought to control their people, and the people were beginning to notice.

Some of them, anyway—enough that as the government tried to hold onto their power against the defectors, both inside and outside the nation, more and more people were asking for the truth and finding the government's answers lacking.

As the *Perdition* directed forces around the world, further breaking the URS off from their bases and labs, the end of their power was becoming more of a possibility.

Exton glanced out the window as he walked by. He faltered in his footsteps, stopping short as he watched the world below.

Aerie is the reason for all of this, he thought. He had never been able to see past the pain of his past, only seeing a bleak future where he was destined to meet the same fate as his father.

Not until he saw her. Since Aerie came into his life, everything had changed. Now, she was his. And now, everything was better.

Even the world seemed to be in better shape. Exton saw the thick band of clouds coiled almost protectively around the middle of the world. Since the last battle at Petra with the Craftcarrier, it seemed that the clouded belt around the middle of the world, the one that had chilled the equator and killed off several ecosystems, had shrunk some, both in size and density. He could see little patches of the world through the bulky foam; he could see little patterns of breaking fractals as rain once more poured down on the earth below.

Exton's attention turned toward Petra, the stronghold of his community in Antarctica, where he knew Emery was helping his aunt and the other leaders.

While he was sure she was immersing herself in the day to day needs of Petra's citizens, Exton was almost sorry Emery wasn't onboard the *Perdition* with him. She had regularly been his confidant, and he missed her counsel. Especially since he had General St. Cloud under his guard.

His mood darkened instantly, as his mind swept itself away to his meeting with St. Cloud in the small room that had been arranged into a prison cell.

"I assume you're not here to ask me what I think about my accommodations?"

Exton grimaced; it had been three days since they'd left Petra to board the *Perdition*, and even the afterglow of celebrating Aerie's return and their wedding was not enough to leave him unaffected by the sound of St. Cloud's voice.

He looked at his foe now, frowning at him from the doorway, as St. Cloud sat at the small table. It was a standard room, with a kitchenette close by. Exton was glad, on several levels, that St. Cloud had not broken his confinement, and that he hadn't given Exton any grief over the arrangements.

Over the years, St. Cloud had given him enough grief over other things.

Other things I want to discuss.

Even though he was determined to get the answers he wanted, Exton found himself only too willing to hesitate.

His old mentor was drinking coffee from a mug, and for the first time it hit Exton that he was looking at his father-in-law.

God certainly has a weird sense of humor, Exton thought wryly.

St. Cloud cleared his throat. "I can keep talking if it would make you feel better. Getting acclimated to life's inconveniences is—"

"Is not a privilege, but a necessity, for the warrior," Exton finished. He remembered St. Cloud's teachings more than he liked to admit.

A spark appeared in St. Cloud's eyes, and Exton had a hard time wondering if it was a sign of hope or because St. Cloud wanted to disconcert him.

Well, Exton thought, *nothing would disconcert me more than to be his protégé again.*

If only he'd had the same feeling when he was younger, when St. Cloud originally extended the offer to be a career mentor.

If he'd turned down the offer, Exton knew he might have never gotten into university early; he might not have even tried. Instead of going to university to be an engineer, he might have joined the URS military in hopes of gaining fame as a top officer, finally taking out the last MENACE remnant, and quickly advancing in rank.

His father might even still be alive, mass producing more weapons, fighters, and life-saving technology for Dictator Osgood.

"Never mind," Exton muttered to himself. He had plenty of possibilities to wonder about later. He had to deal with the realities right now.

"How is Aerie?" St. Cloud asked slowly.

Exton nearly choked on his words. "She's doing well."

He hated that Aerie was stuck in the middle of their feud, but it couldn't be helped. She was St. Cloud's daughter—even if Exton was sure she hated it almost as much as he did—and now she was also his wife.

His beautiful, loving, compassionate wife.

Exton felt his hardened stance soften, minimally, as he thought of her.

"I'm glad to hear that."

Exton snorted disdainfully. "After decontamination, you're probably glad to hear of anything that resembles news."

St. Cloud frowned. "I have a right to know my daughter's being treated well."

"That certainly didn't bother you when you signed her over to be tortured under Osgood's orders, and by Lieutenant Dubois, no less."

St. Cloud waved the matter away with a flick of his hand. "I expect that sort of thing from Osgood and his ilk," he said. "After years of dealing with him, I know how Osgood thinks and how he operates. Thankfully, the Ecclesia has a different standard."

"You're not dealing with the Ecclesia."

"But I am dealing with you, and you were raised in the community of believers, even if you don't agree with them on everything," St. Cloud replied. "With all their teachings, I know you have received a set of morals I know you won't discard as easily. That's part of the reason I knew you would be a good leader, believe it or not."

Exton said nothing as he fumed.

St. Cloud's eyes gleamed again, this time with cunning. "I know you, Exton. I taught you well, and you learned your lessons better than I could have ever hoped."

"You taught me how to be a fighter," Exton said. "Nothing more."

"I taught you how to be a fighter," St. Cloud agreed, "but one with honor."

"For all the good it did me."

"I didn't tell you what to believe," St. Cloud said. "That is where we differ, you know."

"What do you mean?" Exton flustered over. "You were a

part of the Ecclesia once, too—and still are, according to what you told me at Petra."

"And I am."

"I wouldn't advertise that too loudly. Dennis wouldn't like to hear that."

"You're right. It drives him crazy, you know. Merra's grown on him over the years, but he never warmed up to me." St. Cloud took a sip from his mug.

"I can't imagine why," Exton snarled.

Dennis, known as Reverend Thorne, always seemed too wise and too aloof from the world. While the older man tried to act like a second father to him, Exton never appreciated his efforts. Of course, Exton never wanted his efforts in the first place.

"Even you agree with me, Exton, that inside the Ecclesia there are people who disagree with each other on what to do with the truth." St. Cloud continued, "But we don't disagree that there *is* truth, and that includes the fact that there are things worth protecting and worth risking our lives for."

Exton nodded.

St. Cloud smiled humorlessly. "I knew you would agree with me on that."

"What makes you so sure?" Exton grumbled.

"Aerie."

"You leave her out of this." Exton felt his hand curl into a fist. He had to force himself to remember the empty feeling that had come over him at Petra when he struck St. Cloud before. It was too tempting to think that physically overpowering his enemy would heal his heart.

"See? You want to protect her," St. Cloud said. "You believe in beauty, truth, love, and goodness. Just as I do."

Exton felt his fingers dig into his palms. "I guess so."

"I'm trying to tell you, Exton, that we agree on truth. But we disagree with what to do with it. A long time ago, Merra and I both infiltrated the URS government and used our positions to gain intel and resources and connections that would eventually help us overthrow it."

"I don't believe you."

"Yes, you do, but you still want to hate me." St. Cloud arched an eyebrow at him.

"You don't have any proof."

"I can get some, if you'll let me out of this room."

"You're not going anywhere right now."

St. Cloud laughed dryly. "I had a feeling that was going to be your answer. We won't get far if you can't see past your anger. And we won't get any further if you can't believe me when I say I have been a member of the Ecclesia, even while working directly under Osgood."

Exton grumbled to himself. Playing with possible scenarios was an exercise in imagination and discipline. Sometimes, he knew, it was easier to see truth of a situation if its result was applied to reality.

"For the moment," Exton finally said, "I'll give you the benefit of the doubt. But I don't see why you're explaining this to me."

"You're the one who came to me looking for answers. I didn't say that they would be easy, or that you would like them. I only told you I would tell you why I killed Silas, and this is part of that."

Exton scowled. "I'm not going to change my mind about hating you for it," he said.

"I grieve his loss, too, you know."

"Then why are you telling me this?" Exton asked. "I'm still captain of this ship. I can make you walk the plank, if you'd like to prove me more pirate than warrior."

"I'm not here to ask for your mercy," St. Cloud said. "I'm here at your mercy only because I chose to be. I'm here because even if I don't deserve your mercy, I want your trust."

"Ha!" Exton laughed, but he was caught off guard by St. Cloud's admission.

"I want your trust as an ally," St. Cloud clarified. "Not as a father-in-law, and not as a former mentor or family friend. I will agree to leave Aerie out of it as much as I can."

"Good. I don't want her mixed up in this."

"That is something we can also agree on." St. Cloud smiled. "She doesn't have the temperament for war. I hope you gave her an easier job while she's here."

"She's working in the Biovid," Exton replied, instantly regretting his admission when he saw St. Cloud's obvious pleasure at the news. Before he could say anything, Exton continued, reasserting control over the conversation, "I trusted you before, and I know how that ended. I won't make that mistake again."

"You might not trust me, but I still know you very well. I know you blame yourself for Silas' death," St. Cloud said quietly.

Exton's eyes widened in surprise and fear at his words. His gaze shot up to meet St. Cloud's, betraying his inner turmoil.

St. Cloud nodded as he watched him. "But you should know, as I tried to explain to you afterward, that it is not your fault. The cause is mine, but the fault is your father's."

Exton felt his throat tighten as he stopped himself from shouting. "Why would you say that?"

"The day everything happened—the day you weren't supposed to be there, I'll remind you—I had orders from Osgood to investigate the reasons that there was a delay in the construction of the *Paradise*. Silas was in charge, and he made several changes to the final model right up until the very end. I know he was a prominent figure in the Ecclesia, and to this day I know several of the workers and engineers and designers had 'special orders' from him. The Ark is proof of that," St. Cloud said. "And you know that. You were the one who told me about it, in the beginning."

His fists clenched, hard and fast; Exton wouldn't be surprised if he'd drawn blood. "Yes," Exton agreed reluctantly. "I remember. My mom said it was at the orders of the URS that he added in several of the changes off-record."

"That's what he told her. *I* know that was a lie." St. Cloud straightened in his chair.

"I don't believe you."

"I don't have anything to gain by lying to you now," St. Cloud said. "Aerie is safe, my family is safe, and I am in exile from my forces."

"You and Merra have been playing a deep game," Exton reminded him bitterly. "You'll have to excuse me if I seem skeptical."

St. Cloud smirked. "I always liked your sense of humor," he murmured. "It was one of the other reasons I chose to mentor you."

"There is nothing funny about this."

"I agree, which is why it's all the more amusing. When everything is on the line, and you've been dealt a bad hand, a dark sense of humor can be sustaining, even if it is hollow in the end."

Exton turned away and looked back at the door. "I have other duties to attend to," he said. "If you're going to tell me why you killed my father, you might as well get it over with."

"You know I killed him on Osgood's orders," St. Cloud said. "But I also did it because he was going to destroy us."

Exton whirled around. "Excuse me?"

"The URS commissioned the *Paradise* to be a military research hub," St. Cloud said. "Silas convinced them to make it into a lifeboat of sorts. Osgood was the one who wanted it to be able to house weapons, eventually. Remember, at the time, Osgood had been the dictator for over a year."

"I know that," Exton snapped. "But he was the second in command, just like you, for years. He'd already had a lot of oversight on the project from what I remember."

"Silas didn't like that."

"No, he didn't," Exton agreed. "I remember that. He used to brood over it."

A memory of his father came into his mind. His father often stood at the window of their small unit, looking out toward the shipyard where the *Paradise* resided. His hands, with consistently bruised knuckles and blisters forming on his palms, curled around his Bible, his lips moving in silent, frustrated prayer.

What had happened to his Bible? Exton wondered, suddenly intrigued. He made a mental note to ask Aunt Patty about it. It was possible she had it somewhere at Petra, since she'd been the one who inherited his mother's things.

Exton blinked as St. Cloud shifted in his chair. The memory faded away instantly, replaced by the cold black and red room, where he stood only a short distance from his greatest enemy.

"Osgood gave his orders, but I carried them out," St. Cloud said, not realizing Exton had slipped away for a few long seconds. "I wanted to give Silas a chance to escape, believe it or not. But when he told me the truth, I shot him."

"Why?"

"He was going to gather up the Ecclesia inside of the *Paradise* and then use the weapons to destroy New Hope and other URS outposts."

"That's a lie," Exton yelled. "My father would never do that."

"I'm not the only one who played a deep game," St. Cloud argued back. "Silas was just as tired as the rest of the Ecclesia were, and he knew from Evelyn's research they were pushing for more war, even back then. Merra knew it too."

"Her word won't validate your own."

"I know. I'm telling you I didn't want to, but I did. Silas wouldn't let it go. I tried to reason with him. But he would've been risking too much, including the lives of our friends and allies."

"So you killed my father to save yourself?" Exton asked incredulously.

"To protect others. Merra and I have both watched several of our friends taken into Reeducation and tortured until their will and resolve was broken. Aerie's *lucky* that they have designed a way to control people through their memories and rewiring their brain since then. They have moved on from outright killing the dissenters to rewiring them into mindless monsters, like Gerard."

"He was far from mindless when he was torturing Aerie," Exton said, thinking of the burned skin and twisted scars on her body where the electrodes had been placed. Her nightmares, when she woke up shivering and moaning muffled words, gave him further clues about the pain she'd suffered.

"She'll be fine," St. Cloud said. "She was only there for one session."

His mouth dropped open in immediate outrage. "How dare you," Exton shouted. "How dare you trivialize her suffering!"

"What is the suffering of one person against the rest of the world?" St. Cloud shouted back.

"But it's *Aerie* you're talking about," Exton insisted.

"*Everyone* has someone they've lost," St. Cloud retorted.

"I know! I lost my father."

St. Cloud paused for a long moment. "Aerie was innocent, Exton. *Is* innocent, truth be told. Your father was not."

"I don't believe you."

"Silas was trying to give Eden back to the world, Exton. He saw *Paradise* as a way to return to the good times, but he was wrong." St. Cloud stiffened in his chair, placing his now-empty mug down on the table with impeccable calm. "He was wrong. There is no going back. We can only press on, going forward."

"My father did *not* want to destroy the world, especially not in order to save it," Exton insisted.

"He had no qualms about it, Exton. Remember Noah?"

It took a moment for Exton to recall the story from the Bible about Noah, a man who was righteous in the eyes of God. He was told to build an ark and collect the animals of the world, two by two, and gather them inside while the world was washed away by rain and floodwaters.

"Silas saw *Paradise* as a present-day ark. He wasn't destroying the world in his mind. He was saving the Ecclesia while the world would be purified by fire."

Exton forced himself to breathe in and out as evenly as possible.

"He had a lot of people in the Ecclesia who supported him, Exton, but he was smart enough to know that there would be plenty of people—in fact, pretty much everyone—who would be against him. I even believed him for a long time, until I saw the truth. I firmly believe that's how he convinced so many people to help. Many did come to join the Ecclesia when we had to contract out work to new places."

Somehow, St. Cloud saying that his father's goodness remained, despite all the alleged badness, stung worse than the accusations altogether. Exton felt a moment of resignation as he realized he wouldn't be able to fight St. Cloud over every bit of information he gave.

"So he cloaked his words in secrecy, and—"

"And secrets, while necessary, can destroy you," Exton murmured, remembering another one of St. Cloud's favorite sayings.

St. Cloud nodded approvingly.

Disgust sparked inside of him. "I still think you're lying," Exton said.

"What if I'm not?" St. Cloud asked. His voice grew quiet and contemplative again, forcing Exton to change directions.

"If you're not," Exton said slowly, "then you've been misinformed."

"What if you're the one who's been misinformed?" St. Cloud's expression was almost amused now.

"It's not like you can prove it," Exton replied.

"*I* can't, while I'm in here. If you want proof I'm telling the truth, all you have to do is locate the Boötes system."

"Boötes?" Exton frowned. "That's a constellation, not a star. It doesn't have a system."

"Not the stars, Exton. That's its name. Boötes is the name of an intranet that the underground agents of the government use to communicate. The URS has known for the last several years, after you began intercepting our fights and our shipments to various places, that you and your crew were able to monitor our comm systems. That's why we had the NETech designed for our fighters and our military comms. Before that, there was another system in place that was used to keep out foreign interceptors. It's a shadow web."

"We've already had access to several of the State's military communications."

"This is more of an archive; it was used as a place for our space program, specifically."

Exton frowned. "What do you mean by 'our?'"

St. Cloud rolled his eyes. "The State's. I would've thought that was obvious."

Exton considered the matter carefully. He'd forgotten that the URS would have had a record of the plans for the *Paradise*. He knew from Tyler that the URS had planned to expand their weapons to make them space-capable, as they had done with the MENACE fighters. But other than that, there had been no news on what the State was planning as far as their space program. There were no additional projects in the hacked files they did have regarding that. Exton had heard the rumors that it was shut down after he and his friends had stolen the *Perdition* from them. He was more than willing to believe them, too.

Maybe too willing, he admitted to himself. St. Cloud's shadow web could possibly provide some insights into what exactly had happened.

"What's on there that would prove you were right about my father, especially if he was as secretive and deceptive as you say?" he finally asked. If—*if*—St. Cloud was telling the truth, there would have to be something very specific, very incriminating, to serve as his proof.

"The plans for *Paradise*. The ones he originally submitted for the military development division in the URS government," St. Cloud replied.

Tyler would probably be able to handle scouting for that, Exton decided. "Fine. I'll order an investigation. But you will remain here until I have my answers."

"I have chosen to abide by your wishes—for now." St. Cloud gave him a small, shrewd smile. "You can always come and talk with me about other things if you get bored."

The thought of visiting St. Cloud of his own accord held no appeal. Exton shook his head.

Before he left, there was one other thing that made him pause. "Boötes was my father's nickname," Exton said softly. "Why is it named after him?"

"You can thank Osgood for that," St. Cloud said. His amber eyes, so similar to Aerie's, darkened with an ominous shadow. "I wasn't the only one Silas managed to fool."

"They were friends." His words came out as more of a statement than a question. "I remember he had a lot of meetings with him. I'd forgotten about that."

"Yes. Osgood named it after him to remind himself not to trust anyone, ever again," St. Cloud said. "They used to be good friends, the two of them. It fell apart after Osgood became dictator. While I never knew the exact reason why, my guess is that politics drove them apart. Both of them were unhappy with the last dictator, but I suspect Silas felt bitter once Osgood took up the title."

Exton only nodded. He'd known a lot of defectors from the URS who also had trouble keeping friends because of political disagreements.

St. Cloud cleared his throat. "If you look for the Boötes system, their shadow web, you'll find the nation's most carefully guarded secrets. It should prove that Silas' designs for the *Paradise* were ultimately different from the ones the URS ordered. If you're half the engineer he was, you'll see the reasons why they were changed."

At his words, Exton felt a rush of pure hatred rekindled inside of him.

Even if it was true, that alone doesn't mean my father deserved to die. Even if I have been misinformed, my father is still dead. Even if St. Cloud killed Papa to stop him from doing bad things, he took away all the good things he could've done, too.

His father had been silenced, and he wasn't able to

defend himself. Exton owed his memory more than a quick, cursory condemnation, provided by the very man that had robbed his father of his life.

"You're not telling me the truth," Exton insisted as he headed for the door. He'd had enough of this conversation. He had known it would not be an easy one, and he knew it was time to leave.

"It is the truth, Exton, whether you believe it or not."

St. Cloud's last words hung in the air before Exton slammed and locked the door behind him.

Exton blinked and found himself still glaring out the window of the *Perdition*, seeing past the world before him.

He thought about the argument he'd had with Aerie that morning, and for the first time since that conversation with St. Cloud, he felt a small quiver of doubt.

What if St. Cloud was *telling the truth?*

The truth mattered—to him, and to others. It was nothing for him to play along with the URS's narrative that he was the ghost of Captain Chainsword, his father's remnant. It was the only way his father was capable of having revenge on the world, after all, and Exton had no trouble assuming the responsibilities of that calling. Besides, what did it matter to establish a fitting role for himself in a world where the truth was what the State said it was, and nothing else?

Here, in his own community, and on the *Perdition*, he knew he wasn't really a ghost working with MENACE.

But that was the problem, wasn't it? He knew what he *wasn't*. What was he? *Who* was he, really?

He'd always looked up to his father, even if they had, only naturally, disagreed on some points. His papa was a loving husband, a diligent worker, and a brilliant engineer. His mother idolized him, wholeheartedly championing his idealism, seeped in religious conviction and strong against the tides of reality's derision.

The thought that his father had become radicalized by his ideals, ones his mother even denied, was startling; the idea that he died because he was willing to do anything to obtain his own paradise was unfathomable.

Or at least, *nearly* unfathomable.

The idea that his father would hijack a state science and military endeavor, only to send it into space and use it as a weapon against his home nation, a nation that was threatening to take even more away from him than it already had … Never in a million years would he have thought his father capable of doing that.

Exton also knew he'd never guessed *he* was capable of that, either. Yet, there he was, the captain of the starship he'd stolen from the State, the one he could have used to destroy his enemies, only stopped by what he would call a miracle.

Exton rubbed his temples, distressed.

Who am I, really?

Exton knew the answer to that question, and he didn't like it.

As he quietly resumed his steps, Exton admitted to himself that he was suddenly afraid. If what St. Cloud said was true, Exton was too much like his own father for comfort—and he was afraid of what Aerie would think of him if she knew the truth.

He barely noticed that his stride had lost its confidence as he turned onto the Command Bridge.

♦3♦

"Here's the report you asked for, ma'am."

Aerie smiled and wiped the dirt off her face with her arm as she looked up at the towering figure behind her. "Thank you, Bruce."

"The orchids look much better already."

"Yes, it was a good call," Aerie agreed. She ran her fingers through the soft leaves. "They'll have a little more room now, before we prune them again."

"Yes, ma'am."

Aerie grinned up at the large man. "There's no need to call me ma'am. Aerie is fine."

Bruce blushed through his reddish beard as he shyly looked down at his feet. "But you're the captain's wife now, ma'am. 'Tis only proper."

"I'm still a member of the community, same as you, even if I am just substituting in the Biovid for Emery."

"Director Caldwell," Bruce corrected softly.

Aerie laughed. "I guess that is her correct title here. I guess I thought everyone was a lot more informal."

"Not everyone is like that. Director Ward insisted on using titles down in Petra." He shrugged. "I've gotten used to it from her."

"I wonder why people use titles so much?" Aerie wondered aloud, as she busied herself with cleaning up some of the mess she'd made in transferring the plants while thinking about the differences between the URS and the *Perdition.* Growing up in the URS, things had always been more formal. Students were told to address each other as "Comrade," and instructors were "Master," and even her father preferred "General." Family unit members were also discouraged from using names, unless it was from the unit leaders to their subordinates. Exceptions were only made for good friends or colleagues, but there never seemed to be many exceptions.

"Sometimes people put walls—and titles—up to keep

people away. Others do it to see who will knock them down."

She paused for a moment in her workmanship. She had heard enough stories from others around the city to know that the rural areas of the nation were less centralized around the federal government.

"Interesting idea," Aerie finally said. Before she came aboard the *Perdition*, Aerie assumed that things outside of New Hope were not as strict.

It is not a good practice to make assumptions of these things, I guess.

"Well, call me what you'd like," Aerie finally replied a moment later. She stood up next to him. "But I still prefer Aerie."

Bruce blushed again, red enough that his face was only a shade lighter than the flannel jacket he wore over his uniform. "Aerie it is, then."

"Good. I was hoping I wouldn't have to call you 'Director' or whatever your title is, myself. I've forgotten it, actually," Aerie admitted.

Bruce laughed hard enough to send his whole body shaking. "It's 'Doctor,' although there are some I know who like to call me 'Treebeard.'"

"I think I'll stick to Bruce, if that's okay with you," she replied, unsure of the reference that caused him such great amusement.

Aerie met Bruce when she first agreed to step in for Emery as one of the Biovid's caretakers. Bruce was the lead caretaker, with several years of experience as an arborist. His taciturn manner had prevented her from asking too many questions, but once he began to talk, his shyness slowly faded into a friendly countenance.

She watched as he turned his attention toward the flowers she had spent the last hour repotting. Aerie pressed down on the soil gently, giving it a final pat down. "What do you think?" she asked. "Are they ready to go?"

Bruce nodded. "Much better. Orchids need special attention to flourish. I'll move them into the pollination chambers. The new pots will help, even if there's not a lot of space in the chambers."

Aerie thought of the small rooms below the Biovid. Several of them were used for different purposes, including pollination. Emery and Exton had both recently warned her not to investigate them on her own. When she asked why, Exton had been firm, telling her there were lots of things besides plants and tools below the Biovid, and many of them were dangerous.

Aerie brightened. "Can you show me?" she asked. It was one thing to go on her own, she thought, and another to have a guide. "I'd love to see it."

Bruce nodded, picking up the newly planted orchids. "Sure. We can't be long; I've got to go and check the water supply and take care of some water stripping still."

"I guess I'll need those reports from you soon enough, too, so you'd better get them done."

Bruce nodded. They had arrived on a small landing in the middle of several rows of plants when he passed Aerie the flower pot.

"Here," he said. "Step back. The pollination room is here, underneath the Biovid. It's a steep staircase down, so watch your step."

"Got it."

Aerie felt her fingertips tighten against the smoothness of the flowerpot she held as Bruce pulled open the door. "I was wondering if these were storage rooms," she said. "I remember how, during the harvest celebration, there were rooms where you had to climb to get to them."

"This is similar to that," Bruce said. "The ship was all designed by one man, and he was very good at maximizing the space available."

Aerie nodded, briefly forgetting Bruce couldn't see her past the orchid pots she carried as she thought about Exton's father.

Silas Shepherd seemed to be more of a myth than a man to her. Aeric had known some of the specifics of his story from her school days in the URS, even though she knew him as Captain Chainsword. It was said he'd been betrayed by those who loved him best, and he had been insistent on causing trouble for the URS by working with MENACE, an old enemy from several decades ago.

While she knew some of the story had been embellished and propagated between Exton and the General, and other high-ranking members of the State, she didn't know too much about the actual man himself. Hearing Bruce speak of his skill seemed to give more credence to his memory.

Or maybe just his legend, Aerie thought.

"Keep your eyes open on the way down," Bruce warned, as he took one of the pots from her.

Aerie nearly sputtered an apology at finding herself off in one of her musings, but Bruce didn't seem to notice.

She stepped carefully down each step, her boots making a soft *clank* on the hard metal. Aerie had to remind herself to watch her steps, as she found herself in the middle of a small room. "Wow," she uttered.

The room was small, but it seemed to be filled with wonders. The walls were covered with shelves, and the shelves were filled with delicate plants. Small, bright lights were placed on all surfaces, and there was a smell in the air that reminded Aerie of the times she spent with her mother as she tended their unit's small garden. There was much more humidity in the air, enough to make her feel like she was walking into a steam room. Her uniform seemed to cling to her as she spun around, gaping at the room in amazement.

"This is wonderful," Aerie said. "It's almost like a rainforest is growing around the room in here."

"That's what the Biovid is for, but in the smaller room I think it creates more of that effect," Bruce said, as he took the plants from her and set them down on a cluttered shelf.

"It is small," Aerie agreed. "You weren't kidding about that."

"I don't kid about my plants much," Bruce said, his voice muffled as he ducked down and pulled out a few bottles.

"I thought maybe you were mistaken since you're so tall," Aerie explained apologetically. She shuffled a step back from Bruce, but there was hardly any more room for her to maneuver.

Bruce chuckled. "I guess I can understand that. The *Perdition* is a grand ship, but it does seem much smaller on the inside. Part of that is because there's so much to fit, and then part of it's like that because it was built to last."

Aerie watched as Bruce sprayed down the orchids with water and pressed some fertilizer feeds down into the soil. "How long do you think it will last?"

Exton had told her before about the stories of his father and how he'd set out to take the *Perdition* back. But she was surprised to find that it was in such good condition, especially after the URS—and her father—had ordered attacks against it in the past.

"Oh, it could last for several decades, if not centuries, with proper upkeep."

"So it's pretty indestructible?"

Bruce considered the question for a long moment before nodding. "Yes, I would say so," he said. "The *Perdition* was built to withstand a lot," Bruce said. "I worked with the designer, the Captain's father, on some of the Biovid's final additions. The greenhouse glass is part of my addition. You want to have enforced paneling for sunlight, but it's got to be able to withstand high pressures, heat for reentrance, and a whole plethora of other potential problems."

"So you're not scared of the URS up here? You're not worried about them trying to attack?"

Bruce waved the matter aside, his arm nearly hitting Aerie in the face as she stood behind him. "The designer thought of that, too. Biovid, for all its size, is well protected by the ship's design. The rooms below are especially protected, because of the different designs. They easily double-up as extra escape pods."

"They're that strong?"

"Certainly. Plants and water are necessary for human life.

If they're gone, we're not going to be far behind. While the designer wanted to safeguard some of the more exotic plants from Earth in the Biovid, he sold the idea to the URS as having a farm of sorts or a research plant in the URS-approved designs. It's natural to think he wanted to protect that, and he wanted to provide for the possibility that there would be extra people onboard."

Aerie nodded. "What do the other rooms have in them?"

Bruce shrugged as he turned around, indicating he was finished. "There aren't a lot, but there are some larger ones. I know I am not allowed in them, and the Ark especially."

"The Ark?" Aerie asked. They climbed out of the pollination chamber back into the Biovid.

"Yes. It's where some of the seedlings are preserved and animal DNA is housed. I wouldn't need in there anyway, for the work I do with the trees and the plants. The only time I have seen it at all was several years ago. I had a tall tree, a *cashapona*, and it was dying, unable to be supported by even the deepest plots available here in the Biovid. I gathered its seedlings, and one of the researchers here, Cordelia Harrick, took them and placed them in the Ark for preservation."

"Harrick?" Aerie frowned, recognizing the name. "I wonder if she's related to one of my old school instructors."

"T'wouldn't be surprising," Bruce said. "A lot of our workers, especially the ones who have been here for years, are former residents of New Hope."

Aerie was about to ask if she could be introduced to Cordelia when a new voice called out to her.

"There you are, Aerie."

Recalling that she was told not to go exploring through the Biovid chambers, Aerie felt a rush of guilt. The feeling dissolved quickly when she saw it was her mother, and there was a grin on her face that told Aerie she was not about to get in trouble for bending the rules to satisfy her curiosity.

After all, her mother bent rules for worse reasons with bigger costs.

"Mom."

♦4♦

Aerie felt the strangeness of greeting her mother, her uneasiness even more exaggerated by her hesitancy. Exton had warned her that her mother was here to get something, and she had been reunited with Merra long enough to know she wasn't above using her children for her agenda.

If Merra had been suspicious of her hesitation, she didn't show it. "Aerie," she called as she came up to her. "I had a feeling you would be in here."

"It's my job here now," Aerie said stiffly.

"I know that, but you're drawn to this place in ways that have nothing to do with your job," Merra said. "I can tell." Her green eyes, lovely and sharp as ever, flickered to the pollination chamber as Bruce sealed it off.

Aerie felt her discomfort increase. *How did she know?* Aerie wondered. Was it something only a mother could see?

Before she could ask, Merra nodded toward her arm, where the URS had branded her during her time in the Reeducation Program. "How's your wrist doing since the surgery?" she asked.

Aerie glanced down at the very visible scar on her wrist, where the new skin graft was still settling in. When she was captured by the URS and held in the Reeducation Center, her arm was branded, marking her as a patient, as well as allowing them to track her movements. The med team on the *Perdition* had been able to remove the device from her body. While the remaining scar would fade over time, she would likely have the mark all her life.

"Decontamination was easier," Aerie admitted.

"And how's your shoulder? Is it doing better now that the Ecclesia's medics have been able to realign the ligament?"

"All better," Aerie said, her voice in clipped tones as her discomfort increased. She hated that it seemed unnatural for Merra to inquire after her condition; after nearly seven years of her absence, there was a strange opposition to each other, and Aerie hated it as much as she enjoyed it.

"Ma'am?" Bruce looked back at her and gave her a formal nod. "I'll go and check up on the water systems now. I'll have the reports to you soon."

Aerie caught the formality. "Thank you, Doctor," she replied, hoping he would see her gratitude.

He seemed to catch it, because he gave her a quick smile from under his beard, before ducking away into the depths of the Biovid.

Merra smirked ruefully as he disappeared. "I see Exton's warned his crew about me."

"He knows you're good at manipulating people," Aerie remarked, recalling her own conversation with him earlier.

"Good to know you've been warned, too," Merra said. "I guess a regular conversation is out of the question?"

"We've hardly ever had those, even before you faked your death and left me with the General," Aerie said. At the ire in her own words, she nearly flinched in surprise, but Merra took it in stride.

"I see you're still working through processing it," she said. "Good. I'd hate for you to be unaffected by it. If you are, it's because you care, one way or another, and I'll take what I can get."

Aerie bit her lip to keep herself from snapping back.

"Emery wanted me to say hi to you from her," Merra said. "She's hoping you'll touch base with her again soon."

"I talked to her last week," Aerie said. "I haven't been able to get back to the Bridge much since then."

"She understands. She's hoping you'll come down and visit, too."

"I don't think I can do that."

"Sure you can," Merra said. "You're the Captain's wife, now. You can do what you want, within reason, and with proper pretext."

"I don't want to abuse my position," Aerie muttered back.

"But chances are you will at some point," Merra said, crossing her arms. "There's no need to be so high and mighty about it."

Aerie's feet shifted nervously. "How is Emery doing?"

"She's well. Baby's fine, too, I suppose. She's still not showing. You'd never know she was pregnant by looking at her. Of course, the first baby doesn't usually show that quickly. If this was her third or fourth kid, she'd be out to here already." Merra moved her hand out in front of her own stomach a good foot, and despite everything, Aerie smiled.

"I'm glad to hear she's good. I was worried she wouldn't be happy after Director Ward assigned her to help you with the Craftcarrier wreckage."

"We've had a nice time combing through the water samples and sending in the robotic sub explorers," Merra said. "We've already managed to find several booby traps. Only a few have gone off on our watch."

"The ship is still there then?"

"Nearly all of it," Merra said with a nod. "It's not leaking anything toxic, but it will need a lot of clean up. For now, I'm happy it's still there. We might be able to pull more weapons out, and it'll be good shield for any other Craftcarriers that might decide to fight against us."

Aerie's heart clenched. She was the one who had been raised in a largely utilitarian household, where the need for human compassion was never prioritized over the good of the collective and the State. Despite that, she was surprised at the lack of sympathy and grief at her mother's statements.

Merra didn't seem to notice Aerie's discomfort as she looked around. "You know," she said, her voice softer, "I can see why you'd like this place. I always envied Evelyn for her gardening talents."

"Evelyn?"

"Exton and Emery's mother," Merra said. "She was a short woman, and even I stood about a foot taller. Emery looks a lot like her, but this room almost feels like her."

"I think Exton feels that way about the ship and his father," Aerie admitted quietly.

"Evelyn and I were friends, even if we weren't close,"

Merra said, barely acknowledging Aerie's words. "She was a year or two ahead of me in school, and this was before I had joined the Ecclesia. I was upset when she was picked to lead one of the research teams we were assigned to work on. But she won me over in the end, and I ended up wishing I was more like her than hating her for being different from me."

"Did you know Exton's father, too?" Aerie asked.

"Of course. Not very well, though," Merra said. "He was good friends with Victor, though."

"Then why did he shoot him?"

Merra's eyes gleamed, and at once Aerie knew she shouldn't have said anything. "Exton didn't tell you what Victor told him?" she asked.

"It's not like we're not busy," Aerie murmured.

"There's always plenty to do when there is nothing to talk about," Merra muttered. She gave Aerie a thoughtful look. "Why don't you go see him and ask him yourself?"

"I … " Aerie let her voice trail off. She didn't want to tell her mother her real answer to that question. "Exton said he lied. That was all he told me. I … I figured he just didn't want to dignify the General's comments by repeating them."

Merra snorted. "I'm sure," she replied mockingly. At Aerie's frown, she sighed. "I'm sure he has his reasons," she said, this time more softly.

"What did the General tell you?" Aerie asked.

"Silas was a good man, and Evelyn was a dreamer through and through," Merra said. "Dreamers and workers do well together, especially when they share a vision. Their vision was probably just too big."

"This coming from a woman who's determined to overthrow the most powerful government in the world?" Aerie asked, her own sarcasm surprising her.

Merra only nodded, as if she knew that taking Aerie at her words, rather than her jeering, she'd make more trouble. "Of course. Silas was a brilliant man. I don't doubt that he started the *Paradise*'s construction without malice. But then, Silas saw an opportunity to save his community, and he took it. I can't blame him for that, to be honest."

"So why did the General kill him?"

"Victor had been training Exton for a couple of years at that point," Merra said. "This was before I left, remember? Evelyn and I were working, secretly, on trying to prevent the URS from developing eco weapons. That was when we moved quite a bit of our research to Chaya."

"That's not answering my question."

"I'm getting to it. Context matters, remember?"

Aerie made a face at her.

"Exton was the one who told Victor about the various modifications to the ship as it was built," Merra explained. "He knew they were friends. He trusted Victor. He loved his father, even if he wasn't sure of him."

"What do you mean?"

"I'm sure he doesn't like to think about it," Merra said, "but Exton was very different from Silas. They clashed over a lot of things before Silas was killed."

"You still aren't answering my question," Aerie grumbled.

"Maybe it's better you ask your father for the information about it, then," Merra replied. "Silas wanted paradise. He got it, just in a different way from what he was thinking."

"That's cruel," Aerie gasped, as angry tears came to her eyes.

"Yes, it's cruel, but that's life for you."

A long moment passed as Aerie just stared at her, unable to believe what she was hearing. Seeing her mother now, listening to her now, the compassionate, caring mother she remembered from her youth seemed to be completely gone. Aerie half-wondered if her mother had died and the woman who stood before her was merely an intruder wearing her mother's skin.

But then, Aerie recalled, her mother had been interested in plants, too. It was at the URS's own rules, rules which would have prevented her younger brother, Marcus, from being born, which had caused Merra to fake her own death. If her mother was different from what Aerie remembered, it was because of what the government had done to make her this way.

Merra shrugged and turned her attention toward the curved ceilings. "Just look at this place. Even if I hadn't known Silas personally, I would know this place was constructed to be a new Eden. *This* is why so many of the Ecclesia volunteered to help him, you know. The Ecclesia is not so fond of war. They are always looking for earthly deliverance; odd, really, since heavenly deliverance has already been given."

"Exton told me that his father refused to let the URS have it for their purposes," Aerie said, trying to get more information.

"But he still had it for his own, Aerie. The Biovid and the Ark are proof of that."

"You know about the Ark?" Aerie asked.

"Of course. Evelyn was my friend, remember? She was in charge of coordinating a lot of the seed transfers from the Norwegian research labs."

Aerie glanced around curiously. "What else do you know about the ship?"

"I know some of the other rooms house bombs. Some of them are pretty wicked, too. I remember that because it was something that convinced Victor he had to act."

"I would think the weapons were put there by the URS before they were ordered by Exton's father," Aerie said.

"This is where sentimentality can lead to ruin," Merra said. "Evelyn was more than a fool to believe everything he told her. You're more than a fool, too, if you can't see that Exton has his own flaws, and some of them are much worse than his father's."

"Why did you let me marry him, then?" Aerie nearly shouted.

"His flaws are bad, but that doesn't mean he isn't without honor, or that he has no potential." Merra shrugged. "Everyone has problems, Aerie. His father, while well-intentioned, was overprotective and overbearing at times. I'm just telling you to watch for it so you won't be so disappointed or trapped when you finally do see it."

Aerie shook her head, torn between leaving and arguing. "I don't see why you think you can tell me how to feel about my husband. It's not like you and the General have a loving relationship," she said.

"Your father and I trust each other more than you will ever know," Merra told her, a hardened edge coming into her voice.

"He got a new unit director fairly quickly," Aerie reminded her, deliberately provoking her. "Director Phoebe was in the unit less than a month after you were gone."

"He had to do that, to appease Osgood," Merra snapped, her temper flaring.

"I'm just saying it's unusual, now that I think about it."

"You can forget about her. Phoebe was selected by Osgood himself. He wanted a spy in our unit, and he took advantage of my absence quickly enough."

"She was a spy?"

"Of course she was," Merra snarled. "She is one of his cousins."

"Really?" Aerie felt her mouth drop open in surprise. She'd never paid much attention to her new unit director, and she was shocked to realize that Phoebe might have done that intentionally.

"Yes, it's true. Now you can forget about her. I don't like thinking of her," Merra admitted. "But as for her presence in the unit, that was a necessity Victor had to face, much as he had to sign the warrant for your arrest."

"I still don't see how you can trust him so much."

"Who do you think told me about Exton taking you to Nova Scotia, and who do you think told me you were being sent to the Reeducation Program?"

Aerie said nothing. The idea that her father was a man on his own mission was not surprising, but it was hard for her to picture her mother working with him in tandem.

"He was the one who called me, Aerie. So I could send a

rescue team." Merra reached out and put her hand on Aerie's shoulder. "I trust him with my life, entirely, and the feeling is mutual. Our trust in each other is one of the many ways we love each other. You have no idea how much I have missed him in these last several years."

Realization dawned. "That's why you're here," Aerie said. "That's what you want. You want Exton to let him go."

"Of course."

Aerie bit her lip, nervous. "I don't think he'll let him go," she said.

"I'm up for the challenge of convincing him," Merra said. "And between you and me, I have an ace up my sleeve. Right now, Victor is in perfect position to inherit the title and return the world, albeit slowly, to a constitutional, democratic republic.

"We have already put the necessary rumors in place, saying that Osgood is working with MENACE and St. Cloud tried to stop him. When we kill Osgood, we can easily blame MENACE, tie up some loose ends, and have the people's trust."

"But you're lying to them," Aerie said, shocked. She stepped back out of reach, letting her mother's arm fall off her shoulder into empty air.

"Aerie, you're young. You don't know how war is played out in real time. You have to know the rules to break the rules," Merra said. "Dying for something's easy; living for something, that's harder. But killing for something? Even harder. Truth is rarely something people will die for. So instead, we tell them a good story."

"But it's not the truth."

"Some stories are true, even if they never happened," Merra said. "Like I said, you're young. You'll understand it later. Of course, only if you want to."

"But what you're doing is wrong," Aerie said, scowling in confusion. "You're taking advantage of people's trust."

Merra laughed. "That's what government does, Aerie. That's what *people* do. There are no perfect forces this side of

Heaven. But we have to uphold ideals even if we can't help but break them."

"You're breaking them intentionally."

"If a leg breaks and needs to be straightened, what does a doctor do? He breaks it again."

"Yes, he doesn't smash it to bits," Aerie argued, her voice rising in frustration and fury.

"The world has already been smashed to pieces. The URS is only a symptom of a broken world. The government before was broken too, and the ones before that. You think truth alone will heal it? Don't be so naive, Aerie. Exton's living proof that the truth doesn't heal people."

Aerie thought about Exton. She had always known he had pain inside of him, and she had always wanted to soothe it. *No*, she thought. *Truth doesn't heal people. Not completely. But it's part of it. Truth and trust have to work together.*

She lowered her eyes. "Exton doesn't trust either of you," she told Merra. Aerie didn't say she sometimes wondered if he trusted her, too. He'd told her before that he did, but he certainly acted strange about telling her about what the General had to say.

"We are family now, thanks to you." Merra's eyes gleamed happily. "Exton might hate Victor, but we have known each other a long time. He will come around."

"I wouldn't count on it."

"He's come around to some things already, thanks to you," Merra reminded her pointedly. "I, for one, won't give up on it. Just like I've never given up on the idea that our family will be reunited one day, and we will be able to live in peace." Merra suddenly reached out and took Aerie's hand in hers, rubbing her thumb over the back of it. "Your wedding day was a great gift for me, Aerie."

Aerie softened at the old gesture from her childhood. There was something unspeakably comforting about her mother's presence as she held her hand, as much as Aerie might have hated to admit it.

"Speaking of which, I hope you have found peace with

my own decisions that relate to our family," Merra added.

The old gesture, one of trust and love, seemed even more hollow against their conversation. Aerie, distracted from Exton's family concerns, recalled how she felt the moment that she learned her mother was still alive.

It was not the joy she might have thought she would feel, especially at how much she'd loved her mother as a child.

She ruined the moment by saying something, Aerie thought bitterly. She tugged her hand free. "Not peace," Aerie said, "but acceptance."

"For now?"

"For now."

"Then I'll take it. I know you've been lied to, plenty, and disappointed by the very people who are on your side. I know I have a lot to atone for," Merra said. "And I will try. But I won't let the imperfect stop me or you from being a step better than what we were before. There's no quick fix for things like these."

Aerie bristled.

"Well, I suppose you know that already, thanks to Exton," Merra said.

Before Aerie could tell her mother not to concern herself with her relationship with Exton, a tiny beep emitted from Merra's pack.

"Speaking of which, I get to go see him, finally," Merra said, as she examined her device.

"Well, bye then," Aerie murmured.

"I'll try to come and see you before I leave. I love you, Aerie."

Aerie felt her heart, despite all its anger and turmoil, warm with hope. She waited until she was sure her mother was out of earshot. "Love you too … Mom."

♦5♦

Exton felt his body shake with fury as he studied the guileless look on his best friend and brother-in-law's face. Realizing there was no reason to suspect Tyler of lying to him, the strong flood of emotion inside of him threatened to overwhelm his self-control.

Tyler glanced up from the file he had in his hand. "What?" he asked. "What is it?"

There was a loud *bang!* as Exton slammed his fist into the nearest cabinet.

Tyler sighed. "This has to do with St. Cloud, doesn't it?"

Exton welcomed the stinging numbness running up his knuckles as Tyler watched him with concern.

Of all people, Tyler knew how much he had wrestled with the guilt and anger over his father's death and his own questions about life, faith, and the pursuit of the truth—and payback. Exton couldn't name one moment in particular that he was more grateful for than the others.

The pain in his fist pumped furiously, but he returned his attention to the file still innocently held in Tyler's hand. "Are you absolutely sure the report checks out?" Exton asked. He was determined to make his tone poised and controlled, even if his mind was reeling in raging anger and strange sadness.

"Positive," Tyler said, running a hand through his blond hair uneasily. "NETech was easy enough to crack, once me and the other techs had some time to devote to it. This system was even easier, which was good, since, you know, you asked me to handle this by myself."

"Not *too* easy, right? No chance this is a conspiracy of sorts? Something designed to lead us astray?"

"Come on. You know as well as I do that there are endless ways to speculate the truth, but we have to follow the facts. This is what I found."

"I know, but … " *But I was hoping you wouldn't find anything.*

Exton was silent as he tried to process everything. He didn't doubt Tyler's skill when it came to working with technology, and he would never question his integrity or his loyalty.

But it was still hard to believe that St. Cloud had been telling him the truth.

Or at least enough of the truth to make me think he is the good guy.

"The URS has been pretty good about keeping the NETech stuff under wraps," Tyler pointed out. "If you're worried about misinformation being a problem, you should recall that they know we've been able to hack their comm feeds for several years, and we've cut off a large portion of those, too, sometimes just for fun. We've already been given a misinformation source."

"No chance this is just … insurance? A set-up?" Exton looked down at the file. He didn't have to see his face to know there was a glum look on it.

"No, I checked for authenticity. The Boötes system has an automatic backlogging record. It dates back more than ten years with no obvious alterations found in its data bank. There are references to certain events in its data, too, and it's intricate enough to where any manipulation would be unlikely."

"So you're saying it's real? Completely real?"

"I'd have to do a deeper run, but overall it checks out."

Exton put his head in his hands. "Great. And here I thought meeting with Merra would be the worst part of my day."

"I thought you'd be happy to hear your intel was correct," Tyler said, his tone rueful. "It has a lot of information on the *Paradise* from when it was under construction, including your dad's notes. I thought you would be happy to see those at least."

"I might be, if it wasn't proof that St. Cloud was right about my father."

"What do you mean?"

Exton sighed. "St. Cloud told me that my father wanted to use the *Paradise* as a sort of Noah's Ark, saving the Ecclesia and destroying the URS. He said the Boötes system would have proof of what my father was planning, and that was why he killed him."

Tyler said nothing for several moments. Exton watched as he processed the information and weighed it, glancing from the floor to the file, and then finally back up to Exton's gaze.

"Flooding the world with fire, I guess?"

Exton sniffed. "It's not funny."

"Sorry," Tyler said. "I guess it's not hard to see you're unhappy about that."

"Is that really what you're worried about?" Exton glared at him. "Aren't you more worried that St. Cloud feels justified in murdering my father?"

"Well . . . well, it's just that—"

"What it is?" Exton asked.

"I never met your dad," Tyler reminded him. "But I know you argued with him over a bunch of stuff quite frequently."

"Not a *whole* lot," Exton argued.

"Emery told me that he got onto your back all the time for reading novels and spending all your free time with St. Cloud and his military assignments. She knew you didn't get along as well as you'd like to think."

"I still did my work," Exton said through clenched teeth. "Remember? That's how I got into University early."

"And I know you took his death hard. Maybe you even blamed yourself, and I know you hate St. Cloud for it."

"No kidding," Exton scoffed.

"I'm glad you can admit it." Tyler glanced over at him thoughtfully. "But you and I both know you're more than willing to believe the worst in St. Cloud. I'm only pointing out that you forgot the worst of your father, too."

"My father had his faults and his devotion to his ideals," Exton conceded. "And you're right, we didn't see eye to eye a lot on certain things. But he was not radicalized or crazy."

Exton once more thought of how his father, would stand by the window of their unit. He would do that often, late at night, after a hard day's work down at the plant or the mill, or even touring through different offices for updates and meetings—the "boring part of the job," as he'd explained it to Exton.

But while he'd said it with a kind smile on his face, Exton remembered the look in his own ice-blue eyes; beneath the disguise, there had been a smoldering anger, a deep frustration, and maybe even a feeling of being trapped.

"Don't tell me you think St. Cloud was right," Exton scoffed, saying it to himself as much as he was to Tyler.

"I'm not sure about St. Cloud," Tyler said, pulling back. "I'm just saying that this information on the Boötes system, with all its military intel, is something we can use, now, as we fight. And we'll need to use it if we're going to finish the war. You should be glad that St. Cloud told us about it, even if it's not what you would have wanted."

"I can be glad for the information and still hate what it means."

"Can you?" Tyler shook his head. "You're already upset over it."

Exton shot him an angry look.

Tyler pushed on carefully. "Don't forget, even if St. Cloud said that there was proof in the system, we haven't found it yet. I took care of it privately, as you requested."

"All I need are the original designs for *Paradise*," Exton said. "According to St. Cloud, that's where I'll see what he wants me to. Emery and I found some of my dad's other blueprints for the ship down in Aunt Patty's stuff."

"Even if it is true that your father was going to destroy the world with the *Paradise*, you are not your father, Exton." Tyler hesitated. "And Aerie will still love you, regardless."

Several moments passed in silence. "How do you know?" Exton finally asked, his voice soft against the walls of the small room.

Tyler's response came at once. "Because even if it is true, I still love Emery," Tyler said. "You are still my best friend. And we are still fighting a war, and it is still worth fighting."

"What if Aerie doesn't see it that way?"

"She won't. She is not her father—or her mother, either. If anyone could understand about having parents who do crazy things, it's Aerie."

"That's true." Exton felt calmer as Tyler's counsel anchored into his mind. "I guess it is silly to worry over what she will think of my family when I have you and Emery to round out the rough sides."

"I knew she would be good for you once I saw how much you cared for her."

"Trying to take credit for it?"

Tyler seemed relieved at the attempt at levity. "Well, Emery and I did help you get her back, thanks to asking Meredith for her assistance."

It was Exton's turn to struggle to find the right words to say. He glanced down at the floor, his gaze solemn and steady. "I owe Meredith for that, too, as much as I owe you. On top of everything else I owe her already."

"Meredith is glad to help you get your own happy ending, even while she is still waiting for hers. Love and friendship are not about *owing* people, Exton."

"That's what people say when they can't pay their debts."

"It's also what people say when there is something more important between people and their debts."

Exton arched his brow. "You like being the morally superior one between us, don't you?"

Tyler grinned. "It can't be helped," he said with a laugh. "You make it too easy."

Exton rolled his eyes. "Well, at least I don't have to worry about Emery in your care."

"And I no longer have to worry about the world in yours."

"That's good," Exton grumbled. "I wasn't going to change my mind because of you anyway."

"Thankfully, we'll never know for sure," Tyler said. He picked up the file. "I'm going to head down to the hangar, okay?"

"What are you going down there for?"

Tyler grinned. "I'm headed down to Petra. Jared came back from Chaya, since Kamalo's in charge there for now. Jared's going to be taking over the Command Bridge with Henry for a while, so I can spend some time with Emery."

"Oh." Exton nodded. "Well, thanks for your help."

"No problem." Tyler stopped at the door to the Records Room. "I'll send you what I find on this." He waved the file around.

Once more, the image of his father, standing beside the window, looking at the horizon with an angry expression in his eyes, called to him.

"Can you do me one more favor?" Exton asked.

Tyler nodded. "Sure. What do you need?"

"When you find the information, can you see if my father's old Bible is there, too?" Exton recalled his father's tight grip on the old Bible. He had been adamant about keeping it close in the housing unit, even though it was forbidden. *Maybe there was something there*, he thought.

"You got it. I can have it shipped up if I see it."

"No need," Exton said. "Just put it with the rest of the other stuff Emery and Aunt Patty found, the stuff my father left behind. I'll take a look at it when I come down."

"Don't put it off forever."

"I doubt I will be able to," Exton said with a small smile. "Aerie will want to see Emery and Moona before too long. And the rest of her family is down there, still."

"Some of her friends, too," Tyler reminded her. "Emery told me the other day that Alice has taken over nannying for Marcus when Merra is busy. Sometimes she helps Alice out just to see what it's like. It's been a long time since Emery and I have babysat kids."

"You should take a turn when you get down there," Exton remarked, nearly laughing at the mental image.

Tyler grinned. "Don't tell Emery that, or she'll get ideas. Anyway, see you later."

He was nearly out the door when he paused.

"What is it?" Exton asked.

"You know, God works out all things for good in the end," Tyler said. "I know you don't like to hear things like that, but there's no hope left if all you have is despair."

"You know I don't like hearing things like that," Exton said slowly, "but keep saying them."

Tyler grinned, clearly relieved. He nodded and clapped his hand on Exton's shoulder. "I know you're just saying that because you have to meet with Aerie's mother today."

"You're right," Exton said. "Better start the prayer vigil now. I'm on my way to meet her next."

♦6♦

Merra St. Cloud never failed to find her footing, even when she was denied her prize.

The small conference room still echoed with her barely-concealed fury. When Merra came to discuss things with him, she requested privacy for their discussion, and Exton readily agreed, knowing she would be more than happy to use the crew's eavesdropping to her advantage if she could.

Now, he was glad he had agreed to that for more than just his sake. Her passion, even in arguing for St. Cloud's release, would have easily inspired some of his crewmembers, spiriting them away from their duties and the war's demands. She might have even managed to recruit some members to her own cause.

Exton watched Merra in reluctant half-admiration as she continued to argue, even after he'd given his decision on the matter. Exton had to give her credit for her tenacity; he might have even ended up agreeing with her, if Tyler hadn't just vindicated St. Cloud moments earlier.

It was just too much of a risk. There was a reason he'd preferred to keep Aerie in the dark when it came to how he felt about her father; there were so many uncertain things, and it was dangerous to expose doubt to the wrong person.

He was almost relieved, really, in dealing with Aerie's mother instead. He knew he would not be tempted to divulge any of those details with her.

Merra is definitely the wrong person to confide in, he thought grimly.

"You can stop," Exton said, interrupting her between arguments. "I'm not letting St. Cloud go. I told you why. I don't trust him."

"That's a silly reason. The world will end before that happens," Merra replied. "You don't even trust me, but I'm here."

"You weren't the one who killed my father," Exton said through gritted teeth.

"That's also a failing argument. You've made your own fair share of mistakes," Merra remarked. "Victor hasn't forgotten about Silas, any more than you've forgotten about Gerard and his father."

Exton felt his breath leave him in a rush of air at her words.

"See?" Merra looked over at him haughtily. "You know what it is to be a leader, Exton, because you've lost people who trusted you. That's why you make a good captain."

"That was low," he finally managed. "I never told you about Gerard and his dad."

"I knew Brother Jean-Luc just as you did," Merra said, her arrogance softening only slightly. "Jean-Luc was imprisoned and killed for failing to reveal his son's guilt after you launched the *Perdition.* I heard about it, even though I never put the two together before Victor told me about Gerard."

Shame colored Exton's face as he remembered how it felt to win against the URS, to have his father's ship in his possession, only to find out it had come at the cost of a friend.

He deliberately turned away from Merra's scrutinizing gaze. "I'm still not letting him go."

"You shouldn't let your feelings compromise your judgement."

"I fail to see how letting him go is good for the war, let alone his own safety," Exton insisted, facing her once more. "He tried to kill Osgood, according to what we've heard. If he didn't stage it."

"So?"

"So, he's not exactly trustworthy to Petra, and Osgood wants him dead now. There are not a lot of other places I can send him without a guard or where people will listen to him. He's better off here."

"He's *useless* here."

"He's *safe* here."

"That should give you all the more reason to release him

to me," Merra said. "It would be fitting revenge, after everything, to let him go and confront Osgood with your blessing."

"I haven't decided what is 'fitting revenge,' yet," Exton snapped. "But it isn't going to be sending him off with you."

Merra scowled. "You're being foolish. Victor is certainly capable of escaping from here. He is only here because he wants to be."

"He already told me that, but I think he'd find escaping more difficult than you say."

Exton almost smiled, thinking of how he'd assigned the Reverend Thorne himself to the task of monitoring St. Cloud's movements. While the leader of the Ecclesia had been unwilling to lend the full force of their following, he had promised to lend a hand where he found it appropriate. Guarding a controversial prisoner seemed to be the perfect request, and Exton considered it a bonus that he managed to anger both St. Cloud and Dennis with the guard assignment.

"You should let him go to earn his trust."

If Merra hadn't said it so seriously, Exton might have laughed. "I *don't* want his trust," he asserted. "If anything, he told me that he wants to earn mine."

"That's a mistake."

"No. The mistake is thinking that I'm the one who has to do something."

"No, it's a mistake thinking that trust between two people is a one-way street."

"It starts out that way, Merra, and if he wants my trust, he's going to have to abide by my rules." Exton held his ground firmly. "And that means staying here. For now."

If not forever, he added silently.

Exton couldn't stop himself from smirking as Merra stewed in angry silence. He finally scored a victory against her, and one that was big enough to get her to give up.

She pursed her lips in bitter resignation. "Fine. But this is not the last time I will argue with you over this."

"Fine. We can always reevaluate the situation later,"

Exton said, keeping his tone detached, even while he was relieved. Arguing with Merra could be more draining than physically fighting. He had a feeling it was more dangerous than an actual fight, too.

It wasn't that she didn't have good principles. He knew her well enough to know that she fought for others more than herself, and nothing she asked for was completely unreasonable. Even letting St. Cloud go wasn't an irrational move.

The problem, Exton thought, *is that there is too much that is uncertain right now.*

It wasn't just doubts about St. Cloud's charges against his father, or even St. Cloud himself. As Merra began pacing around the small conference room, furiously running her fingers through her gray-streaked hair, Exton glanced out of the window, looking down at the world.

It didn't look much different, since he'd been staring out the window the night of Emery's wedding, imagining throwing the world into the bowels of hell.

If anything, Exton knew he was the one who had changed. The old derision, the bitterness at the world, the pain and guilt he carried for it—all of it had been transformed. He felt a strange sense of protectiveness, and he wanted to honor that connection as much as his promises to Aerie.

It helped knowing that he did have support in Merra, his family, and the others who were working around the world with the *Perdition* and the other defectors from the URS.

But even with all of that, he could not just abandon his own inner demons.

"We'll reevaluate this situation later," he repeated, his voice sounding hollow and brusque against the silence in the room.

Before Merra could reply, his comm device went off. He jerked his attention toward it, slightly jarred from its sudden interruption. He answered it out of habit more than anything else.

"Yes?"

"Hey, Cap." Jared's voice came in clear. "I've got a few issues for you here on the Bridge. Trust me, you'll want to come see this."

Exton glanced over at Merra. "I'll be there in a moment," he said.

"Roger that."

He clicked off the device. "I have to head back," he said. "Was there anything else you needed?"

"Fine time to ask me that, right before you're leaving," Merra scoffed. "But no. I have nothing more to ask of you."

Exton narrowed his eyes in suspicion. It seemed like a long way to come for the trouble. *Maybe she figured she would get her way in person rather than over the comm system,* he mused.

Still, he had other matters to attend to. "Alright," he said. "I know Tyler's headed back down to Petra with you. The ship should be ready for you."

"Thank you," Merra said. She drew herself up proudly, giving him a dazzling smile. "I can see myself out."

Exton watched as she whirled around and waltzed angrily out the door. He had a feeling she was going to cause him further trouble. That smile, as pretty as it was and as brilliant as he remembered it from his youth, suddenly seemed sinister.

"I can't do anything about it now," he grumbled to himself, as he headed toward the Command Bridge nearby.

As he came up on the Bridge once more, he was glad Merra had taken her leave; there was an air of frenzy about the room. Just from looking at the focused expressions on his crew, Exton could tell there was trouble coming.

Was Osgood up to something? Exton wondered. Or maybe it was something else. He knew from reports on the ground there was a lot of confusion in the URS, including the capital.

While Jared was examining reports with Thora, the large monitor on the screen was filled with another familiar face. Exton stepped forward, smiling in warm greeting.

"Kamalo," he said. "Nice to see you again."

Kamalo had joined Exton in liberating Chaya only a few weeks before, saving Exton's life in a critical moment during the battle. Exton was grateful for Kamalo's actions, and he was also glad Kamalo had risen up as a leader among the Chaya camp.

The man's darkened wrinkles contrasted sharply with the whiteness of his grin as he saw Exton. "Always a pleasure, *boet.* Or should I stick to Captain, now that you're back on the *Perdition*?"

"Either or is fine," Exton assured him. "What can we do for you?"

"Our sensors are picking up some unusual movement in the Caribbean," Kamalo informed him. "We have weapons shipping out to different camps, and one of our ships—"

"Hold on," Exton said. "What ships? Chaya doesn't have any ships registered, let alone any for weapons transport."

"Once we took over the camp, we were able to claim two of the ships the URS had brought over here. We're using one to ship the research equipment to Petra, and the other is headed out to the rendezvous point in the Caribbean."

Exton was stunned. "I wasn't informed of this. And why would you send them out, with weapons?" Exton asked. "There was no order."

Exton was suddenly half-tempted to call Merra up from the hangar to ask if she was behind this. Deciding it was best to be prudent, he was just about to call for her when Kamalo answered him.

"Chaya has its own governing structure in place," Kamalo said. "I stayed back to help with aid and relief, and to keep you informed of our team's progress. I didn't know about this myself until a few hours ago. I was only informed, too, when it was clear the ship was missing."

"Great," Exton muttered. He knew they would have to find the ship first, before it was lost, or even worse, before it was found by the URS. He would deal with Chaya's secrecy after the ship was under their surveillance.

"Jared." Exton turned toward the copilot. "Hold Tyler's

ship."

"I'll send the transmission now, Captain," Jared said, hurrying over to the console.

"What information do you have so far, Thora?" Exton asked.

"We're trying to locate the ship based on Kamalo's estimates," Thora said, pushing a loose lock of her long black hair out of her face as she studied the portable screen in her hands. "With the new program to locate the Craftcarriers, we've been able to push back against a lot of the static in that part of the world. I've adjusted it for the ship, so we should have the results soon."

"Keep me updated."

"Will do," she said with a quick nod.

Exton looked back at Kamalo. "We're on it. What else has the community been doing that they don't want us to know about?"

"Nothing that demands as much attention as this, *boet.* I'm disappointed, too. I'll see what else I can find and report back to you."

"Thank you. I'll have Thora send you the reports when she delivers them to me."

"I'll look for it."

The monitor went blank as Kamalo signed off.

"Captain," Jared called. "Commander Caudwell has delayed his takeoff."

"Excellent. Have him report to the Bridge along with Aerie's mother."

"You mean Mrs. St. Cloud?"

There was something about the way Jared said her name that irritated Exton. He felt the old familiar hatred for people who couldn't keep their mouths from flapping when it came to discussing other people's business, even if he knew he often depended on rumors and gossip for intel and insights. Exton was certain the *Perdition* was buzzing about with discussions of St. Cloud's family drama. While it was expected, he could only hope Aerie wouldn't be hurt by it.

"Yep, that's her," Exton replied, turning back toward the main monitor, avoiding Jared's eyes. "I have some more questions to ask her, apparently." He rubbed his temples, already exhausted from the day's work.

Glancing at the clock, he knew he still had hours to go before he could sink himself back into Aerie's warm and welcoming embrace.

A thought struck him as he gazed at the information on the screens, all of it pouring onto the monitors at once, like a mystical form of dance.

"Jared." He held up his hand. "Just delay Tyler's ship. I'll meet with Merra later when we know more."

The younger man nodded. "You got it, Cap."

"Good." Exton hid a grin. If he was going to be stressed and angry and disappointed, he was going to make sure Merra was, too. There was no point in attacking her with no proof, and there was no proof so long as Kamalo and Thora were still gathering it up.

She can wait for us, just as I have to wait for them. Knowing she would not be pleased in the meantime, and that it would likely have her beyond frustration by the time he was ready to talk with her, gave him a smug half-sense of satisfaction.

The other half of his satisfaction came with the thought of inviting Aerie to accompany him on his rounds.

He nodded toward Jared, giving him full control of the Command Bridge, as he headed out to find his bride.

♦7♦

Aerie stared at the door in front of her. The uneasiness of her decision pressed into her again, juxtaposing against the curiosity inside of her.

It was no surprise to her, in the end, that curiosity won out. She knocked on the door, loudly enough not to feel like a coward, and waited.

Aerie had decided a long time ago that curiosity wasn't just about being intelligent; it was about being brave, and she knew she would need to be brave if she wanted to be accepted into the New Hope Military Academy.

How long ago and far away that life seems now, she thought, amused and grateful for the twists and turns her life had taken in recent months.

A voice called out from the other side of the door. "Come in. It's open."

Aerie wasted no time in opening the door. She came into the room just in time to see the flicker of surprise on her father's face. "General," she said in greeting.

"Aerie." The surprise mutated into amusement. "To what do I owe the honor?"

"Huh?" Aerie frowned. "I just wanted to come and … "

What did I want to do? Aerie wondered. She hadn't actually considered that she would be able to see her father. She had taken up her mother's suggestion without thinking it through.

The General stopped her. "Would you like something to drink?" he asked. "I've got plenty of tea here, although your husband was kind enough to make sure I had coffee."

"He doesn't really oversee that," Aerie murmured.

"I don't doubt on a regular basis that he has more important things to do. But I suspect I am the exception in this case."

"Why?" Aerie narrowed her eyes. "Do you think you're that special to him?"

"Not at all," the General admitted. "But if I had a prisoner, one who was only a step down from an uninvited guest, I would make him happy so he wouldn't bother me further."

"Exton doesn't think like that," Aerie said.

"I've known him much longer than you have," he reminded her. "And I taught him to think just like that, too. So, chances are I am the one who is correct between the two of us."

"Maybe he just did it to prove he's the better man," Aerie offered.

"He already is. There's no need to show it or prove it."

At his admission, Aerie sighed. "I don't understand you or Mom."

"Is that why you came to see me?" Her father's eyes focused on her intently, and Aerie felt the old, squeamish feeling she had when she was going to get into trouble.

"Mom said I should ask you about Exton's father," Aerie said, "and about what you told Exton."

"He didn't tell you?"

"Don't be surprised," Aerie bit back. "If you taught him, you would know why he wouldn't."

"Your mother and I have always been open with each other," the General said. "So this is actually surprising to me."

"Well, *we* have never been open with each other, and it's still surprising to me, too." Aerie glanced down, suddenly wondering if Exton and her father found her able to handle the truth. Maybe it was more her fault than theirs, she realized.

She turned her gaze back to the General. "Mom told me that you were the one who contacted her about my arrest."

"Do you want an apology for that?"

Aerie shook her head. "No. Ultimately, I was able to be rescued. And I'm glad for that."

"Do you want me to apologize for the Reeducation Program?"

"No." She shook her head again. "I would suffer anything to be with Exton," she admitted. "After I remembered him, I couldn't stop thinking about him."

"It's good to see you love him," the General said quietly. "I would've stopped you from marrying him if I didn't think he was good for you."

"You didn't stop me from getting married," Aerie pointed out. "You came after we said our vows."

He waved his hand, brushing the matter aside. "Do you think I didn't know? Your mother let me know. That's part of the reason I failed to kill Osgood, believe it or not."

"What do you mean?" Aerie asked. "What happened?"

"She contacted me and my comm device went off," General St. Cloud explained. "I have it set to alert me even if I have it turned off. I was caught sneaking into Osgood's office in New Hope because it went off. As much as I love your mother, I should have left it behind. Rookie mistake, but then, love will unravel the greatest of champions."

"So you really did try to kill Osgood?"

"Yes. I barely managed to escape. Apparently, even before my comm went off he had been expecting me. He said it was because of your arrest, but signing the form should have derailed his suspicion some."

"How did he know?" Aerie asked.

"I have an idea. He said after you had escaped, he was right, and he would go and take care of you next," he said.

Aerie felt a chill go down her spine. She didn't know much about the dictator of the URS, but she knew enough about him to know he was a threat.

Dictator Osgood, sometimes fondly called "Daddy Dictator" by some of his more adoring circles, was an older man who seemed professional as much as he was congenial. Aerie had never given him much consideration before, other than to think about how he wasn't nearly as handsome as people seemed to think he was. It was only when she' was captured that she started to think of him as evil.

"When I fought with him, it was a very dramatic confrontation. I won't share the details with you. It's too graphic for your temperament."

"Why do you think that I can't handle it?" Aerie asked through gritted teeth. "I placed high in my combat classes."

"This is different from combat," he replied. "Which is good, really. Your mother's death managed to scar you much more than your brothers and sister. You, out of all our children, have the most compassion."

"Thanks, I think," Aerie murmured.

"It is a high compliment," General St. Cloud assured her.

There was a strange look on her face that made her even more uncomfortable. "If you think that means we'll be able to get along, don't count on it," Aerie warned him. "I know Mom is here because she wants you back down at Petra with her, but I won't betray Exton to help you."

"I am content to stay here for now," he said. "The food is decent, the room is small but comfortable, and I can still listen to the news. I am safe here."

"Oh. Well. Good."

The two of them lapped into silence. Aerie stayed by the door, barely entering the room. She glanced around it, taking it in; it reminded her a lot of her old room aboard the *Perdition*, only it was smaller.

General St. Cloud relaxed, sitting back in the chair at his desk.

Aerie was almost relieved when he broke the silence. "I had fun at your wedding," he said. He gave her an uncharacteristic smile as he added, "The part I was there for, anyway."

"Thank you," Aerie replied stiffly.

"It was really nice to see Marcus again, too," he said. "And to have everyone there, even though it was only for a few short hours … well, it was something I never could have asked for or hoped for."

Aerie bit down her lip to keep from replying. She knew the only reason that he didn't have that already was because he'd chosen to forsake his family's happiness for something else. *It was his own fault*, Aerie thought to herself.

"There is such hope when we get things we don't

deserve," the General continued. "I didn't think I would get any time with my family, and at such a happy occasion, too. Maybe one day I'll get the other thing I don't deserve—something I hope for, even though I can't hope to ever have it."

"What's that?" Aerie asked, her voice hard. "Your freedom?"

"No. Your forgiveness," he said.

Aerie did a double-take, before she balked. "You've got to be kidding me," she said.

"No. I'm not." He met her gaze. "Can you forgive me for injecting you with Memory Serum, for lying to you about your injuries, for being overprotective, and sending you to the Reeducation Program, where Gerard tortured you?"

"I already told you, I don't need an apology," Aerie hissed.

"I'm not apologizing. But still I need your forgiveness," her father said.

Something inside of her retched at the thought of forgiving the General for all his atrocities. She wasn't just going to give him a free pass, even if he apologized, and even if in some strange, twisted, unlikely way he had done all those things for her own good.

"You're a liar," Aerie said quietly. "Exton was right not to trust you. I won't trust you either. This is a power play of some kind. You can't be serious, and even if you are, I can't trust you."

"I wasn't lying when I told Exton the truth about his father," the General said. "He'll find that out soon enough."

Aerie said nothing. She turned on her heel and opened the door. "I knew I shouldn't have come," she whispered.

"Aeris," the General called.

Aerie nearly jumped at the sound of her name. "What?" she asked.

"I understand that you're upset, but you and I still have things to discuss."

"Like what?" Aerie retorted.

"I wanted to know about your escape," he said.

"What is there for you to know?" Aerie swiveled around and faced him. "Brock came and broke me out of there, and then we escaped with Serena, and Cal mentioned you had told them to stick with Brock so we all … "

Aerie paused as she considered what the General had told her.

"I wanted to know why Comrade Rearden came to get you," General St. Cloud said. "I informed Merra of your capture, but he went in to save you before Exton arrived."

"You know Brock wanted to cohabitate with me," Aerie said, her cheeks flushing over red. She never liked to think about that, especially now that she had married Exton.

"But why did he rescue you?"

Aerie watched her father's face as he asked that question, and instantly grew irritated. It was clear he already knew the answer, and he wanted to see if she did, too.

"Because he thought he loved me," Aerie insisted. "And I'm willing to bet you sent him … to … "

Scenes from her rescue, as harsh and terrifying as they were, popped up inside her mind.

Brock had rescued her, even though the General informed Merra. He would have known Exton was coming. So why send Brock? And why have her brothers follow him?

"You didn't send Brock to rescue me," she breathed.

"No, I didn't." General St. Cloud sat up in his chair and sighed. "I should have guessed Osgood was behind it all sooner. I might have managed to kill him if I had anticipated that, too."

"How would Osgood have—"

"Don't be naïve, Aerie. Brock might have loved you, but he was trained to follow orders from the day he was born. And he did an exceedingly good job of it. Osgood has used some of his other subordinates to contact him about military training for years."

Aerie remembered the rumors about Brock's PAR assessment, saying he'd been in touch with the military for over a year. She considered the rumor an exaggeration at the time.

"Brock freed you on Osgood's orders."

"That's ridiculous," Aerie said.

"How else would Brock have known about Petra?" the General asked. "He was flying here from the capital, wasn't he?"

Yes.

"I don't know how he figured it out, but Osgood found Petra, even before the Craftcarrier attack." General St. Cloud sighed. "I'll have to find out."

Aerie's mind reeled at the possibility Brock had been secretly recruited by Osgood. He was currently working down in Petra, with all her friends and Exton's family. Emery had told her not to worry about him when she left for the *Perdition*, since she would watch over him, and Serena and her brothers.

"I'll watch over them and take care of Moona and the Memory Tree for you while you're gone," Emery said. She smiled. "Hopefully, you can check in on the Biovid for me."

Aerie relaxed just the slightest. There was no proof the General was telling the truth; everything was circumstantial.

This isn't the first time he's done this to me, either.

Aerie remembered that moment on top of New Hope, standing on the surface of the forbidden world. She saw the Memory Tree had vanished, and the Memory Serum she now knew about was unable to hold back the memories of getting captured by Exton and his crew.

I will not let my father lie to me anymore, Aerie thought determinedly.

She opened her mouth to berate him, but then she stopped. She barely stopped herself from screaming, instead choosing to take a deep breath. There was no use in arguing over this. She needed proof, and once she had it, she would be able to condemn him.

"I have to go," Aerie finally blurted out, before she hurried out and slammed the door behind her. She didn't even say goodbye.

The old scars from her broken relationship with her father seared against her heart in new disappointment.

He would have to make me doubt.

She was just thinking about going to find Exton to tell him what the General had told her when, as if he'd known she was up to no good, she heard him call out to her.

"Aerie."

The edge in Exton's voice, even from down the hall, was sharp with his own anger. She froze, mid-step, and struggled not to stumble as she swiveled around.

It was an act of self-torment to look into his eyes. "Exton. What are you doing here?"

He crossed his arms. "I could ask you the same question."

"I was just talking to my father," Aerie said, her face flushing over in knowing guilt. She forced herself to straighten her posture. "I'm *allowed* to see him. He is my father."

"I didn't give you permission."

At his words, she was barely able to contain her aggravation. "He's my *father*, Exton. I don't need permission from you," Aerie argued.

"He's a prisoner of war, whether he's your father or not."

"You can't order me not to see him."

"I can, too," Exton replied, stepping toward her. He took her arm and started walking with her away from the General's quarters. "I'm the captain of this ship. You don't get special treatment just because you're my wife."

"Ha! I probably got better treatment as a guest," Aerie bristled. She jerked her hand free of his and pulled back, stopping him.

"Being a guest is different from being an active member here," Exton said, his voice still brittle, even as his gaze softened.

It was not enough to calm her rage. "Maybe I should go back to being a guest, then."

"You can't," Exton pointed out. "There's no escaping that when you joined us—and when you became part of my family—you took on responsibilities. Part of that is a commitment not to endanger our crew."

"Talking to the General was not putting the crew in danger," Aerie snapped. She brightened. "If anything, I'm one of the only people who can really connect with him, and we can use that to gain access to more information."

"You don't know what kind of information we need. And I'm guessing that he didn't decide to tell you about anything Merra was planning or what sort of plan Osgood has to try to destroy us." Exton frowned. "I'd bet anything that you just went in there to satisfy your own curiosity, and little else."

Aerie put her hands on her hips. "I wouldn't have to if you would just tell me," she shot back.

She held her breath as he came close to her, almost trapping her. His face, etched in exhaustion and stress, was inches away. Just as she had before, she met his gaze, willing herself not to lose her courage or her common sense as she stood against him.

"I told you I would tell you later," Exton muttered, softly. "You waited for me all this time, and then the instant you don't get what you ask for, right when you want it, you go running off? There was no need, Aerie."

Aerie was just about to tell him about the General's suspicions about Brock when Exton drew back from her.

"I have rounds to make," he said. "I can't be here all day. I was going to ask you to join me, but I can see that would likely be a bad idea."

"Why?" Aerie scowled, insulted at his disregard. "Afraid that your crew will see that we're fighting?"

"It is bad for morale," he said. His voice was flat, and Aerie knew that if he hadn't been so upset with her, he would've laughed at her remark.

Aerie turned away from him with a huff. "Well, we wouldn't want that," she said. "I'll leave you to your work then."

As she started walking away, he called out, "You're still not allowed to go and see General St. Cloud, Aerie."

"What? Why?" Aerie glared over her shoulder. "I wasn't going to go see him again anytime soon, but that's still taking it too far, Exton."

"You're the one who took it too far," he replied, "by going in the first place."

"I told you, you can't just order me to stay away from my father. That's not how being married works, and even I know that. I can't imagine Tyler forcing Emery to stay away from her family."

"First of all, Tyler and Emery are also not allowed to see St. Cloud without my permission, so there's no need to pretend that you're being treated differently because of that. You are my wife, yes, but you're also under my command as captain."

"Oh, so that's how it's going to go down, is it?" Aerie sniffed. "Good to know you can always pull the 'Captain' card out while we're stuck here."

"It's not like—"

"What? That you don't trust me?" Aerie felt a rush of surprise at her own words.

"Come on, Aerie—"

"No, that's it, isn't it?" Aerie's eyes briefly sparkled with angry tears, before she blinked them away. "I should've known you were lying to me about that."

"Aerie, that's—"

"No. We're done talking, *Captain.*"

Before Exton could say anything else, Aerie stomped off, determined to get away from him.

♦8♦

Exton as watched Aerie stormed away from him, angry and amused and befuddled by her all over again. She was a woman of spirit, and she was beautiful even when she was angry.

She is even beautiful when she is being careless, too, he added silently to himself. What had she been thinking, going to see St. Cloud, especially without him or even anyone else? St. Cloud could have told her anything, and there would be no one stop him from corrupting her mind.

She's already on his side, anyway, he thought, recalling their argument that morning. At this point, it was more prudent to worry that he would solidify her resolve.

With a sigh, he turned back to the duties at hand. After all, duty first," he muttered to himself, not surprised at how wearing the words sounded against the ship's corridors.

As he walked through the ten levels of the *Perdition,* checking in with the different managers and directors and officers, he found himself returning to that mental picture of Aerie walking away from him.

He wondered why it seemed familiar to him.

Granted, it was always upsetting when Aerie did finally allow herself to fight with him; Exton knew she was facing a lot of new changes, with their marriage—probably more than half of that coming from just discovering the difference between a marriage and a unit partnership or cohabitation under the URS—and with trouble from the war.

Exton had hoped that working in the Biovid would distract her from some of the harsher uncertainties of their situation. It wasn't like everyone onboard the *Perdition* was involved with the war; only a couple of levels had been affected by the militant activity. While there were still plenty of people who would gather over whispers and rumors, outside the med ward and the Command Bridge there were few places where the war took priority. Many still went about their usual business, just as they had for the last six years.

As she disappeared down the hallway, ducking out of his sight, he knew that his plan hadn't worked; even the mystical, otherworldly appeal of the Biovid was not enough to relieve Aerie's worry.

Exton made his way through the ship, his eyes taking in the sleekness of the design, the quality of the workmanship, and the blend of the efficient and the elegant.

The dark luminescence of his father's ghost.

Papa didn't have this kind of trouble with Mama, Exton thought. *Or at least, he never seemed to.*

He thought of his father once more, standing in the house back down on Earth, staring out into the far distance as he gripped his Bible.

Exton thought of his mother, recalling her own stubborn gentleness. She was the one who had all the tenderness between them. She was also the one who'd helped him stash his books, the ones Papa didn't like, in a safe and secret place.

When his father would stare out the window, sometimes his lips moving in silent prayers, his mother would come and kiss his cheek, and then head to bed.

There was no doubt his father loved his mother, and that he loved his family. He taught Emery and Exton how to fly, his favorite pastime, and as they grew older, he allowed them to pursue their own interests. Exton worked in mechanics and design, always relishing the days when he could go to the shipyard with his papa, and Emery stayed close to their mother, working with special botany and horticulture curriculum.

He stopped and glanced around, surprised to see he was already halfway through his rounds. *Time flies,* he thought bitterly. Exton nodded to the maintenance crew members he passed on Level 5 as he headed to the elevator.

But as he stepped into the elevator, he decided against going up to the next level. Instead, he pushed the button for Level 10, where his room, and now Aerie's, too, was located.

Whether St. Cloud was telling the truth or not, Exton knew his father did keep secrets—secrets he kept from others, even those closest to him.

"And secrets, while necessary, can destroy you," he murmured. He had faced the darkness alone for long enough, and now that he had Aerie to give his soul some sunshine, he had to be just as brave to face the light as he had been to confront the night.

He wasn't his father. He didn't want Aerie to be kept in the dark, even when it came to sharing the deepest parts of himself.

Slipping past the hustle and bustle of the nearby hangar, Exton slowly opened the door to their room. "Aerie?" he called. "Are you in here?"

Silence answered him. She wasn't there.

He checked the time. *I suppose it's possible she is in the commissary.* Both of them had been running too late to get a proper breakfast that morning, and there never seemed to be an appropriate moment to stop for lunch.

Exton sighed and left the room. Before he could think of what to do next, his comm beeped. When he answered it, Jared's voice came in as clearly as his concern.

"Captain, we found the ship."

"Let me guess. There's trouble," Exton said.

"Yep."

"I'll be right there." He gripped the comm device tightly. *Aerie will have to wait.*

It was never easy to prepare for trouble. But as Exton stepped onto the Bridge, he quickly saw the situation had devolved beyond even his expectations.

There were crew members hurrying around, while Jared was once more talking with Kamalo on the main monitor, and Merra was tapping her foot impatiently against the hard floor. As he came up to the helm, Thora glanced up from her station. "Two minutes to confirm my results, Captain," she called.

"You have it," Exton approved.

"Exton," Merra said, nodding curtly as she came up beside him. "I'm curious as to why you delayed my flight, but I guess I know why now, from just looking around."

It was not the most ideal of situations, Exton thought. He nodded. "Tell me what you know about the ship."

"I doubt I know anything important about it," Merra replied breezily. "I don't have the specifics."

"You've been in Chaya for a long time. Surely you know enough to guess," Exton said, trying hard to have patience. He kept his gaze forward, determined not to let Merra distract him.

"Hey, Cap," Jared called. "Come over here and talk to Kamalo. He's got some news you're going to want to hear."

"What is it?" Exton asked as he hurried over. "Anything good?"

"*Ag*, good news and bad news, I'm afraid," Kamalo said. "We were able to get a partial emergency transmission from the ship called the *Freedom*. It said it was blown off course due to equipment failure, and it was looking for a port."

"So the ship's okay," Exton clarified. "Were you able to find out what they were carrying or who ordered the shipment?"

"I was told it's military," Kamalo said. "I was given a comm address to talk with the commanding officer, but I wasn't able to connect with him. It's classified, though the governor here assures me it's likely just supplies."

"I was hoping for more," Exton said. "We'll try to establish a firm connection with them from up here. Thora, can you handle that?"

Thora nodded as she stepped up beside him. "Absolutely," she said, jotting down notes on her report screen. "But we'll have to wait on that."

"What? Why?"

"There's the bad news," Kamalo reminded him.

"What's the bad news?" Exton asked.

"They've also been picking up warning signals on their

radar."

"Which we can confirm to be accurate," Thora said. Holding out her reports, she pointed to the Eastern Caribbean Sea. "From the flight patterns and the jetstream currents, we've been able to see that the there's another Craftcarrier headed to meet the ship."

Merra came up next to the screen. "Greetings, Kamalo," she said cordially. "It's nice to see you again."

"Always nice to have the Redbird call," Kamalo replied with an easy smile. "They've been telling me stories here about you."

"I'll have to refute them later," Merra said with a small chuckle. "So there's a Craftcarrier headed over to attack the ship?"

Thora, standing on the other side of Exton, cleared her throat. "Yes. The ship is now heading up toward the Panama Canal."

"Excellent," Merra said. "I'll be happy to lead a small force and take out the Craftcarrier myself."

"How exactly would that be helpful?" Exton asked, irritated at Merra's interference.

"Well, for one, it would get me off of the *Perdition*, so you wouldn't have to worry about me anymore," Merra said.

"Unlikely," Exton muttered.

"And it would also help distract the Craftcarrier while we can get a shuttle or two to load up the crew."

"There's no telling how many people are on the—"

"Chaya's settlement is relatively small compared to the other camps," Merra said, cutting in. "I doubt there's more than a skeleton crew on there."

Exton studied the innocent expression on her face for a long moment. "You wouldn't happen to know the details of this? Or have anyone down at Chaya who could give us more insight?"

"Of course I do," Merra said. "I can direct them to Kamalo immediately, if you like. But that won't change the fact that there are people onboard who will need protection from the URS and their Craftcarrier."

Thora sighed. "She has a point. The Craftcarrier has been picking up speed since the ship passed Puerto Rico."

"If we move quickly, we can get to the Craftcarrier before it reaches the Northbound Canal," Merra said. "There's a port there."

"A state-occupied port," Exton reminded her. "Panama might be far from New Hope, but they still have connections."

"If we can take down a Craftcarrier, surely we can protect a small ship like the *Freedom* from the States' reserves." Merra smirked. "Besides, isn't that your calling card? Protecting 'freedom?'"

Before Exton could reply, Kamalo interrupted. "I can send some fighters from here. Ali has been eager to fight again."

"He'll get himself killed with that kind of attitude," Exton grumbled.

"He considers you one of his heroes, so it's on you, *boet.*" Kamalo laughed.

The sound, rich and full of joy, sounded distinctively and absurdly out of place. Exton had to force himself to remain stoic.

"What do you think, Exton?" Merra asked. "Let me go and help them."

He nodded. What other choice did he have? Chaya, even long before the United Revolutionary States officially annexed large parts of the western hemisphere, had been a freedom-loving ally. They had fought off MENACE, the real one, before the URS began to encroach on their territory and sovereignty. The small, stubborn nation of Chaya had drifted off the record the same time the URS began pushing their national narrative, the one which focused so much on surviving that it forgot about living.

Exton even remembered his parents discussing the rumors that the URS wanted to capture Chaya's settlement.

"Alright," he said. "We can send some fighter pilots and a

shuttle, too, to get the passengers off the ship."

"I'll head to Petra immediately, then," Merra declared. "I'll see to the arrangements myself, and I'll chat with Director Ward about seeing to the new arrivals. Kamalo, how many fighters can you send out to meet us?"

Exton was only half-listening as Kamalo and Merra discussed troops. He watched as Thora slipped back to her station, while Jared asked Merra if he could pilot a fighter as well.

He recalled an older conversation down at Petra, one in which Emery had informed that the URS had a significant number of troops in Panama. It was the largest area likely to attack Petra.

There was no way that ship just left Chaya, either. It would have to have left port at least three days ago.

Merra, working with his aunt and Petra's resources, would have been able to maintain her contact with Chaya.

What is she up to?

Did she purposely put citizens of Chaya at risk in order to establish cause for an attack?

He glanced back at Kamalo and Merra, still talking stats and available resources. He wasn't going to be able to verify things here. He would have to check the comm logs at Petra.

"Merra," he said, interrupting them. "Count me in. I'll join you on your way to Petra."

He was gratified to see her face fall, ever so slightly.

"You don't have to go," Merra said. "I can handle this."

"No, you're right. We need to do something, and I can coordinate our forces. It'll help to have the *Perdition* on standby."

"Can't you just do that from here?"

"The *Perdition* is not just about war; there are other activities here which are monitored, Merra. It's better to have my aunt ready to step in and advise, too."

"I don't think that really justifies—"

"We need to do what we can to help Chaya," Exton pushed, glad that it was his turn to interrupt her. "Not to mention to protect Petra. That means I'll want to interview the ship's crew myself, to see exactly what happened."

"Alright then," she replied.

"I'll start the transport prep," Exton offered, before he headed toward the exit. "I'll meet you down in the hangar in two hours. That should give us enough time."

"Fine. See if you can get there sooner." Merra nodded brusquely and then turned her attention back to Kamalo. Before she said anything, she glanced back at him. "You might want to go and tell Aerie," she said. "She hates to be left out of these sorts of things."

I can't imagine why, he thought, keeping his sarcasm to himself.

"I know," Exton replied. "I've got to call Henry anyway, if Jared's going to be leaving the *Perdition*. Never a good thing to leave a ship without a pilot."

♦2♦

Aerie sighed against the window, letting out a partially squashed giggle as her cloudy breath obscured a small portion of the window in the Captain's Lounge.

There were no windows in her room. It was a shame, she thought. Aerie remembered her time in the med ward, when she first came aboard the *Perdition*. There, up on Level 1, the room had plenty of small windows, allowing the patients to look up into the nearby surrounding space.

Perhaps that was what compelled her to come and visit the Captain's Lounge, she mused, feeling like a child again, with her legs crossed and her forehead pressed against the steel-enforced glass. There was some comfort in feeling younger, feeling less burdened with the responsibilities of adulthood.

More likely, she admitted to herself, *I came here because I wanted to feel close to Exton again.*

Even if she was angry at him, she still loved him. And this was his room, the one he'd claimed for himself as captain of the ship.

He'd never had a problem sharing it with her. The Captain's Lounge was where she first felt him kiss her with that devastating passion, where she allowed herself to admit to him she'd wanted to kiss him as badly as he'd wanted to kiss her, where she first felt the strange mixture of vulnerability and braveness as she faced him.

Aerie stared down at the world, remembering the day she'd spent in this same room with Exton as they worked on getting to know each other.

We still only barely know each other, she thought. Of course, there were some days when she barely knew herself.

"Knowing an entire person entirely is likely a difficult thing," she told herself.

But at what point did knowing someone lead to love? And from what point did love allow for trust? Or were they all separate things, or things that all worked together in different ways?

"I don't know what to think," she murmured, looking once more down at the world.

The world was full of mystery and beauty, but it held no certain answers for her. When she thought about God, about what she had heard from Emery and even Exton, and others in the Ecclesia, she wondered if it was the same with him.

Probably, she thought. God was, after all, immortal. Getting to know him would take a literal eternity.

But loving him? Trusting him?

Those were harder questions, she decided. It was easier to answer that question when it was about Exton.

Of course she loved Exton. There were so many things about him she loved, so many good things inside of him she wanted to bring out, and so many bad things she wanted to protect him from. It was hard to pinpoint the exact moment that she knew she loved him, but when she recalled the entirety of their relationship, it was impossible to say when she had *not* loved him. Even as she pictured him in his pirate's costume, with his chainsaw sword ready to cut down her Memory Tree, she could only sigh wistfully.

Another round of her breath blocked up the window. She smiled. Using her finger, she started drawing little squiggles in the foggy mist. She barely registered the sound of the door as it opened.

"I thought I might find you here."

Exton's voice sent shivers up her spine. It was soft and gentle, but still strong. If there was any trace of anger in it, Aerie couldn't find it.

She slowly turned to face him. "Why were you trying to find me?" she asked. He might not be angry anymore, but she still felt the last singes of her fiery temper. "I thought you'd prefer to be alone."

"I've already been alone for a very long time," he told her.

"Is that an excuse for why you're not good at being around people like me now?"

He shook his head. "Not an excuse." He shrugged. "I suppose it's more of an explanation."

"An attempt at one."

"It's vague enough to work," he said. His tone was still light as he came into the room, shutting the door and leaning against the wall opposite of her.

"You might as well tell me what you want," Aerie said after a long moment of silence. "I can't imagine that you would come here just to enjoy the view."

"I'll admit, I enjoy any view when it comes to looking at you," he teased, "but I came to see if you wanted to make another deal with me."

At his words, she felt herself stiffen ever so slightly. He always was good at charming her, she remembered. "I don't want to play any games with you."

"It's not a game. You know I don't do that."

"You're treating our deals like they're some kind of game."

"Believe me, if they were games, I wouldn't play them. There would be too much at risk. And I couldn't bear to think of losing."

"Losing what?" Aerie snapped. "Your pride? Ego? Control?"

"No. Losing you." He straightened. "And everything that comes with you that I no longer want to live without—your respect, your compassion. Your love."

Aerie still felt haughty, but she said nothing. Remembering their earlier arguments, a sense of wariness took hold of her.

"I know it's been a while since we've made a deal," Exton continued, his eyes holding fast to hers. "It seems we're about due."

Aerie felt the coolness of the window glass behind her. "What is it?" she asked. "What kind of deal do you want?"

"If you forgive me, I'll forgive you," he said. When she didn't move to reply, he added, "Or I will promise to apologize, if you promise to apologize. What do you think?"

"It's too hard to tell if I have to apologize first," Aerie replied. "Besides, you already broke our other deal."

"What do you mean?" Exton frowned. "I didn't break any of our deals."

"You said you wouldn't lie to me."

"What did I lie about?"

"You don't trust me." She shifted, jumping down from the window seat to stand before him. She immediately stepped back against the wall, but she met his gaze boldly, daring him to contradict her.

"I do trust you, Aerie." He sighed. "I don't trust your father."

"What about before? Why won't you tell me what happened when you first went to go meet with him?"

"Because," he said, "it's … it's something that would be really hard to explain without going into detail over some of the more unpleasant parts. It's been more than ten years, Aerie, since my father died, and I can still step into that moment like it just happened."

She felt her anger begin to wane. She watched as he clenched his fists, leaning further into the wall behind him.

"That's part of the reason. There are others, too. I don't want to share some of that with you because it is quite terrible, and I don't want to scare you or burden you with that sort of thing."

"I married you so I could do that," Aerie reminded him.

Exton glanced down.

"Maybe if you tell me, you'll be able to feel better about it," Aerie added. "Emery told me once that joy that is shared multiplies, and grief, when it's shared, divides."

"There's always an exception to prove the rule," he replied.

"I don't care. If you trust me, tell me. Tell me the whole story. That's a deal I'll take."

For a long moment, she wondered if he was just going to leave. But then the moment passed, and he nodded. "Alright."

Aerie felt her breath rush out in relief. She didn't even realize she had been holding it in.

Exton uncurled his fists and looked down at them. "There were a million moments that led up to that one," he said. "And I—"

"Wait." Aerie reached forward. "Come and sit with me," she said. With the smallest hint of a smile, she added, "It's a little cold in here."

He came over without question, but there was a visible veneer of happiness in his eyes as he glanced down at her. As they sat down on the floor, Aerie moved his arm so it wrapped around her shoulders, he leaned over and pressed a small kiss on the top of her head. "Thank you," he said.

"Well, go on," Aerie muttered, angry that she felt her face flush over with embarrassment.

"I was fourteen when it happened. As you know, St. Cloud had been acting as a mentor to me in addition to teaching his class and working under Osgood," he said. "Osgood hadn't been the dictator long. There were rumors that he'd killed the previous one, but there was no proof. Some said it was poison."

"I can believe that," Aerie decided, thinking of the man who ruled over the URS as its dictator. She hadn't seen him since her graduation day—the day she met Exton—but the more she thought about him, the more he seemed like the perfect person to murder someone and then try to convince other people that it was only a natural phenomenon of some kind, and that people should rejoice that it happened.

"St. Cloud knew about the *Paradise*. It was almost complete. My father was obsessed with it and kept requesting changes or asking for more contractors to work overtime. One day I saw the blueprint for what he had, and I, as an engineer under his direct tutelage, noticed that he was making a lot of changes on his own. I knew of his requests, but the transition from paper to actuality held vastly different results."

"What did he say when you asked him about it?" Aerie

asked.

"I didn't ask him about it, not really," Exton admitted. "My father and I didn't get along all the time. As much as I liked working with him and his team, which included a lot of members from the Ecclesia, I didn't care about him or his life that much. He was angry at me, I think, for choosing the military over engineering, and preferring St. Cloud's agenda to his."

"Emery told me that you didn't want to join the Ecclesia like she did."

"No, I didn't. I wanted fame and advancement opportunities," Exton said. "I grew up surrounded by religion and community and informality. I didn't see anything wrong with it. I even agreed that there were a lot of good reasons to hold to those beliefs. But seeing that it was outlawed, and that there was no usefulness in it when it came to my career, I really only played along, going through the motions when I felt like it.

"I saw it as something you did differently in different people's company. When St. Cloud became my mentor, it was hard to maintain that line, since I knew he'd at least known about the Ecclesia. I never saw him emotionally connected with it, but then I never knew he had a family he loved, either."

Aerie snorted. "I didn't know that either, especially after my mom left, to be honest."

She felt better at the sound of Exton's small laugh. "Who knew our parents were such complicated people?" he wondered aloud.

Aerie laughed at that and snuggled into Exton's arm further. "Tell me more. What happened after you noticed the differences in the design and the product?"

He heaved a deep sigh, one that seemed to come from the very center of his soul. "After one particularly bad fight with Papa, I mentioned the changes he was making to St. Cloud. He was surprised, likely both at the news and at my anger. I didn't think my father was committing treason—well, that blatantly, anyway; the religion stuff didn't bother me, though, on a practical level. When I told St. Cloud about the changes, he said he would look into it."

Aerie tightened her arms around him, as if she could sense what was coming.

"Weeks passed and he said nothing else about it, so I assumed he found nothing to worry about or it was possible he even forgot about it."

"He didn't," Aerie said. Suddenly, she knew what her parents had been trying to tell her without really saying it: Exton was the reason St. Cloud had ultimately been forced to dispose of his father.

Exton nodded. "No, he didn't. He told me one day that he had special orders from Osgood and he wouldn't be able to meet with me for one of our sessions. He gave me some work to do, but I finished much earlier than expected. I headed home."

"And you saw him confront your father."

"I came home in time to see him put the bullet through his heart. I held him as he bled out. I think I was in shock as much as he was."

At the detached quality of his words, Aerie gripped him harder. "It wasn't your fault," she told him. "There was nothing you could have done."

He gripped her arm tightly and let her hold onto him for a long, silent moment, as silent tears wet his cheeks. "I wish that were the truth," he said.

Aerie brushed the tears off his face. She felt him struggling not to be overwhelmed, as deep breaths wrecked through him.

She lay her head down against his heart, listening as it beat furiously while he fought to regain his self-control.

"You can cry if you want to," Aerie told him softly.

"Not if I want to finish the rest of the story," he replied. He cleared his throat. "The rest of it is much less … less emotional, I guess. My father died, my mother went into a deep depression, and Emery and I were not sure what to do.

I backed away from St. Cloud once my shock turned into anger. I did it trying to be as inconspicuous as possible, telling him I changed my mind, and that I wanted to be an engineer instead of a military figure."

"He must've wondered if you were lying," Aerie said. "I can't see him backing down on something like that."

"He knew I was lying for sure when I managed to lead a group of defectors, mostly from the Ecclesia, but also some who were not religious, either, and steal the *Paradise*. It was, somewhat jokingly, renamed *Perdition* as I took over as Captain Chainsword."

"I already knew a lot of that," Aerie said, thinking it through. "What else did the General tell you when we came here? Tell me."

This was the information she was waiting for. Aerie held her breath as she waited for him to speak.

"He said my father was going to use the *Paradise* to attack the URS and destroy a good bit of the nation. Papa made it big enough to house their entire community and still allow them a generation or two to wait until the nuclear fallout was over, or they could find a new place to settle."

Aerie felt her eyes go wide. "Is that true?"

"I don't know," Exton admitted glumly. "He said there was proof in the old plans of the *Paradise* in the Boötes system. It's another web intranet the government in the military uses. Tyler hacked it for me this week."

"Have you seen it yet?" Aerie hoped she didn't seem too eager to know, since it was something that caused him pain. But she knew, as he'd taught her before, that only the truth could provide the answers that would truly satisfy the seeker.

"No," he admitted. "I'll take a look at it once I get down to Petra."

"You're going to Petra?" Aerie asked. "Am I going too?"

"No," he said. "I was going to ask you to stay here and watch over the ship for me."

Before she could argue with him, he reached down and caressed her cheek. "I need to leave it in the hands of someone I trust," he told her.

"I don't know," Aerie said. "I'd rather be with you there, if you need support or something. I mean, I don't want to believe the worst of your father, but … but if it's true, then you might need me."

"I always need you." He sighed. "That was part of the reason I hesitated to tell you about all this, to be honest. I didn't want you to be disgusted and leave."

"I'm not married to your father," Aerie said. She looked up at him and grinned. "Just like you're not married to my mother."

He gave her a tired smile back. "Well, that's true. I never thought I would think that your parents deserved each other, but stranger things have happened."

"Emery says that God is a god of miracles," Aerie said. "Maybe my parents finding each other is proof of that, in some weirder way."

Exton laughed this time, the sound hard against the ever-present pain she knew was still inside of him. "You are my miracle," he said. "So I guess I should take comfort in the fact that someone I hate as much St. Cloud has one, too. Maybe there is hope for me yet."

"You've already known there is," Aerie told him. "You just keep forgetting, for some reason."

"I married one smart lady." He reached down and pulled Aerie up against him, then he pressed his lips against hers. "I love you."

"I love you, too." She shifted her legs, allowing her to sit in his lap comfortably. "But you are *not* going to kiss me so I'll forget we're in the middle of an argument."

Exton fisted his hands into her hair. "Oh, we're arguing? About what?" Before she could answer, he kissed her again. And again. And then again.

"Come on, we need to talk about you heading down to Petra," Aerie said, as she pushed her hand against his chest. His mouth gently brushed against hers once more, and before she could regain her senses, they were all swept up into passionate silence. Her fingers curled around his shirt as she felt her brain turn to mush.

♦10♦

Exton squeezed Aerie's hand in his as they walked through the corridors of the *Perdition*, heading for the hangar. He watched, amused, as she used her other hand to straighten out her hair.

"You don't have to worry about your hair," Exton told her with a smirk. "You look beautiful."

"That's easy for you to say," Aerie grumbled, pulling free from him so she could pull back her hair into a haphazard ponytail.

He grinned shamelessly. He knew she was right; it was much easier for him to come away from their interludes with less incriminating evidence. Looking at her now, he doubted it would be hard for anyone to see she had recently been kissed, and quite fervently. Her lips were swollen, her hair was mussed, and her eyes were still steamy.

Of course, that could have been due to frustration as much as passion, he admitted. She was still determined to talk with him about his plans.

As if on a cue, she turned their conversation to that very topic. "Now, tell me why you're going to Petra. Even if Tyler did find something for you, shouldn't you be here to watch over my father?"

"That's not the only reason I'm heading down," Exton replied as they reached the elevator. "There's been some developments. Another Craftcarrier seems to be moving to attack."

"Petra's in trouble again?" Aerie dropped her hands from her hair.

"No, not Petra this time. There's a ship that deployed from Chaya that's caught the attention of the Craftcarrier. My analysts have agreed it's trouble, and Merra has offered to attack the carrier while we stage a rescue mission."

"You're not going to be flying, are you?" Aerie asked.

"No." Exton shook his head. "I'm going down to Petra to help coordinate the mission, and to watch over your mother. She came to negotiate St. Cloud's release today, and she was upset with me for denying her request. I want to make sure she's not up to something."

"She'll like the attack mission, probably." Aerie sighed as they stepped in the elevator. "Before we left for the *Perdition*, I talked with Alice some. She was impressed with my mom's flying and leadership skills."

Exton watched as Aerie's face filled with worry. "I can vouch for her skills. I'm sure she will be okay."

"I'm more worried about you," Aerie said. "I know my mother can handle herself. I mean, really, she's been doing it for a longer time than I even knew about. I don't want you to get hurt."

"I'm not actually going to be fighting alongside her." Exton took her hand once more, lacing his fingers through hers. The joy of feeling the delicate strength of her hands and the smoothness of her skin against his rough palms washed over him.

Love was certainly a strange thing, he thought. How could something so deceptively simple shift the whole world from under his feet?

Loving his family as he was growing up was both a choice and a duty. He was grateful that his parents were, for the most part, easy to love; they loved him, and he loved them back. Emery was a sister and a friend, and he knew he would not be half the man he was without her. His family life had been stable and full of jubilance, allowing the darkness of each human heart to easily slide by the wayside. Between his family and their friends, Exton had thought he'd learned everything when it came to love.

Aerie was still so much of a surprise to him.

Exton watched her as she bit her bottom lip, glancing all around as they headed toward the shuttle at the end of the hangar. He pulled her hand up and kissed her knuckles. "I trust you, Aerie," he said. "The *Perdition* will be in good hands while I'm gone."

"What should I do?" Aerie asked. "I don't know how to

be captain."

"You're not going to be captain, don't worry. You're only going to be my representative onboard. The rest of the crew can handle the job without my interference, but if they need help, I'll be able to tell you what to do."

"Okay. If you're sure."

"I'm sure."

"I'd still rather go with you," Aerie admitted, "but I am glad you trust me." She gave him a bright, brave smile. "I will do my best."

He nodded. *I'm glad she's okay with this. Even if it's the first time we'll be apart since we found each other again …*

At the thought of physically leaving her, being so far away, he faltered. Exton knew it was a precarious situation. There was an attack underway, and a counterattack and rescue mission to follow. He would be concerned with these issues while keeping watch over Merra, making sure she wasn't up to anything mischievous, and he had the chance to check into St. Cloud's claims about the Boötes system at the same time.

Out the corner of his eye, he saw Merra coming down the gangway, and Tyler was making his way from across the runway.

Exton took a deep breath. He decided it would be okay to leave Aerie on the *Perdition.* She would be safe. His crew knew how to handle themselves and act accordingly. They would support Aerie and help facilitate any needed action.

After all, he had put Henry on duty, he had called up Rhodey to be on attack watch, and, for no other reason than unavoidable self-compulsion, he'd alerted Reverend Thorne and his brother, Don, to inform the Ecclesia. He had included limited details to them, to prevent any possible information leaks; overall, he was still reluctant to directly ask for divine intercession, but he still wanted them to know what was going on.

He barely heard Aerie greet her mother as he tightened his grip on her hand, allowing himself a long moment to memorize the feel of her palm against his, her fingers twined between his own.

It was only when Tyler clapped him on the shoulder and nudged him that he forced himself to let her go.

"I'll see you soon," he promised. "I'll be in contact shortly. Keep your comm with you at all times."

"Roger that, Captain," she said, giving him a small giggle.

Then he reached over and cradled her face between his hands, resting them on the silkiness of her hair and the softness of her cheeks. "I love you," he whispered, gently pressing his forehead against hers.

She closed her eyes against the tender embrace. Before he pulled away, she reached up and pressed her lips into his. "I love you too," she replied, her voice breathless.

Exton released her and slowly backed away. He felt a robotic quality in his legs as he walked up the ramp to the shuttle's cockpit; each step was only a little easier than the one before, as he slowly stepped out of the light of his life and into the darkness of the world before him.

But, I'm not going out to join it, he reminded himself. *I'm going out to face it, head on, and find out the truth. Whatever it may be.*

He waved at Aerie as he started up the engines, and then he turned away from her. He didn't want to watch as she headed out of the hangar.

"I can take care of the flying," Tyler offered.

"No thanks," Exton said. "It'll give me something to focus on besides Aerie." Before Tyler could tease him, he asked, "Is everyone here?"

"Jared just stepped in," Tyler said. "Give us a couple of moments to settle in."

"We don't have much time to play around."

Merra laughed. "Don't worry. I think we can make time for safety. Patty is already working on scouting out some pilots for us down in Petra. She said Aerie's friend Brock is happy to join us."

"I hope you can avoid telling Aerie," Exton said. "She's already worried enough for you."

Merra blinked in surprise. "Well, that's sweet," she murmured, before focusing her attention on strapping herself into her seat.

As Exton gave the reports to the crew and they headed out into space, another rush of protectiveness came flooding out of his heart. The earth had seen happy days before the war, Exton thought, and he would do his best to bring those days back.

But first, that meant dealing with other things.

Quiet stillness seemed to permeate through the landscape of Petra's community as Exton sailed through the nearby skies. It was early in the morning for them, but, just as it was with the *Perdition*, there were always some people running around. The rest of the area seemed dark with sleepiness; the outlines of the mountains and hills, and even the Memory Tree, seemed to blur into the night with an unspeakable sigh.

Once he landed the shuttle, Exton wasted no time in seeing Merra off as she headed to meet with his aunt and reminding Jared of the rules when it came to working with the other pilots and their fighters.

His only deviation from his plan was to go and see Emery along with Tyler. And since family was family, he didn't mind postponing his search through the URS military system for her.

"Do you want a moment to see her alone first?" Exton asked as he walked with Tyler.

Tyler laughed. "You might need to wait longer than a moment if you let me," he joked. "I haven't seen her since your wedding."

"It's only been a little over two weeks."

"You're already despondent after leaving Aerie on the *Perdition*," Tyler replied. "I'm looking forward to seeing how you last for two weeks."

"It might not take that long," Exton told him. He held up

the file Tyler had handed him earlier. "This is all I have to check, and then I can go back."

"If you say so," Tyler said. "But I'm more than willing to bet you'll stay here for longer than that."

"Why?"

"You don't like St. Cloud, and you feel like you have to practically babysit Merra."

"How did you know I'm here to check on her?" Exton said with a frown.

"I can just tell sometimes. I've known you for a long time, even before we committed treason against the URS." Tyler grinned. "Besides, you were looking like you were ready to just strangle her while we were on the shuttle here."

"She seems too eager to engage in warfare."

"She is. I think she's bored, partly."

"And the other part?"

"Ugh. The other part is understandable if disconcerting," Tyler admitted. "I think she likes watching the URS scramble around. After all those years she had to play along with them, living up to their imposed rules and how she left everything behind so she could keep her family alive, I can't exactly blame her for enjoying their increasing desperation."

"Even if it's at the expense of others' lives?"

"She'd probably argue they weren't living that great of lives anyway." Tyler shook his head sadly. "Tough situation."

Exton only nodded, but he was pretty sure Tyler missed it as Emery came around the corner.

Exton caught the split-second look of surprise on her face before it transformed into joy. "You're here!" Emery cheered. She raced up beside them, throwing her arms around Tyler. "I'm so happy to see you."

"I can tell," Exton remarked with a wry smile.

His younger sister gave him a teasing smirk as she looked over Tyler's shoulder at him. "You'll get your hug in a moment."

"I'll pass," Exton said. "Or maybe I'll defer the pleasure to Tyler."

"Noted," Emery replied with a laugh as she gave Tyler another squeeze.

"I have business to discuss with you later, but I'll need both of you to keep tabs on Merra while I'm preoccupied."

"She's back already?" Emery sighed. "I was hoping she would stay away longer."

"She hasn't been too bad, has she?" Tyler asked. "She seemed to be okay when I was with her."

Emery made a face. "Oh, she's not terrible, I guess. She's been occupied in the spare office Aunt Patty gave her, but she comes out and does her rounds. She always seems to have Marcus around to distract me when I want answers from her. Then she asks questions and has ideas that would make even Aerie suspicious of whose side she is on."

"Well, we know which side she's on," Exton said. When Emery and Tyler both gave him the same surprised look, he sneered. "Hers."

"Ha! True enough." Emery crossed her arms over her chest. "Aunt Patty doesn't seem to question her loyalty."

"Your aunt's glad for her expertise and friendship. She was your mother's colleague, too. I imagine running this place is actually quite lonely." Tyler shrugged. "I wouldn't put it past her to see Merra as a friend. She is pretty reliable."

"Still, Tyler, I'm going to need you and Emery watching her while I'm working through the Boötes system stuff," Exton said.

A wary look came into Emery's eyes. "Are you sure you don't want me to help you sort through all that?"

Instantly, Exton glared at Tyler. "Come on, man. You didn't have to tell her."

"We were worried," Tyler said, his voice sheepish as he took a step back. "I mean, I was worried. I figured I'd run the information by her. Besides, Emery's involved, too."

"If St. Cloud is telling the truth, you're not the only one who has to deal with the fallout," Emery insisted. "I'm his daughter, just as you are his son."

"But you're not the one—" Exton stopped. *You're not the*

one who got him killed in the first place. He felt his fingers flex involuntarily, as fear and shame snapped through him viciously.

Emery arched her brow. "I'm not the one who set out to avenge him? So what? I still mourned him."

Exton shook his head, breathing out slowly. "Well, since you know," he said, "I'll need to have the rest of Papa's stuff."

"I've set up a small office for you near the hangar," Emery said. "I moved all his stuff in there."

"Does anyone else know?"

"No. I did it myself," Emery told him.

"Are you sure you should be doing that?" Tyler asked. "Some of those boxes are heavy."

"It's fine," Emery said, brushing the matter aside. "I'm pregnant, but I'm still healthy. And I am certain of that actually, since Serena has been checking on me constantly."

"Aerie's sister?"

"Yeah. She said she's never seen a pregnant patient before," Emery said.

"I'm glad you found an inauspicious way to keep watch over her." Exton thought of Aerie's older sister. She reminded him of Merra much more than Aerie did. He knew it would be a mistake to underestimate her.

"She's been getting along with the other med techs nicely," Emery said. "Tyra's been supervising her under Aunt Patty's direction. She's been earning her keep just nicely. She even seems to have softened toward us somewhat."

"Somewhat."

"Exactly." Emery smiled ruefully. "She's disappointed that she's not encouraged to date her patients, and her bedside manner has been cited as 'overly friendly.'"

"I can imagine," Exton grumbled. "Aerie told me Serena's a bit of flirt. I was almost hoping she would start dating Brock while they were stuck here."

"Almost hoping?" Tyler asked.

"I was actually hoping he would leave, period," Exton

admitted. "I am indebted to him for rescuing Aerie from the URS, but he wore out his welcome after he tried to escape with her."

"In his defense, he said he was taking her away so she wouldn't get hurt by the Craftcarrier attack," Tyler said. He gave Emery a wink. "I know how easy it is to want to be the hero."

"He's still more of a villain in my book."

"He's been doing well here," Emery said. "I've been coordinating the reports from our managers. He's been working with Aerie's brothers a lot. Nothing seems to be out of the ordinary."

"What are they doing?"

"They fly out supplies or work in maintenance," Emery said. "We don't have a lot of shuttles or fighters here, so we're making sure we can keep up what we have."

Exton frowned. "Did Merra or anyone else say anything about a ship coming here?"

"A ship like a shuttle or—"

"A ship like a boat, on the ocean."

"Oh." Emery shook her head. "You mean like the one that's gone missing?"

Exton glared at Tyler again.

He threw up his hands. "What? She's still your Coordinating Director," Tyler said. "She's allowed to hear this sort of information."

"Just as long as other people don't," Exton reminded him.

"Emery and I have our own comm frequency. I set it up myself. You don't have to worry about that."

"Fine." Exton rolled his eyes. He knew better than to try to argue technology with Tyler. Exton turned back to Emery. "What about the ship?"

"Nothing," Emery said. "Aunt Patty hasn't heard anything, either. At least, not that I'm aware of, but I'm pretty much aware of everything here."

Exton knew that was no exaggeration. He was glad to

know Emery was excelling at her job. He'd wanted to keep her somewhere safe while the war was going on, and while Petra still had its vulnerabilities, the *Perdition* was more isolated by being up in space.

The downside of individualism, Exton thought wryly. He had more appreciation for Merra's critique of their movement since the *Perdition* and Petra had been attacked.

"If I hear anything otherwise, I'll let you know right away," Emery said. She nudged him on the shoulder. "Now, go ahead and get started on your project. Tyler and I will take care of the rest."

"You do make a good team." Exton ruffled her hair affectionately, surprised to notice it was much longer than he remembered it. "Is your hair getting longer?"

"Prenatal care," Emery explained, pushing her tresses back down. "It hasn't grown that much."

"It's almost to your shoulders. You usually keep it shorter."

"I'll take care of it later if it bothers you so much."

"I like it," Tyler said.

Exton shrugged. "If you're happy with it, that's all that matters, really. I just didn't realize … "

Emery laughed. "Time goes by quickly. "Sometimes, anyway. It usually goes by quicker when you're not paying attention. I'm more than willing to bet you've had other, more demanding things to pay attention to than the fact that I'm pregnant and my hair has gotten longer."

"I guess so," Exton said. He thought of his project, the one where he would have to go through all of his papa's things, searching through the Boötes system for the URS files, trying to find evidence for the truth. Beyond that, he still had the war and his community to handle. He sighed. "I can't let that get in the way of family, though."

Emery patted his arm. "I'll make sure you don't," she promised. "And I'm willing to bet Aerie will keep you in line, too. That's the first job of the wife, you know."

"What's the first job of the husband?" Exton asked.

"To give the wife a job to do," Tyler answered. He smiled wickedly. "So the wife will have something else to worry about."

"Excuse me?" Emery cleared her throat. "What do you mean by that?"

"I think I'll take off now, so you can discuss that amongst yourselves," Exton said, struggling to keep his laughter down. He knew Emery wouldn't appreciate it, especially since he had done exactly that, by leaving Aerie to act as his representative on the *Perdition.*

♦11♦

"Are we almost finished for today, Bruce?" Aerie glanced up from the foliage, looking for the large, familiar shadow of her friend and coworker. She was surprised, and slightly irritated, to see that he was nowhere in sight.

Sighing, she stood up and began to brush the dirt off her uniform. She studied the stains on her outfit ruefully, knowing Olga would give her one of her famous "you can do better, Aerie" expressions.

But, Aerie thought, *it would be nice to see Olga again.* She was one of the first people she met when she first came to the *Perdition*, and she enjoyed her company. Since Exton left the ship two days ago, some of the other crewmembers had been almost too kind, checking up on her every so often. Aerie could tell some of it seemed forced, though she would likely guess that it was more out of guilt than actual force.

Sometimes it was just too kind, too, she thought, remembering how tired she'd been, staying up late to have dinner or heading all over the ship for visits.

Not that she minded the time with others. She appreciated their efforts to make her feel welcome and supported as the wife of their captain. But she still missed Exton, and even dinner with Olga and her husband, Sean, and four of their six children was not enough to relieve her heart of that burden, even if her attention had been necessarily diverted.

"Bruce?" Aerie circled around, glancing over the pots of smaller trees and plants, hoping to catch sight of Bruce's flannel jacket.

"Over here, Aerie," he called back a moment later.

Good. I was just about to give up and leave. Aerie carefully made her way over to the small clearing, where Bruce was checking the pH levels of the water system.

"Sorry 'bout that," he said. "Didn't mean to leave you for so long."

"Oh, it's no trouble," Aerie assured him. "I just noticed

the shift's almost over."

"If you want to head out early, you can go with my blessing," Bruce said. He gave her a kind look.

"I would appreciate it," Aerie said. "I wanted to go and see how things were on the Command Bridge. I know Henry said that my mother's attack force launched a few hours ago, and they should already be at the rendezvous point. I figured they would have something to report by now, anyway."

"'Tis not a problem," Bruce assured her. He waved her away. "Go. I'll finish up here and I'll see you in here tomorrow."

"If you're sure."

"I'm sure." Bruce's beard twitched in amusement. "The Biovid will still be standing if you leave a few moments early. And since you're doing more than one job, it's only right that you should consider it a break."

"Well, when you put it like that, I don't have any reason to worry at all." Aerie giggled. "Alright. See you tomorrow."

She returned Bruce's wave as she headed toward one of the exits. Upon reviewing her destination, Aerie decided to head over to the forward portside exit. It was a smart move, she thought. It would get her closer to the front of the ship where the Command Bridge was located, and it would allow her to walk through the rest of the Biovid.

She passed through a small clearing, where there was a fresh hill of soft soil piled. Aerie recognized it immediately; it was where Exton had planted the Memory Tree in the ship, after he decided to save it for her, and before he had his lumberjack crew transfer it down to Petra.

Aerie took a moment to gaze at the dirt. It was dark and dry, and part of her wondered if she could use the area to plant some new seedlings.

Footsteps approached her from behind, startling her.

"Forgive my intrusion, Miss. I didn't mean to startle you."

Aerie turned to see the familiar old face of Reverend Thorne, the leader of the Ecclesia on the *Perdition.* Exton told her before that he always imagined himself to be a father figure of sorts, and he was more insulted than appreciative of his efforts.

It must have been something Exton saw that she didn't. Aerie gave the reverend a kind smile. "No problem."

"You look more like your mother when you smile," Reverend Thorne said. "I see St. Cloud's features otherwise."

Aerie laughed, nervously running her hand through her hair. "My mother's hair is darker," she said. "I always thought I looked more like her than my father."

"You have his eyes. And his penchant for the adventurous."

"I never thought of him as adventurous," Aerie admitted.

Reverend Thorne shrugged. "Most children don't know their parents very well, outside of the role of being a parent," he said. "But you need not look any further than your mother to see St. Cloud's sense of adventure."

"That's sweet, I guess," Aerie murmured. She frowned. "Have you talked to him recently?"

"I talk with him every once in a while," Reverend Thorne said. "Everyone likes having company. My brother and I go to visit him sometimes."

"Did he tell you I went to go see him?" Aerie suddenly felt suspicious. Exton had warned her he didn't trust Reverend Thorne much; it wasn't that he wasn't a good man, but there always seemed to be too much that the older man knew and he wouldn't divulge. It was irritating, Exton had told her.

She had been hesitant to accept that; she knew Exton had a different perspective on a lot of the people she met on the *Perdition*, and the Ecclesia especially.

On some level, she wondered if Exton didn't blame them for his father's death, too.

"No," Reverend Thorne answered. "I like to walk through the Biovid. We call it Eden here, sometimes."

"My mother had a small garden she called Eden, too," Aerie said.

"Yes, I know. She loved to garden. She said it was

something peaceful to balance the rest of her out."

"I remember her doing it a lot before she died—I mean, before she left the URS," Aerie corrected herself.

"She did a lot of it at Chaya, too," the reverend said. "She stepped down to work with your family unit soon after you were born, but she always came and volunteered with our scientists. Merra has been a great asset to Chaya."

"What about to the Ecclesia?" Aerie asked. "Has she been good to the Ecclesia, too?"

"We are a religion," he replied. "Our religion doesn't fall based on one person." He smiled. "Or at least, it's not based on Merra. But to answer your question more fully, she has never failed to call upon us to help people in need."

"I can't tell if that's a backhanded compliment or not," Aerie said.

"It is true that we can be overburdened, like any community," Reverend Thorne said. "But we can always pray."

Aerie nodded. "Have you been praying for Exton and the war?"

"Of course."

"Why hasn't God answered your prayer for that?" Aerie asked. "It's still going on."

"That's a more complicated question that it seems," he said. "Are you sure you'd like an answer?"

Aerie thought about the Command Bridge, and how she had a job to do. But … she was curious. "I can spare a few moments," she replied.

"Okay. Then let me start to answer your question by asking you another one." Reverend Thorne took a step closer to her. "Have you ever played the piano? Or have you learned music of any kind?"

"No," Aerie admitted. She had never been comfortable with music in the URS, and even if she'd liked it, she would never have admitted it.

"There are some pretty basic elements to music," the reverend said. "When you look at a sheet of music, it's written out in a special way. There's the melody and the harmony, and the scales of the different notes."

"Uh-huh," Aerie said, nodding. She squirmed slightly; she didn't know much of anything about music.

"Just imagine for a moment that the melody is all you hear to a song. The melody is often considered the most pleasing part of the song. It tends to lead the rest of the parts.

"Now, the harmony is lower than the melody. Its notes are deeper, and its accents, without being in combination with the melody, seem incomplete."

"Okay." Aerie sighed. "I'm not sure how this is tied into war."

"Think of the melody as joy and goodness, and think of the harmony as depth and darkness. The melody by itself can be lovely, but with the harmony, a new level is added to the final product. The lower tones contrast the good, giving them even more emphasis, and the higher pitches become weighted, keeping the melody grounded. Music is a product of living between worlds, with the ideal and the real coming together to form something even more beautiful."

Aerie still felt confused. "I'm not sure I get it."

"We see God as the grand composer," Reverend Thorne said. "All of the good and evil in this world are still subject to him, and as humans, we are still subject to it and the consequences of sin. The high notes—the good, the beautiful, and the truth—and the low notes—the pain, the sadness, the uncertainty—all of this is still within his power to redeem. It's not a perfect metaphor, since I know plenty of excellent harmonies just as beautiful as melodies. But this war, while it is unpleasant and we cannot understand its full impact, can still bring about goodness. We believe that has been the answer the Ecclesia has been given for now."

"I see it more now," Aerie said, nodding slowly. "Maybe I should've had you use a plant metaphor."

"That would've been better, seeing as you are Merra's daughter," the reverend said. He chuckled. "I thought mine was pretty clever, still. I didn't want to forget it."

"You seem to have a pretty good memory, from what Exton's told me," Aerie said. "You recognized me as Merra's daughter right away, didn't you?"

"Not *right* away," Reverend Thorne said. "But nearly so. I have talked with her before. She was at Chaya for many years, and it is one of our favorite camps to visit."

"Why didn't you tell him about her?" Aerie asked. "Why didn't you reveal me when you did realize the truth?"

"I am bound by my vows to silence when it comes to certain things, such as secrets I am entrusted with," the reverend explained. "Your husband has little appreciation for that."

"No, he wouldn't like that," Aerie agreed. "Not when information can save people's lives."

"Some secrets can still protect people," Reverend Thorne said. He nodded toward her. "That's part of the reason I kept yours. I knew you deserved a chance to see our world. And once I saw Exton's reaction to you, I had a feeling you could help him, too."

Aerie said nothing, knowing that he was right on both accounts. She was grateful for his silence on her behalf, allowing her to stay onboard the *Perdition* and find out the truth of the world herself. And she knew Exton felt the same way—he'd called her his miracle.

"If you want," the reverend said, "come to the sanctuary sometime. We have plenty of people who can discuss your questions there."

Aerie nodded. "I will," she said. She brightened. "I know Olga and her family would like that. They've invited me before."

"Well, then hopefully I'll see you there soon," Reverend Thorne said. His face wrinkled even more as he gave her a wide smile. "It was nice talking to you."

"Thank you. It was nice talking to you too," Aerie replied. *Even if I didn't get all of it.* As she watched him walk away, Aerie suddenly wondered if he'd known Exton's father, too.

That's a discussion for another time, she thought, remembering she had her own task to accomplish. She turned and headed back toward the exit, determined to get to the Bridge before the shift change.

♦♦♦♦

"I'm pulling up the latest information right now, milady."

Aerie smiled and nodded, almost watching in wonder as Henry and the other crewmembers worked in unison around the controls. There were so many buttons and screens, Aerie thought as she admired the Bridge.

The computers and stations crowded the immediate area, but Aerie knew there were even more areas where different protocols were undergone. There was the Records Room, where she knew they kept all the files and monitored the ship, and there were conference rooms for group meetings. Engineers and techs working on everything from electricity to systems to sanitation would come in once in a while, but mostly it was the same cast of crewmembers who greeted Aerie as she entered the area.

The first day she showed up as Exton's representative there had been a lot of curious glances and some staring. But by the second day, most people seemed satisfied by their captain's choice of ambassador.

For her part, Aerie was relieved. She knew she hadn't struggled the same ways that the crew had. They had been in space, hovering around the world and circling the moon for nearly seven years. Some of them had transferred from Petra or other ally camps around the world from time to time, but she knew from the few times she'd been there that only a few had done that. And of those, many of them had come back after a few years or even a few months.

Henry was one of them. For the past three years, he had been Jared's understudy, working on learning how to pilot the ship. He told Aerie he came back to the *Perdition* after he got bored being on Earth.

"At least up here, you know you're doing your part to

resist the evil the world has to offer," he'd said. "Being down there, it was too easy to forget to fight, especially if I worked somewhere comfortable."

Aerie had been impressed by his dedication, especially for his young age, and she said so. Henry had instantly transformed from ally to friend when she told him. He even gave her the "milady" moniker as an affectionate tribute.

He glanced at the screen before him. "Well," he said. "It looks like they're making their first run."

"I've established the comm," another voice spoke up from a station behind him.

"Thanks, Thora," Henry called.

"I'm not Thora, I'm Greer," the woman retorted.

"Apologies, Greer." Henry shot her an apologetic look. "I'm used to Thora."

"I've noticed." Greer smirked back. "This is the third time today I've had to correct you."

"Apologies, apologies. I'll make it up to you if I do it again."

This seemed to satisfy Greer, who sat back in her chair and smiled brightly.

Aerie put a hand up to her mouth, hiding her own smile at the exchange. Even in the midst of war, people still found a way to make friends.

"Well, milady," Henry said, turning back to her, "if you'd like to listen in, we can give you a headset."

"Oh. Well, thank you." Aerie hesitated as Henry tossed her a headset. She hadn't worn one since that awful two weeks when she was stuck in the URS, back when she was having trouble remembering the *Perdition.* Part of her was repulsed by the headset itself.

The other part of her told her other people were counting on her to be brave.

She put the headset on. Instantly, she fell into the world of warfare. She glanced at Henry, who nodded toward the monitor, where she could see the satellite feeds from the area.

Different leaders were chatting with each other across the

lines.

Aerie instantly recognized her mother's voice, and she even thought she recognized Jared as he talked over the comm.

"Headed toward the target," Merra said. "No interference so far."

"Any chance this will be a clean discharge?" another pilot asked.

"There's always a chance." Merra's voice was cheery enough. "Still, let's make sure the shuttle can pick up the crew."

"What about the ship?" Jared asked. "Aren't we going to try and save it?"

"No, too risky," Merra said. "We're going to cut our losses and chalk it up to Chaya's irresponsibility this time."

"But—"

"But nothing, Jared," Merra insisted. "We're at war and the target is close to a State-held base. We're lucky we haven't seen any missiles coming our—"

Blip! Aerie glanced up as a blinking light suddenly appeared on the monitor. The instant it turned red, she gasped.

"Bogies, headed your way," Greer said. There was a catch in her voice. "Multiple POs, most centered at zero degrees north, seventy-two west."

"Targets locked," Merra responded. She started calling out orders to her small crew, working on a group strategy.

Aerie turned away from the main monitor, too worried to watch. She turned toward Greer, who was typing so fast her fingers blurred over.

"Where are the missiles coming from?" Aerie asked. Her classes on military combat never seemed more further away as she watched the bustling room around her.

"Close to the old city of Cartagena," Greer told her. "It's been a quiet base for years, but they've been moving around a lot since Panama became more active a couple of years ago."

"What's going on at Panama?" Aerie asked.

"It's a military base for the URS right now," Greer said. "It's been hit hard by the ecological disaster, and by the fact the country has been compelled to rent out the space to the States."

"What's the state of the canal there?"

"The Panama Canal? It's still being run, though there are not as many shipments as there used to be. No one likes to travel by sea under the cloud cover. It's too thick, there's a lot of discharge, and it's turbulent. Too easy to get off course."

"Like Chaya's ship."

"Exactly." Greer gave her a big smile. "Even with all the algorithms we have in place from up here, it would be hard for one of ours to navigate the oceans well."

"Bogies are headed toward the ship," Henry called.

"Intercept," Merra ordered. "Intercept, now!"

"Doesn't the ship have scrambler tech?" A new voice came over the intercom. Aerie was surprised to hear Brock.

"I'd rather not find out the hard way," Merra told him. "Henry, what's our status? Where's our critical target?"

Aerie watched, transfixed, as red lights lit up the screen. More missiles were being shot out different areas south of Panama.

"The URS Craftcarrier is oh-five-four from your current position," Henry called. "It's moving slower than it was before."

"Maybe with all the missiles launching, it's working on gaining a strategic advantage POV?" Cal retorted. "*That* would slow it down some, especially considering who it's dealing with here."

"I doubt the carrier's the one attacking us," Merra said. "The missiles are first-line defenses we likely triggered just by passing into the area. The Craftcarrier defenses are less economic."

Dorian's voice chimed over the intercom. Aerie knew it was his voice, rather than Cal's, because he was always the less obnoxious between the two of them. "We need to split up. Some of us should to stay here and protect the ship, while some of us need to go and take care of the Craftcarrier."

"Good idea," Merra commended, her voice proud. "I'll lead the attack on the Craftcarrier. Jared, take command of running interference."

"Roger," Jared replied, his voice eager.

"Dorian," Merra called. "You and Cal protect the ship. The shuttle should be there in a few moments to get the crew."

"We're better marksmen than protectors," Cal said, interrupting. "We'll follow you. Someone else can stay with the ship."

"You need to learn your place, Cal," Merra said. "That is an order. Brock, come up and flank me. Stay close on the approach."

"The Craftcarrier has stopped its advance," Henry said. "It's hovering now, over the old Colombian air space."

"Would that be where the missiles are coming from?" Aerie asked Greer.

"Huh?" Greer looked up at her. "Oh. It's possible. But it's more likely the missiles are ground attacks from the angle we're reading. The Craftcarrier has stalled."

Aerie brightened. "Can you open the comms?" she asked. "We might be able to communicate with them."

Greer raised her eyebrows. "That's a good idea," she said. "Henry, get this girl a station."

Henry jerked around, surprised, but didn't question Greer's order. He hurried Aerie to the far side of the room. "Here, you go," he said, booting up the monitor.

Aerie hurried to get to work. *I guess on some level,* she thought, *it's good I went back to the URS long enough to figure out their comm system.*

She almost laughed at the thought of her old boss, Director Anand. He would be pacing the floor, slowly and loudly going mad if he knew she was just about to use her skills against the URS.

Serves him right, for making me work late and overtime so much.

Aerie quickly dismissed her cranky boss from her

concerns and began pulling up the Comm Sec information. She was surprised to see that it was full of static; only a few frequencies were clear for use in the South American region. She switched over her headset to block out her mother's forces and focused on finding the URS.

"Well, at least this will be easy," she told herself, already flipping through the open channels with a hailing frequency. She could tell she was getting a little rusty, but her confidence was quickly returning.

Her mood elated at once as her hailing frequency was answered.

"Identify, identify," she called. "This is the *Perdition*, calling for identification and cease-fire."

A voice answered her a few moments later. "Identification response. This is the *Morgan Soromsky*. Cease-fire declined."

Aerie froze. She might have cheered, if the voice didn't sound so familiar …

"This is General Dubois speaking."

Aerie said nothing as Gerard continued to talk, listing off his titles and accomplishments. Her voice caught in her throat as her nightmares came rushing back over her. Her hands shook slightly, as the memory of lightning racing up her body exploded into her mind.

Aerie breathed in deeply, trying to remind herself Exton was relying on her, just as her mother's crew was, and just as the rest of the *Perdition* was now, too. There was no time for a panic attack, no matter how much she wanted to curl up into a ball and scream.

She was about to abandon the project when he spoke again.

"Well, it's good to know that you're a coward, just like your precious captain," Gerard snarled.

Aerie sucked in her breath sharply, angry as much as she was afraid. Was it possible he'd recognized her voice?

"Your crew has two minutes to leave this airspace, or we will bring them down ourselves. We will not tolerate another theft of our military prowess," Gerard said. "And this time, we will have *our* revenge. You can tell Captain Chainsword that's a promise from me to him, directly."

He laughed, cackling along as the static overtook the airway once more.

Aerie forced herself to sit back in her chair. She glanced over at Henry and Greer and the others as they moved through the Command Bridge with purpose and grace. Aerie suddenly felt like an outsider, as if she didn't belong with these people. She was broken and confused and terrified.

How do they do it? Aerie wondered to herself. She was at a loss as to how they managed to cope with the pressure, especially when people's lives where hanging in the balance.

She blinked, watching as another round of missiles were launched on the monitor.

What am I supposed to do now?

Aerie thought about calling Henry. She glanced down at the computer controls in front of her, ashamed to wonder if she would be able to explain what happened without looking like a fool.

An idea struck her as she studied her controls. She switched her comm line over to her mother's forces.

At the first crackle of connection, Aerie felt a wave of relief wash over her. "Mom? Can you read me?"

"Roger, Aerie," Merra called. "What's up?"

"Gerard's on the Craftcarrier," Aerie said. "He's further south from your position, but he seems to be coordinating the mission."

"What did he say? Tell me, specifically. Hurry." Merra grumbled and let out a string of curses. "Sorry. This isn't easy, Aerie."

"Right." Aerie sighed. "He said you have two minutes to get out of there or he would bring you guys down."

"Ha!" Merra laughed. "I'd love for that sleazy maggot to try."

"I … I'm worried." Aerie blurted out the truth before she could think about whether or not she would regret it.

"Don't worry," Merra told her.

As if it was that easy, Aerie thought grimly. "But don't you think—"

"Hang on, Aerie. Something's stuck. I'm going to have to complain to Henry some. Exton told him to check the systems for bugs before we left."

"What—"

"No!" Merra's cry penetrated the deep recesses of Aerie's heart, and then went silent as the line was cut off.

"Mom?" Aerie felt her heart pumping as furiously as she moved her fingers, trying to type in the frequencies.

"I've lost the comms," Aerie called. She glanced up to see Henry was staring at the screen as the seven dots representing the fighters went dark.

"Something's happened," Greer called. "We've lost the comms, and several fighters are down."

"Did we miss any bogies?" Henry asked. Aerie could hear the strain in it as he glanced around at the others.

Another crew member stepped forward. "No, sir," he said.

"Where are the fighters?" Aerie asked. *Where is my mother? And Brock? And what about my brothers?*

Henry didn't look at her. He bowed his head.

Greer put her head in her hands.

"We lost them," Henry finally said.

"How?" Aerie asked, using her anger to steady herself. She leaned over the surface of her desk, fighting to find a way through the situation.

"I don't know. But the ships are down." Henry glanced up at the monitor again. The satellite imaging was cluttered with clouds and smoke.

Aerie gripped her fingers into the controls. "Let me see if I can communicate with any of them," she said slowly.

"Aerie." Greer's voice was soft. "I don't know what you think you'll find, but—"

"No buts," Aerie snapped, shoving the headset back on. She rerouted the comm and tried different frequencies, all in the hopes of hearing familiar whispers inside the impersonal static.

A crackle on the main monitor came alive. Two lights flickered back on, indicating the fighters were back online.

"Report in," Henry called.

The static hummed for a long moment, before Brock's voice came in clear. "It's Brock," he said. "I'm heading back to base."

"Brock!" Aerie called. "You're alive!"

"Aerie? Is that you?" She could almost see the surprised look she knew was on his face.

"Brock, what happened?" Henry cut in. "What happened to the rest of you guys?"

"Cal and I are still flying," Brock said. "But a static bomb discharged, and then the radios needed to be booted up. Before I could reconnect, the rest of the crew went down. Dive-bombed. Some hit the water. One hit the *Freedom.* A couple hit ground, but I don't know where exactly. I flew over them."

"The ship is on fire, and it's sinking," Brock said. "The Craftcarrier is currently firing at it more."

Henry sighed. "Call off the rescue shuttle," he said. "We can't offer any protection now."

"I don't know if the crew will be able to get out into lifeboats. I'd keep watch for them from there."

"We will," Henry pledged. The defeat in his voice was too painful for Aerie. She cringed as he turned back to Greer. "What is your analysis, Greer?"

"Kamikaze," Greer said in hushed tones. "Forced kamikazes."

"How would that happen?" Henry asked, his tone torn between confused and skeptical.

"I'm working on a theory," Greer said. "Give me a few moments."

"Well, I don't know what happened," Brock offered. "I wasn't able to talk to the rest of them when it happened. If Cal wasn't flying next to me, I wouldn't know he was alive, either."

"Did any of them eject?" Aerie asked. "Did you see anyone alive?"

"No one other than Cal and me." Brock paused a moment before he added, "I'm sorry, Aerie."

Aerie shook her head and ignored him. She sat back down and tried swapping out frequencies, working to enlarge the range and trying to cut off interference, all while trying not to think about how very much she wanted Exton there with her.

♦12♦

As he stared at the screen in front of him, a cold sense of dread tingled down his body, chilling him all the way to his fingers.

I can't believe he was telling me the truth.

As he read and reread over the notes and numbers, Exton felt his chest convulse, as if his father's ghost—a sad, almost benevolent figure in his mind over the last decade—had stuck a knife into his back and twisted it.

He had spent the last several days, as Merra and her selected volunteers prepared for their venture and headed out, sorting through the States' military intranet and finding his father's matching scribbles. In between breaks for rest and food, he had been able to piece together a tentative timeline of the *Paradise* and its construction, and his father's evolved designs. As an engineer, he was able to read the notes from Osgood and other military leaders, asking for different elements to be included or the plans adapted a certain way. There was nothing explicit about his father's defection.

Not until his note.

2122528—see Lu for details. Tell Exton about Ark.

The Ark was placed below the Biovid, only able to be accessed through the Biovid. The Ark on the ship was where different seedlings and animal DNA had been gathered for preservation and study. Exton already knew that, thanks to Emery and others, and their work within the Biovid.

He'd only gone down there a few times in all the years he'd been onboard the *Perdition.* It had been nothing to assume that the URS had ordered the Ark to be built. The room was small, cold, and impersonal; animal DNA was stocked in small test tubes, labeled with terrifying efficiency, while seeds were vacuum-sealed and packed away.

After his papa's funeral, Exton remembered his mother's voice, full of venomous trepidation, as she told him the URS wanted to use the *Paradise* for destruction rather than research.

He almost envied her, that she was gone, too. She didn't have to process a fresh, foreign layer of grief.

He looked down at the blueprints and mock-ups of the *Paradise* prototype again. He knew, as he held the prints between his fingers, that the official URS design hadn't called for the Ark. His father added it of his own initiative. According to the dates, that note was the first one that mentioned the Ark, and there was no reason for anyone other than a member of the Ecclesia to call it that.

"Lu" was proof of that—it was an easy reference to Luke 21:25-28, where the end of the world was foretold by Jesus himself. The references to the signs in the stars, distress among the nations, the seas full of roaring waves while men's hearts were full of fear—all of these things, before the people were told to "look up, for redemption is at hand," seemed to point to deliverance.

Exton sighed, done double-checking his data for the last time.

What does this mean?

He knew part of the answer: He knew he didn't know his father as well as he originally thought, for one. He also knew that St. Cloud had just cause in punishing him, even if shooting him seemed excessive.

Did he really have to kill him for all of this? Exton shook his head. He knew the URS officials could use brutal tactics. St. Cloud would have likely had to threaten to use his family or torture to get the job done.

Papa was the best engineer in the whole nation, he thought. It would have been necessary to get him to cooperate. Maybe St. Cloud was, in his own way, being merciful.

"No!" Exton slammed his fist down on the Bible before him. "No, I will not vindicate him for this."

He knew instinctively that he still wasn't ready to forgive St. Cloud, either.

Exton heard St. Cloud's voice, almost as if he was whispering in his ear:

You've ruined my plans before, but I won't let you ruin them again.

St. Cloud had been working to overthrow the URS government. He told Exton that he had worked alongside Merra for years, as they undermined the power of the government.

It didn't make sense. Why kill his father? To show his loyalty to Osgood? St. Cloud was never working for Osgood.

"He had another plan," Exton murmured, thinking of his old mentor's ways. There was always a plan and a backup plan, and at least two different motives for every movement. As much as he had a feeling St. Cloud was content to stay onboard the *Perdition* for the meantime, he knew there was likely another reason for his motive, too.

But what was it this time?

That is what I need to figure out next.

There was a quick, sharp knock at the door. Exton nearly fell out of his seat when his aunt opened the door to the darkened office. When he saw she was looking down at him with a hard look, he almost dismissed her.

Exton could never clearly remember a time when his aunt seemed genuinely happy, and from the look on her face as she came into his makeshift office, he knew today would be no spectacular exception.

But then she caught his gaze, and he was shocked to see the sheen of unshed tears.

He was in no mood to share in her obvious despair; he had enough of his own to work through. His father's old Bible was in his hand, the old pages musty with settled use. He had been flipping through the book, often switching between it and the Boötes web, almost as often as he switched between fear and anger and despair as he sorted through the information.

But family was family, and he knew what it meant to do his duty. "What's wrong?" he asked, his voice croaking from fatigue.

"The mission failed," Patty told him.

Exton blinked, uncertain if he'd heard her correctly. "What?"

"The mission failed," Patty repeated. "Aerie's been trying to reach you for several hours now."

"Aerie." At the mention of her pain, Exton forgot his own. He stood up, banging his knee on the edge of the desk as he straightened. He ran his hand through his hair, scowling as he realized it was getting scruffy again. "Where is Emery?"

"She just came on duty," Patty said. She stepped to the side, allowing him out of the room, and then walked beside him as they started down the hall. "I have been reporting in with different leaders around the globe, trying to figure out the next move. We lost a good bit of our fighters along with our pilots."

Agony ran through him, thinking of all the people he would never see again. "This is terrible."

"Agreed, from a personal and practical standpoint," Patty said. "And we lost some of our best fighters. Aerie's mother and her one brother among them."

Dread came over him once more. He forced himself to ask the question. "Dead or missing?"

Patty pursed her lips. "Most likely dead, but we are not sure."

"I doubt Merra's gone," Exton said. "If anyone could survive an attack from the URS, it would be her."

"Reports are coming in that suggest it wasn't from the URS exactly."

"What? Who else would it be from? MENACE hasn't really existed in decades now." Before he could comb his mind for other nations and communities capable of attacking his people, Patty interrupted him.

"It seems it was sabotage of some sort," Patty said. "The fighters all went down on their own, according to the analysts on the *Perdition*. Petra's forces are examining the fighters who did come back."

"Down … dive-bombed?"

"Yes."

Exton frowned. "The survivors?"

"Aerie's other brother and Brock Rearden are the only

two that survived, so far as we know."

Brock. Exton mentally consigned Aerie's old friend to the grave, and then thought that was too kind. Brock had to know something about this, Exton thought. "Call them up. I want to talk to them."

"They're both in the med ward," Patty told him. "But just to warn you, you might want to find out what happened first. Neither one of them seems to have much of an idea."

"Of course they wouldn't," Exton grumbled. "Where's Tyler?"

"Comms. He's waiting for sunrise in New Hope. He wanted to contact his family today for updates. His parents have been keeping tabs on Osgood for us."

"Oh, good." Exton nodded. He knew that he was one of the leaders around Petra and the *Perdition*, but any of his success at it stemmed from his family and their organization. He had forgotten, lost in a world of URS military schematics and blueprints and notes, just how demanding it was.

They walked on in stifled silence before Exton let out a weary sigh. "Do you think the war will end soon?"

Patty shrugged. "There is always a war going on, Exton. It never truly ends, so long as people seek power. All that changes are the players."

"I agree. But I meant this war, the one we're fighting."

"I know what you meant." She gave him a quick smile. "Honestly, it depends. If we can take out Osgood, we can end it much sooner."

"I doubt that," Exton muttered, softly enough his aunt wouldn't hear. Exton knew that with St. Cloud out of the picture, it was Gerard who was next in line to take over as dictator. While he didn't know who followed him, he had a feeling it was going to be nearly impossible to maintain order. The war might be over soon, Exton thought, but there would still be plenty of battle lines to be drawn.

They entered into the forward command center, and as soon as Exton entered, Emery called out to him.

"There you are," she said. "Here." She tossed him a

comm device. "I should have made sure you had one when we left you the other day. Aerie's on the line. We have more information to discuss once you're done."

"Thank you." As Exton stepped off to the side of the room, he thought about telling Emery he would be quick. But he didn't want to take anything away from Aerie, especially while he was so far away from her. He didn't know what she needed, but he had a feeling he wouldn't be able to do much, other than listen while he was on Earth and she was onboard the *Perdition.*

"Aerie?"

"Exton."

He nearly grimaced at the sound of her voice. It was flat and sad, deflated and defeated—nothing like the sunlit music he'd come to associate with her presence. "I'm here," he said. "How are you holding up?"

"I'm trying to be strong for the crew. I don't think I'm doing a good job," Aerie admitted. "I'm worried about my family."

"I know." He sighed. "I'll see what I can find out from down here. I haven't been briefed on everything just yet."

"Gerard is onboard the Craftcarrier," Aerie said. "I was able to intercept a message from him."

"He is?" Exton frowned. "Are you okay? I know hearing from him couldn't have been easy."

"I'm fine."

"I'm glad to hear that, and I'm glad you told me. With Gerard onboard the Craftcarrier, it's likely we'll hear from them soon. He never liked to wait. That was part of the reason he escaped the *Rothsburton* before, too. He's quick to fight, but he's also quick to run away."

"I wonder why Osgood promoted him then," Aerie scoffed. "He seemed to enjoy his time torturing people in the Reeducation Center."

"If I had to guess, I would say it's your father's fault."

"Seriously? Do you think *everything* is my father's fault?"

He would have laughed if he didn't think she was

seriously concerned. "My judgment on this matter is entirely impersonal," he told her. "St. Cloud told me that Osgood has a history of not trusting people, even him. He likely promoted Gerard in hopes that he would help watch over your father. Gerard and the General were never close."

"I guess that makes sense. Sorry."

"It's okay."

There was a moment of silence, and Exton hated that he couldn't see her. They were both strained by their circumstances. It was hard enough to guess whether or not she was sad or angry with him.

"I'm sorry to disturb you," Aerie said.

He thought he heard a sniffle.

"I know you have your own family crisis at the moment. I don't want you to think that you were wrong to leave me here to help."

"Of course I don't think that." He gripped the comm. "No one could have expected this, Aerie. I certainly didn't."

As he said it, he realized that this was the first big mission failure. The reality of it hit him hard all over again. They'd lost friends as well as family. *Jared had been among them,* he remembered. He struggled to try to find something to say to Aerie, and he suddenly regretted leaving her.

"I'm going to have Tyler come and get you," he said. "He's on duty right now, but I'll have him come and get you and we can be together."

"No. I don't want to fail you up here," Aerie said. "I'll be okay. I already lost my mom once, didn't I?"

"We both know this is different," Exton replied, wishing that he didn't sound so angry. "Please, Aerie, just come down here. I need you, too."

"Did you find something?" Aerie asked.

Exton thought about the papers and notes he had been able to see on the older designs of the *Paradise*. "I'm still searching," he finally said. He felt awful, but he couldn't tell her the truth about what he'd found just yet. "Papa had his codes for things and it's been years since I worked with him."

"I see."

They lapsed into silence once more.

What else could he say? Exton wondered. There was no use in telling her how strange it had felt to leaf through his father's Bible; to find the little notes tucked into its pages from his mother; to see the secret prayers his papa prayed, for him and Emery and their future; to feel the anger and confusion and desperation of his father's spirit as he held the old leather book between his hands. The only other thing he could tell her was what he saw in the Boötes system, and there were too many ties to his own past to choose where to begin.

"I miss you," he said instead.

"I miss you, too." Aerie's words were a soothing whisper over his wounded soul.

"I'll call you back when I find out more," Exton said. "I'll make sure I have a working comm."

"Thank you," Aerie said. "I'm going to check in at the Biovid. I'm going on duty here in a little while."

"Don't overwork yourself."

"I won't."

"I love you."

"I love you, too." Exton was reluctant to click off their communication, but he had no choice when Aerie left the line. He sighed. Had it really been two whole days since he'd last seen her?

A month ago, not seeing her was the purist form of torture. Thanks to St. Cloud, he had once more been taken prisoner by his past.

Exton shook his head, disappointed in himself as he headed over to Emery once more.

"Updates," he requested.

"What? No, 'Hi, sis, how are you?'" Emery's attempt at levity fell flat as she handed him a file. "Here. This is the information we have so far. Brock and Cal are being checked over in the med ward. They've talked with some onboard the *Perdition*, but I know that they didn't survive unscathed. We don't know where the rest of our fighter pilots are, if they survived. But it doesn't look good."

"Did we miss enemy fire? Anything slip through our radars?" Exton glanced through the file, thinking back to the different diagrams on the Boötes web as he glanced through the data. There wasn't anything he could remember that would have prevented Petra or the *Perdition* from picking up their deployed weapons.

"No. There was only a quick system disruption from what we could tell. Aerie talked to me a little while ago. She said Greer told her it was a forced kamikaze."

"How though? Did they hack the fighters?"

"It's possible," Emery told him. "But it's terrifying to think they would have had the access to everything they needed to do that, especially without our forces noticing."

"They already do that, through NETech," Exton reminded her. He paused as he put it all together in his mind. "What about the NETech? Could that work? Aerie told me before they can send signals to their pilots."

"I don't know if that would work either. But it is an idea." Emery glanced down at her desk. "Cal and Brock were the only ones who didn't crash."

"When we went to go rescue Aerie, one of her brothers told me that he'd turned off his NETech," Exton said. "I don't think it would be hard for Brock to do it. He was in their military classes with them, even though they were older students."

Emery tapped her fingers against her desk thoughtfully. "It would make the most sense," she agreed. "I can send a message up to Aerie and ask her about it."

As she reached for the communication settings, the line beeped. "Impeccable timing," Emery murmured.

Exton gave her a playful grin. "Just in time to ruin your plans."

Emery answered the call. "Petra, main control station, Director Caldwell speaking."

"I was told I would be speaking to the captain." Kamalo's

voice came over the line seconds before his picture popped up.

"I'm here," Exton said, nudging Emery over. She gave him a quick frown, but she hurried to the side.

"Ah, there you are. I have the information you requested about the *Freedom*."

"I'm guessing from your tone I'm not going to like it," Exton said with a sigh.

"Doubtful. The *Freedom* was never scheduled for departure. It seems a small group of pro-State rebels took it. They were apparently headed for Panama in hopes of joining the URS military outpost there. The States has a reserve base there."

"We know that from the missile launch sites," Emery said. "We've located what we believed to be the main holding, just southeast of the Canal, inside Old Columbian borders."

"So we attempted to rescue a captured ship?" Exton shook his head. *This was a bad mission from the start.*

"It gets worse. The ship was carrying weapons. Chaya's research specializes in weaponizing the environment. It looks like it took off with several ecobombs in its cargo hold."

"Great," Exton muttered. "Emery, can you see if Henry has been able to pull up any data on the attack? We need to know if any of the bombs were activated."

"Roger that," Emery said. "I'll go see Aunt Patty. She should be in contact with the *Perdition* now."

"Thanks." Exton glanced back at Kamalo. "That will give us something to look for, definitely."

"I heard something else," Kamalo said. "I thought you should be aware of it."

"Well, you have my attention. Go on."

"There's talk that the Redbird was behind the ship's capture. It is said she orchestrated it and made sure that it was carried out. My sources are highly credible, especially now that the disruptive faction we had here is upset that their shipmates are lost at sea."

Exton felt his hands turn into fists. "You mean that Merra is the one who is behind this?"

"I knew you did not trust her, *boet.*" He gave Exton a sympathetic smile. "It seems you were right about her. Some of the friends I've made here have a saying from back home: He who marries beauty marries trouble. And there is no denying you have a very beautiful bride."

Exton nodded. "I wouldn't think the trouble would be proportional to her beauty," he said, making Kamalo chuckle. "Or that it would be her parents causing the trouble."

"Every generation leaves trouble for the next one to take care of," Kamalo said. "It cannot be avoided. Doing nothing would only make it worse."

"It can get worse if we do something, too," Exton pointed out.

"True, true enough," Kamalo replied. "We often find enough trouble on our own, too. Even if you left the world in perfect peace, it wouldn't take long for it to fall back into broken apart."

"Very optimistic of you to say, Kamalo. I can see why you left the URS."

Kamalo chuckled. "True. But don't despair, *boet.* I've known of you for a long time. I know you are very careful about these things. No one is perfect. We must do the best with what we've been given."

Exton nodded, grateful for the encouragement even if he didn't have time to fully appreciate it. "Thank you. Keep me posted on any updates."

"Roger that."

Exton cut off the signal and hurried to catch up with Emery. He would have to let them know to look for evidence that an environmental bomb of some sort went off near the Panama Canal, in addition to looking for survivors.

He recalled his earlier suspicions about Merra's involvement with the ship at Chaya. Kamalo's information seemed to prove that he had been right.

It wouldn't be the first time she's done something underhanded to get what she wanted, he thought, thinking of Aerie's younger brother, Marcus, and how she had manipulated so many into believing she had died in order to save him.

This time, however, he found nothing to admire about her maneuvering.

He forced himself not to think about what he would yell at Merra the next time he saw her—if he saw her at all.

He thought about Merra's determination. If she knew the ship was being run by forces loyal to the States, why did she insist on going to rescue the ship? And why would she risk their fighters?

"Merra likes to play a deep game," Exton reminded himself. He thought about the time when he'd gone with her to attack the captured Chaya outpost. She knew there were weapons; he'd personally attacked one of the shuttles that carried an ecobomb. Merra had only admitted it, too, he recalled, because that was the reason Chaya had been attacked and captured in the first place. Their weapons research had accidentally poisoned their water resources—

"Poison." He heard himself say the word aloud and nearly stumbled.

If she did organize the capture of the Freedom, *along with the weapons onboard, she could have been going to make sure that the weapons went off near the States' military station.*

The ecobombs would go off, and the URS would be in a very vulnerable position. With the last of their major forces depleted, it would be easy for the defectors' forces to go in and call for their surrender.

But what about the fighters? What had happened to them?

Exton turned around and headed in the direction of the med ward. He didn't want to further indebt himself to Brock, and he didn't want to deal with Aerie's belligerent brother, but he needed to know what had happened.

As he passed through the hallways of Petra, a sense of angry urgency took a hold of him. The St. Cloud family seemed to be destined to give him trouble, no matter where he turned.

It looked like General St. Cloud had been telling the truth about the Boötes system, if not about his father as well. Merra was tied to secret operations, and now she was missing, along with one of her sons. He was going to go and try to talk with another one. He would probably run into Aerie's sister, too, while he was there.

They are all a headache in and of themselves, he thought grimly. *Thank God I don't have to worry about Aerie causing me trouble right now.*

♦13♦

Aerie rubbed her eyes, exasperated as she sat up in her bed. She was tired, but she was also tired of trying to fall back asleep. It was the middle of the night shift, or probably past the middle of the night, and even though she had managed to get a few hours of sleep, she was unable to find real rest. She glanced at the cold, empty sheets next to her and sighed.

Exton was still down at Petra, and it had been hours since she'd talked with him. She was tempted to go to the Command Bridge to see if there was any news.

A wry smile crept onto her face. She was interested about what was happening, but she had a feeling there was more bad news than good news waiting for her. It was good to see her curiosity had some limits, she thought.

Unlike my courage.

Aerie felt her face flush over in shame as she recalled her reaction to the battle. From hearing Gerard's voice again, taunting them, to listening as her mother's voice died away with her comm line, and possibly the rest of her as well, Aerie knew she had a long way to go before she would be battle ready.

"I'm already battle weary," she muttered to herself. Disgusted by herself, she pushed the sheets away, reaching for a new uniform. She decided to force herself out of bed and head down.

It was the same strategy she'd used when she was in school. If she was frightened of something, she would ignore it and force herself to confront the fear. Aerie had already lost her mother at that point, and the only hope she had for feeling like life was worth living at all was to earn her family's esteem.

"Ha," Aerie muttered under her breath, laughing at her own naivety. Even with her family safe at Petra, they hardly considered her little more than a nuisance. She wouldn't be surprised if she found out they had contingency plans, if the URS were to somehow invade the community and capture them; she could see them now, telling Dictator Osgood how everything had been her fault, and they were only collateral damage caught in her extensive treason.

No, it wouldn't surprise me at all.

She almost wondered if Brock would say the same, but decided against it. He would offer to work off his punishment, most likely, or he would find a way to get out of it altogether.

He did that a few times in school, she remembered, thinking of when they were several years younger.

She'd fallen behind on one her training courses. Even years later, she felt the shame of that moment, as her instructor—a faceless blob in her memory, with a name just as lost—yelled at her, degrading her in front of the rest of the class.

Aerie still recalled the recoil at the outburst. It had been close to the anniversary of her mother's disappearance, and Phoebe, her new unit director, had recently moved into the unit. Her focus had been off since meeting the woman who was supposed to replace her mother. Aerie thought about how happy she was that Phoebe's young appearance, along with her dark brown eyes and her black hair, contrasted sharply with Merra's dark red hair and bright green eyes. Merra's intelligence was unmistakable; Phoebe's was subtle, and Aerie shuddered, wondering how much of a mistake she had made in largely ignoring her.

Her mind never let her settle on Phoebe for too long. Aerie knew she hated the situation, and it was far from Phoebe's fault she was in it. Since she'd met her, Aerie was certain she barely said more than ten words to her at a time. Phoebe, for her part, never seemed willing to push herself onto Aerie's affections; she mostly gave Aerie her silent frowns of disappointment, her slow shakes of her head, and her long looks of resignation. Most everything that Aerie remembered about her was how she would stare off into space. From the expression on her face, it seemed as though Phoebe was taking in everything even as she removed herself from everything simultaneously.

Maybe that's what she really was doing, Aerie thought. Some of the short remarks Serena made about their stepmother, about how she would avoid interacting with Aerie because Aerie reminded her of Merra, suggested Phoebe was not as harmless nor as inobservant as Aerie had tried to believe.

Either way, the instructor had no sympathy for her plight. Phoebe's addition to their unit was routine, and therefore nothing worth failing over.

Aerie blushed, thinking of how Brock had come up to stand beside her as she was reprimanded. When the instructor asked what he thought he was doing, Brock said he was protecting his team. *Those are the rules, Brock had insisted. We can only be as strong together as we are weak individually.*

Aerie had been further angered by the implication she was weak to notice he was interpreting the rules differently than the instructor was.

Now, she saw Brock's kindness; it was just cruel enough he got away with it, and flexible enough she was never sure if he was on her side or not.

He'd always been a stickler for rules, Aerie thought with a grimace. She slipped her feet into her boots as she turned to face the door.

With a sigh, she forced herself forward, her feet noticeably dragging as she headed toward the Command Bridge. The moment she stepped out of the elevator next to the small forward room, she knew it was better that she had come.

"Aerie?" Henry's usually kind voice was sharpened with disconcerted concern as he greeted her.

"Henry." Aerie nodded to him cordially, but inwardly she knew something was going on. She knew that tone, whether it came from Exton or her father or someone else; something was going on, and they hadn't wanted her to know about it just yet.

She glanced around the room, watching as other familiar faces and some new ones hurried around, taking notes and studying the screens. Back at her station, Greer was pressing her hands against her headset. Aerie briefly saw, out of the corner of her eye, her knuckles were white. She turned back to Henry. "What is it?"

"I was just coming to get you," he said. "We've been hailed from Panama. The Lieutenant General wants to talk to you."

"Gerard?" Aerie felt his name brush past her lips involuntarily, as if the name itself was mocking her.

"Yes." Henry's young face seemed to age a decade as he looked at her. "The night commander, Phil, told me the lieutenant general said he won't talk to anyone else."

Aerie vacillated between disgust and fear as Henry added, "We are hoping he'll tell you about the fate of our fighters, milady."

Disgust won out. "Put him on over the speakers," Aerie ordered. "That way everyone can at least hear him."

"We don't have to hear him to know how despicable he is," Henry remarked, offering her a comforting pat on the shoulder. "Come this way."

Aerie steeled herself, bracing for the moment when she would hear Gerard's sadistic drawl once more.

"Aerie, my friend," he said. "It's nice to know your mother wasn't lying when she said you were on the *Perdition*."

Aerie swallowed a gasp at the news. She breathed in quietly as she asked, "You've talked with my mother?"

"Of course. We've had some lovely chats while I was deciding what to do with her. You can speak from personal experience how *electrifying* making my acquaintance can be."

"I want to talk to her," Aerie demanded, trying to keep her voice from shaking.

"There's no need for that," Gerard said. "She's quite comfortable here down at the URS's Panama base. We have every luxury onboard here, including the ones you were fortunate enough to experience at the Reeducation Center."

Aerie froze, shuddering at the thought of her mother, trapped and helpless, in a prison as she waited to be tortured.

Gerard interrupted her thoughts as he continued to gloat. "There are even some here which you weren't able to enjoy before your rather surprising exit," he said.

"I escaped," Aerie said, reminding herself she was safe from Gerard as much as she was reminding him.

"Ha! We let you go," Gerard insisted. "We could have stopped you if we wanted."

"What do you want now?" Aerie asked. "You have my mother, or so you say."

"It's not a matter of what I want," Gerard replied. His voice was smooth, but from the gleeful tone, Aerie knew she had asked the right question. "It's a matter of what's right."

"What do you want?" Aerie asked again. "I don't want to waste my time here talking to you."

Henry nudged her arm. "Keep him talking," he whispered. "Greer's locking onto his position as we speak. If we can track the *Morgan Soromsky*, we'll have an advantage."

"Since you're in a hurry," Gerard said, "I'll just tell you. If you want your mother back, you need to turn General St. Cloud and Exton Shepherd over to me."

"What? No."

"I have it on good authority that your mother is still the love of your father's life, even more than the State. He will do anything for her, even give his life."

"Who told you that?" Aerie asked.

"Your stepmother," Gerard replied simply. "Director Phoebe has been placed in your mother's care. She was very grateful for the chance to make your mother's experience here even more … *exciting.*"

"I still don't have a reason to believe that you have her," Aerie said. "I would never agree to a deal with you, even if you think General St. Cloud would agree to it."

"He will agree with it," Gerard said. "I know him well."

"Even if he does, Exton won't," Aerie pointed out. "I don't know why you think he would."

"Then you'll never see your mother again. Shame, too, since you just lost your brothers in that mess of an attack too, didn't you?"

Her blood ran cold at the thought of Dorian. A moment later, after the ache inside lessened its grip on her heart, Aerie straightened. Cal had returned to Petra, but Gerard didn't seem to know that.

"I'm sure you know as a former Comms Sec worker that rewiring the NETech for suicide missions was necessary," Gerard said.

So, it was the NETech. Aerie glanced over at Henry. He gave her a slight nod and a sympathetic look.

"How did my mom survive then?" Aerie asked.

"She managed to eject herself," Gerard said. "I happened to be the one who picked her up."

"I doubt you did any of the heavy lifting." Aerie felt herself starting to grasp for anything, anything that would give her a position of strength over Gerard. She glanced over at Henry again, hoping he would have something for her. He only gave her a thumbs up, and Aerie knew he had managed to get the location of the Craftcarrier.

That's not going to help me now.

"Well, I ordered it, so it's technically the same thing," Gerard said.

"I want proof that you have her. I want to talk to her. I'm not going to do anything until I'm sure you have her and she's unharmed," Aerie said. She glanced at Henry again, but he had turned his attention toward the monitors.

Silence clicked over the comm line for a long moment.

"Hello?" Aerie frowned. "Hello? Are you there still?"

"Aerie?" Merra's voice came over the comm, and Aerie almost fainted from the shock.

"Mom," Aerie whispered back. *Thank God, she's alive.*

"I'm here," Merra told her.

"Are you alright?"

Aerie could see the smile of self-assurance on her mother's face. "Of course I am. I know how to take care of myself, Aerie."

"Did anyone else … make it?" Aerie asked.

Before Merra could reply, Gerard's voice cut in once more.

"I'll give you three days to reconsider your decision," Gerard said. "Until then, you have some thinking to do, I'd say."

The line went dead.

♦14♦

Exton slammed the door behind him carelessly. "I can't believe this," he muttered.

He had hoped—foolishly, he now knew—that in seeking Tyler out, he could permanently delay a conversation with Cal and Brock. Finding Tyler had taken him longer than he'd liked, but in between updates on Meredith and the rest of Tyler's family, Exton had not been able to find any useful information about what went wrong in the rest of the fighters, or if anyone else was thought to have survived.

Grudgingly and gingerly, he made his way down to the med ward to have the conversation he'd hoped to avoid.

Only to be turned out of the room by Petra's own medical team as they finished checking up on Brock and Cal's conditions. He was told he would have to wait while the techs were finished removing some of the steel-enforced glass that had managed to wriggle its way up Cal's arm. It could take up to an hour, Tyra said.

Two hours and multiple rounds around the ward later, he was still waiting.

"Well, it's real, whether or not you like it."

Exton narrowed his eyes over at Serena, as she leaned against the counter in the med ward. "You might look like Merra," he said, "but she would at least be a little bit nicer about telling me no."

Serena smirked. "I'm glad to hear there are significant differences between me and my mother, thanks. Besides, I don't know what you're complaining about. It's not me that's stopping you," she said. "It's your other medical supervisors."

"You're part of the team now, too, whether you like it or not."

"Well, I don't like that I'm stuck on the same 'team' as you," Serena countered, "but I don't actually mind helping people who need it."

"Well, good. You might learn to disregard me one day." Exton frowned at the door, where, only moments earlier, he'd been told that he would have to wait while the patients were in the process of getting treated for their injuries. "Just like some of my medical staff has, apparently."

"I thought you were in charge," Serena said. She turned and started putting away the med supplies she'd brought in from the hangar.

Exton knew by just looking a new shipment had come in from some of their traders.

"I am, which makes this all the more irritating," Exton assured her. "I wanted to ask Brock and Cal some questions. Both of them seem more worried about their cuts and scrapes than giving me potentially vital information."

"Well, they did answer your questions and the others on the way back from Panama," Serena pointed out. "They probably figure that they've done their part."

"I just wanted to make certain," Exton said.

"They just lost their comrades in arms," Serena replied. She continued to unpack the supply cart she had behind her with methodical precision. "Among them was my mother and another brother. You might as well let them rest a bit longer and give them a day."

"Why aren't you taking the day off?" Exton scoffed.

"The URS has done a brilliant job in training me," Serena said. She gave him a sneer, but it was a sad one this time. "We are trained in the medic professions to disregard human life. We fight for it, and we strive to keep it, but we are taught not to get emotionally attached to it."

"That doesn't sound much different from the military," Exton said, thinking of his time under St. Cloud's tutelage.

"Of course it's different. In the military, you're putting your life on the line to either save someone else or destroy someone else. It's hard not to think of life as vital, and to even take pride in it," Serena said. "But as a doctor, or nurse, or combat medic, I can only help someone survive. It's not me in the end who has the final say. So there's no emotional connection."

"I'm surprised you would choose it then," Exton said,

making her turn around.

There was a stricken look on her face.

"You seem too willing to emotionally engage in things here."

"I guess it is nice," Serena admitted after a moment of silence. "I wasn't allowed to do this at home much. I would sneak out with my friends to loosen up before."

"We still need you to do your job, and to keep the peace as much as possible with the people here," Exton said. "But other than that, it would be nice to see more of who you truly are."

Serena's mouth opened and closed a few times before she responded. When she finally replied, it was with a contrite look in her eyes. "I can see why Aerie wanted to keep you."

Exton winced at her words, saying nothing as she finished unpacking her supplies. When she was done, she nodded to him; it was the slightest, smallest hint of a nod, but Exton managed to catch the respect behind it.

He felt a sense of relief, in many ways, but he had to wonder if it was his office or his marriage to Aerie which had earned her respect.

Finally, seemingly hours later, the door behind him opened. "Captain?"

Exton looked over his shoulder to see Tyra, one of the many med technicians, as she came out of the room. Others, no doubt students from the Ecclesia, followed her.

"We're finished, sir," Tyra said. "We had to remove some fragments from Cal's arm. You can go and see them now."

"Thank you," Exton said, his voice brusque as he hurried inside.

One look from Brock and Cal's face clearly told him that his visit was undesired. In fact, Exton thought, he had a feeling he didn't want to be there anymore than he suspected Brock and Cal wanted to see him.

"Gentlemen," he said, trying to start out on more professional footing. It was too easy to see that Brock, while his arm was bandaged and there was an IV in it, was more than willing to put up a fight. And Cal had always been the more blustery brother; he'd never enjoyed answering any of Exton's questions without going off-topic or insulting him.

Exton hoped that the untimely demise of his family members and his other comrades in arms might temper that impulse some.

It was a stretch, he knew.

"What are you doing here?" Brock spat. "I was hoping to rest some. We've had a long two days, if you haven't heard."

"I've been informed of the mission," Exton replied sharply. "I'm trying to figure out why it happened."

Cal snorted softly. "The other ships all lost control while we were protecting the target," he said. "Seems like a systems failure to me."

"Your ships didn't go down," Exton pointed out. "Everyone else's did."

"So?" Cal shrugged. "Maybe ours were the only ones that were working properly."

"Or maybe your ships were the only ones which *weren't* working properly."

When Cal only gave him a scowl, and then turned his gaze to stare at the far wall, Exton turned to Brock.

"I wanted to ask about the NETech," Exton said. "Can you tell me if it was activated in your fighters?"

Brock frowned and ignored him, while Cal sank deeper into the thin sheet on his bed.

"Well?" Exton sighed. "I need to know, so we can see about protecting others."

"Mine wasn't," Cal finally said. "I know because when the comm lines were going fuzzy, I wasn't able to connect to the others with the NET system."

"I thought Dorian had deactivated his a while ago," Exton said.

"He did. We just switched ships," Cal admitted. "We like to play games like that sometimes. We don't have a lot of fun in the URS. We were able to get away with switching from time to time."

Brock snorted. "Not all the time."

"I never said all the time," Cal snapped. He turned back to Exton. There was an apologetic look in his eyes. "We didn't mean any harm. It was our way of having fun."

For a long moment, Exton felt old. He was nearly three years older than Aerie's brothers, and even older than Brock. He had forgotten how it felt to be free from the control—the seemingly endless, all-consuming ways the State managed to exhort its influence on the young and old alike. Even before that, he knew he'd had the advantage of the protection offered from his own family, and their community. Aerie's family, and her friends, had no such protection; if anything, because of their family's position under Osgood, they likely had even less.

"I can imagine that it's hard to come by fun when everything is about survival," Exton said quietly. "I know from experience how it's never considered a priority. Either way, it's not your fault that Dorian's ship went down."

"If anything, it's the State's fault," Brock said. "After all, they are your enemy, aren't they? It would have to be their fault that they killed a bunch of our people by hacking their planes. Maybe you should have thought about that possibility before sending us out to die in compromised fighters."

Before Exton could ask him what he thought happened, Cal turned to Brock. "You were the one who told me to make sure the NET was disable in the fighter. You should've checked the rest of them."

Exton narrowed his eyes at Brock. "Why did you tell them to disconnect the NETech?"

Even from behind, Exton knew Brock was radiating fury as he searched for the right words. "I know the URS can use it to spy on people," Brock admitted.

"You know they can spy on us?"

Cal shot up straight in his bed. "You knew they could use the NET to do a bunch of other stuff, too, didn't you? That's why you told me and Dorian to disable ours. I thought mine was already disabled, and he thought his was already disabled, too, but his wasn't. That's why he died, isn't it?"

When Brock said nothing, Cal lunged out of his bed and onto Brock. The IV in Cal's arm ripped free, and blood spotted the floor as Exton fought to separate them.

Tyra and several other med techs came rushing in at the noise.

"That's enough," she yelled, and the whole room seemed to stop at her announcement. "You two need to rest. Captain, if this is taking up too much of their energy, then I must insist you wait to ask them any further questions."

He frowned, but seeing Cal's seething expression and Brock's shameful blush, he decided he had enough information for now. He had been right about the NETech, and there was nothing to suggest that anything else had been the cause. For now.

"Alright," he said, nodding to Tyra. "I'd get these guys in separate rooms, however. On top level lockdown, too, please."

"Yes, Captain."

Exton headed out of the med ward, glad to be free. He never liked to be in a med ward, unless it was to go and visit Aerie.

He pulled out his own comm device again, wondering if he should call her. Looking at the time, he knew she was supposed to be asleep still, resting up for the day shift.

Exton was glad when, a moment later, the comm started beeping. He almost laughed, startled by the noise. He answered it with expectation. "Aerie?"

"It's me," she replied.

"I was just thinking of you," he said. He felt his face tighten as he smiled, thinking of how long of a day he'd had. And it wasn't even over yet. He knew he still had plenty to do, but hearing Aerie's voice was a tonic to his shattered world. He glanced at the time again and realized how tired she sounded. "Did you have trouble sleeping?"

"Yes," she admitted. "But it's okay. I was going to have a bad night as it was."

"I'm sorry I'm not there."

"No, it's not that. I mean, it would be really nice if you were here, but Gerard ended up hailing the *Perdition* and he wanted to talk to me."

"To you?"

"Yes."

Exton felt his grip on the comm device tighten, and he wished he could do something equally vicious to the man who caused his beloved wife such pain. "What did he say?"

"My mom is alive."

"Oh. Well. That's good." He bristled at his own detached tone. Hadn't he just been talking to Serena about the very same thing? It was good Aerie's mother was alive, and he shouldn't have to berate himself into sounding like it.

Aerie didn't seem to notice his flippancy. "I don't think my brother is, though," she said. "I know Brock said Cal was the only one who was with him."

"I'm sorry," Exton said. He was just about to tell her he had just come from meeting with them, but she continued on before he could tell her.

"I don't want to think about it now," Aerie said. "I know if I do, I'll likely go crazy. I don't know how you did this for so long."

"We didn't do so much active warfare before," he said, trying to brush it off.

"Still, I don't know how you did it."

"I don't either." He didn't want to tell her the truth; he'd only done it to survive, and now that she was with him, that she was safe, there was something greater than just revenge waiting for him at last. Exton knew she would be happy that he had something more to hope for now, but he didn't want her to realize how deeply the monster inside of him lay, and how close it had been to devouring the rest of him. "Tell me what else Gerard told you."

"He said they used the NETech to do something to the fighters that made them crash."

Exton shook his head, feeling silly as he realized Aerie

couldn't see him. "I know," he said. "I had a feeling that was it, anyway. I just talked to Brock and Cal about it. They more or less confirmed that theory."

"You saw them? Spoke to them? How are they?" Aerie asked. "I wasn't close with my brothers, but I know Cal is probably upset. He and Dorian have never been apart for very long. And I don't even know how Brock would feel."

"Probably like it is his fault, which it is," Exton replied, trying to hold back his snarl. He thought of Brock's attempts to brush off the incident and felt a wave of anger stir inside him once more.

"What? Why would it be Brock's fault?" Aerie asked. "He was with them when it happened. There's no way he could've known about anything."

She was upset and likely shocked; Exton decided it was better to direct her away from that conversation. Petra was built to withstand incidents of rebellion and treason; Aerie was not, especially when it was one of her oldest and dearest friends at the center of controversy.

"Never mind," Exton said, interrupting her as she listed off reasons why Brock was the victim, rather than the victimizer. "He's fine, too. They just moved him into his own room to get some rest."

"Are you sure? Because I know that you don't exactly trust him or anything like—"

"I'm sure," he said. "Back to Gerard, please. What else did he say?"

"He said that he was willing to trade Merra for you and the General." Aerie sighed. "I told him no. He's given us three days to think it over."

"Well, I'm tempted to give him your dad," Exton said. "But I do think he's asking for too much. He doesn't even know how we feel about Merra."

"She's my mother," Aerie said, her voice flat with disappointment. "And he knows how much my father cares for her, thanks to my stepmother."

"Your stepmother?"

"Yeah. She's apparently with him at Panama right now."

Exton thought about the ecobombs that had likely gone off at Panama. "I think he's trying to force our hand," he said. "I'll have Emery pull up the maps, but I'm willing to bet the bombs went off."

"Bombs? What bombs?" The shock in Aerie's tone returned, this time underscored by worry rather than suspicion.

Exton had a feeling he wasn't going to be able to tell her the truth. She wasn't going to be able to stomach it—not without blaming him.

Well, I am to blame. Aren't I? Exton hung his head. If he'd been more diligent, he would have waited to find out more about the ship before sending in their small squadron of fighters and a rescue shuttle. Had he known Merra had most likely been the one to organize its departure, he wouldn't have sent anyone to rescue it.

"Exton? Tell me the truth."

It was almost as if she knew he was finding a way to keep it from her, he thought. Sometimes Aerie seemed to know him too well.

"We found out that there were ecobombs on the *Freedom*," he told her. "According to my sources, your mother was the one who organized everything, including its destination."

Aerie said nothing, and instantly, he was concerned.

"Are you okay?" he asked her a moment later.

"She said she had a way to make you release my father," Aerie said.

"What? When did she tell you that?" Shock hit Exton, hard and fast.

"When she came up here to see you," Aerie answered. "She talked to me some in the Biovid before going to see you."

"Why didn't you tell me?" Exton felt the rising tide of rage inside of him, and he knew there was very little that would hold it back at this point.

"I didn't think anything of it at the time," Aerie continued. "I know you can be very effective at putting your foot down, Exton. But now, Gerard has her and he's asking for my father and you as a hostage swap. I didn't think she would do something this extreme, but—"

"But nothing," Exton growled. "She managed to get herself captured and nearly the rest of the fighter pilots killed, too. I lost some of my best people, Aerie."

"I know this is terrible, Exton—"

"This is more than terrible," he argued, cutting her off. "This is *dangerous*. Your family is dangerous, Aerie. Your mother didn't count on Gerard using the NETech to override her legion, and because of that, we lost people and we lost the battle. And because the ship was in the Caribbean in the first place, the ecobombs have detonated and now it's leaking poison through the URS camps."

"My mother was only trying to win the war against them," Aerie pushed back. "She's on your team."

"She might be on our team, but she's playing by her own rules."

"She still had good intentions."

"You're really going to defend her, knowing she caused a lot of people to die needlessly? That's weak, Aerie, and not worthy of you."

"Isn't that the same thing that your father tried to do?"

Her rebuttal was striking, and Exton felt his heart barely survive the blow.

"Well?" Aerie demanded. "Isn't it?"

"That was low," he growled. "My father is the only reason that we're alive today."

"Well, he still wanted to kill a few hundred thousand people," Aerie argued, her voice clearly edged by her own anger. "He was planning on it, according to what the General told you. I don't see how your father is that much different from my mother."

"My father still didn't deserve to die. Your mother is getting exactly what she deserves," Exton snapped.

"How can you say that?" Aerie's tone was sharper now. Exton was glad he couldn't see her face, because he was certain that her eyes were full of angry tears.

"This is real life, Aerie," he said. "This is war. And this is the price you pay when you're fighting the world for something you want! You risk everything—*everything*—for a slim chance at what you want. And in the end, you still might not get it, even if you still pay for it."

"You're talking in circles, Exton. You're not making sense. By your own logic, it would seem that the General did the right thing in stopping your father."

He had to take another deep breath to steady himself. "Even if it's true that my father was planning on attacking the URS with the *Perdition*, he was stopped. We're not dealing with hypotheticals. Your mother was not stopped, and now an ecobomb is likely poisoning half the Caribbean. And our fighters are still gone."

"It's still the same, Exton. Your father wouldn't have been killed if he wasn't doing something wrong," Aerie insisted.

"You don't know that!" Exton shouted into the comm. "You don't even know if he was doing something wrong."

"My father told me what he told you," Aerie said. "I know you don't believe him, but I do, after hearing what he had to say. Don't you?"

Exton gritted his teeth together. "I'm not talking about that with you," he growled. "I'm not talking about it. Go and talk about it with St. Cloud if you want to talk about it."

"We wouldn't be talking about it if you would just do something about my mom. Who gets to decide who has to die, Exton? Who decides who has to pay?" Aerie asked.

Exton tried to brush her question aside, but it was difficult. He knew that she had a point, but he didn't want to face the reality of it right now. He had other priorities that demanded his attention, and as much as he felt for Aerie, seeing her mother's capture, he had to assess the damage that came along with the events leading up to her capture.

"We have to rescue my mother," Aerie continued. "Gerard has her imprisoned. They're going to torture her. Just like they did to me, Exton."

He sighed. He didn't want her thinking that he didn't care about her. But there were other factors to consider.

"Right now, we can't do anything. We're still collecting information here," Exton said. "We are still deciding what to do. No definite plans have been made."

"My mother doesn't deserve to be tortured, Exton," Aerie insisted. "I know that for sure."

"I'm sorry, Aerie."

Aerie must have caught the lack of sympathy in his voice. "You're not seriously thinking of leaving her there, are you?"

He sighed. "Aerie, this is war. Sometimes people get left behind. You're the one who told me earlier that you'd already lost her once."

"I can't believe you," she hissed

"I'm just telling you the truth," Exton snapped. "We have to wait for more information to come in. There's plenty we need to know before we do anything at all. Maybe if I had known sooner that your mom wanted to poison the Caribbean Sea, we wouldn't be where we are now."

Aerie sank into a bitter silence, saying nothing in reply.

"I've lost people, too, Aerie. Gerard is proof of that."

"I don't care about that right now," Aerie said. "What are we going to do?" There was a hint of desperation in her voice now.

He said nothing. He had already given his answer. He rubbed his forehead, trying not to hate her in that moment; he was sorely tempted to yell at her some more, trying to hurt her as much as she had hurt him. Silence was the easiest answer for now, and also the least condemning.

"Well?" Aerie demanded. "Are we going to attack? Stage a rescue mission? What?"

"We don't have the resources to do that," Exton said.

"I can do it then," Aerie offered.

"No." Exton's voice was sharp and scalding. "No, you

will not do anything, Aerie. Do you hear me? I will *not* have you put yourself in harm's way. Not after everything we've been through, and especially not after all the trouble your mother has caused."

"But she's my mother!" Aerie insisted.

"I know, but the answer is still no. Do not disobey me on this, Aerie. You've seen what Gerard can do."

"Exactly! That's all the more reason to do something!"

Exton scoffed. "If you go, you could just make things worse for us, Aerie. You might have some training, but you still don't know what to do or what kind of powers you're up against."

"But—"

It was time to hang up before he said something he would regret even more. "There is no easy answer for these things, Aerie," he said. "I'll talk with you later."

Exton didn't say goodbye before he clicked off the comm.

♦15♦

The second the comm line went silent, Aerie felt something inside of her snap.

"Augh!" Aerie screamed as she tossed the small communications device across the room. Her hands were shaking as she ran them through her loosened hair. She fell to her knees and wondered if the anger and betrayal would ever cease.

There was nothing he could do. *No*, Aerie corrected herself bitterly, *there was nothing he* would *do*. Angry tears fell down her flushed face, and she was very glad she was alone. Her frustration was almost manifest, and she did not want to be face to face with Exton's cruel reality.

In the back of her mind, Aerie knew that Exton was probably right. Aerie had never thought of her mother's recklessness when she was a child, but since she had found her mother not only alive but coordinating a worldwide revolt against the States, she had wisely reevaluated her mother's character. But …

But she's my mother! Aerie's hand flew up to her heart as she felt the hollow ache in her chest. Shame filled her as she thought about how reluctant she had been to forgive her mother for leaving her. Even if she could understand it, even if she had a younger brother now, she had been unwilling to overlook her mother's abandonment of her as a young child.

But now, it seemed silly. Of course she loved her mother, and of course she forgave her. It was a miracle she even had a second chance to be with her.

And now, Aerie thought, *I'm back where I started. She's gone, and I'll likely never see her again.*

Gerard was cruel, whether he tried to hide it or flaunt it alongside his so-called charm. There was no telling what he would do—or, apparently, what Phoebe would do—when it came to making her mother pay.

Aerie recalled all too vividly the feeling of lightning lashing through her body, the dark energy drilling into her body all the way down into her bones. Reliving the memory made the dull shadow inside of her roar once more.

As she slumped against the ground, she shook her head. "He's not going to do anything," she whispered to herself, as shocked disbelief sank into her skin and permeated her soul.

She knew she had fought Exton's reasoning with everything she had; Aerie knew she had overstepped a line in bringing up Exton's father. She was distressed and fuming and frantic, but she was also right. What was the difference, really, between her mother and Exton's father? Why should one be exonerated while the other one is condemned?

Something has to be done.

Exton wasn't planning on doing anything.

As soon as that thought, that harsh resonance of truth, crossed her mind, Aerie sat up and pushed herself off the floor. Her knees buckled at the sudden rush of blood, but her resolve was reignited.

This feeling had come to her before—this feeling that Exton was wrong. It was the same feeling she'd had as she sat on the shuttle when he took her back to see the General at Nova Scotia.

Back then, she was hoping against all hope Exton would change his mind and allow her to stay with him, even if it meant angering her father. He had been unhappy, but resigned. He had been so concerned with Petra that he didn't realize he was ultimately putting the rest of the world in more danger by turning her back over to her father.

Aerie had been understanding. She didn't want to cause Exton's community to be devastated with attacks from the URS, and she didn't want to force him to admit that he loved her more than he feared the death of his friends. Aerie had willingly submitted to his commands, proving that she could do so as much as she would, if it was the only thing that would prove to Exton she loved him.

But in the end, they had been wrong; all of them had been brutally wrong. They had both been laboring under false assumptions—namely, that the General wouldn't try to kill

Exton, and that Aerie wouldn't be harmed. And they paid the price for it.

Aerie knew Exton was wrong now.

Yes, her mother had been involved in some shady dealings before. And yes, it wouldn't surprise Aerie to find out that she had coordinated the attack on Panama from the start. But she did know what Gerard and his cohorts were capable of, and Aerie knew that her mother didn't deserve *that.*

Her breath provided a steady beat alongside the furious beating of her heart.

"Exton's not going to do anything," Aerie told herself, steeling herself. "So I will."

It was the right thing to do.

At that realization, Aerie faltered; she didn't want to lose Exton. She knew she would be going against her word, and Exton's orders, and she knew even in the best case scenario, she would lose Exton's trust, and possibly his love.

But she also wanted her mother back. She had to tell her mother that she forgave her, and that she loved her. And if it was possible to free her, Aerie would do whatever it took to do just that.

If she was going to do this, she thought, she needed help. An idea, rebellious as it was brilliant, came to her instantly.

She was going to see the General.

If there is anyone who will be able to help me do this, it's the General. Aerie had a feeling he would relish the chance to help Exton see he was wrong.

There was still some hesitation inside of her as she glanced around the room. Aerie felt the full weight of her condemnation as she slipped out the door of her room, willingly leaving the last of her innocence behind.

Aerie worked through the rest of her shift with terrifying efficiency. She kept her eyes innocent and clear, and her expression engaged. She made sure there was nothing to suggest she was planning a quiet rebellion of her own as she attended meetings, read reports, and managed the staff.

Emery would be proud, Aerie thought, as even Olga left their meeting without demonstrating any inkling of suspicion.

Exton tried to contact her more than once throughout the day, but she ignored his calls. She made excuses, dodged crewmembers, hid from messengers—anything that was necessary to avoid the fight she knew would come the next time she talked with her husband.

She saw the time, and headed off the Command Bridge with a few moments to go on the shift. Due to the late night, Henry had passed the console to Phil, another copilot, after the midmorning break. Aerie quickly excused herself by implying she need to take care of female trouble, and that was that. Phil nodded at once, and there was no awkward questioning or any particular inquiry after that.

She was left to walk the long hallway of betrayal alone, with no one the wiser to her thoughts or feelings or plans. Aerie did feel guilty enough for lying that she stopped at the restroom briefly, but only long enough to wash her hands and stare at her reflection, steeling herself for another visit to her father.

When she came to the General's door, she considered turning back one last time.

She was a second away from knocking when the door opened, and she was face to face with her father.

"General," she greeted, surprised and unsure.

"Get in," he said, grabbing her arm and pulling her inside the room.

"I can get in by myself," Aerie huffed, as she struggled to regain her ground. If she was going to be breaking all the rules, she was going to assert herself to the last of who she was to everyone, and that included her father. "There's no need to be so pushy about it."

"I know what's happened," the General told her. "We don't have a lot of time. And I know Exton's far from foolish enough to allow you to see me again. If we're going to escape from here, you're going to have to follow my lead as we get out of here."

"What?" Aerie's attempt at reorienting herself flailed even further off course. "What are you talking about?"

"Merra," he said. "Your mother. We're going to rescue her."

"What have you heard?" Aerie asked. She folded her arms. "I'm not doing this 'you-take-the-lead' stuff. Not after what you did to me last time with the Memory Serum. You have to tell me what you know." She gave him a hardened look. "You owe me that at least."

"I don't owe you anything," the General snarled back. "But if it'll gain your cooperation and make my life even the least little bit easier, I'll give you that."

Aerie was beginning to regret her decision to come see him.

"I've been in constant contact with your mother since she left for Chaya years ago," the General said. "When she was captured by Gerard, we were cut off. I know she's alive."

"Gerard has her down near Panama," Aerie said. "He called the *Perdition* last night. He had the URS sabotage the MENACE fighters by hacking their NETech."

"Figures. That was always a last resort for using that technology."

"You knew?" Aerie's eyes widened.

"I knew and I didn't know. It was never fully tested. Some people had ethical issues with testing it, especially on the MENACE fighters. Don't forget, when the URS made those, MENACE was already less than a threat. All we needed the fighters for, in theory, was propaganda. It was decided that a testing of the kamikaze feature would be a waste of resources and money, especially since we were not supposed to use them for anything that amounted to anything other than fearmongering."

"So you didn't know."

"I didn't know they would actually do it," the General

clarified. "I was one of the people who ruled against testing the kamikaze hack to begin with."

"Dorian's gone."

The General finally stopped and stared at her, as though he was trying to figure out the meaning of the words she'd just told him. Then he put his hand over his heart and sat down at the small table.

"I was shocked, too," Aerie admitted, trying hard not to let her emotions overcome her again. She knew she was already at a disadvantage when it came to working with her father. She needed her wits sharp and alert, and there was no way crying over the loss of her brother, again, would help her.

"What else?" the General asked.

"Cal and Brock are the only ones who made it back to Petra. The rescue mission was foregone. Exton said that he'd been told the ship, the *Freedom*, had ecological weapons on it."

"It did."

Aerie sat down across the table for him. Her fingers tightened around the edge. "Did Mom actually plan for that to happen?"

"You already know she did," General St. Cloud said. "The ecobomb she was working on along with Evelyn, Exton's mother, had been further developed over the last couple of years."

"So she did all that? Why did she need to lead fighters to the ship then?" Aerie asked.

"So she could ensure the bomb would go off. The ship only had a skeleton crew, and there was no way to know if they would make it down there. Merra took off to ensure that the bomb went off."

It all formed a picture inside her mind, one that was painstakingly coordinated. From her conversation on the *Perdition* with Merra before, it all somehow came together like clockwork. Aerie could see it clearly, and she realized just how elegant and terrifying her mother's plans could be.

"I see," Aerie said quietly. She felt bad when her resolve

to rescue her waned ever so slightly.

"The crew was originally headed for Petra. It was a good thing that she managed to get it to head for Panama instead. When the bomb explodes, it will unleash a poison into the water system near Panama. We were aiming for the Canal, so it would do the most damage. The URS, when it ships things, still uses the Panama Canal quite a bit. Slowing their supply train would open up a new black market and it would force trade routes to be redrawn."

"Not to mention we would kill a bunch of the URS forces that remain near Panama," Aerie interjected.

At her gloomy tone, St. Cloud raised an eyebrow. "It's war, Aerie. It's kill or be killed, or even worse—you could get to live while you watch others get killed. Or they don't even have to be killed. You just watch their souls quietly morph into a twisted form as their humanity is slowly killed off by the sheer stress of it all."

"There are other ways to win a war, aren't there? Couldn't we could still negotiate with Osgood—"

"That's a laugh. Osgood knew from day one of his dictatorship that the world was nearly his. All he had to do was undermine our allies and tie up all the loose knots. What he didn't realize was that Silas had already been aiming to stop him."

"Why did you kill Silas then?" Aerie asked. "If you have no problem killing other people, and he was going to kill people, then why bother?"

"He grew reckless in the end," the General said. "It's one thing to kill in all-out war, Aerie. It's another thing entirely to kill the truth to gain power and to maintain the narrative."

"The narrative?"

"Every side in a war has a story they want to be true. You know Exton is a man of honor. I do, too. But he's working with people like Silas and Merra, people who will stop at nothing to win this war, so they can make their ideas into reality. But the truth is, people like that fight the other side by *becoming* the other side. So there's a story, like a fairy tale, that they tell themselves, to keep themselves from realizing it."

"So Mom and Exton's father fell victim to the narrative?"

"No. They fell victim to their own impatience and self-serving attitude," the General said.

Aerie gaped at him. "Mom still doesn't deserve to die."

"We all deserve to die, Aerie," the General said dejectedly.

"So you won't help me rescue Mom?"

"No, I didn't say that. On the contrary, you're going to help me rescue her, and not the other way around."

Aerie was confused. "Why are you going to rescue her if you think she deserves to die?"

"Because I love her, of course." The General's gaze softened as he looked at Aerie. "I have always, always loved her. She has always been my best friend and the one person with whom I could be free."

"Even after all her meddling and her … relentless fighting?"

"Yes."

Aerie felt a new level of shock as she watched her father's eyes, so similar to her own. She could almost see her father as he met Merra for the first time, she could almost feel the thick layer of conviction as he married her, and she could almost sense the disorientation he felt in being kept from her.

Once she realized she was staring at him with her mouth open, Aerie cleared her throat. "Well, Gerard talked to me," she said. "And he said he would give up Merra in exchange for you and Exton."

"He seems to have developed quite the vendetta against the two of us," General St. Cloud mused. "I'm not surprised."

"He told me that Phoebe is with him, helping to take care of Mom."

The General's eyes held a sudden sparkle. "I can't imagine that he's doing either of them a favor. I told you before I was married to Phoebe against my will. I only agreed to it because Grant—Dictator Osgood—insisted it would be better for me and you kids."

"I didn't think you cared enough to like her," Aerie admitted.

"I didn't care at all," the General assured her. "But I knew she was a spy. She was handpicked by Osgood, and it would have warranted even more concern if I refused him. I'd managed to keep him at bay for a year with excuses. She was the ultimate punishment in many ways."

"I see." Aerie felt much better knowing her father loved her mother and hated her stepmother. "I guess that's why Mom hates her, too."

"More or less. I'm sure she can fill you in on the specifics later," General St. Cloud said. "She'll likely be happy to. I never enjoyed listening to her complain about her. There was very little I could do. Another death in my family would have—"

"—warranted concern." Aerie did a double-take, as she finished his sentence and another revelation came to her. "That's why you wouldn't let me stay with Exton initially."

"You're *young*, Aerie. I know you love him, but you're going to find out the hard way that marriage and true love have their price."

"There's no need to worry about me there," Aerie said, thinking of her earlier conversation with Exton. "Exton's already warned me."

"I can assure you, whatever he said before, he was being nice about it. He's a man who has a duty to fulfill, and he knows it. You'll never be satisfied being number two in his life. Right now he has to choose between the war and you, and you're upset about it. But if it'll get us out of here so we can save your mother, I'm willing to use it to my advantage."

Aerie shifted uncomfortably in her seat. Before she could ask her father if it would be better for her to leave, he changed the subject.

"Now," he said. "Let's go over the plan."

Aerie said nothing. She had spent the better half of her shift trying to formulate a plan of her own, but she had come up with nothing substantial. A part of her knew she was still hoping to talk herself out of it, but she knew the General was right. She didn't agree with Merra's methods, and her mother definitely wound up in a trap she had set herself. But she still loved her, and there was nothing else to be done.

She gave him a small nod. *Time to step up,* she told herself. "Okay."

♦16♦

It had been many hours since the sunlight gracing Petra's landscape slipped under the horizon when Exton headed into the main hangar.

He sighed and put his comm device in his pocket, but not before he fought off the urge to throw it away. It had been too many times that he'd tried to get a hold of Aerie, only to get a bunch of half-muttered excuses or blatant ignorance. Even his own crewmembers were too curious as to why they needed to help him get ahold of his wife.

Exton looked down from his position on the walkway over Petra's hangar. He considered powering up his shuttle and flying to the *Perdition* just to find her and demand they finish their earlier argument before they moved onto a new one about communication etiquette.

Exton was just imagining the look on Aerie's face when he heard footsteps behind him.

"What's wrong? Missing your sweetheart?" Tyler asked, as he came up beside him.

"Shut up."

Tyler gave him a wicked grin. "Oh, I guess I'm right."

"I said shut up about it."

The smile fell away from his face. "I guess I was wrong," Tyler said. "You're not missing her. You're upset with her."

"More myself, but yes, I'm upset with her." Exton glared at him from over the railing. The two of them were on the second level of Petra's hangar, looking down at the small array of fighters and shuttles, as any NETech was getting disabled. The ships would then be refitted with frequency scramblers and monitors, just to make sure that they would never face another Panama situation.

"What did you do?" Tyler asked.

"Why are you assuming it's my fault?"

"Because Aerie's still in that honeymoon phase, and you've been forced out of it," Tyler replied. When Exton gave him a quizzical look, he explained, "When I see or hear about her, she's always trying to help you, or to keep you from getting upset. She wants you to be happy that you married her."

"I *am* happy that I married her," Exton growled.

"But you're both stuck in an international conflict. It's bound to get in the way of some things."

Exton snorted. "You have a point."

"So it's more than likely your fault. After she's tried to be so appeasing, you likely pushed her too hard and she pushed back."

"That's about right," Exton agreed, thinking of Aerie's harsh words about her father, and how she was quick to compare her mother's actions with his father's. There was still a soreness he felt when he thought about that. He tried to call her earlier to see if they could work things out in a more civilized way, but he had to commend her on her wisdom in turning his messages away. He was still ready to fight.

"I imagine it's hard on her, too," Tyler said. "She's upset about her mother and her family."

"At least know I called it right, way back at the beginning. She wants her family's acceptance still, even if she has our affections."

"Who doesn't want both of those things?" Tyler laughed. "She'll try for both, until she sees that it's pointless, or until she's hurt too much to continue to be disappointed."

"That is the way she seems to work." Exton waved his hand down at the ships. "I'll try to call her again later, after dinner. In the meantime, what are we going to do about Merra?"

"I know your aunt is pretty distressed," Tyler said. "She's been twice as snappy today."

"Must be a family trait," Emery said, as she came up behind them. "I heard you've had a fight with Aerie, Exton."

"Shut up," Exton said, before he stuck his tongue out at her, like they used to when they were younger.

"See? Family trait. Good thing it skipped over me."

"It's none of your business."

Emery didn't give him a pass. "Really? You're going to try to charm your way out of this mess?"

"Hasn't failed me yet."

"There's a first time for everything."

"How did you hear about it anyway?" Exton asked. "I didn't think I was broadcasting my relationship throughout the community."

"I have friends other than you," Emery reminded him. "Olga's daughter told Alice that Aerie was upset today. Alice mentioned it to me, hoping that Aerie was doing okay."

"We really need to stop the gossip lines between Petra and the *Perdition*," Exton muttered.

"It's not my fault everyone's always enjoyed commenting on your personal life."

"I would make the argument that it is a security concern."

Tyler laughed. "You know my friends would catch any disruption," he said. "There's nothing to worry about."

"I know that," Exton assured him. "But it would stop a lot of the chatter."

"Well, if that's all you have to worry about, it seems that I'm leaving Petra in good hands while I'm away," Emery said.

Exton frowned. "Where are you going?"

"I'm going up to Cartagena," Emery told him. "There's a small research team I've been checking in with here while keeping up with your demands. They're the ones who are making sure that the nuclear waste isn't leaking from the Craftcarrier," she explained, nodding toward the open hangar doors, where a sliver of the fallen Craftcarrier could be seen in the shadowy waters.

"*Why* are you going?"

"I *asked* to go," Emery said, mimicking his irritated tone. "You know I've missed studying horticulture. This is a chance for me to assess the area, to see what Merra's ecobomb has done, if anything, and to see what kind of effect it's having on the environment."

"Will you be able to even see anything from Cartagena?" Tyler asked. "Panama is still pretty far out."

"From the data we gathered, it's a safe place for us to land for a few days. We'll be able to send out divers from there."

"I don't like this," Exton said. "We just lost a bunch of our fighters."

"It's a small group, with plenty of armed guards," Emery insisted. "And anyway, the URS won't be looking for scientists. From what I know of the ecobomb, they'll likely be looking for a cure. If they can still move."

"I still can't believe Merra had the nerve to do that," Exton said with a sigh.

"I'm not surprised she did it now that it's done," Emery said. "But I didn't see it coming ahead of time."

"Hindsight is twenty-twenty," Tyler offered.

Exton leaned down on the railing, looking down at Captain Chainsword's shuttle as it was inspected. "Aerie said Merra's actions weren't any different from Papa's, except Papa was stopped."

"She said that?" Emery frowned. "Seems a bit harsh."

Tyler shrugged. "We can't know for sure," he said. "No matter what St. Cloud told you, we don't have much evidence to suggest he was going to attack New Hope."

"I saw the evidence," Exton said. "I found it in his notes. He was planning on making the *Paradise* the Ecclesia's new home while the nuclear radiation effects wore off."

Tyler shrunk back ever so slightly. "Oh."

"Exton." Emery reached over, rubbing his back with her hand, just like their mother used to.

It did little to comfort him; rather, he felt even worse now that he was missing his mother as well. "St. Cloud was right."

"It didn't mean that he was right to kill Silas," Tyler said.

"I agree with you there," Exton said. "But I'm not sure I would agree with you if I was considering Merra's actions."

"You think she should die for it?" Emery looked thoughtful. "I wouldn't object to putting her in prison for war crimes, especially if the ecobomb is as devastating as I've heard. But death? I'm not sure … "

"Even if your father was planning terrible things," Tyler said, "you have to consider that he might not have gone through with it in the end."

"You mean like I didn't?" Exton retorted.

Tyler skipped over his derision and nodded. "Merra actually went through with her plans. So that's different."

"I don't know if it's different enough," Exton admitted. "Maybe Aerie is right."

"If that's what made you mad at her, I can understand. But she is upset about her mother and her family," Emery said. "So give her some time. Although," she added with a smirk, "ten years might be too long."

"Gerard gave us three days to decide what to do with his offer. He said he would trade Merra for me and St. Cloud."

"Well, you're not going to take that deal," Emery said. "So what are we supposed to do?"

"I don't know. We don't know enough to make a solid move. And with things as they are, I'm not sure there is something we can do that will make any difference. Gerard can easily force our hand, like St. Cloud did at Nova Scotia."

"Well, we know some things. We know Merra was behind the ecobomb," Tyler said.

"And the URS was behind the fighters' kamikazes," Exton said.

"And now Gerard has Merra at the base in Panama?" Emery asked.

"Yeah."

"Why don't you just try to go and rescue her?" Tyler asked. "Seems like a small group could infiltrate the base there easily enough."

"We don't exactly have the layout."

"Don't you? It would be in the Boötes system."

Exton glanced over at him. "That's true," he said. He'd forgotten about that. "The blueprints would be in there, just like the ones for *Paradise* are in there."

"You have three days, right? We can buy you some time there, too, if you need it. We'll just ignore his hailing frequency, or even better, reroute it," Tyler said. "It'll be some good fun, trying to watch him communicate with the *Perdition* only to end up hearing something from some other URS outpost."

"Can your tech guys do that for—"

"Okay, I think that's my cue to head out. I'm leaving," Emery interrupted. "I've got to get packed and ready for tomorrow."

"Please promise me you'll be careful," Exton said. He wrapped his arm around her neck and rubbed her hair affectionately.

"I will. I know you can't survive without me for long." Emery grinned. Her gaze softened for a moment. "In return, you can promise me that you'll make up with Aerie. She's my family too, now."

"I'll talk to her," Exton said, careful to keep his tone even. He was still hurt.

"Fine," Emery said. She gave him a smile. "I'll be in contact with you and Aunt Patty soon." She turned around and headed out of the hangar.

"She'll be okay," Tyler said. "I have a list of the people going with her, and I know she'll be good. Serena even volunteered to go with her, just to help keep track of her health, believe it or not."

"Emery said Serena was warming up to her."

"It's always a matter of trust," Tyler said with a shrug. "New people, especially people from the URS, have become cynical when it comes to trust. And we still fail to meet every expectation. It takes a while for expectations to become more realistic and for bonds to build, so when there is an infraction, it can be overcome."

Exton said nothing to that, privately wondering if Tyler was trying to make a secondary point to him about Aerie. He decided not to focus on it; he hated how Tyler seemed like some relationship guru at the worst times. Of course, Exton was glad Tyler was around to help him out, too, but he hated that he was glad for all the help.

Just because you don't believe it is a bad thing for a person to accept help doesn't mean you want to be the one who needs it.

He pulled out the comm device again, fiddling with it as he turned back to Tyler. Before he reached out to Aerie once more, he had other things he wanted to discuss. As important as she was, he had other priorities to attend to.

"I wanted to ask you about your family," Exton said. "How are they doing? Tell me what you found out when you talked to them."

"They're doing as well as can be expected," Tyler said. "There is still a crackdown going on in New Hope, but their community center is pretty tight. No one has said anything, and they're able to get by without much hassle."

"That's good."

"Yeah. Meredith said to pass on her hello to you and Aerie."

"I'll take it." Exton pursed his lips. "How is she, since seeing Gerard again?"

"She's been worse, even though she won't say anything," Tyler said. "My mother told me Mer's been having a hard time sleeping, and she's been losing weight since she's so worried. She thinks something is going to happen because St. Cloud has been outed as a defector. She knows, firsthand, how many people on our side are skeptical of him."

"I don't know what to do with him still," Exton admitted. "Keeping him away from all of this is the only low-risk solution. Considering how much trouble Merra's given us, especially now that she's been captured, it seems to be the wise thing to keep him where he's at."

"He might be able to help us with Gerard," Tyler offered. "He's at Panama now, as we know. Meredith's keeping an ear to the ground for information about him. She said he's been promoted to General St. Cloud's old position."

"We know that too."

"She also said he was expecting a transfer again, one after Panama. Any ideas?"

"Nope." Exton shook his head. "Where he goes, I don't

care right now. I just wish it was away from Aerie and the rest of her family."

"Well, you know better than most you don't always get what you wish for."

"I'm careful about what I wish for. I know what it means to pay for my pleasures. I know how to count the cost of my decisions."

"I don't know what to tell you then, since you seem to have it all figured out." Tyler's tone was teasing, but Exton knew that he was serious.

Exton, thinking of Dorian and Jared, and all the others they'd lost at Panama, said nothing in reply. He knew Tyler had a point, but he didn't think he was entirely wrong, either.

He'd tried to follow the path where the prize was worth the cost. He thought he'd lost Aerie for good after General St. Cloud captured her at Nova Scotia. He'd gone to war not only to make the URS pay for his pain, but also to pay on his own debt toward Meredith. Merra's information, and her contacts with other nation-state leaders around the world, proved that there were enough weak points in the States' military strategy that it would be easy to take them out. Everything seemed to work out after they liberated Chaya. He even managed to get Aerie back, and they were able to fight off one of the Craftcarriers, easily the States' largest military investments.

But now, weeks later, with failure finally hitting home, Exton wondered if he had made the right choice, even if it had been a choice which seemed to be thrown on him at the time.

"I don't have life all figured out," Exton finally said. "I would be less surprised by it if I did."

"Sometimes there are better things in store for us." Tyler smiled. "I'm going to go and catch up with Emery. I don't want her going up to Cartagena, either, but it's hard for me to say no to the things she wants."

"I warned her before about that," Exton said, as his mind swept away to the night of Emery's wedding. "I told her that you're a fool when it comes to her."

"I might be a fool, but I'd be even more a fool if I let her go. But you're probably right about this trip. I don't really want her to go, but I did check through the itinerary. It doesn't seem dangerous, and the crew has contingency plans. For now, I'm learning how to argue with her," Tyler said. "It's a process."

"I'll keep that in mind when it comes to Aerie," Exton promised.

Tyler nodded. "There isn't anything I wouldn't do for Emery, Exton. And she knows it, for better or for worse. And you know, she's had a lot of practice with the divers from the Craftcarrier inspection, over in Palmer Bay. So it's only logical that she was asked to go along with the Panama crew."

"Well, I'm glad to hear it's not a hazardous mission." He tossed the comm device up in the air and caught it playfully. "I'm going to try Aerie again and then get some work finished up. I'll see you tomorrow."

"Bright and early, no doubt."

Exton watched as Tyler disappeared from the hangar, leaving him to watch the activity below, as mechanics and cleaners and all sorts of workers ran around. In the late night, there were plenty of bright lights on, illuminating the small hangar. In some ways, he felt like a ghost again, hovering over the world as its time continued on without his input.

He sighed as he caught sight of the Memory Tree, the choppy top of the tree just barely visible at the edge of light. Exton thought about finding Aerie there, tucked in its trunk, her hair twisted around the twigs.

Aerie had already told him, after hearing the story about his father, and his own temptations to destroy the URS, that she still loved him. Could she still love him if he denied her mother passage home?

Probably not if he denied it, he thought. But if he at least tried to find a way to work with Gerard, that was one thing. He thought about his conversation with Tyler over his family, and suddenly Exton wondered if it would be possible to find a way to free Gerard in all of this, too.

The idea began to form in his mind as he turned away and headed toward his room, just as a small passenger shuttle came gliding down into the far corner of the hangar.

♦17♦

Aerie watched as the General shut off the engines and turned off the cabin lights. Outside the front window of the small shuttle, she could see Petra was as busy as it usually was, and she was glad none of the mechanics seemed to take notice. She was worried that they wouldn't be able to get out of the camp once they landed; it was a calculated risk, and she was not as optimistic about it as her father seemed to be.

Even from where she was sitting, only a few meters away from the General, she could almost see a charged energy around him, emitting from his quick, precise movements. Aerie wondered if he was nervous at all, or if he as just relieved to be out of his small cell of a room.

"Are you sure about this?" she asked. Even as she spoke the words, she knew it was the wrong thing to say, especially since it was about the tenth time she'd asked the question. "I mean, I don't see why we can't just go to Panama now. Why stop at Petra?"

"Aerie, just pretend this is combat class," the General replied smoothly. "We need to get some supplies. We're not going to go barreling into a well-guarded military base to free your mother with no weapons."

"I wasn't talking about that part of the plan, necessarily," Aerie retorted. "I was talking about getting Cal. I don't know if that's a good idea."

"Believe it or not, it's the best sort of therapy. He's going to have to get over his fear of getting back into battle, or he'll never recover. The sooner, the better, and the faster he'll get used to it." General St. Cloud glanced over at her. "It's not going to be hard to get him. This is the night shift at Petra, and you should have enough of your mother's natural talent to be able to sneak down to the med ward and find your brother without drawing attention to yourself."

Aerie thought of how Merra had come to see her as she worked in the Biovid with Bruce. She had come unannounced, choosing to reveal herself when she saw fit.

"She did warn me that I would fail to follow Exton's instructions one day," Aerie said with a loud sigh, thinking of what her mother had said to her that day.

"You're the one who decided to do it, so stick to the plan. We're already too far in this to go back."

That was true, Aerie conceded to herself as she tightened the utility belt around her waist. Sneaking her father out of the ship had been tricky enough; there was little hope she would be able to get him to go back to his room. Once they found out she was gone, and then that he was gone, there would be no escaping punishment.

What that punishment was, Aerie didn't want to know. She could only hope that she would be able to rescue her mom before anything went wrong, and that would allow Exton, and the others in charge, to overlook her malfeasance.

At the thought of her mother, strapped down to a parrilla and being shot through with bursting streams of electricity, Aerie pushed herself forward.

"I'm going to get our supplies," the General told her. "I can borrow a mechanic's jacket and start loading up the ship. You go and get Cal from the med ward."

"What do I do if he's not there?" Aerie asked.

"Find him. We'll likely need another man around if we're going to make it a quick trip."

Aerie took a deep, steadying breath, allowing herself to pretend that it was a combat mission; she could even imagine Master Browning's thick eyebrows boring into her back as she stepped out of the small shuttle and headed toward the shadows of the hangar as naturally as she could.

Several moments later, Aerie was surprised as much as she was relieved to find out the General had been correct. As she stepped into the room she was certain belonged to Cal, she breathed a silent sigh of relief.

Here's hoping the rest of this plan goes just as smoothly.

It hadn't taken long for the General to formulate a master plan. It was simple enough, but complicated at different points. Sneaking down to Petra, unnoticed, or at least with a plausible story, was difficult. Aerie was glad that the only people who had caught her were Reverend Thorne and his brother, Don. They were bound by their vows of silence when it came to secrets. Just to make it official, both of them had taken the time to pray over them.

That was actually really nice of them, Aerie thought, remembering the soft-spoken prayers offered as a supernatural quality seemed to encapsulate them. She felt much more at peace with her decision after that.

It was good to know that God would still accept her, especially since she was pretty sure Exton was going to be upset with her.

The interruption by the reverend and his brother had proved to be even more fortuitous, as they were able to point Aerie in the direction of an empty shuttle.

"What are you doing here?"

Aerie whirled around to see Serena behind her, her hands on her hips and an eyebrow raised in hardened disdain. Aerie's optimism, the little that remained, completely died. "Serena."

"Yeah, nice to see you too," Serena replied. "Now, what are you doing here? I heard from Alice that you've had a fight with your precious husband. Did you come here to kiss and make up?"

"That's none of your business," Aerie said, her cheeks running red.

"Well, you're in my med ward, during my shift, so it's at least a little bit of my business."

Aerie straightened, forcing herself to stand up to her older sister. "I'm looking for Cal. I wanted to see how he was doing, if you must know." It was a small lie, one that was mostly of omission; Aerie didn't need to tell Serena she was looking for Cal to see if he was up for a half-revenge-fueled rescue mission.

Aerie hoped Serena would believe her; she didn't want to answer any more questions, especially ones that would force her to lie and immediately convict her.

At the mention of their brother, Serena softened ever so slightly. She dropped her hands from her hips and sighed. "He's in the room down the hall and to the right," she said. "Brock's across the hall, if you want to go and visit him, too."

"Cal is my primary concern," Aerie said curtly, "but thanks for letting me know."

Before she turned away, Aerie stopped herself. "How are you doing?" she asked Serena. "You know, with everything?" It was the kindest way of saying their mother's imprisonment and their older brother's death.

"Life goes on," Serena said, rolling her eyes. "We've been training for the day when we give up our lives for the URS. Dorian was trained to do what he ended up doing, and he liked doing it. So what difference does it make?"

Aerie blinked, jarred by the rational absurdity of Serena's comments. She was right, Aerie realized. Dorian had been brought up in the URS, and his skills as a pilot had been refined to be an instrument of warfare. Even if he was fighting against the URS, his life's mission had an appropriate ending. But the hollowness of such a life, and such a purpose, and the meaninglessness of his fate against everything—one that several other pilots in the URS and now in Petra's camp still faced—was still too sad to properly contemplate.

He might have died doing what he'd been trained to do, and even something that he loved to do. But why die for something you don't believe in? Why die for a cause that means little to nothing to you?

Aerie sighed. There were some questions she knew she would never get the answers to. She decided to switch topics. "You're not worried about Mom?"

"If Mom's reappearance has taught me anything, it's that Mom can take care of herself," Serena said. "If she is alive, I pity the people who think they've won."

Aerie smiled, giggling a little at the thought. Serena was most likely right. Their mother was a fighter.

"I do think I'll miss Dorian," Serena added a moment later. "He was a good brother. Tolerable. Cal's the one who always seemed more abrasive."

"I feel like I didn't know him very well," Aerie admitted.

"Well, he was several years older than you," Serena said. "We didn't know you very well, either, I think. Maybe now that we're all adults, and we're stuck here working for the *Perdition*, we'll start to understand each other better."

It was the closest thing to a compliment Aerie could recall hearing from Serena. She reached over and gave Serena a quick, fervent hug. "Thank you."

Serena frowned, but she did not attempt to pull away from Aerie's embrace. "I said understand each other better, not like each other."

Aerie laughed again as she stepped back. "I think I like you just fine," she said, "even if I don't agree with you all the time."

Serena's expression was obviously perplexed, and Aerie forced herself to keep from laughing. Did her sister never really figure out familial love?

Before Serena could recover from her admission, Aerie headed down the hall. "Thanks for the help," she called back, hoping her voice wouldn't carry too far. She heard Serena snort, before her footsteps disappeared down the hall once more

Aerie quickly found Cal's room and slipped inside. After she closed the door behind her, she was glad no one was in the room checking in on him; she'd forgotten to check before she opened the door.

I've got to be more careful. There's no such thing as luck at this point.

"Aerie?"

At the sound of Cal's voice, Aerie stepped forward.

Her older brother turned around to face her. As much as Serena had been surprised by her visit, there appeared to be no shock on Cal's face as he looked at her.

"Hi, Cal." Aerie came up beside him with soft footsteps.

Cal took one look at her, sizing her up. "You're here to break me out of here, aren't you?" he asked.

Aerie blinked. "How did you know?"

"Come on, Aerie. I know about Mom, and I know Dorian's gone. You're here to ask me to go help you rescue her."

Confusion briefly derailed her. "Did the General contact you ahead of our arrival here?"

"Dad's here too?" Cal shot up in the bed, a new eagerness in his movements. "Alright then, I'll actually go."

Aerie frowned. "You mean you were going to refuse me if it had been just me?" she asked.

"You're smart, Aerie," Cal said. "As much as the rest of us picked on you, we knew you were smart. But if I'm going to go sweeping through a military base for the URS, I want someone with experience leading the charge."

Aerie watched as Cal grabbed his boots from under the mattress, stupefied as to how to respond. Between getting told that her siblings knew she was smart and then getting told she wasn't capable of pulling off a rescue mission on her own, she wasn't sure if she should be angry or insulted or both.

She just scowled at him, only stopping as they made their way down through the halls of the med ward, and headed back toward the hangar.

"Where is Dad?" Cal asked.

"We have a small shuttle from the *Perdition*," Aerie said. "The General's loading up supplies and weapons now." She checked the time. "We should have another twenty minutes before anyone grows concerned."

"That's plenty of time. What model of ship? Can I pilot?"

As Aerie filled Cal in on the details, she felt herself glancing around, an uneasy feeling settling on her shoulders. She hoped no one else would see her. She'd pulled back her red hair, tucking into a tight bun, similar to the one she used to sport at the Education Center.

Some part of her wondered if she didn't feel like a child enough already, playing hide-and-seek with her husband and playing pretend war games with her father.

No, Aerie told herself. *Stop thinking that.*

She had no choice. Exton didn't have a plan to rescue her mother. He was not going to surrender to Gerard. Their hands were tied, and there was no other option than organizing a rescue mission. With the recent casualties from the battle at Panama, there were just not enough people to go and storm the area. And, as he'd said, he thought Merra deserved her imprisonment as payment for her recklessness.

If I don't do anything, Mom will be killed or tortured. She could end up like Gerard, her mind so warped she wouldn't know the true enemy when she saw it. I can't just do nothing. Not when my mother needs help.

"Alright, good job, kids." General St. Cloud's voice cut through her inner thoughts as Aerie blinked. She was surprised to find that she had made it back to the shuttle without a hitch. Cal stood beside her, giving the General a formal salute.

"Sir," Cal said in greeting. His mouth formed a hard line. "I'm here to accept my role in this mission."

"Excellent," the General replied. "Let's get going then. I've got the ship stocked with what we need. Are you up to piloting the ship, Cal?"

"You know it," Cal replied, a spark of his old self shining in that small moment. "I've got a legacy to uphold, for Dorian as well as the rest of my family."

Aerie watched as Cal trotted up the ramp into the shuttle, heading for the cockpit. She felt a half-smile curl on her lips, glad to see the General had been right. There was no doubt that her brother was going to enjoy the chance to fight the forces responsible for Dorian's loss. She was also glad to see that he was using the word "family" over "unit."

A flickering light at the opposite end of the hangar caught her attention. She saw no one hailing their ship, no one approaching the ship to ask about unloading cargo or running an inspection.

Aerie knew enough about Petra's black market arrangements to know that there was little chance someone would pay them any significant attention. But Aerie also knew it was time to go.

The supernatural quality she'd felt earlier, as Reverend Thorne and Brother Don asked for a blessing on the mission, was still there, but it felt as though it had dimmed.

Moments later, as Aerie was snuggled into the shuttle seat and buckled in, while her brother cheered at being in the air once more and her father oversaw things with an enviable amount of self-assurance, she admitted to herself she almost wished someone *had* caught them.

She watched, transfixed by her own thoughts, as the clouds gradually began to lighten, as their shuttle flew over the curved belly of the world; the almost cheerful atmosphere of the sky was at odds with her somber mood.

Exton had told her that all pleasures, all desires—all of them came with a price. She never thought that her displeasure would have an even higher cost.

♦18♦

"What do you mean, she's not there?" Exton's voice repeated Henry's words with startling detachment, even as there was a feeling inside of him, one that he recognized as much as he dreaded.

He narrowed his eyes, glancing around his small office, where his father's files and different reports were scattered slapdashedly on his desk, as if he was looking for any other possibility than the one stirring around in his gut. He had been using some of the papers as an unwitting pillow, until the call from Henry came through.

"I've had the ship searched," Henry continued. Over the comm, his voice was full of weariness, but there was a strong undertone of worry that was distinct. Exton was glad to see that the crew had taken to Aerie as quickly as they had; he didn't notice until that moment how much Aerie meant to them.

Exton sincerely hoped that whatever game Aerie was playing, she wasn't going to risk that relationship with the crew.

"I'm sorry, Captain. She's nowhere to be found. I have some of the techs checking through the cams."

She's gone.

Exton felt his blood run cold with certainty. He thought about their earlier argument, when he'd been angry and upset and devastated by their losses, and even more infuriated to know it was because of Merra's own interference.

What in the world does she think she's up to now?

He didn't even have to ask himself that question. He knew immediately what she was doing.

Instinctively, Exton's hand flew to his chest, landing on his side, right over the ribs Aerie had bruised the first time he'd met her. As she pushed against her injuries and her fatigue, she'd fought with him over the fate of the Memory Tree and Moona, determined to protect what was hers. She was more than willing to damage everything that got in her way.

He reeled in a new level of indescribable pain as he realized that she was not only willing but determined to put herself in danger—even if it meant she threw away their relationship in the process.

"What should I do, Captain?" Henry asked.

Good question, he thought bitterly. Exton tasted bile as he seethed, calling on the last reserves of his self-control to keep his voice calm. "For now," he said, slowly and carefully, "just keep an eye out for her. And let me know if the techs spot her on the cams at all. I want to know as much as I can so we can take care of her."

If I don't strangle her for her insolence, he thought. His fingers flexed, as if he could reach out into the empty air and grab onto her.

"Roger that." Henry sighed. "I should've watched her more carefully. I know she was more upset about her family than she let on. I could see it in her eyes."

Those eyes, Exton thought bitterly to himself. So innocent, so lovely—or so they once were.

"No need to blame yourself, Henry," Exton told him. "I'll have a team start searching down here, and I'll get Aunt Patty—sorry, Director Ward—to check in with our ships. Hopefully something will come up."

"I hope so."

Exton felt his heart harden inside of him. "Me, too." He clicked off his comm device before he threatened to go up there and tear the ship apart himself.

He knew he might have considered doing that anyway, if he was nearly a hundred percent sure she was there anyway.

What could she be thinking?! Running off to save her mother was all very noble, but it was just plain nonsensical, especially when she would have no support or anyone else with her to help, and she had done this right as he'd finalized his plans for getting Merra and Gerard out of the hands of the URS.

Exton turned on his feet and headed out the door. He knew he didn't have long until Emery left, and he had no one else he could turn to.

He was hailing her on his comm when he caught sight of her heading down to the med ward. "Emery!" he called out.

"Exton," Emery said, nodding a greeting. She smiled. "Come to try to talk me out of going to Cartagena? Did Tyler put you up to it?"

"What? No. No, I need to talk to you." He took her arm, annoyed to see his hands were shaking slightly.

"What's wrong?" Emery's smile disappeared. "What happened?"

"Aerie's gone missing from the *Perdition*."

Emery's blue-green eyes widened at the news. "Huh. Well, that's surprising. Are you sure?"

"I'm pretty sure that Henry's sure. He had the ship checked over."

"Even the Biovid? She always liked it in there, same as I did. Maybe you can ask Henry to check with Bruce once more?"

"I don't think she's there."

Emery nodded as realization dawned. "You think she left because she was angry with you, don't you?"

"I left her there to keep in touch with the crew for me," Exton said, dodging the observation.

"Did she leave because of her mother?" Emery pressed.

Exton grumbled to himself before replying. "I think so. No, that's not right. I *know* so. I know her, and this is exactly the sort of idiotic thing she would do." Exton slammed his fist into the nearby wall, gratified to see the wall stand up to his pain. He gripped his knuckles in further anger. "We've got to do something before she gets into any more trouble."

"More trouble?"

"She's going against my orders, Emery. Of course she's going to get more trouble once I'm through with her!"

"Oh, I see where this is going." Emery sighed. "You told her there was nothing we could do about her mom, didn't you?"

"Of course. There *is* nothing we can do right now. I was

going to put something together, but that's—"

"That's not good enough for Aerie," Emery finished. She sighed.

"I'm not going to lie to her," Exton insisted.

"I didn't say anything about that," Emery replied. "But I know how you feel about failure, Exton, and I know how much Merra aggravated you. You're the only other person that likely came close to understanding how I felt about her. I'm going to take a wild guess here and bet that you didn't handle the situation very well."

"Aerie knows how I feel about her mother," Exton snapped. "The fact that she has good intentions means nothing to me, especially when her actions suggest that lives are somehow expendable."

"But Merra is not our mother," Emery retorted. "You don't get to insult her in front of Aerie, even if Aerie feels the same way about her as you do. She's still Aerie's mother, for goodness sake."

"Are you saying that it is my fault Aerie's gone?" Exton huffed. "She was the one who left! I told her to stay there and I'd get back to her later about her mom."

"It might have been her choice, but it was clearly your words," Emery scoffed. "You can't talk to your wife like that."

"You're supposed to be on my side, Em."

"You're supposed to be on your *wife's* side, Exton!"

"We're in the middle of a war!" Exton heard his voice rise in the small corridor. "I can't just prioritize Aerie's needs. Not over everyone else's. Not over Petra or my crewmembers."

"I know it's hard." Emery lowered her voice as she wrapped her arm around her brother.

"She's gone." Exton held onto Emery's arm, remembering how their mother used to comfort them. "What am I supposed to do now?"

"The same thing you did last time," Emery told him. "Go and find her."

"What about here?"

"How many times are you going to have to go and rescue Aerie before you realize we're here?" Emery waved her free hand around. "We're your family. We can take care of the war while you're gone."

"This isn't fair to other people."

"*Life* isn't fair, Exton. We know that." Emery shrugged. "You might as well work with what you have. Lucky for you, you have me and Tyler and Aunt Patty, and all the rest of your friends here and onboard the starship."

"That's true." Exton sighed. "You're right." *I guess we're going to be moving up the plans we made.*

"Of course I am." Emery giggled.

"This is serious. Aerie manages to get herself into the worst situations."

"But you always seem to get her out of them, just like she always makes your life better."

Exton snorted. "I don't know about better."

"More interesting? More worth the while?" Emery offered.

"I don't know. Doesn't matter. I've got to get some work done I guess."

"What else have you found out?"

"Henry just called me with the news," Exton told her. "I had him continue searching the cams, and he's going to send out messages to the other ships and shuttles nearby."

"Did anyone else go missing?"

Exton started. "I didn't think to ask," he said. "I doubt Henry checked on that, either."

"If she's missing from the *Perdition*, she would've had to take transportation," Emery said. "Any chance she's in the hangar on the *Perdition*?"

"I don't know. I'll call and check."

Emery patted his shoulder. "That's the spirit."

"What do I say to her?" He ran his hands through his hair.

"Are you going to need me to counsel you through

everything?" Emery smiled. "Come on. You can figure that out. Besides, I've got a shuttle to catch, and I promised I'd come and get Serena when we were leaving."

"Yeah, you did, and I'm ready to leave."

Exton had to stop himself from jumping as Serena stepped up beside Emery from out of nowhere, with a small med pack on her back. Between her resemblance to Merra, and her sudden appearance, Exton was caught off guard.

"Good," Emery said. She turned back to Exton. "Are you okay if I head out now?"

"Yeah, go ahead. But put your pilot on standby. We're going to have to redo some of our plans, but the lead team and I will go ahead with them for now. I'll let you know if I hear anything about Aerie."

"Are you looking for Aerie?" Serena asked. "She was here earlier. Haven't you seen her yet?"

Exton and Emery exchanged surprised glances.

Seeing their expression, Serena started laughing. "Oh, I get it. Aerie's causing trouble for you again. I knew something was off when she came down here looking for Cal last night."

"Why didn't you tell someone you'd seen her?" Emery asked. "She wasn't supposed to be here at all."

Serena shrugged. "I watched her as we came here with Brock in that cargo ship," she said. "She's a lot more determined than I would've thought. Last night she wanted something, and I didn't want to be the one who stood in her way."

"Where is Cal now?"

"I thought he was still in his room," Serena muttered, as she turned down the hall and started walking in the direction of the med ward.

Exton and Emery followed behind her, but Exton had a feeling there was no need to check and see if Cal was there or not. He had a feeling he was gone.

His comm beeped, and he quickly answered it, hoping against all hope that Aerie had been found in some obscure location onboard.

"Captain," Henry's voice greeted him once more. "I have some bad news."

"Let me guess. You found proof Aerie's not onboard."

"Good guess, but that's not everything," Henry said. "She left here last night with General St. Cloud."

Exton felt another round of frustration run through him. "I guess that means our earlier plans are going to have to be significantly revised," he muttered.

"Yes. She left in one of the smaller shuttles. I've checked in with Petra, and it seems there are some shipments missing this morning."

"I could've guessed," Exton said. "Great. Can you put a tracker on the ship?"

"Thora's working on it now," Henry said.

"Alright. Thank you." Exton clicked off his comm and turned back to see Serena and Emery arguing as Brock was standing up in the doorway of his room.

Brock was fastening the sleeve of the new uniform. He kept his attention away from Serena, who was trying to tell him he wasn't ready to get out of bed, and Emery, who was trying to order him back to bed. He focused on Exton.

"Aerie's in trouble, isn't she?"

Brock's question made Exton even more irritated. As he looked at Brock, he saw nothing short of resignation in his eyes.

"Yes," Exton admitted. "Big trouble. She's gone to try to rescue her mother from Gerard."

Brock sighed. "Not a good idea."

"She has General St. Cloud with her."

"Still not a good idea," Brock said, "but at least it's better than nothing. I guess taking Cal was a good idea. He wanted the chance to make the URS pay for making us look like fools."

"How do you know about Cal's role?"

Brock shrugged. "I went to go see him earlier and he wasn't in the room. I knew he wouldn't have gotten out earlier than me. Not with his arm wounded as badly as it was."

"You're right," Serena said. "He shouldn't have left. And you need to get back in bed too. You didn't have as much damage, but we are still monitoring your condition."

"Go monitor someone else, Serena," Brock said. He glanced over at Exton. "I'm going with you."

"What? No," Exton snapped. "Aerie's my wife, and I'll take care of her. You need to get back to your room and listen to the med techs."

"Believe me, if you want her back, and you want her to be safe, you'll take me with you," Brock said. "I'm the only one who will be able to find her."

"Why?" Emery asked. "Why only you?"

Brock seemed to realize he had an audience all of a sudden. He seemed to struggle for the words as he finally said, "Because … because I can get in contact with the URS and their forces."

"What are you talking about?" Exton's voice went low and dangerous.

Brock looked at his feet, before he unbuttoned his uniform jacket, letting them watch as he peeled away a small patch of synthetic skin from the area just underneath his collarbone.

Once the skin was ripped away, there was a small, clear device revealed, one barely able to be seen against his skin. Brock pointed to it, then he ran his finger over it, trying to dislodge it. "Aerie wasn't the only one was who was tracked by the URS."

Before Exton could think to stop himself, he lashed out, grabbing Brock by the shoulders. He didn't even see his fist as it sunk into the younger man's face.

"Exton," Emery said, stepping forward. She managed to grab hold of his fist before he launched it at Brock again.

"Step back, Emery," he yelled. "He's putting all of us here in danger, and he did it willingly."

"That's true," Emery said. She used her free hand to pull out a small gun from its hidden holster at her side. "But we have other ways of dealing with this sort of thing. We don't need you to punch him. I'm perfectly capable of shooting him."

"Stop!" Brock rubbed his face where Exton's fist had connected. A bruise was already forming underneath his eye. "Calm down," Brock shouted back. "It's a manual tracker. I can turn it on and off at my discretion."

Serena stepped forward. "I can verify that," she said. "I recognize the model. We put them in troops for special assignments. Sometimes they forget to schedule a removal surgery."

Exton glared at her, and then turned his gaze back to Brock's. "Why do you have it in the first place?"

Brock scowled at him, his expression awkwardly contorted due to his blackening eye. "You of all people should know why," he said. "I was handpicked from my class to serve the URS in its military."

"I know that much," Exton retorted. "It's one of the only reasons I kept you here after you tried to kidnap Aerie before. In fact," he growled, "it was the *only* reason."

"No it's not," Serena huffed. "He's Aerie's friend, and you wouldn't have sent him home if you thought she would be upset by it."

Exton said nothing to her remark, but the bitter silence surrounding them let Serena know she was right.

Brock continued. "I was approached by Osgood himself a couple of years ago. He knew I was at the top of my class. He said he wanted to mentor me."

"Osgood is your mentor?"

"Yes," Brock admitted. He frowned. "Just like St. Cloud was yours."

Exton felt his frown deepen. He was glad that Emery was the one holding the weapon, because at the mention of Aerie's father, he was more than willing to bet that if he was the one holding it, Brock would be dead—or at minimum, severely injured.

"Dictator Osgood told me he had a mission for me. He

wanted me to get close to Aerie's family. When he found out I was interested in her … " Brock's face flustered over red, making his swollen cheek turn an ugly shade of purple.

"Why did he assign that to you?" Exton asked curtly. "Go on."

"I'm trying," Brock muttered. "When he realized I liked her, he said he would approve cohabitation for us once she was eighteen, should she accept. But he said he wanted to keep a closer watch on St. Cloud."

"Why?" It was Serena's turn to ask the question. "The General did all the work he was supposed to. Even Phoebe told me that he had been doing more than he had to for work."

"Osgood doesn't trust anyone," Exton answered. "That's why."

"He's suspected St. Cloud for years," Brock admitted. "But I didn't see anything that was really a concern. I mean, I know he seemed okay with religion, but I thought that was more unfortunate than terrible. I didn't think that was a lot to worry about when I sent in my reports on St. Cloud to Osgood."

Exton shook his head. All the connections had been in front of him, and he had not seen it. "Osgood was the one who sent you in to save Aerie from the Reeducation Center, wasn't he?"

Brock nodded. "Yes. He wanted to know where the Ecclesia's secret outpost was. He didn't know specifically, but once he found out that Aerie had been in contact with them and she was determined to find them again, he had her arrested."

"He was hoping to get St. Cloud to admit he'd known," Exton continued, recalling how St. Cloud had been the one who signed her arrest warrant. "But he followed orders and didn't give anything away."

"So he had me chipped, and I went in to rescue Aerie. He knew Gerard was too happy to torture someone to be ready to defend himself, let alone win against someone like me."

Brock shrugged. "So I took her and we left. I asked Serena to come because I was actually worried about Aerie's wounds."

"For a military guy, you are weirdly adverse to blood and needles," Serena said with a playful smirk.

"That's enough," Exton snapped at Serena. He turned back to Brock. "So you lied to her, to us, and you infiltrated Petra. Tell me why I shouldn't just shoot you now and get you out of my way for good."

"I can contact the Craftcarrier near Panama," Brock said.

"Why didn't you do it earlier?" Emery asked. "Why did you go off to fight them?"

Brock shuffled his feet, reminding Exton how much younger and how much more inexperienced at life he really was. "I … I sort of like it here," he admitted bashfully. "I mean, I'm mad that Aerie's not here." He glared at Exton briefly, before adding, "But I like the people here. Cal and Dorian and I managed to make a few friends, and we all had more freedom here. The other day, Cal and Dorian and I all went ice fishing with some of the other guys around here, and I realized I'd never had a lot of real friends like that—people who would argue with me freely or force me to think about new ideas. It was … weird. And nice."

He lowered his gaze. "After the Craftcarrier went down in the bay, I realized that I didn't really want the URS to win. I didn't want to return to a life where survival of the State was everything. I felt bad about calling them before."

"You were the one who contacted Osgood with the location of our post." Exton closed his eyes. *How blind could I have been?*

Part of him suddenly hated how much he had fallen in love with Aerie those few weeks on the *Perdition.* His heart had done him a great disservice. He was a better fighter when he had his heart in cold stasis, dead to the concerns of the world and only a servant to his own inner darkness.

He even hated that he had to go and rescue her from her own recklessness. He was beginning to wonder how much she was like Merra, and what that would mean for the two of them.

Could they live with each other? She had told him she didn't judge him based on his father's choices, but what about his own? Exton knew he had difficult decisions to make, especially when it came to war. She didn't seem to understand how much her mother had messed things up, and how difficult it was for him to act as both a leader and a husband in this matter.

"Well, yeah," Brock replied, interrupting Exton's worries. "But I didn't think he would try to kill me along with everyone else. He told me to stay there, and when everything was over, he would send a scouting team out for me."

"He used you," Emery remarked. "He wouldn't have trusted you."

"I realize that now," Brock said with a nod. "So I clicked off my device after the Craftcarrier was shot down. I'd hoped he would think that I was killed in action. But I promise you, sincerely, on anything that you want, I did not contact them after that. I swear. If I'm lying, you can kill me with my full approval."

After a long moment of considering Brock's eager, still-swelling face, and glaring into his eyes as he searched for some semblance of a soul, Exton groaned. "Fine," he said. "I'll take you with me to go and get Aerie. But you're piloting the ship, and you're going to take the fall once Osgood alerts his minions that you're no longer on his side."

"He might figure that out anyway," Serena pointed out. "After all, why would you come back just as Aerie's gone missing?"

"He might not have found her yet," Emery said. "You have some time, but you have to decide whether or not to take it now."

Exton felt a rush of shame as he realized he wasn't completely willing to go. Some part of him wanted Aerie to learn the hard way how much she couldn't disobey his orders; he even rationalized that she was stronger than most people gave her credit for. He even thought she might succeed, especially since St. Cloud was with her. And there were other things that required his attention. His father's files, Petra's fighter force was down, and he had no clear plan of how to rescue Merra anyway.

There were a lot of reasons to stay away. The more pragmatic side of him said there were more than plenty of reasons to at least wait until he knew the full extent of his options. It was almost too easy.

Almost.

The temptation to allow Aerie to run away from him, even for what she saw as a justifiable reason, went against everything good and principled inside of him.

He nodded. "It's always now or never," Exton said. "Emery, before you go, alert Aunt Patty of the situation. I'm going to go take care of Aerie and Merra. And St. Cloud, too."

Emery gave him a small smile. "She'll be happy to help out," she said. "She wanted Merra back too, almost as much as Aerie did."

Exton snorted. "Not enough to risk her life or the fate of this community, obviously. Give me your weapon, please, so I can take Brock down to the hangar."

"I'm not going to fight you," Brock said.

"I just punched you," Exton reminded him, as he knocked the gun into Brock's back, forcing him to march down the hall. "I'm not about to let my guard down now."

♦19♦

Aerie felt the shuttle land hard, and for a moment she had to wonder if Cal was allowing his shoulder to affect his flight skills. When she saw him laugh and give their father a high five, she realized he'd done it on purpose.

"Hey!" she snapped. "There's no need to try to be 'cool' here, Cal. We still need this ship to be able to take off once we've rescued Mom."

"Lighten up," Cal bit back. "This is a standard rescue mission for me. Maybe if you'd made it into the military, you would have more appreciation for my attempts to have fun."

"I'm risking my marriage for this," Aerie hissed back. "There's nothing *fun* about that."

"If you're risking all of that, it's your fault," Cal replied, as he stuck his tongue out at her.

"Kids, calm down," General St. Cloud said. His voice was deep but bland, and Aerie knew he was more focused on the scene before them. "Cal, you need to prep the ship for another takeoff. Even if it's a standard mission to you, we're not going to be taking our time. It's already been over a full day since Merra was taken, and there's no telling what the State will do to her. They have a problem with people who just won't die, you know."

Aerie caught his expression and knew he was talking about Exton's father. Once Silas had been killed, Exton had resurrected him as the ghost of Captain Chainsword. At her graduation, she remembered Osgood's hopeful, almost sadistic delight that the *Perdition* was going to attack New Hope.

Under the coils of clouds, the Panama Canal appeared to be hemorrhaging blood, but Aerie knew it was just a rare form of red algae.

Or at least that's what I hope it is. She glanced back at the General.

"It's poison," he said, answering her inquiring gaze. There was a happy gleam in his eyes. "The URS will have to evacuate before too long. The algae is growing to the point where it will easily contaminate their water supply."

"Where is their base?" she asked.

"Further east from here," the General replied. He turned toward Cal. "You'll need to make sure you keep your communication line open while you wait. You also need to keep watch on our scope. No screw ups, Cal."

Her older brother huffed. "We went over it several times already. I got it."

The General held his gaze for a long moment, as if he was sizing up Cal's resolve. Then he nodded slowly. "Alright, son. I'm counting on you."

"You're fine," Cal said, brushing him off. "Now, get going before Aerie changes her mind. She doesn't want to get in trouble with her husband, remember?"

Aerie was about to insult him back, but her father stepped between them. "If I know Exton, it's already too late for that," the General said, and Aerie felt her heart sink. "Now, let's grab our packs and go, Aerie."

Aerie nodded, determined to keep going. *The General is right. What other choice do I have? I need to save my mother, no matter what Exton says.*

Recalling their earlier argument made it easier for Aerie to climb down from the shuttle and step into the chilly mountain air.

"I thought we were going down into Columbia," Aerie said. "Why are we at Panama?"

"All militaries have weaknesses, Aerie." General St. Cloud took out his binoculars and looked around.

Aerie could tell from his sweeping movements he was getting a digital reading of the nearby area.

"You're looking at Panama. This is where the main docking station for the URS forces is located. They might be concentrated in the Columbian boarders, but they still use the isthmus as a central hub for their supply runs."

Aerie glanced around, surprised. She saw the large canal docking stations, the water that was weaving its way into the wounded earth, and the sturdy mountains closing in on the manmade structure. "Makes sense," she muttered, relishing the taste of the saltwater in the air.

"This is where the Old Republic blasted through the mountains during the Canal's construction," the General said, as they overlooked the small mountain range.

"Is this place close to where is Gerard keeping Mom?" Aerie asked. "I don't see their base."

"The base is underground here, same as New Hope. It has several tunnels and channels, among other things, running down into Columbia."

"Even New Hope has some parts that remain above ground."

"The reasons are the same," General St. Cloud told her. "You have the outcasts aboveground, before you decide to kill them or use them for test subjects, and then everyone else who is able to follow orders stays below."

Aerie's eyes widened. "They really killed all the homeless people at New Hope?"

"If you're not useful," the General said, "they find a way to make you useful. It's not pretty, Aerie, when the world works on a purely utilitarian scale."

"I've noticed," Aerie said, wrinkling her nose.

A few moments passed while they walked on in silence. Aerie watched the General as he muttered to himself, looking around and taking mental notes. He would sometimes use the comm to ask Cal a question.

She decided she was glad, even if it was reluctantly, that her father had come with her. He was comfortable taking the lead, and Aerie didn't feel half as prepared as he looked.

She squatted down on the path and squinted across the way. From where she was, she could just make out the slim waterway where the red algae continued to feed its way into the canal. Towers of smoke drizzled in the distance, and for the first time, Aerie wondered if she was looking at the remains of the *Perdition*'s fighters.

"I've located an entrance," the General told her. "We

need to get down onto the Ustupo plains. That's where their main base hangar opens up to air shipments. It's going to be a bit of a hike, so stay close to me."

"I can manage," Aerie assured him. She clung to the straps on her pack, trying to show him she was up to the task. "As you said, this is just like combat class so far."

Several hours and several miles later, Aerie regretted her proud assertion. She was still determined to go on strong, but with the aches in her legs and the strain on her back, she was starting to wonder how much longer it was going to take. She had been on the *Perdition* for weeks, and while the ship had its artificial gravity generator, Aerie could tell she was back on Earth.

"Cal," the General said, startling Aerie as he spoke into his comm. It had been a long time since either of them had said anything. "Can you hear me?"

"Clearly," Cal replied. "I'm keeping the engines warm enough to be ready to go when you are."

"Good. How's the lookout?"

"Clear, for the most—wait."

Aerie felt her breath rush out as there was a sound scraping against the sky.

"I have some ships approaching the landing strip to the south of your position," Cal said. "It looks like some from back home."

"I see them," the General replied. He didn't sound surprised.

"Petra?" Aerie grabbed her own binoculars out and whirled around, looking for the ships. Her heart started beating terribly fast, as she wondered if Exton was on his way to stop her.

"No, not Petra," Cal said. "Home, Aerie. New Hope."

Aerie almost dropped the binoculars in surprised relief. She let out a nervous laugh, right before she felt her right foot fall through the ground.

"Hey!" she yelled in surprise as she lost her balance.

"Watch it!" Her father grabbed her arm.

As he hauled her up to level ground once more, Aerie quickly saw she'd stepped on a concealed reservoir cover. It was empty now, except for a thick layer of mud topped with an icy sheen.

She took a deep breath and saw the General had saved her from nearly a ten-foot drop. "Thank you," she murmured. "That was close."

General St. Cloud didn't seem to hear her. He turned his attention back to Cal. "Do you have a clear shot of the ships?"

"No," Cal responded. "I wouldn't take it anyway. There's no way I have enough power to take down the flagship. It looks like a C-Class shuttle, with enhancements."

The General frowned. "Can you see who it is that's getting off?"

Aerie was just about to ask him why it made a difference when she heard Cal choke out, "It's Osgood."

"What's he doing here?" Aerie asked. She felt another rush of sudden fear. With the dictator himself here, there had to be something else going on. "Could he be here about the ecobomb?"

The General sighed. "I doubt it. He watches over everything, and all the reports are given to him. If he heard the water supply was poisoned, he wouldn't act on it right away. He's not very proactive."

"He did try to get the Emergency Responders up for when Exton came to New Hope," Aerie reminded him. "That was something, at least."

"That's true, but it was hardly a battle."

Aerie watched her father as he took off his backpack. "What's wrong?"

"We're going to have to hurry," he said. "The base will be on lockdown with Osgood here. We might not be able to rely on my memory to get to your mother if they have special orders."

"What should I do?" Cal asked. "I can fire at them, if you want."

"No," the General replied. "Don't do anything. We can only hope they don't see you and the shuttle."

"I have the shields on."

"Shields on that shuttle are a joke compared to what the URS has here."

Aerie watched as Osgood and his legion of guards walked down the landing strip. They were headed to a small building, one that was half-buried into the mountain base. She adjusted the focus on her binoculars. "From the look on his face, I can't tell if he looks angry or if he is airsick," she said.

At the sound of the low rumble in General St. Cloud's throat, Aerie nearly jumped. She was surprised to see him smile down at her.

"You're right," he said. "That's a hard call."

Aerie giggled herself. As the two of them shared a laugh, Aerie realized it was the first time she felt as though she was actually having fun with her father.

It only took a world war, my mother's kidnapping, and the destruction of my marriage to get us here. Her eyes fell to the ground in shame.

As she was glancing down, something caught her eye. "Look," she said. "There's a small stream of water still running through the reservoir."

"So?"

"Even from here, I can tell it's contaminated." Aerie had to wonder just what her mother and the other scientists at the Chaya settlement had put in the bomb. "Looks like the bomb definitely went off."

The General turned and followed her gaze. "You're right. Better be even more careful then."

As she watched the small trickle of pinkish water push through the rusty pipe, Aerie frowned. "You can stop the poison from spreading, right?"

"We have the cure for it at our research center," General St. Cloud assured her. "Merra actually tested it herself."

Aerie saw the softening of his expression for the quickest second. She turned back to the landing strip. "Good. She can be in charge of cleaning up this mess once we get her back."

"We won't get her if we just stay here. Let's get moving again. We need to find a quiet way in, especially with Osgood's arrival."

Aerie followed him closely as he started moving down the bare mountains.

♦20♦

Brock's face was still slightly puffy as Exton piloted his shuttle through the clouds over the Old Columbian atmosphere. Despite feeling as though he'd been fully justified in hitting him, Exton was glad the mark under his eye seemed like it was slowly settling in.

Just like the guilt, Exton thought bitterly. He had been sitting next to Brock for hours, wondering about Emery and watching for reports from Henry, and he was starting to feel guilty about punching Brock—well, at least punching him as hard as he had.

It was hard for him to believe that he felt sorry for Brock. Exton had a feeling it was Aerie's influence, because compassion was not one of his stronger reflexes. He knew compassion was good, and even necessary, and he knew he needed it as much as other people did. But Brock had deliberately placed Petra—along with Aerie—in danger by hiding the truth from them. He had been able to reach out and contact the URS ever since he came, and he came on specific orders from Osgood himself.

Exton felt his compassion wane as he thought of how Brock had tried to kidnap Aerie several weeks ago, while the Craftcarrier was on its way to attack Petra. Brock had been overcome, and he relented to Exton's decision. He even seemed to falter in his loyalty to the URS as he talked with Aerie in the command room, watching as Patty and the others coordinated their counterattack.

Time continued to pass slowly as Exton forced himself to consider the whole situation as logically as possible. Since the *Rothsburton* had fallen, Brock said he hadn't contacted the URS. He had worked on Petra's grounds and he had even signed up for the fighter squad with Cal and Dorian. Was it possible he had changed his mind, at least somewhat, since he arrived? It seemed so, Exton thought, considering he admitted everything in the med ward that morning.

It's certainly been a day for confessions.

Exton was briefly distracted from Brock's bruise and his own inner reflection as he recalled his earlier conversation with the Thorne brothers.

Dennis had been unrepentant, while Don was at least somewhat apologetic.

"We're sorry we didn't tell you sooner," Reverend Thorne had said. "But you have to understand, Exton, we are bound by our order to keep silent on the secrets others share with us in prayer."

"Speak for yourself," Don scoffed. "We are under no jurisdiction to keep secrets for Victor, no matter what Merra or our orders say."

"We didn't tell him about Aerie before," Reverend Thorne pointed out to his brother. "I didn't think there was any real reason for alerting him about their behavior this time, either."

"How in the world did you come to that asinine conclusion?" Exton retorted angrily. "You know St. Cloud was under our watch, and you know I didn't want Aerie to be put in danger. That seems pretty simple, *and you still messed it up*."

"You do not have the support of the Ecclesia for this war, even if we agreed you could do as you wanted."

"That's even more convoluted." Exton frowned. "I gave you the specific responsibility of watching over him. Why would you allow him to leave, and with Aerie at his side, no less?"

Reverend Thorne crossed his arms over his chest. "People will do what they want to, Exton, even if you leave them under guard and under orders."

"Good to know you're on St. Cloud's side, then," Exton said. "I'm ordering you down to Petra for further questioning."

"Both of us?" Don asked.

"Yes," Exton snapped. "See if Sister Katalina or someone else can come and relieve you. I need someone up there who knows the difference between my orders and following your calling."

"I don't think *you* know the difference," Reverend Thorne shot back with a scowl.

His anger was somewhat uncharacteristic, Exton noticed. In all the years that he'd known the Reverend, and worked with him on the ship, Dennis had never been the one to lose his temper before Exton had. Don rambled on, talking about the price one took for following the Lord, and how a war among nations could not usurp the right of the individual, and how they had warned Exton before they weren't going to be compelled to follow him if they didn't want to …

Exton largely ignored it, choosing instead to reiterate his orders, telling them he would be ordering Henry to get them onto a shuttle to Petra just in case they decided not to listen to his orders now, and then signed off.

Sitting in the cockpit of his shuttle, with Brock brooding at his side, Exton suddenly wondered if the Reverend Thorne knew his father's secrets as well.

It was possible. Papa did know both of them well before. They were close with him.

Maybe they knew the truth of Silas's plans for the *Paradise.*

He decided that would be the first thing he would ask them when he got back.

There was another small *beep.* At the sight of the Craftcarrier on the radar, Exton finally addressed Brock directly. "How is the pain?"

"Shut up, before I hit you just as hard, so you know what it feels like."

Exton grimaced. "I'm sorry I hit you so hard." The words tasted like bile on his tongue, but he spat them out in as much as a poised manner as possible.

Brock rolled his eyes. "Just shut up. I don't like you, and I don't want to talk to you. The only reason I'm agreeing to this is because Aerie's in trouble, and I don't want her to get hurt."

"At least we have that in common." Exton glanced down

at the controls. "We'll be coming up on the Canal soon. Are you going to hail the URS?"

"Why don't you try to call Aerie again?" Brock snapped back. "I'd prefer to hear from her first, before we decide to go all suicidal with this mission."

"We've had her movements confirmed," Exton reminded him. "Henry, the *Perdition*'s pilot, managed to find her on the ship's cams as she and General St. Cloud stole a shuttle. There's no doubt where she's headed, either, since my analysts were able to track the shuttle's movements until they passed the Tropic of Capricorn."

He felt his fist clench tightly as he added, "Besides, there's no reception for our comms out here. The cloud cover prevents us from signaling her."

Brock kept his mouth in a tight frown as he fiddled with the miniature comm. He'd had Serena pull it out from under his skin completely before they left.

He punched in a code before a responding siren emitted softly from the device. "Beacon One, hailing Beacon One. This is Comrade Rearden of New Hope. Do you copy?"

"Copy"

"This is Comrade Rearden," Brock said. He glanced over at Exton. "I'm approaching the Panama area. I am experiencing engine troubles with my craft."

"We do not have you on scope, Comrade."

"I'm approaching from the southeast quadrant."

A moment of silence passed. Exton saw the *Morgan Soromsky* as they approached. He nudged Brock's arm, pointing to the approaching Craftcarrier.

"I'm in the vicinity of a Craftcarrier," Brock added, giving Exton another dirty look. "That could be preventing you from catching my ship on radar."

"Roger that. We have confirmed with Dictator Osgood that you have the required security clearance to land at Panama. He has directed you to land at the Ustupo landing site. He will personally come out to meet you once you land."

Exton and Brock exchanged quick glances. "His

Excellency is at the Panama base?" Brock asked. "Repeat for clarification."

"Yes. His Excellency arrived this morning," the voice on the other end confirmed.

As the air traffic controller read off the landing site's coordinates, Exton leaned back against his seat.

It had been many, many years since he'd seen the dictator in person. Over the years as Captain Chainsword, he'd made some calls with the man, taunting him when possible. Osgood made his threats and ranted appropriately for a man who hated having anything outside of his control. Exton knew he was in his late fifties, or even possibly older, and he had never been one who did his own dirty work.

As the communication link between Brock and the base was once more severed, Exton sighed. "I wonder why Osgood is here."

"It's pretty unusual for him to leave New Hope," Brock agreed. "I've only ever seen him leave a few times. Most of the time it was for on-site verification, from what I know."

"On-site verification?"

"Not all bases and communities are connected by the same systems," Brock said. "If there was a record he wanted to check or a follow-up inspection he wanted to make in person, that's when he would leave."

"I see." Exton had to wonder if he had gone to Nova Scotia after St. Cloud betrayed him there. *That would be one way to catch St. Cloud in a lie*, he thought. He knew St. Cloud had altered medical records for Aerie's sake.

"Well, this throws a wrench in our plan to land quietly," Brock said. "I don't think we'll be able to hope no one cares if I'm there or not."

"I won't be able to hide," Exton said. "Osgood will recognize this shuttle. He'll likely have it stripped for parts by the time he's done pulling it apart."

"Well, we better think of a new plan. We're closing in on the base; only about another twenty minutes."

Exton reached up and grabbed the comm. "That gives

me only a few moments to get this sorted out. Here." He tossed Brock Emery's weapon, the one he'd used on Brock earlier.

"What's this for?" Brock asked.

"You're going to need it," Exton said.

"I don't think we're going to be able to hold off an entire base of soldiers. Especially Panama. I've never been there myself, but it's supposed to be pretty big," Brock said.

"That's not how you're going to use it," Exton replied. He gave him a humorless smile. "But you are going to get what you wanted."

"What do you mean?" Brock's expression was curiously interested.

"You're going to get a chance to hit me after all." Exton turned his attention back to the comm, as Kamalo's voice came over the line. "Kamalo, can you read me?"

"Loud and clear." Despite the time difference, Kamalo was alert and engaged. "What can I do for you?"

"You might be sorry you asked that question," Exton replied. "We have a new mission, and I need you to put it together, stat. I'm going to try to patch in my aunt and Henry too. We're going to need everyone on board for this one."

"Sounds exciting," Kamalo cheered. "I'm ready."

"I'll need more than that," Exton said. He glanced over at Brock, who was still slightly confused. "Osgood is in Panama, and if we can capture him, we'll be able to finish the war. Brock and I are here right now, and if you and the others can give me a sizable distraction, that will give Brock and me the cover we'll need to get in and get out."

"And save Aerie," Brock added.

Exton nodded, jolted he'd almost forgotten. "Yes, that too."

He could almost see Kamalo's smile at the thought. "Well, *boet*," he said, "then let's finish this war."

♦20♦

"Ugh, this stinks," Aerie muttered, as she made her way past another pile of laundry.

"We're in Panama now," the General reminded her. "In New Hope, it is easier to keep the temperatures regulated. Here in Panama, this close to the equator and with all the humidity in the air, the soldiers here are more likely to sweat more."

Aerie pinched her nose shut even more tightly. "Thanks," she muttered, her voice nasal. *I was taught to fight and shoot and survive,* she thought. *I was not supposed to deal with this amount of terrible body odor!*

It wasn't like she had a whole array of other options, and this was the least troublesome of the others she had discussed with the General. They had managed to do a quick survey of the surrounding environment as they made their way out of the mountain trails. It was then that, after a few rounds of arguing, they decided to move in through the ventilation.

Aerie was happy to know her experience with slipping in and out of air vents was coming in handy; it was all too easy to recall the rush she felt when she would climb up an old, broken shaft to get to Moona and the Memory Tree, to allow herself a few moments to escape New Hope's underground city. When they came across an older vent, Aerie found a similar set up.

She almost smiled, despite the smell in the air as they made their way through the sanitation center of the base. The General had commended her with a nod as he struggled to shimmy down the tube after her.

"Aerie." Her father's voice was soft and sharp against the atmosphere. "Something is wrong."

"What is it?"

"No one is here," the General said. He glanced at his watch. "It's mid-shift."

"Well, Osgood is here," Aerie said. "Maybe they are reporting to him?"

"Doubtful, but possible." He sighed. "We'll need to find an informant."

Aerie picked up a relatively clean-looking uniform. It looked close enough to her size that she had an idea. "Do you think we can blend in by playing along?"

"We'll have to leave our packs here if we disguise ourselves," the General said. "They'll know someone is here."

Aerie scowled. "You're the one who said this would be quick," she reminded him. "I think we'll be able to last between here and getting Mom out."

"We don't know how long it will be until we find her," General St. Cloud said. "Anyway, I wasn't disagreeing, I was just letting you know the risks."

"The risks of this mission are already too much for some people," Aerie snapped, her patience nearly gone. "We might as well finish it." She put her pack down and started to pull the URS uniform over her own.

The General put a hand on her arm. "Everything will be alright, Aerie," he said. "You can just tell Exton that everything was my idea, and I coerced you into going along with it."

"What?" Aerie shook her head. "No. That won't work. He already told me not to go and meet with you. I'm already breaking his orders and disobeying him; there's no need to add to my betrayal with dishonesty."

"If you had a good enough reason to disobey him, he'll likely be able to forgive you."

"Like he forgave you for killing Silas?" Aerie shot back. She wrinkled her nose. "No, you're mistaken. Exton doesn't forgive people very often, and especially not people like you … or maybe I should say like us."

She was surprised at the lump that formed in her throat as she spoke the words. *Is this really what is in my heart?* Aerie wondered.

"He's hurting himself more than anyone else," the General said. "You can't change things like that. You can only go forward."

Aerie stiffened. "He might forgive you if you were a little more sincere about things like this, you know."

"And the moon might fall into the ocean, or the sun might suddenly burn blue." The General shook his head before searching through another pile of uniforms to find one he could borrow. "There's no point in wondering about what could be, when you already know what it won't be."

Aerie said nothing else as she finished zipping herself into the uniform. She tucked her hair up under the hat as much as she could, hoping that she would be able to sneak around without her long, red hair giving her away.

"Here." The General handed her a small gun. "Tuck this into your belt. Make sure you can reach it easily."

"I have my own weapon," Aerie reminded him.

"You're smaller, and even in that uniform disguise, it'll stick out. Take the smaller one."

Aerie tightened her lips, irritated he was ordering her around, and further irritated that he had a point. "I wish there was a mirror in here," she murmured, pushing her bangs out of her face.

"Don't obsess over your hair. It's longer than the URS would like, but you'll pass. That being said, don't be surprised if someone says something about your uniform or your boots. Those always were your bigger problems when it came to presentation."

Aerie shot him a scowl, but she was surprised to see him smile back at her. She lost her confrontation air as he explained, "Your mother had the same issues, Aerie. It was never something that bothered me, even if it was too unkempt for the military."

Warmth in her heart seemed to trickle through her body, making her more confident at once. Some part of her wondered if she'd always had her father's approval, even though he felt he had to protect her from the truth. "I wish you would have told me that after Mom left," Aerie said quietly. "I missed her a lot."

"You did a good job of hiding it," the General told her.

"And I guess I did a good job of not looking for it."

It was surprising when, despite his past and her grief, Aerie realized she could forgive him, too. He was more like Exton than she'd realized—a man of honor, charged with a responsibility too great for one person to bear alone.

The General nodded toward the door. "We'd better get going. We're going to have to—"

Before he could finish the rest of his sentence, an alarm blared throughout the complex, gutting Aerie's ears with its instant power.

"Augh," she moaned. "What's going on?"

The General peeked out of the room. "I see some other soldiers," he said. "Let's follow them. You go first; I'm the one who is more likely to be recognized between the two of us."

Aerie nodded and took the lead. They fell in line easily between different groups of guards, but no one seemed to notice their presence.

Good, Aerie thought. She didn't want to have to fight. They had a limited supply of shots and a close fight in the labyrinthine corridor would give them the advantage. Several moments passed, but Aerie barely realized it; she glanced between the guards, wondering if Gerard was close. The few whispers she was able to catch all spoke about Osgood, not his lieutenant commander.

She almost fell over when a door opened and the sunlight, as little as it was, lit up the hallway. She could see the landing strip from earlier as she peeked outside. There was even a shuttle landing on it.

A shuttle she recognized.

Aerie felt her mouth drop open as her heart stopped. She might have gasped, if she had been able to speak, if her body had been able to work properly. As the line of guards walked outside, the General pulled her back, diverting her to an area off to the side where they could watch without being noticed.

It was a good thing, too, Aerie decided. Her legs went numb, her arms went limp, she almost tripped, and she struggled to breathe in that moment.

She watched as Exton came down the gangway of his chainsword shuttle, the very same one she'd been picked up in months before. She could see from where she was there was blood slowly dripping out of his nose.

He was followed by Brock, who held something tucked under his one arm. In his other hand, he held a weapon steady, pointing directly at Exton's heart.

Exton! No, not him! God, no, please no …

Beside her, the General nodded approvingly. "I told you Brock was probably a traitor," he said. "Looks like I was right."

"This is not the time to remind me of that," Aerie snarled. Her annoyance blossomed into full self-disgust, as she realized she could have told Exton about the General's suspicion of Brock, but she didn't. And now he was captured.

The General raised his eyebrows at her. "What's wrong?"

"He's got Exton," Aerie whimpered, her head falling into her hands. "And this is all my fault."

"If you were going to put yourself in danger, you should've at least considered that someone would come and get you," the General told her. "Even your mother likely knows we're coming for her."

"We can't leave without him," Aerie insisted. She felt her face flush over while she watched her husband as he suddenly stood before Dictator Osgood, with Brock still at his back.

She leaned forward, already reaching for the concealed weapon at her side. "We have to—"

"Don't," the General snapped. "Stay here with me. Right now is not the time to attack. Take a deep breath and steady yourself, Comrade."

Aerie tried to swallow the lump in her throat. She gave the General a barely perceivable nod as she tried to control herself.

The General is right. This is not the time to lose it. Mom needs me, Exton needs me, and now Brock is a traitor. I have to do something. But I have to wait.

She sighed to herself. That was exactly the reason she'd gotten into this mess in the first place. Her mind reeled as she realized that her combat classes had done little to prepare her for events such as this.

But why would they? Aerie thought disdainfully. There was nothing in the URS that was supposed to have a hold on her heart more than her mission. She had been emotionally compromised.

"You need to keep it together," the General whispered to her. "If you step out and try to save him, we could easily be signing Merra's death warrant as much as his."

"But—"

"But nothing." The General turned his attention back to Osgood, who was obviously confused by Exton's appearance. "This is for the best, despite what you might think. Once Osgood realizes who Brock's captured, he'll likely lead us straight to Merra in the prison ward."

"I think Osgood already knows who Exton is," Aerie whispered back. She watched from here as Brock nudged Exton forward, with his gun pressing into Exton's back. Brock handed Osgood the object he'd carried down from the shuttle.

Even from where she was, Aerie recognized the pirate hat Exton had worn that first time she'd fought with him.

"I hope he doesn't do anything foolish."

At the dry amusement in his voice, Aerie frowned. "What do you think he can do at this point?" She watched Osgood as his face twisted into a pleasurable smile, while Exton was forced down onto his knees as Brock elbowed him in the ribs. "He's trapped."

"You're watching the wrong person," the General told her. "Look at Exton's face. He's not worried about Brock. He's barely able to stop himself from attacking Osgood."

Aerie turned her attention to Exton's face. She had trouble watching him; her heart was screaming that this was all her fault, and there were a million things she would trade to have him safe. But despite her anxiety and despair, she saw that the General was right. He was composed, even if she could see he was seething with rage inside.

"It's only going to be a matter of time before something happens," the General said. "We need to be ready for it."

"What should we do?" Aerie asked. Her hands were starting to shake; her mind was racing with a hundred different scenarios at once. The cruel voice inside of her just wanted to laugh at the absurdity of everything—how she had decided to take matters into her own hands, how she had caused all of this to happen, and how she would pay the ultimate price for her arrogant foolishness.

As her inner voice grew louder, she looked to her father for direction.

"Follow them," the General said, flexing his fingers as they hovered close to the weapon hidden in the folds of his uniform. "If we're lucky, they'll lead us right to Merra."

♦21♦

In all his years of taunting Osgood from the *Perdition*, Exton wasn't sure if he'd ever heard the dictator laugh. Even if he had, the communications between them had been from a distance, half way from the earth to the moon. There had been plenty of filters between them.

In person, the experience was harrowing.

Grant Osgood, for all he was a meticulous man, always so neat in his appearance, guffawed with laughter as he looked down his pert nose at Exton. His snickers were a strain of exacting syllables, sounding almost like a robot that had been pushed into a musical loop; it was almost as if, having been confronted with a situation in which he could not program himself for a proper reaction, his voice automatically tried to make up the difference.

As Exton knelt on the ground, gritting his teeth at the pain from Brock's blow, he was torn between which punishment was worse.

I should have told Brock to take it easy on me, he thought. That punch in the stomach could have been avoided, or at least better executed. On the other hand, even Exton had to admit, if the situation had been reversed, he would have had trouble stopping himself from celebrating, too.

Osgood's laughter stopped as abruptly as it started. "Well, well, Captain Chainsword," he rasped. "It's good to finally see you unmasked."

Brock straightened. "His real name is Exton Shepherd," he said. "He's the leader of the defectors and their forces."

"I should've known," Osgood said. "Silas Shepherd's boy, am I right?"

Exton felt his eyes narrow as he looked up at Osgood.

Osgood nodded.

Age had not been kind to the older man, as much as he knew Osgood had tried to hold off old age. He remained very similar to the man he remembered talking with his father over the monitors, and even the one he remembered seeing at his own graduation ceremony. The small wrinkles around his mouth and eyes hinted at cosmetic surgery, and from this close, Exton could see the roots of his graying hair, receded significantly from his forehead. His teeth were perfectly white and perfectly straight, sparkling in the dim sunlight.

"You look too much like him to be otherwise," Osgood continued, his smile fading somewhat as Exton refused to answer. "You even seem to have his attitude. He never said much to me, especially after the last dictator retired. He always thought he was too good for me, too good to talk to a political leader."

Exton said nothing. Osgood was looking for an excuse to have him punished further, and he wasn't going to give it to him.

"I should have remembered you," he drawled on. "I remember searching through the records after the *Paradise* was taken. I didn't find anything. But then, you've got some good hackers on your side, don't you? I've noticed several other records have been altered or have gone missing in recent years."

Exton was once more thankful for Tyler's recommendations on that course of action. He had been wondering if Osgood knew who he was. St. Cloud had remembered, but Exton knew he'd said nothing to Osgood about his identity. It gave him a small advantage, and he hoped he would get the chance to use it.

Osgood huffed. He turned his attention to Brock. "Comrade Rearden," he said. "Congratulations on your capture and completing your mission. I do believe a promotion with a nice-sized bonus is in store for you."

"Thank you, sir," Brock replied.

Exton almost rolled his eyes. Despite the fact Brock was on their side, his prompt response and his apparent pleasure at pleasing his boss were more than irritating. He wasn't going to be able to deal with Brock changing sides again.

I'll have to talk to him about his wishy-washy attitude later, he thought to himself.

"I'm glad to see you were able to come out of Petra largely unscathed," Osgood continued. "Although your eye could use some medical attention by the looks of it."

"The pain is nothing," Brock assured Osgood. "I am glad to have this *filth* taken care of."

"What happened to Comrade St. Cloud?" Osgood asked. "Did she end up fully defecting? Or did the *Rothsburton* manage to take a few defectors down with its demise?"

"Oh, uh … " Brock faltered, and Exton breathed a sigh of relief. While they had not discussed Aerie's role in their scheme, it was good to know Osgood had no idea of her plan to rescue her mother.

Exton almost wondered if Aerie had turned around and went to Petra after all. It was not a simple plan, rummaging around a large military base. As he watched Brock and Osgood, he certainly hoped so, even though Emery had made it a point to tell him there was no sign of her, returning or otherwise. It would be nothing for him to escape with Merra, if only he knew she was safe.

Brock cleared his throat. "Comrade St. Cloud did not defect at all, sir. Actually, she helped me take this defector down. She was playing along with them. It was pretty easy to do, really. A lot of them don't seem to want to question who is really on their side. They seem to think it will help make them appear nicer or something silly like that."

"I know she was captured after the attack on New Hope."

"She deliberately planned it," Brock asserted. "She told me that since she was not approved for entrance into the New Hope Military Academy, she wanted to get close enough to the defectors to take them down to show her worth as a soldier. Comrade Rearden, once she was captured, gained their trust and then used it to find out all about their plans. She even convinced them to let her stay there as one of them so she could gain more intel."

"Remarkable. She never seemed the type to succeed other than by blind luck."

Exton was glad he was looking at the ground, or Osgood would've seen his eyes widen in surprise. It was a good story, he thought. Brock's plan had that eerie quality of sounding true, without really being true. If he didn't trust Aerie, he might have believed it himself.

After all, what better way to capture him than by lies and deceit, especially when he'd been so willing to give her the benefit of the doubt? It wasn't hard to see the story fall into place; just like St. Cloud and Merra, Aerie could have been trained to lie as much as she had.

He nearly smiled, discarding the idea almost immediately after its conception; Aerie might have been similar to her family at some points, but there were some very pronounced distinctions. For one, he trusted her. And he knew she had not lied to him since they'd struck their deal back in the Captain's Lounge on the *Perdition.*

Where are you, Aerie?

Exton could only pray she was safe.

"I can personally vouch for Comrade St. Cloud's determination, sir," Brock said. "We trained together for years. She was devastated when she did not get assigned to the military. She acted with desperation."

That's where I can also vouch for her, Exton thought humorlessly.

"I see. But her plans didn't work, did they? I know she came back afterward by St. Cloud's maneuverings," Osgood said. "He was the traitor in all of this."

"He remains at large," Brock said. "I wasn't able to get to him. The defectors do not trust him, and plenty of them want him dead as well."

"Good, good." Osgood smiled. "I am glad to hear it. Hopefully he won't be much of a problem."

"I understand his first wife is here," Brock continued. "That's how I was able to get this scum to come with me. He wanted to try to rescue her, and I planned everything else."

"You've heard about Merra St. Cloud?" Osgood's smile grew. "You've been a busy worker, Comrade. Excellent. And this is perfect timing. We're about to finish off the defectors, once and for all, and once they're gone, the rest of the world will soon follow."

Exton caught Brock's hesitation as he paused for the slightest second. "Good," he said.

"It's time you completed your training," Osgood said. "I'm going to need more dedicated soldiers like you at my side as we launch the GPI."

"What's the GPI?" Exton asked, unable to stop himself.

As if to answer him, Brock slammed his weapon over Exton's head. "Keep quiet," he barked.

As Exton struggled to keep his balance from the pain, Osgood laughed again. The mechanical quality of his mirth was even less humane than the previous time. "Nothing you need to know about, Captain," he replied. "After all, you'll be dead soon enough."

He turned and called up another comrade behind him. "Private, take this prisoner to his new quarters. We'll need to have a special announcement for the rest of our troops to let them know of our captive."

"Yes, sir," the man intoned, saluting the dictator before turning to face Brock and Exton.

"Here," Brock said, stepping forward and gripping Exton's arm tightly. Exton wondered if he was trying, in some way, to reassure him their plan was working, or if Brock was getting in one last round of retaliation against him. "*Move.*"

He shoved Exton forward, and Exton allowed himself to be led away. He glanced back at Osgood, watching him as his wrinkled mouth curled into a smirk. Beside him, Brock stood, clearly uncomfortable but trying to be brave.

Brock had been at the top of his class. *Time to prove it,* Exton thought grimly. They hadn't planned to be separated before getting to Merra. He knew he was going to run into trouble, too, because it was going to be harder to overpower any guards or obstacles on his own. Brock, too, would face his own set of problems.

But, Exton thought, it was good that he was at least able to get some insight on Osgood's plans.

What was the GPI he was talking about? Exton wondered again. There was something familiar about that plan, too. Of course, the URS had always been planning on taking over the world, eventually; it wasn't hard to see from the battles they'd engaged in, and the things they'd done to reorganize everything from communities to continents. But at the mention of the GPI, coupled with destroying the rest of their enemies … Exton was pretty sure he had read about it somewhere before.

He knew his first goal in being at the base was to free Merra, but if possible, he knew he should try to find more information.

If only my head didn't hurt so much, he thought. Brock's bludgeon hadn't drawn blood, but there was definitely a bump forming on the back of his head.

"Keep moving," the guard behind him ordered.

Exton said nothing, but quickened his steps, realizing he had slowed down his pace as his thoughts had taken off.

He was actually grateful for the guard's interruption. He needed to pay attention if he was going to need to recall how to escape. He knew he also had to watch for guard changes and their routes, and any signals or codes that might be necessary along the way.

Several floors and several steps later, Exton found himself directed down a dark hallway. It was full of doors, guarded by other sentries, as they were spaced out every couple of meters. He could hear some other people screaming on the other side, but there was no voice that he could clearly recognize.

Keeping an ear out for Merra, he waited patiently while his guard handed him off to another, before he was thrown into his own cell.

Before he could ask any questions, or get one last look around, the door was slammed in his face.

Glancing around, he saw a small room, stripped of

everything but a dim, flickering light. There was no bed, no running water, and nothing to suggest that he would be getting out anytime soon.

"Great," he muttered sarcastically to himself. "This is just great."

He leaned against the door, pressing his ear to the slippery metal. The sounds he heard earlier had faded, and part of him had to wonder if the screaming was real. He did this to each wall of the room, and the weeping and the shrieking were even more muffled.

Exton sat down against the wall, tucking his knees under his chin as he thought. As he sat there, he almost smiled, thinking of the Captain's Lounge. Aside from the missing window and its window seat, the cell was nearly the same dimension.

If Osgood thinks this is going to break me, he's in for a surprise.

For the moment, Exton knew he had to play the waiting game and hope his aunt, Emery, and Kamalo were almost ready to take down the Panama base.

♦22♦

"Are you sure this is going to work?" Aerie asked, as she pushed the cart back down the increasingly familiar hallways.

"Either it will work, or we'll make it work," the General told her. "Now, stop talking. We're almost back at the prison ward. There are ten guards in the hallway, and we're going to have to play this smart. No stupid mistakes, Aerie."

"Okay," Aerie murmured. "If you say so."

As her father shot her a frown, she sighed. She knew they had been extremely fortunate so far. Once Osgood had ordered Exton away, they had followed at a distance, enough to know where he was being held. They had backtracked their steps, doubling around the area, looking for other clues as to where Merra might be being held.

Aerie had gotten used to walking around the base like she deserved to be there, like she had earned her way in. There had been a few glances in her direction, but she managed to stare them down. She was glad when the General told her they had to find a place to hide as the shifts changed.

Once he saw the protocol, he knew it would be easier to rescue Exton, and possibly Merra, during the middle of the shift. There was less of a chance reinforcements would be ready, and there was a better chance at surprising them.

"Ahem." The General gave her the signal, and Aerie nodded.

She took a deep, steadying breath one last time and then pushed the cart forward into the hallway of prisoners.

"What are you doing?" another guard asked, stepping forward.

"I, uh, must've gotten lost," Aerie replied, the flush in her cheeks genuine as she looked around. She leaned in closer to him, trying to place herself at a good angle. He was much taller than her, and if she was going to knock him out, she needed to be closer. "Can you help me?"

The guard fell right into her trap. The instant he was close enough, Aerie gave him a swift uppercut, aided by her hidden weapon. He fell over almost immediately, and she backed up enough that his body hit the floor flat.

"Oh, no!" she yelped, calling out in the direction of other guards. "Can you help me?"

She saw a couple of them exchange glances, unsure. She went over to the unconscious guard and made fake attempts to haul him up to his feet. Aerie knew it would be hard for them to resist helping her if they believed she was truly helpless.

It worked.

As they made their way over, a brief second of melancholy overcame her as she remembered how frequently her siblings declared her to be helpless. She snapped back to the situation at hand, slipping back out of the guards' way. It was the General's turn to get to work, she thought, as she headed toward the doors.

Loud noises of screaming guards, breaking bones, and clattered weapons echoed behind her. She could hear her father as he rose up from the cart and began fighting.

Aerie was almost sorry she wasn't beside him, helping him. But she knew he made the better distraction between the two of them.

Before she could reach Exton's door, another alarm went off in the building. Aerie jolted and turned back to face the General.

"The *Morgan Soromsky*!" A cry came rushing down from the other end of the hall. "She's been hit!"

Before she could ask if he thought they were in trouble, a large explosion rippled around the hallway.

Aerie felt the floor slip out from under her, and the remaining guards fighting with her father were shaken off their feet. The mountain of support around the building was not enough to isolate them from the blast.

"What's going on?" Aerie called back to her father.

"Nothing we can stop," the General hollered back as he clawed his way up to a standing position. "Check the rooms."

"Oh, right," Aerie grumbled. The shaking walls gradually

stilled as she raced down the hall, and she knew she would be able to fight if she was careful.

"Exton?" she called. "Mom?"

She made her way through the hallway, banging on the doors and shouting out for her family to hear her. Aerie pushed past another round of guards, barely managing to knock them out, when she heard a roughened voice call back.

"Aerie? Is that you?"

She broke out into a wide smile and wriggled her butt in triumph. "Exton!" Aerie scrambled to the door. "Keep talking. I'm coming to get you."

"No," Exton called back. Seconds later, the door just off to her right slammed open. "If anything, *I'm* the one who's here to get *you*."

Aerie felt her cheeks burn as his eyes met hers; she wasn't sure how much he was teasing her—if he was teasing her at all. "I guess that's a good point," she conceded. She was about to curse her pride and rush into his arms anyway, when he stepped forward and grabbed her arm.

With a swift tug, he jerked her across the hall, just as another guard came up behind her. Aerie watched, taken aback, as Exton managed to get the guard in a headlock.

"Hold him," the General called out.

Exton and Aerie both turned to see him as he appeared behind them. Before either of them could say anything, the General punched the guard, knocking him out cold.

General St. Cloud shook out his hand as Exton dumped the limp body onto the ground. "Thanks for the assist," he said.

Aerie held her breath, hoping Exton and her father would be able to work together for the moment. Tension raged between the three of them as they stood perfectly still, while the alarms kept blaring and other guards were being called to their stations.

Finally, Exton relaxed, ever so slightly. "I guess I could say the same thing."

Aerie felt her breath rush out.

"Where's Merra?" Exton asked. "Why isn't she with you?"

"We didn't find her yet," Aerie said. "We saw you when you … when Brock … at the hangar."

Exton turned to the General for clarification, and he obliged. "We saw Brock bring you in," he said. "We figured we better rescue you first, so we could see where the important guests were being held."

"Let's split up and look for her then," Exton said. "And then we've got to get Brock and get out of here."

"You really want to save Brock?" Aerie felt her fury ignite. "After what he did to you?"

"He's on our side, Aerie," Exton snapped. "I would've thought you would know that by now."

"But he turned you in."

"Brock was following orders, unlike someone else I can think of."

Aerie's face burned in shame. "You're telling me that you ordered him to turn you in?"

The General said, "I see. You came here to turn yourself in so you could find Merra."

Exton nodded.

"Good idea," the General said. "Worthy of my protégé, even."

"No thanks," Exton scoffed. "I'm just glad it worked."

Aerie sniffed angrily. "Well, it's good to see you care about my mother's fate *now*."

"I care more about yours," Exton argued back. "Which is the main reason I'm here in the first place."

"I would've thought you would have just let me go," Aerie said. "After all, I would be getting what I deserve, wouldn't I?"

The General stepped between them. "I'm going to go and search for your mother," he told Aerie. "You two have five minutes, and then we need to get back on schedule. If we're going to rescue Brock while we're here, that's going to take longer."

"We'll have the extra time," Exton assured him. "I called in Kamalo and Petra's remaining forces."

"Why?" the General asked.

"Osgood is here. If we can take him out, we'll be able to end the war," Exton explained.

"That's how the Craftcarrier was hit," Aerie exclaimed. At Exton's inquiring gaze, she clarified, "I heard one of the guards say the *Morgan Soromsky* was hit."

"That loud explosion we heard?" Exton nodded. "Good to hear they got here so quickly. I thought it would take longer." He turned back to St. Cloud. "Gerard is here, too, in addition to Merra. If we can capture him, rescue her, and take down Osgood and the GPI, we'll be in a position to call for unconditional surrender."

Aerie watched as her father considered Exton's information. She was glad to see his expression was thoughtful and even impressed. She was about to say something when Exton added, "If there's anything that would make the trip out here worth it, it's that."

Her anger sparked again. "Any chance it's miraculous?"

Exton frowned at her. "I'd say it was, especially after you deliberately disobeyed your orders."

"I'm not one of your soldiers," Aerie shot back.

"Alright, that's my cue. I'm going to get Merra," the General said, stepping back. "Three minutes now, kids."

At the smirk on his face, Aerie wondered if he was getting some sort of sick pleasure watching the two them snip at each other. She let him go, though, as he began kicking open doors, calling for her mother. Aerie turned to face Exton.

"Well, you heard my father," Aerie retorted. "You've got three more minutes to yell at me."

"I'll need more than that to feel like you've been properly chastised," Exton replied. "Do you know how awful it has been, knowing that you went out and foolishly risked your neck for your mother?"

Aerie held her ground. "Do you know how awful it feels to know you weren't even going to rescue her?"

"I didn't have a plan in place," Exton grumbled. "It didn't mean that I wouldn't, eventually. Maybe."

"Ha! You see?" Aerie bristled. "That is just your problem, you know. You didn't have a plan when we met, either. It's any wonder you didn't throw me off the *Perdition* the first time we met."

"Don't make me regret it," he murmured.

"And then you didn't have any idea of how to deal with the General," Aerie pressed. "You were wrong to send me back to him before. I know it, you know it, we all knew it."

"Aerie—"

"No," Aerie insisted. "Look, your plans don't always go according to plan, and—"

"And they wouldn't anyway, if you're not willing to follow orders," Exton cut in. "That was *your* problem, even before we met. You admitted it, and the military confirmed it."

"Well, it's your fault for marrying me anyway then," Aerie told him. "You knew what you were getting into, at least. I didn't. I knew we should have waited longer, just to make sure it could work between us."

"Aerie—"

"Because this is awful," Aerie continued. "How is this really going to work, Exton? If you get angry every time things don't go your way and I don't listen, I don't see how you'll be happy unless you're free from me. And my family."

She looked up at him, watching as an odd expression suddenly came over his face. *This is it,* she thought. She'd told the truth about what she thought of their marriage, and after all the trouble she'd caused him, he had no choice but to agree with her.

Aerie looked down at her borrowed boots, feeling the awful weight of the pain inside of her.

I am not *going to let him break my heart,* she vowed to herself. *If anything, I did the breaking.*

Shame and self-disgust, mingled with the residue of her righteous fury, all forced her to face the truth, and she would pay the price for her transgressions against him—even if it meant letting him go.

Several seconds passed; they had only moments, as the missiles screeched through the air outside and more explosions echoed through the empty hallways.

Suddenly, finally, she heard his response—and then she was immediately angry. He was laughing!

Under the thundering chimes of the nearby battlefield, Aerie was surprised to hear Exton's quiet laugh, the one that always made her think of the time she'd first met him. There had been a great deal of pain in him, pain she had wanted to absolve, but in the end, she had only made it worse for him. And now, he was being an idiot by just standing there, laughing at her.

She balled her fists and stamped her foot. "I'm being serious. It's not funny," she said defensively, narrowing her eyes at him. "There's nothing funny about our situation."

"You're right. There's nothing funny about it, and you're also right that we probably did rush into things." Exton shook his head. "But be that as it may, I could never be free of you, Aerie, any more than you could be free of me."

Aerie was momentarily stunned. She felt a rush of confused tears and forced herself to make them recede as she faced him.

"In a world where love is easily discarded and causally dismissed, I guess it would seem we are not a great match. We have different ideas and different backgrounds, and some of them will not be reconciled."

"Then why were you laughing?" Aerie asked, hurt by his comments. "Don't you care that I don't think we should be together? That I put you in danger? That I put the world in danger, apparently?"

"I laughed because … because I never quite got it, you know." Exton reached up and scratched his head nervously.

Aerie could tell he was searching for the right way to say what was on his mind; she knew he never sought to explain himself to others. She waited for him to go on as patiently as she could, only arching her brow in expectation.

He caught the hint and shrugged. "The Ecclesia have taught that God loves us, no matter what we do, no matter how terrible we are. I thought when my father died, and I walked away from God, I left behind the last of the little area of my life I'd left to him and I believed he would just give up on me. I didn't see how he would keep loving me, even if I didn't love him. But now I get it."

He reached out and took her hand. Still upset, Aerie grabbed it back instantly. "Get what?" she asked.

"I'm telling you that I get it. I love you. I can't name the moment I started loving you, but since the moment I met you, my life has never been the same. You brought my heart back to life. You gave me hope for the future. And you don't give up on something you love because of pain."

He came closer, putting his arms around her in an embrace. She stiffened against him, unable to believe he had been arguing with her in front of her father only moments before. He'd been so upset and bitter. *What had changed?* Aerie wondered.

"You have caused me much trouble, Aerie, but I could no more stop loving you than I could stop time from moving forward. And because of that, I'll never be free of you. I would never want to be free of you, either. Even though I am, understandably, upset at your poor decision-making skills and patience."

"Shut up." But Aerie felt her nose prickle as she finally looked up into his eyes.

"There's the charm," he said with another laugh. "And your stubborn pride. You could just apologize, if you really felt badly enough."

"Never!" Aerie declared, sticking her nose up in the air. But even as her posture remained defiant, Aerie knew she was relieved he still wanted her. As he held her, her fingers pressed into his chest, and her body began to sway along with his.

"I never understood Christ's love for his church until

you," Exton said. "You were always a miracle to me, whether I knew it or not. And now you are so much more to me, whether I like it or not."

"That's not nice."

"I didn't mean that in a bad way. You know what I meant."

Aerie couldn't stop herself. Her arms reached up and circled around his neck. "I know," she said, laying her head down over his heart. "I just wanted to make you suffer."

"I'll return the favor later once we're back home," he warned, "by kissing you senseless until you're begging me for more."

"You're a monster," Aerie moaned, but she was already pushing herself further into his arms, standing up on her tiptoes to kiss him.

At the touch of his lips on hers, she felt her heart nearly break apart, bursting open with pure joy and even her own laughter, as some part of her was fully aware that they were in a secure URS base as a battle was raging outside. But the musky air of Exton's body beckoned to her, wrapping her up in a world that belonged to just the two of them.

Before she could lose herself completely, the General interrupted them as he cleared his throat. "Well, I wasn't able to find Merra. She's not here."

Aerie nearly jumped out of Exton's arms at the sudden reappearance, but he held onto her, keeping her close.

"Where else would she be?" Exton asked.

"Is there another prison ward here? Maybe somewhere else?" Aerie suggested.

"Panama's base is the biggest base for the URS outside of New Hope," he said. "But the building only has one prisoner cell block, and she's not here." General St. Cloud glanced back at Exton. "What were you saying earlier about the GPI?"

"Osgood talked with Brock and me," he said. "He said he was going to destroy the last of his enemies and launch the GPI. He didn't say anything else about it, but it sounded familiar to me. I've been trying to think of where I've heard of it."

"How thoroughly did you sort through the Boötes system?" General St. Cloud asked. "It's a military project. GPI stands for the Global Planethood Initiative. And if Osgood is going to launch it, we need to make sure we do everything possible to stop him."

♦23♦

Exton gripped Aerie's hand in his as they headed down the hall. He knew he had to concentrate on the mission, and he was, mostly, as he followed behind St. Cloud. But there was still a ringing quality in his mind, almost like his heart was humming. He was still in a mild state of shock, or maybe it was more of a complete overhaul of his life.

He'd known he'd fallen in love with Aerie as surely as he knew he was the one who had jumped. But in that moment, as she finally allowed herself to tell him the darkest truth in her heart, after she inspired the worst inside of him, something had clicked and come together.

It was as though the heavens had opened up, all so God himself could reach down and smack him in the head, pressing into him a lesson his heart couldn't even fully translate into words. It was something divine, and something he wouldn't soon forget.

Exton looked over at Aerie now, and the unabashed longing rushed through him in turbulent waves, despite all the trouble she gave him. There was a special kind of magic in knowing he could still choose to love her, even as there were moments where his love for her chose her all over again.

"Are you okay?" Aerie asked. "You have a strange look on your face."

"I'm just so glad we're back together," he told her quietly.

"I'm glad you're safe," Aerie replied. Her amber eyes turned solemn, and her footsteps slowed ever so slightly. "I was really scared when I saw Brock turn you over to Osgood."

He tightened his hand around hers. "Keep pace," he said. "And don't worry about that now. Brock's the one who needs your worry, if anything."

Her lips flitted into a small smile. "Do you always feel the need to order people around?"

"After so many years, it's a hard habit to break," Exton

admitted.

"After so many years of not listening, it seems like it would be a hard habit to start."

Exton nearly laughed. "We'll have to meet somewhere in the middle, I guess."

"It won't be easy."

"But we have time." He could see the question in her eyes, and he answered it before she asked. "We'll make it enough, Aerie."

"Stop talking," the General said with a sigh. "You're starting to make me sick, and this is a military mission."

Exton sent a triumphant smirk in his direction. "It would serve you right, too, for all the trouble you caused me. Aerie wouldn't have gotten this far if it weren't for you."

"Be grateful we're here," St. Cloud said. "The GPI is dangerous. It was a new project Osgood ordered after he took office, but after you stole the *Perdition*, all the space program initiatives were supposedly canceled."

"Maybe Osgood saw it as more of a military endeavor," Aerie said. "That would explain why it was on the Boötes system?"

"Probably," St. Cloud said. "But only the plans were on it, last I checked. There wasn't any budget and there weren't any allocations for the project."

"It wouldn't be the first time a politician engaged in fraud or corruption," Exton pointed out.

"True." St. Cloud nodded up ahead. "Either way, we need to target it."

"If we can get back to my shuttle, I'll be able to contact the *Perdition*," Exton said. "I left my comm behind when Brock and I were allowed to land. Even if they've stripped the ship, I'll be able to call them from the shuttle."

"We don't need your ship," St. Cloud said. "Aerie's with us. All the comms here are the same as the NETech and the systems we use in Comms Sec. She'll be able to contact your friends if we can get to a comm terminal."

Exton felt Aerie's surprise at hearing the General say her

name. From the look on her face, he had a feeling she was grateful for the compliment. He rolled his eyes. It looked like Aerie was warming up to her father once more. Exton knew he would have to be extra vigilant if he was going to make sure she didn't get hurt by him again.

They hurried to the hangar, only to find it full of activity. Outside the hangar doors, Exton could see the outline of a few MENACE fighters and a couple of other fighter jets as they fought off the URS forces.

Miles away, Exton watched as another missile launched, its piercing shriek wailing as it shot up into the air.

He frowned. Why were they using larger missiles? The fighters were smaller, and they wouldn't need a lot of ammunition to take down.

Before he could ask St. Cloud about it, the General interrupted him.

"There," St. Cloud called out. "There's the lieutenant's shuttle. Spilt up and get onboard."

"Why?" Aerie asked.

"This is not the time to question orders, Aerie," St. Cloud reminded.

"I'm just curious."

"Come on, Aerie," Exton said, grabbing her arm. "Let's just go."

"Gerard is here," St. Cloud said. "He's likely keeping watch over Merra, since he wasn't there to greet Brock when he came in with Exton. If they are launching the GPI, they'll need a shuttle to get the launch site. That means we stay close to his ship."

"Oh." Aerie nodded and then hurried after Exton.

"Did you really have to know that to follow orders?" Exton asked. "We're already suspicious enough, considering I'm supposed to be in a cell."

"I happen to like knowing why," Aerie insisted. "After everything my father's done, for good or for bad, I'm not just letting him call the shots."

"I guess I can see your point. As antithetical as it is to

military protocol."

A shot rang out beside them, and Exton pushed Aerie behind a loading station. "Watch out," he said. "I think we've been found out."

"Ouch," Aerie murmured, as she pulled herself up onto her knees. "Oh well, better than shot, I suppose." She pulled out the gun tucked into the folds of her uniform. "I only have one," she said.

"I'll watch your back," Exton told her.

He wondered if she was nervous. She peeked up over the small ledge the loading station lent them with some reserve. But a moment later, she took aim and began to fight back. He grinned as he turned to watch out for other possible ambushes.

They were in a battle for their lives and the lives of others. Behind him, Aerie continued to fire, never stopping to do more than aim. He saw a number of guards downed.

"Aerie," Exton called over his shoulder. "You're doing well, keep going."

"I'm almost out of rounds," she yelled back. She ducked down again.

"We might be able to grab some of the guard's weapons," he said. "We'll need a distraction."

Where is St. Cloud with all of this? Exton wondered. It would be the perfect distraction, to have two battlefronts.

More shots followed, before a sudden stop. Aerie was just loading her last round when a guard called out, "Come out with your hands up. You're surrounded."

"What do we do?" Aerie whispered.

Before Exton could say anything, a scream cried out through the hangar, effectively interrupting their resistance.

"Victor!"

Aerie nearly bounced up, but he grabbed her and kept her down. "Mom!" she cried. She recovered her balance and looked over toward Gerard's shuttle.

Exton followed her gaze. He saw Gerard and another woman as they were leading Merra toward the shuttle. St.

Cloud had stepped in their path, his weapon raised.

"I'm here for my wife," he said. Even several meters away, Exton could hear the undertone of cold rage.

"Which one?" the woman beside Gerard asked.

"You know which one, Phoebe." His gaze flickered to her, dismissive and unimpressed. "I never considered you my wife. You were just a unit director."

Phoebe held her gun to Merra's face. "We were still married according to the URS laws. Say anything else, and I'll make sure this one is properly dead this time."

St. Cloud hesitated.

Before anyone could do anything else, Gerard yawned, blatantly bored. "This is stupid," he said. "You can't win, St. Cloud. You're outnumbered."

The other guards, as if broken from a spell, suddenly left Aerie and Exton behind and hurried over.

"I might be outnumbered," St. Cloud said, "but I've never been outmatched when it came to you, Gerard. I know your training and everything you could ever hope to think of. I'll be the winner in this battle. Besides, you're forgetting something."

"Oh, really?" Gerard laughed. "What's that? Your daughter?" He turned and caught Aerie's eyes. "I've already had the pleasure. And Exton's, too."

"You're forgetting the rest of my family," St. Cloud told him easily. He held up his comm device in his other hand.

Exton felt a rumble. His eyes darted to the ceiling, where rubble began to break and fall. He hurriedly grabbed Aerie. "Run for cover."

A large *blast!* echoed in the distance, before the weight of the sound came crashing down on them the same time the roof of the hangar crumbled in.

In the quick seconds that followed, Exton pushed Aerie into a nearby hallway and covered her, protecting her as the guards were scattered and squashed. He squinted through the rubble to see St. Cloud fight with Gerard, as Merra, free from Phoebe's full attention, made for a fallen weapon.

"It's Cal," Aerie murmured behind him.

Exton turned his eyes away from the fight to see one of Petra's smaller supply shuttles as it came down into the hangar. It hovered over the debris. Even from where he was, he could see Cal's grim determination.

It couldn't have been an easy feat to get here, Exton thought. There was still an airship battle going on outside the hangar.

A cry of pain shot out from among the noise.

"Mom!" Aerie cried, hurrying over.

Exton flew after her as she ran for her mother. Merra landed hard on her knees as blood ran out from her shoulder.

Phoebe stood over her, her confidence shaken, her dark hair unkempt and dusty, but a final triumphant gleam in her eye. "This is the end," she said.

Exton heard, rather than saw Aerie as she took aim and fired. Phoebe crumbled and fell to the floor, limp and pliant against the floor, her body in a broken position.

"Sorry, Director," she mumbled. Before Exton could assure her that she did it to protect her mother, Aerie turned to him. "We have to get her out of here."

Behind him, St. Cloud and Gerard were still locked in a fierce battle, while Cal managed to open his ship's cargo bay doors. "Let's move," he said. He came up beside Merra, who was doing her best to hold off going into shock.

"Mom," Aerie called. "I'm so glad to see you."

Merra relented to Aerie's embrace, as she turned her attention to Exton. "Hello, Exton," she said. "My favorite son-in-law. I knew you wouldn't let an innocent woman suffer."

"Unless you're talking about Aerie, you can give up the act. I know about the ecobomb," he told her, as Aerie took off her uniform jacket and used it to hamper the bleeding in her shoulder. "Which we will discuss later."

"I'm not sure I could survive that," she rasped.

"I'll see to it that you do," he replied. He carefully arranged her arms and then hoisted her over his shoulder.

She was barely any taller than Aerie, and even with her awkward position, he was able to manage the extra weight. "Cal's waiting for us."

Merra grunted in pain. "I heard about Dorian," she said. "I'm glad Cal survived. He's doing his brother proud."

Aerie nodded, pressing into her shoulder as Exton hurried toward the ship. "You need to stay with us," she said. "For all of us. Marcus still needs you as a mother, and so do I. Even Serena needs you."

Merra gave her a pained smile. "I'm not a fool, Aerie. I know I owe it to you to survive. Who else would let Victor free and convince her space pirate husband to come rescue me?"

"Oh, Mom." Aerie sighed.

Exton clutched at his mother-in-law's body as he carried her into the awaiting shuttle. He settled Merra into the small sick bay area. As Aerie tended to her wounds, Exton hurried to the cockpit.

He saw Cal and nodded in greeting. "Nice shooting."

Cal's arrogant smirk came quickly enough. "I might be able to teach you how to do it one day. If you ask nicely."

"I'll keep it in mind," Exton replied. "Even though I am the second-best pilot in all of Petra. Maybe I'll be able to teach you a thing or two as well."

"I guess I still have to figure out how to catch a skydiver in midair," Cal replied. "Now, buckle up. We're getting out of here."

"We still need St. Cloud," Exton said. "And Brock is here, too."

"I have orders from the General," Cal said. "Get Mom out of here." He adjusted the thrusters and began to take flight.

"Just fly over to where he and Gerard are fighting," Exton said. "I want to take Gerard with us."

"What? Why?"

He grimaced. "I can tell you and Aerie are related," he grumbled. "Just do it. I'm going to go down to the loading dock."

Cal snarled back, but he was silent as he took the aircraft over to the other side of the hangar.

This was going to be tricky, Exton thought, as he headed toward the back the of ship once more. He could hear Aerie and Merra's muffled voices, as they crammed into the small ward behind him. He almost smiled as he heard Aerie scold Merra as she attempted to bandage the wound.

Gerard's yell cut through Exton's concentration. He turned to see St. Cloud as he held Gerard down against the floor, his weapon trained on Gerard's heart. The General was breathing hard.

We might be able to save him this time, Exton thought. For the first time in what seemed like forever, hope sparked inside of him.

"St. Cloud," he called. "Bring him here and get onboard."

"I can't."

Exton frowned. "What are you talking about?" he asked. "Just grab him and let's go."

"He's bleeding out, Exton."

At his words, Exton didn't stop to think. Terror rushed through him as he grabbed the spare med pack and jumped down off the ramp, hurrying over.

"Here," he said. "We've got to hurry."

St. Cloud, as exhausted and sweaty as he was from the battle, didn't question his assertion.

Exton saw Gerard was bleeding heavily. "What happened?" he asked, suddenly wishing he had been trained to save lives better than he had been trained to take them.

"I shot him, Exton," St. Cloud told him, clearly unapologetic. "I managed to get him just under the ribs."

"Help me," Exton said. "Apply pressure while I see if this temporary bandage will stick."

"Why are you trying to save me?" Gerard asked, his voice wheezy.

"Sounds like I broke a rib or two," St. Cloud said.

"We've got to save you because of Meredith," Exton told

Gerard, feeling like he was screaming as his hands kept pressing down on the bandage. "I promised her."

"You promised my med tech you would save me?" Gerard asked. His eyes were blinking fast, and his breathing was getting more labored.

"Yes!" Exton bit his lip, watching as Gerard's face went white. He clapped Gerard's cheek. "Stay with us!"

"Why?"

"We were friends once," Exton told him. "Don't you remember? You were friends with me and Tyler and Meredith, and she loves you. You gave us the codes so we could steal the *Perdition* from the URS."

"We were friends?" Gerard coughed.

"Yes," Exton yelled, silently cursing as the bandage slipped off again. There was too much blood, he realized. "Stay with us for Meredith. We'll help you. We can help you get back to your old self."

"Is that so?" Gerard's eyes cleared a second later. Exton was just about to see if St. Cloud would help move him when Gerard laughed.

Exton frowned. "What are—"

Gerard spat at him, his salvia mixed in with blood. "I'll die before I'll help you." His arm came out and ripped away the last of the makeshift tourniquet Exton had arranged on his chest.

Exton stood there, stricken, with Gerard's cloud of bloody spit still sprayed on his chest. He felt the world seem to stop and fall silent, as Gerard breathed his last breath, allowing death to take his defiant spirit away.

He's gone. I failed. Exton felt numb as he sat back on his knees and glanced over at St. Cloud.

"He deserved it, Exton. If nothing else, he deserved it for what he did to Aerie." St. Cloud stood up and turned toward the waiting ship.

Exton felt his heart take St. Cloud's words like a blow. He knew he had to hurry, and there was nothing he could do for Gerard now. But something inside of him cried out, words failing him as he felt just how wrong it was that Gerard was gone. Part of him was tempted to scream out at God, asking why, why this terrible thing had happened and demand justice.

But he already knew Gerard would not come back if he did that. Exton knew the answer, or at least part of the answer, as to why Gerard was gone. He knew Gerard died because of his own choices and actions, and Exton knew he was partially to blame.

The full answer to that question was complicated. Likely too complicated for him to fully know or understand.

And as for justice, Exton thought, it was already served.

"Exton, come on," St. Cloud called from behind him. "We have other people to save now."

Exton slowly stood up as he nodded. He took one last look at Gerard, saluting him, and then hurried back to the ship.

I failed to save Gerard, but I will not fail to stop Osgood. I won't let him destroy my friends and allies.

St. Cloud reached out a hand for him. Exton took it, and before he could thank him for his support, Cal shut the cargo bay doors and took off.

♦24♦

Aerie nearly fell over as Cal hit the accelerator and shot up out of the hangar. She almost yelled at him, but before she could say anything, she caught sight of Exton's face.

The look of defeat on his stark face was unnerving and awful. She turned toward the General. "Dad."

St. Cloud nearly jumped. "What is it?"

"Come here and watch over Mom," Aerie said as she hurried past him, trying to get to Exton.

She reached for him as he sat on the floor. "Exton," she murmured, the hard and fast flight making it easy for her to sit beside him.

"I'm okay," he said.

"That's good to hear," Cal called out from the cockpit. "Because I need all of you to buckle up. We're still in the middle of the battle, and the ship's got a target on it.

"I know you're not okay," Aerie told Exton. She gave him a quick hug. "But we'll be okay." She tugged on his hand, trying to get him to strap into a seat, but he resisted.

"I wasn't able to save Gerard." Exton looked down at his hands.

Apparently, he wasn't concerned about flying through a battlefield. Aerie gripped his hands. "You can't save everyone, Exton," she told him softly.

"Some people don't believe that."

She almost smiled. How did Exton manage to get this way? Aerie wondered. To feel responsible for the whole world, when the whole world seemed to be against him. She was amazed at his heart, even if she knew she objected to his logic.

"Some people don't even try to save others," Aerie reminded him. "Now, let's get settled. My mom's going to need a lot of medical attention. She's lost a lot of blood."

"We need to get her to a medic as soon as possible," her father called from the med ward. "We're out of med supplies."

"What can we do, Exton?" she asked. "We still have to stop the GPI, don't we?"

"Yes, we do," the General said. "There's nothing more important than stopping him. If we don't, he'll crush Petra and Chaya and the rest of our allies."

Aerie watched as Exton shook his head, as if he was clearing it of his troubles. From his expression, she knew it was not the end of his sorrow. Aerie vowed to get him to talk about Gerard later. While she was not sad he was gone, she was sad that he'd had his life taken away from him so tragically.

But now, she knew Exton's heart, and even Merra's wounds had to be pushed back in order to defeat Osgood.

"If we can stop Osgood now," Aerie said, "we'll be able to free the URS from his control."

Exton stood up and turned toward Cal. "We need to know what's happening," he said. "Cal, I need you to head toward Cartagena. Emery's there, with Serena, so we'll be able to get Merra some care while I find out how Kamalo and Aunt Patty are doing on the battlefield front.

"What about the GPI?" the General asked. "It's better to stop it from launching. If it gets into space before we shoot it down, it'll put the entire world at risk."

Aerie frowned. "What is the GPI exactly?"

"It's an advanced model of the *Perdition*," the General explained. "It was made with military enhancements. While Silas wanted to make the *Paradise* a place of education and refuge, the URS wanted a battle starship."

"So Osgood really will be able to conquer the world," Exton muttered darkly. "That sounds about right."

Aerie felt a shiver go down her spine. She didn't need her father to explain every detail about the GPI's weapon capabilities, but she knew what the *Perdition* was capable of. She recalled the nukes that were protecting the Biovid hanging off the bottom of the ship.

Cal cheered. "Alright, we're past the battlefront and Cartagena's ten minutes from here if I push it."

Aerie watched as her father frowned. "You're sure about this, Exton?"

"We can drop Merra off with Emery," Exton replied. "Serena will be able to take care of her. We'll have to leave her there, but once I figure out where everyone is, we'll be able to stop the GPI. Turnaround time will cost us some, but it's negligible. It's worth it if we can save Merra."

Aerie felt warm as he looked over at her. "That's what we came here for in the end, right?"

"I'm grateful," the General said. "Thank you."

Exton shrugged. "The feeling is mutual. If it weren't for Cal and your ship, we might not have made it out of the hangar."

Aerie put her hand on his shoulder. "Let me try to get a hold of Emery," she said. "Maybe we can save some more time that way."

"Good idea."

"What's she doing in Cartagena anyway?" Aerie suddenly asked.

"The *Morgan Soromsky* was hit when the *Freedom* was attacked. She was going with a bunch of botanists and other scientists to test the waters and see if there were any nuclear leaks, among other things."

"Oh. That sounds like fun, actually," Aerie said.

"You can stay with her if you want," Exton remarked. "You can watch over your mom and help Serena. Your father and I can take care of Osgood."

Aerie would've laughed if the stakes weren't so high. "Never," she declared. "I know you and my father have a common goal in defeating Osgood, but there's no way I'm going to leave you two alone. You need a referee, and you know I can help with other things, too."

Exton smirked. "I should've known it was pointless to try to argue with you."

"Where you go, I will go," Aerie whispered softly, reminding him of their wedding vows.

"That's not meant to be quite that literal," he replied.

"Doesn't matter." Aerie put her hands on her hips. "After all the fighting we've done, it's time for us to fight for something greater, together."

Aerie felt her face blush over as he stared into her eyes for a long moment. She was about to argue further when he just nodded.

"Alright," he said. "But only if you agree to obey my orders."

She sighed. "Fine. But only because I don't know Osgood that well. I know you and my father know him better, so you'll be able to anticipate his movements."

Exton shook his head. "Good to know you trust me."

"I do," Aerie insisted. "I just … struggle with trusting you more than trusting myself, I guess."

"Survival instincts are one thing, Aerie. But they do not have the primary position when it comes to war." Exton glanced behind her. Aerie followed his gaze to see Merra and Victor, as he laid his head down next to hers. Aerie could see there were small tears leaking out of the corner of her mother's eyes. "Maybe that's true in relationships, too."

It didn't even take the full ten minutes for Cal to land the shuttle on the beach at Cartagena. Exton took a good look around, glad to see they were not far from Emery's camp. He could see their temporary housing tents easily against the rotting cityscape in the distance.

Cartagena had been a beautiful city once, he remembered, thinking of the data he'd downloaded on different parts of the world. It was a bustling hub for a variety of business enterprises, most of which fell away once the city's skies clouded over with nuclear ash and toxic discharge.

As St. Cloud and Aerie helped Merra out of the small shuttle, Exton hurried over toward the camp. They were going to take care of Merra, and he had to take care of his role. If they were going to stop the GPI, he knew he would have to coordinate efforts with the rest of his allies.

"Exton!"

At the sound of Emery's cry, Exton braced himself. The impact came a moment later, as she came rushing into his arms. "Hi, Em."

"I was so happy to get Aerie's call," she said. "Are you okay?"

"Gerard is gone."

At his words, Emery shrunk back. "Oh, Exton."

"He died fighting St. Cloud."

"You don't blame him for his death, though, do you?"

"No."

"I knew it." Emery shook her head. "It's not your fault, either, Exton. Gerard knew the risks when he helped us take back the *Perdition*."

"I doubt he thought he would wind up a tool for the States and their torture program," Exton said, surprised at how normal his voice seemed to sound. From all the turmoil inside of him over his anger at Gerard's treatment of Aerie, he would have thought it would have come storming out, full of vitriol and spite. "Let alone face the reality of forgetting all about his true love and his friends."

"Don't forget that he still did terrible things," Emery said. "I know you told me that Aerie's forgiven him for what happened in New Hope, but there's no reason that because he had been forgiven, judgment is not just or necessary."

Exton nodded. "That's probably why I am not sad," he said. "When people die, you think of the good things first. I'm more angry that the whole thing happened that way to begin with."

Emery took his arm. "I'll have Tyler tell Meredith the news," she said. "It's his right, anyway, as her brother."

"I should tell her myself. I'm the one who promised her I would save him."

"He was saved," Emery said. "You know as well as I do that sometimes death is kinder. He is now free from the URS and their games."

"It's not the same thing. It's not what I wanted."

"It's not all about you," Emery said, chastising him lightly. "If you're upset because he died when you might not have been able to save him anyway, you are only fooling yourself."

"I know."

"Gerard knew as we did that there was something greater to live for. Don't be so conceited, Exton. You're just going to dishonor his memory in the end, if you think you could have saved him, or that you condemned him to his fate."

"I guess I am glad he's finally at peace, if for no other reason than I don't have to worry about Aerie running into him any more."Emery nodded. "Good. She's your main concern now."

Exton sighed. "But I wanted to make Meredith happy again. Gerard was our first loss, and were good friends when we were younger. Then there is the fact Meredith is Tyler's sister, and she did help save Aerie's life. She had such hope for him all those years working beside him, and she helped us out when we needed her. I wanted to keep my promise to her and see her get her happy ending, too."

"Meredith will understand," Emery assured him in a firm voice. "She has known for a long time not everyone gets a happy ending on this side of Heaven. And she will not regret helping you get Aerie back, even if you were not able to bring Gerard back to her."

"I'll argue with you about this later, probably multiple times."

"I'll warn Aerie to expect it, too," Emery said with a quick smile. "Maybe between all of us, we'll be able to get it all out of your system in record time."

"You mean before I do something stupid or reckless?"

"We're already at war," Emery said. "Can't be much worse at this point."

"We'll see about that." Exton frowned. "I need to get in touch with Aunt Patty and Kamalo to see what's going on at Panama. I wasn't able to observe a whole lot from the half-imploded hangar."

"Come with me," Emery said. She glanced over her shoulder. "It looks like the others will be using my tent for Merra, so let's go ahead and go to the ship."

Exton glanced behind him to see Aerie and St. Cloud as they carried Merra's passed-out body. Serena led the way. She sent him a quick wave, and he returned the gesture before he caught up with Emery.

It looks like Merra will be okay, he thought. He doubted Serena would have been so calm if there was something to worry about, even if she had been trained to disregard her feelings when it came to her patients. *Good.*

Exton didn't want to see Aerie hurt anymore. He knew that in the long run, Merra was likely going to bother him for years to come as they had a new chance at being close. And he decided that, while he was no doubt going to be constantly angry and frustrated with her schemes and half-truths, it was still more than he deserved.

But he was going to demand that she find her own accommodations to reside in when she came to visit. There was no need to make it easy for her to be completely comfortable.

Exton's concerns about Aerie's family visits were immediately hijacked as soon as he started talking to Henry.

"I had a feeling you wouldn't exactly be happy with the news," Henry said. "Miguel and Rhodey told me not to worry about it."

"You allowed them to drive the *Perdition* into the airspace above Panama," Exton said. "Of course I'm not happy. If we lose the *Perdition*, we lose everything."

"Not everything," Henry said.

"Now's not the best time to argue with me," Exton told him through gritted teeth.

"We've already ordered evacuations," Henry said. "The people are still going to be fine. Director Ward already has her staff on standby to recover them. I've programmed it so that every pod is headed for Petra."

"What about the workers?" Exton asked. "You still need to pilot the ship."

"So far, a handful of volunteers have offered to stay behind," Henry said. "Rhodey and Miguel both have all the veterans working to replace them. They know what they're risking."

Exton sighed, miserable all over again. The veteran division on the *Perdition* had been a collection of the remaining soldiers from the Old Republic. They had signed on to the *Perdition* for situations just like this one.

But this shouldn't even be happening, he thought. "Why did Miguel and Rhodey agree to this?"

"Kamalo and Director Ward's forces weren't able to get to Panama as quickly as the *Perdition* was," Henry explained. "I thought it prudent to make sure you and milady were safe. When we found out Osgood was there, we knew we'd made the right choice."

Exton put his hand over his eyes, rubbing his temples. He hated that Henry had a point.

"Rhodey used one of the smaller nukes on the last Craftcarrier, too," Henry said. "So even if Osgood gets away, we have at least downed their last major Craftcarrier. And don't worry, I already warned Director Caudwell about it, so she's aware of the situation."

Exton hoped Emery had taken precautions, but he was also glad to hear the Craftcarrier was down. Besides being a threat to their forces, they had been a major deterrent for some of the *Perdition*'s suppliers.

His fingers gripped the top of the monitor. "What did Rhodey or Miguel say about the GPI?"

"We haven't seen any significant development regarding that," Henry said. "I only have a few reports from our forces fighting down in Panama. Some have said something big is coming."

"It is, and we need to stop it." Exton's mind raced with questions. How much longer would it take for Osgood to launch the battle starship? Was it possible to hit it before it launched? Would they be able to ensure its complete destruction?

All of the questions faded as the answer came to him. Exton had a plan.

"Anything else I can do for you, Captain?" Henry asked.

"Send me the coordinates and hailing frequency for the *Perdition*, and then get to an escape pod," Exton said. "I'm coming back up to relieve you."

♦25♦

Aerie gripped onto her mother's hands. She watched as her mother's eyes blinked open, and instantly Aerie felt a weight of relief fall off her heart and shoulders. "Mom," she said. "How are you feeling?"

Merra tried to move her right shoulder, where Phoebe had managed to clip her. "Stiff," she replied softly. Her face was beyond pale, but there was some color starting to come back into it.

"Serena said that you lost a lot of blood, so you should already be feeling some of the medication taking effect," Aerie said.

Merra gave her a tired smile. "I can tell. If I say anything loopy right now, I don't mean it."

"You got it," Aerie said. She watched as Exton came into the room and signaled for the General to follow him. Aerie was surprised when her father left without protest.

Merra's eyes followed him as he headed out of the tent. "I'm almost surprised those two are getting along," she said. "I had a feeling they would learn to live with each other, eventually."

"Don't get too excited," Aerie said. "They'll still take years to learn how to get along. Just to spite us, I think."

"You were the one who let him free, aren't you?" Merra asked. "You did it to save me."

"I didn't do it without thinking it all through," Aerie told her.

"I was right. You disappointed Exton."

"Yes," Aerie admitted grudgingly. "But we'll be okay." Her cheeks warmed as she thought of how Exton, even as he was furious with her, told her that he would never leave her. Her heart raced and she knew a helpless, dreamy look had come over her face a moment later when Merra chuckled.

"You always were a daydreamer," Merra said. "I always liked that about you."

Aerie grimaced. "My instructors never liked it much, and

I can't imagine it helps with the war effort a whole lot. I know I'm not a lot like you."

"Aerie, you're a lot *better* than me," Merra told her. "I am sorry I wasn't around during your teenage years, but I am very proud of how you've turned out."

Aerie leaned down and wrapped her arms around her mother's neck. "I love you, Mom."

"I love you, too, Aerie." Merra pulled back. "Now, go get Serena. I'm going to have her load me up on more meds so I can try to get some sleep. As much as I'm feeling better than before, I know I'm going to need to get to Petra before I'll be able to get my shoulder properly fixed up."

"Alright," Aerie said, letting a small laugh escape.

"And please watch out for your father. I'm not happy about my shoulder," Merra said, "but it was well worth the pain, now that I never have to deal with Phoebe again. Still, I'd like another several years with Victor."

"You got it, Mom."

Aerie walked out of the tent, nearly running into Serena. "Mom's going to rest," she said.

"Good. She needs to," Serena replied. "And you'd better hurry. Your husband and the General are about to head out for the *Perdition*. Don't let them leave you here."

"Thanks," Aerie said. "I can see Exton trying to leave me behind."

"It won't work," Serena said.

Aerie was touched her sister was so concerned about her. "Thank you, Serena. I appreciate the notice. I didn't know you cared about me so much."

Serena wrinkled her nose. "With all of our staff, and Cal, too, we don't have room to take you back to Petra," she said. "Frankly, even dealing with Cal will be hard in addition to the other six people, considering all the extra stuff I packed for Emery."

"Cal's staying with you?" Aerie asked.

"Yeah, he promised to keep watch for us. Exton told him to stay here anyway, since he wanted to make sure we were well guarded in case any of the fighting from Panama leaks out over here."

"Oh. Well, that's good to know. I'm glad you'll have the extra protection."

"Don't get all mushy on me." Serena gave her a light push toward the shuttle. "You've got more work to do."

Aerie twisted away from her, before circling back and giving her a hug. "Thank you," she said. "For everything."

Serena bristled at the embrace, but eventually patted Aerie on the back. Aerie knew she was surprised by the sisterly affection, but she was also glad Serena didn't push her away. If there was one thing rescuing her mother had taught her, it was that family was even more important in times of trouble.

Aerie let her go and waved, heading over to the shuttle, where her husband and her father were already arguing.

"Time to referee," she said, steeling herself for the coming confrontation.

Her efforts to prepare hadn't taken long, but they were a waste. Aerie watched as Exton and her father both scowled at each other, before turning and facing her.

"What are you arguing about now?" she demanded to know. She put her hands on her hips. "Come on, tell me. We can take it to a vote."

"That wouldn't work," Exton said.

"Why not?" Aerie asked. She was confused, until she realized it likely had to do with her. "I'm part of this team, too."

The General shook his head. "Aerie, we both think it would be best for you to stay here."

"You can't make me stay," Aerie insisted. She turned to Exton. "You know I'll just make things worse if I get the chance to."

"That's why I was telling St. Cloud ordering you to stay here wasn't a good option," he said. "I was all for just leaving."

"Hey," Aerie objected. "I'm your wife. You have to protect me."

"This is protecting you," Exton insisted.

"You have to take me, and you have to protect me," Aerie said. She glanced over at the General. "Same goes for you."

Neither of them were happy, but Aerie pressed on. "I already told you, I can help. And I will. I have friends who are on the *Perdition* just as much as you do, Exton. And you," she said, turning toward her father, "you owe me still, for all the trouble you caused me."

He sighed. "We don't have time to argue this," he said. "Come on, but if you get into any trouble, don't expect Exton or me to always come rushing."

"Speak for yourself," Exton snapped.

"You know as well as I do that you can't compromise this mission," St. Cloud shot back. "Once Osgood launches his battle starship, all he has to do is strike us where we're vulnerable. And that means Petra and Chaya, among others. We're here to protect our world."

"Aerie is my wife."

"And she's my daughter," St. Cloud yelled back.

"You just spent the last two days trying to rescue Merra," Exton said. "Who are you to tell me what my priorities should be?"

"I am your commanding officer."

"No, you're not!"

"Stop!" Aerie yelled. She was appalled by their arguments, and even more by the fact that the only thing they could agree on was that she was the one who would hold them up, when they clearly had their own issues. *I'll show them who is useless,* she thought determinedly.

"That's enough, you two. We have to go. We're all in this together. I can take care of myself, and even you if I need to. So stop your arguing and get moving!"

Exton and the General turned their angry glances on her, but Aerie remained firm. "Now," she said pointing to the ship.

After another second of bitter silence, the two of them

turned around and marched onto the shuttle, neither saying anything else.

Aerie breathed a sigh of relief. *This better not be how the rest of this mission is going to go.*

♦♦♦♦

Exton switched over to autopilot support as soon as the shuttle left Earth's atmosphere, allowing himself a brief moment of rest.

He was tired from the long, long day, and there were no indications it was going to end anytime soon. There were also no indications it was going to get any easier.

Exton glanced over at Aerie as she sat in the copilot's chair, watching her as she ignored him. In retrospect, he thought, it probably hadn't been the best idea to try to keep her from coming. He could tell she was already mulling over how to make his life more difficult because he'd wanted her to be safe.

Despite everything, he almost smiled. It wasn't enough for her to pledge her life to him; she was actually going to physically do it, and do it to the most nerving-racking degree, likely using up the last of his patience and testing every last inch of his faith in the process. As fearful as he was for her, he was also relieved to be with her.

He thought about engaging her in conversation, testing the waters of her amity, but he decided to let her stew for the moment. Exton knew that she had to be even more tired than he was.

Exton's gaze turned to his other side, where St. Cloud sat in a passenger chair, seeming to follow in Exton's footsteps, with his gaze mindlessly wandering among the world's face.

As he watched his father-in-law, Exton couldn't help but wonder if he was thinking of Merra. Before they'd left, Exton had returned to Emery's tent in hopes of saying goodbye. He'd been surprised to see St. Cloud tenderly embracing his wife.

St. Cloud had squeezed his eyes shut as he whispered in Merra's ears, while Merra was actually crying. She almost never seemed to show her fear, but it was clearly written on her face as she gripped him back.

Exton was too stunned to slip out right away. He knew part of him was fascinated, as he saw how both of Aerie's parents, people he had been wary of for a variety of valid reasons, were capable of such a strange range and mixture of emotions. He hadn't thought it possible. Or, he admitted to himself, he hadn't wanted to. There was something terribly practical in thinking St. Cloud and Merra were less than human.

He turned his attention back out the window, as the ship curved along with the edge of the earth, and the *Perdition* came into sight. It was much closer to Earth, hanging in the middle of the broken belt of clouds.

He watched as several of the escape pods rushed out of the starship from all directions, and he was glad Henry had the foresight to do that. Exton didn't want to risk the lives of the people onboard.

The silence in the shuttle's cabin was killed with St. Cloud's astonished whisper.

"It's starting," he said, as he pulled up an enhanced image on the nearby monitor.

Exton looked out of the front window to see a gigantic oval of fire burning on the land just below Panama, the tip of it reaching into the Old Columbian borders. As the fiery cloud grew, he was briefly reminded of his own experience launching the *Perdition*, north of the New Hope Military base. He'd watched the blackened earth beneath him liquefy into mud and metal as his ship left a sizeable scar across state lines.

"The GPI looks much bigger," he admitted, his discomfort increasing.

"It is," St. Cloud said. "Silas was the best engineer in the Revolutionary States, but Osgood still had quite a few at his disposal."

"Let's hope it's not too different from the *Perdition*," Exton said. "It'll be easier to search for weaknesses." He turned to Aerie. "See if you can get Henry on the line."

Aerie nodded and went to work with the comm system, while Exton studied the images coming in over the monitor. From the outline of the darkened ditch in the middle of the world, he could tell that the body of the GPI had been elongated from the *Perdition*'s design.

"Any idea of how many weapons are on it?" he asked St. Cloud.

St. Cloud snorted disdainfully. "Osgood wants to destroy the world. It's likely packed with firepower."

"Great." Exton sighed.

"Exton," Aerie called. "Phil's on the line for you."

"Where's Henry?" he asked.

Phil's familiar face came up onto his comm monitor. "Henry's prepping your report so he can meet you face to face when you land," Phil replied. The gruff sound of his voice was oddly comforting against the coming tide of trouble.

"We're only a few moments out," Exton replied, checking the ship's ETA. "What can you tell me about the GPI?"

"We're watching it. It looks like between the toxic clouds and the Craftcarrier signals, we weren't able to pick up on its construction. I've been studying the roads leading into some of the station points in Columbia. They've been doing this for a long time—likely since the *Perdition*'s blueprints were finished by your father."

"What else can you tell me?"

"We're going to have to be very careful," Phil said.

"No kidding," Exton retorted. He already knew that. He silently cursed himself; after all the years he'd flown around the world on the *Perdition*, he still considered St. Cloud to be the bigger threat between him and Osgood. He knew St. Cloud well—or at least, he thought he did. Exton could only hope he would be able to outmaneuver Osgood.

"I'm deadly serious," Phil said, doubling down. "If

Osgood has even packed it with half as much weaponry as I think he has, we're going to have an ELE coming."

"Of course we are," Exton muttered darkly. Only the URS would see that an Extinction Level Event would be a good thing.

"What are the analysts saying?"

"Greer's the only one left right now," Phil said. "When Henry ordered the evacuations, Thora took her kids and her family and left."

Exton nodded. "Good. Greer's got the better military experience anyway. What does she think?"

"Here she is."

"Captain." Greer's voice, with its cheerful New England accent, cut in through the link. "I've taken things into consideration and talked with Rhodey. We're going to have to use the last of the nukes, but if we can hit the ship at some designated marks, we'll be able to break up the ship into small enough parts to where they won't cause catastrophic damage to the earth."

"What's the catch?" Exton asked.

"We're going to have to make sure they don't get past the earth's atmosphere," Greer told him.

"So we don't have a lot of time."

"Miguel's gone down to ready the bomb release," she said. "We'll be ready for your orders."

"No," Exton said, his sharp tone sudden and brusque. "Go and get to an escape pod, Greer. Rhodey and I will handle things from here on out. If we fail, we lose."

"But what if—"

"You've been relieved of duty," Exton said. "Petra will need you if we fail. Please go."

There was a slight pause before Greer, her cheerful voice now full of trepidation, agreed. "Yes, Captain."

"Give me back to Phil," Exton said. When Phil spoke up a moment later, Exton said, "I'll be there soon. Hold the Bridge for me, and when I get there, you will also exit the *Perdition*."

"Yes, Captain," Phil said. The gruffness was gone, with only a solemn somberness left.

Exton signed off before he could get caught up in the risk they were taking. When he was younger, he had wanted to grow up and be a military hero.

What I wouldn't give to go back and slap my younger self, Exton thought grimly. He could no longer see anything glorious about being a hero.

The rest of the trip passed in silence, as Exton watched the GPI's fiery takeoff from the surface.

"Prepare for docking," Aerie said a few moments later.

"Thank you," Exton said, reaching over and taking her hand. He hated how, now that he knew it was possible he would meet the horizon of his life, the sentimentality was unavoidable. His young wife's eyes glittered with pride as she looked back at him, but he couldn't help but wonder if he would live to see another day with her. She had been the sunshine, calling to him from the dark recesses of space in his own heart. He didn't want her to be part of his life's sunset.

Aerie gave him a quizzical look. "What are you thinking?" she asked.

He sighed and pulled back from her. "Time to go."

"Yes," St. Cloud said behind him, forcing Exton's attention back to their present situation. "It is."

♦26♦

"Come on, Exton," Aerie said, stamping her foot against the floor. "I want to stay with you and help with Osgood."

Aerie hated how much like a child she sounded, especially considering the gravity of the situation they were in. But her old instincts refused to back down; Exton was not going to order her around like she was one of the soldiers. She was his equal, and she had equal say in her fate.

Going through the ship and releasing the supply capsules was not a job she wanted.

"Greer told us that we don't have a lot of time," he reminded her. "We need to strike the GPI, and fast. That means I need to have it ready for battle, and there are things that need to be done before that happens."

"It still seems like something that you could have anyone do."

Exton shook his head. "Look," he said, "I trust you, remember? This is a dangerous job, and I need to make sure someone does it; you're the best candidate for the job, because I know I can rely on you. The supplies contain everything from medical supplies to the extra food we've stored from the Harvest. There's even some research stored away, just in case of circumstances like this one. If the *Perdition* is in danger, we need to make sure Petra will still survive."

Aerie frowned, watching him for the longest moment she could manage. She hated how much it seemed like such an important job when she knew she had other skills. When he didn't so much as blink, her resolve crumbled. "Fine," she said.

"Good. Start with the outer plantations," Exton said. "If you go to mid-ship, Level 5, there will be several release stations. You'll need to type in the code and then push the button. There will be a light to indicate the capsules have been released."

"Fine," Aerie repeated again. "Consider it done, Captain."

He grabbed her arm, holding her back as she tried to hurry off. Before she could object, he kissed her. It was brief but passionate, and Aerie felt her breath leave her in a rush.

"Exton," she murmured, her mouth against his.

"That's better. I like how you say my name," he said. "*Now* you can go."

Aerie nodded and hurried off, not trusting herself to say anything else as she left him in the hangar. *That man,* she thought. He knew just what to do to get his way, didn't he?

"On the bright side, at least he seems to know me well enough," Aerie murmured to herself, as she stepped off the elevator and turned onto the ship.

It felt strange walking through the *Perdition* this time. She had never been in it with so few people on it. She knew Henry promised Exton he had ordered all civilian evacuations. That left a skeleton crew of close to a hundred Veteran Masters, all who had volunteered to stay behind.

Exton was on his way to meet with their leader, a man she knew from listening to his conversations was named Rhodey. Aerie didn't know what exactly Exton had in mind for destroying the GPI, but from what she'd heard of Rhodey and his impressive reputation, she had a feeling he and his league of military retirees were preparing for a massive offensive.

Well, she thought, *they need to. If Osgood has his way, the free world will die.*

The echoes of the empty hallways made her uneasy as she ran through the ship, looking for the mid-ship emergency release stations. Level 5 had been one of the first places she'd explored on the ship, she recalled, remembering her time with Olga and Alice as they made their way through the ship, cleaning and taking care of the smallest details.

Aerie wondered if she would ever see Olga's face again, as she worked through her tasks one at a time, as careful as she was thorough.

Before she allowed herself to get swept up in her memories, or too pressed by her worries, Aerie saw the release station room. She wriggled her butt in happiness and then hurried inside.

There were twenty-four release stations, some lining the wall, and some in the middle of the room. Each was marked with a different name and section number. Aerie wasted no time. She knew Exton wanted the plantation supply rooms, the capsules where the extra food from the Harvest was stored, deployed first. By the look of it, she thought, all she had to do was work around the room and then finish off with the center stations.

Finding the right kiosk station, Aerie pulled out the handle, twisted it open, and tugged hard. The panel came back to reveal a keypad and a button.

"Just as Exton said," she cheered to herself. She typed in the code and then pressed the button.

Seconds later, she thought she felt the rest of the ship sway; Aerie wondered if it was because the capsule was freed, or because of something else.

Either way, she decided, it was best to hurry. She was eager to get back to Exton's side on the Command Bridge, where there were other people, so she could have a better view of what exactly was happening.

Her plan was delayed when she got to the last release station. She opened the panel and typed in the code. She pressed the button.

Nothing happened.

She frowned. "What's wrong? Why aren't you working?"

Aerie typed in the code again and pressed the button. Still nothing.

"Ugh!" She hit the panel with her fist, frustrated. *What am I supposed to do now?*

She knew the Ark was important, and part of the special design Exton's father had included in the ship's design. Aerie didn't want to disappoint him.

Aerie reached up to type in the code once more, when an explosion rocked through the ship.

"Augh!" Aerie cried out as she slammed against the far

wall. Down the hallway, alarms began going off. Aerie moaned briefly as she rubbed her shoulder and neck, trying to assuage the sudden pain of impact.

As she stood up, Aerie heard the automatic public service announcement calling for evacuation and identifying a breech in the haul.

She glanced back at the defiant kiosk, where she was unable to initiate the release of the Ark. As the sirens continued to sound off, Aerie made her choice: She would go back to the Command Bridge, before it was too late. There was nothing else she could do, she realized.

Aerie could only hope it would be okay, and that Exton wouldn't be upset.

"But I guess he's going to have other problems to worry about, especially if there's been a breech," she said to herself as she spurred onward to the Bridge.

Exton grumbled as he pulled himself off the floor. "How did we miss those?" he asked, glaring over at St. Cloud.

He felt his anger growing as he saw the smile on St. Cloud's face. "We were just hit! What's your problem? There's nothing funny about it."

"It was the latest model of the Redbird-FTK," St. Cloud said. "You'll have to pardon my poor sense of humor, same as always."

"What's so funny about that?" Exton asked again. "And how would you know what it is anyway?"

"The latest model leaves a small red streak of residue from burning the neon inside of its thrusters," St. Cloud replied. He pointed out the nearest window, where there was a slim line of red, just as he'd said, glinting off the half-hidden sunlight in the distance.

"It's funny," St. Cloud continued, "because I was the one who ordered the update after I launched the one at you, trying to warn you of Osgood's retaliation on the *Perdition* for stealing the Memory Tree."

"He's never said anything about it to me," Exton said. "I thought that attack was just you."

"It was, and it wasn't. I convinced him to attack once I knew I had to get your attention," St. Cloud replied.

"You know that one could have ended much differently," Exton said, as he initiated the PSA one last call for evacuation. "It's a wonder you didn't kill Aerie and the rest of us."

"Osgood is old-school, if you think about it," St. Cloud said. "He wants too much done too quickly, and he never thinks about the costs. He hated that you managed to escape New Hope with the Memory Tree, but more because you managed to live through it without any damage. He didn't care about the tree at all, really, but he was smart enough to grind into some people that patriotic nonsense. Once they were up in arms, I only had to pacify them with the right doubts, and then when I wanted them stirred up again, it was only a matter of letting them loose once more."

"Sometimes it's terrifying hearing how you talk about people."

"I'll take that as a compliment," St. Cloud said. "In many ways, the elite will disregard a man who goes to war over one who reads books; but it's men like me, who have seen men at their least humane, who know more about the dark side of the human heart than those professors and students will ever comprehend."

"I can understand that," Exton said quietly. "I've lived through enough of that myself."

"Don't romanticize it, Exton," St. Cloud replied curtly. "You've never been so far gone from being a man of honor that you've really experienced what it is like to be without it."

"I'll take that as a compliment," Exton retorted, slightly stung but also surprised by St. Cloud's assessment of him. He didn't *want* to want his father-in-law's approval, but somewhere, deep down inside of him, Exton was afraid that he did.

Exton watched the monitors as they began reporting different sights of the damage the Redbird had done to the ship. It was small, but it managed to hit one of the outer plantation rooms. He was glad to see the supply capsule had already been released, so there was nothing left there. Aerie had done her job. Hopefully, he thought, she was on her way back to them.

"It doesn't matter if I have your approval or not," Exton said, turning his attention back to St. Cloud as he was thinking of Aerie. "I'm married to Aerie now, so it's too late for you to give your blessing."

Exton had just keyed in Rhodey's comm frequency when St. Cloud spoke.

"I already gave you my blessing," St. Cloud said.

Exton froze. "What?"

"I didn't call you just to protect them, you know," he said. "That was an excuse. I could have easily let you land and captured you. But I called, because after all the trouble you were determined to cause for her, I knew you would find her and keep her safe."

He remembered that call. St. Cloud was taunting and awful as usual—but he was right, too. He could have easily let Exton land at New Hope, and he could have taken him prisoner.

"I guess I'm not doing that great of a job of protecting her while she's up here with us," Exton said.

St. Cloud's eyes lit up. "Aerie has always been a handful," he said. "So I won't judge you too harshly, even if this is going to end up a suicide mission."

Exton turned back to the comm and pressed the button for Rhodey. "I was worried about that, too. I would appreciate it if you didn't mention that to her."

"It won't be a suicide mission for her," St. Cloud told him. "I'm—no, *we're*—going to protect her."

Rhodey answered Exton's call before he could affirm the General's statement.

"That you, Captain?" Rhodey asked. "We're right and

ready down here by the manual release."

"Rhodey, do you have a clear shot where you're at?" Exton asked. "The URS is firing missiles up at us and we won't get any second chances with any of them."

"Felix is the sharpshooter here," Rhodey replied. "He's ready on my mark. All I'm waiting for, whether I think it's ridiculous or not, is your approval."

"You have it. Fire away when you have an opening. I'll keep watch for more bombs."

"We've done this hundreds of times, Captain," Rhodey told him. "Felix and I were in the first battalion of UNA's most decorated legion."

Exton almost rolled his eyes. There was nothing Rhodey and his friends liked more than war. He appreciated their skills, but keeping them busy on the *Perdition* for the last several years had been a chore.

"Where's Miguel?" Exton asked. "Is he there, too?"

"Miguel chose to evacuate," Rhodey said. "He's in love with a pretty little lady, and I told him it was his moral duty to follow his heart."

Exton was surprised at the news, but he took it in stride. Miguel and Felix had tended to the bombs under the Biovid for years. He was certain Rhodey had control of the situation.

"Once the bombs are all released, Rhodey," Exton said, "I want you and your crew to leave."

"We have our transportation ready," Rhodey confirmed. "See you on the other side, Captain."

Rhodey signed off, and Exton felt a strange mix of fear and hope inside of him. He knew he could count on his crew, but there was still so much at risk.

Before he could turn his attention back to the GPI, Aerie burst into the door.

"There you are," St. Cloud said, chastising her. "What took you so long?"

"I had trouble with the Ark's release," Aerie admitted. "I couldn't get it, so I came up here."

"There's a manual release on the Ark," Exton told her.

"I'm not going to worry about it now. I know it was designed with a lot of reinforcement. But the rest of them are out?"

"Yep." Aerie gave him a smile. "What's next?"

"Rhodey and the others are about to release the nukes," Exton said. "We just have to wait."

"Do you want me to try to contact Osgood?" Aerie asked. "Offer him one last chance to repent and surrender?"

"No," St. Cloud scoffed. "But watch the comms. He might try to do that sort of stunt with us."

Aerie obeyed at once, while Exton watched as his starship's monitor beeped. The first nuke had fallen away.

He watched the bomb as it came into sight, barreling through the edge of the atmosphere, heading for the GPI.

"We have a hit!" Exton called, as the warhead hit the port side. "Three more to go."

"Next one is away," St. Cloud said. "Headed for the starboard engine."

As the warheads were released, Exton held his breath, hoping they would be enough to stop Osgood. He watched as the larger starship, hovering miles off the ground, wondering if the missiles would be enough to stop the GPI entirely.

Aerie called out to him a moment later. "Exton," she said. "He's hailing our ship."

"Answer it," he said.

"Don't," St. Cloud said. "Let him suffer in silence."

After looking to Exton, Aerie answered it.

"Hello?"

At the familiar voice, all of them turned.

"Brock?" Aerie asked. "Is that you?"

"Yes, it's me," Brock said. "I'm on the GPI. This is the first I've been able to get to the control room to talk with you."

"You need to get out of there," Aerie told him. "We're trying to stop the GPI before it gets out of the atmosphere."

"I noticed," Brock said. "The ship's crew is determined to give you a run for your money. Osgood has the lambs going out."

Exton shook his head. "I can't believe he's really sending people out to their deaths like that." He glanced over at Aerie's confused glance. "Fighters are going out to try to stop the bombs from hitting the GPI. They'll likely die."

Aerie's eyes softened. "That's terrible."

Brock spoke up again. "I wanted you to know Osgood has set course for Petra first. Even if you do stop him from getting out into space, you'll need to make sure he's safe. I'm trying to alert Director Ward."

"All the escape pods are headed there," Aerie gasped. She glanced back at Exton.

His mouth set into a grim line. He knew Osgood was after the defectors.

"Brock, it's Exton," he said. "You need to get out of there, now. We have a plan, and it will work. But the GPI will be destroyed completely. Get out of there now."

Brock's tone shifted slightly. "Alright, Captain," he finally said. "I'm going."

There was something entirely surreal about Brock finally acknowledging him as his captain. Between Brock's respect and St. Cloud's blessings, Exton's silent, buried concern finally metamorphized into acceptance as he realized the truth: He was going to die today.

There was no other possible explanation.

But, Exton decided, he was ready. He faced the front of the ship as if it was his future, and he clung to the faith inside of him. *God, let your will be done at last. No longer mine first.*

His only other prayer was that Aerie would be safe.

"Brock, I'll keep the lines open," Aerie said, "so if you land somewhere outside of our allies' camps, we'll be able to come and find you."

"Don't try to sabotage the ship anymore," Exton told Brock, snapping back to the scene before him. "We'll take care of it. Just get to the escape pods in the hangar; it's the safest place for you to leave from right now."

"Got it. See you guys soon. And Aerie?" Brock sighed.

"I'm sorry I wasn't a better friend."

"You were the best," Aerie assured him. "Be careful."

The comm line went down, and Aerie stared at it, unsure of what to do or say.

"He'll be alright," St. Cloud finally said. "He was the top of the class for good reason."

Time seemed to slowly resume, before it picked up the pace exponentially. Exton watched as the GPI began to fall, as panels broke off, and as escape pods jettisoned out of its heart, like fireworks bursting against the clouds.

"Let's hope it's enough," Exton said.

Aerie came up beside him, placing her hand on his shoulder. "It'll be alright," she told him.

He barely heard her; all he saw was the last nuke explode, his eyes fixated past the mushroom cloud that reached up into the blackness of space. As the cloud dispersed and the light faded, Exton frowned.

The GPI was still rising. It was still rising, like a dying phoenix refusing to quell itself into its ashes.

Exton closed his eyes. There were no more warheads.

He was almost too depressed to answer Rhodey's signal.

"Captain?" Rhodey called. "We let the lions go free. Was it enough?"

Exton slowly let out his breath. "No," he said. "No, they managed to stop the last one."

"Anything else we can do?" Rhodey asked. "Felix and I would be happy to go out with a bang."

"There's only one thing you can do for me," Exton said. "Get to your escape pod."

Rhodey was silent for a moment.

"Rhodey? Did you hear me?"

"Captain, there are only two left," he said. "Felix and I can take the one, but that will only leave you with—"

"You have your orders, Rhodey."

"Yes, Captain."

"It was a pleasure," Exton said, and then he hung up the line. He couldn't bear to hear anything else. War was a weird thing, he thought. It made men tougher, but it also made them strangely sentimental. He knew he felt the same way at times, but he would allow himself to indulge in it later.

If later ever came.

Exton turned to face St. Cloud. "It's time for the GPI to go to hell, don't you think?"

St. Cloud nodded. "Set the course for the middle," he said. "Right through the heart. That'll take care of that. Like a heart attack."

"I can extend the plank," Exton told him with a wry grin.

"I'm not interested in seeing if it will hold me, before you make some stupid joke about making me walk it first," St. Cloud warned cheerfully.

"What's wrong with you two?" Aerie asked. "This isn't a game."

"I'm glad you know that, Aerie," Exton said quietly. "Because we're about to lose."

She went very still. "What do you mean?"

"It wasn't enough to stop them. Even if we delayed them, there's always the possibility Osgood will run if we don't do something quickly."

The comm line crackled. Aerie answered it at once. Exton had to guess from her expression that she was tempted to tell them to call back later, but she stopped a second later.

"So, Captain Chainsword." Osgood's voice was dark and cutthroat, coy enough Exton was reminded of Gerard. "This is the end."

"For you," Exton replied.

"Tell Victor I'm sorry things had to end this way. It's nothing personal; it's just business. I've planned this for too long for him to stop it now."

St. Cloud scoffed. "I'm here, Grant, and you can cut the melodramatics. I've known for some time that you wanted to rebuild the world from its remains."

"Think of how neat and organized it could be," Osgood said. "It would be so perfect and beautiful, like my own little cultivated garden of humanity. No more guessing, no more wondering about the questions of life. An answer for every question, an arbitrator for any disputes, everyone looking to follow my lead. Population control would be no problem; production would be streamlined. Everyone would have a job, and everyone would have an education. Everyone would be cared for, and there would be no more war."

"Those might sound good," St. Cloud retorted, "but no one would be free."

"Freedom is overrated," Osgood said. "Look at all the trouble your freedom has brought you. You're going to die, your ship will be destroyed, and your community will be completely leveled. It seems as though you've wasted your life."

Exton shook his head. "You're wrong, Osgood," he said. He glanced at Aerie, unable to quite look her straight in the eye, and then he looked at St. Cloud, who gave a firm nod. "We still have time."

♦27♦

Aerie was glad when the communication line cut itself off. "What are you going to do?" she asked, as she turned to face her husband.

"You already know," he told her simply.

And that was the truth. But Aerie was not going to give him the easy way out of it.

"Tell me," she said. "In your own words. I want to hear out of your own mouth that you're going to kill us all."

"Well, actually," Exton said, standing up, "that's not what I was thinking at all."

Aerie took a step back, confused but relieved. "Good."

"Give me one moment, and then we'll leave," he said. He pressed several buttons, making his way around the Command Bridge.

A beep came from the control board next to her. "Exton," she called, "there are more missiles coming our way."

"Don't worry about it. I'll put more power to the front shields."

Aerie watched him move from station to station, still unsure of what he was going to do. Her eyes shifted to her father, who was standing around, shifting on his heels. He seemed bored, she thought.

Exton then reached out a hand to St. Cloud. "Can I borrow your weapon, sir?" he asked.

St. Cloud smiled eerily. "Of course." He handed Exton the weapon at his side.

"What are you going to do?" Aerie asked, stepping forward. She was growing more concerned by the moment. Her husband and her father were not natural allies. She was afraid she was deliberately being left out of the loop.

"I'd find something to grip onto if I were you," Exton called back, before he shoved the controls of the ship forward. The ship shot out, fast and hard, rushing forward back down toward Earth.

Rushing as it headed straight for GPI.

Aerie felt her whole body quake, and not from the sudden onset of pressure. "You're going to ram them?" she called out, watching in shock as Exton shot several rounds through the control panel, firmly planting the controls forward. "But the whole ship will blow up. We're all going to die."

"It's called a Pyrrhic victory, Aerie," Exton told her. He grabbed her by the arm. "The GPI has to go. Osgood has to go. This is the perfect chance we have of getting to him."

"What about Brock?"

"We told him to escape," Exton argued. "If he left when we said, he will likely get out just fine."

"But what about us?" Aerie asked.

"Right now, we have to go. We have to get to the escape pods."

Aerie's eyes lit up. "But Rhodey said there was only one left!" she recalled. "I thought you said you weren't going to kill us."

"I know." Exton turned to St. Cloud. "I'm going to die. You and your father are going to return to Petra."

"What?!" Aerie gasped, nearly choking. "No, you said I could stay with you. I'm not leaving you, Exton. If for no other reason than to assure myself you suffer, for tricking me with your semantics all over again."

"When did I do it before?" Exton asked.

"When you told me the *Perdition* didn't house any nuclear weapons," Aerie said, exasperated.

"Aerie, calm down," the General said, as Exton handed him back the gun. "You're making yourself look like a fool. You know the realities of war."

"But … But … " Aerie felt dizzy. She couldn't say goodbye to Exton!

Before she could put up another fight, he grabbed her hand. "Come on," he said. "I'm going to make sure you get into that pod. I told you that I'd never lie to you, Aerie, and I told you that I trust you. But this is one thing that I know I can't trust you with. You'll have to excuse me."

"There has to be another way," Aerie asserted, as she found herself in the elevator, heading down toward the hangar.

Her eyes grew wide as she took in her last view of the *Perdition*'s halls. She saw the edge of the Biovid, she saw the commissary and the endless hallways, where children once played while the adults gathered in the sanctuary for teaching and singing, the games and the med ward, as all of them flashed through her memory like a dream she never wanted to leave.

"No," she whispered, recalling the day Emery had tried to go over the emergency protocols with her, when she'd learned the truth of Exton's family and the reality behind the MENACE warmongers.

Tears flew down her cheeks easily as Exton and her father pushed her to the remaining pod; it was just across the way from the room she'd shared with Exton, where he'd shared everything with her—his world, his books, and his love and his body. His future.

"No," she repeated, more firmly this time, as Exton gently shoved her into the escape pod and stepped back.

"Yes," he told her. "I can't let you die here, even if it means I have to. I need you to go on with the world. And the world, once it's free of Osgood, will need the General. They'll look to him to lead the world once it's fallen apart."

He glanced back at St. Cloud. "Isn't that right?" he said.

General St. Cloud nodded. Aerie felt his full betrayal stab into her heart once more. "Exton's right," he said. "You need to go. I'm getting tired of listening to your fighting."

Aerie felt herself fall backward into the escape pod. "Ouch," she shouted, as she hit her head against the back wall.

As Exton rushed forward to help her up, that's when it happened.

A shot rang out from directly behind him, and Exton fell to the side. He cried out in agony, and his hand went immediately to the left side of his body, where blood was pouring out freely.

"Exton!" Aerie cried out. She caught him, but then she fell back again; this time, the *clunk* she heard was not her own head hitting the wall, but Exton's. She reached up, cradling his head and calling his name, as his body fell further on hers. She briefly felt the bump on his head, from where Brock had hit him before, and hoped it would not grow any bigger.

She glanced past Exton to see her father's cruel smile. "You can thank me, Aerie, by being a good wife to him," he said. He sighed and lowered his gun, tossing it onto the ground. "After all I've done to him, he deserves someone who will make his life better. Now, don't wait; get to Petra and have them take care of your husband. He'll need it, especially if he's going to nurse a new vendetta against me after this."

Aerie felt her mouth open in shock as the General reached forward and shut the door to the escape pod, squeezing the two of them inside.

Aerie met her father's amber eyes with hers. She finally looked away and hugged Exton even more tightly to her chest. "I love you, Daddy."

"I love you, too, Aerie."

Aerie could barely see as the escape pod doors closed, and her father disappeared, while she and Exton were shuttled out of the *Perdition.*

She brushed the tears out of her eyes just in time to watch as the *Perdition*, looking like a great knight lunging forward with its plank-like bowsprit extended, sliced through its grand enemy. The GPI and its menacing shadow collapsed and shattered in a supernova of fire and light.

♦28♦

The shadows came back to haunt him one last time. They fell swiftly over him, as pain shot out from his head and he felt himself slip away into the place where worlds overlapped and dimensions were interwoven.

He found himself in a dark world, standing alone. There was nothing cold, but nothing warm, and there was no one around. The pain in his head faded into memory, and even there, a barrier came between him and the recollections of the real world. A *thump!* called back from his memory, and it was accompanied by jarring sensation.

"What happened?" he heard himself say, and his voice seemed to cry out into the void forever.

Exton realized, at that moment, he was unconscious to the physical realm. He had been brought here through pain.

Before he could claw himself out of the darkness, a light sparked against the starless night. He watched as his hands formed out of the shadows, before they came up to protect his eyes. But the light wasn't stopped; it seemed to have a life of its own as it grabbed hold of him, pulling him forward into the place where there was no darkness. He watched, terrified, as the light bent around his fingers, twisted around his arms, and finally took him captive.

There was nothing he could do to resist.

He felt his mouth open, and he felt himself scream silently. His eyes closed in preparation for the worst.

Nothing happened.

There was no strike of lightning, no charring of his flesh, no gnashing of the teeth.

Nothing.

He finally opened his eyes and gasped at the scene before him.

It was his father—Silas Shepherd—on the night before his death. He watched as he stared out the window in their unit, looking past the small kitchen and its homey decorations. The old leather Bible was in his roughened hands. His black hair was streaked with gray and speckled with white, and in need of a trim. The ice blue of his eyes, so similar to Exton's own, gleamed with acceptance and faith.

Exton felt himself reach out, wondering if he could touch him. Wondering if he would be able to talk to him, to feel his father's strength, to hear his father's voice.

He was surprised when his father turned and looked right at him. Tears prickled into his eyes. "Papa?" he whispered, in near disbelief.

His father didn't answer. He bowed his head and resumed his prayers.

Exton took a step closer. "Papa, can you hear me?" His hand reached out again to touch his shoulder.

Silas's head suddenly came up, as his face turned toward the ceiling. "Thy will be done, Lord," he spoke, the husky timbre of his voice sending a dizzying new reality between them.

Exton watched as his father's words rippled into the air, the very fabric of time altering at their touch. A new world came forth from the power of the words, and Exton watched as his father began to disappear.

"No," he cried. "No, Papa, come back. Don't leave me." The guilt over his death, mixed with shock and loss and anger, roared along with his cry.

As he watched, his father's form continued to fade away, while he slipped through death's door and time passed.

Exton stood there, his hand still reaching out. He watched as the shadowy figure of his father, fading away into the ghost of his spirit, grabbed his hand. Instantly, the figure transformed.

As Exton watched, his father was suddenly replaced by St. Cloud. Out of his father's fluffy bearded face came the clean-shaven formation of the General's features, complete with the stark lines of his cheeks and the hard jut of his chin as his thin lips curled into a smirk.

"This isn't a game, Exton," he said. "Life is not a game."

Exton fell into speechlessness, as St. Cloud's grip on his

hand became more solid, more firm, and the rest of world before him slinked back into the recesses of his heart and mind.

Patches of the physical world crept back into his sight. Exton watched, helplessly transfixed. He could see the darkness of space, with the starlight twinkling with its iridescent inner fire. The earth in the background gleamed, with both pollution and divine prosperity. The sea shook with storms, the ice glittered with simulated sunlight, and the Memory Tree stood over it all, as a man stood at its base, beckoning him to come back home.

And then, it was over; the darkness returned, and sank, still helpless, into the nothingness awaiting him; the only thing Exton was still certain of, as he tread upon the last lines of his awareness, was the feeling of a hand holding onto his.

The hand sustaining him remained strong and tight, but the feel of it became smaller and softer, and infinitely more welcome and familiar. Other sensations began to creep back into his mind, as if a million markedly tiny alarms were all going off inside his brain at the same time in hopes of waking him up, almost like he'd decided to use Christmas tree lights instead of a lamp to light a room.

Exton's eyes blinked open, and he nearly squinted at the bright light above him. "That's bright," he murmured.

"Exton? Are you awake?" Aerie's voice was sunlight against the clouds.

"I think so," he replied, surprised to find his voice sounded scratchy.

"If you want to go back to sleep, it's okay," Aerie said, squeezing his hand in hers reassuringly. "It's been quite an adventure getting here."

He had a feeling, from her words and the remainder of his dream—vision?—that she was grossly understating their situation.

"Where is here?" Exton struggled to sit up as he glanced around. At once, he recognized the various medical displays and supplies. "Oh. We're at Petra."

"Yes. That's where all the escape pods were programmed, remember?"

Images flooded through him, as he stepped back into the moment before he was taken away to see his father—the escape pod. St. Cloud, standing over him, smirking. Aerie's weepy voice, whispering in the distance, as even further back explosions and bright flashes of bombs went off. The end of the *Perdition*, as it collided with the GPI, that monstrous beast of a technological wonder, determined to be the end of the free world.

The last second of his energy as he struggled to fight off the pain of his body and his already-bruised head, all in order to save Aerie and her father from the fiery end they were determined to meet alongside him.

"What happened?" Exton asked. "Did we win? Did the plan work?"

"The GPI is gone," Aerie said. "Emery and your aunt have been celebrating with the rest of our friends down in the command center. It was awful. A lot of the wreckage burned up and broke up at the top of the atmosphere. We're still tracking the debris."

"So Osgood is finished."

"Yes."

At her answer, Exton relaxed into the cot once more. Aerie watched as frown crossed his brow. "Why don't I remember it?"

"Well … my father … shot you," Aerie said carefully.

At her words, the pain in his torso, on the left side of his body, suddenly screamed, as if his body was already giving him the verification he would have asked for.

He groaned. "I remember now."

"You fell over and hit your head again. I was upset at what my father did," Aerie said, "but he picked you up, after you passed out, and put you and me into the last of the escape pods. And then … we left, and he stayed behind."

There was a sadness in her voice that told Exton all he needed to know; St. Cloud was gone. He had sacrificed himself so they would be able to get away. He squeezed her hand back. "I'm sorry," he said.

Aerie nodded, but he could see her eyes were full of sadness. She swallowed hard before she continued. "I wasn't sure if you were going to make it for a few moments," she admitted.

"I would never leave you," he said, bringing her hand up to his lips.

"You promised me once you would never lie to me."

"I haven't. I wouldn't leave you." He pressed his hand against his heart. "You're in here."

With her free hand, she cupped his cheek. "You know, this never would have happened if I had just stayed onboard the *Perdition*, way back in the beginning."

He reached up and pulled her close to him, burying his face in her hair. "We saved the world from Osgood's Planethood Initiative," he said. "Your recklessness saved millions of people, including Petra and Chaya."

"But so many people died," Aerie murmured, close to tears. "Gerard's gone, Dorian's gone, and so is my father. And I almost lost you."

He held her close, running his hand through her hair and down her back. He wasn't sure there was anything that he could say. Exton knew he could tell her that there was a price for standing up in the face of evil, that there was still hope for goodness to triumph in a fallen world, that it was too big of a miracle to contemplate, that humans had any chance at all to alter their lives; he could tell her that she was rightfully worried about protecting her mother, that she had been driven by good things to do something that went wrong and right in different ways, that she wasn't alone in her blame.

But he knew, from his own experience with Reverend Thorne in the days following the loss of his father, that those words meant nothing when divorced from his love for her.

And she needed that first.

He pulled back from her ever so slightly. He looked deeply into her eyes, those eyes that haunted him as much as he pursued them. He took the moment to memorize the distinct shades of amber, basking in the glow that hinted at her inner fire. And when he felt his own soul latch onto hers a moment later, he said, "I still love you. And so do many others."

His voice was hoarse and husky, and he was pretty sure his pain medication was keeping him from being fully awake; but as Aerie teared up again, he knew, for now, his love was the best he could offer her, and he knew, for now, it would be enough.

Aerie scooted back from him a moment later. "Sorry," she said. "I know I wasn't cut out for war." She gave him a tiny smile and a small attempt at a laugh.

"You don't have to apologize," he told her. He sat up against his pillows more, trying to focus on her completely. "I can imagine that you'd enjoy this part, though, right?"

"What do you mean?"

"The role reversal," he explained. "I'd say you probably like being the one outside of the bed, rather than in it yourself."

Aerie's smile widened a little at his words. "You do have a point," she conceded.

"All I need now is Moona on my lap," he told her.

"Ha!" Aerie laughed. "Moona wouldn't be willing to wake up from her nap in Emery's room to come and see us. She apparently spends the majority of her time on the cat bed Tyler bought for her."

"Tyler always liked animals," Exton said. "I'm not surprised he managed to find a way to get Emery to like her."

Silence came back after their laugh. As Exton woke up, he thought about telling Aerie about his dream, where he saw his father. Some part of him wanted to keep that for himself, as a secret between him and God, but as he watched Aerie, as she lovingly tended to him, he eventually told her what happened.

She frowned. "I wonder what it means," she said.

"Could be nothing," Exton replied. "I never took stock in things like dreams and visions from God. At least, not for myself. But he seemed determined to prove me wrong with miracles when it came to you, so I have to admit, I'm not sure what it means."

"But it does mean something."

"I guess so."

"Huh." Aerie sat back thoughtfully. "Well, if that was a message to you from your father or mine, it at least certainly sounds like him. He used to tell me survival wasn't a game all the time."

"I know him well enough to take him at his word," Exton said. "I wouldn't be surprised if it was something he wanted to tell me. It was a good way for him to die, from his perspective. He finally found a way to atone for his sins against me."

"And me," Aerie said with a smile. Her eyes glistened with tears. "He shouldn't have bothered. I would've forgiven him anyway."

Exton held her against him, allowing himself to enjoy the feel of her underneath his hand. "Me, too," he admitted. "I still feel like my father didn't need to die. But war claims a lot of victims, both in the mind and on the battlefield. Maybe my father did go mad at the end."

"There are some things we will never know," Aerie agreed quietly.

The door to the room opened. "If you're talking about Papa, I don't think he went mad," Emery said as she walked into the room.

"Emery." Exton reached out with his free hand and took hold of his sister's.

"Yes, brother dear," Emery said, her tone ever practical, but her eyes full of sisterly affection. "I've been keeping tabs on everything for you, and I will be happy to fill you in on everything you've missed in the last couple of days."

"Tell me about Papa first," he said. "What did you mean, he didn't go mad?"

"I had a feeling you wouldn't be distracted from that, even though there's a lot to report," Emery said. "I had Tyler comb through the Boötes system some more. He caught a few more details about Osgood's plan for the GPI. He was going to start his onslaught at Chaya. Apparently, he has been planning this for several years."

"He wouldn't have liked that."

"No, he wouldn't have," Emery said. "Once the initial plans for the GPI were submitted, the anomalies began appearing in Papa's designs for the *Paradise*."

Everything suddenly became clear. "Once he found out about it, Papa decided to steal the *Paradise* and save the Ecclesia."

Emery nodded. "That's best guess, anyway," she said. "There are a few more things we likely won't ever find out."

"Why is Chaya so important?" Aerie asked. "It seems like an unusual place to start destroying the world."

"Before Petra was created, Chaya was one of our smaller allies, but it was also one of the most resourceful," Emery explained. "They had a lot of leading scientists there, including the botanists and geoengineers who are now going to work on cleaning up the earth's atmosphere. And in addition to that, it is considered part of the Holy Lands from the history of the Ecclesia."

"So your dad wanted to protect it," Aerie said. "Osgood threatened it, and your dad stood up to protect it. Just like you did, when Petra was threatened." She brushed a lock of his dark hair out of his eyes.

"Your father wanted to stop him, because he wanted to get the URS onboard and then blow it up," Emery added. "At least, that's what Merra told me yesterday when I went to babysit Marcus for her."

"I guess Merra is doing okay, by the sound of it," Exton said.

"She's more than fine, physically," Aerie answered.

"Emotionally, I think it will take more. Right now she's working on healing, but she's planning a memorial for my brother. She was very upset to learn about Dorian's death."

Emery shook her head, her fingers resting protectively over her own belly, where a small bump was minimally protruding. "I can't imagine the pain of losing a child," she said. "This one is not even here, and I worry for him."

"Him?" Exton asked.

"DNA testing," Emery said, a smile returning to her face. "It's a boy."

"Oh, congratulations," Aerie cheered. "That's wonderful, Emery."

"I was thinking it would be nice to name him after Papa," Emery said, as she looked back over to Exton. "Tyler's already agreed to it."

"Silas is not a bad name," Exton replied. "And there's not even a bad legacy to go with it. But I'd recommend making sure he's well grounded in reality. I'd hate for Papa's idealism to be his downfall, too. Especially since that seems to be the truth after all, and much more so than we thought."

Emery laughed again. "He'll have his cynical uncle to do just that."

"Exton will have his work cut out for him because I'll be there, too," Aerie said. "And hey, maybe Marcus, too. He's close to five. He might enjoy having a younger friend around."

"He's been getting along with the other babies and younger kids," Emery said. "I talked to Alice and his other nanny, Joya, just the other day. They've been watching him almost exclusively since Merra's capture. Even since she's been back, they've been taking care of him."

"Remember, this is my mother we're talking about," Aerie said. "She might be sad about Dorian, but I doubt anything would keep her down for long."

"How is she taking the loss of St. Cloud?" Exton asked quietly. "I know it can't be easy for her."

There was a short pause, before Emery shrugged. "Well,

actually, St. Cloud is alive," she said.

Silence rocked through the room, as Aerie and Exton looked back and forth between each other and Emery sharing the same bewildered expression.

Emery nodded. "Come on, Exton," she teased. "You should know the St. Cloud family well enough by now to know they're apparently very hard to kill."

"I can't believe it," Aerie said. "My father is alive."

"What happened?" Exton shifted on the medical cot, nearly knocking Aerie out of the bed. "How?"

"Merra brought him here earlier today," Emery said. "She told me about his plans to convince me to let her leave with one of our shuttles. He contacted her while he was up on the *Perdition*. He managed to stow away inside the Ark."

"The Ark?" Exton felt his mouth drop open in shock.

"The Ark is protected by the Biovid. It was designed to withstand reentry pressures, and it has its own manual release. When the *Perdition* slammed into the GPI, it managed to stay intact."

Aerie's face lit up. "I remember now," she said. "Bruce told me that the different rooms beneath the Biovid were designed to be extra escape pods, in case of an emergency."

"Did St. Cloud know about it ahead of time?" Exton asked. "Did he know that was how he was going to cheat death?"

"I don't know," Emery said. "Why?"

"I want to know if he was up for sacrificing himself on purpose or if it was planned," Exton said. "I'm curious."

Morbidly curious, he admitted to himself.

"Come on, Exton," Aerie said. "You can't keep thinking that my father is some kind of mad genius plotting to take over the world. We just dealt with Osgood, and Osgood and my father are nothing alike."

"Then it doesn't strike you as odd that he's now in position to be Dictator of the Fair World?" Exton asked.

Aerie faltered. "Well … well, at least we'll be able to hold him accountable," she finally replied.

"And we can make him transition the nation back into a free market republic," Emery said. "I've already been assured by Merra that's what he intends to do."

"Really?" Exton put a hand to his forehead. "This is just a day for surprises, I guess. I think I'm starting to get lightheaded from it all."

"Well, you do need your rest, Captain," Serena called as she came into his room. There was a med screen in her hand and she was making notes with a stylus as she came over to him. "All these people need to go away."

"I'm staying," Aerie told her, giving her a stubborn look.

"Fine, but no funny business," Serena replied.

Emery giggled. "Well, I think I'll go ahead and take my leave," she said.

"Emery, wait," Exton said. "I had to ask … how is Meredith doing?"

Emery's blue-green eyes lost their sparkle. "She's doing better than we expected," she said slowly. "Tyler went up there, to be with his family when he told them the news of everything that happened. He told her about Gerard earlier today."

Exton wasn't entirely sure if he knew what he wanted to ask, or if what he wanted to ask was able to be answered. "Did he say anything … did she say anything to him?"

Emery nodded. "She wanted you to know she knows it was not your fault, and she's glad that he didn't die alone."

"He might as well have," Exton muttered. "He didn't know who we were in the end anyway."

"Maybe that's for the best," Aerie said. "So he didn't die with regrets. And, if I've learned anything from watching Don and Dennis run around, I know that he's in a better place."

"We can't know that," Exton scoffed.

"We're told not to judge," Emery said glumly. "But it's too easy to do just that sometimes, isn't it?"

The room went silent again, until Serena spoke up. "Alright, let me get a new IV bag for you, Captain, and then

I'll be finished with you for now."

"Thank you," Exton replied, his tone automatous.

"You're welcome." Serena winked. "I'll get out of here and then you can canoodle with Aerie some more."

"Serena," Aerie snapped. "Boy, you really don't have any respect for people's privacy, do you?"

Serena's eyebrows arched, and she looked too much like Merra in that moment for Exton to allow himself any illusion to the contrary. He thought he heard her laugh as she walked out of the room and headed down the hall.

Emery sighed. "Shift change is coming soon," she said, "so you won't have to put up with her for much longer."

"Good," Exton murmured. "I know there were some reports about how she is overly friendly in her duties, and I would hate to see them up close."

Aerie snuggled into his shoulder, scooting down next to him on the small cot. "I'll protect you," she promised. "Just like you protect me."

"That reminds me," Exton said. "How is Brock doing? Did he manage to get off of the GPI before it fell apart?"

"He's fine. He arrived here in Petra before you did," Emery said. "Right now, he is actually with Tyler. He wanted to go back to New Hope and see his friends and family."

Exton thought about Brock being back in New Hope. After everything he'd seen and fought and nearly died for, it would be interesting to see what Brock thought of his old home. Exton knew better than most that it was hard, if not impossible, to see home with the same eyes after a long journey.

"Any other news I should know about?" he asked.

"Plenty," Emery said, "but you need your rest first. Aunt Patty and I are, as ever, ready to relieve you, Captain." She gave a taunting bow and then headed out the door.

Finally, Exton thought. He was alone with Aerie again.

"How are you really feeling?" Aerie asked. "Are you okay with Meredith and the *Perdition* and everything?"

"I'm okay," he said. The words sounded almost strange

to him as they came out of his mouth. And, he decided, it was true. And if it wasn't entirely true, he knew it would be, one day. The old wounds, the past regrets, the fierce desire for revenge … all of them were still there and still a part of him. But there was something more in his life now. The past had finally released him—or maybe, he had finally been able to let it go—and he could see a new life for himself at last. He wanted to tell Aerie about it, about how he knew he had another chance to make a real life for himself, and for her, and for whatever family they made together.

As he looked up at her, his dizziness returned; Exton decided to wait until later, when he had more energy. He had a feeling he might not need to tell her anyway; she seemed to sense the change in him as she watched him, and for the moment it was enough.

Aerie laid her head in the crook of his shoulder and pulled the sheet up higher. "I'm going to miss the *Perdition*," Aerie said. "But I'm glad Osgood is dead, and the URS has a chance for a new era of peace."

"Me, too," Exton said. "This is a big day."

"It doesn't really feel like it, in some ways."

"I think if it did, we would be too overcome to really appreciate it."

"Good point. I never thought I would experience anything like this," Aerie whispered. "This is a new beginning for the world as much as it is for the URS, isn't it?"

"It is." Exton kissed her cheek softly, allowing himself a moment to breathe in the scent of her. "And it is a new one for us as well."

"I'm going to get relationship whiplash if we keep getting new beginnings. We haven't even been married for two months," Aerie said with a giggle.

"We'll figure it out," Exton promised, as he allowed his drowsiness to catch up with him, to seep into him until his whole being was sure he'd never felt so physically, emotionally, and mentally drained. "But maybe not today. And for that, I'm sorry, Aerie."

"You're sorry for what?" Aerie's expression softened with mild confusion. "You don't have anything you need to apologize to me for."

"Yes, I do," he replied. "I promised you I'd kiss you senseless when we got back. I'm going to have to do that later."

"Don't worry," Aerie told him with a bright smile. "We have enough time."

Yes, Exton mused as he made his way back into sleep, *yes, we do. At last.*

♦Epilogue♦

The years that followed the official end of Grant Osgood's leadership were marked with long days of uncertainty, short months of victory, and lots of environmental cleanup. General St. Cloud, whether he had planned for his own dictatorship or not, was instantly welcomed back by the people who had, just weeks ago, believed that he'd tried to murder the previous dictator.

Aerie thought that it was complicated, once upon a time, but apparently that was all part of the narrative. That was according to what her father had told her, anyway, during one of their monthly family dinners. He'd told her, quite arrogantly, that if enough people believed it, or at least if enough people didn't question it, everyone else would soon fall into line. "That's the power of a good narrative," he said. "And useful idiots, too, when you think about it."

Narrative or truth, life immediately began to get better for nearly everyone. The defectors were allowed to return to their homes, bringing with them plenty of new suppliers and new sellers. The controlled markets of the URS were suddenly overwhelmed, and it was a good thing, as new laws were written while the old ones were struck down. The nation, which had been so divided by the things which were said and even more so by the things left unsaid, gradually came together. Where they could, anyway. It was still a battle, as courts were called in and police were overworked, but things managed to settle some. People were glad to be free to worship outside of the State's demands, and other people were just glad to have the government out of the news industry. Several other members of the newly reborn private sector, most of them former pirates of sorts, were also cheerful, as they were able to make a living without risking arrest.

Aerie knew she was certainly happy. As she'd learned from her own experience on the *Perdition*, real change happened at its own pace, as people let it, and one person at a time.

As much as things didn't change, and others changed entirely, time still passed.

It was years after that day, the day she'd been thrown back to the world by her father's commanding sacrifice, when Aerie sat down outside in the garden behind her home.

She was tired, but she wanted a few moments of peace and serenity before the day began. After all the events in her young life, Aerie knew there wasn't enough time for peace in the world.

Once the war was declared over, and St. Cloud negotiated peace through strength with Captain Chainsword, the URS went back to its normal routines, although there were a few less than normal attitudes. The forefront belief that survival was the most absolutely necessary thing took a backseat to the expansion of educational programs, social events, and new skills development initiatives St. Cloud and his followers introduced in the newly elected legislative branches. Slowly, people were beginning to see that survival was all very well and good, but it was not the goal of a life, but rather part of its foundation.

A republic was not quite there, but it was close. Her father was getting older, and he wanted to retire so he could spend more time with his wife and his kids.

And now his grandkids, too, Aerie added to herself, thinking of the small, sleeping pair of twins she'd finished nursing an hour ago. She smiled and, despite her fatigue from the late-night feedings, kept looking for signs of the vegetables she'd planted earlier that year.

The door opened behind her. "I thought I heard you leave the house."

Exton's voice still called out to her with its irresistible quality, as if his heart was talking directly into hers.

And, Aerie thought, her heart still answered with enraptured joy.

"I thought I would get a few moments to myself," Aerie explained to him, as her husband came and sat down beside her. "Well, a few moments with me and Moona," she said, chuckling as Moona stood up from her hidden spot in the soil. Moona stretched and yawned, and Aerie had to wonder if her kids were interrupting the large cat's sleeping habits as well. "I feel like I haven't had a real moment to myself in years. Those kids filled my heart with love, but they took all my energy."

"I can go if you want."

"No," she said. She took his hand. "I haven't gotten enough time with just you, either, since they came."

Exton came up beside her and ran a hand through her loose hair. "Emberly looks just like you when she sleeps," he said. "Except with curls."

"Callen looks more like you," Aerie replied. She wrinkled her nose. "And they both act like you. Stubborn and demanding and high-handed."

"Those would easily describe both of us, I'm afraid," Exton pointed out.

"They're not even six months old, and they already seem to think I'll do whatever they want."

"Let's hope they get it out of their system before they're teenagers," Exton said. "Or they'll have just as many problems with their parents as we had with ours."

Aerie laughed. "Oh, that does remind me," she said. "Mom is coming over today. She said she wants to help with the Harvest this year. She just got some new seedlings from the University."

"It's time for the Harvest already?"

"What do you mean, 'already?'" Aerie laughed. "I've been waiting forever for New Hope's winter to come. I don't think I've ever been this warm here for so long."

"Either way, we'll make the best of it, my love." He planted a kiss on her cheek.

"What are you talking about? The weather has been really warm, but it has been more than bearable."

He grinned. "I meant your mother's visit."

Aerie gave him a playful punch on the shoulder, but she

couldn't hold back her smile. "Seriously, though. You did remember today's the Harvest's festival day?"

"How could I forget?" Exton rolled his eyes. "Reverend Thorne has been leaving me messages all week."

"He's been calling me too," Aerie said. "He just wants to know if we want the kids dedicated while everyone's together. Tyler and Emery are bringing their new baby up from Petra."

"Emery's going to have to stop having kids one day," Exton said with a sigh. "I can't remember all their names as it is."

"It's only her fourth."

"They've only been married for five years, Aerie."

"Are you saying they need to slow down, or we need to catch up?" Aerie teased.

"Well, when you put it like that … " Exton ran his eyes down her body, and then reached for her. After nearly tripping over Moona, he caught hold of Aerie. His hands framed her face before he kissed her soundly. Then, probably thinking of the terror he'd faced in watching her birth his son and daughter, and the twins' subsequent demands on his being, he pulled back from her. "I guess we'll just have to go visit them more."

Aerie grinned. "I would love that. I don't talk to Emery enough."

"She talks to you every week, and sends you plenty of photos besides."

"I'd also like to see how Cal's doing. He apparently has a new girlfriend. And there are all our other friends besides."

"Plenty of them are in New Hope, Aerie," Exton reminded her. "Alice and Brock are working with St. Cloud, and Serena's become good friends with Meredith at the new hospital."

Aerie continued on, ignoring him. "And I would love to see how Petra is doing, now that it's not an official defector camp."

"Aunt Patty is always busy, so you know she's happy. I swear, she and my mom were nothing alike." Exton gestured to around the garden. "You remind me of my mother, when you're out here. Mama would've liked you."

"This is where I was always meant to be," Aerie said. She glanced around, thinking of her family, her children, and her husband. Her appreciation for the permanent things in her life, the anchors she had always clung to, whether she knew them or not for what they truly were, had only increased since the end of the war. "My mother had a garden she called Eden, you know, when I was younger. This is my Eden. It might be a small garden in a fallen world, but this is the place where I know I belong."

"When I was on the *Perdition*," Exton said, "I never pictured this kind of beauty was possible. I knew hell was real; but now I know that Heaven is too, because of this place."

Aerie tightened her grip around him, as he ran his fingers through her long hair. She thought of that day, the day he'd first kissed her, and felt that same longing inside of her stir. "You're right. Hope grows here, and God knows we don't deserve any of it."

Exton took her hand and lead her back to the house, as the pristine peace of the moment was ruined by Callen and Emberly, as they once more woke up. "Come on," he said. "Our children need us again from the sound of it. How about a deal? I'll change them while you take care of the feeding?"

Aerie allowed her gaze to fall over her various flowers. In the center of the garden was a tiny tree, one that she'd planted when they first came to live in Exton's old community. It was a seedling from the Memory Tree, one that Emery had given to her, and as she watched the sunlight peek over the mountaintops, she reminded herself all over again that she had survived war, even as much as she hated it. Now, here in this place, with the right people by her side, until the end of the world, she was determined to thrive.

Aerie smiled. "You know there's no one I'd rather make a deal with than you."

THANK YOU FOR READING!

Please leave a review and check out
https://www.csjohnson.me
for updates and more!

www.ingramcontent.com/pod-product-compliance
Lightning Source LLC
Chambersburg PA
CBHW030345310726
48979CB00001B/189

* 9 7 8 1 9 4 8 4 6 4 6 0 4 *